D0848956

edgeworks.4

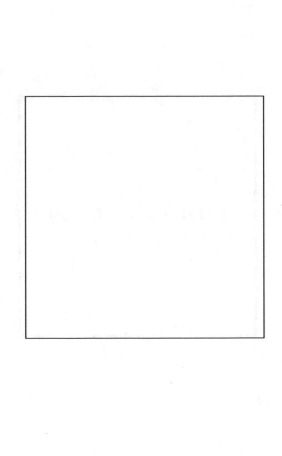

harlan ellison

edgeworks.4

love ain't nothing
but sex misspelled

the beast that shouted love
at the heart of the world

BOOKS BY HARLAN ELLISON

NOVELS:	WEB OF THE CITY [1958]
THE SOUND OF A SCYTHE [1960]	SPIDER KISS [1961]
SHORT NOVELS:	
DOOMSMAN [1967]	ALL THE LIES THAT ARE MY LIFE [1980]
RUN FOR THE STARS [1991]	MEFISTO IN ONYX [1993]
GRAPHIC NOVELS:	
DEMON WITH A GLASS HAND (ADAPTATION WITH MARSHALL ROGERS) [1986]	
NIGHT AND THE ENEMY (ADAPTATION WITH KEN STEACY) [1987]	
VIC AND BLOOD: THE CHRONICLES OF A BOY AND HIS DOG [1989] (ADAPTATION WITH RICHARD CORBEN)	
SHORT STORY COLLECTIONS:	THE DEADLY STREETS [1958]
SEX GANG [1959] (AS PAUL MERCHANT)	A TOUCH OF INFINITY [1960]
CHILDREN OF THE STREETS [1961]	GENTLEMAN JUNKIE AND OTHER STORIES OF THE HUNG-UP GENERATION [1961]
ELLISON WONDERLAND [1962]	PAINGOD AND OTHER DELUSIONS [1965]
I HAVE NO MOUTH & I MUST SCREAM [1967]	FROM THE LAND OF FEAR [1967]
LOVE AIN'T NOTHING BUT SEX MISSPELLED [1968]	THE BEAST THAT SHOUTED LOVE AT THE HEART OF THE WORLD [1969]
OVER THE EDGE [1970]	DE HELDEN VAN DE HIGHWAY [1973] (DUTCH PUBLICATION ONLY)
ALL THE SOUNDS OF FEAR [1973] (BRITISH PUBLICATION ONLY)	THE TIME OF THE EYE [1974] (BRITISH PUBLICATION ONLY)
APPROACHING OBLIVION [1974]	DEATHBIRD STORIES [1975]
NO DOORS, NO WINDOWS [1975]	HOE KAN IK SCHREEUWEN ZONDER MOND [1977] (DUTCH PUBLICATION ONLY)
STRANGE WINE [1978]	SHATTERDAY [1980]
STALKING THE NIGHTMARE [1982]	ANGRY CANDY [1988]
ENSAMVÄRK [1992] (SWEDISH PUBLICATION ONLY)	JOKES WITHOUT PUNCHLINES [1995]
ВСЕ ЗВУКИ СТРАХА (ALL FEARFUL SOUNDS) [1997] (UNAUTHORIZED RUSSIAN PUBLICATION ONLY)	ROUGH BEASTS [FORTHCOMING]
THE WORLDS OF HARLAN ELLISON (AUTHORIZED RUSSIAN PUBLICATION ONLY)	
SLIPPAGE [1997]	
OMNIBUS VOLUMES:	
THE FANTASIES OF HARLAN ELLISON [1979]	DREAMS WITH SHARP TEETH [1991]

COLLABORATIONS:

PARTNERS IN WONDER collaborations with 14 other wild talents [1971]

THE STARLOST: Phoenix Without Ashes (with Edward Bryant) [1975]

MIND FIELDS 33 stories inspired by the art of Jacek Yerka [1994]

NON-FICTION & ESSAYS:

MEMOS FROM PURGATORY [1961]

THE GLASS TEAT essays of opinion on television [1970]

THE OTHER GLASS TEAT further essays of opinion on television [1975]

THE BOOK OF ELLISON (edited by Andrew Porter) [1978]

SLEEPLESS NIGHTS IN THE PROCRUSTEAN BED Essays (edited by Marty Clark) [1984]

AN EDGE IN MY VOICE [1985]

HARLAN ELLISON'S WATCHING [1989]

THE HARLAN ELLISON HORNBOOK [1990]

SCREENPLAYS, ETC:

THE ILLUSTRATED HARLAN ELLISON (edited by Byron Preiss) [1978]

HARLAN ELLISON'S MOVIE [1990]

I, ROBOT: THE ILLUSTRATED SCREENPLAY (based on Isaac Asimov's story-cycle) [1994]

THE CITY ON THE EDGE OF FOREVER [1996]

"REPENT, HARLEQUIN!" SAID THE TICKTOCKMAN [1997]
(rendered with paintings by Rick Berry)

RETROSPECTIVES:

ALONE AGAINST TOMORROW A 10-Year Survey [1971]

THE ESSENTIAL ELLISON A 35-Year Retrospective [1987]
(edited by Terry Dowling, with Richard Delap & Gil Lamont)

AS EDITOR:

DANGEROUS VISIONS [1967]

NIGHTSHADE & DAMNATIONS: THE FINEST STORIES OF GERALD KERSH [1968]

AGAIN, DANGEROUS VISIONS [1972]

MEDEA: HARLAN'S WORLD [1985]

The Harlan Ellison Discovery Series:

STORMTRACK [1975]
by James Sutherland

AUTUMN ANGELS [1975]
by Arthur Byron Cover

THE LIGHT AT THE END OF THE UNIVERSE [1976]
by Terry Carr

ISLANDS [1976]
by Marta Randall

INVOLUTION OCEAN [1978]
by Bruce Sterling

THE WHITE WOLF SERIES:

EDGEWORKS.1 [1996]

EDGEWORKS.2 [1996]

EDGEWORKS.3 [1997]

EDGEWORKS.4 [1997]

edgeworks: volume four	harlan ellison
layout and typesetting	kathleen ryan
editor for white wolf	anna branscome
editorial consultant	michael d. toman
cover illustration	john k. snyder, III

Edgeworks: Volume Four The Collected Ellison
Love Ain't Nothing but Sex Misspelled
The Beast That Shouted Love at the Heart of the World

A White Wolf *Borealis* edition by arrangement with the Author, and the Author's agent, Richard Curtis Associates, New York.

White Wolf Publishing
735 Park North Blvd, Suite 128
Clarkston, GA 30021
www.white-wolf.com

Printed and Bound in the United States of America.
First White Wolf Omnibus Edition: November 1997
Second Printing: May 1998

10 9 8 7 6 5 4 3 2

Copyright acknowledgments appear on pages vii, viii, and ix, which constitute an extension of this copyright page.

COPYRIGHT ACKNOWLEDGMENTS

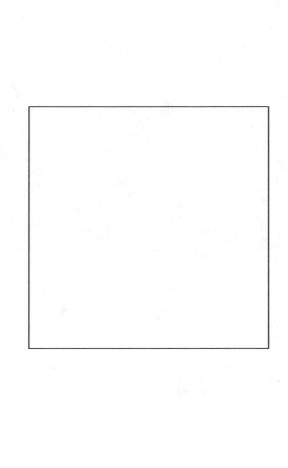

This one, with affection
and friendship, is for 2
of the best writers inna world,

BILL AND ELIZABETH KOTZWINKLE AND GUNDY

in deliquescent memory
of the coldest I've ever been,
the morning my piss
froze into an arcing icicle
as it left my blue body.

EDGEWORKS 4:	

**"The best love is like a knife.
It cuts through anything."**

Christopher Fowler
MENZ INSANA, 1997

INTRODUCTION

Dealing With the Lot of Y'all

(Part One)

In that attenuated moment just before the chute opens, as you're falling 32.2 feet/second/second, the thought occurs, *maybe this wasn't such a hot idea, after all.*

Zzzzz. As I sit down to write this introduction, I look up, waiting for the chute to blossom, waiting for the Parafoil canopy to pull out of the sleeve and the lines to pull taut. Paramnesia, that illusion of remembering events you haven't previously experienced. I have been in this elevator before.

Without doubt, this one is going to get me in trouble.

I have mild arthritis in some of the oft-busted places on my weary carcass, and I can feel the rain coming. Right now, in some of those oft-busted places in my memory, I'm feeling mild paramnesia; and I know—as certainly as I know I've packed my chute badly—I'm gonna regret the hell out of writing this introduction.

So why do it. Sheeesh, if I had half a working brain in my skull, you think I'd be hanging here at the end of this bungee cord, head-down under the Tacoma Narrows Bridge, eyeball-to-eyeball with the icy waters of Puget Sound? I do it for the same reason most of you have done cabbage-stupid stunts: it seemed like a good idea at the time.

Then again, coupled with a truly suicidal inability to suffer the mewling bullshit that passes for "honesty" in these days of bonding, sharing, opening-up and confiding, I have come to accept the tenebrous truth that I'm now too old and set in my ways to much give a fuck. Whip them dice, Silky; eight the hard way's yer point.

So as my velocity increases, I'll just get into it.

This guy I met, I think, once in my life—and don't even remember *that* encounter—recently died. Miserable death, not one I'd wish on anybody, even someone I didn't like as much as I didn't like this guy. Couldn't stand the sonofabitch, but if Fate, or Destiny, or Neil Gaiman, or whoever it is that runs the Universe, had come up to me and offered me the opportunity to get even with this guy for what he'd done to me, actually faced with the responsibility of tripping the guillotine, actually ordering up this guy for the Blue Plate Special, I know for certain I'd visit on him maybe a perpetual hangnail, or a case of the runs that would start right in the middle of his address to the Daughters of the American Revolution, and would end a year from February. But nothing nastier than that. Now, don't get me wrong: I hold grudges (still working on several from 1961), but I'm no Tim McVeigh. At some proper remove from the *schwishhh* of the dropping blade, simple sense and decency take possession of my dementia, and I can't bring myself actually to drop them piranhas into some schmuck's sauna.

But he died, and a mutual friend called to tell me about it. I wish I could dissemble, and advise you that I had a *frisson* of sorrow because he was gone (after all, his *was* a human life), but in truth I merely sighed and thought, *he got his*.

Now. . .I understand with paper-cut sharpness that this is a revelation that will not, in any smallest way, endear me to you. But to plead otherwise, to affect a lachrymose lamentation, to pretend—as Queen Elizabeth recently did when delivering her eulogy for Princess Di—to a great mourning—when I'd be willing to bet she was actually gnashing her mental teeth, deranged behind the certainty that now she would *never* be rid of that little blonde bitch—that Di had outfoxed her in the final moments of the game and would now be deified, something posterity may well deny Her Majesty—is a kind of behavior to which I cannot subscribe. I wish I could tell you that it's a manifestation of unquenchable ethical behavior, but to dig right down to the tap-root of it. . .I just have an embarrassingly low bullshit threshhold. I can't pull off the crocodile-tears thing.

So he died, and I wasn't happy he'd suffered, but I was not unhappy that he no longer walked the earth. I'm not going to go into even the smallest detail about what he did to me, because that would reveal of whom I'm speaking. (The mutual friend will know, but he's had me figured out since he was fourteen years old.) What I *will* say is this: what he did to me he did gratuitously, and it cost me. Cost me pretty much big-time, lost me friends, obliterated a valuable business liaison, held me up to ridicule. . .and here's the point of my relating all of this. . .he did it out of that fan-boy set of mind that is half slavering sycophancy and half vicious boiling-lava loathing. The behavior of *some* of y'all that makes this public commingling of ours so frequently murderous.

I never even knew what it had been, that had set this dude on me. Never had a clue what I'd done or said or maybe believed in, that turned him into a vengeful Fury, bent on making me look like a piece of shit. It wasn't until a couple of years ago that I had a casual conversation with the mutual friend, who told me that the guy had finally copped to the basis of his active antagonism for me. And I'll tell you what that worm of enmity was in just a moment, but as usual, we depart from our scheduled broadcast to bring you this chickenshit self-justification.

As best I can tell, after sixty-three years of. . .well. . .sixty-three years. . .it looks to me as if most people spend a lot of their time trying to be "well-liked" (in the words of Arthur Miller, out of Willy Loman's mouth). I can't fault the attitude, because it is certainly a lot easier plowing the field of one's life *without* enduring the rancor of those one encounters, than it is trying to get through the day's work while *also* having to duck and dodge the rain of arrows and the reign of the shit-rain.

But, as those of you who've run this race with me for many years know, I don't spend much time worrying about being "well-liked." (More on *that* concept of life at a somewhat later remove from these here-now comments.)

I learned very early on—right there in the playground of Lathrop Grade School—that unless you choose to be as bland and as invisible as Caspar Milquetoast, there is absolutely no way you're going to get through The Game without pissing someone off, without incurring some casual acquaintance's wrath, without making an enemy by the most innocent of misunderstandings.

It can't be done, because the world is full of assholes.

Now, look, we both know I'm not talking about you and I. You, me, the both of us, hell. . .we're as close to perfect as the mold could produce. It's all the *rest* of those jamooks. The idiots that put the soft stuff at the bottom of the grocery bag instead of on top; the creep who makes a right turn from the left lane and nearly collapses your lung; the tight-assed little pecksniff who tells you s/he would "love" to give you that loan, or remove that erroneous charge from your credit card bill, or let you have that extra muffin. . .but, well, he (or she) is just going by the rules, I'm truly sorry.

There are simply a greater number of *them* out there, for us to bump into every day, than there are of us—rational, fair-minded, decent and honest. Sad truth, but truth for alla that.

So, it's inevitable. We're going to fall in the path of some of these people all through our days. And some of them are going to spray Nazi graffiti on your wall, or key-slash the shiny surface of your new car, or write an anonymous note to your landlord telling him you're selling crack out of the apartment, or. . .

Well, you get where I'm going here.

You simply cannot escape the irrational who chug along in our midst, looking normal till you catch the psychotic gleam in their eyes, or until they run amuck, go postal, and shoot half the kindergarten class before offing themselves.

So I decided, long long ago, not to play The Game, not to pretend to an equanimity of nature that would allow such people to vent their animosity on me, while I pretended I was turning the other cheek. This guy, of whom I was speaking, dicked me; and he dicked me good. And I hated the muthuh. Not enough to travel cross-country, as I have done on several occasions, just to plant one on the creep, but enough to send him—every five years or so, over several decades—a Xerox copy of the piece he had caused to be published about me, with a one-line note that said: *Just to let you know I haven't forgotten*.

That was my way of getting even. It was the equivalent of the hang-nail or the perpetual runs, rather than the guillotine, which I reserve for those five or six of you out there Who Know Who You Are. And so, when he croaked, I felt well-rid of him, and I could not then, nor can I now, pretend to a false sorrow, which would make me look a lot better in your eyes, I know; but which I cannot even *pretend* to pull off. Because the guy dicked me, in a serious way, and after *years* it still ranked me.

And you know why he did it?

He did it—he told our mutual friend—because twenty years earlier, when he'd been a fan-boy, he'd gone to some comic-book or science-fiction convention, and I was a guest at the Big Do, and I'd been speaking on the lecture platform for about two hours, and I'd been signing books and stuff for another hour after that, and finally—as it comes to all men—I had to go to the bathroom. No, let me be more specific: I hadda take a piss. I was in anguish. And so I begged away from the crowd wanting autographs (mister big-time superstar) and motored as fast as I could toward the convention hall's facilities. On the way to the toilet, apparently, this now-dead guy, who was then a teenager, tried to get me to stop, to ask me a question or get me to sign a paperback or somedamnthing (who the hell can remember minuscule specificities after thirty, forty years?) and I blew him off. I may have been polite, I may have been brusque, I may have just blown past him without taking notice.

I have no memory of the encounter.

It was that fleeting an incident.

But this guy was honked at me. In his fucked-up head, here's how it played:

Who the hell d'you think you are, Mister big-time superstar? I'm as important as you! I bought your fuckin' book, didn't I? You *owe* me, I'm your audience! I made you who you are, if it weren't for me, you'd be out diggin' ditches! Who the hell do you think you are, ignoring me, treating me like shit? Well, fuck you, Mister Superfuck, I'll get even with you, if it takes me a million years.

Hell hath no fury like that of a fan-boy ignored.

And so, ten, twelve, fifteen, whatever, years later. . .he dicked me. And he did it big-time. So he's dead, and I cannot pretend to that disingenuous claptrap breast-beating that phony baloneys perform with such ease and regularity.

He was a part of the audience that is deadly, simply murderous. And that's what I want to talk about in this Introduction that will, fer shure, get me in hot water with you.

But not now. Now, I am in some physical pain, and I discover I cannot keep writing this Introduction to the inordinate length I usually do in these little get-togethers of ours. But I won't lie to you. I am simply unable to do it now. No serious problem, not another "coronary episode," and no problem floating the words. I'm just having a bad deadline crunch, I've got to be physically somewhere else and, startling as I am as a human dynamo, I haven't yet parsed how to be in two place at the same time. So I'm cutting this short. This will have to serve as unavoidable set-up, a prologue, if you will. Yes, I know you've grown fat and lazy expecting long, rambling, but incredibly incisive and ultimately brilliant, introductions. . .but *this* time (if I want to keep my sanity, make the printing deadline, and retain any degree of health that will permit me to write the *next* introduction) you'll have to settle for something over 2000 words. And I make you this simple promise:

I'll finish this one, and write a *second* one, at acceptable length, in Volume 5. So if you deign to honor me with your money and your presence in the next volume—which is a mere six months away as I write this today, on 12 September 1997—you will get what's coming to you.

Which is what the Introduction is all about, anyhow.

Getting what's coming to you.

Harlan Ellison / 15 Sept 1997
Los Angeles

"The gap between the public and the most advanced forms of art is eternal; but never before has the lowest common denominator been so enshrined, institutionalized, and popularized in its place, so widely disseminated and so skillfully sold on such a major scale."

Ada Louise Huxtable

THE UNREAL AMERICA:
ARCHITECTURE AND ILLUSION
(1997)

harlan ellison

edgeworks.4

love ain't nothing but sex misspelled

ACKNOWLEDGMENTS

The Author wishes to acknowledge the kindness and encouragement of Messrs. Ralph Weinstock, Bentley Morriss; Raymond F. Locke and Jared Rutter of *Knight* and *Cad* magazines; Paul Neimark; the late Hans Stefan Santesson; Damon Knight and Kate Wilhelm; Brian Kirby, formerly of the *Los Angeles Free Press* and *The Staff*; Arthur Kunkin, former publisher of the *Free Press*; G. Barry Golson of *Playboy*; and Frank M. Robinson, whose editorial and critical proclivities ran more toward giving the Author freedom than directing his words into acceptable channels. And to Andy Ettinger and Herb Alexander, formerly of Trident Press, who were not only critical but kind. And most particularly to my agents at the time, the late Robert P. Mills (in New York) and the still-with-us Marty Shapiro (in Hollywood), who refused to let the Author sell his birthright for a mess of pottage, and because of whose efforts this book became a wonderful reality for the Author who seldom knows what's good for him.

have always been matters of very special attention for me. I don't show auctorial respect and/oraffection casually. But time passes and things change, and sometimes those who were prominent in the loop, have gone long time away. Even so, a nod should be given to memory.

In 1968, the first edition of this book carried the following dedication:

> *"These are the Fates,*
> *daughters of Necessity. . .*
> *Lachesis singing of the*
> *past, Clotho of the present,*
> *Atropos of the future."*
>
> PLATO, *The Republic*

FOR SHERRI, WHO PICKED UP THE PIECES

Eight years later, in February of 1976, when it came time to revise this book for the updated paperback edition, I retained the Plato quote, and reconfigured the dedication thus:

FOR SHERRI, WHO PICKED UP THE PIECES.

FOR LESLIE KAY, WHO ARRANGES THE PIECES.

FOR LORI, WHO IS OPTING TO BE ONE OF THE PIECES.

It is now twenty-one years later, close on three decades since this book was first published. I've had one or two brief phone conversations with Sherri in the last twenty years; Lori is long gone and married to someone else, and one hopes she's happy and content; and Leslie Kay is still my long-time friend. I'm not going to recycle the dedications and add someone new. Let it stand, with a gentle smile for Clotho, Lachesis, and Atropos.

Harlan / 2 Aug 97

There is an inscription on the lintel over the octagonal portal to Ellison Wonderland. It says:

ALWAYS LOOK UP.
NEVER LOOK DOWN;
ALL YOU EVER SEE
ARE THE PENNIES
PEOPLE DROP.

There is a seven-headed dog guarding the octagonal portal to Ellison Wonderland. If you aren't nice, it will bite you in the ass.

LOVE AIN'T NOTHING BUT SEX MISSPELLED

KILIMANJARO IS A SNOW-COVERED MOUNTAIN 19,710 FEET HIGH, AND IS SAID TO BE THE HIGHEST MOUNTAIN IN AFRICA. ITS WESTERN SUMMIT IS CALLED THE MASAI "NGÀJE NGÀI," THE HOUSE OF GOD. CLOSE TO THE WESTERN SUMMIT THERE IS THE DRIED AND FROZEN CARCASS OF A LEOPARD. NO ONE HAS EXPLAINED WHAT THE LEOPARD WAS SEEKING AT THAT ALTITUDE.

THE SNOWS OF KILIMANJARO

BY ERNEST HEMINGWAY

INTRODUCTION

Having an Affair with a Troll

(Written in 1976)

One evening I met a young woman for whom I quickly developed carnal desires. We met at a party, I think. I don't remember now. It was a while ago. And I cut her out of the crowd and finally we got back to my house and it started to go wrong. Oh, not wrong in the way that once we were alone the sexual thing didn't seem to be working out: quite the contrary. She began getting misty-eyed. I could see that she was forming a fantasy view of the man who had swept her away to this strange and colorful eyrie. She was thinking ahead: *can this one be* THE *one I've been looking for?* And I didn't want that.

No point here in going into the *reason* I didn't want that; perhaps I was the wrong one for her on more than a casual basis, perhaps she was wrong for me permanently, perhaps it was a hundred different little things I sensed in the ambience of the evening. Whatever it was, I wanted to discourage the fantasy, but not the sexual liaison. I'm not sure there's anything wrong with that. But maybe there is. It depends where your concepts of morality lead you. For me, it was better to be upfront about it, to say *there's tonight, and maybe other nights, but under no circumstances is this permanent.*

And I tried to tell her, gently.

And *that* was wrong. Because it was hypocritical.

I wanted to have my picnic, but I didn't want to have to spend the time necessary to putting the picnic-grounds back in the same condition I'd found it.

(That isn't a casually conceived metaphor; and it's quite purposely not coarse in its comparisons. To love well and wisely, I now believe, we must attempt to leave a situation with a love-partner with the landscape and its inhabitants as well off, or better off, than they were when We arrived. Like this:

(Walter Huston and Tim Holt and Fred C. Dobbs [sometimes known as Humphrey Bogart] are about to leave the mountain from which they've clawed their gold. And Huston says to Holt and Bogart,

"We've got to spend a week putting the mountain back the way we found it." And Bogart looks amazed, because they are running the risk of being set upon once again by Alfonso Bedoya and his *bandidos*. So Huston explains very carefully that the mountain is a lady, and it has been good to them, and they have to close its wounds.

(And finally, even flinty, paranoid Bogart understands, and he agrees, and they spend a week repairing the ecological damage they've done to the mountain that was good to them.)

So instead of trying to weasel and worm my way through an explanation that would have been no real explanation at all, I asked her if she would mind my sitting down and writing something for her. She said that would be nice, and I did it, trying to say as bluntly as possible with fantasy images what words from the "real world" would not adequately say. And this is what I wrote:

> She looks at me with eyes blue as the snow on Fuji's summit in a woodblock print by Hiroshige. She says, "You're really different, really unique." Beneath the paleness of her cheeks the blood suddenly rushes and she only knows her nervousness has increased in the small room, though nothing has altered from the moment before. She does not understand that her skin and survival mechanisms have registered the presence of an alien creature. Her blood carries the certain knowledge. Like the sentient wind, she perceives only that she has crossed an invisible border and now roams naked and weaponless in a *terra incognita* where wolves assume the shapes of men and babies are born with golden glowing eyes and the sound from the stars is that of the very finest crystal.

To her fingertips come the vibrations of flowers singing in silent voices, telling of times before the watery deeps carried the seed of humanity. Her skin: absorbing the vibrations of unicorn's hooves as they beat the molten earth into gold. Her nostrils: bringing to her the scents of dreams being born. Her delicate nerve-endings: vital and trembling with expectation of oddness.

She sits with a troll, with another kind of creature, and her uneasiness grows. Cellular knowledge assaults her in wave after wave, and she cannot codify that knowledge.

"Let me tell you a story," I say, and in few words explain the horizons of the land into which she has wandered.

Will she understand that mortals and trolls cannot mate?

It didn't go well with her. It was a sour relationship from the start. I wound up doing her damage, hurting her; she didn't hurt me. I don't brag about it, I'm certainly not proud of it, there was no notch cut in the stock of the weapon from the encounter. *Machismo* wasn't part of it: I hurt her and she didn't hurt me only because it didn't mean as much to me. I was a hard thing. Colder. She was vulnerable. It had to happen, I suppose. If I'd been a nicer person I'd have forgone the sex and sent her away at the start. I explain it now, by way of justification, by saying she is a born victim: someone waiting to be savaged by love. But the truth is simply that I am precisely like everyone else when it comes to love. . .I am a child. I want my picnic, and I hate cleaning up the mess.

Pause. Go back to page **VIII** of this book, just before the beginning of this new introduction. Read the quote from Hemingway's "The Snows of Kilimanjaro." Do you know what it was the leopard was seeking? Do you understand why the creature climbed to that altitude and what happened to it? The answer to the riddle is the answer, I think, to understanding how to travel the road of love. I put the quote there, what has become a powerful literary metaphor since Hemingway first wrote it exactly forty years ago in 1936, because it seems to me to contain the truest thing one can know about traveling that difficult road. Friends of mine, around this house as I assemble this book for a publisher's deadline, don't seem to understand why that little parable, riddle, metaphor, whatever the hell it is, seems so eloquent, and so right for this book of kinda sorta love stories. I hope these words will clear it up for them. Probably not, though. I'm not too clear on this subject of love myself.

In fact, some years ago, when I was writing the introductions to the stories in an anthology I edited called DANGEROUS VISIONS, I found myself writing these words about myself and Theodore Sturgeon:

"It became clear to Sturgeon and myself that I knew virtually nothing about love but was totally familiar with hate, while Ted knew almost nothing about hate, yet was completely conversant with love in all its manifestations."

That was in 1966. Ten years ago. I've revised my estimates of both Ted's and my understandings of hate and love. It's been an interesting ten years for both of us, and if I were to take the toll today I'd have to admit grudgingly that I've had some of the parameters of the equation of love drilled into me by experts. And so now, ten years later, I set down these first few tentative thoughts about the subject, offering as credentials the stories in this collection.

I can tell you many things love is *not*. Telling you what it *is* comes much harder to me. When one feels like a novice, it becomes an act of arrogance to pontificate. Much of what I think changes from day to day. And I suppose by the accepted standards of success, I'm a poor spokesman. It seems the more experience I get, the less sure I become about anything where love is concerned. (I'm not talking about my three marriages and divorces. That's another thing, and peculiarly, it has less to do with my caution about this subject than more "informal" relationships.)

Lori and I were talking about this several weeks ago, and with what I take to be the normal curiosity of anyone merging his or her life with someone else's, she asked me how many women I'd been with. For a few days I wouldn't answer her. I wasn't hiding anything, I just didn't think she'd care to hear the real answer. Finally, I told her. "I tried to count up, one time about six years ago," I said. "And I used snapshots and correspondence and phone lists I found lying around in old files and desk drawers, and I had to stop when it got over three hundred. I suppose I've been to bed with maybe five hundred different women."

She didn't say anything for a long while, but I could see she was shocked. When I'd tried to take the tally half a dozen years ago, I'd been shocked, too.

I realize there will be guys out there who'll read that figure—five hundred—which I think is pretty accurate, and they'll react in one of several different ways. There will be assholes who'll think that's pretty terrific. There will be amateur Freudians who'll think it's sick. There will be professional sympathizers who'll feel sorry for me. There will be guys who can't get laid who'll think I'm lying, trying to trumpet some kind of bogus swashbuckler image.

Each view has some validity going for it.

But mostly, since I went *through* all those days and nights and people, since I was *there* (or as much of me as I had control of was there), I subscribe to the view that I was looking for something very hard, perhaps with uncommon desperation. I think I understand the psychological reasons I was on that endless hunt, and I submit there was less of deviation, perversion or obsession than of loneliness and a determination to find answers. I'm constantly perplexed at the dichotomous position of people who laud a student's seeking everywhere to find the answers to life, or creativity, or the existence of God, or the direction of the student's career. . .who cluck their tongues and badrap the same attempts to discover the answers to interpersonal relationships by those who seek in every area that presents itself. If the true purpose of living a fulfilled life is in establishing meaningful liaisons with people, if it's part of that fulfillment to seek and find and give and accept love, then why should the search be looked on with such moral disapproval?

Perhaps I'm advocating profligacy, but I don't think so. Discovering the nature of love is infinitely more complex and exhausting than, for instance, learning how to be a brain surgeon. But the smug, self-satisfied moralists think it's precise and proper for someone to spend fifteen years learning how to ease a subdural hematoma, yet twisted, sick and sad for someone to spend the same fifteen years learning how to ease his or her loneliness. Answers to the former can be found in medical textbooks and in O.R.s all over the world; answers to the latter slide and skitter and avoid discovery save by chance and steady application to all possibilities.

The search is as important as the discovery.

(And therein lies the core of the answer to Hemingway's riddle about the leopard.)

Lori seems to feel as I write this, that even if I don't have the answers, at least I've had a greater opportunity to *find* the answers than those who deny the search, settle for whatever's handiest, and then spend the rest of their lives with secret thoughts and open frustration.

On the basis of her view, and the fact that I trust her opinions most of the time, I'm plunging ahead with this essay on love. I hope to God she's right. If she's wrong, and I've been merely a profligate, indulging myself in adolescent sex-antics, I'm going to look like a righteous *shmuck* by the time this introduction is completed. If I don't already.

Ambrose Bierce has two definitions of "love" in THE ENLARGED DEVIL'S DICTIONARY (Doubleday, 1967, and a sensational book). Bierce, a cynic beside whom *I* look like Pollyanna, writes this:

> **Love**, *n*. The folly of thinking much of another before one knows anything of oneself.

> **Love**, *n.* A temporary insanity curable by marriage or by removal of the patient from the influences under which he incurred the disorder. This disease, like caries and many other ailments, is prevalent only among civilized races living under artificial conditions; barbarous nations breathing pure air and eating simple food enjoy immunity from its ravages. It is sometimes fatal, but more frequently to the physician than to the patient.

People reading my books, most particularly the introductions *in* my books, think I am the reincarnation of Bierce: that I am a mean, pugnacious, constantly depressed or alarmed sonofabitch into whose life the sunshine of affection has never cast its effulgent glow. Fuck you, I say politely.

Even the most drooling of the Jukes or the Kallikaks* should be able to perceive that someone who manifests such volatile feelings about injustice, racism, stupidity, mediocrity and general negative bullshit in the Universe has his times of joy and happiness and noble

* In my ongoing efforts not only to entertain but also to uplift my readers, this note about the Jukes and the Kallikaks. Many of you may have wondered where the word "jukebox" came from. Many of you may not. For those who *have* wondered, be advised "Jukes" was a fictitious family name used in THE JUKES: *A Study in Crime, Pauperism, Disease and Heredity* (1877), on the life histories of the descendants of a family of sisters who lived in New York, written for a prison association. It is now a common-coin term used to indicate those of low mentality; and because of the often less-than-ennobling music to emanate from Wurlitzers and Rock-Olas ("Sugar, Sugar" / "Yummy, Yummy, Yummy, I've Got Love in My Tummy" / "How Much is That Doggie in the Window?" / "Mairzy Doates" / "Fwee Widdle Fishies" / and "Run, Joey, Run" surge instantly to mind), the term came to be applied generically to coin-operated phonographs in public places. There are those who contend the word "juke"' comes from jute, the fiber used for cordage and binding, and by vulgarization to have been first applied to the drinking and dancing places in the Southern U.S. where field workers went to relax; thus, "juke joints." Since juke joints played music, and juke boxes were found there long before they became omnipresent in every roadside restaurant and roadhouse, the term slopped over onto the music machine itself. I prefer my etymological derivation. Nonetheless, the reason for this footnote originally was to make a subtle point about the name Kallikak, which is usually used, erroneously, as meaning the same as Juke. "Kallikak" was, again, a fictitious name used in a sociological study of a New Jersey family of which one branch was predominantly intelligent and successful, another subnormal and prone to crime. Used without this distinction being made, as a label meaning persons of low mentality, it is inaccurate. So when I referred to drooling Jukes and Kallikaks earlier, I meant the *drooling* ones, not the ones whom I might one day meet in the audience of some college lecture I'd been giving, who would stand up with a Remington XP-100, scream, "You maligned my family, you muthuh-fuckuh!" and blow me in half. Does that explain why I've taken this seemingly pointless digression? No? Well, I wouldn't be so goddam paranoid if all you creeps weren't after me!

dreams that soar aloft as one with the greatest aspirations of the human race. Those who read my works and remember only the stories and essays that deal with blood, lust, violence, death, disfigurement, pain, depression, smarmy sex and ka-ka do me a disservice. Also, they are sick and ought to be "put away," if you catch my drift. I have written dozens and dozens of kind, gentle, happy, funny stories and introductions. But do they remember *those*? Do they? Huh, I ask you, *do* they!?! Not on your cryogenic crypt, they don't! All they remember are stories such as "I Have No Mouth, and I Must Scream" or "The Prowler in the City at the Edge of the World." All they recall when my work is mentioned are the shrieks of torment coming from my characters.

When the truth of the matter is that I'm basically a *very* happy fellow. Funny, too. I adore small children, dogs of all breeds, *Barney Miller* and Richard Pryor and George Carlin and *M*A*S*H*, noodles, the humorous novels of Donald Westlake. (Noodles have always seemed hilarious to me, go figure it.) For instance, I got a letter today from Debe (No Last Name Given) at Millikin University in Decatur, Illinois; and she went on you wouldn't *believe* about being a fan of my writing, but how disturbing it all was, how I always seem to write sad or mean stuff. "Is there another side?" she asked. "We all have our demons. But tell me more of you. You must have some light, some happiness, something good that you cherish?"

Now, see! There you go. A perfect example. Here's this young woman (I presume she's fairly young from the writing and the content) who encounters me in a series of books and gets all grunched out of shape because she thinks I'm downcast, and she wants me to spill the beans on myself, to tell her what makes me smile and laugh and love.

And apart from wanting to keep *some* personal feelings to myself—Gawd, you're a greedy bunch, no matter how much I blather and reveal, you're never satisfied—the things I *do* unleash are frequently as happy as they are miserable. But when I try to look on the bright side, and pass along the lucent limbus of my personal joy, everyone who remembers those screams of anguish comes down on me like a *tsunami*, accusing me of being maudlin and saccharine.

So if the observations I make about love seem just a tot on the pragmatic, even cynical, side. . .well, it's purely an attempt to walk the tightrope: to indulge an uncommon (to my readers) softness of spirit without spastically lurching into a hideous rigadoon of wretched and nauseating mawkishness; to be as tough-minded as possible (and thereby as useful as possible) about something as worrisome and intangible as love, without sounding bruised or discouraged; to avoid cliché without purposely bumbling about like a boob in the glades of perversion.

So I have consciously eschewed "diary" or "reminiscence" and shunted my observations over into fiction. It's in the story-form that I feel most at ease writing my views of love. Unless one is Shelley, a Nuñez de Arce or La Rochefoucauld, one has no business publicly shooting off one's mouth about something as mysterious and ethereal as love. Unless one is *le* Marquis de Sade, in which case one has a personal vision of love that defies all strictures.

But in fiction, even a groping dullard like myself can stumble upon a truth or two; or at least a rule-of-thumb that seems to work in certain situations, among certain kinds of people. So when I pass along these remarks, I'll try and couch them in anecdotal terms, all the better to entertain you, my dears, and not coincidentally to alleviate my own nervousness in this area.

So here is just about all I know concerning love. Some of it light and happy, some of it cynical, perhaps some of it even accurate and truthful. One never know, do one.

The minute people fall in love, they become liars.

You'd think such good feelings in the gut and other places would make people want to ensure the continuance of those feelings. But their fears overcome their good sense, not to mention their ethics. They begin to lie, virtually from the first moment they feel the stirrings in the aorta. . .or wherever it is love is supposed to make itself felt.

They lie in a hundred different ways. From the first tentative social conversations that bore them silly, they lie by pretending to be interested in inanities. This is a generality, but I think it holds: if it's guys, they listen to banal bullshit just on the off-chance they'll get laid. If it's women, they listen to the blown-out-of-proportion nonsense of men so they can reinforce the guy's need to be a Big Man. They lie to one another with looks and with words, and only the body-language tells the truth.

They lie to keep the upper hand, even before they're threatened. The fear of rejection is so ingrained, from the schoolyard, from the locker room, from the parties, from the Homecoming Dance, from the years of seeing lithe tanned women in bikinis and feral muscular men with shirts open to the sternum up there on four-color billboards; they fear the unknown outer darkness of someone saying, "No."

So they lie to one another. Granted, it's akin to the social lying we all do at parties, in restaurants, at social events: putting up with trivia to be politic or civilized or "gracious," whatever that means. Nonetheless, it is lying. And by feigning interest in that which bores or turns one off, they set up artificial grounds for a potential relationship that they have to maintain all through the rest of the association. I know a young woman who met a guy at a party. He turned her on, and he started voicing some of his rustic views on busing. She had worked for the integration legislation as a regional attaché to one of the senators pushing the facilitation of busing. She came out of ten years of hard and thankless work trying to achieve racial balance. He was a divorced businessman with two kids, who was, at heart, a man who feared and hated blacks. Though he would have gone to his grave swearing there wasn't a scintilla of bigotry in his well-clothed body. But they turned each other on, and she listened and nodded, and said nothing. They started dating. It lasted six months. Then it fell apart. When his narrow view of the world became too much for her, she started to fight back. Now he tells everyone she was a "castrating bitch" and she harbors guilt feelings for her own intransigence. False and untenable rules for the relationship had been the order of their mating from the git-go. It was doomed to fail.

Earlier, I passed along a generality. There are, of course, exceptions. There are women who listen to the crapola put out by guys at parties because *they* want to get laid, and there are guys who put up with women's inanities because they want to be polite. It happens. But the point still holds. They do it because they want to be liked. They lie and listen to lies so they'll be accepted. The first faint stirrings of love—barely codified, still inarticulate—force them into the role of liar.

And then the lies, once having been freed from Pandora's Hope Chest, begin to breed. They multiply like maggots and riddle a relationship like a submarine hit by a depth charge. Consider just the most obvious ones we've all either used or been victimized by:

You walk into a room and she (or he) is brooding.

"What's the matter, something wrong, something bothering you?" That's what you say.

Then he (or she) replies, "Nothing."

A lie, a bald-faced lie. You know damned well there's something wrong. The way the legs are crossed, the way the arms are folded, that telltale pursing of the lips, the vacant, abstracted stare, the peremptory way the words are bitten off. There's *something* wrong. But she (or he) says, "Nothing."

Is it because the brooding party really *has* something heavy to brood about and, out of love, chooses to lie rather than to lay it on the other person? Is it (more likely) that the brooder has been brought down by something the other party did, and wants to whip a little unconscious, free-floating guilt on the perpetrator before spilling the load of shit being carried in the gut? Is it part of the stylized ritual of hide-and-seek so many lovers play? Is it a physical manifestation of the brooding party's having done something they mutually consider "wrong" (like going out and getting laid on the sly), and getting him or herself set to rationalize it in such a way that the other member of the team feels like the criminal, using the brooding dark mood as a kind of head start in the argument that will follow?

What does it matter? What we're dealing with here is dishonesty, cupidity, misdirection, acting-out. . .lying.

Here's another one. And you've *all* been on one or the other end of *this* one:

"No, I have a headache."

"No, I'm tired."

"No, I'm a little inflamed."

"No, I have a hard day tomorrow."

"No, it isn't right."

"No, I'm still in love with [fill in appropriate name]."

Now *none* of those oldies but goodies is being spoken by a man or woman on a first date. I'm talking about their use in an already ongoing relationship. But a relationship in which one of the partners has been turned off, and won't cop to it! So he or she lies. Again and again and again. Instead of simply saying, "You have bad breath," or "I'm not sexually turned on by you any more," the lies are ranked like MIRV missiles and fired off, one each time an enemy approach is sighted.

Here's another one. Before they met, he was attracted to medium-height, auburn-haired females between the ages of seventeen and twenty-eight with high conical breasts and very thin legs. She was attracted to guys with tight little asses and an almost total absence of chest and arm hair; guys with blue eyes and heavy torsos and English accents and thin, aquiline noses. But one time he made the error of going on admiringly about one of those fantasy-women just a few seconds too long, as they sat there watching the hair-coloring commercial in which the woman appeared, and she got extremely uptight. And one time *she* made the error of spending a half-hour in a corner at a party talking to a guy just like the kind she lubricated for, and *he* (her boy friend) went into a towering Sicilian *machismo* rage about her flirting.

So now, they purposely turn away from the somatotypes that attract them, when they're out driving, when they're walking in the shopping mall, when they go to the movies, when they spend an evening at the bowling alley, when the tv camera pans across the bleachers at the football game, when they're at a party. She'll test him by drawing his attention to a girl he's already clocked and turned away from, by saying, "Do you think she's attractive?" And he'll glance over quickly, and with feigned disinterest mumble, "Legs're too skinny." But he has a stack of beaver magazines hidden away in his work bench, each magazine containing 372 unretouched shots of girls *just* like the one he dismissed. He'll test *her* by introducing her to a guy at the office party who fits her secret sex fantasies, and later asking, "What'd you think of Ken?" And she'll go right on basting the roast or drawing up the blueprints for the new museum wing or finishing the sketches for that children's book, and she won't even look up as she says, "He's nice enough, I suppose. Not very bright, though, is he?" But half the time when she's fucking *him*, she's envisioning Ken.

These are only a few. There are others, many others. Add your own at leisure. Talk it over with your mate or love-partner. See if you can get further examples to convince yourself that what I'm talking about here is hypocrisy and fear, not standards of sexual conduct. What I'm talking about is the title of this book: love ain't nothing but sex misspelled. The perversion of sex in the name of love, using two quite clearly separable needs as reinforcements of one another, because you're not secure enough in either to think they stand by themselves and take care of themselves and enrich through their separate powers. The perversion of love to obtain sex as a commodity. The lies that are told because honesty might well mean rejection. And the unbelievably crippling fear of rejection that moves most of us more than we care to admit. Thus doth love make liars of us all.

An obnoxious woman is a strong man's "limp."

(I'm sure there's a reverse to this, as seen from the viewpoint of a woman; but being a man, I'm most familiar with this side of it. You'll forgive me if I report this section only from what I know, even if it is one-sided. Female readers can mentally write an addendum in which they project what I'm about to say for the flip-side.)

Here's this really sensational sweet guy. He's gentle, fair, moderately talented, seems to be happy with his life and what he's doing; and he's involved with a woman who is a righteous phony. She's loud, she drinks too much, she's a fucking pain in the ass at a dinner table: name dropping, interrupting, belittling him in front of his friends, cutting the other women who try to show some warmth to the guy because they're embarrassed for him, interrupting everyone, rearranging the environment to suit herself ("I have to sit here, not there". . ."Would you ask the *maître d'* to lower the air conditioning". . ."There's absolutely *nothing* on this menu, would you ask the waiter if they can find me an abalone steak". . ."Sid, would you mind not smoking, I washed my hair this afternoon").

And you ask yourself, how can this terrific guy hang out with such a creep?

(It occurs to me that the reverse, a sensational woman tied to a *shmuck* guy, is more clearly changing these days. The incidence of women splitting from their husbands, initiating divorce or dissolution of a living-together situation, is very much on the rise. Female-initiated divorces have risen in this country alone by three times what they were even fifteen years ago. Now it's the men who try to hang in there with a lousy relationship while the women, I suppose because of widespread consciousness-raising that has advised them it's *feasible* to break up without social stigmatization, are taking off. But that's just a guess.)

I've fiddled around with trying to come up logical on this one, finding some kind of Universal Truth why strong people should harness themselves to albatrosses, but this is one of those aspects of love that I've seen again and again, and every time it's for a different reason. In one case it was that the guy wasn't sufficiently secure in his ego-strength, sufficiently filled with feelings of his worthiness to love and be loved in return. In another case it was because the woman was devoted to the guy in private, absolutely revolved around him. In yet another case the guy felt guilt about how he and his woman had gotten together, and he hung in there because he was paying dues.

Lori shrugs and says, "Love is blind."

Maybe that's the best answer. I don't know. It's one of those troublesome areas that defies pat answers.

All I know for sure is that there are many, many women and men who are hanging out—because of "love"—with partners who are clearly their inferiors.

Shit, maybe it's that one of the selfish aspects of love is that we be able to feel we're the dominant love-partner in the link-up. I don't know. Think about it; maybe you can write a critical study, then we'll both know.

Love weakens as much as it strengthens, and often that's very good for you.

The operable part of that aphorism is that vulnerability is a good and enlarging thing. When you fall in love, you start to need. For people whose self-sufficiency or fears of life have made them encysted creatures, love opens them.

For instance, the other day Lori and I were talking about what a prick I am when someone tries to chop me conversationally. Being a "fast gun" in a verbal encounter has always been a stance I believed to be extremely pro-survival. There aren't too many people who have as vicious and insulting a manner as I can manifest when I'm annoyed. That's because in some ways I'm conversationally suicidal: I'll say anything. There are no bounds to how deeply I'll cut to win. That's simultaneously one of my strengths and one of my weaknesses. I won't go into how it got started, it goes 'way back. I'll just say that it makes me a very enclosed individual a lot of the time. I'm constantly on the alert for the attack.

So Lori put forth the proposition that I was stronger than she in such situations, and I said, "No, we're evenly matched." And then she said, with considerable disbelief, "But you could cut me up in a minute and we both know it."

Which led me to think about it and I responded, "Then why don't I?"

"Because you love me," she said.

"Right," I said.

Then she grinned and made the perfect point. "You're handicapped."

Right!

Willingly, gladly, joyously handicapped. A mercurial sprinter happily tying a bag of cement to his left leg so he can race with fairness to the competition, because he loves the race, not the winning.

Love can do that. It can make you dull those savage aspects of your nature so you become more nakedly ready to accept goodness from your love-partner. It is even *more* pro-survival, if one accepts the theory that life is a string of boredoms, getting-alongs, sadnesses and just plain nothing-happening times, broken up by gleaming pearls of happiness that get us through the crummy stretches on that string.

Weakness becomes strength.

After you've had the Ultimate Love Affair that has broken you, leaves you certain love has been poisoned in your system, then, and only then, can you be saved and uplifted by the Post-Ultimate Love Affair.

Because that's when you're most uncertain, most self-doubting, most locked into a tunnel vision of love and life. And that's when new experiences come out of nowhere to wham you.

I guess this ties in with what I was saying about pain in the introduction to PAINGOD and about how we cannot savor the full wonder of joy unless we've gone through some exhausting, debilitating times of anguish. No one *likes* pain (and please be advised I'm *not* advocating S-M or any of the torture-games some people need to get them off; I'm talking about life-situation pain; enemas and *shtupping* amputees and whips 'n' chains may be superfine for *Penthouse* and other sources of communication for those who're into such things, but I'm not, and so when I talk about pain I mean getting your brain busted, not your body shackled; okay?) but it seems to me that we spend so much time *avoiding* pain of even the mildest sort, that we turn ourselves into mollusks. To love, I think, one must be prepared to get clipped on the jaw occasionally.

Otherwise, one would always settle for the safest, least demanding, least challenging relationship. Wouldn't we?

I think that makes sense.

And so, having been destroyed by an affair, knowing one has had the Ultimate Love, one wanders lost and broken in a new place. And then, from out of nowhere—and I've seen it happen time and again—comes this whirlwind that sweeps you up and carries you along, and three, four, five months later you realize it isn't a rebound affair, it's the

Post-Ultimate Affair, and you're whole again, and stronger than ever.

So go find the greatest love of your life, the one that burns and sizzles and chars everything around it, and fling yourself into it like a child in a playground. Drain all you can from it, and then get your back broken. Suffer and stumble around and weep and piss and moan. And then look out! Because here comes The Lone Ranger or Wonder Woman, ready to make it all good again. . . and this time probably for keeps.

Here are a few more things about love I think work.

Friendship is better than passion.

As Richard Shorr says, if you can say to your partner, even when you hate him or her the most, I wish you well, then you've got a chance to make it. Lust works wonders, it puts apples in your cheeks (and sometimes crabs in your bed), but it ebbs and flows. Friendship sustains and enriches and stays constant.

Hate and love have the same intensity of emotion.

Hate ain't nothing but love misspelled.

But you know that one already.

You can't go home again.

If you were sweethearts after college, and had a thing going, and one or the other of you took off and did your number and it went sour—the marriage dissolved, the career didn't materialize, discovering yourself turned out to be a drag filled with Tantric Yoga and Kahlil Gibran platitudes—and you fantasize what it would've been like if you'd stuck with that Great Love of Your Youth. . .forget it. He's changed, she's changed, you've changed, and the best you can have is a quick fuck and a lot of recycled memories. It just doesn't play.

Next to telling your lover what turns you on precisely, the best thing to bring to bed is a sense of humor.

Nothing is more tiresome and capable of creating tension in bed than heavy breathing *el serioso*. God save us from the men and women who need to hear all the artificial "I love you" jingoism, even when they know it's bullshit, said at the moment and having substance no longer than it takes to use a Kleenex and dash to the shower. But laughter, taking the hangups and inconveniences and wonky awkwardnesses as sources of mirth. . .wow, how bright that can make it.

Please yourself and be selfish about it.

In love and sex, it's every man and woman in a one-person life raft. If you don't go'n'get it, no one'll stake you to a free ride. Concern for each other goes without saying, and attention to detail; but when it comes right down to it, you've got to satisfy yourself. If the guy ain't doing it right, lady, bite his nose and tell him *how* to do it. And if you've got a premature problem, fella, let her know about it before the fact so arrangements can be made. And don't clutter up your pleasure by swallowing that outdated nonsense about, "Oh, it seems too clinical that way; it takes all the romance out of it." Romance is one of those ephemerals they whip on you so you won't know that sex is *supposed* to be sweaty!

And finally: *love ain't nothing but sex misspelled.*

Which is an ironic title. It means people confuse one for the other. They think passion alone makes love. And so the relationship flares while they explore each other's bodies, and when it's gone, so is their affection for one another.

Love is being utterly honest, even when it's ground-glass painful. Tell the truth *all* the time! All the truth! Not just that part that you can get away with. Go the limit. And the answer to Hemingway's riddle is that the leopard lost his way. He took the wrong path. And that's what so many of us do in love.

Keep aware, keep wide open, and remember everything that's ever happened to you, everything that's ever been said, every motion and change of tone and subtle hint. We'll read a long, essentially dull book on how to get through probate with our skin intact, or take a correspondence course in electrical wiring just so we don't have to pay an electrician to do our house, or go to college for four years to acquire the obscure knowledge that will permit us to make a living in one or another proscribed field of endeavor. But about the most mysterious subject of all, love, we bumble and careen and hope for the best; without proper education, without proper tools, without even a goal that can be named. And more often than not it poisons our lives. The wrong men and the wrong women get together and proceed to kill each other piece by piece.

This is all I know of love: like the leopard we must pick the right path, and we must never confuse what the body needs with what the soul demands. Beyond these idle thoughts, I know no more than you.

As a troll, as an alien creature, I know that having an affair with me is not the same as having an affair with an orthodontist or a salesman of mobile homes or a guy going for his degree in P.E. That's my arrogance.

I hope to god you have yours.

Final words about this book.

In the original edition of LOVE AIN'T NOTHING BUT SEX MISSPELLED, published in hardcover in 1968, there were twenty-two stories. For the revised paperback edition in 1976, I dropped nine of those stories. They were (and are) good stories. . .and some of them I consider among my best. But they are either currently available elsewhere in one or another of the EDGEWORKS series, or in other books of mine currently in print. Twenty years ago, I became highly sensitive to one reader's random remark about duplications of stories in my collections. And so I have taken extra-special pains to make sure there are **no** duplications in these new EDGEWORKS editions.

In '76 I added three new, then-uncollected pieces to the thirteen from the original version of this book. Usually, a short story collection bulks out at about 60,000 words. LOVE, first time around, came to 165,300 words, almost the equivalent of three books. I've deleted

51,900 words of stories and added 21,400 to the remaining 115,400 words' worth of material from the hardcover. That makes a total of 136,800 words of stories, plus this introduction of approximately 8500 words, for your money's worth of 145,300. Something well over two ordinary collections' size. And no room for complaints from those who've bought my other books.

And since there were three minor duplications of items on the 1976 table of contents in *this* 1997 edition, I bounced *them* (two are in EDGEWORKS, Volume 3. . .in THE HARLAN ELLISON HORNBOOK) (the third one will be found in GENTLEMAN JUNKIE *and Other Stories of the Hung-Up Generation,* one of the two titles to appear in EDGEWORKS, Volume 11, scheduled for publication in May of the year 2001; patience, I commend thee to patience!) and I've added a previously uncollected story for which I have great fondness—"Passport"—and I've even revised it strenuously. Also, I've added a new, previously unpublished teleplay based on a short story to appear in EDGEWORKS, Volume 7, in May of 1999. And you thought we were just a flash in the pan!

Now: to the underlying theme of these wry fictions. There *is* a theme, *pace* the title of the book. A few of these tales may seem to you less thematic than others. Oh, cynical you. "Blind Bird, Blind Bird, Go Away from Me!" (for instance) is a war story, and I suppose might easily have gone into another sort of collection. But I intended this book to cover a *broad* spectrum on the subject of love; and friendship, a sense of duty, love of those who depend on you. . .that's love, too. As is the love-turned-to hate demonstrated in one of the new pieces, "Moonlighting," and "The Universe of Robert Blake" (not the actor, though we're friends and I probably used the name unconsciously years before we met) and "A Prayer for No One's Enemy." These are all stories peripherally concerned with love, and they are included here because this book was, and remains, one of my personal favorites. And each tale to be told reflects another part of my fumbling attempts to understand the mystery of love.

These stories have helped change my opinion of myself where human knowledge is concerned. They total over 145,000 words of groping in the dark to find the answer.

For a troll, groping in the dark is second nature.

Here's hoping they shed a little light.

Harlan Ellison
Los Angeles
12 September 75 and
2 August 97

INTRODUCTION TO THE FIRST EDITION

The Introduction to the first edition was dumb, and I've dropped it. You wouldn't have liked it, anyway. Trust me.

THE RESURGENCE OF MISS ANKLE-STRAP WEDGIE

(DEDICATED TO THE MEMORY OF DOROTHY PARKER)

HANDY

In Hollywood our past is so transitory we have little hesitation about tearing down our landmarks. The Garden of Allah where Benchley and Scott Fitzgerald lived is gone; it's been replaced by a savings and loan. Most of the old, sprawling 20th lot has been converted into shopping center and beehive-faceted superhotel. Even historic relics of fairly recent vintage have gone under the cultural knife: the Ziv television studios on Santa Monica, once having been closed down, became the eerie, somehow surrealistic, weed-overgrown and bizarre jungle in which tamed cats that had roamed sound stages became cannibals, eating one another. At night, passing the studio, dark and padlocked, you could hear the poor beasts tearing each other apart. They had lived off the film industry too long, and unable to survive in the streets, lost and bewildered, they had turned into predators.

That may be an apocryphal story. It persists in my thoughts when I remember Valerie Lone.

The point is, we turn the past into the present here in Hollywood even before it's finished being the future. It's like throwing a meal into the Disposall before you eat it.

But we do have one recently erected monument here in the glamour capital of the world.

It is a twenty-three-foot-high billboard for a film called *Subterfuge*. It is a lighthearted adventure-romance in the James Bond tradition and the billboard shows the principal leads—Robert Mitchum and Gina Lollobrigida—in high-fashion postures intended to convey, well, adventure and, uh, romance.

The major credits are listed in smaller print on this billboard: produced by Arthur Crewes, directed by James Kencannon, written by John D.F. Black, music by Lalo Schifrin. The balance of the cast is there, also. At the end of the supplementary credits is a boxed line that reads:

ALSO FEATURING MISS VALERIE LONE as Angela.

This line is difficult to read; it has been whited-out.

The billboard stands on a rise overlooking Sunset Boulevard on the Strip near King's Road; close by a teenie-bopper discothèque called Spectrum 2000 that once was glamorous Ciro's. But we tear down our past and convert it to the needs of the moment. The billboard will come down. When the film ends its first run at the Egyptian and opens in neighborhood theaters and drive-ins near you.

At which point even *that* monument to Valerie Lone will have been removed, and almost all of us can proceed to forget. Almost all of us, but not all. I've got to remember. . .my name is Fred Handy. I'm responsible for that billboard. Which makes me a singular man, believe me.

After all, there are so few men who have erected monuments to the objects of their homicide.

1

They came out of the darkness that was a tunnel with a highway at the bottom of it. The headlights were animal eyes miles away down the flat roadbed, and slowly slowly the sound of the engine grew across the emptiness on both sides of the concrete. California desert night, heat of the long day sunk just below the surface of the land, and a car, ponderous, plunging, straight out of nowhere along a white centerline. Gophers and rabbits bounded across the deadly open road and were gone forever.

Inside the limousine men dozed in jump seats and far in the rear two bull-necked cameramen discussed the day's work. Beside the driver, Fred Handy stared straight ahead at the endless stretch of State Highway 14 out of Mojave. He had been under the influence of road hypnosis for the better part of twenty minutes, and did not know it. The voice from the secondary seats behind him jarred him back to awareness. It was Kencannon.

"Jim, how long till we hit Lancaster or Palmdale?"

The driver craned his head back and slightly to the side, awkwardly, like some big bird, keeping his eyes on the road. "Maybe another twenty, twenty-five miles, Mr. K'ncannon. That was Rosamond we passed little while ago."

"Let's stop and eat at the first clean place we see," the director said, thumbing his eyes to remove the sleep from them. "I'm starving."

There was vague movement from the third seats, where Arthur Crewes was folded sidewise, fetuslike, sleeping. A mumbled, "Where are we what time izit?"

Handy turned around. "It's about three forty-five, Arthur. Middle of the desert."

"Midway between Mojave and Lancaster, Mr. Crewes," the driver added. Crewes grunted acceptance of it.

The producer sat up in sections, swinging his legs down heavily, pulling his body erect sluggishly, cracking his shoulders back as he arched forward. With his eyes closed. "Jeezus, remind me next time to do a picture without location shooting. I'm too old for this crap." There was the murmur of trained laughter from somewhere in the limousine.

Handy thought of Mitchum, who had returned from the Mojave location earlier that day, riding back in the air-conditioned land cruiser the studio provided. But the thought only reminded him that he was not one of the Immortals, one of the golden people; that he was merely a two-fifty-a-week publicist who was having one helluva time trying to figure out a promotional angle for just another addle-witted spy-romance. Crewes had come to the genre belatedly, after the Bond flicks, after *Ipcress*, after *Arabesque* and *Masquerade* and *Kaleidoscope* and *Flint* and *Modesty Blaise* and they'd all come after *The 39 Steps* so what the hell did it matter; with Arthur Crewes producing, it would get serious attention and good play dates. *If*. If Fred Handy could figure out a Joe Levine William Castle Sam Katzman Alfred Hitchcock *shtick* to pull the suckers in off the streets. He longed for the days back in New York when he had had ulcers working in the agency. He still had them, but the difference was *now* he couldn't even *pretend* to be enjoying life enough to compensate for the aggravation. He longed for the days of his youth writing imbecile poetry in Figaro's in the Village. He longed for the faintly moist body of Julie, away in the Midwest somewhere doing *Hello, Dolly!* on the strawhat circuit. He longed for a hot bath to leach all the weariness out of him. He longed for a hot bath to clean all the Mojave dust and grit out of his pores.

He longed *desperately* for something to eat.

"Hey, Jim, how about that over there. . .?"

He tapped the driver on the forearm, and pointed down the highway to the neon flickering off and on at the roadside. The sign said SHIVEY'S TRUCK STOP and EAT. There were no trucks parked in front.

"It must be good food," Kencannon said from behind him. "I don't see any trucks there; and you know what kind of food you get at the joints truckers eat at."

Handy smiled quickly at the reversal of the old road-runner's myth. It was that roundabout sense of humor that made Kencannon's direction so individual.

"That okay by you, Mr. Crewes?" Jim asked.

"Fine, Jim," Arthur Crewes said, wearily.

The studio limousine turned in at the diner and crunched gravel. The diner was an anachronism. One of the old railroad-car style, seen most frequently on the New Jersey thruways. Aluminum hide leprous with rust. Train windows fogged with dirt. Lucky Strike and El Producto decals on the door. Three steps up to the door atop a concrete stoop.

Parking lot surrounding it like a gray pebble lake, cadaverously cold in the intermittent flashing of the pale yellow neon EAT off EAT off EAT. . .

The limousine doors opened, all six of them, and ten crumpled men emerged, stretched, trekked toward the diner. They fell into line almost according to the pecking order. Crewes and Kencannon; Fred Handy; the two cameramen; three grips; the effeminate makeup man, Sancher; and Jim, the driver.

They climbed the stairs, murmuring to themselves, like sluggish animals emerging from a dead sea of sleep. The day had been exhausting. Chase scenes through the rural town of Mojave. And Mitchum in his goddam land cruiser, phoning ahead to have *escargots* ready at La Rue.

The diner was bright inside, and the grips, the cameramen and Jim took booths alongside the smoked windows. Sancher went immediately to the toilet, to moisten himself with 5-Day Deodorant Pads. Crewes sat at the counter with Handy and Kencannon on either side of him. The producer looked ancient. He was a dapper man in his middle forties. He clasped his hands in front of him and Handy saw him immediately begin twisting and turning the huge diamond ring on his right hand, playing with it, taking it off and replacing it. *I wonder what that means*, Handy thought.

Handy had many thoughts about Arthur Crewes. Some of them were friendly, most were impartial. Crewes was a job for Handy. He had seen the producer step heavily when the need arose: cutting off a young writer when the script wasn't being written fast enough to make a shooting date; literally threatening an actor with bodily harm if he didn't cease the senseless wrangling on set that was costing the production money; playing agents against one another to catch a talented client unrepresented between them, available for shaved cost. But he had seen him perform unnecessary kindnesses. Unnecessary because they bought nothing, won him nothing, made him no points. Crewes had blown a tire on a freeway one day and a motorist had stopped to help. Crewes had taken his name and sent him a three-thousand-dollar color television-stereo. A starlet ready to put out for a part had been investigated by the detective agency Crewes kept on retainer at all times for assorted odd jobs. They had found out her child was a paraplegic. She had not been required to go the couch route, Crewes had refused her the job on grounds of talent, but had given her a check in the equivalent amount had she gotten the part.

Arthur Crewes was a very large man indeed in Hollywood. He had not always been immense, however. He had begun his career as a film editor on "B" horror flicks, worked his way up and directed several productions, then been put in charge of a series of low-budget films at the old RKO studio. He had suffered in the vineyards and somehow run the time very fast. He was still a young man, and he was ancient, sitting there turning his ring.

Sancher came out of the toilet and sat down at the far end of the counter. It seemed to jog Kencannon. "Think I'll wash off a little Mojave filth," he said, and rose.

Crewes got up. "I suddenly realized I haven't been to the bathroom all day."

They walked away, leaving Handy sitting, toying with the sugar shaker.

He looked up for the first time, abruptly realizing how exhausted he was. There was a waitress shaking a wire basket of french fries, her back to him. The picture was on schedule, no problems, but no hook, no gimmick, no angle, no *shtick* to sell it; there was a big quarterly payment due on the house in Sherman Oaks; it was all Handy had, no one was going to get it; he had to keep the job. The waitress turned around for the first time and started laying out napkin, water glass, silverware, in front of him. You could work in a town for close to nine years, and still come away with nothing; not even living high, driving a '65 Impala, that wasn't ostentatious; but a lousy forty-five-day marriage to a clip artist and it was all in jeopardy; he had to keep the job, just to fight her off, keep her from using California divorce logic to get that house; nine years was *not* going down the tube; God, he felt weary. The waitress was in the booth, setting up the grips and cameramen. Handy mulled the nine years, wondering what the hell he was doing out here: oh yeah, I was getting divorced, that's what I was doing. Nine years seemed so long, so ruthlessly long, and so empty suddenly, to be here with Crewes on another of the endless product that got fed into the always-yawning maw of the Great American Moviegoing Public. The waitress returned and stood before him.

"Care to order now?"

He looked up.

Fred Handy stopped breathing for a second. He looked at her, and the years peeled away. He was a teenage kid in the Utopia Theater in St. Louis, Missouri, staring up at a screen with gray shadows moving on it. A face from the past, a series of features, very familiar, were superimposing themselves.

She saw he was staring. "Order?"

He had to say it just right. "Excuse me, is, uh, is your name Lone?"

Until much later, he was not able to identify the expression that swam up in her eyes. But when he thought back on it, he knew it had been terror. Not fear, not trepidation, not uneasiness, not wariness. Terror. Complete, total, gagging terror. She said later it had been like calling the death knell for her. . .again.

She went stiff, and her hand slid off the counter edge. "Valerie Lone?" he said, softly, frightened by the look on her face. She swallowed so that the hollows in her cheeks moved liquidly. And she nodded. The briefest movement of the head.

Then he knew he had to say it just right. He was holding all that fragile crystal, and a wrong phrase would shatter it. Not: *I used to see your movies when I was a kid* or: *Whatever happened to you* or: *What are you doing here*. It had to be just right.

Handy smiled like a little boy. It somehow fit his craggy features. "You know," he said gently, "many's the afternoon I've sat in the movies and been in love with you."

There was gratitude in her smile. Relief, an ease of tensions, and the sudden rush of her own memories; the bittersweet taste of remembrance as the glories of her other life swept back to her. Then it was gone, and she was a frowzy blonde waitress on Route 14 again. "Order?"

She wasn't kidding. She turned it off like a mercury switch. One moment there was life in the faded blue eyes, the next moment it was ashes. He ordered a cheeseburger and french fries. She went back to the steam table.

Arthur Crewes came out of the men's room first. He was rubbing his hands. "Damned powdered soap, almost as bad as those stiff paper towels." He slipped onto the stool beside Handy.

And in that instant, Fred Handy saw a great white light come up. Like the buzz an acid-head gets from a fully drenched sugar cube, his mind burst free and went trembling outward in waves of color. The *shtick*, the bit, the handle, ohmigod there it is, as perfect as a bluewhite diamond.

Arthur Crewes was reading the menu as Handy grabbed his wrist.

"Arthur, do you know who that is?"

"Who *who* is?"

"The waitress."

"Madame Nehru."

"I'm serious, Arthur."

"All right, who?"

"Valerie Lone."

Arthur Crewes started as though he had been struck. He shot a look at the waitress, her back to them now, as she ladled up navy bean soup from the stainless steel tureen in the steam table. He stared at her, silently.

"I don't believe it," he murmured.

"It is, Arthur, I'm telling you that's just who it is."

He shook his head. "What the hell is she doing out here in the middle of nowhere. My God, it must be, what? Fifteen, twenty years?"

Handy considered a moment. "About eighteen years, if you count that thing she did for Ross at UA in forty-eight. Eighteen years and here she is, slinging hash in a diner."

Crewes mumbled something.

"What did you say?" Handy asked him.

Crewes repeated it, with an edge Handy could not place. "Lord, how the mighty have fallen."

Before Handy could tell the producer his idea, she turned, and saw Crewes staring at her. There was no recognition in her expression. But it was obvious she knew Handy had told him who she was. She turned away and carried the plates of soup to the booth.

As she came back past them, Crewes said, softly, "Hello, Miss Lone." She paused and stared at him. She was almost somnambulistic, moving by rote. He added, "Arthur Crewes. . .remember?"

She did not answer for a long moment, then nodded as she had to Handy. "Hello. It's been a long time."

Crewes smiled a peculiar smile. Somehow victorious. "Yes, a long time. How've you been?"

She shrugged, as if to indicate the diner. "Fine, thank you."

They fell silent.

"Would you care to order now?"

When she had taken the order and moved to the grill, Handy leaned in close to the producer and began speaking intensely. "Arthur, I've got a fantastic idea."

His mind was elsewhere. "What's that, Fred?"

"Her. Valerie Lone. What a sensational idea. Put her in the picture. The comeback of. . .what was it they used to call her, that publicity thing, oh yeah. . .the comeback of 'Miss Ankle-Strap Wedgie.' It's good for space in any newspaper in the country."

Silence.

"Arthur? What do you think?"

Arthur Crewes smiled down at his hands. He was playing with the ring again. "You think I should bring her back to the industry after eighteen years."

"I think it's the most natural winning promotion idea I've ever had. And I can tell you like it."

Crewes nodded, almost absently. "Yes, I like it, Fred. You're a very bright fellow. I like it just fine."

Kencannon came back and sat down. Crewes turned to him. "Jim, can you do cover shots on the basement scenes with Bob and the stunt men for a day or two?"

Kencannon bit his lip, considering. "I suppose so. It'll mean replotting the schedule, but the board's Bernie's problem, not mine. What's up?"

Crewes twisted the ring and smiled distantly. "I'm going to call Johnny Black in and have him do a rewrite on the part of Angela. Beef it up."

"For what? We haven't even cast it yet."

"We have now." Handy grinned hugely. "Valerie Lone."

"Valerie—you're *kid*ding. She hasn't even *made* a film in God knows how long. What makes you think you can get her?"

Crewes turned back to stare at the sloped shoulders of the woman at the sizzling grill. "I can get her."

HANDY

We talked to Valerie Lone, Crewes and myself. First I talked, then he talked; then when she refused to listen to him, I talked again.

She grabbed up a huge pan with the remains of macaroni and cheese burned to the bottom, and she dashed out through a screen door at the rear of the diner.

We looked at each other, and when each of us saw the look of confusion on the other's face, the looks vanished. We got up and followed her. She was leaning against the wall of the diner, scraping the crap from the pan as she cried. The night was quiet.

But she didn't melt as we came through the screen door. She got uptight. Furious. "I've been out of all that for over fifteen years, can't you leave me alone? You've got a lousy sense of humor if you think this is funny!"

Arthur Crewes stopped dead on the stairs. He didn't know what to say to her. There was something happening to Crewes; I didn't know what it was, but it was more than whatever it takes to get a gimmick for a picture.

I took over.

Handy, the salesman. Handy, the *schmacheler*, equipped with the very best butter. "It isn't fifteen years, Miss Lone. It's eighteen plus."

Something broke inside her. She turned back to the pan. Crewes didn't know whether to tell me to back off or not, so I went ahead. I pushed past Crewes, standing there with his hand on the peeling yellow paint banister, his mouth open. (The color of the paint was the color of a stray dog I had run down in Nevada one time. I hadn't seen the animal. It had dashed out of a gully by the side of the road and I'd gone right over it before I knew what had happened. But I stopped and went back. It was the same color as that banister. A faded lonely yellow, like cheap foolscap, a dollar a ream. I couldn't get the thought of that dog out of my mind.)

"You like it out here, right?"

She didn't turn around.

I walked around her. She was looking into that pan of crap. "Miss Lone?"

It was going to take more than soft-spoken words. It might even take sincerity. I wasn't sure I knew how to do *that* any more. "If I didn't know better. . .having seen all the feisty broads you played. . .I'd think you *enjoyed* feeling sorry for your—"

She looked up, whip-fast, I could hear the cartilage cracking in her neck muscles. There was a core of electrical sparks in her eyes. She was pissed off. "Mister, I just met your face. What makes you think you can talk that way. . ." It petered out. The steam leaked off, and the sparks died, and she was back where she'd been a minute before.

I turned her around to face us. She shrugged my hand off. She wasn't a sulky child, she was a woman who didn't know how to get away from a giant fear that was getting more gigantic with every passing second. And even in fear she wasn't about to let me manhandle her.

"Miss Lone, we've got a picture working. It isn't *Gone With the Wind* and it isn't *The Birth of a Nation*, it's just a better-than-average coupla-million-dollar spectacular with Mitchum and Lollobrigida, and it'll make a potful for everybody concerned. . ."

Crewes was staring at me. I didn't like his expression. He was the bright young wunderkind who had made *Lonely in the Dark* and *Ruby Bernadette* and *The Fastest Man*, and he didn't like to hear me pinning his latest opus as just a nice, money-making color puffball. But Crewes wasn't a wunderkind any longer, and he wasn't making Kafka, he was making box-office bait, and he needed this woman, and so dammit did I! So screw his expression.

"Nobody's under the impression you're one of the great ladies of the theater; you never were Katharine Cornell, or Bette Davis, or even Pat Neal." She gave me that core of sparks look again. If I'd been a younger man it might have woofed me; I'm sure it had stopped legions of assistant gophers in the halcyon days. But—it suddenly scared me to realize it—I was running hungry, and mere looks didn't do it. I pushed her a little harder, my best Raymond Chandler delivery. "But you *were* a star, you were someone that people paid money to see, because whatever you had it was *yours*. And whatever that was, we want to rent it for a while, we want to bring it back."

She gave one of those little snorts that says very distinctly *You stink, Jack*. It was disdainful. She had my number. But that was cool; I'd given it to her; I wasn't about to shuck her.

"Don't think we're humanitarians. We *need* something like you on this picture. We need a handle, something that'll get us that extra two inches in the Wichita *Eagle*. That means bucks in the ticket wicket. Oh, shit, lady!"

Her teeth skinned back.

I was getting to her.

"We can help each other." She sneered and started to turn away. I reached out and slammed the pan as hard as I could. It spun out of her hands and hit the steps. She was rocked quiet for an instant, and I rapped on her as hard as I could. "Don't tell me you're in love with scraping crap out of a macaroni dish. You lived too high, too long. This is a free ride back. Take it!"

There was blood coursing through her veins now. Her cheeks had bright, flushed spots on them, high up under the eyes. "I can't do it; stop pushing at me."

Crewes moved in, then. We worked like a pair of good homicide badges. I beat her on the head, and he came running with Seidlitz powders. "Let her alone a minute, Fred. This is all at once, come on, let her think."

"What the hell's to think?"

She was being rammed from both sides, and knew it, but for the first time in years something was *happening*, and her motor was starting to run again, despite herself.

"Miss Lone," Crewes said gently, "a contract for this film, and options for three more. Guaranteed, from first day of shooting, straight through, even if you sit around after your part is shot, till last day of production."

"I haven't been anywhere near a camera—"

"That's what we have cameramen for. They turn it on you. That's what we have a director for. He'll tell you where to stand. It's like swimming or riding a bike: once you learn, you never forget. . ."

Crewes again. "Stop it, Fred. Miss Lone. . .I remember you from before. You were always good to work with. You weren't one of the cranky ones, you were a doer. You knew your lines, always."

She smiled. A wee timorous slippery smile. She remembered. And she chuckled. "Good memory, that's all."

Then Crewes and I smiled, too. She was on our side. Everything she said from here on out would be to win us the argument. She was ours.

"You know, I had the world's all-time great crush on you, Miss Lone," Arthur Crewes, a very large man in town, said. She smiled a little-girl smile of graciousness.

"I'll think about it." She stooped for the pan.

He reached it before she did. "I won't give you time to think. There'll be a car here for you tomorrow at noon."

He handed her the pan.

She took it reluctantly.

We had dug Valerie Lone up from under uncounted strata of self-pity and anonymity, from a kind of grave she had chosen for herself for reasons I was beginning to understand. As we went back inside the diner, I had The Thought for the first time:

The Thought: *What if we ain't doing her no favors?*

And the voice of Donald Duck came back at me from the Clown Town of my thoughts: With friends like you, Handy, she may not need any enemies.

Screw you, Duck.

2

The screen flickered, and Valerie Lone, twenty years younger, wearing the pageboy and padded shoulders of the Forties, swept into the room. Cary Grant looked up from the microscope with his special genteel exasperation, and asked her *precisely* where she had been. Valerie Lone, the coiffed blonde hair carefully smoothed, removed her gloves and sat on the laboratory counter. She crossed her legs. She was wearing ankle-strap wedgies.

"I think the legs are still damned good, Arthur," Fred Handy said. Cigar smoke rose up in the projection room. Arthur Crewes did not answer. He was busy watching the past.

Full hips, small breasts, blonde; a loveliness that was never wispy like a Jean Arthur, never chill like a Joan Crawford, never cultured like a Greer Garson. If Valerie Lone had been identifiable with anyone else working in her era, it would have been with Ann Sheridan. And the comparison was by no means invidious. There was the same forceful *womanliness* in her manner; a wise kid who knew the score. Dynamic. Yet there was a quality of availability in the way she arched her eyebrows, the way she held her hands and neck. Sensuality mixed with reality. What had broken that spine of self-control, turned it into the fragile wariness Handy had sensed? He studied the film as the story unreeled, but there was none of that showing in the Valerie Lone of twenty years before.

As the deep, silken voice faded from the screen, Arthur Crewes reached to the console beside his contour chair, and punched a series of buttons. The projection light cut off from the booth behind them, the room lights went up, and the chair tilted forward. The producer got up and left the room, with Handy behind him, waiting for comments. They had spent close to eight hours running old prints of Valerie Lone's biggest hits.

Arthur Crewes's home centered around the projection room. As his life centered around the film industry. Through the door, and into the living room, opulent beneath fumed and waxed, shadowed oak beams far above them; the two men did not speak. The living room was immense, only slightly smaller than a basketball court in one corner where Crewes now settled into a deep armchair, before a roaring walk-in fireplace. The rest of the living room was empty and quiet; one could hear the fall of dust. It had been a merry house many times in the past, and would be again, but at the moment, far down below the vaulting ceiling, their voices rising like echoes in a mountain pass, Arthur Crewes spoke to his publicist.

"Fred, I want the full treatment. I want her seen everywhere by everyone. I want her name as big as it ever was."

Handy pursed his lips, even as he nodded. "That takes money, Arthur. We're pushing the publicity budget now."

Crewes lit a cigar. "This is above-the-line expense. Keep it a separate record, and I'll take care of it out of my pocket. I want it all itemized for the IRS, but don't spare the cost."

"Do you know how much you're getting into here?"

"It doesn't matter. Whatever it is, however much you need, come and ask, and you'll get it. But I want a real job done for that money, Fred."

Handy stared at him for a long moment.

"You'll get mileage out of Valerie Lone's comeback, Arthur. No doubt about it. But I have to tell you right now it isn't going to be anything near commensurate with what you'll be spending. It isn't that kind of appeal."

Crewes drew deeply on the cigar, sent a thin streamer of blue smoke toward the darkness above them. "I'm not concerned about the value to the picture. It's going to be a good property, it can take care of itself. This is something else."

Handy looked puzzled. "Why?"

Crewes did not answer. Finally, he asked, "Is she settled in at the Beverly Hills?"

Handy rose to leave. "Best bungalow in the joint. You should have seen the reception they gave her."

"That's the kind of reception I want everywhere for her, Fred. A lot of bowing and scraping for the old queen."

Handy nodded, walked toward the foyer. Across the room, forcing him to raise his voice to reach Crewes, still lost in the dimness of the living room, the fireplace casting spastic shadows of blood and night on the walls, Fred Handy said, "Why the extra horsepower, Arthur? I get nervous when I'm told to spend freely."

Smoke rose from the chair where Arthur Crewes was hidden. "Good night, Fred."

Handy stood for a moment; then, troubled, he let himself out. The living room was silent for a long while, only the faint crackling of the logs on the fire breaking the stillness. Then Arthur Crewes reached to the sidetable and lifted the telephone receiver from its cradle. He punched out a number.

"Miss Valerie Lone's bungalow, please. . .yes, I know what time it is. This is Arthur Crewes calling. . .thank you."

There was a pause, then sound from the other end.

"Hello, Miss Lone? Arthur Crewes. Yes, thank you. Sorry if I disturbed you. . .oh, really? I rather thought you might be awake. I had the feeling you might be a little uneasy, first night back and all."

He listened to the voice at the other end. And did not smile. Then he said, "I just wanted to call and tell you not to be afraid. Everything will be fine. There's nothing to be afraid of. Nothing at all."

His eyes became light, and light fled down the wires to see her at the other end. In the elegant bungalow, still sitting in the dark. Through a window, moonlight lay like a patina of dull gold across the room, tinting even the depressions in the sofa pillows where a thousand random bottoms had rested, a vaguely yellow ocher.

Valerie Lone. Alone.

Misted by a fine down of Beverly Hills moonlight—the great gaffer in the sky working behind an amber gel keylighting her with a senior, getting fill light from four broads and four juniors, working the light outside in the great celestial cyclorama with a dozen sky-pans, and catching her just right with a pair of inky-dinks, scrims, gauzes, and cutters—displaying her in a gown of powdered moth-wing dust. Valerie Lone, off-camera, trapped by the lens of God, and the electric eyes of Arthur Crewes. But still in XTREME CLOSEUP.

She thanked him, seeming bewildered by his kindness. "Is there anything you need?" he asked.

He had to ask her to repeat her answer, she had spoken so softly. But the answer was *nothing*, and he said *good night*, and was about to hang up when she called him.

To Crewes it was a sound from farther away than the Beverly Hills Hotel. It was a sound that came by way of a Country of Mildew. From a land where oily things moved out of darkness. From a place where the only position was hunched safely into oneself with hands about knees, chin tucked down, hands wrapped tightly so that if the eyes with their just-born-bird membranes should open, through the film could be seen the relaxed fingers. It was a sound from a country where there was no hiding place.

After a moment he answered, shaken by her frightened sound. "Yes, I'm here."

Now he could not see her, even with eyes of electricity.

For Valerie Lone sat on the edge of the bed in her bungalow, not bathed in moth-wing dust, but lighted harshly by every lamp and overhead in the bungalow. She could not turn out those lights. She was petrified with fear. A nameless fear that had no origin and had no definition. It was merely *there with her*; a palpable presence.

And something else was in the room with her.

"They. . ."

She stopped. She knew Crewes was straining at the other end of the line to hear what followed.

"They sent your champagne."

Crewes smiled to himself. She was touched.

Valerie Lone did not smile, was incapable of a smile, was by no means touched. The bottle loomed huge across the room on the glass-topped table. "Thank you. It was. Very. Kind. Of. You."

Slowly, because of the way she had told him the champagne had arrived, Crewes asked, "Are you all right?"

"I'm frightened."

"There's nothing to be frightened about. We're all on your team, you know that. . ."

"I'm frightened of the champagne. . .it's been so long."

Crewes did not understand. He said so.

"I'm afraid to drink it."

Then he understood.

He didn't know what to say. For the first time in many years he felt pity for someone. He was fully conversant with affection, and hatred, and envy, and admiration and even stripped-to-the-bone lust. But pity was something he somehow hadn't had to deal with, for a long time. His ex-wife and the boy, they were the last, and that had been eight years before. He didn't know what to say.

"I'm afraid, isn't that silly? I'm afraid I'll like it too much again. I've managed to forget what it tastes like. But if I open it, and taste it, and remember. . .I'm afraid. . ."

He said, "Would you like me to drive over?"

She hesitated, pulling her wits about her. "No. No, I'll be all right. I'm just being silly. I'll talk to you tomorrow." Then, hastily: "You'll call tomorrow?"

"Yes, of course. Sure I will. I'll call first thing in the morning, and you'll come down to the Studio. I'm sure there are all sorts of people you'll want to get reacquainted with."

Silence, then, softly: "Yes. I'm just being silly. It's very lonely here."

"Well, then. I'll call in the morning."

"Lonely. . .hmmm? Oh, yes! Thank you. Good night, Mr. Crewes."

"Arthur. That's first on the list. Arthur."

"Arthur. Thank you. Good night."

"Good night, Miss Lone."

He hung up, still hearing the same voice he had heard in darkened theaters rich with the smell of popcorn (in the days before they started putting faintly rancid butter on it) and the taste of Luden's Menthol Cough Drops. The same deep, silken voice that he had just this moment past heard break, ever so slightly, with fear.

Darkness rose up around him.

Light flooded Valerie Lone. The lights she would keep burning all night, because out there was darkness and it was so lonely in here. She stared across the room at the bottle of champagne, sitting high in its silver ice bucket, chipped base of ice melting to frigid water beneath it.

Then she stood and took a drinking glass from the tray on the bureau, ignoring the champagne glasses that had come with the bottle. She walked across the room to the bathroom and went inside, without turning on the light. She filled the water glass from the tap, letting the cold faucet run for a long moment. Then she stood in the doorway of the bathroom, drinking the water, staring at the bottle of champagne, that bottle of champagne.

Then slowly, she went to it and pulled the loosened plastic cork from the mouth of the bottle. She poured half a glass.

She sipped it slowly.

Memories stirred.

And a dark shape fled off across hills in the Country of Mildew.

3

Handy drove up the twisting road into the Hollywood Hills. The call he had received an hour before was one he would never have expected. He had not heard from Huck Barkin in over two years. Haskell Barkin, the tall. Haskell Barkin, the tanned. Haskell Barkin, the handsome. Haskell Barkin, the amoral. The last time Fred had seen Huck, he was busily making a precarious living hustling wealthy widows with kids. His was a specialized con: he got next to the kids—Huck was one of the more accomplished surf-bums extant—even as he seduced the mother, and before the family attorney knew what was happening, the pitons and grapnels and tongs had been sunk in deep, through the mouth and out the other side, and friendly, good-looking, rangy Huck Barkin was living in the house, driving the Imperial, ordering McCormick's bourbon from the liquor store, eating like Quantrill's Raiders, and clipping bucks like the Russians were in Pomona.

There had been one who had tried to saturate herself with barbiturates when Huck had said, "À *bientot.*"

There had been one who had called in her battery of attorneys in an attempt to have him make restitution, but she had been informed Huck Barkin was one of those rare, infuriating, "judgment-proof" people.

There had been one who had gone away to New Mexico, where it was warm, and no one would see her drinking.

There had been one who had bought a tiny gun, but had never used it on him.

There had been one who had already had the gun, and she *had* used it. But not on Huck Barkin.

Fearsome, in his strangeness; without ethic. Animal.

He was one of the more unpleasant Hollywood creeps Handy had met in the nine Hollywood years. Yet there was an unctuous charm about the man; it sat well on him, if the observers weren't the most perceptive. Handy chuckled, remembering the one and only time he had seen Barkin shot down. By a woman. (And how seldom *any* woman can *really* put down a man, with such thoroughness that there is no comeback, no room to rationalize that it wasn't such a great zinger, with the full certainty that the target has been utterly destroyed, and nothing is left but to slink away. He remembered.)

It had been at a party thrown by CBS, to honor the star of their new ninety-minute Western series. Big party. Century City Hotel. All the silkies were there, all the sleek, well-fed types who went without eating a full day to make it worthwhile at the barbecue and buffet. Barkin had somehow been invited. Or crashed. No one ever questioned his appearance at these things; a black mohair suit is ticket enough in a scene where recognition is predicated on the uniform of the day.

He had sidled into a conversational group composed of Handy and his own Julie, Spencer Lichtman the agent and two very expensive call girls—all pale silver hair and exquisite faces; hundred and a half per night girls; the kind a man could talk to afterward, learn something from, probably with Masters earned in photochemistry or piezoelectricity; nothing even remotely cheap or brittle about them; master craftsmen in a specialized field—and Barkin had unstrapped his Haskellesque charm. The girls had sensed at once that he was one of the leeches, hardly one of the cruisable meal tickets with wherewithal. They had been courteous, but chill. Barkin had gone from unctuous to rank in three giant steps, without saying, "May I?"

Finally, in desperation, he had leaned in close to the taller of the two silver goddesses, and murmured (loud enough for all in the group to overhear) with a Richard Widmark thinness: "How would you like me down in your panties?"

Silence for a beat, then the silver goddess turned to him with eyes of anthracite, and across the chill polar wastes came her reply: "I have one asshole down there now. . .what would I want with you?"

Handy chuckled again, smugly, remembering the look on Barkin as he had broken down into his component parts, re-formed as a puddle of strawberry jam sliding down one of the walls, and oozed out of the scene, not to return that night.

Yet there was a roguish good humor about the big blond beach-bum that most people took at face value; only if Huck's back was put to the wall did the façade of affability drop away to reveal the granite foundation of amorality. The man was intent on sliding through life with as little effort as possible.

Handy had spotted him for what he was almost immediately upon meeting him, but for a few months Huck had been an amusing adjunct to Handy's new life in the film colony. They had not been in touch for three years. Yet this morning the call had come from Barkin. Using Arthur Crewes's name. He had asked Handy to come to see him, and given him an address in the Hollywood Hills.

Now, as he tooled the Impala around another snakeback curve, the top of the mountain came into view, and Handy saw the house. As it was the *only* house, dominating the flat, he assumed it was the address Barkin had given him, and he marveled. It was a gigantic circle of a structure, a flattened spool of sandblasted gray rock whose waist was composed entirely of curved panels of dark-smoked glass. Barkin could never have afforded an Orwellian feast of a home like this.

Handy drove up the flaring spiral driveway and parked beside the front door: an ebony slab with a rhodium-plated knob as big as an Impala headlight.

The grounds were incredibly well-tailored, sloping down all sides of the mountain to vanish over the next flat. Bonsai trees pruned in their abstracted Zen artfulness, bougainvillea rampant across one entire outcropping, banks of flowers, dichondra everywhere, ivy.

Then Handy realized the house was turning. To catch the sun. Through a glass roof. The front door was edging past him toward the west. He walked up to it, and looked for a doorbell. There was none.

From within the house came the staccato report of hardwood striking hardwood. It came again and again, in uneven, frantic bursts. And the sound of grunting.

He turned the knob, expecting the gigantic door to resist, but it swung open on a center-pin, counterbalanced, and he stepped through into the front hall of inlaid onyx tiles.

The sounds of wood on wood, and grunting, were easy to follow. He went down five steps into a passageway, and followed it toward the sound, emerging at the other end of the passage into a living room ocean-deep in sunshine. In the center of the room Huck Barkin and a tiny Japanese, both in loose-fitting ceremonial robes, were jousting with sawed-off quarter staves—*shoji* sticks.

Handy watched silently. The diminutive Japanese was electric. Barkin was no match for him, though he managed to get in a smooth rap or two from moment to moment. But the Oriental rolled and slid, barely seeming to touch the deep white carpet. His hands moved like propellers, twisting the hardwood staff to counter a swing by the taller man, jabbing sharply to embed the point of the staff in Barkin's ribs. In and out and gone. He was a blur.

As Barkin turned in almost an *entrechat*, to avoid a slantwise flailing maneuver by the Oriental, he saw Handy standing in the entranceway to the passage. Barkin stepped back from his opponent.

"That'll do it for now, Mas," he said.

They bowed to one another; the Oriental took the staffs, and left through another passageway at the far end of the room. Barkin came across the rug liquidly, all the suntanned flesh rippling with the play of solid muscle underneath. Handy found himself once again admiring the shape Barkin kept himself in. *But if you do nothing but spend time on your body, why not?* he thought ruefully. The idea of honest labor had never taken up even temporary residence in Huck's thoughts. And yet one body-building session was probably equal to all the exertion a common laborer would expend in a day.

Handy thought Huck was extending his hand in greeting, but halfway across the room the robed beach-bum reached over to a Saarinen chair and snagged a huge, fluffy towel. He swabbed his face and chest with it, coming to Handy.

"Fred, baby."

"How are you, Huck?"

"Great, fellah. Just about king of the world these days. Like the place?"

"Nice. Whose is it?"

"Belongs to a chick I've been seeing. Old man's one of the big things happening in some damned banana republic or other. I don't give it too much thought; she'll be back in about a month. Till then I've got the run of the joint. Want a drink?"

"It's eleven o'clock."

"Coconut milk, friend buddy friend. Got all the amino acids you can use all day. Very important."

"I'll pass."

Barkin shrugged, walking past him to a mirrored wall that was jeweled with the reflections of pattering sunlight streaming in from above. He seemed to wipe his hand over the mirror, and the wall swung out to reveal a fully stocked bar. He took a can of coconut milk from the small freezer unit, and opened it, drinking straight from the can. "Doesn't that smart a bit?" Handy asked.

"The coconut mil—oh, you mean the *shoji* jousting. Best damned thing in the world to toughen you up. Teak. Get whacked across the belly half a dozen times with one of those and your stomach muscles turn to leather."

He flexed.

"Leather stomach muscles. Just what I've always yearned for." Handy walked across the room and stared out through the dark glass at the incredible Southern California landscape, blighted by a murmuring, hanging pall of sickly smog over the Hollywood Freeway. With his back turned to Barkin, he said, "I tried to call Crewes after you spoke to me. He wasn't in. I came anyway. How come you used his name?" He turned around.

"He told me to."

"Where did *you* meet Arthur Crewes!" Handy snapped, sudden anger in his voice. This damned beach stiff, it had to be a shuck; he had to have used Handy's name somehow.

"At that pool party you took me to, about—what was it—about three years ago. You remember, that little auburn-haired thing, what was her name, Binnie, Bunny, something. . .?"

"Billie. Billie Landewyck. Oh, yeah, I'd forgotten Crewes was there."

Huck smiled a confident smile. He downed the last of the coconut milk and tossed the can into a wastebasket. He came around the bar and slumped onto the sofa. "Yeah, well. Crewes remembered me. Got me through Central Casting. I keep my SAG dues up, never know when you can pick up a few bucks doing stunt or a bit. You know."

Handy did not reply. He was waiting. Huck had simply said Arthur Crewes wanted him to get together with the beach-bum, so Handy had come. But there was something stirring that Barkin didn't care to open up just yet.

"Listen, Huck, I'm getting to be an old man. I can't stand on my feet too long any more. So if you've got something shaking, let's to it, friend buddy friend."

Barkin nodded silently, as though resigned to whatever it was he had to say. "Yeah, well. Crewes wants me to meet Valerie Lone."

Handy stared.

"He remembered me."

Handy tried to speak, found he had nothing to say. It was too ridiculous. He turned to leave.

"Hold it, Fred. Don't do that, man. I'm talking to you."

"You're talking *nothing*, Barkin. You've gotta be straight out of a jug. Valerie Lone, my ass. Who do you think you're shucking? Not me, not good old friend buddy friend Handy. I know you, you deadbeat."

Barkin stood up, unfurled something over six feet of deltoid, trapezius and biceps, toned till they hummed, and planted himself in front of the passageway. "Fred, you continue to make the mistake of thinking I'm a hulk without a brain in it. You're wrong. I am a very clever lad, not merely pretty, but smart. Now if I have to drop five big ones into your pudding-trough, lover, I will do so."

Handy stopped moving toward him. Barkin was not fooling. He was angry. "What is all this, Barkin? What are you trying to climb onto? No, forget it, don't answer. What I want to know is why?"

Barkin spread hands as huge as catcher's mitts. The fingers were oddly long and graceful. And tanned. "She is a lovely woman who finds the company of handsome young men refreshing. Mr. Crewes, sir, has decided I will brighten her declining years."

"She is a scared creature who doesn't know where it's at, not right now she doesn't. And turning you loose on her would be a sudden joy like the Dutch Elm Blight."

Barkin smiled thinly. It was a mean smile. For the time it took the smile to vanish, he was not handsome. "Call Arthur Crewes. He'll verify."

"I can't get through to him, he's in a screening."

"Then go ask him. I'll be here all day."

He stepped aside. Handy waited, as though Barkin might surprise him and leap back suddenly, with a fist in the mouth. Huck stood grinning like a little boy. Ain't I cute.

"I'll do that."

Handy moved past and entered the passageway. As he walked hurriedly down the length of the corridor, he heard Barkin speak again. He turned to see the giant figure framed in the blazing sunlight rectangle at the other end of the dark tunnel. "You know, Fred chum, you need a good workout. You're gettin' flabbier than hell."

Handy fled, raising dust as he wheeled the Impala out of the driveway and down the mountainside. There was the stink of fusel oil rising up from the city. Or was it the smell of fear?

4

When he burst into Arthur Crewes's office at the studio, the reception room was filled with delight. All that young stuff. A dozen girls, legs crossed high to show off the rounded thigh, waiting to be seen. As he slammed in, Twiggyeyes blinked rapidly.

He careened through the door and brought up short, turning quickly to see an unbroken panorama of gorgeous young-twenties starlets. Roz, fifty and waspish, behind the desk, snickered at his double-take. Handy recognized the tone of the snicker. He was a man periodically motivated from somewhere low in his anatomy, and Roz never failed to hold it against him. He had never asked her out.

"Hello, Fred," one of the girls said. He had to strain to single her out. They all looked alike. Teased; long flat blonde hair; freaky Twiggy styles; backswept bouffant; short mannish cuts; all of them, no matter what mode, they all looked alike. It was Randi. She had had a thing about touching his privates. It was all he could remember about her. Not even if she'd been good. But a publicist must remember names, and with the remembrance of her touching his penis and drawing in her breath as though it had been something strange and new and wonderful like the Inca Codex or one of the Dead Sea Scrolls, the name of Randi popped up like the NO SALE clack on a cash register.

"Hi, Randi. How's it going?"

He didn't even wait for an answer. He turned back to Roz. "I want to see him."

Her mouth became the nasty slit opening of a mantis. "He's got someone in with him now."

"I want to *see* him."

"I *said*, Mr. Handy, he has someone in there now. We *are* still interviewing girls, you know. . ."

"Bloody damn it, lady, I said get your ass in there and tell him Handy is coming through that door, open or not, in exactly ten seconds."

She drew herself up, no breasts at all, straight lines and Mondrian sterility, and started to huff at him. Handy said, "Fuck," and went through into Crewes's office.

He said it softly, but he made noise entering the office.

Another of the pretties was showing Arthur Crewes her 8x10 glossies, under plastic, out of an immense black leather photofolio. Starlets. Arthur was saying something about their needing a few more dark-haired girls, as Handy came through the door.

Crewes looked up, surprised at the interruption.

The starlet smiled automatically.

"Arthur, I have to talk to you."

Crewes seemed puzzled by the tone in Handy's voice. But he nodded. "In a minute, Fred. Why don't you sit down. Georgia and I were talking."

Handy realized his error. He had gone a step too far with Arthur Crewes. Throughout the industry, one thing was common knowledge about Crewes's office policy: any girl who came in for an interview was treated courteously, fairly, without even the vaguest scintilla of a hustle. Crewes had been known to can men on his productions who had used their positions to get all-too-willing actresses into bed with promises of three-line bits, or a walk-on. For Handy to interrupt while Crewes was talking to even the lowliest day-player was an affront Crewes would not allow to pass unnoticed. Handy sat down, ambivalent as hell.

Georgia was showing Crewes several shots from a Presley picture she had made the year before. Crewes was remarking that she looked good in a bikini. It was a businesslike, professional tone of voice, no leer. The girl was standing tall and straight. Handy knew that under other circumstances, in other offices where the routine was different, if Crewes had been another sort of man and had said, *why don't you take off your clothes so I can get a better idea of how you'll look in the nude shots we're shooting for the overseas market*, this girl, this Georgia, would be pulling the granny dress with its baggy mini material over her head and displaying herself in bikini briefs and maybe no brassiere to hold up all that fine young meat. But in this office she was standing tall and straight. She was being asked to be professional, to take pride in herself and whatever degree of craft she might possess. It was why there were so few lousy rumors around town about Arthur Crewes.

"I'm not certain, Georgia, but let me check with Kenny Heller in Casting, see what he's already done, and what parts are left open. I know there's a very nice five- or six-line comedy walk-on with Mitchum that we haven't found a girl for yet. Perhaps that might work. No promises, you understand, but I'll check with Kenny and get back to you later in the day."

"Thank you, Mr. Crewes. I'm very grateful."

Crewes smiled and picked out one of the 8x10's from a thin sheaf at the rear of the photofolio. "May we keep one of these here, for the files. . .and also to remind me to get through to Kenny?" She nodded, and smiled back at him. There was no subterfuge in the interchange, and Handy sank a trifle lower on the sofa.

"Just give it to Roz, at the desk out there, and leave your number. . .would you prefer we let you know through your agent, or directly?"

It was the sort of question, in any other office, that might mean the producer was trying to wangle the home number for his own purposes. But not here. Georgia did not hesitate as she said, "Oh, either way. It makes no difference. Herb is very good about getting me out on interviews. But if it looks possible, I'll give you my home number. There's a service on the line that'll pick up if I'm out."

"You can leave it with Roz, Georgia. And thank you for coming in." He stood and they shook hands. She was quite happy. Even if the part did not come through, she knew she had been *considered*, not merely assayed as a possible quickie on an office sofa. As she started for the door, Crewes added, "I'll have Roz call one way or the other, as soon as we know definitely."

She half-turned, displaying a fine length of leg, taut against the baggy dress. "Thank you. 'Bye."

"Good-bye."

She left the office, and Crewes sat down again. He pushed papers around the outer perimeter of his desk, making Handy wait. Finally, when Handy had allowed Crewes as much punishment as he felt his recent original sin deserved, he spoke.

"You've got to be out of your mind, Arthur!"

Crewes looked up then. Stopped in the midst of his preparations to remark on Handy's discourtesy in entering the office during an interview. Crewes waited, but Handy said nothing. Then Crewes thumbed the comm button on the phone. He picked up the receiver and said, "Roz, ask them if they'll be kind enough to wait about ten minutes. Fred and I have some details to work out." He listened a moment, then racked the receiver and turned to Handy.

"Okay. What?"

"Jesus Christ, Arthur. Haskell Barkin, for Christ's sake. You've got to be *kid*ding."

"I talked to Valerie Lone last night. She sounded all by herself. I thought it might be smart therapy to get her a good-looking guy, as company, a chaperon, someone who'd be nice to her. I remembered this Barkin from—"

Handy stood up, frenzy impelling his movement. Banging off walls, vibrating at supersonic speeds, turning invisible with teeth-gritting. "I *know* where you remembered this Barkin from, Arthur. From Billie Landewyck's party, three years ago; the pool party; where you met Vivvi. I know. He told me."

"You've been to see Barkin already?"

"He had me out of bed too much before I wanted to get up."

"An honest day's working time won't hurt you, Fred. I was here at seven thir—"

"Arthur, I frankly, God forgive my talking to my producer this way, frankly don't give a flying *shit* what time you were behind your desk. Barkin, Arthur! You're insane."

"He seemed like a nice chap. Always smiling."

Handy leaned over the desk, talking straight into Arthur Crewes's cerebrum, eliminating the middleman. "So does the crocodile smile, Arthur. Haskell Barkin is a crud. He is a slithering, creeping, crawling, essentially reptilian monster who slices and eats. He is Jack the Ripper, Arthur. He is a vacuum cleaner. He is a loggerhead shark. He *hates* like we *urinate*—it's a basic bodily function for him. He leaves a wet trail when he walks. Small children run shrieking from him, Arthur. He's a killer in a suntan. Women who chew nails, who destroy men for giggles, women like *that* are afraid of him, Arthur. If you were a broad and he French-kissed you, Arthur, you'd have to go get a tetanus shot. He uses human bones to bake his bread. He's declared war on every woman who ever carried a crotch. This man is death, Arthur. And *that's* what you wanted to turn loose on Valerie Lone, God save her soul. He's Paris green, he's sump water, he's axle grease, Arthur! He's—"

Arthur Crewes spoke softly, looking battered by Handy's diatribe. "You made your point, Fred. I stand corrected."

Handy slumped down into the chair beside the desk.

To himself: "Jeezus, Huck Barkin, Jeezus. . ."

And when he had run down completely, he looked up. Crewes seemed poised in time and space. His idea had not worked out. "Well, whom would *you* suggest?"

Handy spread his hands.

"I don't know. But not Barkin, or anyone like him. No Strip killers, Arthur. That would be lamb to slaughter time."

Crewes: "But she needs *some*one."

Handy: "What's your special interest, Arthur?"

Crewes: "Why say that?"

Handy: "Arthur. . .c'mon. I can tell. There's a thing you've got going where she's concerned."

Crewes turned in his chair. Staring out the window at the lot, a series of flat-trucks moving scenery back to the storage bins. "You only work for me, Fred."

Handy considered, then decided what the hell. "If I worked for Adolf Eichmann, Arthur, I'd still ask where all them Jews was going."

Crewes turned back, looked levelly at his publicist. "I keep thinking you're nothing more than a flack-man. I'm wrong, aren't I?"

Handy shrugged. "I have a thought of my own from time to time."

Crewes nodded, acquiescing. "Would you just settle for my saying she once did me a favor? Not a big favor, just a little favor, something she probably doesn't even remember, or if she does she doesn't think of it in relation to the big producer who's giving her a comeback break. Would you settle for my saying I mean her nothing but good things, Fred? Would that buy it?"

Handy nodded. "It'll do."

"So who do we get to keep her reassured that she isn't ready for the dustbin just yet?"

Again Handy spread his hands. "I don't know, it's been eighteen years since she had anything to do with—hey! Wait a bit. What's his name. . .?"

"Who?"

"Oh, hell, *you* know. . ." Handy said, fumbling with his memory, ". . .the one who got fouled up with the draft during the war, blew his career, something, I don't remember. . .aw, c'mon Arthur, you know who I mean, used to play all the bright young attorney defending the dirty-faced delinquent parts." He snapped his fingers trying to call back a name from crumbling fan magazines, from rotogravure coming-attraction placards in theater windows.

Crewes suggested, "Call Sheilah Graham."

Handy came around the desk, dialed 9 to get out, and Sheilah Graham's private number, from memory. "Sheilah? Fred Handy. Yeah, hi. Hey, who was it Valerie Lone used to go with?" He listened. "No, huh-uh, the one that was always in the columns, he was married, but they had a big thing, he does bits now, guest shots, who—"

She told him.

"Right. Right, that's who. Okay, hey thanks, Sheilah. What? No, huh-uh, huh-uh; as soon as we get something right, it's yours. Okay, luv. Thanks. 'Bye."

He hung up and turned to Crewes. "Emery Romito."

Crewes nodded. "Jeezus, is he still alive?"

"He was on *Bonanza* about three weeks ago. Guest shot. Played an alcoholic veterinarian."

Crewes lifted an eyebrow. "Type casting?"

Handy was leafing through the volume of the PLAYERS DIRECTORY that listed leading men. "I don't think so. If he'd been a stone saucehound he'd've been planted long before this. I think he's just getting old, that's the worst."

Crewes gave a sharp, short bitter laugh. "That's enough."

Handy slammed the PLAYERS DIRECTORY closed. "He's not in there."

"Try character males," Crewes suggested.

Handy found it, in the R's. Emery Romito. A face out of the past, still holding a distinguished mien, but even through the badly reproduced photo that had been an 8x10 glossy, showing weariness and the indefinable certainty that this man knew he had lost his chance at picking up all the marbles.

Handy showed Crewes the photo. "Do you think this is a good idea?" Handy looked at him.

"It's a helluva lot better idea than *yours*, Arthur."

Crewes sucked on the edge of his lower lip between clenched teeth. "Okay. Go get him. But make him look like a knight on a white charger. I want her very happy."

"Knights on white chargers these days come barrel-assing down the streets of suburbia with their phalluses in hand, blasting women's underwear whiter-than-white. Would you settle for merely *mildly* happy?"

5

Cotillions could have been held in the main drawing room of the Stratford Beach Hotel. Probably had been. In the days when Richard Dix had his way with Leatrice Joy, in the days when Zanuck had his three rejected scenarios privately published as a "book" and sent them around to the studios in hopes of building his personal stock, in the days when Virginia Rappe was being introduced to the dubious sexual joys of a fat kid named Arbuckle. In those days the Stratford Beach Hotel had been a showplace, set out on the lovely Santa Monica shore, overlooking the triumphant Pacific.

Architecturally, the hotel was a case in point for Frank Lloyd Wright's contention that the Sunshine State looked as though "someone had tipped the United States up on its east coast, and everything that was loose went tumbling into California." Great and bulky, sunk to its hips in the earth, with rococo flutings at every possible juncture, portico'd and belfry'd, the Stratford Beach had passed through fifty years of scuffling feet, spuming salt-spray, drunken orgies, changed bed-linen and insipid managers to end finally in this backwash eddy of a backwash suburb.

In the main drawing room of the Stratford Beach, standing on the top step of a wide, spiraling staircase of onyx that ran down into a room where the dust in the ancient carpets rose at each step to mingle with the downdrifting film of shattered memories, fractured yesterdays, mote-infested yearnings and the unmistakable stench of dead dreams, Fred Handy knew what had killed F. Scott Fitzgerald. This room, and the thousands of others like it, that held within their ordered interiors a kind of deadly magic of remembrance; a pull and tug of eras that refused to give up the ghost, that had not the common decency to pass away and let new times be born. The embalmed forevers that never came to be. . .they were here, lurking in the colorless patinas of dust that covered the rubber plants, that settled in the musty odor of the velvet plush furniture, that shone dully up from inlaid hardwood floors where the Charleston had been danced as a racy new thing.

This was the terrifying end-up for all the refuse of nostalgia. Hooked on this scene had been Fitzgerald, lauding and singing of something that was dead even as it was born. And so easily hooked could *anyone* get on this, who chose to live after their time was passed.

The words tarnish and mildew again formed in Handy's mind, superimposed as subtitles over a mute sequence of Valerie Lone shrieking in closeup. He shook his head, and not a moment too soon. Emery Romito came down the stairs from the second floor of the hotel, walking up behind Handy across the inlaid tiles of the front hall. He stood behind Handy, staring down into the vast living room. As Handy shook his head, fighting to come back to today.

"Elegant, isn't it?" Emery Romito said.

The voice was cultivated, the voice was deep and warm, the voice was histrionic, the voice was filled with memory, the voice was a surprise in the silence, but none of these were the things that startled Handy. The present tense, *isn't it*. Not, wasn't it; isn't it.

Oh my God, Handy thought.

Afraid to turn around, Fred Handy felt himself sucked into the past. This room, this terrible room, it was so help him God a portal to the past. The yesterdays that had never gone to rest were all here, crowding against a milky membrane separating them from the world of right here and now, like eyeless soulless wraiths, hungering after the warmth and presence of his corporeality. They wanted. . .what? They wanted his *au courant*. They wanted his today, so they could hear "Nagasaki" and "Vagabond Lover" and "Please" sung freshly again. So they could rouge their knees and straighten their headache bands over their foreheads. Fred Handy, man of today, assailed by the ghosts of yesterday, and terrified to turn around and see one of those ghosts standing behind him.

"Mr. Handy? You *are* the man who called me, aren't you?"

Handy turned and looked at Emery Romito.

"Hello," he said, through the dust of decades.

Jefferson once said people get pretty much the kind of government they deserve, which is why I refuse to listen to any bullshit carping by my fellow Californians about Reagan and his gubernatorial gang-banging—what I chose to call government by artificial insemination when I was arguing with Julie, a registered Republican, when we weren't making love—because it seems to me they got just what they were asking for. The end-product of a hundred years of statewide paranoia and rampant lunacy. That philosophy—stripped of Freudian undertones—has slopped over into most areas of my opinion. Women who constantly get stomped on by shitty guys generally have a streak of masochism in them; guys who get their hearts eaten away by rodent females are basically self-flagellants. And when you see someone who has been ravaged by life, it is a safe bet he has been a willing accomplice at his own destruction.

All of this passed through my mind as I said hello to Emery Romito. The picture in the PLAYERS DIRECTORY had softened the sadness. But in living color he was a natural for one of those billboards hustling Forest Lawn pre-need cemetery plots. *Don't get caught with your life down.*

He was one of the utterly destroyed. A man familiar to the point of incest with the forces that crush and maim, a man stunned by the hammer. And I could conceive of *no one* who would aid and abet those kind of forces in self-destruction. No. No one.

Yet no man could have done it to himself without the help of the Furies. And so, I was ambivalent. I felt both pity and cynicism for Emery Romito, and his brave foolish elegance.

Age lay like soot in the creases of what had once been a world-famous face. The kind of age that means merely growing old, without wistfulness or delight. This man had lived through all the days and nights of his life with only one thought uppermost: let me forget what has gone before.

"Would you like to sit out on the terrace?" Romito asked. "Nice breeze off the ocean today."

I smiled acquiescence, and he made a theatrical gesture in the direction of the terrace. As he preceded me down the onyx steps into the living room, I felt a clutch of nausea, and followed him. Cheyne–Stokes breathing as I walked across the threadbare carpet, among the deep restful furniture that called to me, suggested I try their womb comfort, sink into them never to rise again. Or if I did, it would be as a shriveled, mummified old man. (And with the memory of a kid who grew up on movies, I saw Margo as Capra had seen her in 1937, aging horribly, shriveling, in a matter of seconds, as she was being carried out of Shangri-La. And I shuddered. A grown man, and I shuddered.)

It was like walking across the bottom of the sea; shadowed, filtered with sounds that had no names, caught by shafts of sunlight from the skylight above us that contained freshets of dust-motes rising tumbling surging upward, threading between sofas and Morris chairs like whales in shoal, finally arriving at the fogged dirty French doors that gave out onto the terrace.

Romito opened them smoothly, as if he had done it a thousand times in a thousand films—and probably had—for a thousand Anita Louises. He stepped out briskly, and drew a deep breath. In that instant I realized he was in extremely good shape for a man his age, built big across the back and shoulders, waist still trim and narrow, actually quite dapper. Then why did I think of him as a crustacean, as a pitted fossil, as a gray and wasted relic?

It was the air of fatality, of course. The superimposed chin-up-through-it-all horseshit that all Hollywood hangers-on adopted. It was an atrophied devolutionary extension of *The Show Must Go On* shuck; the myth that owns everyone in the Industry: that getting forty-eight minutes of hack cliché! situation comedy filmed—only the barest minimally innervating—to capture the boggle-eyed interest of the Great Unwashed sucked down in the doldrum mire of The Great American Heartland, so they will squat there for twelve minutes of stench odor poison and artifact hardsell, is an occupation somehow inextricably involved with advancing the course of Western Civilization. A myth that has oozed over into all areas of modern thought, thus turning us into a "show biz culture" and spawning such creatures as Emery Romito. Like the cats in the empty Ziv Studios, nibbling at the leftover garbage of the film industry, but loath to leave it. (Echoes of the old saw about the carnival assistant whose job it was to shovel up elephant shit who, when asked why he didn't get a better job, replied, "What? And leave show biz?") Emery Romito was one of the clingers to the underside of the rock that was show biz, that heavy weight dominating like Gibraltar the landscape of Americana.

He had forfeited his humanity in order to remain "with it." He was dead, and didn't know it. *What, and leave show biz?*

The terrace was half the size of the living room, which made it twice as large as the foyer of Grauman's Chinese. Gray stone balustrades bounded it, and earthquake tremors had performed an intricate calligraphy across the inlaid and matched flagstones. It was daylight, but that didn't stop the shadowy images of women with bobbed hairdos and men with pomaded glossiness from weaving in and around us as we stood there, staring out at the ocean. It was ghost-time again, and secret liaisons were being effected out on the terrace by dashing sheiks (whose wives [married before their men had become nickelodeon idols] were inside slugging the spiked gin-punch) and hungry little hopefuls with waxed shins and a dab of alum in their vaginas, anxious to grasp magic.

"Let's sit down," Emery Romito said. To me, not the ghosts. He indicated a conversation grouping of cheap tubular aluminum beach chairs, their once-bright webbing now hopelessly faded by sun and sea-mist.

I sat down and he smiled ingratiatingly.

Then he sat down, careful to pull up the pants creases in the Palm Beach suit. The suit was in good shape, but perhaps fifteen years out of date.

"Well," he said.

I smiled back. I hadn't the faintest idea what "well" was a preamble to, nor what I was required to answer. But he waited, expecting me to say something.

When I continued to smile dumbly, his expression crumpled a little, and he tried another tack. "Just what sort of part *is* it that Crewes has in mind?"

Oh my God, I thought. *He thinks it's an interview.*

"Uh, well, it isn't pre*cise*ly a part in the film I'm here to talk to you about, Mr. Romito." It was much too intricate a syntax for a man whose heart might attack him at any moment.

"It isn't a part," he repeated.

"No, it was something rather personal. . ."

"It isn't a part." He whispered it, barely heard, lost instantly in the overpowering sound of the Santa Monica surf not far beyond us.

"It's about Valerie Lone," I began.

"Valerie?"

"Yes. We've signed her for *Subterfuge* and she's back in town and—"

"*Subterfuge?*"

"The film Mr. Crewes is producing."

"Oh. I see."

He didn't see at all. I was sure of that. I didn't know how in the world I could tell this ruined shell that his services were needed as escort, not actor. He saved me the trouble. He ran away from me, into the past.

"I remember once, in 1936 I believe. . .no, it was '37, that was the year I did *Beloved Liar*. . ."

I let the sound of the surf swell inside me. I turned down the gain on Emery Romito and turned up the gain on nature. I knew I would be able to get him to do what needed to be done—he was a lonely, helpless man for whom *any* kind of return to the world of glamour was a main chance. But it would take talking, and worse. . .listening.

". . .Thalberg called me in, and he was smiling, it was a very unusual thing, you can be sure. And he said: 'Emery, we've just signed a girl for your next picture,' and of course it was Valerie. Except that wasn't her name then, and he took me over to the Commissary to meet her. We had the special salad, it was little slivers of ham and cheese and turkey, cut so they were stacked one on top of the other, so you tasted the ham first, then the cheese, then the turkey, all in one bite, and the freshest green crisp lettuce, they called it the William Powell Salad. . .no, that isn't right. . .the William Powell was crab meat. . .I think it was the Norma Talmadge Salad. . .or was it. . ."

As I sat there talking to Emery Romito, what I did not know was that all the way across the city, at the Studio, Arthur was entering the lot with Valerie Lone, in a chauffeured Bentley. He told me about it that night, and it was horrible. But it served as the perfect counterpoint to the musty warm monologue being delivered to me that moment by the Ghost of Christmas Past.

How lovely, how enriching, to sit there in sumptuous, palatial Santa Monica, Showplace of the Western World, listening to the voice from beyond reminisce about tuna fish and avocado salads. I prayed for deafness.

6

Crewes had called ahead. "I want the red carpet, do I make my meaning clear?" The studio public relations head had said yes, he understood. Crewes had emphasized the point: "I don't want any fuckups, Barry. Not even the smallest. No gate police asking for a drive-on pass, no secretary making her wait. I want every carpenter and grip and mail boy to know we're bringing Valerie Lone back today. And I want *deference*, Barry. If there's a fuckup, even the smallest fuckup, I'll come down on you the way Samson brought down the temple."

"Christ, Arthur, you don't have to threaten me!"

"I'm not threatening, Barry, I'm making the point so you can't weasel later. This isn't some phony finger-popping rock singer, this is Valerie Lone."

"All *right*, Arthur! Stop now."

When they came through the gate, the guards removed their caps, and waved the Bentley on toward the sound stages. Valerie Lone sat in the rear, beside Arthur Crewes, and her face was dead white, even under the makeup she had applied in the latest manner—for 1945.

There was a receiving line outside Stage 16.

The Studio head, several members of the foreign press, the three top producers on the lot, and half a dozen "stars" of current tv series. They made much over her, and when they were finished, Valerie Lone had almost been convinced someone gave a damn that she was not dead.

When the flashing red gumball light on its tripod went out—signifying that the shot had been completed inside the sound stage—they entered. Valerie took three steps beyond the heavy soundproof door, and stopped. Her eyes went up and up, into the dim reaches of the huge barnlike structure, to the catwalks with their rigging, the lights anchored to their brace boards, the cool and wonderful air from the conditioners that rose to heat up there, where the gaffers worked. Then she stepped back into the shadows as Crewes came up beside her, and he knew she was crying, and he turned to ask the others if they would come in later, to follow Miss Lone on her visit. The others did not understand, but they went back outside, and the door sighed shut on its pneumatic hinges.

Crewes went to her, and she was against the wall, the tears standing in her eyes, but not running down to ruin the makeup. In that instant Crewes knew she would be all right: she was an actress, and for an actress the only reality is the fantasy of the sound stages. She would not let her eyes get red. She was tougher than he'd imagined.

She turned to him, and when she said, "Thank you, Arthur," it was so soft, and so gentle, Crewes took her in his arms and she huddled close to him, and there was no passion in it, no striving to reach bodies, only a fine and warm protectiveness. He silently said no one would hurt her, and silently she said my life is in your hands.

After a while, they walked past the coffee machine and Willie, who said hello Miss Lone it's good to have you back; and past the assistant director's lectern where the shooting schedule was tacked onto the sloping board, where Bruce del Vaille nodded to her, and looked awed; and past the extras slumped in their straight-backed chairs, reading Irving Wallace and knitting, waiting for their calls, and they had been told who it was, and they all called to her and waved and smiled; and past the high director's chair which was at that moment occupied by the script supervisor, whose name was Henry, and he murmured hello, Miss Lone, we worked together on suchandsuch, and she went to him and kissed him on the cheek, and he looked as though he wanted to cry, too. For Arthur Crewes, in the sound stage somewhere, a bird twittered gaily. He shrugged and laughed, like a child.

Someone yelled, "Okay, settle down! Settle down!"

The din fell only a decibel. James Kencannon was talking to Mitchum, to one side of the indoor set that was decorated to be an outdoor set. It was an alley in a Southwestern town, and the cyclorama in the background had been artfully rigged to simulate a carnival somewhere in the middle distance. Lights played off the canvas, and for Valerie Lone it was genuine; a real carnival erected just for her. The alley was dirty and extremely realistic. Extras lounged against the brick walls that were not brick walls, waiting for the call to roll it. The cameraman was setting the angle of the shot, the big piece of equipment on its balloon tires set on wooden tracks, ready to dolly back when the grips pulled it. The assistant cameraman with an Arriflex on his shoulder was down on one knee, gauging an up-angle for action shooting.

Del Vaille came onto the set and Kencannon nodded to him. "Okay, roll—" Kencannon stopped the preparations for the shot, and asked the first assistant director to measure off the shot once more, as Mitchum stepped into the position that had, till that moment, been held by his stand-in. The first assistant unreeled the tape measure, announced it; the cameraman gave a turn to one of the flywheels on the big camera, and nodded ready to the assistant director, who turned and bawled, "Okay! Roll it!"

A strident bell clanged in the sound stage and dead silence fell. People in mid-step stopped. No one coughed. No one spoke. Tony, the sound mixer, up on his high platform with his earphones and his console, announced, "Take thirty-three Bravo!" which resounded through the cavernous set and was picked up through the comm box by the sound truck outside the sound stage. When it was up to speed, Tony yelled, "Speed!" and the first assistant director stepped forward into the shot with his wooden clackboard bearing Kencannon's name and the shot number. He clacked the stick to establish sound synch and get the board photographed, and there was a beat as he withdrew, as Mitchum drew in a breath for the action to come, as everyone poised hanging in limbo and Kencannon—like all directors—relished the moment of absolute power waiting for his voice to announce action.

Infinite moment.

Birth of dreams.

The shadow and the reality.

"Action!"

As five men leaped out of darkness and grabbed Robert Mitchum, shoving him back up against the wall of the alley. The camera dollied in rapidly to a closeup of Mitchum's face as one of the men grabbed his jaw with brutal fingers. "Where'd you take her. . .tell us where you took her!" the assailant demanded with a faint Mexican accent. Mitchum worked his jaw muscles, tried to shove the man away. The Arriflex operator was down below them, out of the master shot, purring away his tilted angles of the scuffling men. Mitchum tried to speak, but couldn't with the man's hand on his face. "Let'm talk, Sanchez!" another of the men urged the assailant. He released Mitchum's face, and in the same instant Mitchum surged forward, throwing two of the men from him, and breaking toward the camera as it dollied rapidly back to encompass the entire shot. The Arriflex operator scuttled with him, tracking him in wobbly closeup. The five men dived for Mitchum, preparatory to beating the crap out of him as Kencannon yelled, "Cut! That's a take!" and the enemies straightened up, relaxed, and Mitchum walked swiftly to his mobile dressing room. The crew prepared to set up another shot.

The extras moved in. A group of young kids, obviously bordertown tourists from a *yanqui* college, down having a ball in the hotbed of sin and degradation.

They milled and shoved, and Arthur found himself once again captivated by the enormity of what was being done here. A writer had said: ESTABLISHING SHOT OF CROWD IN ALLEY and it was going to cost about fifteen thousand dollars to make that line become a reality. He glanced at Valerie beside him, and she was smiling, a thin and delicate smile part remembrance and part wonder. It really never wore off, this delight, this entrapment by the weaving of fantasy into reality.

"Enjoying yourself?" he asked softly.

"It's as though I'd never been away," she said.

Kencannon came to her, then. He held both her hands in his, and he looked at her: as a man and as a camera. "Oh, you'll do just fine. . .just fine." He smiled at her. She smiled back.

"I haven't read the part yet," she said.

"Johnny Black hasn't finished expanding it yet. And I don't give a damn. You'll do fine, just fine!" They stared at each other with the kind of intimacy known only to a man who sees a reality as an image on celluloid, by a woman confronting a man who can make her look seventeen or seventy. Trust and fear and compassion and a mutual cessation of hostilities between the sexes. It was always like this. As if to say: what does he see? What does she want? What will we settle for? I love you.

"Have you said hello to Bob Mitchum yet?" Kencannon asked her.

"No. I think he's resting." She was, in turn, deferential to a star, as those without marquee-value had been deferential to her. "I can meet him later."

"Are there any questions you'd like to ask?" he said. He waved a hand at the set around him. "You'll be living here for the next few weeks, you'd better get to know it."

"Well. . .yes. . .there are a few questions," she said. And she began getting into the role of star once more. She asked questions. Questions that were twenty years out of date. Not stupid questions, just *not quite in focus*. (As if the clackboard had not been in synch with the sound wagon, and the words had emerged from the actors' mouths a micro-instant too soon.) Not embarrassing questions, merely awkward questions; the answers to which entailed Kencannon's educating her, reminding her that she was a relic, that time had not waited for her—

even as she had not waited when she had been a star—but had gathered its notes in a rush and plunged panting heavily past her. Now she had to exercise muscles of thought that had atrophied, just to try and catch up with time, dashing on ahead there like an ambitious mailroom boy trying to make points with the Studio executives. Her questions became more awkward. Her words came with more difficulty. Crewes saw her getting—how did Handy put it?—uptight.

Three girls had come onto the set from a mobile dressing room back in a dark corner of the sound stage. They wore flowered wrappers. The assistant director was herding them toward the windows of a dirty little building facing out on the alley. The girls went around the back of the building—back where it was unpainted pine and brace-rods and Magic Marker annotated as SUBTER'GE 115/144 indicating in which scenes these sets would be used.

They appeared in three windows of the building. They would be spectators at the stunt-man's fight with the assailants in the alley. . .Mitchum's fight with the assailants in the alley. They were intended to represent three Mexican prostitutes, drawn to their windows by the sounds of combat. They removed their wrappers.

Their naked, fleshy breasts hung on the window ledges like Dali-esque melting casabas, waiting to ripen. Valerie Lone turned and saw the array of deep-brown nipples, and made a strange sound, "Awuhhh!" as if they had been something put on sale at such a startlingly low price she was amazed, confused and repelled out of suspicion.

Kencannon hurriedly tried to explain the picture was being shot in two versions, one for domestic and eventual television release, the other for foreign marketing. He went into a detailed comparison of the two versions, and when he had finished—with the entire cast of extras listening, for the explication of hypocrisy is always fascinating—Valerie Lone said:

"Gee, I hope none of *my* scenes have to be shot without clothes. . ."

And one of the extras gave a seal-like bark of amusement. "Fat chance," he murmured, just a bit too loud.

Arthur Crewes went around in a fluid movement that was almost choreography, and hit the boy—a beach-bum with long blond hair and fine deltoids—a shot that traveled no more than sixteen inches. It was a professional fighter's punch, no windup, no bolo, just a short hard piston jab that took the boy directly under the heart. He vomited air and lost his lower legs. He sat down hard.

If Crewes had thought about it, he would not have done it. The effect on the cast. The inevitable lawsuit. The Screen Extras Guild complaint. The bad form of striking someone who worked for him. The look on Valerie Lone's face as she caught the action with peripheral vision. The sight of an actor sitting down in pain, like a small child seeking a sandpile.

But he didn't think, and he did it, and Valerie Lone turned and ran. . .

Questions that were not congruent with a film that has to take into account television rerun, accelerated shooting schedules, bankability of stars, the tenor of the kids who make up the yeoman cast of every film, the passage of time and the improvement of techniques, and the altered thinking of studio magnates, the sophisticated tastes and mores of a new filmgoing audience.

A generation of youth with no respect for roots and heritage and the past. With no understanding of what has gone before. With no veneration of age. The times had conspired against Valerie Lone. Even as the times had conspired against her twenty years before. The simple and singular truth of it was that Valerie Lone had not been condemned by a lack of talent—though a greater talent might have sustained her—nor by a weakness in character—though a more ruthless nature might have carried her through the storms—nor by fluxes and flows in the Industry, but by all of these things, and by Fate and the times. But mostly the times. She was simply, singularly, not one with her world. It was a Universe that had chosen to care about Valerie Lone. For most of the world, the Universe didn't give a damn. For rare and singular persons from time to time in all ages, the Universe felt a compassion. It felt a need to succor and warm, to aid and bolster. That disaster befell all of these "wards of the Universe" was only proof unarguable that the

Universe was inept, that God was insane.

It would have been better by far had the Universe left Valerie Lone to her own destiny. But it wouldn't, it couldn't; and it combined all the chance random elements of encounter and happenstance to litter her path with roses. For Valerie Lone, in the inept and compassionate Universe, the road was broken glass and dead birds, as far down the trail as she would ever be able to see.

The Universe had created the tenor of cynicism that hummed silently through all the blond beach-bums of the Hollywood extra set. . .the Universe had dulled Valerie Lone's perceptions of the Industry as it was today. . .the Universe had speeded up the adrenaline flow in Arthur Crewes at the instant the blond beach-bum had made his obnoxious comment. . .and the Universe had, in its cockeyed, simple-ass manner, thought it was benefiting Valerie Lone.

Obviously not.

And it would be this incident, this rank little happening, that would inject the tension into her bloodstream, that would cause her nerves to fray just that infinitesimal amount necessary, that would bring about metal fatigue and erosion and rust. So that when the precise moment came when optimum efficiency was necessary. . .Valerie Lone would be hauled back to this instant, this remark, this vicious little scene; and it would provide the weakness that would doom her.

From that moment, Valerie Lone began to be consumed by her shadow. And nothing could prevent it. Not even the wonderful, wonderful Universe that had chosen to care about her.

A Universe ruled by a mad God, who was himself being consumed by his shadow.

Valerie Lone turned and ran. . .

Through the sound stage, out the door, down the studio street, through Philadelphia in 1910, past the Pleasure Dome of Kubla Khan, around a Martian sand-city, into and out of Budapest during the Uprising (where castrated Red tanks still lay drenched in the ash-drunkenness of Molotov cocktails), and through Shade's Wells onto a sun-baked plain where the imbecilically gaping mouth of the No. 3 Anaconda Mine received her.

She dashed into the darkness of the Anaconda, and found herself in the midst of the Springhill Mine Disaster. Within and without, reality was self-contained.

Arthur Crewes and James Kencannon dashed after her.

At the empty opening to the cave, Crewes stopped Kencannon. "Let me, Jim."

Kencannon nodded, and walked slowly away, pulling his pipe from his belt, and beginning to ream it clean with a tool from his shirt pocket.

Arthur Crewes let the faintly musty interior of the prop cave swallow him. He stood there silently, listening for murmurings of sorrow, or madness. He heard nothing. The cave only went in for ten or fifteen feet, but it might well have been the entrance to the deepest pit in Dante's Inferno. As his eyes grew accustomed to the gloom, he saw her, slumped down against some prop boulders.

She tried to scuttle back out of sight, even as he moved toward her.

"Don't." He spoke the one word softly, and she held.

Then he came to her, and sat down on a boulder low beside her. Now she wasn't crying.

It hadn't been that kind of rotten little scene.

"He's an imbecile," Crewes said.

"He was right," she answered. There was a sealed lock-vault on pity. But self-realization could be purchased over the counter.

"He *wasn't* right. He's an ignorant young pup and I've had him canned."

"I'm sorry for that."

"Sorry doesn't get it. What he did was inexcusable." He chuckled softly, ruefully. "What *I* did was inexcusable, as well. I'll hear from SEG about it." That chuckle rose. "It was worth it."

"Arthur, let me out."

"I don't want to hear that."

"I have to say it. Please. Let me out. It won't work."

"It *will* work. It *has* to work."

She looked at him through darkness. His face was blank, without features, barely formed in any way. But she knew if she could see him clearly that there would be intensity in his expression. "Why is this so important to you?"

For many minutes he did not speak, while she waited without understanding. Then, finally, he said, "Please let me do this thing for you. I want. . .very much. . .for you to have the good things again."

"But, why?"

He tried to explain, but it was not a matter of explanations. It was a matter of pains and joys remembered. Of being lonely and finding pleasure in motion pictures. Of having no directions and finding a future in what had always been a hobby. Of having lusted for success and coming at last to it with the knowledge that movies had given him everything, and she had been part of it. There was no totally rational explanation that Arthur Crewes could codify for her. He had struggled upward and she had given him a hand. It had been a small, a tiny, a quickly forgotten little favor—if he told her now she would not remember it, nor would she think it was at all comparable to what he was trying to do for her. But as the years had hung themselves on Arthur Crewes's past, the tiny favor had grown out of all proportion in his mind, and now he was trying desperately to pay Valerie Lone back.

All this, in a moment of silence.

He had been in the arena too long. He could not speak to her of these nameless wondrous things, and hope to win her from her fears. But even in his silence there was clarity. She reached out to touch his face.

"I'll try," she said.

And when they were outside on the flat, dry plain across which Kencannon started toward them, she turned to Arthur Crewes and she said, with a rough touch of the wiseacre that had been her trademark eighteen years before, "But I still ain't playin' none of your damn scenes in the noood, buster."

It was difficult, but Crewes managed a smile.

Meanwhile, back at my head, things were going from Erich von Stroheim to Alfred Hitchcock. No, make that from Fritz Lang to Val Lewton. Try bad to worse.

I'd come back from Never-Never Land and the song of the turtle, and had called in to Arthur's office. I simply could not face a return to the world of show biz so soon after polishing tombstones in Emery Romito's private cemetery. I needed a long pull on something called quiet, and it was not to be found at the studio.

My apartment was hot and stuffy. I stripped and took a shower. For a moment I considered flushing my clothes down the toilet: I was sure they were impregnated with the mold of the ages, fresh from Santa Monica.

Then I chivvied and worried the thought that maybe possibly I ought just to send myself out to Filoy Cleaners, *in toto*. "Here you go, Phil," I'd say. "I'd like myself cleaned and burned." *You need sleep, Handy*, I thought. *Maybe about seven hundred years' worth.*

Rip Van Winkle, old Ripper-poo, it occurred to me, in a passing flash of genuine lunacy, knew precisely where it was at. I could see it now, a Broadway extravaganza

RIP!
starring Fred Handy

who will sleep like a mother stone log for seven hundred years right before your perspiring eyes, at $2.25 / $4.25 / and $6.25 for Center Aisle Orchestra Seats.

The shower did little to restore my sanity.

I decided to call Julie.

I checked her itinerary—which I'd blackmailed out of her agent—and found that *Hello, Dolly!* was playing Pittsburgh, Pennsylvania. I dialed the Olady and told her all kindsa stuff. After a while she got into conversations with various kindly folks in the state of Pennsylvania, who confided in her, strictly *entre-nous*, that my Lady of the moist thighs, the fair Julie Glynn, *née* Rowena Glyckmeier, was out onna town somewheres, and O-lady 212 in Hollywood would stay right there tippy-tap up against the phone all night if need be, just to bring us two fine examples of Young American Love together, whenever.

As I racked the receiver, just as suddenly as I'd gotten *into* the mood, all good humor and fancy footwork deserted me. I realized I was sadder than I'd been in years. What the hell was happening? Why this feeling of utter depression; why this sense of impending disaster?

Then the phone rang, and it was Arthur, and he told me what had happened at the Studio. I couldn't stop shuddering.

He also told me there was an opening at the Coconut Grove that night, and he thought Valerie might like to attend. He had already called the star—it was Bobby Vinton, or Sergio Franchi, or Wayne Newton, or someone in that league—and there would be an announcement from the stage that Valerie Lone was in the audience, and a spontaneous standing ovation. I couldn't stop shuddering.

He suggested I get in touch with Romito and set up a date. Help wash away the stain of that afternoon. Then he told me the name of the extra who had insulted Valerie Lone—he must have been reading it off a piece of paper, he spoke the name with a flatness like the striking trajectory of a cobra—and suggested I compile a brief dossier on the gentleman. I had the distinct impression Arthur Crewes could be as vicious an enemy as he was cuddly a friend. The blond beach-bum would probably find it very hard getting work in films from this point on, though it was no longer the antediluvian era in which a Cohen or a Mayer or a Skouras could kill a career with a couple of phone calls. I couldn't stop shuddering.

Then I called Emery Romito and advised him he was to pick up Valerie Lone at six-thirty at the Beverly Hills. Tuxedo. He fumphuh'd and I knew he didn't have the price of a rental tux. So I called Wardrobe at the Studio and told them to send someone out to Santa Monica. . .and to dress him *au courant*, not in the wing-collar style of the Twenties, which is what I continued to shudder at in my mind.

Then I went back and took another shower. A hot shower. It was getting chilly in my body.

I heard the phone ringing through the pounding noise of the shower spray, and got to the instrument as my party was hanging up. There was a trail of monster wet footprints all across the living room behind me, vanishing into the bedroom and thence the bath, from whence I had comce.

"Yeah, who?" I yelled.

"Fred? Spencer."

A pungent footnote on being depressed. When you have just received word from the IRS that an audit of your returns will be necessary for the years 1956–66 in an attempt to pinpoint the necessity for a $13,000 per year entertainment exemption; when the ASPCA rings you up and asks you to come down and identify a body in their cold room, and they're describing your pet basset hound as he would look had he been through a McCormick reaper; when your wife, from whom you are separated, and whom you screwed last month only by chance when you took over her separation payment, calls and tells you she is with child—yours; when World War Nine breaks out and they are napalming your patio; when you've got the worst summer cold of your life, the left-hand corner of your mouth is cracked and chapped, your prostate is acting up again and oozing shiny drops of a hideous green substance; when all of this links into one gigantic chain of horror threatening to send you raving in the direction of Joe Pyne or Lawrence Welk, then, and only then, do agents named Spencer Lichtman call.

It is not a nice thing.

New horrors! I moaned silently. *New horrors!*

"Hey, you there, Fred?"

"I died."

"Listen, I want to talk on you."

"Spencer, please. I want to sleep for seven hundred years."

"It's the middle of a highly productive day."

"*I've* produced three asps, a groundhog and a vat of stale eels. Let me sleep, perchance to dream."

"I want to talk about Valerie Lone."

"Come over to the apartment." I hung up.

The wolf pack was starting to move in. I called Crewes. He was in conference. I said break in. Roz said fuckoff. I thanked her politely and retraced my monster wet footprints to the shower. Cold shower. Cold, hot, cold: if my moods continued to fluctuate, it was going to be double pneumonia time. (I might have called it my manic-depressive phase, except my moods kept going from depressive to depressiver. With not a manic in sight.)

Wearing a thick black plastic weight-reducing belt—compartments filled with sand—guaranteed to take five pounds of unsightly slob off my drooling gut—and a terry cloth wraparound, I built myself an iced tea in the kitchen. There were no ice cubes. I had a bachelor's icebox: a jar of maraschino cherries, an opened package of Philadelphia cream cheese with fungus growing on it, two tv dinners—Hawaiian shrimp and Salisbury steak—and a tin of condensed milk. If Julie didn't start marrying me or mothering me, it was certain I would be found starved dead, lying in a corner, clutching an empty carton of Ritz crackers, some fateful morning when they came to find out why I hadn't paid the rent in a month or two.

I went out onto the terrace of the lanai apartments, overlooking the hysterectomy-shaped swimming pool used for the 1928 Lilliputian Olympics. There were two slim-thighed creatures named Janice and Pegeen lounging near the edge. Pegeen had an aluminum reflector up to her chin, making sure no slightest inch of epidermis escaped UV scorching. Janice was on her stomach, oiled like the inside of a reservoir-tip condom. "Hey!" I yelled. "How're you fixed for ice cubes?" Janice turned over, letting her copy of Kahlil Gibran's THE PROPHET fall flat, and shaded her eyes toward me.

"Oh, hi, Fred. Go help yourself."

I waved thanks and walked down the line to their apartment. The door was open. I went in through the debris of the previous evening's amphetamine frolic, doing a dance to avoid the hookah and the pillows on the floor. There were no ice cubes. I filled their trays, reinserted them in the freezer compartment, and went back outside. "Everything groovy?" Janice yelled up at me.

"Ginchy," I called back, and went into my apartment.

Warm iced tea is an ugly.

I heard Spencer down below, shucking the two pairs of slim thighs. I waited a full sixty-count, hoping he would pass, just once. At sixty, I went to the door and yowled. "Up here, Spencer."

"Be right there, Fred," he called over his shoulder, his moist eyeballs fastened like snails to Pegeen's bikini.

"The specialist tells me I've only got twenty minutes to live, Spencer. Get your ass up here."

He murmured something devilishly clever to the girls, who regarded his retreating back with looks that compared it unfavorably to a haunch of tainted venison. Spencer mounted the stairs two at a time, puffing hideously, trying desperately to do a Steve McQueen for the girls.

"Hey, buhbie." He extended his hand as he came through the door.

Spencer Lichtman had been selected by the monthly newsletter and puff-sheet of the Sahara Hotel & Casino in Las Vegas, Nevada, U.S.A., in their August 1966 mailing, as Mr. Charm. They noted that he was charming whether he won or lost at the tables, and they quoted him as saying, after picking up eleven hundred dollars at craps, "It's only money." The newsletter thought that was mighty white of Spencer Lichtman. The newsletter also thought it was historically clever of him to have said it, and only avoided adding their usual editorial (Ha! Ha! Isn't old Spencer a wow!) with a non-Vegas reserve totally out of character for the "editor," a former junior ad exec well into hock to the management of the hotel, working it off by editing the puff-sheet in a style charitably referred to as Hand-Me-Down Mark Hellinger.

Spencer Lichtman was, to me, one of the great losers of all time, eleven hundred Vegan jellybeans notwithstanding. That he was a brilliant agent cannot be denied. But he did it *despite* himself, dear God let me have it pegged correctly otherwise my entire world-view is ass-backwards, not *because* of himself.

He was a tall, broad-shouldered, well-fried, blue-eyed specimen, handsomely cocooned within a Harry Cherry suit. Light-blue button-down shirts (no high-rise collars for Spencer, he knew his neck was too thick for them), black knee-length socks, highly polished black loafers, diminutive cuff links, and a paisley hankie in the breast pocket. He might have sprung full-blown like Adolph Menjou from the forehead of *Gentleman's Quarterly*.

Then tell me this: if Spencer Lichtman was good-looking, mannerly, talented, in good taste, and successful, why the hell did I know as sure as Burton made little green Elizabeths, that Spencer Lichtman was a bummer?

It defied analysis.

So I shook hands with him.

"Jesus, it's hot," he wheezed, falling onto the sofa, elegantly. Even collapsing, he had panache. "Can I impose on you for something cold?"

"I'm out of ice cubes."

"Oh."

"My neighbors are out of ice cubes, too."

"Those were your neighbors—"

"Right. Out there. The girls."

"Nice neighbors."

"Yeah. But they're *still* out of ice cubes."

"So I suppose we'd better talk. Then we can go over to the Luau and get something cold."

I didn't bother telling him I'd rather undergo intensive Hong Kong acupuncture treatments with needles in my cheeks, than go to the Luau for a drink. The cream of the Hollywood and Beverly Hills show biz set always made the Luau in the afternoons, hustling secretaries from the talent agencies who were, in actuality, the daughters of Beverly Hills merchants, the daughters of Hollywood actors, the daughters of Los Angeles society, the daughters of delight. The cream. That *is* the stuff that floats to the top, isn't it? Cream?

No, Spencer, I am not going with you to the Luau so you can hustle for me, and get me bedded down with one of your puffball-haired steno-typists, thereby giving you an edge on me for future dealings. No, indeed not,

Spencer, my lad. I am going to pass on all those fine trim young legs exposed beneath entirely too inflammatory minis. I am probably going to go into the bedroom after you've gone and play with myself, but it is a far far better thing I do than to let you get your perfectly white capped molars into me.

"You talk, Spencer. I'll listen." I sat down on the floor. "That's what I call cooperation."

He wanted desperately to undo his tie. But that would have been non-Agency. "I was talking to some of the people at the office. . ."

Translation: I read in the trades that Crewes has found this *alta-cockuh*, this old hag Valerie Whatshername, and at the snake-pit session this morning I suggested to Morrie and Lew and Marty that I take a crack at maybe we should rep her, there might be a dime or a dollar or both in it, so what are the chances?

I stared at him with an expression like Raggedy Andy.

"And, uh, we felt it would be highly prestigious for the Agency to represent Valerie Lone. . ."

Translation: At least we can clip ten percent off of this deal with Crewes, and she ought to be good for a second deal with him at the Studio, and if *anything* at *all* happens with her, there're two or three short-line deals we can make, maybe at American–International for one of those *Baby Jane/Lady in a Cage* horrorifics; shit, she'd sit still for *any* kind of star billing, even in a screamer like that. Play her right, and we can make thirty, forty grand before she falls in her traces.

I segued smoothly from Raggedy Andy into Lenny: *Of Mice and Men*. Except I didn't dribble.

"I think we can really move Valerie, in the field of features. And, of course, there's a *lot* of television open to her. . ."

Translation: We'll book the old broad into a guest shot on every nitwit series shooting now for a September air-date. Guest cameos are perfect for a warhorse like her. It's like every asshole in America had a private tube to the freak show. Come and see the Ice Age return! Witness the resurrection of Piltdown Woman! See the resurgence of Miss Ankle-Strap Wedgie! Gape and drool at the unburied dead! She'll play dance hall madams on *Cimarron Strip* and aging actresses on

Petticoat Junction; she'll play a frontier matriarch on *The Big Valley* and the mother of a kidnapped child on *Felony Squad*. A grand per day, at first, till the novelty wears off. We'll book her five or six deep till they get the word around. Then we'll make trick deals with the network for multiples. There's a potload in this.

Lenny slowly vanished to be replaced by Huck Finn.

"Well, *say* something, Fred! What do you think?"

Huck Finn vanished and in his stead Spencer Lichtman was staring down at Captain America, bearing his red-white-and-blue shield, decked out in his patriotic uniform with the wings on the cowl, with the steely gaze and the outthrust chin of the defender of widows and orphans.

Captain America said, softly, "You'll take five percent commission and I'll make sure she signs with you."

"Ten, Fred. You know that's standard. We can't—"

"Five." Captain America wasn't fucking around.

"Eight. *Maybe* I can swing eight. Morrie and Lew—"

Captain America shifted his star-studded shield up his arm and pulled his gauntlet tighter. "I'll be fair. Six."

Lichtman stood up, started toward the door, whirled on Captain America. "She's got to have representation, Handy. Lots of it. You know it. I know it. Name me three times you know of, when an agent took less than ten? We're working at twelve and even thirteen on some clients. This is a chancy thing. She might go, she might not. We're willing to gamble. You're making it lousy for both of us. I came to you because I know you can handle it. But we haven't even talked about *your* percentage."

Captain America's jaw muscles jumped. The inference that he could be bought was disgusting. He breathed the sweet breath of patriotic fervor and answered Spencer Lichtman—alias the Red Skull—with the tone he deserved. "No kickback for me, Spencer. Straight six."

Lichtman's expression was one of surprise. But in a moment he had it figured out, in whatever form his cynicism and familiarity with the hunting habits of the scene allowed him best and most easily to rationalize. There was an angle in it for me, he was sure of that. It was a sneaky angle, it had to be, because he couldn't find a trace of it, which meant it was subtler than most. On that level he was able to talk to me. Not to Captain America, never to old Cap; because Lichtman couldn't conceive of a purely altruistic act, old Spence couldn't. So there was a finagle here somewhere; he didn't know just where, but as thief to thief, he was delighted with the dealing.

"Seven."

"Okay."

"I should have stuck with eight."

"You wouldn't have made a deal if you had."

"You're sure she'll sign?"

"You sure you'll work your ass off for her, and keep the leeches away from her, and give her a straight accounting of earnings, and try to build the career and not just run it into the ground for a fast buck?"

"You know I—"

"You know *I*, baby! *I* have an eye on you. Arthur *Crewes* will have an eye on you. And if you fuck around with her, and louse her up, and then drop her, both Arthur and myself will do some very heavy talking with several of your clients who are currently under contract to Arthur, such as Steve and Raquel and Julie and don't you forget it."

"What's in this for you, Handy?"

"I've got the detergent concession."

"And I thought I was coming up here to hustle *you*."

"There's only one reason you're getting the contract, Spencer. She needs an agent, you're as honest as most of them—excluding Hal and Billy—and I believe *you* believe she can be moved."

"I do."

"I figured it like that."

"I'll set up a meet with Morrie and Lew and Marty. Early next week."

"Fine. Her schedule's pretty tight now. She starts rehearsals with the new scene day after tomorrow."

Spencer Lichtman adjusted his tie, smoothed his hair, and pulled down his suit jacket in the back. He extended his hand. "Pleasure doing business, Fred."

I shook once again. "Dandy, Spencer."

Then he smirked, suggesting broadly that he knew I must have a boondoggle only slightly smaller than the Teapot Dome going. And, so help me God, he winked. Conspiratorially.

Tonstant weader fwowed up.

When he left, I called Arthur, and told him what I'd done, and why. He approved, and said he had to get back to some work on his desk. I started to hang up, but heard his voice faintly, calling me back. I put the receiver up to my ear and said, "Something else, Arthur?"

There was a pause, then he said, gently, "You're a good guy, Fred." I mumbled something and racked it.

And sat there for twenty minutes, silently arguing with Raggedy Andy, Lenny, Huck and old Captain America. *They* thought I was a good guy, too. And *I* kept trying to get them to tell me where the sleazy angle might be, so I could stop feeling so disgustingly humanitarian.

Have you ever tried to pull on a turtleneck over a halo?

7

Valerie Lone had only been told she would be picked up at six-thirty, for dinner and an opening at the Grove. The flowers arrived at five-fifteen. Daisies. Roses were a makeout flower, much too premeditated. Daisies. With their simplicity and their honesty and their romance. Daisies. With one rose in the center of the arrangement.

At six-thirty the doorbell to Valerie Lone's bungalow was rung, and she hurried to open the door. (She had turned down the offer of a personal maid. "The hotel is very nice to me; their regular maid is fine, Arthur, thank you.")

She opened the door, and for a moment she did not recognize him. But for her, there had only been one like him; only one man that tall, that elegant, that self-possessed. The years had not touched him. He was the same. Not a hair out of place, not a line where no line had been, and the smile—the same gentle, wide pixie smile—it was the same, unaltered. Soft, filtered lights were unnecessary. For Valerie Lone he was the same.

But in the eye of the beheld. . .

Emery Romito looked across the past and all the empty years between, and saw his woman. There had been gold, and quicksilver, and soft murmurings in the night, and crystal, and water as sweet as Chablis, and velvet and plumes of exotic birds. . .and now

there was arthritis, and difficult breathing, and a heaviness in the air, and perspiration and nervousness, and stale rum cake, and the calling of children far away across the misty landscape, and someone very dark and hungry always coming toward him.

Now there was only now. And he lamented all the days that had died without joy. Hope had sung its song within him, in reverie, on nights when the heat had been too much for him and he had gone to sit at the edge of the ocean. Far out, beyond the lights of the amusement park at Lick Pier, beyond the lights of the night, the song had been raised against dark stars and darker skies. But had never been heard. Had gone to tremolo and wavering and finally sighed into the silent vacuum of despair, where sound can only be heard by striking object against object. And in that nowhere, there was no object for Emery Romito.

"Hello, Val. . ."

Tear loneliness across its pale surface; rend it totally and find the blood of need welling up in a thick, pale torrent. Let the horns of growth blare a message in rinky-tink meter. Turn a woman carrying all her years into a sloe-eyed gamine. Peel like an artichoke the scar-tissue heart of a lost dream, and find in the center a pulsing golden light with a name. She looked across yesterday and found him standing before her, and she could do no other than cry.

He came through the door as she sagged in upon herself. Her tears were soundless, so desperate, so overwhelming; they made her helpless. He closed the door behind him and gathered her to himself. Shrunken though he was, not in her arms, not in her eyes. He was still tall, gentle

Emery, whose voice was silk and softness. Collapsed within the eternity of his love, she beat back the shadows that had come to devour her, and she knew that now, *now* she would live. She spoke his name a hundred times in a second.

That night, *her* name was spoken by a hundred voices in a second; but this time, as she stood to applause for the first time in eighteen years, she did not cry. Emery Romito was with her, beside her, and she held his hand as she rose. Fred Handy was there; with the girl Randi, from the office that afternoon. Arthur Crewes was there; alone. Smiling. Jubilant. Radiating warmth for Valerie Lone and the good people who had never forgotten her. Spencer Lichtman was there; with Miss American Airlines and an orange-haired girl of pneumatic proportions starring in Joseph E. Levine's production of *Maciste and the Vestal Virgins*. ("You've got a better chance of convincing the public she's Maciste than a virgin," Handy muttered, as they passed in the lobby of the Ambassador Hotel.)

Valerie Lone! they cried. Valerie Lone!

She stood, holding Romito's hand, and the dream had come full circle.

Like the laocoönian serpent, swallowing its own tail. Ouroboros in Clown Town.

The next day John D.F. Black delivered the rewritten pages. The scenes for Valerie were exquisite. He asked if he might be introduced to Valerie Lone, and Fred took him over to the Beverly Hills, where Valerie was guardedly trying to get a suntan. It was the first time in many years that she had performed that almost religious Hollywood act: the deep-frying. She rose to meet Black, a tall and charming man with an actor's leathery good looks. In a few minutes he had charmed her completely, and told her he had been delighted to write the scenes for her, that they were just what she had always done best in her biggest films, that they gave her room to expand and color the part, that he knew she would be splendid. She asked if he would be on the set during shooting. Black looked at Handy. Handy looked away. Black shrugged and said he didn't know, he had another commitment elsewhere. But Valerie Lone knew that things had not changed all *that* much in Hollywood: the writer was still chattel. When his work on the script was done, it was no longer his own. It was given to the Producer, and the Director, and the Production Manager, and the Actors, and he was no longer welcome.

"I'd like Mr. Black to be on the set when I shoot, Mr. Handy," she said to Fred. "If Arthur doesn't mind."

Fred nodded, said he would see to it; and John D.F. Black bent, took Valerie Lone's hand in his own, and kissed it elegantly. "I love you," he said.

Late that night, Arthur and Fred took Valerie to the Channel 11 television studios on Sunset, and sat offstage as Valerie prepared for her on-camera live-action full-living-color interview with Adela Seddon, the Marquesa of Malice. A female counterpart of Joe Pyne, Adela Seddon spoke with forked tongue. She was much-watched and much-despised. Impartial voters learned their politics from her show. Wherever she was at, they were not. If she had come out in favor of Motherhood, Apple Pie and The American Way, tens of thousands of noncommitted people would instantly take up the banners of Misogyny, Macrobiotics and Master Racism. She was a badgerer, a harridan, a snarling viper with a sure mouth for the wisecrack and a ready fang for the jugular. Beneath a Tammy Grimes tousle of candy-apple red hair, her face was alternately compared with that of a tuba player confronting a small child sucking a lemon, and a prize shoat for the first time encountering the butcher's blade. She had been married six times, divorced five, was currently separated, hated being touched, and was rumored in private circles to have long-since gone mad from endless masturbation. Her nose job was not entirely successful.

Valerie was justifiably nervous.

"I've never seen her, Arthur. Working out there in the diner, nights you know, I've never seen her."

Handy, who thought it was lunacy to bring Valerie anywhere near the Seddon woman, added, "To see is to believe."

Valerie looked at him, concern showing like a second face upon the carefully drawn mask of cosmetics the Studio makeup head had built for her. She looked good, much younger, rejuvenated by the acclaim she had received at the Ambassador's Coconut Grove. (It had been the Righteous Brothers. They had come down into the audience and belted "My Babe" in her honor, right at her.)

"You don't think much of her, do you, Mr. Handy?"

Handy expelled air wearily. "About as charming as an acrobat in a polio ward. Queen of the Yahoos. The Compleat Philistine. Death warmed over. A pain in the—"

Crewes cut him off.

"No long lists, Fred. I had one of those from you already today. Remember?"

"It's been a long day, Arthur."

"Relax, please. Adela called me this afternoon, and *asked* for Valerie. She promised to be good. Very good. She's been a fan of Valerie's for years. We talked for almost an hour. She wants to do a nice interview."

Handy grimaced. Pain. "I don't believe it. The woman would do a Bergen-Belsen on her own Granny if she thought it would jump her rating."

Crewes spoke softly, carefully, as if telling a child. "Fred, I would not for a moment jeopardize Valerie if I thought there was any danger here. Adela Seddon is not my idea of a lady, either, but her show is *watched*. It's syndicated, and it's popular. If she says she'll behave, it behooves us to take the chance."

Valerie touched Handy's sleeve. "It's all right, Fred. I trust Arthur. I'll go on."

Crewes smiled at her. "Look, it's even live, not taped earlier in the evening, the way she usually does the show. This way we know she'll behave; they tape it in case someone guests who makes her look bad, they can dump the tape. But live like this, she has to be a nanny, or she could get killed. It stands to reason."

Handy looked dubious. "There's a flaw in that somewhere, Arthur, but I haven't the strength to find it. Besides," he indicated a flashing red light on the wall above them, "Valerie is about to enter the Valley of the Shadow. . ."

The stage manager came and got Valerie, and took her out onto the set, where she was greeted with applause from the studio audience. She sat in one of the two comfortable chairs behind the low desk, and waited patiently for Adela Seddon to arrive from her offstage office.

When she made her appearance, striding purposefully to the desk and seating herself, and instantly shuffling through a sheaf of research papers (presumably on Valerie Lone), the audience once again transported itself with wild applause. Which Adela Seddon did not deign to acknowledge. The signals were given, the control booth marked, and in a moment the offstage announcer was bibble-bibbling the intro. The audience did its number, and Camera No. 2 glowed red as a ghastly closeup of Adela Seddon appeared on the studio monitors. It was like a microscopic view of a rotted watermelon rind.

"This evening," Adela Seddon began, a smile that was a rictus stretching her mouth, "we are coming to you live, not on tape. The reason for this is my very special guest, a great lady of the American cinema, who agreed to come on only if we were aired live, thus ensuring a fair and unedited interview. . ."

"I *told* you she was a shit!" Handy hissed to Crewes. Crewes shushed him with a wave of his hand.

". . .not been seen for eighteen years on the wide-screens of motion picture theaters, but she is back in a forthcoming Arthur Crewes production, *Subterfuge*. I'd like a big hand for Miss Valerie Lone!"

The audience did tribal rituals, rain dances, ju-ju incantations and a smattering of plain and fancy warwhooping. Valerie was a lady. She smiled demurely and nodded her thankyous. Adela Seddon seemed uneasy at the depth of response, and shifted in her chair.

"She's getting out the blowdarts," Handy moaned.

"Shut up!" Crewes snarled. He was not happy.

"Miss Lone," Adela Seddon said, turning slightly more toward the nervous actress, "precisely *why* have you chosen this time to come back out of retirement? Do you think there's still an audience for your kind of acting?"

Ohmigod, thought Handy, *here it comes*.

EDITED TRANSCRIPT OF SEDDON
"LOOKING IN" / 11-23-67
(. . .*indicates deletion*)

VALERIE LONE: I don't know what you mean, "my kind of acting"?

ADELA SEDDON: Oh, come on now, Miss Lone.

VL: No, really. I don't.

AS: Well, I'll be specific then. The 1930s style: overblown and gushy.

VL: I didn't know that was my style, Miss Seddon.

AS: Well, according to your latest review, which is, incidentally, eighteen years old, in something called *Pearl of the Antilles* with Jon Hall, you are, quote, "a fading lollipop of minuscule talent given to instant tears and grandiose arm-waving." Should I go on?

VL: If it gives you some sort of pleasure.

AS: Pleasure isn't why I'm up here twice a week, Miss Lone. The truth is. I sit up here with kooks and twistos and people who denigrate our great country, and I let them have their say, without interrupting, because I firmly believe in the First Amendment of the Constitution of these United States of America, that everyone has the right to speak his mind. If that also happens to mean they have the right to make asses of themselves before seventy million viewers, it isn't my fault.

VL: What has all that to do with me?

AS: I don't mind your *thinking* I'm stupid, Miss Lone; just kindly don't *talk* to me as if I were stupid. The truth, Miss Lone, that's what all this has to do with you.

VL: Are you sure you'd recognize it?
(*Audience applause*)

AS: I recognize that there are many old-time actresses who are so venal, so egocentric, that they refuse to acknowledge their age, who continue to embarrass audiences by trying to cling to the illusion of sexuality.

VL: You shouldn't air your problems so openly, Miss Seddon.
(*Audience applause*)

AS: I see retirement hasn't dampened your wit.

VL: Nor made me immune to snakebites.

AS: You're getting awfully defensive, awfully early in the game.

VL: I wasn't aware this was a game. I thought it was an interview.

AS: This is *my* living room, Miss Lone. We call it a game, here, and we play it *my* way.

VL: I understand. It's not how you play, it's who wins.

AS: Why don't we just talk about your new picture for a while?

VL: That would be a refreshing change.

. . .

AS: Is it true Crewes found you hustling drinks in a roadhouse?

VL: Not quite. I was a waitress in a diner.

AS: I suppose you think slinging hash for the last eighteen years puts you in tip-top trim to tackle a major part in an important motion picture?

VL: No, but I think the fifteen years I spent in films prior to that *does*. A good actress is like a good doctor, Miss Seddon. She has the right to demand high pay not so much for the short amount of time she puts in on a picture, but for all the years before that, years in which she learned her craft properly, so she could perform in a professional manner. You don't pay a doctor merely for what he does for you *now*, but for all the years he spent learning how to do it.

AS: That's very philosophical.

VL: It's very accurate.

AS: I think it begs the question.

VL: *I* think *you'd* like to *think* it does.

. . .

AS: Wouldn't you say actresses are merely self-centered little children playing at make-believe?

VL: I would find it very difficult to say anything even remotely like that. I'm surprised you aren't embarrassed saying it.

AS: I'm hard to embarrass, Miss Lone. Why don't you answer the question?

VL: I thought I *had* answered it.

AS: Not to my satisfaction.

VL: I can see that not being satisfied has made you an unhappy woman, so I—

(*Audience applause*)

—so, so I don't want to dissatisfy you any further; I'll answer the question a little more completely. No, I think acting at its best can be something of a holy chore. If it emerges from a desire to portray life as it is, rather than just to put in a certain amount of time in front of the cameras for a certain amount of money, then it becomes as important as teaching or writing, because it crystallizes the world for an audience; it preserves the past; it lets others living more confined lives, examine a world they may never come into contact with. . .

AS: We have to take a break now, for a commercial—

. . .

VL: I'd rather not discuss my personal life, if you don't mind.

AS: A "star" has no personal life.

VL: That may be *your* opinion, Miss Seddon, it isn't mine.

AS: Is there some special reason you won't talk about Mr. Romito?

VL: We have always been good friends—

AS: Oh, come *on*, Valerie dear, you're starting to sound like a prepared press release: "We're just friends."

VL: You find it difficult to take yes for an answer.

AS: Well, I'll tell you, Miss Lone, I had a phone call today from a gentleman who volunteered to come into our dock tonight, to ask you a few questions. Let's go to the dock. . .what is your name, sir?

HASKELL BARKIN: My name is Barkin. Haskell Barkin.

AS: I understand you know Miss Lone.

HB: In a manner of speaking.

VL: I don't understand. I don't think I've ever met this gentleman.

HB: You almost did.

VL: What?

AS: Why don't you just let Mr. Barkin tell his story, Miss Lone.

She came offstage shaking violently. Romito had seen the first half of the interview, at his hotel in Santa Monica. He had hurried to the studio. When she stumbled away from the still-glaring lights of the set, he was there, and she almost fell into his arms. "Oh God, Emery, I'm so frightened. . ."

Crewes was furious. He moved into the darkness offstage, heading for Adela Seddon's dressing room/office. Handy had another mission.

The audience was filing out of the studio. Handy dashed for the side exit, came out in the alley next to the studio, and circled the building till he found the parking lot. Barkin was striding toward a big yellow Continental.

"Barkin! You motherfucker!" Handy screamed at him.

The tall man turned and stopped in mid-step. His long hair had been neatly combed for the evening television appearance, and in a suit he looked anachronistic, like King Kong in knickers. But the brace of his chest and shoulders was no less formidable.

He was waiting for Handy.

The little publicist came fast, across the parking lot. "How much did they pay you, you sonofabitch? How much? *How much, motherfucker!*"

Barkin began to crouch, waiting for Handy, fists balled, knees bent, the handsome face cold and impassive, anticipating the crunch of knuckles against face. Handy was howling now, like a Confederate trooper charging a Union gun emplacement. At a dead run he came down on Barkin, standing between a Corvette and a station wagon parked in the lot.

At the last moment, instead of breaking around the Corvette, Handy miraculously *leaped up* and came across the bonnet of the Corvette, still running, like a decathlon hurdler. Barkin had half-turned, expecting Handy's rush from the front of the sports car. But the publicist was suddenly above him, bearing down on him like a hunting falcon, before he could correct position.

Handy plunged across the Corvette, denting the red louvered bonnet, and dove full-out at Barkin. Blind with fury, he was totally unaware that he had bounded up onto the car, that he was across it in two steps, that he was flying through the air and crashing into Barkin with all the impact of a human cannonball.

He took Barkin high on the chest, one hand and wrist against the beach-bum's throat. Barkin whooshed air and sailed backward, into the station wagon. Up against the half-lowered radio antenna, which bent under his spine, then cracked and broke off in his back. Barkin screamed, a delirious, half-crazed spiral of sound as the sharp edge of the antenna cut through his suit jacket and shirt, and ripped his flesh. The pain bent him sidewise, and Handy slipped off him, catching his heel on the Corvette and tumbling into the narrow space between the cars. Barkin kicked out, his foot sinking into Handy's stomach as the publicist fell past him. Handy landed on his shoulders, the pain surging up into his chest and down into his groin. His rib cage seemed filled with nettles, and he felt for a moment he might lose control of his bladder.

Barkin tried to go for him, but the antenna was hooked through his jacket. He tried wrenching forward and there was a ripping sound, but it held. He struggled forward toward Handy awkwardly, bending from the waist, but could not get a hold on the publicist. Handy tried to rise, and Barkin stomped him, first on the hand, cracking bones and breaking skin, then on the chest, sending Handy scuttling backward on his buttocks and elbows.

Handy managed to get to his feet and pulled himself around the station wagon. Barkin was trying frantically to get himself undone, but the antenna had hooked in and out of the jacket material, and he was awkwardly twisted.

Handy climbed up onto the hood of the station wagon and on hands and knees, like a child, came across toward Barkin. The big man tried to reach him, but Handy fell across his neck and with senseless fury sank his teeth into Barkin's ear. The beach-bum shrieked again, a woman's sound, and shook his head like an animal trying to lose a flea. Handy hung on, bringing the taste of blood to his mouth. His hand came across and dug into the corner of Barkin's mouth, pulling the lip up and away. The fingers spread, he poked at Barkin's eye, and the beach-bum rattled against the car like a bird in a cage. Then all the pains merged and Barkin sagged in a semiconscious boneless mass. He hung against the weight of Handy and the hooking antenna. The strain was too great, the jacket ripped through, and Barkin fell face-forward hitting the side of the Corvette, pulling Handy over the top of the station wagon. Barkin's face hit the sports car; the nose broke. Barkin fainted with the pain, and slipped down into a Buddha-like position, Handy tumbling over him and landing on his knees between the cars.

Handy pulled himself up against the station wagon, and without realizing Barkin was unconscious, kicked out with a loose-jointed vigor, catching the beach-bum in the ribs with the toe of his shoe. Barkin fell over on his side, and lay there.

Handy, gasping, breathing raggedly, caromed off the cars, struggling to find his way to his own car. He finally made it to the Impala, got behind the wheel and through a fog of gray and red managed to get the key into the ignition. He spun out of the parking lot, scraping a Cadillac and a Mercury, his headlights once sweeping across a row of cars in which a station wagon and a Corvette were parked side by side, seeing a bleeding bag of flesh and fabric inching its way along the concrete, trying to get to its feet, touching softly at the shattered expanse of what had been a face, what had once been a good living.

Handy drove without knowing where he was going.

When he appeared at Randi's door twenty minutes later—having dropped her off from their date only a few hours before—she was wearing a shortie nightgown that ended at her thighs. "Jesus, Fred, what happened?" she asked, and helped him inside. He collapsed on her bed, leaving dark streaks of brown blood on the candy-striped sheets. She pulled his clothes off him, managing to touch his genitals as often as possible, and tended to his needs, all sorts of needs.

He paid no attention. He had fallen asleep.

It had been a full day for Handy.

The columns had picked it up. They said Valerie Lone had carried it off beautifully, coming through the barrage of viciousness and sniping with Adela Seddon like a champ. Army Archerd called Seddon a "shrike'" and suggested she try her dictionary for the difference between "argument" and "controversy," not to mention the difference between "intimidation" and "interview." Valerie was a minor folk heroine. She had gone into the lair of the dragon and had emerged dragging its fallopians behind her. Crewes and Handy were elated. There had been mutterings from Haskell Barkin's attorney, a slim and good-looking man named Taback who had seemed ashamed even to be handling Barkin's complaint. When Handy and Crewes and the Studio battery of lawyers got done explaining *precisely* what had happened, and Taback had met Handy, the attorney returned to Barkin and advised him to use Blue Cross to take care of the damage it would cover, get his current paramour to lay out for the facial rebuilding, and drop charges: no one would believe that a hulk the size of Haskell Barkin could get so thoroughly dribbled by a pigeonweight like Handy.

But that was only part of the Crewes-Handy elation. Valerie had begun to be seen everywhere with Emery Romito. The fan magazines were having a field day with it. To a generation used to reviling their elders, with no respect for age, there was a kind of sentimental Gene Stratton Porter loveliness to the reuniting of old lovers. No matter where Valerie and Emery went, people beamed on them. Talk became common that after all those years of melancholy and deprivation, at long last the lovers might be together permanently.

For Emery Romito it was the first time he had been truly alive since *they* had killed his career during the draft-dodging scandal. But that was all forgotten now; he seemed to swell with the newfound dignity he had acquired squiring the columns' hottest news item. That, combined with his rediscovery of what Valerie had always meant to him, made him something greater than the faded character actor the years had forced him to become. The fear was still there, but it could be forgotten for short times now.

Valerie had begun rehearsals with her fellow cast-members, and she was growing more confident day by day. The Seddon show had served to fill her once again with fear, but its repercussions—demonstrated in print—had effectively drained it away. These rises and fallings in temperament had an unconscious effect on her, but it was not discernible to those around her.

On the night of the second day of rehearsals, Emery came to pick her up at the Studio, in a car the Studio had rented for him. He took her to dinner at a small French restaurant near the Hollywood Ranch Market, and after the final Drambuie they drove up to Sunset, turned left, and cruised toward Beverly Hills.

It was a Friday night.

The hippies were out.

The teenie-boppers. The flower children. The new ones. The long hair, the tight boots, the paisley shirts, the mini-skirts, the loose sexuality, the hair vests, the shirts with the sleeves cut off, the noise, the jeering. The razored crevasse that existed between *their* time, when they had been golden and fans had pressed up against sawhorses at the premieres, to get their autographs, and *today*, a strange and almost dreamlike time of Surrealistic youth who spoke another tongue, moved with liquid fire and laughed at things that were painful. At a stoplight near Laurel Canyon, they stopped and were suddenly surrounded by hippies hustling copies of an underground newspaper, the *L.A. Free Press.* They were repelled by the disordered, savage look of the kids, like barbarians. And though the news vendors spoke politely, though they merely pressed up against the car and shoved their papers into the windows, the terror their very presence evoked in the two older people panicked Romito and he floored the gas pedal, spurting forward down Sunset, sending one beaded and flowered news-hippie sprawling, journals flying.

Romito rolled up his window, urging Valerie to do the same. It was something Kafkaesque to them as they whirled past the discothèques and the psychedelic book shops and the outdoor restaurants where the slim, hungry children of the strobe age languished, turned on, grooving heavy behind meth or grass.

He drove fast. All the way out Sunset to the Coast Highway and out the coast to Malibu.

Finally, Valerie said softly, "Emery, do you remember The Beach House? We used to go there all the time for dinner. Remember? Let's stop there. For a drink."

Romito smiled, the lines around his eyes gathering, in gentle humor. "Do I remember? I remember the night Dick Barthelmess did the tango on the bar with that swimmer, the girl from the Olympics. . .you know the one. . ."

But she didn't know the one. That particular memory had been lost. He had had the time to nurse the old memories—she had been slinging hash. No, she didn't remember the girl. But she did remember the old roadhouse that had been so popular with their set one of those years.

But when they came to the spot, they found the old roadhouse—predictably—had been razed. In its stead was a tiny beach-serving shopping center, and on the spot where Dick Barthelmess had danced the tango on the bar with that swimmer from the Olympics, there was an all-night liquor store, with a huge neon sign.

Emery Romito drove a few miles down the Coast Highway, past the liquor store, more by reflex than design. He pulled off on a side road paralleling the ocean, and there, on a ridge that sloped quickly down into darkness and surf somewhere below them, he stopped. They sat there silently together, the car turned off, their minds turned off, trapped in the darkness of loneliness, the landscape and their past.

Then, in a rush, all of it came back to Valerie Lone. The rush of thoughts waiting to be reexamined after twenty years. The reasons, the situations, the circumstances.

"Emery, why didn't we get married?"

And she answered her own question with a smile he could not see in the darkness. It was possible he had not even heard her, for he did not answer. And in her mind she ticked off the answers, all the deadly answers.

It was the dreams each of them had substituted for reality; the tenacity with which they had tried to clutch smoke and dream-mist; the stubborn refusal of each of them to acknowledge that the dream-mist and the smoke were bound to become ashes. And when each had been swallowed whole by the very careers they had thought would free them, they had become strangers. They were frightened to commit to one another, to anyone really, to anything but the world that stood and called their names a hundred times in a second, and beat hands in praise.

Then Emery spoke. As though his thoughts had been tracking similarly to her own, heading on a collision course for her mind and *her* thoughts hurtling toward him.

"You know, darling Val, you always made more money than me. Your name was always star-billing. . .at best, mine was always 'Also Featuring.' It wouldn't have worked."

She was nodding agreement, at the complete validity of it, and then, in an instant, the shock of what she was accepting without argument, believing *again* as she had the first time, the insanity of it hit her. Twenty years ago, in the fantasy-world, yes, those *might* have been real reasons—in the lunatic way that blasted and twisted logic seems rational in nightmares—but she had spent almost two decades in another life, and now she *knew* they were false, as specious as the life that claimed her on the screen.

But for a moment, for a long moment she had accepted it all again. It was the town, the industry, the way the show biz life sucked one under. For those in the industry it had rapidly become that way, as they had fallen under the spell of their own weird and golden lives; it had taken more than twenty years to catch on completely, to permeate the culture. But now it was possible never to come up from under that thick fog of delusion. Because it hung like a Los Angeles smog across the entire nation, perhaps the world.

But not for Valerie Lone. Never again for her.

"Emery, listen to me. . ."

He was talking softly to himself, the sound of moths in the fog. Talking about screen credits and money and days that had never really been alive, and now had to be put to death fully and finally.

"Emery! Darling! Please, listen to me!"

He turned to her. She saw him, then. Even dimly, only by moonlight, she saw him as he really was, not as she had wished him to be, standing there in the doorway of the bungalow at the Beverly Hills Hotel that first night of her new life with him. She saw what had happened to the man who had been strong enough to deny war and say he would lose everything rather than fight against his fellow man. Emery Romito had become a willing prisoner of his own show biz life. He had never escaped.

She knew she had to explain it all to him, to unlearn him, and then teach him anew. An infinite sadness filled her as she readied her arguments, her coercion, her explanations of what the other world was like. . .the world he had always thought of as dull and empty and wasted.

"Darling, I've been out in the desert, out in nowhere, for almost twenty years. You've got to believe me when I tell you, none of this matters. The billing, the money, the life at the studios, it doesn't *matter*! It's all make-believe, we always said it was that, but we let it get us, grab hold of us. We have to understand there is a whole world without any of it. What if the show *doesn't* go on? What then? Why worry? We can do other things, if we care about each other. Do you understand what I'm saying? It doesn't matter if your picture is in the PLAYERS DIRECTORY, as long as you come home at night and turn the key in the door and know there's someone on the other side who cares whether or not you were killed in the traffic on the Freeway. Emery, *talk to me!*"

Silence. Straining on her part, toward him. Silence. Then, "Val, why don't we go dancing. . .like we used to do?"

The shadow came again to devour her. It showed its teeth and it prodded her, looking for the most vulnerable places, the places still filled with the juice of life, which it would eat to the bone, and then suck the marrow from the bone, till it collapsed into despair as had the rest of her.

She fought it.

She talked to him.

Her voice was the low, insistent voice she had cultivated in the star years. Now she turned it to its full power, and used it to win the most important part of her career.

We have a chance to make it together at last.

God has given us a second chance.

We can have what we lost twenty years ago.

Please, Emery, listen.

Emery Romito had been falling for many years. A great, shrieking fall down a long tunnel of despair. Her voice came to him down the length of that tunnel, and he clutched for it, missed, clutched again and found it. He let it hold him, swaying above the abyss, and slowly pulled himself back up that fragile thread.

Pathetically, he asked her, "Really? Do you think we can? Really?"

No one is more convincing than a woman fighting for her life. Really? She showed him, really. She told him, and she charmed him, and she gave him the strength he had lost so long ago. With her career burgeoning again it was certain they would have all the good things they had lost on the way to this place, this night.

And finally, he leaned across, this old man, and he kissed her, this tired woman. A shy kiss, almost immature, as though his lips had never touched all the lips of starlets and chorus girls and secretaries and women so much less important than this woman beside him in a rented car on a dark oceanside road.

He was frightened, she could feel it. Almost as frightened as she was. But he was willing to try; to see if they could dredge up something of permanence from the garbage-heaps of the love they had spent twenty years wasting.

Then he started the car, backed and filled and started the return to Hollywood.

The shadow was with her, still hungry, but it was set to waiting. She was no less frightened of the long-haired children and the sharp-tongued interviewers and the merciless lights of the sound stages, but at least now there was a goal; now there was something to move toward.

A gentle breeze came up, and they opened the windows.

HANDY

My first premonition of disaster to come was during the conversation Crewes had with Spencer Lichtman. It was two days before he was to shoot her initial scenes for the film. Spencer had made an appointment to discuss Valerie, and Crewes had asked me to be present.

I sat mute and alert. Spencer made his pitch; it was a good one, and a brief one. A three-picture deal with Crewes and the Studio. Sharpel, the Studio business head, was there, and he did some of the finest broken-field running I've ever seen. He suggested everyone wait to see how Valerie did in *Subterfuge*.

Spencer looked terribly disturbed at the conversation as he left. He said nothing to me. Neither did Sharpel, who seemed uneasy that I'd been in the room at all.

When they'd gone, I sat waiting for Arthur Crewes to say something. Finally, he said, "How's the publicity coming?"

"You've got the skinnys on your desk, Arthur. You know what's happening." Then I added, "I wish *I* knew what was happening."

He played dumb. "What would you like to know, Fred?"

I looked at him levelly. He knew I was on to him. There was very little point in obfuscation. "Who's got the pressure on you, Arthur?"

He sighed, shrugged as if to say *welllll, y'found me out*, and answered me wearily. "The Studio. They're nervous. They said Valerie is having trouble with the lines, she's awkward, the usual succotash."

"How the hell do *they* know? She hasn't even worked yet; only rehearsing. And Jimmy's kept the sessions strictly closed off."

Crewes hit the desk with the palm of his hand, then again. "They've got a spy in the crew."

"Oh, *c'mon*, you're kidding!"

"I'm *not* kidding. They've got a pile tied up in this one. That ski troops picture Jenkey made is bombing. They won't get back negative costs. They don't want to take any chances with this one. So they've got a fink in the company."

"Want me to sniff him out?"

"Why bother. They'll only plant another one. It's probably Jeanine, the assistant wardrobe mistress. . .or old Whatshisname. . .Skelly, the makeup man. No, there's no sense trying to pry out the rotten apple; it won't help her performance any."

I listened to all of it with growing concern. There was a new tone in Crewes's voice. A tentative tone, one just emerging for the first time, trying its flavor in the world. I could tell he was unhappy with the sound of it, that he was fighting it. But it was getting stronger. It was the tone of amelioration, of shading, of backing-off. It was the caterpillar tremble of fear that could metamorphose easily into the lovely butterfly of cowardice.

"You aren't planning on dumping her, are you, Arthur?" I asked.

He looked up sharply, annoyed. "Don't be stupid. I didn't go all through this just to buckle when the Studio gets nervous. Besides, I wouldn't do that to her."

"I hope not."

"I *said* not!"

"But there's always the chance they can sandbag you; after all, they *do* tend the cash register."

Crewes ran a nervous hand through his hair. "Let's see how she does. Shooting starts in two days. Kencannon says she's coming along. Let's just wait. . .and see how she does. . ."

How she did was not good.

I was on the set from the moment they started. Valerie's call was for seven o'clock in the morning. For makeup and wardrobe. The Studio limo went to get her. She was in makeup for the better part of an hour. Johnny Black showed up as she was going into Wardrobe. He kissed her on the cheek and she said, "I hope I do justice to your lines. It's a very nice part, Mr. Black." We walked over to the coffee truck and had a cup each. Neither of us spoke. Finally, Black looked down at me and asked—a bit too casually—"How's it look?"

I shrugged. No answer. I didn't have one.

Kencannon came on the set a few minutes later, and got things tight. The crew was alert, ready, they'd been put on special notice that these scenes were going to be tough enough, so let's have a whole gang of cooperation. Everyone wanted her to make it.

It was bright-eyed/bushy-tailed time.

She came out of Wardrobe and walked straight to Jim Kencannon. He took her aside and whispered to her in a dark corner for fully twenty minutes.

Then they started shooting.

She knew her lines, but her mannerisms were strictly by rote. There was an edge of fear in even the simplest of movements. Kencannon tried to put her at ease. It only made her more tense. She was locked into fear, a kind of fear no one could penetrate deeply enough to erode. She had lived with it unconsciously for too long. There was too much at stake for her here. The only defense she had was what she knew instinctively as an actress. Unfortunately, the actress who remembered all of it, and who put it to use, almost somnambulistically, was an actress of the Forties. Miss Ankle-Strap Wedgie. An actress who had not really been required to act. . .merely to look good, snap out her lines and show a lot of leg.

They ran through the first shot again and again. It was horrible to watch. Repetition after repetition, with Kencannon trying desperately to get a quality out of her that gibed with the modern tone of the film as a whole. It simply was not there.

"Scene eighty-eight, take seven, Apple!"

"Scene eighty-eight, take seven, Bravo!"

"Scene eighty-eight, take seven, China!"

"Scene eighty-eight, take fifteen, Hotel!"

"Scene ninety-one, take three, X-ray!"

Over and over and over. She blew it each time. The crew grew restless, then salty, then disgusted. The other actors began making snotty remarks off-camera. Kencannon was marvelous with her, but it was a disaster, right from speed and roll it. Finally, they got *something* shot.

Kencannon wandered off into the darkness of the sound stage. Valerie went to her dressing room. Presumably to collapse. The crew started setting up the next shot. I followed Kencannon back into the corner.

"Jim?"

He turned around, the unlit pipe hanging from the corner of his mouth. It was still before-lunch, early in the day, and he looked exhausted.

"Will it be all right?" I asked him.

He started to turn away. He didn't need me bugging him. I guess the tone of concern in my voice stopped him. "Maybe I can cut it together so it'll work."

And he walked away from me.

That afternoon Kencannon got a visit from Crewes on the set, and they talked quietly for a long time, back by the prop wagon. Then they began pruning Valerie's part. A line here, a reaction shot there. Not much at first, but enough to let her know they were worried. It only served to deepen her nervousness. But they had no choice. They were backed against a wall.

But then, so was she.

The remainder of the shooting, over the next week, was agony. There was no doubt from the outset that she couldn't make it, that the footage was dreadful. But we always harbored the secret hope that the magic of the film editor could save her.

The dailies were even more horrifying, for there, up on the projection room screen we could see the naked failure of what we had tried to do. The day's footage went from flat and unnatural to genuinely inept. Kencannon had tried to cover as much as he could with two and three angles or reaction shots by supporting actors, by trick photography, by bizarre camerawork. None of it made it. There was still Valerie in the center of it, like the silent eye of a whirling dervish. Technique could not cover up what was lacking: a focus, a central core, a soul, a fire. Her scenes were disastrous.

When the lights came up in the projection room, and Crewes and myself were alone—we wouldn't allow anyone else to see the dailies, not then we wouldn't—we looked at each other, and Arthur breathed heavily, "Oh God, Fred! What are we going to do?"

I stared at the blank projection screen. There was such a helplessness in his voice, I didn't know what to say. "Can we keep the Studio from finding out, at least till Kencannon cuts it together?"

He shook his head. "Not a chance."

"They move along behind you?"

"Close as they can. I think they've got the labs printing up duplicate sets of dailies. They've probably already run what we just saw here."

Why? I asked myself. Why?

And the answer ran through my head the way those dailies had been run. Behold, without argument, self-explanatory. The answer was simple: Valerie Lone had never been a very good actress, not ever. The films she had made were for an audience hungry for *any* product, which was why Veda Ann Borg and Vera Hruba Ralston and Sonja Henie and Jeanne Crain and Rhonda Fleming and Ellen Drew and all the other pretty, not-particularly-talented ones had made it. It was a nation before tv, that had theaters to fill, with "A" features starring Paul Muni and Spencer Tracy and John Garfield and Bogart and Ingrid Bergman; but those theaters also needed a lower half to the bill, the "B" pictures with Rory Calhoun and Lex Barker and Ann Blyth and Wandra Hendrix. They needed *product*, not Helen Hayes.

So all the semi-talented had made fabulous livings. *Anything* sold. But now, films for theatrical release were budgeted in the millions, for even the second-class product, and no one could risk the semi-talented. Oh, there were still the pretty ones who got in the films without the talent to get themselves arrested, but they were in the minority, in the quickie flicks. But *Subterfuge* was no quickie. It was a heavy sugar operation into which the Studio had poured millions already, not to mention unspoken but desperate needs and expectations.

Valerie Lone was one of the last of that extinct breed of "semi-stars" who were still vaguely in the public memory—though the new generations, the kids, didn't know her from a white rabbit—but she didn't have the moxie to cut it the way Bette Davis had, or Joan Crawford, or Barbara Stanwyck. She was just plain old Valerie Lone, and that simply wasn't good enough.

She was one of the actresses who had made it then, because almost anyone who could stand up on good legs could make it. . .but not now, because now it took talent of a high order, or a special something that was called "personality." And it wasn't the same kind of "personality" Valerie had used in her day.

"What're you going to do, Arthur?"

He didn't look at me. He just stared straight ahead, at the empty screen. "I don't know. So help me God, I just don't know."

They didn't sign her for a multiple.

At the premiere, held at the Egyptian, Valerie showed with Emery Romito. She was poised, she was elegant, she signed autographs and, as Crewes remarked under his breath to me, as she came up to be interviewed by the television emcee, she was dying at the very moment of what she thought was her greatest triumph. We had not, of course, told her how much Kencannon had had to leave on the cutting-room floor. It was, literally, a walk-on.

When she emerged from the theater, after the premiere, her face was dead white. She knew what was waiting for her. And there was nothing we could say. We stood there, numbly shaking hands with all the well-wishers who told us we had a smash on our hands, as Valerie Lone walked stiffly through the crowd, practically leading the dumbfounded Romito. Their car came to the curb, and they started to get into it. Then Mitchum emerged from the lobby, and the crowd behind their ropes went mad.

There had not been a single cheer or ooh-ahhh for Valerie Lone as she had stood waiting for the limousine to pull up. She was dead, and she knew it.

I tried to call Julie that night, after the big party at the Daisy. She was out. I took a bottle of charcoal Jack Daniels and put it inside me as quickly as I could.

I fell out on the floor. But it wasn't punishment enough. I dreamed.

In the dreams I was trying to explain. My tongue was made of cloth, and it wouldn't form words. But it didn't matter, because the person I was trying to talk to couldn't hear me. It was a corpse. I could not make out the face of the corpse.

9

This was the anatomy of the sin against Valerie Lone:

The Agency called. Not Spencer Lichtman; he was in Florida negotiating a contract for one of their female clients with Ivan Tors for his new *Everglades* pilot. He wouldn't be back for six weeks. It was a difficult contract: the pilot, options for the series if it sold, billing, transportation, and Spencer was screwing her. So the Agency called. A voice of metallic precision that may or may not have had a name attached to it, informed her that they were reorganizing, something to do with the fiscal debenture cutback of post-merger personnel concerned with bibble-bibble-bibble. She asked the voice of the robot what that meant, and it meant she did not have a contract with the Agency, which meant she had no representation.

She called Arthur Crewes. He was out.

The Beverly Hills Hotel management called. The Studio business office had just rung them up to inform them that rent on the bungalow would cease as of the first of the month. Two weeks away.

She called Arthur Crewes. He was out.

She called long distance to Shivey's Diner. She wanted to ask him if he had gotten a replacement for her. Shivey was delighted to hear from her, hey! Everybody was just tickled pink to hear how she'd made good again, hey! Everybody was really jumping with joy at the way the papers said she was so popular again, hey! It's great she got back up on top again, and boy, nobody deserved it better than their girl Val, hey! Don't forget your old friends, don't get uppity out there just because you're a big star and famous again, doncha know!

She thanked him, told him she wouldn't forget them and hung up. Hey!

She could not go back to the desert, to the diner.

She had tasted the champagne again, and the taste of champagne lingers.

She called Arthur Crewes. He was in the cutting room and could not be disturbed.

She called Arthur Crewes. He was in New York with the promotion people, he would be back first of the week.

She called Handy. He was with Crewes.

She called Emery Romito. He was shooting a Western for CBS. His service said he would call back later. But when he did, it was late at night, and she was half-asleep. When she called him the next day, he was at the studio still shooting. She left her name, but the call did not get returned.

The hungry shadow came at a dead run.

And there was no place to hide.

Disaster is a brush-fire. If it reaches critical proportions, nothing can stop it, nothing can put out the fire. Disaster observes a scorched earth policy.

She called Arthur Crewes. She told Roz she was coming in to see him the next morning.

There was no Studio limousine on order. She took a taxi. Arthur Crewes had spent a sleepless night, knowing she was coming, rerunning her films in his private theater. He was waiting for her.

"How is the picture doing, Arthur?"

He smiled wanly. "The opening grosses are respectable. The Studio is pleased."

"I read the review in *Time*. They were very nice to you."

"Yes. Ha-ha, very unexpected. Those smart alecks usually go for the clever phrase."

Silence.

"Arthur, the rent is up in a week. I'd like to go to work."

"Uh, I'm still working on the script for the new picture, Valerie. You know, it's been five months since we ended production. The Studio kept up the rent on the bungalow through post-production. Editing, scoring, dubbing, the works. They think they've done enough. I can't argue with them, Valerie. . .not really."

"I want to work, Arthur."

"Hasn't your agent been getting you work?"

"Two television guest appearances. Not much else. I guess the word went out about me. The picture. . ."

"You were fine, Valerie, just fine."

"Arthur, don't lie to me. I know I'm in trouble. I can't get a job. You have to do something."

There was a pathetic tone in her voice, yet she was forceful. Like someone demanding unarguable rights. Crewes was desolate. His reaction was hostility.

"*I* have to do something? Good God, Valerie, I've kept you working for over six months on three days of shooting. Isn't that enough?"

Her mouth worked silently for a moment, then very softly she said: "No, it isn't enough. I don't know what to do. I can't go back to the diner. I'm back here now. I have no one else to turn to, you're the one who brought me here. You have to do something, it's your responsibility."

Arthur Crewes began to tremble. Beneath the desk he gripped his knees with his hands. "My responsibility," he said bravely, "ended with your contract, Valerie. I've extended myself, even you have to admit that. If I had another picture even *readying* for production, I'd let you read for a part, but I'm in the midst of some very serious rewrite with the screenwriter. I have nothing. What do you want me to do?"

His assault cowed her. She didn't know what to say. He *had* been fair, had done everything he could for her, recommended her to other producers. But they both knew she had failed in the film, knew that the word had gone out. He was helpless.

She started to go, and he stopped her.

"Miss Lone." Not Val, or Valerie now. A retreating back, a pall of guilt, a formal name. "Miss Lone, can I, uh, loan you some money?"

She turned and looked at him across a distance.

"Yes, Mr. Crewes. You can."

He reached into his desk and took out a checkbook.

"I can't afford pride, Mr. Crewes. Not now. I'm too scared. So make it a big check."

He dared not look at her as she said it. Then he bent to the check and wrote it in her name. It was not nearly big enough to stop the quivering of his knees. She took it, without looking at it, and left quietly. When the intercom buzzed and Roz said there was a call, he snapped at her, "Tell 'em I'm out. And don't bother me for a while!" He clicked off and slumped back in his deep chair.

What else could I do? he thought.

If he expected an answer, it was a long time in coming.

After she told Emery what had happened (even though he had been with her these last five months, and knew what it was from the very tomb odor of it) she waited for him to say don't worry, I'll take care of you, now that we're together again it will be all right, I love you, you're mine. But he said nothing like that.

"They won't pick up the option, no possibility?"

"You know they dropped the option, Emery. Months ago. It was a verbal promise only. For the next film. But Arthur Crewes told me he's having trouble with the script. It could be months."

He walked around the little living room of his apartment in the Stratford Beach Hotel. A depressing little room with faded wallpaper and a rug the management would not replace, despite the holes worn in it.

"Isn't there anything else?"

"A Western. TV. Just a guest shot, sometime next month. I read for it last week, they seemed to like me."

"Well, you'll take it, of course."

"*I'll take it*, Emery, but what does it mean. . .it's only a few dollars. It isn't a living."

"We all have to make do the best we can, Val—"

"Can I stay here with you for a few weeks, till things get straightened away?"

Formed in amber, held solidified in a prison of reflections that showed his insides more clearly than his outside, Emery Romito let go the thread that had saved him, and plunged once more down the tunnel of despair. He was unable to do it. He was not calloused, merely terrified. He was merely an old man trying to relate to something that had never even been a dream—merely an illusion. And now she threatened to take even that cheap thing, simply by her existence, her presence here in this room.

"Listen, Val, I've tried to come to terms. I understand what you're going through. But it's hard, very hard. I really have to hurry myself just to make ends meet. . ."

She spoke to him then, of what they had had years ago, and what they had sensed only a few months before. But he was already retreating from her, gibbering with fear, into the shadows of his little life.

"I can't do it, Valerie. I'm not a young man any more. You remember all those days, I'd do anything; anything at all; I was wild. Well, now I'm paying for it. We all have to pay for it. We should have known, we should have put some of it aside, but who'd ever have thought it would end. No, I can't do it. I haven't got the push to do it. I get a little work, an 'also featuring' once in a while. You have to be hungry, the way all the new ones, the young ones, the way *they're* hungry. I can barely manage alone, Valerie. It wouldn't work, it just wouldn't."

She stared at him.

"*I have to hang on!*" he shouted at her.

She pinned him. "Hang on? To what? To guest shots, a life of walk-ons, insignificant character bits, and a Saturday night at the Friars Club? What have you got, Emery? What have you really got that's worth *anything*? Do you have me, do you have a real life, do you have anything that's really yours, that they can't take away from you?"

But she stopped. The argument was hopeless.

He sagged before her. A tired, terrified old man with his picture in the PLAYERS DIRECTORY. What backbone he might have at one time possessed had been removed from his body through the years, vertebra by vertebra. He slumped before her, weighted down by his own inability to live. Left with a hideous walking death, with elegance on the outside, soot on the inside, Valerie Lone stared at the stranger who had made love to her in her dreams for twenty years. And in that instant she knew it had never really been the myth and the horror of the town that had kept them apart. It had been their own inadequacies.

She left him, then. She could not castigate him. His was such a sordid little existence, to take that from him would be to kill him.

And she was still that much stronger than Emery Romito, her phantom lover, not to need to do it.

HANDY

I came home to find Valerie Lone sitting at the edge of the pool, talking to Pegeen. She looked up when I came through the gate, and smiled a thin smile at me.

I tried not to show how embarrassed I was.

Nor how much I'd been avoiding her.

Nor how desperately I felt like bolting and running away, all the way back to New York City.

She got up, said good-bye to Pegeen, and came toward me. I had been shopping; shirt boxes from Ron Postal and bags from de Voss had to be shifted so I could take her hand. She was wearing a summer dress, quite stylish, really. She was trying to be very light, very inoffensive; trying not to shove the guilt in my face.

"Come on upstairs, where it's cooler," I suggested.

In the apartment, she sat down and looked around.

"I see you're moving," she said.

I grinned, a little nervously, making small talk. "No, it's always this way. I've got a house in Sherman Oaks, but at the moment there's a kindofa sorta ex-almost ex-wife nesting there. It's in litigation. So I live here, ready to jump out any time."

She nodded understanding.

The intricacies of California divorce horrors were not beyond her.

She had had a few of those, as I recalled.

"Mr. Handy—" she began.

I did not urge her to call me Fred.

"You were the one who talked to me first, and. . ."

And there it was. I was the one responsible. It was all on me. I'd heard what had happened with Crewes, with that rat bastard Spencer Lichtman, with Romito, and now it was my turn. She must have had nowhere else to go, no one else to impale, and so it was *mea culpa* time.

I was the one who had resurrected her from the safety and sanctity of her grave; brought her back to a world as transitory as an opening night. She looked at me and knew it wouldn't do any good, but she did it.

She laid it all on me, word by word by word.

What could I do, for Christ's sake? I had done my best. I'd even watched over her with Haskell Barkin, carried her practically on my shoulders through all the shitty scenes when she'd arrived in town. What more was there for me to do. . .?

I'm not my brother's goddam keeper, I yelled inside my head. Let me alone, woman. Get off my back. I'm not going to die for you, or for anyone. I've got a job, and I've got to keep it. I got the publicity *Subterfuge* needed, and I thank you for helping me keep my job, but dammit I didn't inherit you. I'm not your daddy, I'm not your boy friend, I'm just a puffman in off the street, trying to keep the Dragon Lady from grabbing his house, the only roots I've ever had. So stop it, stop talking, stop trying to make me cry, because I won't.

Don't call me a graverobber, you old bitch!

"I'm a proud woman, Mr. Handy. But I'm not very smart. I let you all lie to me. Not once, but twice. The first time I was too young to know better; but this time I fell into it again knowing what you would do to me. I was one of the lucky ones, do you know that? I was lucky because I got out alive. But do you know what you've done to me? You've condemned me to the kind of life poor Emery leads, and that's no life at all."

She didn't talk any more.

She just sat there staring at me.

She didn't want excuses, or escape clauses, or anything I had to give. She knew I was helpless, that I was no better and no worse than any of them. That I had helped kill her in the name of love.

And that the worst crimes are committed in the name of love, not hate.

We both knew there would be an occasional tv bit, and enough money to keep living, but here, in this fucking ugly town that wasn't living. It was crawling like a wounded thing through the years, till one day the end came, and that was the only release you could pray for.

I knew Julie would not be coming back to me.

Julie knew. She was on the road because she couldn't stand the town, because she knew it would tear her open and throw her insides on the street. She had always said she wasn't going to go the way all the others had gone, and now I knew why I hadn't been able to reach her on the road. It was Good-bye, Dolly.

And the Dragon Lady would get the house; and I would stay in Hollywood, God help me.

Until the birds came to peck out my eyes, and I wasn't Handy the fair-haired boy any longer, or even Handy the old pro, but something they called Fred Handy? oh, yeah, I remember him, he was good in his day. Because after all, what the hell did I have to offer but a fast mouth and a few ideas, and once the one was slowed and the other had run out like sand from an hourglass, I was no better off than Valerie Lone or her poor miserable Emery Romito.

She left me standing there, in my apartment that always looked as though I was moving. But we both knew: I wasn't going anywhere.

10

In a very nice little restaurant-bar on Sunset Boulevard, as evening came in to wipe the feverish brow of Hollywood, across the rim of the bowl, Valerie Lone sat high on a barstool, eating French dip roast beef on a baguette, with gravy covering the very crisp french fries. She sipped slowly from a glass of dark ale. At the far end of the bar a television set was mumbling softly. It was an old movie, circa 1942.

None of the players in the movie had been Valerie Lone. The Universe loved her, but was totally devoid of a sense of irony. It was simply an old movie.

Three seats down from where Valerie Lone sat, a hippie wearing wraparound shades and seven strings of beads looked up at the bartender. "Hey, friend," he said softly.

The bartender came to him, obviously disliking the hairy trade these people represented, but unable to ignore the enormous amounts of money they somehow spent in his establishment. "Uh-huh?"

"Howzabout turning something else on. . .or maybe even better turn that damn thing off, I'll put a quarter in the jukebox." The bartender gave him a surly look, then sauntered to the set and turned it off. Valerie Lone continued to eat as the world was turned off.

The hippie put the quarter in the jukebox and pressed out three rock numbers. He returned to his barstool and the music inundated the room.

Outside, night had come, and with it, the night lights. One of the lights illuminated a twenty-three-foot-high billboard for the film *Subterfuge* starring Robert Mitchum and Gina Lollobrigida; produced by Arthur Crewes; directed by James Kencannon; written by John D.F. Black; music by Lalo Schifrin.

At the end of the supplementary credits there was a boxed line that was very difficult to read: it had been whited-out.

The line had once read:

ALSO FEATURING MISS VALERIE LONE as Angela.

Angela had become a walk-on. She no longer existed.

Valerie Lone existed only as a woman in a very nice little restaurant and bar on the Sunset Strip. She was eating. And the long shadow had also begun to feed.

—Hollywood and Montclair, N.J., 1967

THE UNIVERSE OF ROBERT BLAKE

And this is what Robbie Blake learned that day. . .

On the bus, an old man in an overcoat—so hot for July, that shapeless, whatcolor rag—sat mumbling to himself, next to the window. Occasionally he would rub his palms against stubbled cheeks, a sound like new sandpaper to Robbie's ears.

When the old man got up and left the bus, Robbie Blake saw a small dirty-white card thrust into the window-frame. He moved across the aisle and pulled the card out of its slot in the anodized aluminum frame. It said, very neatly:

BO BO THE CLOWN
Available for Picnics, Clubs

and there was a number, an address. Robbie Blake replaced the card precisely, for even at six years of age, he knew a man has a right to advertise.

Later that day, looking out from behind the billboard at the side of the clothing store, Robbie saw a fat woman with a mustache, carrying a shopping bag at the end of either meaty arm. One of the bags burst as the fat woman passed Robbie's waiting-place, and he watched carefully as she got down on her knees—in stages, like a great beast unhinging itself at a water hole—puffing, sighing. He watched her as she retrieved the packages of frozen foods, the asparagus, the oranges. There was something very natural about the fat woman. Something essential. Robbie Blake watched, and remembered.

A big truck with EMPIRE HAULING on its side went past, and Robbie dashed out from behind the billboard to catch the truck as it stopped by the corner. He pulled himself up onto the lowered tailgate and grasped the anchor chain firmly in both hands as the truck moved with the changing traffic light. Robbie rode along with the smell of his world whipping past; the smell of the rotting gourds in the sidewalk markets; the smell of oil and grease, rainbow puddles among the bricks; the smell of chemicals from some tiny manufacturing company on a side street. He looked and looked and everywhere people dashed and walked, doing things with paper and leather and words. He smiled at the gray sky that promised rain, and he stuck his tongue out when a policeman made a short move to haul him off the fleeing truck as it whipped through an intersection.

Finally, Robert Blake tired of his truck ride, and slid to the edge of the tailgate. When the truck paused for breath at another traffic light, Robbie bounced down and dogtrotted away, in a new place, with wonderful things to see. He saw a shop with bright and coppery bracelets, and a man in a great wide hat. The window of the shop said MEXICO ARTS and Robbie knew where Mexico was. It was someplace downtown, very far downtown in another country.

What it is, to be six years old, is to need to go to the bathroom frequently. That is part of it.

Robbie Blake needed to go to the bathroom, because he had had three papaya juices at 'Nrico's stand, before he had stood behind the billboard, watching the fat woman who might have been his mother or *somebody's* mother, maybe. So he looked for a place to go.

He saw a group of people going into, and coming out of, a big restaurant called FELLOWS' RESTAURANT in red and blue neon lights that went on and off in the late afternoon gray. He decided if all those people were going in and coming out, that at least *one* of them must have had to go to the bathroom sometime or other, and if that was so, then there had to be a bathroom inside. (Never say "I have to go wee-wee"; always say "I have to wash my hands," Moms had said to Robbie.)

Robbie Blake, just like all those other people—well, not quite; shorter, perhaps, but *pretty* much the same—strode purposefully to the restaurant, and went through the revolving door. It was cool inside, and hard to see very well, but he walked around, and listened to the people eating and talking to each other. He stared over the shoulder of a man cutting a baked apple with a fork, and smiled when the man tried to get a piece too big into his mouth. The man half-turned as Robbie smiled (was it a sound, not a smile?) and gave a snort of annoyance. Robbie moved on.

This was a fine world; a fine, fine place to be a little boy, with people eating and talking and taking too big bites of baked apples.

The bathroom was still very important, but in a world as nice as this, well, such things can wait a few minutes longer. After all, one can always cross one's legs and stand hidden in a corner, waiting.

Robbie knew the words to look for, and when he saw the door that said GENTLEMEN, he recognized MEN and went inside. A man with a bow tie and a blue shirt was washing his hands, and he saw Robbie in the mirror, and he chuckled softly, saying, over his shoulder, "Pop, this one yours?" and Robbie saw another man, wearing a white jacket, with a towel ready to be handed to the man with the bow tie.

The man in the white jacket (oh, didn't he look nice and important dressed up that way) gasped, and laid the towel down on the sink next to the fellow with the bow tie. He came to Robbie very quickly, and took him by the shoulder, and dragged him out of the room that said GENTLEMEN. He pulled him through another door, and Robbie suddenly smelled all the wonderful brown and green and pink smells of food. Food that called to him and said *I am meat! I am tossed greens! I am something you don't know, very nice!* It was a kitchen, and Robbie wanted to faint with pleasure. Oh, such a *grand* world.

Then the man in the white jacket was kneeling in front of him, saying, "Boy, watchu doin' here? You crazy or somethin'? You *know* you can't come in here!"

Robbie did not understand. He smiled nicely at the man in the white jacket. "Hello," he said, politely as Moms had taught him to do.

"Don't be smilin' at me that way, chile! I'm tellin' you it's trouble for you in here. They don't allow it!"

Robbie was confused, but he mustered another, tinier smile, and said to the man in the white jacket, "I hadda use the bathroom."

The man took Robbie to the swinging door that led back into the restaurant, and he pulled it open a crack.

"Look." He pointed. "You see alla them people? *They* can use the bathroom, but not you. Now you g'wan get outta here befoah we all get hell!"

Robbie knew what was right. He was just like everyone here. He had a *right* to use the bathroom. He said so.

The man in the white jacket frowned and pulled the swinging door open again. "Now look, boy, I mean *really* look. You see them? They *not* the same's you. They white. Now look at you, look at me. Are we white?'"

Robbie looked at his hand. It wasn't white, that was true. He looked at the man in the white jacket. He wasn't white, either. But what did that have to do with the bathroom? Did it mean he wasn't *ever* allowed to go to the bathroom? It would be very unhappy and painful if that was so.

Then the man in the white jacket—who was very black and almost bald, except for a few curlicues of wispy whiteness that came out of his scalp—was hauling Robbie to the back door of FELLOWS' RESTAURANT, and opening it into the alley, and putting Robbie outside in the growing darkness.

He paused, and bent down, and said, very softly, so the cooks and waiters and busboys rushing would not hear, "Boy, someway you haven't been brought up right; din't yoah parents tell you the way it is? You better learn, boy. You better learn."

And he pushed Robbie gently, out onto a loading dock, and closed the door, the light narrowing to a splinter and then all gone, all gone. Robbie stood in the darkness and waited for something more to happen.

But nothing more happened.

Then he turned, ran to the edge of the loading dock, jumped down, and walked very quickly to the end of the alley.

For a very long time Robbie stood in a doorway, nothing but his eyes seeing out, his body, his strange black body hidden. He watched everyone as they went by. He stared very carefully, as he had stared at the policeman, and the fat woman, and Bo Bo the Clown who was available (which seemed a nice thing to be).

After a very, *very* long time, he felt he understood.

Then he went home.

It had been a full day, a surprising day—and one filled with learning things. Robbie Blake had learned what it meant to know, and what it meant to watch, and what it meant to live. Somehow, his education till then had been love and kindness from Moms, and respect from his sister and his three brothers, and no one had mentioned the Difference. But now he knew.

Robbie Blake had learned many things that day. He had learned which colors were right, and which were wrong; he had learned what color hands must be to open certain doors, and what color thoughts must be employed to exist in the fine, fine nice world. He had learned when to lower his eyes.

And most of all he had learned what it meant to be a nigger.

And most of all he had learned:

It is not enough for a little boy to know his place in the Universe.

He must also know which Universe is his.

And *that* is what Robbie Blake learned that day.

—*New York City, 1962*

G.B.K.—
A MANY-FLAVORED BIRD

So garbled was my secretary's mind, that early in the morning, that I had to call Western Union later in the day, and have them read me the telegram again; even then, in the clarity of a monotoned operator's recitation, the message barely made sense. It read:

> CAMPAIGN MATERIALIZING TO ROCKET YOUR FORTHCOMING MOVIE "THE LATTER LIFE OF GOD" INTO INTERNATIONAL FINANCIAL GOLD MINE.

I had her read it again, and then asked if they would deliver the telegram itself to my hotel. She said Western Union would be pleased to accommodate, and then she said, "This telegram was sent from here in town, by night letter last night, sir." I asked her if it was signed, and she said, "Yes, it's signed G. Barney Kantor, American Association of Fan Clubs."

More bewilderedly than I had any right to feel, I thanked the operator and racked the receiver. I sat there on the edge of the bed in my hotel room in Cleveland, and I tried to make some sense out of the histrionically phrased nonsense I had just heard.

True, one of my magazine short stories, "The Latter Life of God," had been picked up by an independent outfit for production. . .but the script hadn't even been written yet, which was why I was on my way to the Coast, having stopped off in Cleveland merely to see my sister and brother-in-law. Who the hell was G. Barney Kantor, and what the hell was the "American Association of Fan Clubs"?

"Bernice," I yelled into the adjoining room, "do I know a G. Barney Kantor?"

Bernice, festooned with sheaves of press releases, with a pencil behind each ear, emerged from the other room and stood poised in the doorway, cocked onto one hip, thinking. "Not that I know. Is that the business with the telegram this morning?" I nodded. "Dumb sonofabitch whoever he is," she snarled, "waking me up at eight jeezus o'clock! I'd like to get my hands on his throat!" She went back to her room, to that ever-waiting extension of her right hand, the ominously silent telephone, back to ponder arrangements for a local interview show I was going to do over Cleveland television.

It wasn't that important, really, because I knew it had to be a gag, but the peculiar manner of phrasing struck a dim note in my mind, and though I had other things to worry about—the local tv appearances, finishing an article long overdue, the final payment of the option money—for some inexplicable reason my thoughts kept worrying the telegram and the name of G. Barney Kantor, like a dog with a rag doll.

And finally, it came back to me, who he was, and how I'd met him, and what image of him I'd relegated to the back part of my memories. And despite myself, I was forced to smile. After all this time, that he should remember me; I'd been just a kid when I'd met him, however briefly; I'd been perhaps sixteen, seventeen. Now, ten—no, thirteen—years later, Kantor was back in my life.

If anything had saved me from becoming a real flip, from wasting my life and what little talent I had, after my father died and my mother and I moved to Cleveland, it was the science fiction people. I had bought a pulp magazine whose cover had shown a huge robot firing bolts of flame (or something) from its fingertips, and almost immediately had become an aficionado. In due course I met the other science fiction fans in Cleveland, and we formed a club, the Solarians. Not only were they good people, and kind people, but there was a swirl of wonder about them, an unpredictability of imagination that turned my world of mourning sadness and widow's tears into a golden time and space of hyperspatial rocket ships, alien life-forms and concepts of the universe that I'd never even suspected existed.

Inevitably, one of the Cleveland newspapers came to the club rooms to do a feature on us. It was the usual cheapjack yellow pap, tongue firmly in cheek and ridicule replacing reportage. The article appeared in all the editions of that day's paper, and we were more mortified than flattered. Someone suggested iron filings in the reporter's coffee cake. Saner heads prevailed, scolding me for such an uncharitable thought.

All of this was background, however, for the new magic soon to enter our lives, in the person of G. Barney Kantor.

So. On this night that lives in memory, an otherwise undistinguished meeting night, Al Watson (in whose apartment we held meetings) reported a phone conversation he'd had earlier that day. He seemed enthusiastic and genuinely pleased. "So he said his name was Kantor, with a 'K,' and that he was prepared to, uh, how did he put it, 'Lift us from the realm of mediocrity and anonymity to the heights of public awareness.'"

We all stared at Al, and Al beamed back at us. (We sometimes cocked a quizzical eyebrow at Al; he was a member of the Fortean Society, as well as a practitioner of dianetics.) "Isn't that swell?" he asked. "This guy says he has contacts all over the world, and he's coming over this evening to meet us and find out our potentialities for greatness."

Ben Jason, one of the more lucid minds present, had the intemperate presence to ask, "Our potentialities for *what*? Is that another of his remarks?" Al nodded.

We stared at one another, prepared to believe the wildest things.

None of this prepared us, as it turned out, for the actual physical presence of G. Barney Kantor.

At nine-thirty the doorbell rang, and we scurried, rearranging ourselves into positions of respectability and sober world-view sanity, as Al went to answer the door. All we could see when the door was opened was Al, standing there with his hand outstretched in greeting, and then a convulsive widening of the eyes, and the tiniest gasp of disbelief and consternation. We heard Al mumble welcoming words, and then he stepped aside, and for the first time I saw G. Barney Kantor.

As a writer I am affronted by the sterility of imagination and talent that forces some authors to describe their characters as "looking exactly like Gregory Peck, with bigger ears." This recourse to mass consumption identity has always struck me as highly suspect and just short of auctorial bankruptcy. Yet I am compelled, in describing G. Barney Kantor, to take the shortest route to total recognition, by stating simply that G. Barney Kantor looked, looks, will *always* look, precisely like Groucho Marx.

Kantor entered the room, and for an instant I thought his brothers would follow him. He stalked, not walked, in that indescribable half-crouch Marx has patented for the "Captain Spaulding, the African explorer" number (did someone call him *schnorer*?); his moustache was a black, rectangular brush, his hair was wild and manelike. He wore glasses. He smoked a thick, obscene-looking black hawser of a cigar. He was midway between massively impressive and downright comical.

After the first shocking moment wore off, it was possible to detect small ways in which G. Barney Kantor was *not* Groucho Marx, but so studiedly had Kantor sought to mock the Brother's appearance, at no time during the fantastic evening were we free of the impulse to burst into laughter.

(I was later to learn that the RKO Palace Theater in Cleveland occasionally hired Kantor as a sandwich man, strictly on his appearance.)

"A decidedly good evening to you, fellow roamers of the vast, uncharterated Universe!"

No bull, no flummery, that is the way G. Barney Kantor talked. Silver fleeting words of sometimes meaning that were here and gone before you could assemble them in precisely their proper order. Flamboyant phrases slapped together to give a general impression of garrulity, pompousness, absolute phoniness. It has always confused me how people could be gullible enough to be taken in by Kantor, for in the first words from his mouth, it has seemed to me, any rational person could detect sham and the quicksilver maneuverings of the born con man.

Stunned as we all were by this brash and obviously hammy individual from out of nowhere, Ben Jason again made his mark by stepping forward, shaking Kantor's hand and introducing himself. Then he led Kantor around the room, introducing him to Honey Steel, Frank Andrasovsky, Earl Simon and after all the others, finally, me.

"This is Walter Innes," Ben said. "Walter, Mr. Kantor." I took his hand. It was the handshake of the man who is testing the flesh of your body to see if you have worked for a living, or are subsisting on gratuities from a wealthy family. A fleeting thought passed me, and I was glad I wasn't wearing any rings. "Walter is the editor of our club magazine,"—Ben beamed at me; Walter, the mascot—"and quite a promising little writer, too."

Kantor's deep blue eyes stared down at me and he deluged me with words. "A remarkable young man, Mr. Jason. Remarkable. I can tell he has an intuitive grasp of matters both cosmical and naturalistic from the glint of supernal awareness in his lustrous eyes. Remarkable! A man to watch, indeed, a man to watch."

Then he passed on, leaving me stunned to the core, and awash in words whose meanings I was only barely able to fathom.

And so it went all that evening. Kantor the monologist, Kantor the financier, Kantor the *bon vivant* waving his silver-headed walking stick. Amused, bemused, confused and nonplused we sat and listened to his meandering reminiscences of the world in which he had moved, his aspirations, his love of science fiction (and his total unawareness of even the leading writers in the field). . .and we waited for the kicker.

Finally, it came. When we were all wasted and spent by the mere effort of listening to him.

"Fellow Solarians," he blurted, during a three-second lull in what had been entirely *his* conversation, "and I hope I am of a full-hearted enough nature, borne up with recondite camaraderie and bold effusion for you good people of the stars and the night, to call myself so. . .fellow Solarians, I am prepared to make you well-known, nay, say *responsive* to the plucked chords of fickle public sentiment, as you have long adhered to be! Why should men and women of your ilk, your pluck, your boldishness, men and women with so much to give to a world crying out, pleading for light and guidance, be relegated to positions of obscurantivity and idle activity? You, *you* are the brave new future of this land, and I am prepared—for a small fee—to hoist you by the petards of your own magnificence and—"

We were readers of *Startling Stories*, where the hell was he getting this saviors of mankind crap from?

Eventually, we told him we would get back in touch with him, watched the variousness of him exeunt flourishing, and fell back as a group, in absolute exhaustion.

Earl Simon it was, who very simply said it, in a quiet voice, as we all slumped there, drained and confused. "Hey, that guy's a crook."

No one bothered to disagree. We were too exhausted.

And now, thirteen years later, after I had gone my way, the Solarians had gone theirs, and G. Barney Kantor had, presumably, gone his, I was the recipient of a telegram, like a rainbow voice out of the past, like a many-flavored bird of passage that once every thousand years lights and casts its gay gloom over anyone lucky enough to be around.

I put Kantor and his officious, nonsensical 'gram out of my mind till later that night, when we were at one of the local nightclubs, one of the few left in Cleveland's now-ghost-towned downtown. I was with Bernice, my sister Beverly and her husband Jerold, the optician, and we had been joined by the headliner of the show (a well-known male singer who prefers I do not use his name), and three girls out of the go-go chorus.

How Kantor came up, I don't recall now, but I told them of our meeting thirteen years before, when I had been in high school and had not yet written the first book. "And you know, every once in a while," I told them, "when I'd be downtown, I'd see him on the street. He was a sidewalk photographer most of the time. I suppose that's where he made his living."

One of the go-go girls, memory piqued by my comparison of Kantor to Groucho Marx, told me how he had been a sandwich man.

Then my brother-in-law, who is frankly too nice a guy to be married to my sister, added, "You bet your life he remembers you, Walt. When you were in town three years with your book, uh, which one was that—"

"NO MORE FLAMES," I reminded him, always ready to tout my own work.

"Right. NO MORE FLAMES. Well, when you were at that autograph party at Burrows', he found the write-up in the *Press*, with my name in it, and he came around to the shop, and introduced himself. Said he was a good friend, and really came on with me. I managed to get him out of the store, I had a couple of patients, and he was yelling and making an ass of himself."

I grinned, imagining G. Barney Kantor's capers in mild, good-natured Jerry's optical shop.

"But now every time he sees me on the street," Jerry Rabnick continued, "he follows me for blocks with that damned camera of his, yelling at the top of his lungs, 'HEY, THERE GOES DOCTOR RAB, THE BROTHER-IN-LAW OF AMERICA'S FINEST NOVELIST! HEY, DOCTOR RAB, HOW GOES IT?'"

Jerry's voice had climbed in imitation of Kantor's yowl, and heads were turning toward us in the club. He flushed and fell silent. I found myself laughing, at just the mental picture of that colossal fraud, that monstrous charlatan, G. Barney Kantor.

Then my sister chimed in, "We were having a Temple benefit, and he called me, offering something or other, I don't remember what it was now, but I called the Better Business Bureau to check on him and so help me, when I mentioned his name, the girl groaned and flashed the switchboard and said, 'Refer this call to the Kantor Department.'" I broke up completely, then. The singer—who had been listening carefully—also got his jollies, and we sat there for at least a minute till the tears ran down our face, we were laughing so hard.

"He sounds like a real creep," one of the go-go girls commented. "He musta been in an' outta jail a million times. He sounds like a real crook."

I was reminded of Earl Simon's remark so many years before, and it started the juices flowing. "Perhaps not," I replied. "Perhaps G. Barney Kantor lives in his little world of pretense and tomfoolery, believing he *is* a press agent *extraordinaire*. Perhaps he's fooled himself into thinking he's a big man, and these little hangups with the police and people shunning him are just the stupidity of the mass. People who don't recognize his greatness."

I thought that was damned perceptive of me.

Then Bernice shook me by saying, "I think he's pathetic. I feel sorry for him."

"Now what the hell brought *that* on?" I said, the big-time writer who was on his way to Hollywood. "You're the one who wanted to kill him for waking you in the middle of the night."

"It wasn't the middle of the night, it was the early morning, and I feel sorry for the poor little guy."

I snorted. "Rebecca of Sunnybrook Farm, for Christ's sake. Do you take in stray cats and puff adders, too?"

Bernice stuck her tongue out at me. "You've just become too big a deal to remember people like him. Not everybody makes it. This little guy apparently lives a lie, but it's all he's got. I think you stink."

And that was what formed my decision. "All right, Miss Humanitarian, I'll tell you what let's do: let's find out where he lives and go pay him a visit. You'll see him for himself, as he really is, stripped of all the sadness and tarnished glory. He probably lives in some fleabag hotel on Prospect, with crotch shots out of *Playboy* on the walls, and a card file on how to fleece suckers like you."

So we looked it up, and it was in the phone book, but it was an address out on the West Side, in a not too pleasant section of the depressed area. A section getting Poverty Program money.

There were ten of us by the time our cavalcade got to Kantor's street. We had picked up two of the musicians from the combo that backed the Well-Known Male Singer, and all ten of us, in three cars, had turned it into quite a little party. We were all pretty smashed by the time we got out there and it was four or five in the morning.

The street was dark and the houses were paint-peeling, sad-faced, a bit too grim for us really to laugh much. But so intent were we—all of us except Bernice—on revealing G. Barney Kantor as a fraud and a poltroon, that not even the slim neighborhood could really dampen us.

We found the house, and stopped in front. "Here, let me get a couple of my books out of the glove compartment," I said. We had brought them along for the tv show earlier in the day, and I'd shoved them in the compartment when the director of the show said he already had them. "I'll use them to reestablish our 'friendship.' After all, it *has* been thirteen years." The others in the car all smiled and egged me on. All except Bernice.

We got out of the car and walked up the weed-spotted walk, the tiles of the pavement thrust up and cracked from too many changes in temperature, too few repairs.

I rang the bell and didn't really pay any attention to the fact that it was five o'clock in the morning and the house was black. A light came on somewhere inside, and after a moment the door opened a trifle. I looked down at a woman's face. "Yes?" she asked, half-frightened.

"We're friends of G. Barney Kantor. Is he here?"

I thought it must surely be a rooming house.

The door opened a little wider.

"Barney? No, he's out this evening. May I help you? I'm *Mrs.* Kantor."

She was built like a muffin, and had her hair up around her head in a large braid. She was wearing a faded housecoat and a pair of bedroom slippers from which the fuzz had departed. Another figure, a young girl, came to stand behind the older woman.

I suddenly felt very foolish.

"Well, uh, my name is Walter Innes. I'm a writer, and, uh, a friend of Barney's; I—uh—I thought I'd drop by to—uh—" I looked around at the nine others, trying to find some help. They had suddenly developed Little Orphan Annie's Disease: blank eyeballs.

"Oh, Mr. Innes!" the little woman chirped. "Oh, my gosh, yes! Barney has spoken of you many times, won't you come in, it's so cold out there."

She opened the door wide and admonished the young girl to, "Gwen, run and turn on the lights and put on some coffee!"

We came in and she led us into the living room. It was furnished in Early Squalor. I wanted to get out of there very badly.

And yet, at the same time, I was really angry at G. Barney Kantor, really infuriated. Here was his wife and what was apparently his daughter, living in a dump and consigned to a life of poverty, while he ran around Cleveland wasting money sending night letters and playing the poseur. I wanted to tell her what I thought of her blasted husband and his ridiculous antics. I was perhaps a bit too drunk.

"Oh, Mr. Innes, it's such a pleasure to meet you at last. Barney has told us many times how he gave you your start. I'm just sorry he can't be here to see you; he's out on a very big promotion tonight."

I was too amazed by having learned G. Barney Kantor had given me my start to say anything. But the daughter, Gwen, chimed in, "Daddy always said you were his finest hour. Daddy always talks like that." Coffee was apparently on.

I nodded dumbly, and beside me I heard Bernice moving up to whisper, "You bastard!" in my ear.

"Well, uh," I said, apropos of absolutely nothing.

"Please sit down, won't you all," G. Barney Kantor's wife said. I then realized no one had introduced the small army she had let into her living room this wee small hour. As I went around introducing everyone, telling who they were, the two women's faces lit up. They recognized The Singer, immediately, and when he said, "I'm sorry we missed Barney, Mrs. Kantor. He's been a great help to me whenever I play Cleveland," she practically erupted in joy.

Well, it was an agonizing hour and a half. We sat there and heard what a great man G. Barney Kantor was, how this was only a temporary accommodation, how they were going to hit the big time soon, how Barney had connections in Hollywood, how the mayor was thinking of citing him for civic contributions, and on and on and on.

Finally, we made ready to depart. I took out my pen and signed the two books: *To my dear friend, G. Barney Kantor, for all his invaluable help and for showing me a special part of the universe. Walter Innes.*

I gave them to her, and she stood on tiptoe to kiss my cheek. She said good-bye to us all, and we left.

Bernice didn't say anything all the way back to the hotel, but when we left the car with the doorman, and he said, "We watched you on tv today, Mr. Innes. You were great," Bernice snorted and gave me a knowing grin that told me I'd either have to fire her or marry her.

—Cleveland, 1962

NEITHER YOUR JENNY NOR MINE

My first inclination, upon learning Jenny was knocked up, was to go find Roger Gore and auger him into the sidewalk. That was my first inclination; when she called, I lit a cigarette and asked her if my girl Rooney, her roommate, knew about it, and she said yes, Rooney knew and had suggested the call to me. I told her to take a copy of *McCall's* and go to the bathroom, that I had to think about it, and would call her back in twenty minutes. She wasn't crying when she hung up, which was something to be thankful for.

There is a crime in our land more heinous than any other I can think of, right offhand, and yet it goes unpunished. It is the crime of gullibility. People who actually believe the lowballing of used car dealers; people who accept the penciled "2 Drink Minimum" card on their table as law; girls who swallow the line of horse crud a swinger uses to get them in the rack. Like that, yeah. Jenny was a product of that crime wave. She was a typical know-nothing, a little patsy who had been seduced by four-color lithography and dream-images from a million mass media, and she believed the stork brought babies.

In about ninety days her tummy was going to tell her she'd been lied to. And been had.

When I'd started dating Rooney, and had learned that the roommates were two eighteen-year-olds fresh out of nowhere and firmly under Rooney's wing, it had been a toss-up whether I'd try to make them on the sly, or become Big Brother to the brood. As it turned out, Rooney was enough action for me, and I took the latter route.

We started taking Jenny and Kitten (*née* Margaret Alice Kirgen, the second roommate) with us when we went out. Parties, movies, *schlepping*-around sessions in which we put miles on the car and layers on our ennui. Kitten wasn't bad; she was a reasonably hip kid who was actually six months younger than Jenny, but much more aware of what was going on around her. Jenny was impossible. There was a naïve quality about her that might have been ingenuous, if she hadn't been so gawdawful stupid along with it. They are two different facets, naïveté and stupidity, and combined they make for a saccharine-sweet dumb that paralyzes as it horrifies.

Why did we allow them to come along with us, to adopt us someway; or rather, let *us* adopt *them*? Put it down to my past, which was filled with incomplete memories of deeds I did not care to think about. I can't remember ever having been young, not really. On my own as far back as I can recall, there was never that innocence of childhood or nature that I longed to see in others. So Jenny and Kitten became my social projects. Not in any elaborate sense, but it pleasured me to see them enjoy the bounties of the young. . .oh hell, Norman Rockwell and Edgar A. Guest and let's all pose for a Pepsi ad.

Kenneth Duane Markham, thirty years old and a humanitarian. Let's send this child to camp (if we can't roll her in the hay, hey hey!). Call it noble intentions, for all the wrong reasons.

At one of the parties we took Jenny to, I ran across Roger Gore. He was (is) (will be, till I catch his face in my right hand) a good-looking jackpotter with a flair for wearing clothes that would look slovenly on other guys, and a laudable record of having avoided honest labor. His father owned a chain of something or others, and Roger indulged himself by taking jobs as switchman on the railroad, soap salesman door to door, night watchman. He never did any of them for very long; his rationale for taking on such onerous tasks was the same as that of the aspiring novelist. He wanted to be able to say he had done these things. It was all very Robert Ruark and hairy-chested and proletarian. He was a fraud. But a good-looking, smooth fraud with a flair for wearing clothes that would look—but I said that already.

It was one of those parties where some college kid had met a hipster in a downtown black-and-tan club, and had invited him over the following night for "a little get-together." As a consequence, the room was jammed, half with inept, callow UCLA students, half with sinuous spades wrapped up in color. It was one of those scenes where the gray cats felt a sense of adventure and titillation just being in the same time-zone with Negroes, and the blacks were infra-digging, wasting the white boys' Watusi with their own extra-lovely dancing, and mooching as much free juice as possible.

Everybody hated everybody, 'way down deep.

We walked in and I saw Roger first crack out of the bag. He was trying to make the scene with a couple of black dudes I knew from downtown, and they were being indulgent. But they "felt a draft" and Old Rog was about to get frozen out. When they put him down (which could be noted by the way his sappy expression went sour) and he walked away, I took the two girls over and introduced them. To the black guys. Roger would make his own introductions, I had no worries on that score. But the two downtown operators were bad, meaning they were good. One of them was a shipping clerk for a record distributor, and the other was a gopher in an exclusive men's hair salon. (Gopher: "Go for the coffee, Jerry." "Go for Mr. Bentley's shoes, Jerry." "Go for—")

"Hey, baby, what's shakin'?"

"Howya doin', man, it's been time I seen yoah ass."

"Busy."

"Yeah, sheee-it, man, you always busy one thing'n 'nother."

"Gotta keep the bread on the table. . ."

"Got to keep that bread in yoah *pock*et!"

"True."

Jenny was standing there, her face open, and as far as she was concerned, where was she? Rooney was digging, as usual, and loving me with her eyes, which was a groove. I pointed each one out to the guys and named:

"Hey, Jerry, Willis, want you to meet Rooney and Jenny." Kitten had had a date. A CPA from Santa Monica. Wow!

"Very pleased't meetcha." Jerry grinned. That cat had the most beautiful mouthful of teeth known to Western Man, he knew it, and he flashed them like the marquee at Grauman's Chinese. "*Very* pleased't meetcha," Willis said, and I knew he was shucking me, just to make me feel good; he was coming on with Rooney because he knew it would make me feel tall. I gave them each a soft punch on the biceps and we moved off into the crowd. We said our hellos to the host, who was an authentic *schlepp*, and took the coats into the bedroom. A pair of UCLAmnesiacs were making it among the coats, so we laid ours over the windowseat. It promised to be a bad, dull party. The roar of rhythm&blues was coming out of the living room, meeting the bubble-gum music from the dining room head-on, and canceling each other out in the hallways connecting.

We stepped out into one of these eye-of-the-hurricane areas, and started looking for the bar. I saw Roger Gore heading for the kitchen, and I knew immediately where the juice was being dispensed. I turned to Jenny. "See that guy in the gray houndstooth, the one going into the kitchen?"

She nodded.

"Stay away from him. There are ten thousand guys at this party who aren't trouble. That one is. He's clever and pretty fair-looking, but he's a lox, and I tell you three times, one two three, stay out of his reach. That's my only advice for the evening. Now scoot." I gave her a shove on the rump and she moved out.

Rooney grinned at me. "Guardian of the morals of the young."

"Poof you," I answered.

"Not here, surely, sir." There were times I wanted to chomp on her ears. And that damned grin of hers. Heidi. Rapunzel. Snow White. Mata Hari.

We went our way, and nodded to Roger Gore in the kitchen, where he was doing something noxious with martinis and sweet gherkins. What a lox!

About an hour later Rooney was bopping with Willis (that sweet muthuh!) and I was in the corner digging a T-Bone Walker 78 somebody had slipped into the stack. Jenny came up to me: "I'm going out for a drink with Roger. I'll be back in about half an hour."

I didn't even think it was worth getting angry about. I'd known it was going to happen. *Don't go up in the top shelf of the cabinet and take a bean out of the jar and shove it up your nose*, you tell the infant, and when you get back home, there he is, stretched out blue on the linoleum, a bean up his nose. It's the way children are.

She mulched out of there on Roger Gore's arm, and when Rooney was done sweating with Willis, he brought her back and I told her about Jenny's exeunt simpering.

"Why didn't you stop her?" she demanded.

"Who do I look like: Torquemada?" I got hot. "I've got enough trouble governing the habits of you and me without taking on the world at large. Besides, he won't hurt her, for Chrissakes. They'll be back."

We waited six hours. The party was over, we were really drug with the scene, and finally went back to my place to sack out. About five A.M. the phone rang, I groped for it, somehow got it up to my nose and blew into it. After a minute something fell into place and I knew I had it wrong. I tried my eye and my mouth, and by process of elimination got around to my ear. It was Jenny.

"Can you come and get me?"

"Whuhtimezit?"

"I don't know, it's late. Can you come get me?"

"Whereyooat?"

"I'm in a phone booth on Sunset, near Highland. Can you come and get me?" And she started crying. I woke up fast.

"Are you all right?"

"Yes, yes, I'm fine, can you come and get me?"

"Sure. Of course, but what happened to you? We waited till everyone else vanished. What the hell happened to you? Rooney was worried sick."

"I'll tell you later. Can you come get me now?"

"Give me fifteen minutes."

She hung up, I slid out without waking Rooney, threw on a pair of chinos and a jacket, and flew the coop. She was standing under a streetlight where she had said she'd be, and I bundled her into the car, where she immediately broke down. I got her back to my house, and bedded her out on the sofabed in the living room, and went back to sleep myself.

Next morning Rooney cooed over her like Little Orphan Annie. We eventually got the story, and it wasn't that spectacular. He'd taken her to a little bar nearby, tried to get her lushed (which he didn't have to bother doing; Jenny was—putting it politely—not smart enough to avoid being a pushover) and finally told her he had to get the car, which was allegedly his roommate's, back to his house. When he got her there, he proceeded to try The Game, and Jenny swore he hadn't succeeded. In childish retaliation, Roger had fallen asleep. She'd waited around for three hours, but he snoozed on, and finally she'd tried to waken him. Either he couldn't or wouldn't rouse himself, because she finally took to her heels, and an hour and a half later had managed to get to the phone booth.

"Why didn't you call from his house?"

"I was afraid he'd wake up."

"But you wanted him up, didn't you?"

"Well, yes."

"So why didn't you call from there?"

"I was afraid. I wanted to get out of there."

"Afraid? Of what? Of him?"

"Well. . ."

"Jenny, tell me now, tell me true, did he get to you?"

"No. I swear it. He got very angry when I gave him a hard time. He called me. . .he called me. . ."

"I know what he called you. Forget it."

"I can't."

"So remember it. But don't lie to me, did he get in?"

She turned her face away. At the time I thought it was because of my choice of words. "No, he didn't," she said. So I couldn't really bring myself to feel possessively angry at Roger Gore. He'd done what any guy would try to do. He'd tried to make her, failed, and gotten disgusted. His chief sin was in not being a gentleman. In falling asleep and letting her fend for herself; but then, I'd known Gore was anything but a gentleman, anyhow, so there really wasn't provocation enough to go find and pound him. We let the matter drop. I forgot about it, and fortunately, didn't run into Roger Gore again for some time.

Now, eight weeks later, I sat smoking a cigarette, while Jenny languished in the bathroom of her apartment, reading *McCall's*, and the seed grew in her. I felt responsible. The phone rang. I picked it up reluctantly, and it was Rooney. "She told you?" I mumbled something affirmative. "Have you got a solution?"

"Three of them," I answered. "She can have the baby, she can get it aborted, or she can get Roger Gore to marry her. I'd say the first and third are out, the second one the most feasible, and a quick fourth reason altogether possible."

"What's the fourth one?" Rooney asked.

"She can blow her fucking stupid brains out."

All you have to do is get friendly with a couple of jazz musicians, have met a hooker at a party, be on civil terms with a grocer who takes the neighborhood numbers action, occasionally make an after-hours set in the Negro section, and suddenly you are a figure of mystery, a man with "connections" in the underworld; people come to you for unspeakable foulnesses you have never been within spitting distance of. It is a reflex cliché of people who really haven't the faintest bloody idea of what the Real World is like. Since they themselves never slip over the line, anyone who lives beyond the constrained limits of their socially acceptable scene, has *got* to be a figure of mystery, a man with—oh well. . .

Rooney asked me how soon I could locate an abortionist.

"A whaaat?"

She repeated herself, all honey-voiced forthrightness. It was a foregone conclusion. "Spider" Markham, denizen of the murky underworld, familiar of hoods, gunsels and two-bit whores was the man to ask when you needed a butcher.

"What the hell makes you think I know an abortionist?"

"Well, don't you?"

"No. Of course not. I take precautions. I'm not an imbecile like Roger Gore. I've never knocked anyone up, so ergo I don't know any abortionists." I looked at her with unconcealed annoyance, and she stared back blandly. She wasn't convinced. I was, of course, hiding my connections, for obvious reasons.

"Say, you don't believe me, do you?" I was getting highly hacked by this scene. And Jenny just sat there with her face hanging out, and her stomach growing.

"Well, you can call someone, one of your strange friends, can't you?"

I blew higher than the Van Allen radiation belt. "You've got to be putting me on, Rooney! Call who? What 'strange friends'?" My face was so hot I could feel it in my mouth.

She stared at me accusingly.

So I called Candy.

Candy was a muscle for some nameless amalgamation of interests I don't think could be called the Syndicate. Maybe The Group, or The Guys, or Them, but definitely not The Syndicate. To begin with, he was Greek, not Sicilian.

But Candy *was* a furtive figure, I must admit. He collected the payoffs for the numbers banks in East L.A. and I have seen his 340 pounds walk into a deli as lightly as a prima ballerina, and within ten seconds cause more of a stir than a thermite bomb. "There was a lotta hits this week, Candy," the deli proprietor will con him. "The take is tiny. Tiny. I can't pony it all up. I can give ya 'bout half, though, Candy, and the rest next week sometime."

Candy, who is only slightly less prepossessing than Mount Etna, will suck air into his bellows chest, puff up twice again as large as normal, pouter-pigeon fashion, and in a voice soft as strangling babies, will reply: "Angie, you will kindly get it up or I will have to hurt you. Seriously." They scamper. And from some ratty cache beneath a counter, they produce the held-back portion of Candy's pickup money.

So I called Candy, who is maybe the gentlest cat I know.

"Hi," I started. It was not a particularly brilliant opening, but it was all I had available at that moment. "Listen, a friend of a friend of mine has got herself in a family way. Do you know anybody who can, uh, take care of her?"

He was affronted. Practically shrieked at me. What the hell kind of a guy did I think he was? He didn't screw around with those kinda people. Listen, if that was the kinda guy I thought he was, I would kindly honor him by forgetting his unlisted number. The nerve! The gall! What kind of a creep did I run around with, to need a guy who'd do that and finally Good-bye slam!

I turned around to Jenny and Rooney. "He hung up on me. Thanks."

They seemed shocked, and Rooney made devious remarks about the furtiveness of some shady types. I think I groaned.

Then I tried Van Jessup, a character actor who seemed to know everyone. He knew no one. Then I tried a tv director I'd played gin with a few times, and he said he'd get back to me. Then I tried a chick who made the Sunset Strip scene, and she asked a couple of guarded questions and said *she'd* get back to me. Then I called a relative in Pomona and she giggled outrageously, and said *I* should get back to *her*. Then I called The Boffer, who is a writer and a singer and a hustler of personal needs, and the conversation went like this:

"I need a doctor."

"So go to one."

"Not for me, man, for a chick."

"Pregnant?"

"Of course, stupid. You think I'm the Blue Cross or somedamnthing?"

"Rooney?"

"Don't be funny."

"Who then? And does Rooney know you've been playing pattyfingers?"

"I didn't do the knocking-up."

"A likely story."

"Cut it, man. I'm serious. This thing has lost its funny for me. It isn't my woman, and I didn't do the job on her, and I need a D&C man. Now can you help me or not?"

"I suppose so. I've had occasion to—"

"I don't want to know. Everyone agrees you're the finest swordsman in these parts. Can you get me a guy. . .this is a favor I need, Boffer. It's for a friend."

"You know, everybody you call is gonna think it was you."

"I know."

"Since when did you get such humanitarian instincts?"

"A recent malady. What's his name? Is there a number?"

"You're a lot more noble and friendly than I'd be. This kinda scam is liable to ruin your reputation."

"I haven't got a reputation. What's his name? Give!"

There was a pause, as though The Boffer was seriously considering saying no. He's peculiar that way. His reasoning is on a very furry plane, taken up by intricacies even he barely understands, and informed by a scurrying rodentlike deviousness that comes from having been on the Hollywood merry-go-round for too many years. "Take this down. You got a pencil? Okay, take this down: S. Jaime Quintano: the number is—"

He rattled it off twice and I still didn't get it. So he laid it on me slowly, and I wrote it as accurately as I could.

"Thanks, Boffer. You've got one coming."

I gave the information to Jenny, and she stared at it as though it was contaminated. "You'll have to do the calling," I told her. "Apparently he's a good man, has his own clinic, works most of the week in the Miguel Aleman Hospital, that's the big one down there. This friend of mine says he's taken girls down there a couple of times and this man has been very clean, very good. Three hundred dollars."

She continued to stare at the slip of paper.

"This is the number," I emphasized. It was like talking to a statue. "D-U-five-three-three-seven-two, that's in Tijuana, and I think I have his name spelled right. Jenny. . .?"

First her shoulders began to heave. Silently. Then her entire body shook, as though possessed. And in a second she was dry-crying, her head sunk down on her chest almost, the top of her head bobbing like a cork in a rough sea. It had started to get through to her: what she had undergone had not been love, it had been something far more indelicate, something simpler, more destructive. She felt contaminated, felt insulted, in the strictest possible sense of the outmoded term, she felt *sullied*.

I moved over to her and put my arms around her. She was incapable, at that moment, of even knowing I was there. I held her very tightly for what seemed a long time, and slowly the shaking passed, and her head came up. The front of my shirt was soaked.

She came out from the burrow of my arms. "What's the area code to Tijuana?" she said softly.

"Nine-o-three," Rooney said, from the other side of the room. I looked at her, startled. "I've been there, too." Her face was very sad, and I realized: no one comes to anyone untouched.

Everyone goes through fire.

Jenny picked up the receiver and started to dial.

By the time the Thursday rolled around, I had six more names. A doctor in Monterey Park who was rumored to charge between three and five hundred, but had apparently been busted some time before, and was very much under wraps now. It would have entailed a drive out to that suburb. Five more in Tijuana. Two brothers with their own *Enfermería*, who only charged one hundred and fifty, and to whom you had to say, "Nurse Carlotta suggested I call you." Apparently Nurse Carlotta was a swinger in L.A. that the brothers dug. Another was alleged to keep the patient over for eight hours, and that was too terrifying for consideration. Overnight in that town would be worse than the operation for Jenny. There was an American doctor down there, Oswald Tremaine, Jr., who was appended with the title "butcher" by my informant, but he only charged one hundred and twenty-five. We decided Quintano was the best bet. His name had come up again, from a very reputable source, so we held to the date of the appointment Jenny had made that night.

It was tacitly understood that Rooney and I would drive her down. If her parents ever found out, the consequences were too hideous to consider. Jenny never expanded on the remark, but when I suggested that perhaps her parents might be very understanding, if she explained what had happened, she said, "My father has never hit me, but he has a very loud voice, and he wears a belt. My mother would cry."

We left it at that, and spent the week between the phone call and that Thursday getting ourselves ready. I was driving an MG Magnette, a pretentious, cheaper copy of the Jaguar touring sedan. It was a lovely sort of thing, though, with glove-leather upholstery, dual carbs, a solid walnut dash panel that could be lifted out, four doors and the traditional MG red-painted engine. I got it lubed and checked out for the ride down. Rooney worked, of course, so her readying was all interior. As for Jenny, all I could tell of her state of mind, her capacity for handling this thing, as her nineteenth year became a nightmare, was that she did not cry again, and her conversation was not introspective.

When I asked her what had been said on the call to the doctor, she said: "A woman answered. She said, '*Bueno.*' I told her a friend from Fresno had suggested I call Doctor Quintano about consultation. Then she put me through to him, and I said the same thing, and he asked me consultation about what? I said I was having menstrual difficulties, that was what your friend told me to say, and he said just a minute; he said it very quickly, as though he didn't want to talk any more. Then the girl came back and asked me what day I wanted to come down, and I told her Thursday, and she said to call from San Diego when we got that far."

I had a feeling Jenny was going to be all right. She was getting much sharper, very quickly. Sometimes childhood and adolescence pass away just that fast, like morning mist, burned off by the sun or a rotten experience. Markham, the philosopher. You can't miss my ruminations: they're in that purple-bound folio over there.

Three hundred dollars had been the next point Quintano's woman had brought up. "Do you know the Doctor's fee?" she had asked. Jenny said three hundred. Not anymore. That was last year's price. But what with the high cost of this and that, the going rate for Dilation & Curettage was now four hundred. Jenny said all right, to the woman (whose name was Nancy, and who spoke with a faint trace of Spanish accent) and to me, and to Roger Gore when she called him for the money.

She said all right.

But Roger Gore said no.

He also said she was a whore. He also said she was a harpy and a blackmailer and a tramp and slept with dogs in the streets and if she had as many sticking out of her as she'd probably had sticking *in* her, she'd look like a porcupine. He concluded his chivalrous polemic with the comment that she could go peddle her ass on First and Main in downtown L.A. and raise the action that way. His parting line was, "Even if you charge what you're worth, you shouldn't have to make it with more than two or three hundred guys to raise the money."

When she repeated the conversation, I felt my jaw muscles turn to concrete, and I must have scraped a half-dozen layers of enamel off my back teeth. Frankly, I wanted to kill the bastard!

"I'll talk to him," I said.

I took a drive and stopped off at a phone booth in a gas station; while they were putting in a couple of bucks of hi-test I called Roger Gore.

"Is Roger there?"

"Who's this?"

"Ken Markham."

"He's not here."

"You won't be here for long, Gore, if you don't start acting like a man."

"I'll tell him when he comes in."

"Shape up, Gore. The kid's in trouble, and you'd damned well better be ready to take the responsibility."

"Screw you." Click.

I walked back to the car. "You save Blue Chip Stamps?" the gas jockey asked.

"Yeah. I'm saving up."

He grinned pleasantly. Make conversation. Build the clientele. "Oh? For what?"

"A hydrogen bomb."

He was still staring as I tooled out of the lot.

I was right, of course. He *was* trying to split. I drove up his driveway just as he was driving down. He screeched and stalled the Impala, and I slewed the Magnette crosswise across his path. I left the motor running and the emergency brake on, and I was out of the car, dashing toward him, fast as a wad of spit, before he could get coordinated. He was rolling up the windows and locking the doors as I pulled open the rear door on the side away from him. With four doors, four windows, he could only get to so many before I got to him. Logic. Wham!

I yanked open the door and plunged into the rear seat before he could turn around.

My arm went around his neck and yanked him half-out of the driver's seat. I used my free hand to slam the door handle beside him, and flung the front door open. Still holding him, I punched open my door, and reached around. I grabbed the sonofabitch by his jacket and yanked him sidewise. He went sprawl-assing out of the car, and I was on him.

"Let's go see your house," I said tightly.

I took the car keys, and using a bring-along I'd learned at jolly old Fort Benning while doing my two for Uncle Sam, we dogtrotted back to the house. I unlocked the door and shoved him just enough ahead of me to plant my foot in the middle of his butt. I jacked my foot forward as hard as I could and Beau Brummel went flailing across the room, headfirst into the genuine imitation mahogany portable bar. Glassware went in all directions, his right hand swept an ornate cocktail shaker against the wall, and he knocked the caster-mounted shell on its side. He fell in a very untidy heap, and I slammed the door behind me as I moved toward him. His eyes were like a pair of Rolls Royce foglamps.

"Four hundred dollars," I said, very gently, lifting him by his jacket front and his Jay Sebring twelve-dollar razor-cut.

"No, I, listen—" he started. . .

"Curettage," I recited, from reading I had recently done, "is a French word meaning to scrape out. This is the simplest operation performed upon the uterus and consists of scraping the lining of the cavity." I let go of his jacket, still holding him up by the hair, and cocked back my fist. "It is performed under a light general anesthesia." I hit him as hard as I could, just under the left eye. "The normal uterus is a pear-shaped, muscular organ, about three inches long, two inches wide and one inch thick, lying in the midportion of the pelvis." He sagged sidewise, and the skin burned, blued, went gray and he started to bleed from a small cut. His eyes misted.

"The uterus," I continued, slapping him back and forth across the bridge of the nose to revive him, "consists of three layers—a thin, outer, sheathlike coat, a thick muscular layer, and a membranous lining to the cavity which is located in the center of the organ." He came back from wherever he'd fled, and there was a fear of the Furies gibbering in his blue eyes. His tongue peeked out of his mouth, and I slammed him with the palm of my hand, and he bit the tip, screeching at me something I couldn't understand. I cuffed him in the right ear, then the left, and his head bobbled like the top scoop of an unsteady ice cream cone.

"Simply stated, the function of the uterus is to receive the fertilized egg (which travels from the ovary through the fallopian tubes), nourish and contain the egg as it develops through pregnancy and"—I hit him with everything I had, flush in the mouth—"expel the fully developed embryo. Four hundred dollars, Roger." The lower lip tore, teeth bit through the upper, and he went far away again.

Softly, "Four hundred, Roger baby." I let him slip back down on his side. He lay there looking frightened.

I went into the kitchen and drew myself a glass of cold water. He was a lousy housekeeper; I had to rinse my own glass.

It had not been the most methodical of jobs, but then neither was I a schooled pistolero. It had been informed, however, by a classic frenzy and a degree of hatred/brutality I'd never known I contained. I sat there while he sponged off his face with the wet washcloth, and my knees were shaking. He looked as though someone had mistaken his face for ten pounds of dogmeat, and had tried to fry it. His left eye was swollen shut, with thick, red-blue puffy tissue that gleamed in the light. His mouth was raw and cut through by his teeth. He had smaller cuts and contusions all over, and frankly, it would be some time before the hatcheck girl at PJ's winked at him again. I handed him the phone. He looked at it, then at me. The eye was starting to drain blue into his cheek.

He called his father and mouthed some sort of nonsense about needing four hundred dollars to get him out of a very tight spot. I think he knew just how tight that spot was. His old man must have said okay, because I saw Roger Gore visibly brighten at one point midway in the conversation. There was a great deal of "Okay, Dad, this is the last time; I'll be turning over a new leaf, you'll see; you won't be sorry, Dad, thanks a million," and he racked the receiver. I looked at the kid just as hard as I could, and I said:

"It's a shame there's no law protecting girls like Jenny from their own stupidity. It's also a shame there's no law that punishes a guy for not being a gentleman. But anyhow, Roger friend, there are more serious pains than the ones I loaned you. I'm not telling you *not* to swear out an assault and battery on me. That'd be foolish, though; assault means to threaten battery, and since I didn't threaten you, I guess the best you could do would be battery, which might net me about five years in the slam, but there *are* more serious pains, Roger friend, and they are dispensed by much more unpleasant guys than me. I leave you with that thought.

"We'll be taking Jenny down to TJ on Thursday. Get the money to her before then." I stood up and made to leave.

He snarled at me from the floor. "Your Jenny is a tease and a bitch, man! She wanted it as much as I did, that Jenny of yours! So just who the hell you think you're helping? Your Jenny's a dummy and a tramp, and she hasn't got any honor to protect! So take your Jenny and shove—"

I planted my foot with carefully calculated force in his groin. Gently I added, "She is neither your Jenny nor mine. She is her own Jenny, and whatever is wrong there, fellah, she is still a human being.

"Which is a condition I doubt you possess."

He was sucking air like a beached bass when I left.

My engine was still running.

When I got back, Jenny was alone. Rooney had gone over to see her parents; they had bought a new dog, and Rooney was a flip when it came to babies or tiny dogs. It wasn't a vagrant thought: Jenny looked like a little of each. The washed-face pinkness and confusion of a baby; the anxiety and need to love or be loved a small dog wears like a second collar.

"Want to play some gin?" I asked her.

She nodded mutely and went to the sideboard to get the dog-eared deck. We sat down on the sofa, and she shuffled while I lit a cigarette. For a while we played, and didn't say anything. Finally, I knocked on four in a spade hand, caught her with about twenty-five points, and said, "I talked to Roger. He's changed his mind."

"You didn't hurt him!" That was the first thing to cross her mind. Not did I get the money, not was she going to be rescued, but was he all right. I had one of those moments of stomach-muscle-tensing disorientation, as though I had intruded on a personal fight between two people who knew each other better than any interlopers with inclinations of arbitration.

"He's okay. We just. . .talked awhile. I convinced him you were his responsibility. He'll be getting the money to you before Thursday."

She dropped her arms, and I could see her gin hand. It wasn't so hot. "Thank God," she breathed. There was a pale milkiness about her then. As though some vital ingredient in her spirit had been hit by a catalytic agent, had vaporized in her system. She seemed just a little dead, at that moment.

She dropped the cards and lay back against the sofa with her eyes shut. Her hair was a natural blonde, somewhere between hard canary and yellow ocher, and she wore it in a ponytail, usually, a style few girls affect any more. But she wore it well, and there was a pleasantness to her youthfulness. I looked at her, resting there, and something turned over inside me.

She had said something.

I hadn't really heard it, had just imagined I'd heard it, but she had spoken, absently, without realizing what words had been selected to convey her fear and her insecurity, but she had said, "Oh, Kenny. . ."

And it was someone else's voice from another time. I can't remember even now who it was. Another girl I had known, when I was young enough to be able to remember everyone who had said yes, and count them on one hand. Perhaps it was that second girl I'd slept with. I can't recall who she was. There isn't anyone, man or woman, who can't recall the first. But the second. . .ah, that's another matter. And perhaps it was her.

Whoever it had been, this was now, and Jenny had said, "Oh, Kenny. . ." and I was holding her slim body very close to mine, and my hands were locked behind her back, still clutching the gin cards. Her face came up, and there were dust motes spinning in her eyes of whatever color those eyes might be.

I smelled her hair, and it was very clean. It was another reminder of things from before, but they were silly, irrelevant things, like a field of winter wheat I had run through once, on a picnic day, when there had been such things as days right for nothing but picnics. It was a stupid thought, and it passed quickly, but not before I recalled having run and run and finally fallen down on my back, and lain there, completely hidden from all but the sky, staring straight up and feeling sorry as hell for myself. I kissed Jenny, and her mouth was soft, precisely as a woman's mouth should be. I kissed her the way a gentle lover would kiss someone he revered.

"Not like that," she murmured, pulling my face down harshly. "Like this." She opened her lips and worked at me fiercely, as though it was something worth doing and hence, something worth doing well. It was possibly the grandmother of all Soul Kisses, and when she was done, I knew I'd been kissed. My hand was on her thigh, and she moved slightly, so my hand went over the rise, down where her slacks were tightest. I had a mad thought that someone was going to pop out of the clothes closet and take movies of it all, but that thought passed, too, and in a moment we were wriggling with each other's clothes, trying to keep our mouths together, and yet get naked.

Jenny was young, but Jenny was expert. She took me the way Hillary and Tenzing Norgay took Everest: all the way, and chiefly because *it was there*. Anything worth doing was worth doing well. Midway, she arched up and there was a feral gleam on her face, a drawing back of the lips and an exposure of small teeth that reminded me of a timber wolf I'd shot up near North Bay. Sometimes, though, she was a flower, and sometimes she was a hot shower, and sometimes she was a pitch pipe whistling an elegant tune. She had a small habit of twisting her hips sidewise at special times.

When we were over the final hill, and the road behind seemed much too rough for anyone to have crossed alone, much less two people as strangely locked as we had been, I went into the bathroom and took a bath. Not a shower. A bath. I have taken showers since I was sixteen and had a bad back. Baths are a pain, and they leave a dirty ring around the tub.

I felt I needed a bath.

And I wanted to see that dirty ring around the tub.

Thursday was two hells and a decapitation away. Every time Rooney looked at me I could swear she knew. And when Jenny leaned over in a movie we three attended, with her hand on my leg, and whispered, "At least I know for sure you couldn't make me pregnant," I wanted to open my wrists with a beer can opener. What had I stumbled upon: a key to the depravity of the young? Or the key to my own yin and yang? I didn't feel guilty, I felt unclean, which was infinitely worse. I, Kenneth Duane Markham, became a case in point for myself. *This*, I thought angrily, *is how we fool ourselves into thinking we're honorable men.* Jenny's mere existence became a constant reminder of the other side of my nature; an ungovernable side that didn't even have the consistency, the decency or the stamina to be constant. I was a mealy-mouthed, smiling sinner who took his pleasures and pains as they comfortably fit into the regimented scene of everyday life. Dorian Gray be damned! There isn't one of us who isn't in that bag.

But finally we left. Our little caravan moved out onto the road with all the glee and aplomb of a New Orleans funeral that couldn't find a Preservation Hall Dixieland band.

We turned onto the Hollywood Freeway and sped straight down Route 101. Santa Ana Freeway, Pacific Coast Highway, El Camino Real; past Downey and its used car carnivals, past Disneyland and its ludicrous Matterhorn rising out of the surrounding squalor, past Tustin and the art bookstore that faces out on a highway going too fast to give a damn. San Juan Capistrano, and I've never seen a swallow yet, going *or* coming. San Clemente, Del Mar, Pacific Beach, and we were in San Diego. I once asked a resident if they minded the Navy calling it "Dago," and that worthy responded he didn't care if they called it dog-whoopee, as long as they kept spending their money. That, I feel, sums up the beauty and glory of San Diego, a helluva way to end a beautiful state. It is not, I hasten to add, a coincidence that Dago appears at what might metaphorically be termed the backside of the state. We pulled in at a one-arm joint on 101, just before National City, the other side of San Diego, and while Jenny went to phone, Rooney and I had cups of coffee; I worked my neck around, trying to unkink it.

"What's the matter with you today?" she asked, over the lip of the cup.

"What do you mean: what's the matter? Nothing. Why, does something look the matter?" I could feel my nose growing, like Pinocchio's.

"You've been awfully quiet the last forty miles or so."

I shrugged. "Tired. My back aches. That's all."

She didn't answer, but she knew I was lying.

"And this isn't really the pleasure trip of all time," I added. *Keep talking, shmuck,* I told myself. *Dig it a little deeper.*

"Well, it'll all be over soon enough," Rooney said, trying to cover her own awareness of my mood. She knew me too well. I knew we'd be splitting up soon. I couldn't let anyone get that close to the core of me; as long as it was froth and foam it was safe. But the encystment was too marked in me, at age thirty. I smiled across at her reassuringly.

Jenny came back. "Have a cup of coffee and a piece of pie," I told her. She shook her head no. "I'm not supposed to eat before the operation. His girl told me not to eat for about six hours beforehand. I haven't eaten since last night. I'm starving, but you know you're not supposed to eat before this kind of thing."

I *hadn't* known, but I saw no reason for her to make a big who-struck-John of the whole matter. I mumbled something about oh yeah, I knew. And that was that. She sat down next to Rooney, staring at me with open malevolence. Like I was the guy who'd knocked her up. In a philosophical sense, I suppose I was as guilty as Roger Gore, but somehow I couldn't bring myself to eat that particular humble pie. I had a feeling too many strange Jack Horners had already had their thumbs in it.

"Well, what did they say?" Rooney asked.

Jenny pulled her eyes away from me with difficulty. There was actually physical violence in her expression. I chalked it up to her fear and the fact that I was a man the same as Roger Gore, only he wasn't handy for hating.

"She said to drive across the border, into downtown Tijuana, and park behind the Woolworth's at 4:30, there'd be a fellow to meet us. She said his name is Louis—"

"Luis," I corrected her.

"So Loo-ees," she snapped back. "So what?" Then she went on, addressing herself to Rooney. I couldn't have cared less. "She said to dress poorly, not like tourists—"

"*Turistas*," I murmured, under my breath.

"Why don't you *just shut up!*" Jenny was screaming. A man at the counter turned to look at us, and the waitress paused on her way through the swinging doors to the kitchen.

I reached across and grabbed her wrist as hard as I could. "Listen, you little asshole, I've had about as much horseshit from you as I can take. I've had to listen to your miserable bellyaching and whining and complaining for the last week; you may not appreciate the fact that aiding someone in getting an abortion is a prison offense, and that Rooney and I are risking our necks to drag your butt down here, but the least you can do is be civil and keep from being a bigger pain in the ass than you already are." I shoved her wrist away violently and slumped back in the booth. Rooney was staring at us as though we'd both gone insane. Jenny was rubbing her goddam wrist and looking like a whipped spaniel. I drank coffee and pretended I was in Nome, Alaska.

After a long silence in which no one seemed to move, Rooney said, guardedly, "Let's go. It's three o'clock now. It'll probably take us a while to find the Woolworth's."

"I have a terrible headache," Jenny said, rubbing one hand up across her temple. "Do you have an aspirin?"

I threw a half dollar onto the table and slid out of the booth. As I stalked to the car, Jenny was bugging the waitress for an Empirin or somedamnthing. I got into the car and lit a cigarette. It tasted like dust, and so did the day.

Getting into Tijuana, unlike the crossover to Hell, involves no Stygian water-ride, and if one of the border guards be named Charon, at least he has had the good sense to have it Anglicized. At that point, all differences cease.

We drove up to the big white pass-through that stretched across the road. The parking lot on the American side was not filled. Had it been a weekend, with the jai alai, the dog and horse races at Caliente, the bullfights, the lots would have been banged to the fences; but this was

Thursday, and midday was not too far advanced, and traffic was steady, but not a flood, as it would be the next day.

We were waved through without a passing glance from the patrolmen. Does no one smuggle anything *into* Mexico?

A few feet beyond the pass-through, the car told me we were in Mexico, and I knew why most people left their vehicles on the American side (a single reason out of three good ones). The pavement came to a halt, was replaced by a three-foot stretch of open dust-dirt, and then resumed as pavement again. But a return to pavement so marked I knew I had left the United States. The Mexican pavement was in chunks. It was pocked and upthrust as though a decade of cars had gone over it without the most minor attention by repair gangs. We bumped and jounced across the passway, the Magnette clanging like a dinner gong.

(The other two reasons, incidentally, are that if you have an accident involving your car in Tijuana, whether you are right or wrong, struck or striker, the car is impounded, they throw you up *under* the jail, and only a feisty bribe will get you out; the third reason is that hubcaps, car seats, dash clocks, luggage racks, headlamps and other minor items have an uncanny habit of vanishing from the auto in question. Some contend it is the highly spiced atmosphere of the town.)

We passed through the Mexican side with even less event than the Yankee entrance. Fat chance they'd keep out a spendable dollar.

Once through the arch, and a left turn, it was an open scene from Hogarth. Perhaps Hieronymus Bosch. Possibly Dali. Definitely Dante.

Filth.

The word comes unbidden. A hundred, two hundred rickety taxis, all parked in rows, waiting for the *turistas*. The street hard-packed dirt and broken concrete. Dozens of barefoot urchins, scuddy in their dingy rags, clutching cigar boxes full of Chiclets to be sold at a dime or half dollar for a penny pack. Ramshackle buildings, swayleaning as though propped from behind with poles. A miasma of road dust rising turning in the sunbeaten air. A sense of *hurry*, of expectation, of fear and sickness and something about to happen. A faint electric stir of movement *within* the mass gibbering movement of dirty hack drivers and shawl-wrapped women hustling for the dollars. A tone of impending disaster, always omnipresent. Was this perhaps the stench that filled Pompeii before it dissolved in fire? Did Sodom or Gomorrah have to contend with that stink no Air-Wick could ever contain, that color of madness in the wind and in the very horizon line?

I gunned the Magnette and pulled out of the middle of the maelstrom. We banged down the street, between two untidy rows of temporary structures, all of which were selling car upholstery. Tuck and roll shops. Best bargains. Get it here, installed in ten minutes, satisfaction guaranteed. All misspelled.

Cover-up shops for stripping and repainting cars; hot cars; stolen cars; lost cars; impounded cars; and legitimate tucking and rolling, as well. Guaranteed to last at least till you recrossed the border.

A huge sign across the end of the road bellowed:

BIENVENIDAS AMIGOS!

Welcome, suckers. Unfurl your desires and let us see under which banners you skulk. We have it here, guaranteed, satisfaction 100 percent or we give you a dose of the clap free!

A clutch of buildings clogged the roadside on either hand. One of them said MARRIAGE DIVORCE CAR INSURANCE on a sloppily lettered sign. A second advised FULL COVER INSURANCE WHILE IN MEXICO GUARANTEED! A third reversed the order (or perhaps the owner was more of a cynic) by offering DIVORCES QUICK—MARRIAGES—NOTARY. Notary what, I never paused to inquire. We did a dog-leg and turned up another street, in as hideous a condition as the one we'd just left, following a white arrow-sign that said DOWNTOWN TI.

Someone had, perhaps, bitten off the remaining section of the sign. Mad dogs, I am told, are not uncommon in such heavy climates.

Farther into TJ, the incredible poverty and squalor of the people struck us like a hammer blow. "MiGod, it's unbelievable!" said Rooney, as a gaggle of barefooted, dirt-smeared children raced directly across our path, causing me to swerve into a huge chuckhole. They ran across the razor-edged rocks of the road as though their feet were wound with asbestos.

Slat-houses tottered at every curb. Porches boasted fat old women, whose only joys were watching the horrors the young girls had to endure. On every bit of habitable land, someone had thrown up a jury-rigged shack. Garbage cans lived more open lives than the people whose refuse they received. Every half-block there were one or more stores advertising LICORES.

I could understand it; the only way to live and stay sane in such a cesspool, was to stay liquored-up constantly. We drove on.

After what seemed a Minotaur's maze of twistings and turnings, through streets littered with animate and inanimate garbage, with the castoff and the downcast, with the vile and the pitiful, we saw a street of neon lights and brighter buildings. Traffic was incredible. The taxis moved as though their wheels were about to be revoked. Pedestrians leaped out—perhaps hoping they would be struck down by a rich *gringo*—and masses of humanity surged across at intersections which had never known the luxury of a stoplight.

We drove down past the old bullring, the Toreo de Tijuana. The new one was up on the hill overlooking the town, but the *turistas* go there, and for a real bloodbath *corrida*, the townsfolk go to the old ring, where the *toreros* must perform with more skill and passion. A bright, romantic poster outside the ring proclaimed:

6 LA TRASQUILA 6
THE GREATEST BULLFIGHTING FIGURES
CARLOS ARRUZA (The Mexican Cyclone)
FERMIN ESPINOZA MILLITA (The Master of Masters)
AND SILVERIO PEREZ (The Pharaoh from Texcoco)
FIGHTING TO DEATH IMPOSING BULLS FROM
6 LA TRASQUILA 6!!

I did not read this sign all at once, then. Much later I was to have painful opportunity to study it at my leisure, or a copy thereof, while lying on my back. At the time, all I saw was the bright poster color and the word ARRUZA. We continued driving toward what had to be the center of town.

As we drove, seedy-looking men with rolled newspapers leaped out onto the street, trying to wave our car into whatever empty lot they had appropriated as a parking area. We drove straight down into the heart of town. The roads were a little better now, on a par with a neglected side street or country road in the States. I knew I'd have to have the Magnette completely overhauled when I got back. Every seam was sprung; every bolt was loose.

We cruised around, and finally I spotted the Woolworth's. It looked like any plastic-and-chrome eyesore from the States, but among the filthy, falling-down shops and bars and arcades of downtown Tijuana, it was shining, gleaming, sparkling, a reassurance that stability still existed. We rolled slowly toward the big store, and I saw an empty parking place on the street. "She said behind the Woolworth's, in their parking lot," Jenny said.

It was the first sentence out of her mouth since we'd left the coffee shop in National City.

I pulled around the side of the building, and started into the lot. An old Mexican with gold teeth came running out of a rickety guard-shack and tried to take a dollar from me. I asked if this was parking for Woolworth's. My Spanish was passably understandable, but not enough to get elected mayor. He answered in English, almost. "Ess park for no-whan, no Wowlwort's, ees pay for aver'whan!" And he continued to shove his hand through the window. His hand looked as though the last time it had been introduced to soap was when Calvin Coolidge approved the World Court. "I'm waiting for someone, I'll only be here a few minutes," I tried to tell him. I should have known better; it was a stupid thing to say, a *turista* remark. He didn't give a damn if I was there for a minute or the decade. I backed up and found myself on the street, with the old man still screaming imprecations at me, possibly for running my nasty old car across his valuable dust.

The empty parking space was still there. I pulled into it, and as I negotiated the bumper of the car against the high curb, I realized I was being "navigated" from the sidewalk by a little boy of nine or ten. Unasked, he had taken me as his mark. A moment before he had not been there, but like some sort of ambulatory plant he had sprung from the shadows or the sidewalk, and was hand-waving me into the slot. Then he reached into a cigar box he carried, pulled out a penny and leaped at the parking meter. He beat the other four kids to the meter by a split-instant. They were identical in a tragic, sorry way. Each was his own person, but each dwelled within a coat of the same Tijuana dirt, and so they looked alike. The kid that had thrust the penny into the meter was around the car and trying to get my door open before I'd turned off the motor.

Rooney reached across Jenny and unlocked the door Jenny had just locked. "They're just children, Jenny."

She looked as though she'd eaten a ripe persimmon. "But they're so *filthy*!" The Louvre portrait of squeamish. Her nose wrinkled. Her lips vanished.

"It comes from not bathing," I said, snappishly. "And from having to sleep in a doorway. Offensive as hell, ain't it."

She didn't answer. By this time we had parted company for good and always, and for a second a wisp of thought crossed my mind how this adventure had altered all our relationships to one another. Then the kid had my door open and was demanding I pay him for parking my car, for his having waved his hands to steer me in, for his having put a penny in the meter.

"Doe-lahr, Señor," he urged, "doe-lahr!"

I shook my head no. He would not be put off. "Gimme, gimme, gimme!" he kept saying, not shouting, just demanding, in a tone of righteous indignation that was guaranteed to intimidate the sternest soul. And in an instant there was another one beside him, and a third, and then a very little one, no more than five or six, with huge wet eyes like one of the hideously stylized Keane paintings, and all of them with the cigar boxes filled with small change, packets of Chiclets, a knife perhaps.

The tiny one managed to wiggle past me and would not budge;

wedged in between the car seat and the door. I asked him and asked him again, tried, "*Vamanos*," and it didn't work, so I lifted him bodily and set him outside the car, closing the door with my back. His body went rigidly limp, if such a thing makes sense. He was affronted. He demanded money; for what nebulous service I cannot guess.

We managed to elude the kids, and it only cost me a half dollar to the one who had invested his penny. It was a quarter to four. We had forty-five minutes. So we walked up the block.

In the space of two hundred yards, it was a toss-up which deal would be more to my advantage: taking one of the girls offered to me by the sidewalk hustlers, or sell the two I had, turning a tidy profit. Rooney's bemused stares canceled either possibility. We walked through the shops and I decided I wanted to buy a set of steel-rim bongos. The opening price was thirteen dollars. When I left the shop, I had the bongos and was six dollars and fifty cents lighter.

Finally, it came around to 4:30 and we returned to the car. The fog lamps were gone from the front grille. I cursed eloquently, and Jenny mumbled something about replacing them, but I was in no mood for heroics, so I hustled them into the car, and we backed out of the parking slot. I pulled into the parking lot and here came the Old Man once more. I gave him the dollar and pulled into the back.

Jenny had been told to look for a 1962 Imperial, black.

We saw it parked at the other end of the lot, next to an old Ford with a man and woman in the front seat. Loafing against the rear of the Woolworth's was a trio of oily looking juvies overdressed and indolent. "I hope Luis isn't one of them," Jenny whispered. I didn't say anything; he probably was.

We pulled in next to the Ford, and I cut the engine. The man in the Ford was talking earnestly to the girl beside him. She was a wild-looking blonde, and I had the strange premonition that they were there for a familiar reason. "Let's get out, let them know who we are," I said. I got out and went around the car, and very ostentatiously helped Jenny from the car, as though she were an invalid. She looked at me peculiarly, but I didn't feel like explaining.

One of the young hoods detached himself from the group, waved good-bye to his fellow lounge-rats, and ambled across the lot toward us. "Uh-oh, here we go, gang," I said softly. The guy and the blonde got out of the Ford. She was wild. And I thought, *Perhaps they're friends of his, cover sent along in case of trouble.*

"Let's go," the kid said, walking up to the five of us. It was Luis. He had a memorable scar on his right cheek. I doubted he had come by it at Heidelberg.

He opened the doors of the black Imperial, and I helped Jenny and Rooney into the back seat. I started to get into the front seat, and he said, sharply, "In the back."

"I want to follow in my own car," I said. He shook his head. I stared at him for a long moment, and without uttering a sound Luis said, Do you want this thing done, or don't you? I got into the back seat. The blonde and her boy friend got in the front. He was carrying a copy of Kafka's IN THE PENAL COLONY, in a well-thumbed paperback edition, and while I wasn't dead certain, I was inclined to think my original estimate of the couple was correct. Why is it a corollary of being a college student that caution and common sense have been left out of the equation?

Luis backed out of the space, spun the wheel as I imagine he thought Fangio might have done it, and sped across the lot, out a side entrance, and down another street. He drove without saying a word, but flicked on the car radio, and in a moment we were inundated by yay-yays and boom-booms from a San Diego rock 'n' roll station. It was reassuring to know that bad taste was not strictly an American malady.

He drove for a long time, back and forth and around, and at one point stopped to buy a newspaper from a hawker standing on a deserted stretch of road. I surreptitiously glanced behind me as we whipped away down the road, and the newspaper vendor was moving quickly toward a small shack set off the road. I looked for, and found, the telephone lines running into the shack. Signal number one, apparently passing us through.

We drove a while longer, and Luis pulled in at a liquor store that also sold IMPORTED FRENCH PERFUME THE REAL STUFF! He got out, went inside, and I slow-counted to three hundred and eighty-five by thousandcount. He came back with a brown-paper sack twisted at the top, and I knew we'd come through phase two of the clearing process. He was assured—in some indefinable way—not only that we were not being followed, but that we were what we declared ourselves to be: waifs on the sea of intrigue. He roared out of the parking lot of the liquor store, and tooled the big Imperial toward the hills overlooking Tijuana. We roared past Caliente track; I relaxed, and Jenny looked more frightened.

It was a twisty-turny, and I went through a third of a pack of cigarettes. Finally, we pulled down a side street, turned left through an alley, and went right parallel to the street we had just come down. Luis whirled the wheel again, and pulled up into the driveway of an expensive-looking home surrounded by a high polished-wood fence. I could see the house through the close slats of the fence, and it was a big-money pad. Whoever lived there (and don't think for a second it wasn't obvious who lived there), lived well.

Luis braked to a halt before the inner gate, and honked twice, sharply, paused, then honked again. The gate went up, pulled on a chain by a skinny, underfed-looking Mexican youth perhaps a year or two younger than Luis, the pickup agent. He drove the car through, and the rickets case let the gate down again. We were in a narrow passage between the fence and the side of the house. Beyond the house, the passage opened into a large back area that ended in open-face garages. From where I sat, I could see a Bentley, a Thunderbird and what looked to be an Aston Martin roadster, each in its own berth, each a current model, each gleaming and polished.

Luis got out, and I opened the door on my side.

There was just barely enough room to squeeze out, and be wedged against the side of the house. The college students in the front seat could not yet leave the car, the passage was so narrow. Luis came around the car and opened the door beside me, into the house. I stepped back and Jenny and Rooney slipped past me. Luis watched

Jenny's legs as she slid out of the car. Eyes salivate, don't ever let them tell you otherwise. She caught him at it, and smiled coquettishly.

Luis ran a hand through his thick, glistening shock of hair. The Demon Lover strikes again!

We went inside, and were followed by the college students. There were three couples waiting. The girls were all exceptionally attractive, and all under twenty-one, I would have guessed.

It was an anteroom, with two sofas, several large borax modern chairs, and a tv set babbling a moron's guessing game. Something about trusting one another. . .

We sat and waited. Luis vanished through the only door leading into the house. I looked around at the others, and they were all studiously directing their attentions to the two microcephalics vying for prizes on the tv screen. I didn't fool myself that they were interested in what was happening there; they were afraid, unsure of protocol, and suspicious that everyone else was a friend of the Doctor. (The name now had an ominous ring, though by the wealthy surroundings it should have been otherwise.)

Luis stuck his head in, motioned to Jenny, Rooney and myself, and to the college students. The five of us got up and followed him through the door, around a corner, and into a large living room walled with sofas, chairs, an electric heater purring on the floor, and another, larger tv set, tuned to the same channel.

There was another couple sitting close together on one of the sofas. The guy looked more frightened than the chick, and *she* was comforting *him*.

"Seedohn," Luis directed us, and vanished back into the hallway. I paced across the thick carpet to see where he had gone, but the hallway ended in another plain panel door. There was the door through which we had come from the anteroom, and a twin directly across from it. Three doors, the living room, and silence. It hung musty warm in the room, with the electric heater going, the spring sun outside but unseen in the windowless room, and the three table lamps trying to convince us there was neither day nor night.

I sat down on the sofa across from the tv set, and Jenny leaned across. "Are you nervous?"

"No," I answered. "I'm not the one going inside."

She sank back, looking morose. Rooney gave me another of those peculiar stares.

We waited three quarters of an hour, and Luis popped in and out like the changer on a record player. The boredom was starting to get to me. A rerun of *The Lineup* came and went on the tv screen under the name *San Francisco Beat*, and I wondered just how long Warner Anderson and Tom Tully had been in movies. Then a rerun of *Yancy Derringer* came on, and I had to sit through something about a Union officer who had it in for a New Orleans gentleman and had arranged for his early demise by firing squad. I was about to stick my thumb in my mouth, plug up my ears, and blow my brains out through my nose when a nurse in white came into the room. She motioned to the wild-looking blonde, and they went off together. Not a sound. The coward sat and watched the tv set with a whipped expression. *Yancy Derringer* faded into limbo and an early movie came on. It starred Tom Neal (without a moustache), Evelyn Keyes and Bruce Bennett, and had somethingorother to do with Officers' Candidate School in World War Two. It was a drag, but Evelyn Keyes was nice. I yawned perhaps eighty times. Luis did his imitation of a jack-in-the-box several times, and finally, the nurse came back. "Mees. . .com plees. . ." She crooked a finger at Jenny.

Jenny got up reluctantly, clutching her purse with the four one-hundred-dollar bills in it. She gave us each a sickly smile, and we smiled back, rather more bored and struck witless by the heat and the waiting than through any concern. By now my feelings had been assuaged about the Good Doctor's capabilities. A man doesn't live that high from bad butchery. Word of mouth works just as much in D&C as in PR.

Jenny went away, and we settled down alone in the room to wait. After a while I shut off the heater. Tom Neal was better-looking with the moustache.

These are the mechanics of the nightmare:

Doctor's office. Modern desk. Office chair. Straight chair in front of desk. Radio. Telephone with number disc removed. Very bare walls. Doctor Quintano: handsome, early thirties, middle thirties; gray eyes; very impersonal. "Is this the first time you've been pregnant?" Excellent English, no *trace of accent. "What was the date of your most recent period? How do you feel?" Sit waiting, twenty minutes. He comes back. Takes some papers from the desk.* Goes *away. Twenty minutes waiting. See no one. Hear nothing. Sit straight in chair, feel clammy, hot, tired, headache. Nurse returns, asks, "Are you Nancy?" No answer. Nurse indicates without speaking, leave this room, go upstairs. Another nurse waits at head of stairs, march directly into bathroom. Extraordinarily lovely bathroom, gleaming brass fixtures cast in the shapes of lions with open mouths, dolphins, seagulls. Pull off clothes, put on hospital gown open in back, tied with two strings. Down hall to private operating room. Lie down on observation table, light above glowing, eyes hurt. Twenty minutes. Nurse back again, quietly efficient, dark, does not speak. Quintano comes in, asks for money. Give him four crisp bills. Takes money, goes away. Comes back. Takes off underpants, places hand on female stomach. "Your stomach muscles are too tight; go to the bathroom, urinate, relax them."* Goes, *returns, tries again. "Now what you're going to have is a 'curettement,' a very simple operation. It will take about ten minutes, and I'll have to examine you before the operation, don't be afraid." Leaves room. Nurse comes in, follow her to other room. Halls empty, hear no sound. Lie down on another observation table. Quintano returns wearing rubber gloves. Internal pelvic examination. Gentle. Still wearing shoes. Quintano leaves again. Nurse: "Relax, he be right een." Thirty-five minutes. Nurse goes, returns, ties ankles into operating table stirrups with bands of white cloth. Heels in stirrups, uncomfortable angle. Quintano looms above table. "I want to be asleep, please." "That depends on you." "How?" "If you keep your breathing normal and relax." "I can't relax unless you put me to sleep." "Do you want this operation?" Pause, long pause, longest pause, fear, thinking, tottering at the decision's tip, flight, running, trembling,* I must do it! *"Okay. Go ahead." A great black creature coming down from the sky above. Black rubber inhalator mask. Over nose and mouth. Fear of gas, strong, smell to be avoided if encountered on a street, walk in opposite direction, don't die don't fight no sight out light might tight right if you close mouth breathe through nose hose slows goes rose. . .Conversation interchange can't understand allwordsruntogetherlikejelly* GO! *In her, knowing,* I'm not asleep, *feel the first instrument, cry, make a sound, inhale gas and swoon in soft lather down gone deep right leap fight seeeeee thissss wayyyyyy they count in Spanish sweet anesthetist anesthesia anesthetic not sleeping words count in Spanish* uno dos tres cuatro cinco seis siete ocho *Ouch! Oh! Ah! there pain here pain know pain feel it up inside vaguest vaguely vagrant ain pain vain*—nueve diez once doce *dream great white square, huge insubstantial moving great square, cut in four parts, one section all black, the black moves first to one square, then another, then another, around and around and around as dr dr. dR DR. and nurse stand on right, as black square moves from one corner to the other to the other to the next to the next, all clocks stop all clocks silent, every room has a clock,* every room *in the place, every clock has no face just hands that move around and around teasingly teasing* trece catorce. . .*soft scraping down there inside my softness, small creature seeks warm warm warm. . .It's over. Come back up from the world of white squares and black. Quintano and nurse on the right, staring, "How do you feel?" "Dizzy. . ." Pat on the arm. Sit up, naked body stretches out before, open, naked, moist. Cover with the hospital gown. Get off table. Walk out crookedly wobbling a tot on first feet. Into first examination room, lie down on table. Blanket over, warm. Light glowing overhead, "Can you turn that out?" "No." Forty-five minutes go by, one minute, sleep. Nurse comes back. "Get dressed." As door closes hear Quintano saying, "Word word wordword pain word wordword word." What was he saying, pain? Me? Was there trouble? I feel fine, don't I? Yes, a fine feeling. Empty. Nurse with two paper cups. One has water. The other has five pills: two big yellow ones, three small white ones. Take them with difficulty, need second cup of water. Wait again, ten minutes. Nurse and Quintano come back. "You were a fine patient. That damn blonde kept moving her hips, she was scared, nervous; but you were a good patient." Go downstairs with nurse. Other nurse waits at bottom. Hello.*

I had tried to break out for a while, to get some air, to think about something other than nothing. And to wonder why this whole thing with Jenny had come to be so compelling, so *involving* for me, when I was really not the responsible party. I thought I knew why, but I wanted to think about it somewhere other than in the abortionist's front parlor.

I had tried to get out of the house, by the only door I knew for certain led outside, but Luis had been waiting in the outer passage, talking in Spanish with the rickets case. He motioned me back inside. I'd about had it with him. The operation Quintano ran was a clean one, but the scarred, oily appearance of Luis was bad policy. It made the trip to the doctor's home seem more suspicious than was necessary. He instilled no faith or security in the girls coming to get scraped. And his predilection for melodrama was a bit much.

"I want to take a walk," I told him, coming on toward the fence and gate.

"No. You go on back. You wait till she done," and he put his hand in his thigh-length car coat's pocket. I had a feeling the most dangerous item in that pocket was dust, but I saw no sense in hassling with him. I went back inside.

It was only four hours, but it seemed like forever.

I'd gone through my own pack and a half of Philip Morris and was down to smoking Rooney's goddamned Kents or Springs or Passionflowers or whatever those hideous mentholated, perfumed excuses for a self-respecting coffin-nail are called. My mouth tasted like they'd marched the entire Chinese Nationalist Army through it barefoot, with the Dalai Lama in the lead, wearing nothing but a Dr. Scholl's Zino-Pad.

Jenny came in, being helped by a nurse in white, the one we'd seen before, the one who wouldn't talk. I could tell at once something was wrong. Her face looked like a charcoal drawing on papyrus. I got up and moved to help her. She sat down on the sofa beside Rooney and ran her hand up across her temple and into her hair, in that characteristic gesture that meant she was out of it. "How do you feel?" I asked.

"Oh, okay, I guess. I'm glad it's over."

Rooney moved over beside her. “You look a little peaked, are you sure you feel all right?”

She nodded silently, almost numbly.

There was something wrong.

“Was there trouble in the operation?” I directed my question at the nurse. Her face froze over; she was a hard, cold bitch. I asked her again. She didn’t answer.

“You feel be’er eef you put a li’l lisstick on,” the Medusa said. Jenny mumbled something vague at that. I wanted to do something, but didn’t know what.

The decision was taken over by Luis, who appeared magically from the anteroom. “Time to go,” he said. The nurse disappeared back into one of the other doorways, and we stood up, helping Jenny between us. We moved out into the anteroom, and there was a waiting line of five new girls. I was amazed and staggered at the amount of business Quintano had accumulated. If he wasn’t a millionaire, tax-free, he certainly needed a good business manager. The college kids were there, and the blonde looked just fine, just fine.

We left the house and got back in the car and the gate was raised and we drove away, in exact reverse order of the way we had made our entrance. And even though Hot-Rock Luis twisted and turned and drove us back to town by a different route, it didn’t matter: I knew the way to Quintano’s little do-it-yourselfery cold.

Luis left us off at the Woolworth’s lot, and burned rubber getting away. The five of us stood there staring at each other and the cars. “How much was yours?” the college boy asked. “Four,” I replied. He nodded. “Ours, too.” It seemed to make him feel better.

“Can we go?” Jenny said, very softly, beside me. She was feeling weak and strange, I knew it, and so did Rooney. We got into the car and tooled out of Tijuana, heading for the border.

We never made it across.

That part of it happened so fast, it can be told fast. We drove down through the town, getting a noseful and a soulful of dirt and signed testaments to just how miserable the human condition can get to be. We pulled into the long line of cars heading for the check-out point at the border, and watched Jenny from the corner of our eyes. She was shaking slightly, and feeling worse. All I wanted to do was make the trip back to L.A. and get her to her own doctor.

Cars were being passed through one after another.

They stopped us, and the inspector leaned in, asked if I had anything to declare. I figured we were a shoo-in. "Not a thing, sir," I said. "We were just down looking around, didn't buy a thing."

He started to pass us through, when his eye caught the steel-rim bongos I'd bought. He looked from them to me. I looked into the back seat and saw them there. My laugh was as phony as a work of Art by Joseph E. Levine.

"Oh, except those, of course ha ha."

That was our undoing. He asked to see inside the trunk. I opened it and it was empty. Then he tried the glove compartment, under the back seats, and then the girls' handbags. Nothing. Just a bottle of painkiller pills Jenny had had in her purse for weeks, labeled in Beverly Hills and signed with the name of her family doctor.

The inspector took the bottle, put it under my left windshield wiper, and directed me to pull out of line, into an inspection slot. I was hacked. Jenny was about to fall out. But I did as I was told.

I could hear a guy somewhere playing a soft lick on a guitar. It struck me how strange it was: all day in a land where music is supposed to be second nature, I hadn't heard any live music made by the people. A few bastardized notes out of a car radio, some organ background for a quiz show emanating from New York, and silence from the happy, smiling natives of this warm Valhalla. Now, as we were about to leave, a sound of reality from the other world. It was odd.

The inspector came out of his cubicle and examined us. He examined the bottle. Then he asked whose it was. Jenny said it was hers. He asked her to come into the station for a moment to talk to the head man. She looked at me. "I'll come with you," I said.

We followed him across the concrete walkway to the big glass-fronted office. I had to support Jenny very surreptitiously. She was white as the sun at midday.

It went fast. The inspector knew what was happening. One look at her, and you could tell she had been aborted. She was sweating like a shower, hard and hot. He took her in to talk to her. I waited. After half an hour, I got worried. They told me I had to wait.

Rooney came in; she wanted to ask if there was trouble, but I motioned her to wait, I'd tell her later. An hour went by, and suddenly we heard a crash from the next room. The head man came out, panic on his stupid face, and yelled at his aide. "Call the hospital. Miguel Aleman. Have them send an ambulance. Quick!"

I was screaming at him, and was halfway over the counter, my hand tangled in his tie. "You bastard, you stupid fucking bastard! You could see she was sick, you had to pump her, you had to use her all up, didn't you? You bastard!"

He wasn't young, he sure as hell wasn't smart, or decent, or likeable; but he was strong. He whipped his hands up between mine, breaking my hold, and gave me a fast one in the mouth. I went down, and he rushed back into the interrogation room to help Jenny. I crawled off the floor and Rooney helped me up. Through the open door, we could see Jenny's legs kicking as she lay on the floor.

The ambulance came and we rode along to Miguel Aleman Hospital. The waiting room was very clean and very white and Jenny died about four hours later. Blood loss. And it had been on its way to peritonitis.

I stood in the center of the waiting room when they came and told us, and suddenly all the memories I'd wanted to bury in the mud of my subconscious came back. Fran and the baby, sending my wife to the abortionist because I'd been "ill-equipped to handle a child right now, honey." The operation, the fear, and Fran growing to hate me, leaving me, the divorce. It all came back, and I knew then what Jenny had meant to me. Blackness pressed into my eyes.

I ran shrieking out of the hospital, a madman whose passage was unimpeded. They leaped out of my way. I may have been frothing at the mouth, I don't remember.

Then I was back in a dusty Tijuana street, and finding a taxi, and pointing up the hill toward Caliente track, saying, "*¡Vamonos, vamonos!*" I was waving bills under his nose and pointing, and he went. . .

Fast. . .

I directed him through a haze that was thick and red and whining with a high-pitched keen. When I saw the construction of steel and concrete, shaped like a geodesic dome, one of the landmarks I'd carefully noted on my first trip to Dr. Quintano's home, I made the cabbie pull over. Cab fare from any point to any other point in Tijuana is a flat fifty cents. I gave him four dollars, all the bills I had in my hand.

He sped away and I stood looking at the dome, at the sky, at my hands, and for the first time in my life I came to know sin.

I ran down the road, and down a side street, as unerringly as a hound on scent. I found Quintano's home without difficulty. It was one of the most formidable in that neighborhood, and the high fence surrounding it meant nothing to me. I don't know why I was there, what I wanted. Perhaps to hit him, or to get the money back for Jenny at the hospital—but she was gone, she was dead now, wasn't she? I didn't know.

I scaled the fence and hung at the top for a long moment, watching. The rickets case was down the line, near the gate. The door to the house opened and a man came out; he was tall with salt-and-pepper hair, and I thought he was Quintano. I climbed to the top, poised there, let myself go and caught the top of the fence with both hands. I hung for a second, then dropped. The two men saw me, and there was consternation on their faces.

"She died! She died! She and the baby died!" I yelled, and charged them. The older man stepped back, as though to flee into the house, but I went at him in a long flat dive and caught him around the ankles. He went face-forward into the side of the building, and slid sidewise, with my arms still locked around his calves. He was screaming in Spanish, and the rickets case wasn't about to help. He ran past us where we tumbled together on the ground, and into the house. The door was still open and I could hear him yelling for someone, but I was too busy trying to get at the older man's throat. I slid up his body, and locked one hand under his chin. He tried to fight me off and I pummeled him with my free fist. I was choking him, but not very well: his eyes were glazing over, but he kept trying to fight free. I hit him as hard as I could on the side of the head, but he rolled with it, and then he dug his hand into my mouth, catching the soft flesh of my check, and he literally pried my head back. I lost my hold on his throat, and he jacked his knee up into my stomach. All the air went out of me and I flopped back, gasping like a heart case. Then, before I could defend myself, Luis was running through the anteroom, out the door, and was kicking me. His feet were big, and I saw each ripple-soled shoe descend, first right, then left, and he was stomping on my face as if I were a bug. I tried to grab his leg, and caught one pants cuff. I pulled him across and tumbled him, and managed to crawl up his front and hit him once before someone grabbed me from behind, locked his hands around my face and yanked me forcibly back against a knee. My back cracked like an arthritic knuckle and everything bobbled, weaved, swam, dipped in front of me. I started to gray out, and stayed with it just long enough to see Luis and the older man and the rickets case bending down to work me over good.

I was lying on my back, my right hand was loose in a puddle of mud, and I was staring up at a wall that held a bullfight poster. I saw the colors, and the word ARRUZA, and then read the sign very carefully three times before I fainted again.

When I came up the second time, someone was going through my pockets. I didn't stop him. Not even when he pulled my watch off my wrist. I went under again, and when I came back the third time I was very cold, and shivering. I tried to get up, let my legs slide down the wall, where they rose above my head lying in the dirt, and tried to gain purchase on the brick wall. It turned to rubber and peanut butter.

I kept at it, and finally got to my feet.

The world was nowhere to be seen.

Then I realized both my eyes had swollen almost completely shut. I stumbled forward, my hands out before me like a blind man, and came out of the alley into the street. It was noisy and full of people. The lights hurt my eyes. I stared up, and caught a vista of the town, and it was an eye-numbing horizon of neon. I groaned.

A pair of buoyant Mexican girls swinging huge purses went by, and tittered to each other, saying something dirty, but saying it softly, in Spanish. I called them whores, *¡putas!*

I walked the streets for hours, seeing nothing, only feeling a pain far worse than the ache that threatened to split my head open. I must have looked hideous, because I came around a corner suddenly, and came face to face with a heavyset Mexican whose eyes opened wide in amazement. He got a sick look and walked around me. I didn't turn to see if he was still watching.

My pockets were empty, of course. All I knew was that I had to have a drink. My mouth was sandy and my stomach ached. Not entirely from the stomping I'd gotten. Oh, Jenny, oh, Fran!

I wandered into the Blue Fox, and there was a naked girl doing a nautch dance on the bar. Sailors in civvies were trying to grab her crotch. She kept twisting away from them. Then someone announced dinner was served and three broads came out, undressed, and lay down on the bar. Hors d'oeuvres. Three sickies jumped off their bar stools and went to fall down on the goodies. A bouncer tapped me on the shoulder and I left. I was sick.

I went into an alley and puked. Twice. When I was as empty as I was ever going to be, I tried to straighten myself up. I brushed off my clothes, raked my hair back out of my face with a hand, and went in search of a job.

There was a hustler looking for handbill boys at the Rancho Grande, a spieler for one nightclub told me, and I went over there. Three dollars and fifty cents for two hours' work handing out handbills, putting them under the windshield wipers of parked cars. I asked for a half dollar advance and was handed a stack of handbills instead. I went off down the street like a trained monkey, handing pieces of paper to people, pressing them into the hands of strangers. I was giving of myself. It felt wonderful. I wanted to puke again, but that was ridiculous. I knew I was empty.

Finally, all the handbills were gone, and I went back to get paid. The man was gone, and the people at the club didn't know where he could be found. I went looking for him. It took a long time, but I found another handbill-giver, a kid with wide, dark eyes, and told him the man was gone. He told me that was only because I was *gringo*. He grinned and told me where to find the man. I went to the Bum-Bum and there he was, hiring more boys in the service of his cause. I approached him and said pay me. He looked like he didn't want to do it, but I started to make sandpaper noises and my hands became claws and I swear I'd have killed him right then if he'd refused. He'd have gone to his grave with my teeth in his throat. I was more than a little mad.

He pulled out a wad and started to peel off three singles. I reached in and took a ten, and walked away. He started to follow, and started to motion to another man, but I turned my bloody face to stare at them, and he shrugged.

I took the ten and went drinking. I bought a bottle of tequila. It seemed only fitting to drink the wine of the land. I finished the bottle almost by myself. The last dregs were taken by an old Mexican woman sitting in a doorway. She had her legs tied under her so she looked crippled, and her five-year-old son was selling pencils and switchblade knives just down the street while she begged. At one point a well-built but slovenly fifteen-year-old girl came by, swinging her hips, and the old woman told me in broken English that it was her pride, her daughter. "She make *doce*, twelf, *doce* doe-lahr night," she beamed. They lived good. I shared some chili beans with her, and went away.

I was in another place, I think. It was a club. There was a fight and sirens and I ran away. Then I was in the Mambo Rock, and someone was yelling FIRE FIRE FIRE and I turned to see the whole wall blazing. An electrical short, and the whole block was in flames. Twelve feet in the air the flames ate the night sky, and I was helping a shopkeeper pull his bongos and wooden statues of Don Quixote and bead-shirts and *serapes* out into the street, and then there was a Mexican soldier, a member of the National Guard, a *rurale*, something. . .and he was spinning me around telling me to go away. They'd called in the army and half the town was on fire, and I was pulling a woman out of the flames, and her dress was on fire, and I gave her a feel as I beat out the flames with my bare hands. And then they were taking me to the infirmary, and swabbing my hands with cool, moist salve.

Then another place, and I was very drunk and sick and very tired. I walked up Avenida Constitución and saw 287 HOTEL CORREO DEL NORTE and bought a pack of Delicados for seven cents in the booth on the corner, and went back to the hotel.

My room was seventy-five cents for the night. The walls were plywood till they reached five feet, then chicken-wire to the ceiling. I slept with my shoelaces knotted together, so my shoes wouldn't get stolen. I'd have put them under the end-legs of the bed, but I was so tired I knew the bed could be lifted off the shoes and I wouldn't have known it. Someone tried to get in during the night and I screamed about death and snakes and they went away.

I dreamed of jackasses painted like zebras, and *turistas* getting their pictures taken in a cart pulled by the zebra-ass, on street corners, wearing *sombreros* with the name CISCO KID scrawled on the brim. It was a nice dream.

The sign said TÉLEFONO PÚBLICO, and I stood on Avenida Revolución.

I called the hospital, and somehow they found Rooney. She had been looking for me all the day before. I told her where I was, and she came and got me. I was crying, I think. They released Jenny's body, and her parents came down to get it. I don't think I could have borne carrying it back in the Magnette. . .not to Los Angeles. That was forever.

Rooney kept asking me where I'd been, but I couldn't tell her. I wasn't purged, for Christ's sake, but I was tired, and that was almost as good.

Jenny was gone, and Kenneth Duane Markham was gone, and soon enough Rooney would be gone from me. All I wanted to do was get back to Los Angeles and try to be someone else. The taste of tequila was still strong in my throat, and I knew that would help a little.

—Tijuana and Hollywood, 1963

RIDING THE DARK TRAIN OUT

The freight car was cold, early in the morning.

He wore a filthy, ripped suit jacket, with pieces of newspaper and magazines stuffed against his skin, for extra protection; but the chill found him just the same, uncaring.

Feathertop Ernie Cargill brushed a trembling hand back through the silky, almost white baby-hair that tumbled over his forehead. Hair that was smooth, and the slightest breeze picking its way through the shuddering freight made it toss and rise. He cursed dimly, finger-raking it back for the thousandth time. He touched the bottle in his pocket, but did not remove it.

The cotton bales were soft, but the smell of pig shit was strong. He moved gently, making a deeper depression among the stocked bales.

He was a young man, an ex-musician, and down as down could get on his luck.

"No luck, no buck," he would say, hugging himself tightly, shoving his fisted hands into his armpits to keep himself warm. His teeth chattered gently.

He was thin and tall, with a nose that skewed sidewise from a clarinet case across the kisser during his thirty-five-minute gig with a symphony orchestra once. "Bastards," he would say, "all I did was nice; I syncopated Vivaldi and the first chair clobbered me!"

Since then, and since the panther sweat had gotten him divorced from every decent—and even indecent—group from Greenwich Village to the Embarcadero, he had become a sucker-rolling freighter-jumper.

"There ain't nothin' faster, or lonelier, or more direct than a cannonball freight when you wanna go someplace," Feathertop would say. "The accommodations may not be the poshest, but man, there ain't nobody askin' for your ticket stub, neither."

He had been conning the freights for a long, long time now. Ever since the hootch, and the trouble with the Quartet, and Midge and the child. Ever since all that. It had been a very long time that had no form and no end.

He was—as he told himself in the vernacular of a trade no longer his own—riding the dark train out. Out and out and never return again. Till one day the last freight had been jumped, the last pint had been killed, the last measure had been rapped. That was the day it ended. No reprise.

The occasion of Feathertop Ernie Cargill's first killing was an interesting story.

The freight car was cold, early in the morning.

He was pressed far back into the corner of the car on his cotton bales, the rattling and tinning of the wheels striking at the rails almost covering the sound of his ocarina.

He held his elbows away from his body, and the little sweet potato trilled neatly and sweetly as he tickled its tune-belly.

The train slowed at a road crossing, and the big door slid open.

The boy lifted the girl by the waist and slid her into the freight car. She pulled her legs up under her, to rise, her full peasant skirt drawing up her thighs, and Feathertop's music *pffft*-ed away. "Now that is a very nice, a very nice," he murmured to himself, back in his corner.

He took in the girl, in one sharp all-seeing look.

A little thing, but the right twist for the action that counted. Hot, that was the word, hot! Hair like a morning-frightened sparrow's wings, with the sun shining down over them. A poet, yet! His thoughts for the swanlike neck, the full, high breasts, the slim waist, and the long legs were less than poetic, however.

Then the boy straight-armed himself up, twisting at the last moment so he landed sitting, where she had sat.

He was less to see, but Feathertop took him in, too, just to keep the records straight.

Curly hair, high cheekbones, wide gnomelike mouth, a pair of drummer's blocky hands, and a body that said well, maybe I can wrestle you for ten minutes—but then I'm finished. Feathertop went back to the girl. With no regrets.

"We made it, Cappy," the girl said sweetly.

A brilliant observation, thought Feathertop.

"Yeah, seems so, don't it." The boy laughed, hugging her close.

"*Ah-ah!*" Feathertop interrupted, standing up, brushing the pig shit from his dirty pants. "None of that. We run a respectable house here."

They whirled and saw him, standing there dim in the slatted light from the boarded freight wall. He was big, and filthy, and his toes stuck out of the flapping tops of his shoes. He held the black plastic kazoo lightly.

"Who are you?" The boy's voice trembled.

"Come sit," said Feathertop, motioning them toward him. "The crap is softer over here."

The girl smiled, and started forward. The boy yanked her back hard, tugging her off her feet. She landed with a stumbling plop next to him, and he gathered her into the crook of his arm, as he must have seen it done on the cover of some cheap detective magazine.

"Now stay with me, Kitty!" He sounded snappish. "I vowed to take care of you—and that's what I'm gonna do. We don't know this guy."

"Oooo, square bit." Feathertop screwed his face up. This guy was really out of it. But *no*where!

"What is with this *vow* jazz?" Feathertop smiled, lounging against the freight's vibrating wall.

"We—we eloped," Cappy said. His head came up and he said it defiantly. He stared at Feathertop, daring him to object.

"Well, congratulations." Feathertop made an elaborate motion with his hand. These two were going to be easy pickings. They couldn't have much dough, but then none of the freight-bums Feathertop rolled had much. And besides, the chick had a little something the others didn't have. *That* was gonna be fun collecting!

But not just yet. Feathertop was a connoisseur. He liked to savor his meat before he tasted it. "Come sit," he repeated, motioning to the piled cotton bales, over the pig leavings. "I'm just a poor ex–jazz man, name of—uh—Boyd Smith." He grinned at them wolfishly.

"That ain't your name, Mister," the boy said accusingly.

"And you know—you're *right*!" Feathertop aimed a finger at him. "That gets you the blue ribbon banana. But it's safer for anyone riding the redball to know someone else as somethin' other than what he is. Makes it easier all around." He winked.

"Oh, come on, Cappy," the girl said. "He's okay. He's a nice guy." She started to move toward the cotton bales, dragging the reluctant Cappy behind her.

Feathertop watched the smooth scissoring of her slim, trim legs as she walked to the bales. She sat down, tucked her legs beneath her, smoothing the skirt out in a wide circle. He cleared his throat; it had been a long, hot while since he'd seen anything as nice as this within grabbin' distance.

He had it all clocked, of course. Slug the kid, grab his dough—at least enough to get him to Philadelphia—and then have a ball with the doll.

"Where'd you come from, Mr.—uh—Mr. Smith?" Kitty inquired politely, as she maneuvered on the cotton bales. She smoothed the peasant skirt around her again, shaking it off at the same time.

"Where from?" He thought about it. "Out. I been riding the dark train out for a ways now."

"Yes, but—"

Her boy friend cut her off peremptorily. "He doesn't want to tell us, Kitty. Leave him be."

She looked piqued and stepped-on, so Ernie cut in: "I came from Jersey originally. Been a long time, though."

They lapsed into silence, and the freight wallowed up a hill, and scooted down the other side, shaking and clanking to itself like a hypochondriac.

After a while, Kitty murmured something to Cappy, and he held her close, answering, "We'll just have to wait till we pull into Philly, honey."

"What's the matter, she wanna go the toilet?" Ernie found it immensely funny.

The boy scowled at him, and the girl looked shocked.

"No! Certainly not, I mean, *no*, that isn't what I said!" She snapped at him. "I only said I was hungry. We haven't had anything to eat all day."

Joviality suffused Feathertop Ernie Cargill's voice as he reached behind him, pulling out a battered carpetbag, with leather handles. "Whyn't ya say so, fellow travelers! Why we got dinner right here. C'mon, buddy, help me set up the kitchen and we'll have food in a minute or two."

Cappy looked wary, but he moved off the floorboards and followed the dirty ex-musician to the center of the refuse-littered boxcar.

Ernie crouched and opened the carpetbag. He took out a small packet filled with bits of charcoal, a deep pot of thin metal, some sheets of newspaper, a book of matches and a wrinkled and many-times folded piece of tinfoil with holes in it. He put the charcoal in the pot, lit the paper with the matches, and carefully stretched the tinfoil across the top of the pot.

"A charcoal pit, man," he said, indicating the slightly smoking makeshift brazier. "Fan it," he told Cappy, handing him a still-folded sheet of newspaper.

"Yeah, but what're we gonna eat? Charcoal?"

"Fellah," Ernie said, waggling a dirty finger at the younger man, "you try my mutherin' patience." He reached into the carpetbag once more and brought up a cellophane-wrapped package of weiners.

"Hot dogs, man. Not the greatest, but they stick to your belly insides."

He ripped down the cellophane carefully, and laid three dogs on the tinfoil. Almost immediately they began to sizzle. He looked up and grinned with a toothiness that belied his thoughts. Fattening them up for the kill. He blew through puckered lips and his baby hair flew up, only to fall back over his eyes again.

"A Krogers self-serve," he explained. "I self-served."

Kitty grinned and a small, musical laugh fell from her cupid's bow lips. The boy scowled again; it was getting to be a habit.

When they had licked the last of the weiners' taste from their fingers, they settled back, and Cappy offered Ernie a cigarette. *Nice kid*, Ernie thought. *Too bad*.

"How come you're riding the rods, kids like you?" Ernie asked. "There's damned little of that done these days, even by old stiffs like me. Most kids today never even been on a train."

Cappy looked at his wide hands, and did not reply. But surprisingly, Kitty's face came up and she said, "My father. He didn't want us to get married. So we ran away."

"Why din't he want you to get hitched?"

This time even she did not answer. She looked down at her hands, too. After a few seconds, she said, "Dad didn't like Cappy. It was my fault."

Cappy's head came around sharply. "Your fault, hell! It was all my fault. If I'd been careful it never woulda—" He stopped abruptly.

Ernie's eyebrows went up. "What's the matter?"

The girl still did not raise her eyes, but she added simply, "I'm pregnant."

Cappy raged at himself. "Oh he was stupid, her old man! You never heard nothin' like it: Kitty's gonna go have an abortion, and Kitty's gonna go away to a convent, and Kitty's this and Kitty's that. . .like he was nuts or somethin', y'know?"

Ernie nodded. This was a slightly different matter. He remembered Midge, and the child. But that had been a time before all this, a time he didn't think about. A time before the white lightning and the bumming had turned him inside out. But these kids weren't like him.

Oh, crap! he thought. *Pull out of it, old son. These are just another couple of characters to roll. What they got, you get. Now forget all this other.*

"Wanna drink?" Ernie pulling the pint of Sweet Lucy from his jacket pocket.

"Yeah. Now that you offer." The answer came from the open door of the boxcar. From the man who had leaped in from the high bank outside, as the train had slowed on the grade.

Ernie stared at the man. He was big. Real big, with shoulders out to here, and hair all over him like a grizzly. *Road gang*, Ernie thought, staring at the great, pulpy muscles of the man's arms and neck.

"You gonna give me a drink, fellah?" the big man asked again, taking a step into the boxcar.

Ernie hesitated a moment. This character could break him in half. "Sure," he said, and lifted the pint to his own lips. He guzzled down three-quarters of the strong home-blend and proffered the remainder. The man stalked toward them, his big boots heavy on the wooden flooring. He took the bottle with obvious belligerence, and making sucking noises with his thick lips, drained it completely.

He threw back his head, closed his eyes, and belched ferociously. He belched again, and opening his eyes, threw the bottle out through the open door.

"Well, now," he said, and reached into his pocket. "I didn't know I was gonna have company in this box."

"We're going to Philadelphia," Kitty said, pulling her skirt down around her legs all the more.

"No, I don't think so," said the big man, and it was the final clincher for Ernie. He had suspected this guy was trouble, and now he was sure of it, with the first verbal assurance the man had given.

"Maybe you and me will, girlie, but these two bums ain't goin' nowhere but out that door."

He advanced on them, and abruptly there was a shocked electricity in the car. Ernie was screaming inside himself: *No, damn you, you ain't gonna take my meal ticket away from me! I been milkin' 'em for fifty miles. Get outta here, you lousy sonofabitch!*

Usurpation on the high road. He had planned to boot the guy out the door in a few miles when they got to the next little town. That way he wouldn't have far to walk to get to civilization, but far enough so they would be near Philly and he could have enjoyed himself at his leisure with the broad. But now this! *Damn you!*

The newcomer stalked toward them, and Kitty shied back, her hand to her mouth. Her scream split up the silence of the car, accompanied by the rattling of the freight, and then Cappy came off the floor, his legs driving him hard. The kid hit the bigger man with an audible *thwump!* and carried him backward in a linebacker's tackle. They went down in a heap amid the pig scum, and for a long minute there was nothing to see but flailing arms and legs.

The kid showed for an instant, and his arm was cocked back. The fist went down into the pile of flesh, and Ernie heard the bigger man's deep voice: "Aaawww!"

Then they were tumbling again, and the big man reached into the same pocket he had gone for earlier, and came up with a vicious switchblade.

He held the knife aloft an instant—an instant enough to press the stud. The blade came out with a snick; he fisted the knife overhand, and drew back to plunge it into the kid's throat.

Kitty screamed insanely, over and over again, and her face was white as maggot's flesh. She grabbed at Feathertop's sleeve and shrieked in his ear, "Help him! Help him! Do something!"

Do? Do? Feathertop Ernie Cargill was plastered to the cotton bales with fright. He wasn't gonna do a thing. It was the kid's fight. He should of known better than to bring a girl on the freights. It was his own—

The kid grabbed the wrist as it came down, bringing the rusty death with it, and he twisted the arm back back back as far as he could. The big man was off-balance, and at that instant the train hit a curve. The big man fell over, and the kid was on top of him. In one flashing, lightning movement Cappy had the knife in his own hand, and he did not hesitate.

He brought it up and down and up and down again, and there was red on the blade, and red on the big man's shirt, and red on his chest, and red on the floorboards.

Kitty shrieked maddeningly, and fainted.

The kid got off the corpse, and dropped the knife with stunned disbelief. "He—he's d-dead. Ohmigod. . ." the kid murmured. "Who'll believe me? I been in trouble before, but never like this. What'll I do?"

Kitty moaned, and the kid rushed to her side, cradling her head in his lap. "Kitty, we—we gotta get outta here. . .we gotta get away before we get to a town or someth—"

"We're in a town now." Ernie pointed to the rail yards that had taken form around them. His hand froze where it was pointing. It was aimed dead at a railroad switchman who was staring in at them through the open door of the boxcar, who was cupping his hands, who was screeching at a group of gandy dancers farther down the tracks. The men glanced at the freight train slowing to a stop, and they began hopping the tracks, running for the boxcar in a group.

"Rail dicks!" Ernie screamed, and leaped to run.

The kid was rocking back and forth with Kitty's head in his lap, whispering, "Good-bye, honey, good-bye. . ."

Ernie stopped as he pulled open the sliding door on the other side of the boxcar. He stopped, and a strange feeling came over him. He looked at the kids, and memories crowded in on him. He remembered Midge, and the child, and the years in the bands, and all the freights and all the booze, and there was a choking in his throat.

He bent down and lifted the knife from the floor. He wiped the handle—but not the blade—clean on his jacket, and then gripped it firmly.

Stooping, he lifted the boy by his underarms, and stood him on his feet. Then he helped Kitty to rise.

"Go out the other door, and don't stop running till you're a long ways from here. You understand?"

"But I—" Cappy began, looking from Ernie to the body of the big man.

"Go on!" Ernie hit him in the arm. "Go on, and be good to her! You stupid son of a bitch!" He shoved them toward the open door on the opposite side of the boxcar, and as the train came to a shuddering halt, they leaped free, and ran off across the rail yards.

The yard bulls and linemen were running up to the boxcar as Ernie sat down on the cotton bales.

It wasn't so bad. He could holler self-defense. It might be okay. But either way, his time had passed. He was a young man, but he was old, very old; and he was tired. Very tired. Time had made him old folks. It wouldn't of been right for them kids. Not right at all.

Some people are meant to ride the dark train out, and others not. That's the way it's got to be.

He pushed the feathery hair from his eyes.

He was tired, and the dead guy had polished off the last of the Sweet Lucy, damn him. And he smelled of pig shit. But not permanently.

—Elizabethtown, Kentucky, 1959

MOONLIGHTING

FADE IN:

1 BLACK FRAME

CAMERA PULLING BACK OUT OF BLACK while MAINTITLES SUPER OVER. During SLOW PULL BACK we HEAR a VOICE OVER. The voice of MRS. KAY, a middle-aged woman. The voice is filled with heartbreaking anguish and a vengeful madness.

MRS. KAY'S VOICE OVER
You may have made a fool of the law, but you're not going to escape justice. Not if *I* have anything to say about it!
(cold and flat)
All those kids dead...the whole school building collapsed...did you see all those little bodies? *Did you*?

PULL-BACK reveals the BLACK FRAME was looking down the barrel of a handgun. We pull back out of the muzzle as the VOICE OVER CONTINUES. (NOTE: Suggest use of a Colt Automatic "Commander" in the polished nickel model; or alternately a .38 Colt Super or .45 ACP. Suggest 3/4" barrel shorter than standard; polished nickel for shot that follows.)

(CONTINUED:)

1 CONTINUED:

MRS. KAY'S VOICE OVER (CONT'D.)
You cut corners on the material, the construction was rotten... sand in the concrete mix... everybody knows it, even if you bought off the politicians at the hearing...

CAMERA HAS PULLED BACK to feature the handgun LARGE IN F.G. As CAMERA MOVES AROUND the gun we see reflected in the flat, highly-polished nickel surface of its bulk the man at whom the gun is aimed. He looks terrified.

MRS. KAY'S VOICE OVER (CONT'D.)
You don't get away with it, Mr. Canoga...there's a due bill on sixteen dead kids...

CAMERA has PULLED BACK sufficiently to show us the gun held by a tearful, coldly angry, fortyish woman on whose face is written a memory of crushing sorrow. CAMERA AROUND HER and HOLDS HER LARGE IN F.G. to show the man sitting behind the desk, the man we saw reflected in the polished surface of the gun. The large logo on the wall behind him reads:

COLONY CONSTRUCTION COMPANY
Sonny Canoga, Pres.

SONNY CANOGA is in his early forties but retains the rugged self-centered good looks of a college wingback; and he's just that brawny across the shoulders. He is extremely good-looking in the manner of a comic book superhero: blond, expensive haircut, formidable jaw, clear blue eyes, silk shirt open to the sternum, one discreet gold chain: Mr. Wonderful, who could sell sandboxes to Arabs and get away with it. But now he's showing another aspect of his nature: his cowardice.

[MORE]

(CONTINUED:)

1 CONTINUED: - 2

(CONT'D.)

He's terrified with this woman pointing the gun *unwaveringly* at his head. Nervously, he toys with a long LETTER OPENER that has a replica of the distinctive Colony Construction logo at one end. We see now that we are in:

2 INT. CONSTRUCTION OFFICE - NIGHT - ON SONNY

Sweating, toying with the opener, he tries to reason with her, tries to be forthright, but we can tell from his manner that he's lying, just babbling to stop her from blowing him away.

SONNY
(dissembles)
This isn't right, Mrs. Kay...
this isn't fair! You can't come
in here and make threats like
that...I'm not responsible!
(beat)
I didn't pick the land they used
to build on. It was soft
ground, it settled, the school
went down from landfill, not
what my company did!

3 MOVING CAMERA AROUND SONNY TO MRS. KAY IN B.G.

She holds the gun level, straight out in front of her, *not* with both hands gripped around the butt as TV cops do it, but steadily, with one hand.

MRS. KAY
(flatly)
Say: Giselle.

SONNY
(uncomprehending)
What?

(CONTINUED:)

3 CONTINUED:

MRS. KAY
Say it. Say: Giselle.

SONNY
(slowly)
Giselle...

MRS. KAY
Again. Say: Giselle, and say: I'm sorry.

SONNY **MRS. KAY**
(almost together)
Why do you...? *Say it!*

SONNY
Giselle...I'm, I'm sorry...

MRS. KAY
(softly)
My daughter. I want her name on your lips when you die, Mr. Canoga.
(beat)
Her death is on your hands, now I want her name on your lips.

Through preceding dialogue CAMERA COMES AROUND to POV from BEHIND Sonny. Suddenly the door to the construction office bursts open and a large man in uniform, STATE TROOPER FRED LAMONT, smashes through as CAMERA ANGLE WIDENS to FULL SHOT. Another woman is behind him.

4 FULL SHOT - ALTERNATE ANGLE - ON ACTION

As Trooper Lamont wrestles with the slight Mrs. Kay, who seems to possess the deranged power of a dozen lumberjacks. He has grabbed her from behind and wrenches her arm toward the fiberboard ceiling. The gun goes off.

CUT TO:

5 INTERCUT

The logo on the wall above Sonny's head explodes from the random shot. He dives out of the chair.

CUT BACK TO:

6 SAME AS 4 - WITH THE ACTION

Trooper Lamont wrestles the gun away from her.

CUT TO:

7 INTERCUT - THE OTHER WOMAN

Still standing in the doorway, trying to swallow her fist. SARAH BIEBER, an extremely plain-looking, very thin woman of indeterminate years, but past the bloom of youth. She's trying to look years younger with a wildly inappropriate hairstyle. It just looks pathetic. She's what used to be called a lonely spinster. She stares wide-eyed.

CUT BACK TO:

8 MEDIUM SHOT - TROOPER & MRS. KAY

As she lands a hard, short one over his heart. The trooper gasps and manhandles her across the room to the sofa, gets her down with difficulty, and manages to cuff her. She is hysterical now, crying, trying to beg the trooper:

MRS. KAY

Oh please...please don't stop me...please...he *has* to pay...please...

9 WITH SONNY - MEDIUM SHOT TO FULL SCENE

as he gets off the floor, the letter opener still in his hand.

[MORE]

(CONTINUED:)

9 CONTINUED:

(CONT'D.)

He is wild-eyed and furious, reacting to being almost a dead thing. He comes for her, the letter opener held aloft.

SONNY

(wild)

You lousy, crazy, stinking old bat! I oughtta pull your goddamed *head* off!

Trooper Lamont steps in front of him, calms him with his body. He takes the letter opener away from him. He speaks levelly, softly.

LAMONT

It's a good thing Miz Bieber came in late to work on your books, Mr. Canoga. She called us just in time.

SONNY

(furious)

I'm gonna press charges! She tried to kill me! You saw her, both of you saw her; you're witnesses!

Mrs. Kay is slumped over her knees, sobbing softly.

10 ANOTHER ANGLE FEATURING SARAH

as we see the scene shooting past her. Her reactions of intense concern for Sonny underline the action.

LAMONT

Take it easy now, Mr. Canoga. You're okay. This is bad, but no sense in getting yourself all unlaced.

(CONTINUED:)

10 CONTINUED:

Sonny starts to harangue him, but pulls up short. There is a mean twist to his otherwise extraordinary good looks. He breathes deeply, composes himself, and becomes the trained smoothyguts again. He smiles one of those buttery smiles.

LAMONT (CONT'D.)

I'll be takin' her by St. Anne's for a quick stop in the emergency ...and she'll be at the station when you get ready to sign the complaint. If that's what you really want to do.

SONNY

(thin smile)

You're right. Absolutely.

(beat)

And I want you to know the State Police'll be getting some terrific glowing story about you, Trooper. Your commandant's gonna know you saved my life. There'll be a big promotion in this one, you can bet on it. I give you my word!

Lamont frowns at all this unctuousness. He tries to be polite. But he obviously doesn't like the way Sonny is sucking up to him.

LAMONT

Well, that'll be just fine, sir. I'm just glad we got here in time.

(beat)

Oh...here...

He hands him the letter opener. Sonny refuses it.

(CONTINUED:)

SONNY

No indeed. You keep it. A nothing little gift. Just one of our new giveaways with the storm windows. My appreciation.

The trooper places it on the desk with a smile.

LAMONT

Thanks anyway, Mr. Canoga. I don't get much mail.

He goes to the weeping woman and gently, kindly, raises her from the sofa till he's almost hugging her. We get the feeling he is sympathetic to her actions. He turns her to the door and they move off, passing Sarah Bieber, who still stands frozen, eyes wide. As they pass out the door...over his shoulder:

LAMONT (CONT'D.)

I'll see you at the station, sir. If that's what you really want to do.

Then they're gone.

11 LONG SHOT - PAST SONNY TO SARAH

As she stares at him, still wide-eyed. Then suddenly the membrane breaks, and she rushes to him in F.G. She flies into his arms, trembling. She hugs him tightly. Her words of adoration and concern are AD LIB muffled and run-on, incoherent. He kisses her. He pats her back as he holds her, strokes her hair.

SONNY

It's all right...it's okay...I'm fine...you saved my life.

(1/2 beat)

Again.

(CONTINUED:)

11 CONTINUED:

CLOSE ON THEM as they stand together. She comes up for air, looks at him intensely.

SARAH

Oh, my God, I was so frightened. I came in to...you know...to do just a little more work on the loose ends in the books...just in case they subpoena...

His face tightens. He grips her shoulders too tightly.

SONNY

(snake smooth)

Now c'mon, Sarah, honey. You can't just be mentioning that all the time. You gotta make it one of those things we know and don't say. I love you, so it's okay, isn't that right?

She looks away and in EXTREME CU we see she is tormented.

SARAH

(confused)

I...I...don't know...

SONNY

(tougher)

It's *love*, Sarah. I'm not talkin' about what we do here on the sofa, I'm talkin' about *love*!

He has an almost tv evangelist tone to his voice.

SONNY (CONT'D.)

How many people ever feel this in their life, darlin'? How many do you think?

(CONTINUED:)

She's mesmerized. A cobra at a mongoose rally. Sonny keeps pressing.

SONNY (CONT'D.)

I promised you, didn't I? Didn't I give you my bounden word the nights on the sofa would come to an end? Soon as this is all past, I tell Darleen I want a divorce, there's no kids, legally I got it arranged so the settlement won't hurt—

SARAH

But I'm so frightened!

(beat, with awe)

I've *never* been involved in such things...with you...the hearings...now that woman trying to—

SONNY

(getting miffed)

Can't you let it sleep?!?

SARAH

Oh, Sonny...those terrible things she was saying! So many people in town whisper behind my back when I go shoppin' at the stores.

SONNY

(soothes her)

It's okay, dumplin'. It's just nothin' but okay. Commission said I was clean. Nobody can't shake back at that, comes right down to it.

(CONTINUED:)

SARAH

But Sonny, if that's so, why couldn't I find the proper specs on that job, the bills of lading, all the docu—

SONNY

(toughly)

I said it don't *matter*! As long as the books are squeaky, it's just a lotta wind they're raising.

Then he is very businesslike. He puts her from him and starts to roll down his sleeves.

SONNY (CONT'D.)

I build roads, and bridges, and buildings, and whole damned tracts of houses. Let'm say what they want. As long as I got you, you little whiz, I got the world in an egg-cup!

SARAH

(goofy-eyed)

Oh, I *do* love you more than any thing I ever knew, Sonny.

SONNY

(distracted)

And I love you, too, babe. But if I don't get home, Darleen'll be comin' after me with a blowtorch.

(beat)

Now I'm just fine, just *fine*. You stay on, work a bit on those books, and come in late tomorrow.

(CONTINUED:)

11 CONTINUED: - 4

He shrugs into his all-weather padded vest, zips up, and gives her a honey-dripping grin. He opens his arms and, like a puppy, she moves to him, hungry for the smallest touch; and as he embraces her passionately the CAMERA MOVES PAST THEM toward the window of the construction company office, as the first few drops of rain spatter on the pane.

SONNY'S VOICE (OVER)

Can you imagine the *gall* of that damned woman? Makin' me say her dead kid's name!

As Sonny's VO speaks, lightning splits the sky, the rain starts to come down in a torrent, and CAMERA GOES INTO WINDOW as the thunder rattles ominously around the night.

CUT TO:

12 EXT. CONSTRUCTION COMPANY - NIGHT - REVERSE FULL SHOT

From the edge of the woods CAMERA ESTABLISHES the small, three-room construction company offices sitting in the middle of a small clearing at the side of the highway. Tall woods all around. Floodlights illuminate a sign near the road with the Colony Construction name and logo prominent. In the otherwise empty parking area—turning to mud as the rain comes down—we see a fancy current-model pickup truck: a behemoth RV with a rack of spotlights on the cab, wheeled with gargantuan tires. The RV is painted in *very distinctive* candy-flake colors, the Colony logo on the door. There is also a modest sedan, perhaps three years old, sitting very near the RV, looking pathetic next to Sonny's high-rise vehicle. The small grounds of the office are neatly manicured, the lights are on in two of the offices.

[MORE]

(CONTINUED:)

12 CONTINUED:

(CONT'D.)

As we watch, one of the lights goes off, Sonny comes out of the building, pauses a second to gauge the rain as he stands on the porch of the frame office, then he hunches his shoulders, dashes down the steps, rushes through the pelting rain as lightning and thunder crash, leaps up to the runningboard of the RV, gets in quickly. The RV lights go on, throwing cones of brilliance across the highway to the woods. Then the motor revs like a waking dragon and, spewing mud in a wide swath, he tools out of the lot, turns onto the gleaming black highway, and is gone, as CAMERA PANS LEFT to follow the action. Rain falls heavily. CAMERA HOLDS a moment then PANS BACK and BEGINS TO MOVE IN SLOWLY on the office building where the single light glows. Lightning illuminates the woods briefly as CAMERA CONTINUES TO MOVE IN STEADILY toward the window until we can see Sarah inside, poring over the ledgers and we

LAP-DISSOLVE THRU:

13 SARAH - EXT. & INT. SHOTS
and
14 DIFFERENT ANGLE THAN SHOT 12. On the woman working by lamplight, ledgers in duplicate before her, making erasures, altering figures, changing dates. We need not see exactly what she is writing, but should get the impression that time is passing. CAMERA CONTINUES MOVING IN ON WINDOW as we

LAP-DISSOLVE THRU:

INT. OFFICE - ANOTHER ANGLE - SAME SCENE

as she works. Hours have passed. And we CONTINUE

LAP-DISSOLVE TO:

15 EXT. CONSTRUCTION COMPANY - NIGHT

Rain has now turned the parking lot into a venue of small lakes. ANOTHER ANGLE THAN SHOT 12 as the single light goes off in the building, the door opens and Sarah Bieber emerges, locks up quickly, pulls her collar around her neck, and dashes to her car. CAMERA IN as she tries to start the old vehicle. It revs a few times, then catches. CAMERA TO CAR as she pulls away, spraying water, and CAMERA HOLDS on her retreat as she swings onto the highway, going in the same direction Sonny took, and her taillights are lost in the rain.

CUT TO:

16 INT. SARAH'S CAR - NIGHT - HER POV

Past her to show the road barely visible through the sheeting rain. She swabs at the windshield. The wipers work fitfully. Her lights swerve on the road, picking up nothing but rain, and the occasional center-stripe.

17 SERIES OF EXT. ANGLES - TRAVELING SHOTS
thru
19 On her car as it skids. We see her go off the road onto the berm several times. Not many cars pass her going the other way, but each time a car swooshes past, the water from the highway inundates her vehicle. On LAST SHOT of SEQUENCE, CAMERA HOLDS as car passes through to:

20 INT. CAR

as suddenly a gigantic semi looms whale-like in front of the car, its lights glaring. As it booms past, water rises over her like a tidal wave, she starts to skid badly, spins the wheel...

INTERCUT TO:

21 INTERCUT

EXT. HIGHWAY - NIGHT - RAIN

As the vehicle fishtails wildly, swerving across the line and back and we

CUT BACK TO:

22 SAME AS 20

As she struggles with the wheel...the road and trees flashing in the windshield. Then, as she manages to get the car under control, she sees THRU WINDSHIELD the glow of neon lights, red and yellow and flashing at her. She turns toward them, as CAMERA HOLDS HER POV, until she is right under the lights and we can see it's the gaudy road sign of the old sort, circa Forties; the neons flash on and off with the message:

HI OLD TIME
ROADHOUSE DANCING
EATS

23 EXT. ROADHOUSE - NIGHT - HIGH SHOT

On Sarah's car as she pulls past the sign and into the muddy parking lot. Her car is covered with mud, windshield obscured. She pulls into the lot, near the few RVs and cars and 4-wheel-drive vehicles. The Hi Old Time is one of those ratty-looking, utterly disreputable juke joints that features greasy food, redneck music, sawdust on the floor, and probably a congeries of small rooms upstairs in which the totality of furniture is a bed, a hat rack, a bidet and a sink, if you get the meaning. Sarah pulls to a stop near some vehicles.

NOTE: we should not be able to make out one vehicle from another. ANGLE to obscure this element.

24 INT. SARAH'S CAR

CLOSE ON DASH CLOCK. Two A.M. CAMERA PULLS BACK to ANGLE on SARAH as she looks at the Hi Old Time. She makes a disgusted sound, the sort of sound a good churchgoing woman would make at the city limits of Sodom. It is clear that she reviles this sinkhole of depravity. She reaches into her glove compartment, brings out a small squeegee and sponge implement, and opens the door on the rain.

25 EXT. ROADHOUSE PARKING LOT - CLOSE ON CAR - STEADICAM

As Sarah steps out, HAND-HELD CAMERA goes with her. She is lit by the neon that goes on and off with eerie colors washing her. Torrential rain. Cold. She slams the door and begins squeegeeing her windshield, sluicing away the mud covering the glass. Then she stops. CAMERA HOLDS HER as she looks across the hood of the car and CAMERA ANGLE TILTS to show us the vehicle parked next to hers. It rises above her car and as we SHOOT PAST HER we are FULL ON the Colony Corporation logo. It is on the side of Sonny's RV. It can be no other vehicle. We know that trashwagon appearance from Scene 12. She looks around, obviously confused to see the vehicle *here*. Wasn't Sonny going straight home to his wife...or to the police station in town...what's going on here? Concern, querulousness.

CAMERA HAND-HELD - WITH HER

Still holding the squeegee, she slogs through the rain and mud to the roadhouse, opens the front door and steps inside.

26 INT. ROADHOUSE - ANGLE ON DARK ENTRANCEWAY

As Sarah moves out of shadow with the door closing behind her, coming TO CAMERA. CLOSE ON HER as we see her looking into CAMERA. The SOUND of pseudo-disco-cum-country music, achingly bad and cheap music, OVER THIS SCENE. EXTREME CU as she REACTS to what she sees.

CUT TO:

27 REVERSE ANGLE - SARAH'S POV - WHAT SHE SEES

The usual stereotypical roadhouse scene, with neon beer signs bubbling, a bar, booths, tables and chairs, bumper pool, the band platform empty but the jukebox blaring. And in the middle of the room, Sonny is slow-dancing with a pair of, well, to put it politely, a PAIR of BIMBOS. Acres of eyeshadow and blonde hair, short black leather skirts, spiked heels an assassin would envy. Not easy, dancing with two women at the same time. CAMERA MOVES IN CLOSER to show the technique Sonny uses to meet the challenge: his hands where they shouldn't oughtta be, and mouth-to-mouth resuscitation, first one lady, then the other. And heads thrown back with laughter.

CUT BACK TO:

28 SAME AS 26

CAMERA MOVING IN STEADILY, CALMLY, ANGRILY on mousy Sarah's face as she stares in wide-eyed disbelief... then a pain so clear, so obvious, that even an Easter Island statue would melt at her angst...then a rapidly dawning and blossoming and burning hatred. We can see betrayal in her expression, and her clenched fist codifies it for us.

29 CLOSE ON SONNY & WOMEN

They do not attempt to keep their voices down, yet they are saying double-entendres as if they were sotto voce:

SONNY

(lecherously)

Swear I haven't been around such prime beef since I was locked in overnight at the meat market.

(CONTINUED:)

1ST BIMBO
(archly)
You look like a filet mignon type to me, Sonny.

2ND BIMBO
Don'tchoo get no prime filet to home, honey?

SONNY
Ground round, nothin' but ground round.

1ST BIMBO
Dog meat.

2ND BIMBO
Imported kangarooooooo...!

SONNY
Everywhere I put my hands...
(and he puts his hands)
I get hamburger, when my soul cries out for USDA prime cut!

The bimbos squeal and writhe under his pawing, as they dance. Sonny begins to chant, and, after a BEAT, the flashy ladies take it up:

SONNY (CONT'D.)
(chanting)
I wanna double burger...I wanna double burger...I wanna

1ST BIMBO
(joins in)
I wanna double burger...
I wanna double burger...

2ND BIMBO
(joins in)
I wanna double burger...
I wanna double burger...

30 SAME AS 28

CAMERA MOVING IN on Sarah, whose teeth are clenched.

SARAH

(murmurs softly)

"I better get home before my wife comes after me with a blowtorch..."

31 ANGLE PAST SARAH - TO BARROOM

As she stands there. She cannot take her eyes off the squalid scene. Suddenly, the women dancing with Sonny begin to drag him toward the shadowy foyer. Sonny, half resisting, grabs up his padded vest from the back of a chair, screams a goodbye to an unseen bartender, and they all careen toward the spot where Sarah watches. But the spot is empty, and we see the front door slowly closing.

32 EXT. PARKING LOT - THE SCENE

As the reeling trio emerge, the women holding their coats over their heads to protect their "do"s from the rain. They rush to the RV. Sonny is about to unlock the RV when a particularly BRIGHT BLAZE OF LIGHTNING and accompanying thunder illuminate the scene.

33 INTERCUTS BETWEEN SONNY & SARAH IN CU
thru
36 His eyes widen. Rain washes his face as he stares in disbelief.

CUT TO:

ANGLE across the RV and Sarah's car, beside each other, to Sarah staring at him with naked hatred as she stands with her door unlocked and open.

CUT TO:

33 CONTINUED:
thru
36 Sonny dropping the mask. His amazement vanishes and his lips skin back in a rictus of fury. He utters a low growl.

CUT TO:

Sarah throws the squeegee at him and gets in the car, starts it instantly and PULLS OUT OF FRAME as we

CUT TO:

37 FULL SHOT - THE SCENE

As Sonny ignores the women, leaves them standing beside the still-locked passenger door of the RV, dashes around the vehicle as Sarah's car roars out of the muddy parking lot and heads *back toward the office* (and the orientation should be clear from previous shots). He unlocks quickly, jumps up and slams the door, guns the motor and burns rubber, spraying mud everywhichway. He takes off after her as CAMERA COMES IN CLOSE on the two ladies of the evening, now utterly drenched, doing a kind of all-over wet T-shirt performance, furious at his abandonment. The RV's taillights wink, and he's gone.

38 THE HIGHWAY - MOVING SHOT - NIGHT
thru
42 First Sarah's car, careening down the flooded road, skidding, swerving. Sarah in tears if an INTERIOR SHOT is needed. The small car holding the road only by a miracle as she recklessly rushes away from the roadhouse. Then Sonny coming after her, at full throttle, tidal-waving a car that passes him on the opposite side, Sonny cursing, pounding the steering wheel if an INTERIOR SHOT is needed, determined to catch her. End sequence with Sonny as he skids sidewise into the parking area of the Colony Construction offices.

[MORE]

(CONTINUED:)

38 CONTINUED:
thru
42 (CONT'D.)

Sarah's car is close to the front steps, door open, pulled up onto the neatly landscaped display area right in front. The light is on in the car, headlights still flowing, and the front door of the offices is standing ajar. We see all of this in the brilliant glare of Sonny's RV headlights.

43 EXT. CONSTRUCTION COMPANY

As Sonny sluices to a halt, jumps out, rushes up the steps, and through the doorway.

44 INT. SONNY'S OFFICE - THE SCENE - FAVORING DOORWAY

as Sonny rushes in, dripping wet, looking like a raging behemoth. Sarah has the desk lamp on, and she is using the letter opener to prise open a locked desk drawer. As he storms in, big as a house, filling the doorway, lit by the single lamp in terrifying immediacy, she pulls the ledgers from the drawer and looks up. Her face is filthy with tear-tracks and mud.

SARAH
(betrayed, in pain)
Ogod, Ogod, what a fool I am!
Ogod, I believed you!

SONNY
Sarah, darlin', listen to me...

SARAH
No! No more lies!

He comes to the desk, stands on the other side, fists balled, trying to finesse a way out of this.

(CONTINUED:)

SONNY
(smoothly)
Now don't do nothin' with the books you're gonna regret later.

SARAH
(smoothly)
I did terrible things for you. I didn't want to believe them, but I knew, down inside I *knew* ...but I lied for you...
(beat)
All the pain you caused...the dead children...I *saw* them on the TV, and I *lied* for you.

SONNY
No, you're wrong...I...

SARAH
(screams)
You *did*! You did what they said! You shaved the specs, used inferior material, my God, they weren't even galvanized *nails*; the first rain everything ran with rust! Why didn't I see what you are? I'm a decent woman ...what I let you do to me...

Then she gets very cold and calm. She clutches the ledgers and starts around the desk. The letter opener lies there prominently.

SARAH (CONT'D.)
But no more. This is for me and for that poor Mrs. Kay...

As she passes him we

SHARP CUT TO:

45 INTERCUT

as Sonny's hand comes down and picks up the letter opener with its prominent logo of the Colony Corporation sculpted at the end of the hilt.

46 MURDER SEQUENCE - VARIOUS ANGLES
thru
51 (NOTE: suggest this be shot and edited as one would a music video, extreme closeups, tilt angles, slam-cuts, all with misdirection so we never actually see the murder. In much the same way Hitchcock shot the shower sequence in *Psycho*.)

Bodies frozen as Sarah tries to get around him. As she passes, one muscular shirt-soaked arm whips out, grabs her by the hair. He swings her around. The ledgers go flying. The desk lamp is knocked over. The light washes up the wall. The letter opener rises, vanishes from frame. Again. And on the third stroke we see the letter opener is broken off halfway up its length. Sarah falls, the plastic raincoat she still wears streaked and stained with blood *inside*. No blood on the hardwood floor.

52 WITH SONNY
thru
57 As he drops the broken letter opener, the logo shining in the fallen desk lamp's light. He stands there heaving with labored breathing. He wipes his hand over his face, the rainwater still dripping off him. His expressions rush through a gamut of emotions: SERIES OF RAPID LAP-DISSOLVES:

SONNY'S FACE IN MEDIUM CU:

Horror:	I'm a murderer!
Remorse:	Oh, Sarah, you fool.
Panic:	What'll I do?
Fear:	They use the lethal injection in this state.

(CONTINUED:)

52 CONTINUED:
thru
57 And finally...a nasty little smile comes over his face.

SONNY
(calmly)
Well, *okay*. Of course.

58 THE SCENE

as he folds the plastic raincoat around her, leaves her for a moment to exit the office and CAMERA HOLDS ON THE BODY. He comes back quickly from the next room, with a small tarpaulin. He lays it out, rolls her onto it, folds it around her, and tapes it at the ends with industrial strapping tape from a dispenser on the desk. Then he hoists the body and puts her over his shoulder, and leaves through the doorway.

59 BLACK FRAME - INT. CONSTRUCTION SHED - NIGHT

As the overhead swinging-bulb light clicks on. HOLD FULL SHOT OF SCENE as Sonny lays the body down, takes off his vest, rolls up his sleeves, drags out a long, galvanized iron cement trough and begins mixing a six-foot-long troughful. Then, after a bit, he drops the tarp-encased shape into the thickening soup. A few bubbles as it settles. He stares down.

SONNY
Consider it your Christmas
bonus, darlin'.

DISSOLVE TO:

60 EXT. LAKE - NIGHT - FULL SHOT

The black rain slants across frame. The RV is parked at the edge of the lake. Sonny is lowering a large rectangular block of cement onto a small hand-truck.
[MORE]

(CONTINUED:)

60 CONTINUED:

(CONT'D.)

He gets down, tilts it back with some straining of his muscular body, and backs toward the dock. CAMERA MOVES IN to show Sonny easing the block off the dolly, into a skiff tied up at the side.

DISSOLVE TO:

61 EXT. LAKE - LONG SHOT - DAWN

Across the forested area to the body of the lake. It is just coming to light in the sky. We can see a shape out there, and we know it's the skiff. There is movement in the small craft, something goes over, there is a DIM BUT DISTINCT SPLASH and we

DISSOLVE TO:

62 INT. CANOGA HOME - BEDROOM - EARLY MORNING

CLOSE ON SONNY as he sleeps. Birds chirp, the sun shines across his bed. We HEAR the insistent ringing of a strident doorbell. It rings. Rings again. Rouses him from sleep. He turns over and shouts.

SONNY

(yells)

Dammit, Darleen, answer the door!

The ringing continues. No one answers it. Sonny curses and throws the bedclothes off. He sleeps in pajama bottoms, still wearing his discreet gold chain. He snorts, rubs his hair, and goes to the bedroom door.

CUT TO:

63 INT. CANOGA HOME - FRONT FOYER - DAY

As Sonny comes stumbling downstairs toward the front door.

[MORE]

(CONTINUED:)

63 CONTINUED:

(CONT'D.)

The doorbell continues its caterwauling. Barefoot, he reaches the door.

SONNY

Hold yer water, I'm comin'!

He throws open the door. Standing there, very large and ominous, is Trooper Fred Lamont.

LAMONT

Mornin', Mr. Canoga. Got a spare minute?

Sonny looks confused, but gathers his wits.

SONNY

Yeah, sure. Come on in.
(beat)
What's up?

He closes the door. Lamont steps farther inside and removes his Smokey Bear hat.

LAMONT

(question, as statement)
I understand your bookkeeper, Miz Bieber, hasn't been to work for about ten days?

SONNY

(cheerful but careful)
That's right. She went to see her sister in, uh, I think it's Omaha. She's gonna have a kid, and Sarah went to help.

LAMONT

(firmly, shaking his head)
No.

(CONTINUED:)

SONNY
No?

LAMONT
Definitely no.

SONNY
Well, that's what she told *me*.

LAMONT
I don't think so.

Trooper Lamont holds up the broken letter opener. CAMERA ANGLES to include Trooper and Sonny and the doorway to the kitchen nearby.

LAMONT
I found this in the trash barrel behind your office.
(beat)
The other half was rammed through Sarah Bieber's chest, broke off on a rib.

At that moment, a woman in her mid-thirties, once pretty but now a trifle careworn from living with Sonny, comes out of the kitchen carrying a plastic clothes basket filled with wash and clothes pins. She stares openmouthed as Trooper Lamont unships his handcuffs.

LAMONT (CONT'D.)
Let's go, Sonny.

Sonny starts to say something, but Lamont gives him a look.

(CONTINUED:)

LAMONT (CONT'D.)
You really want to make a statement now? *Before* I read you your rights? I don't think so.

Sonny folds. Lamont cuffs him. He opens the door. As they go through the door, Lamont begins:

LAMONT (CONT'D.)
Anything you say may be used...

64 EXT. CANOGA HOME - DRIVEWAY - DAY

FEATURING STATE PATROL CAR IN F.G. as Sonny in cuffs and the Trooper come to it. Darleen stands in the doorway, just watching. They come to F.G. and as Lamont opens the rear door and bends Sonny, protecting his head to put him in the back seat, their faces are very close in EXTREME CU.

LAMONT (CONT'D.)
Damn bone-stupid of you to use your own materials, Sonny.
(beat)
She floated to the top this morning. Fish got most of her face, but I recognized it was Miz Bieber, anyways.
(beat)
Any fool knows that much sand in the mix won't hold together.

Sonny's face falls apart. The horror of his own stupidity overwhelms him. His face slides down the frame in the backseat as the car door is slammed. He stares out the window. He stares back at the house.

QUICK CUT TO:

65 CLOSE ON DARLEEN IN DOORWAY

The veriest hint of a soft smile appears around her mouth and we

CUT BACK TO:

66 STREET SHOT

As the State Patrol car pulls away, with the face of Sonny Canoga, petrified with fear, still staring out at us. On his way to a lethal injection.

FADE TO BLACK
and
FADE OUT

—Hollywood, 1984

WHAT I DID ON MY VACATION THIS SUMMER, BY LITTLE BOBBY HIRSCHHORN, AGE 27

He had begun to smell really rank; and standing there at the side of US Route 1, covered with dust and small bugs, Robert Hirschhorn had begun to suspect There Is No God. All around him the incredible Fairchild Desert sang with mind-frying heat, and the watery horizon devils twittered in the corners of his vision like mad things. Beside him—and on which his good right foot rested—the black sturdyboard suitcase (which he had used to mail home his dirty college laundry) was equally filthy. Yet its binding cords were not as frayed as his nerve ends; and only a close second to his shoelaces, which bulged with knots where they had been rejoined.

Like three eggs basting in a shallow pan, his brains were being steadily fried; his mouth tasted brown, and funky; he was hungry; he had sweated so much it felt like ants on his flesh; his eye sockets flamed from the hundred-watt bulbs burning behind his retinas; he was sick and unhappy.

And a jack rabbit *bdoinged!* across his path.

It took seventeen leaps and was very much gone.

"You are very much gone," Robert said, mostly to the puffs of dust that moved when he spoke. "And I am not far behind you."

His ears went up like the rabbit's, as the Cadillac zoomed out of nowhere on the terribly flat highway, and his thumb went halfway into the air, and the Cadillac whispered away down behind him, toward

Reno, toward San Francisco, toward the Pacific Ocean and all that cool muthuh water.

"Good-bye," he murmured, and fainted.

They had stopped the car almost directly over him—or perhaps had rolled it to him—so that as he fluttered awake, he found himself staring directly up at the canvas water bag hanging from the front fender. A great, chill drop of perspiration water hung precariously from the underside of the bag, and as he watched, it sucked itself free and plummeted down. It struck him directly under the nose. It was tepid.

"Hey, Teddy," a voice came out of the sky, "the yo-yo's comin' to." Robert looked up past the fender. There were three pairs of legs rising directly up out of his vision, continuing, he supposed, to Heaven. "Help him up," said another voice, presumably Teddy's.

Hands reached down, one pair covered by black soft-leather driving gloves, with flex-holes cut in their backs. Robert was drawn unsteadily to his feet, and his eyes focused on the three young men. The one with the Italian driving gloves supported him. "You okay, fellah?" he asked Robert.

"Szmmll." Robert mouthed a cheekful of road dust. He had fallen face-forward; they'd turned him over on his back. He extended his dust-coated tongue and swiped at it with his fingertips. They came away muddy.

"Well? You okay huh?" asked the shortest of the three, and Robert recognized the voice as Teddy's. He found himself nodding yes, he was all right. But he wanted a drink of water, badly. He motioned to the canvas bag, making feeble finger movements in its direction.

"Hey, man," Teddy said to the tallest of the trio, the one with the driving gloves, "dig him out that thermos." The boy reached into the back seat of the car and rummaged through wads of clothing and luggage, till he came up with a thermos bottle. He unscrewed the top, pulled the cork and poured the red plastic cuptop full of a light yellow fluid. He handed it across to Robert, saying, "Lemonade."

Robert took it with both hands, and gulped. The first few swallows were coated with dust and mud, but after that it went down smoothly, and it tasted wonderful.

"Where uh where you headin'?" asked the third boy, a medium-tall, freckle-spotted item with the free-swinging egocentricity that expressed itself in manner before a word could be spoken. The kind of arrogance of personality best connoted by wealthy young men from good families who are Big Men on Campus.

"San Francisco," Robert answered. "I was hitchhiking; I thought it would be a good background experience." He grimaced, and felt the tip of his nose. It was raw where he had scraped it on the ground.

"You scraped it," the one with the driving gloves said. "But it's not bleeding; it just *looks* funky."

Robert murmured something pointless about how it didn't matter. The three young men stood around nervously, until Teddy said, "Listen, we're going to Frisco, too, and if you don't mind a few stops along the way, you can jump in with us." Robert could not quite believe he was hearing properly. It was the sweet chariot, come from beyond the pearly gates to rescue him.

"Robert Hirschhorn," he said, sticking out his hand.

"Theodore Breedlow," said the short boy, returning the gesture. He indicated the tallest boy: "Cole Magnus, and," turning to the third young man, "George Young. They call me Teddy Bear." He smiled sheepishly at his own sophomoronism.

They threw his sturdyboard case into the trunk of the big black Lincoln, and hollowed out a place for Robert among the clothes and packages tossed helter-skelter across the back seat.

And then they were off down the road.

They were from an entirely different social stratum than Robert had known. While he had come from genteel and mildly Puritanical Middlewestern conformity, the three young men in the front seat had been spawned by the harsh, black-and-white hustling of Detroit. Where he chose his words for maximum effect and clarity, they bumbled and shotgunned through the language with rimfire "ain'ts" and copper-jacketed "goddams" and frequent double-barreled scattergunned "muthuh-fuckers." It was not entirely new to Robert, but in such close quarters, and for such a protracted length of time down the road, it became almost a heady experience. They were refugees from an assembly line in Dearborn, ferrying the big black Lincoln to a buyer in San Francisco, and they were GoToHells this week and next. Then, pilot another car back to Detroit, and the lathes and conveyor belts of their waking hours. But this week and next!

"Man, I pushed more'a them goddam Fords down'a line than I got hairs on my head. Sheet, man, it's good to be outta that racket and in the fresh air." And Teddy Bear turned up the air-conditioning in the hermetically sealed Lincoln another notch.

"If my parents could see me now!" George Young chirruped. "They'd crap!" He bounced in his seat. His laughter began slowly, like a dynamo winding up, and in a moment had become so much a part of the charged air, that all four of them were laughing together. "Th-they. . .they. . .think I'm, they think I'm. . .buh. . .back in Dearborn sweating on that fuckin' line an' an' an' here I am out in the m-muh-muh-iddle of Nevaaaaduh. . .!" and he rocked back and forth like an old Yiddish man *dovening* over his Talmud, the tears streaming down his freckled face. Cole Magnus was forced to pull over on the shoulder, as they all capered tightly in the Lincoln. It was a madhouse for a moment.

When they were going again, Cole said suddenly, "Hey, you remember what Roger Sims told us. . .?"

Teddy Bear and George Young looked at him questioningly. "*You* remember: about Winnemucca, Nevada!"

The lights shone out abruptly from their eyes, and Teddy Bear went, "Whoo-eeeee, sheeeet, man! Yeahhh! Now I remember, yeah! Winnemucca, Nevada!"

And George Young clapped his hands together like a delighted child. "Hoo hoo hoo, boy, I'm gonna get me a piece a'tail. . .hoo hoo hoo!"

Cole, without turning around from the wheel, pulled his right shoulder forward allowing his head to move sidewise, as he spoke to Robert. "We got this buddy back in Detroit"—he pronounced it *Dee-troyt*—"and he's almost as big a swordsman as George-O over there, and he took this trip out to Frisco—"

"The natives hate the name Frisco, I understand," Robert stuck in without meaning to be rude. "They prefer it to be called San Francisco. . ."

"Yeah, well," Cole went on without hearing him, "Roger came back and said he stopped off in some little burg called Winnemucca, Nevada, just this side of Reno, and he says they got the next best thing to legalized prostitution there." He pronounced it proz-ti-*toosh*-un. "Wanna stop off there for a little diddly-doo?"

"Aw, that was probably one of Roger's goddam wet dreams," Teddy Bear denigrated the idea. "You know he lies, man. If he says he got laid the night before, it prob'ly means he said hello to some chick on the street and followed her till she called the laws."

"Yeah, well. . ."

George Young stuck in, "No, I think he was shooting straight. He had a ball, I could tell from the way he was talking. Hell, it can't hurt, can it? Just to stop and see. It's on the way, ain't it?"

They pulled out the map and ran fingers down US #1 till they located it. "Right on the way," Teddy Bear said cheerfully. "I guess it can't hurt to try. It'll probably be one of them wet dreams, but what the hell. . ."

"What about you?" Cole asked Robert.

Robert had never been with a whore. In fact, at the age of twenty—perhaps two years older than these three wandering minstrels—he had had only one girl. Sally Gleeson, who had been as virgin as himself, until they had discovered each other the year before. Now Sally had gone off to Radcliffe and was making time with Robert's ex-friend Dave, who had met Sally on a visit to Robert's home, from New Jersey where the family had moved. He was not at all sure he wasn't terrified by the idea. But he could not expose the twitching raw end of that fiber of fear without denying everything he had decided was true of himself:

Robert Hirschhorn came from a small town outside a larger town in central Ohio. He hated the town. Hated it because it did not know what to do with him. He was the one who read Proust and Edward Gorey and MIDDLEMARCH and Ronald Searle and Hobbes and Ian Fleming, and who ignored Morris West and Leon Uris and Daphne Du Maurier and Harry Golden and Irving Wallace and *Time* magazine. He was something other than what everyone else was in town; *he* knew it, and *they* knew it, and there was something more for him than the softly moldering inside of the cocoon called Starkey, Ohio.

He had decided he wanted to be a writer. It came to him not entirely unbidden, for he had contributed a seven-part serial to a kiddies' column in the now-defunct *Cleveland News* when he was still in grade school. He had won a National Scholastic writing award for a short story about a robot that had taken over the world (which he had cribbed in concept from Capek's famous *R.U.R.*). And he had decided that college would be of no use to him if what he needed to know was the world. So Robert Hirschhorn, at the age of twenty, had taken to the road with his black sturdyboard suitcase, and a determination to taste of life in all its sherbet flavors. Which offered, this week, the tantalizing, fraudulent favorite, Cheap Whore. It was a combination of peach, rocky road and lemon. And to turn it away, back to the cooler chest, in return for a triple-dip of the pallidly familiar vanilla on which he had been subsisting for so long, would be to deny all that he had decided about himself.

"I'm game if you are." He grinned widely. Perhaps a trifle too widely.

"Hell, how should I know?" said Teddy Bear. "I suppose you ask a cabbie. Ain't that the way they do it?"

George shook his head. "Listen, stupid, you got to be more uh more undercover, more—"

"Surreptitious?" offered Robert.

"—whatever." George refused to accept the word. "But you can't just go around town asking any dumb hick where the hoo-er-houses are. That's stupid."

"Oh, hell, this isn't Detroit," Cole said. He suddenly braked to a stop by a general store, and leaned out to an old man sitting in a straight-back chair propped against the wall. "Hey, Mister!" The old man looked up disinterestedly. He closed one eye to focus better with the other. "Where's the whorehouses, huh?" Cole asked blatantly.

"Straight down this street till you come to Main, take a left and keep going till you see the veterans' trailer camp. There's a big wood fence behind it. Th'other side is Littletown. That's it, can't miss it." He went back to picking his nose.

Cole rolled the window back up and turned to his companions with a superior grin on his boyish young face. "Morons," he gibed. He slipped the big black Lincoln into D and pulled out.

"I saw it, but I don't believe it. I heard it, but it ain't true," George Young said, amazed.

They followed the old man's instructions and came down the far side of Winnemucca till they saw a cluster of silver trailers, all hunkered together like poor animals in a warren. It was a scene of somehow surpassing squalor, though everything seemed neat and clean. Perhaps it was the lack of grass—just deep brown dirt streets—or the gray and leprous garbage cans tilted and rusting and staved in, right at the edge of the road.

"Helluva place to live, right next'a the cat houses," Teddy Bear remarked. Robert stared out the window as they passed. Yes, it seemed a helluva place to live, and the silent sadness of the little trailer camp abruptly wore down on his spirit. What was he doing here? Going to a house of prostitution, having left college, bumming around the country in search of something intangible, something so remote even that he had no name for it, no way to call it, or think of it. His thoughts leaped bounded fled away.

And he thought of his father.

Was that the reason? Was it his father, who seemed so silent and distant, now that he was away? So importantly silent and distant, without love between them, without communication between them. . .

He knew his mother, perhaps knew her too well. That fine sensitive woman who had to go to Florida every winter for her cough, who took him everywhere, who said: "Wait till your father comes home, will *you* get it!" His mother, who knew she had something strange in the house. The soft, gentle beast that had given birth to the tiger. Where was she now, with his father? The man who went his hurried way, his gray fedora perched on his head with the brim turned up, his face quiet behind his glasses and the thin little sandy moustache, smoking his endless cigars, where were they now? He wanted very much to go to them, no, to *him*, to talk to him, and try to make some connection between them. Before it was too late. He had to talk to that man, to find out who he was, to find out not only who his father was, but who *he*—Robert, me—was also. He wanted simply to. . .simply to *talk* to him, to get the answers.

He wanted to leap from the car, and go to a phone.

"This's gotta be it," said George Young from another world. Robert's thoughts slithered back to him, moaning.

He wrenched himself alert, and stared out the window at the scene in Littletown. They parked at the end of a street. Dirt. It was a long street of dirt. They got out of the Lincoln, and the three Detroiters bunched together as they moved away from the car. Robert stood silently watching them, taking in every facet of the street.

It was an exact replica of some "B" Western street. Dirt down the center, rutted from cars. Clapboard buildings on either side, with hitching rails for horses in front, and slat porches raised a foot off the street.

The buildings ran down either side, and at the far end of the street was a row of the same buildings, identical in their weather-beaten weariness.

The nearest building on his left had a painted sign on its roof-front. It said: THE COMBINATION BAR and under the big red letters it said: DRINKS MUSIC ROMANCE.

He felt ill, but he followed them.

They sauntered down the street, with George Young actually swaggering. He knew his way around. He was the swordsman of the group. And Cole Magnus seemed unsure, but there was breeding in him, some kind of breeding, and it carried him. Teddy Bear had bluff, little-guy bluff, feisty, cocky, and the three of them knew where they were going, knew what they were going to do with their bodies.

Robert closed with them. He was afraid, suddenly; more afraid than he had ever been before. More afraid than the night he had not wanted his parents to go to the party and had sneaked out of the house in his pajamas and ridden on the back bumper of the old green Plymouth, till honking cars had stopped his parents, and he had run away in the dark, and hit the stop sign with his face and neck and chest, and fallen down crying; more afraid than when he had quit college; more afraid than when they had said they were going to the whorehouses. He was bitterly, shiveringly, completely terrified, and he walked with them because they were the only things he had from the past. From before this time.

But they were another kind of boys.

They *knew*!

They knew it, the secret, and he knew none of it. They were younger, but *they* knew, and he did not.

The group walked down the street, and suddenly women began to appear in the windows of the buildings. They leaned out of the openings, their breasts resting on the sills, and they wore ballerina outfits of silk and bright colors, and their meaty arms, also, rested on the sills. Like gossipy middle-aged women in tenement apartments.

"Hey, sweetie, in here!"

"C'mon boys, we know what you want, hey, we'll give it to you. Hey!"

"I can be had, baby, I can be had!"

"Over here, lover. . .c'mon over here, the best THE BEST!"

They walked down the length of the street. In the only lighted building (and suddenly Robert realized it was almost night, the dusk had fallen so swiftly) in the line facing them, at right angles to the main thoroughfare, there was a woman sitting in a large window. She was knitting. She was naked.

They turned around and started back up the street.

Perhaps, Robert prayed, *perhaps we won't go in at all.* He wanted to be somewhere else. With all his soul and spirit he wanted to be somewhere else, far away from this place.

"Well, whaddaya think?" asked George.

"I dunno," said Teddy Bear, "which one?"

"I think that Combination Bar back there's the best one," Cole said. "It looks bigger than the rest, we can probably all get taken care of in there."

"How about you?" Teddy Bear looked at Robert.

He shrugged nervously. "Any one of them's okay, I suppose."

"You got any bread?"

"Huh? What?" Robert was mystified.

"Bread, man, you got any money?"

"Oh, yeah. Yeah, sure, a few bucks." He pulled three silver dollars from his right-hand pants pocket. Teddy Bear nodded. "Okay, let's make it." They walked back down to The Combination Bar and up onto the front porch. Robert suddenly found himself shouldering past the other three, and he was the first to enter.

There was a seedy bar on the right-hand wall, and a dead jukebox against the far wall facing them as they came in, and several doors on the left and right, and off to the far left of the entrance, sitting in the window, was an old, fat woman in a rocking chair. She, like the naked woman at the end of the street, was knitting. Rocking back and forth in a bizarre rhythm, she was knitting. She did not look up as the boys entered, but the girls erupted from the back of the room, and came toward them gladly.

"Must'a been a quiet time," Robert heard Teddy Bear say. Then the girls were on them.

Three of them were fat, bursting out of the silk and satin ballerina costumes that looked ridiculous on them. Their fleshy arms were wattled with excess flesh, and their hair was teased and back-combed into outlandish styles. Two of them had tattoos on their arms. One of them had a black beauty mark, in the shape of a heart, on her cheek. They instantly made for Cole, George and Teddy Bear, but Robert was drawn almost against his will to a smaller, dark-haired girl just coming out of a door on the right, near the bar.

She was exquisite. Really. *I'm ugly, miGod am I ugly,* thought Robert. *I used to have braces, and I still need my glasses for seeing things far away. Oh God!* That fast.

"Hi, sweetie," the girl said, and Robert's terror leaped out of his head through his eyes, like a living creature, and turning, fastened itself claw and fang in his neck.

She had a mass of ebony black hair, piled atop her head. Her features were small, delicate and finely drawn. Her eyes were as dark as her hair, but they gleamed with an inner light. She wore a ballerina costume, like the others, yet somehow it fit her perfectly, was right for her, was proper. She took his arm and led him to the bar. Robert found himself suddenly filled with a great enthusiasm for what was happening. She was lovely. Really.

"How about dancing," he said irrelevantly, turning to the jukebox, "what about it?" She stopped him.

"We can't, sweet baby; it's against the law. We haven't got an entertainment license."

She bounced up onto a stool, and pulled Robert up beside her. "Hey, Jerry," she hailed a tall and red-necked man in a white apron, who had been slumped on a three-legged stool behind the bar, "I'd like a beer." Jerry roused himself, bent down the corner of the page of the double-crostic book he had been working in, and started toward the cooler. The other three girls were at the bar, as well, and they chimed in with Robert's girl. Jerry began pulling splits from the cooler, eight in all, and setting them up for opening. Robert felt put-upon. He didn't want to be hustled; though he had no way of phrasing it to himself. He felt something for this girl, and he didn't want to buy her a beer, like any common patron of The Combination Bar might do.

"No," he said.

"Huh?"

"No. I don't want to buy you a beer."

"Uh."

"Where do we go?"

"Uh, back there, back in uh in my room."

"You don't want to dance, huh?"

"No, we can't, no license."

"Entertainment."

"Yeah, that's right."

"Okay, let's go see your room."

"Yeah huh?"

"Yeah, your room."

"Okay, sweet baby, just follow me."

George looked across from where he was being smothered by his obese tattooed companion. "Lucky bastard," he said, grimacing. Teddy Bear and Cole Magnus stared after Robert as he followed the girl from the bar room. "She was cute," Cole said.

"You just pay attention to me, dahlin'!" said Cole's girl, dragging his head around. Her gold tooth glinted in the light of the Schlitz Beer sign on the back bar.

Robert followed the girl down a short hall, and waited as she took a key from inside her bodice to unlock the door. He looked at her rounded hindquarters as she bent over the keyhole, and was amazed to find that he had never really noticed the way the buttocks joined to the legs of a woman. He was thrilled, and he wondered why he had never looked at Sally Gleeson in the light. They had always made love in the dark—she had wanted it that way—and by the time the lights were turned on again. . .she had always been dressed.

Now she was in the dark with his friend Dave, from New Jersey. It didn't seem fair, somehow, that he had never seen her naked.

"After you, sweet baby." The girl stood aside for Robert to enter the room.

"Oh no, after you," Robert said sincerely.

She gave a small skyward look and preceded him into the tiny room. Robert followed and stopped just within the door. The girl closed the door tightly and turned to his back. "That'll be four bucks. Now," she said firmly.

Without turning around, Robert pulled the three silver dollars from his right-hand pants pocket, and gathered a dollar's worth of change from his left-hand pocket. "On the bureau," she said, from behind him.

Robert placed it on the white lace doily, and was held on a point of fascination by the photographs stuck into the frame of the bureau's mirror. Tony Curtis. Steve McQueen. Steve Reeves. Vincent Edwards. Anthony Franciosa. Paul Newman. An unidentified man with a two-day stubble, a large ten-gallon hat worn at a rakish angle, and a pair of heavily tooled Western boots. A picture of a woman holding a baby holding a teddy bear. Robert thought of Teddy Bear, at the bar outside, pouring beer into the fat woman. A picture of two girls at a seashore, mugging ferociously.

He turned and looked at the rest of the room. There was a bed, with a metal frame, and a very clean, white bedspread. Three dolls, puffed in dirndl skirts, sat up frozen-faced on the pillow. The walls were gray, and covered with pictures in color, cut from movie magazines. There was a preponderance of Paul Newman and Vincent Edwards photos.

The bureau, a closet, a waist-high, overly long sink with rubber tubing connected to the spigot, internal machinery, female machinery, hoses, things without names, whose purposes he could only guess.

"Strip, sweet baby," the girl said, and pulled a zipper on the front of her ballerina costume. She let it fall from her breasts, and shoved it past her waist, over her hips. It fell to the floor and she carefully stepped out of it, being certain not to catch her high heels in it. Robert watched her. She was naked under the ballerina outfit. No bra, no underpants, just her flesh, her pale flesh that filled his vision. He wanted to reach out and touch her, there, or there, on her naked body, but he caught himself; she wasn't Sally Gleeson. She was someone else. He didn't even know her name, and he was going to do with her, that thing he had done only with Sally. "What's your name?" he asked her, softly.

"Terry," she said, and stooped to pick up the satin garment. He watched her as she turned, seeing all of her as she moved, every inch of her, all the dark places only suggested by the folds and wrinkles and postures of women's clothes. She went to the closet and hung the garment on a hanger. There were half a dozen more of other colors hanging there. She took a silver one out, closed the door, and laid the garment across the bureau, covering Robert's four dollars. She turned to him, then.

"Well, c'mon, sweet baby, I haven't got all night, you know." She kicked off her spike-heeled pumps and took a quick step to the bed. She pulled down the spread, carefully removing the dolls and placing them on the bureau. Then without looking at Robert she dumped herself back on the bed, flat on her back, her legs up.

An open cradle. The pillars of love spread to receive him. His thoughts were briefly of Sally Gleeson. They did not match up. This was a girl out of a vision; not his perhaps, but a vision nonetheless.

"Hey, c'mon," she said.

He started to strip, and she watched him as he slipped off his shoes, his socks, his pants. He was standing in his shirt when she said, "That's funny, y'know."

"What's funny?"

"Your pants. You took off your pants first."

"So? Doesn't everybody?"

She shook her head. "Uh-uh. They take off their shirt first, and they all suck in their bellies so they look like some kind of strong man, and they lay the clothes out real neat, like they were going to be here awhile, and then they take off the shoes, and then they turn around and unzip the fly and take off the pants, and lay *them* out real neat, and then they come over and get close before they take off their underpants. Most of them wear either jockey shorts or some kind of loud boxer things. But you took off your pants first. That's funny, y'know?"

It didn't mean much to Robert.

"And they usually come to the bed with their socks on. You ever see how silly a guy looks with nothing but his watch and his socks on?"

Robert unbuttoned his shirt and stripped off his underpants, and dumped them on the floor with his pants and socks. He came to the bed and looked down into the warm dark of her, and felt he should say something: was this the feeling you always got? Was this the way for all men about to know women? He had no idea, but he felt he should do or say something that would set him apart from all the other men who had been inside this girl.

"What's, uh, I mean how uh long am I supposed to be in here for uh four dollars?"

She looked up incredulously.

"Sweet baby," she demanded, "just what the hell are you talking about. . ."

"Well, I—"

"Now, look, will you just kindly lock on here and stop all this laughin' and scratchin'."

She grabbed him by the thigh, and tumbled him onto the bed. His left hand came down hard on her breast, and she went oooof softly, but started moving around till he was firmly positioned. He had the overwhelming urge to talk to her, to make some sort of conversation to keep her from what she was trying to do to him, what he was trying to do to her.

Then she found him, and his body betrayed him as she took him in her hand and guided him. It was like soft polyps, down a slim, slick tunnel, very smooth yet ruffled. It filled him with sensations he had never before known, and all he could think of was that Sally Gleeson, out there in the bushes with New Jersey Dave, his friend, was even a failure at this, as well as a failure at being real to him.

And then she was moving quickly, expertly, but he wanted it to go on and on for a long time. He propped himself up on his elbows and looked down at her lovely face. "Where are you from?" he asked, conversationally.

"Oh, shit! A nut."

"No, really, where are you from? Come on, tell me."

"Texas. West Texas. Okay?"

"How'd you get here?"

"How'd a nice girl like me wind up in a place like this? Oh, shit."

"No, now come on, don't make fun of me. I wouldn't ask you a cliché like that. I know better."

"Oh you do, huh?"

"Sure. I know a little."

"Like that prostitutes are usually dykes, and like they're all fallen girls from good families, and like they never kiss their johns even if they'll screw them?"

"Well, yes, I've heard tha—"

She took his face in both hands and pulled him down to her and kissed him full on the mouth, prying open his lips with her soft, agile tongue, and running it inside hot and moist. She kissed him for a long time, for a very long time, moving her hips in an anticlockwise direction all the while. It was the most thorough kiss Robert Hirschhorn had ever had. In all his twenty years. It did the work of all the women who had come before, how very few there had been.

While she was still kissing him, there was a rude slam on the door, as though someone walking past had idly banged a fist against the panel.

"Oh, shit!" Terry said. "That's the Missus. Come on now, sweet baby, make your seed and let's get outta here before she howls holy hell at me."

So he started working again, drilling and moving as he was expected to do—according to Van de Velde in IDEAL MARRIAGE, which Sally had brought him from her father's library—with too much frenzy and not enough skill. And still he did not finish. On and on he went, in a seemingly endless repetition of the same movements, until Terry slapped him across the backside. "C'mon, sweet baby, do it already!"

And he remembered the screwing scene from James Jones's FROM HERE TO ETERNITY, and the endless conversation the hero had with the whore; and he burst out laughing, falling across her so his face was buried in her deep, rich black hair. "What the hell's so funny?" she demanded. Obviously, she didn't think there was so much funny going on here.

"Nothing. Nothing. Not a single solitary thing." And he continued laughing till she slapped him on the backside again and urged him,

"Pleeeese, sweet baby, she's gonna raise holy hell with me," so he tried very hard, and she did weird things with herself, moving tightly against him, and in a moment it was over.

Then she was up off the bed like a shot, and at the sink performing her rituals with the tubes of rubber. He got dressed quickly, feeling a great affection for her, and said, "Are you coming back to the bar? I'd like to buy you that beer now."

"In a bit, in a bit," she said, without turning.

So he left the room, buttoning his shirt.

In the bar, George and Cole and Teddy Bear were already waiting. "Man, did you get *your* money's worth from *that* sweet piece!" George caroled. "Or couldn't you get it up, Tiger?" They all three laughed.

"How did you guys do with the tattooed ladies?" Robert sneered at them. They shut up. And turned back to their beers. At a dollar a split, they were leaving no dregs. The hogs with the tattoos were elsewhere. Robert decided to take a walk. There were other men in the barroom.

He walked outside and up toward the car, and received a half-dozen offers from the windows across the way. He waved at them in a friendly, magnanimous way. He was truly a man now. He had the secret. It was all warm and delightful, that's what it was. It was serene and lovely, with a lovely girl really. And then the idea hit him. He would ask her if she wanted to come with him to San Francisco.

She had to accept. A girl like that, with a sense of humor, couldn't *really* enjoy this life. He would tell her how he was writing a fine novel, and that he was twenty-four years old. No, better make that twenty-seven. Yes, he was Robert Hirschhorn, age twenty-seven, and he would marry her.

All that black hair.

West Texas.

Lovely. Really.

He sprinted back to the street and to The Combination Bar. He was inside and running through the barroom and down the short hall before the three minstrels realized he was back. He opened the door and stepped through and said, "Hey, listen, Terry, I have a wild ideeeee—"

HARLAN ELLISON

WHAT I DID ON MY VACATION THIS SUMMER

The word shrieked off thinly, as he watched them and he realized how foolish he must have looked doing the same thing. She looked out at him from around the huge, tanned shoulders, and her eyes grew wide.

"Oh, shit!" she exclaimed.

The man's head twisted on the thick red neck, and he yelled, "Say what the fuggin' hell you mean doin' there, boy!" And Robert's tongue balled in his mouth and he felt as though it were full of dust again. And he felt very gone, like the jack rabbit that had crossed his path. Had it been a black jack rabbit? And was that bad luck as well?

He turned and ran from the room, through the bar and out into the chill Nevada night. He kept running till he came out on the main street of Winnemucca, and didn't stop till he had found a phone booth.

Collect. Station. Starkey, Ohio.

"Mom, Mother, hey listen, Mom, let me speak to Dad, will you. It's terribly important, it's awfully important, I have to talk to him. . ."

The sound of his mother's voice was clogged with trembling. "Your father died last night, Bobby."

He wouldn't listen to the words. He wouldn't.

It was foolish. "No, listen, Mom, let me talk to him. . ."

"Our daddy died last night, Bobby. He was sitting right there in his red chair, he was smoking his cigar, and he died, Bobby. He just died."

He *would not* listen! He wouldn't! Screw it NO!

"—thrombosis, that's what Doctor Fisher said. A coronary throm—Bobby, are you there? Bobby darling, are you coming home now, please come home. . ."

"No! No, I'm not coming home now, not now. . ." he cried helplessly, and hung up the receiver. He laid his face up alongside the cool glass of the phone booth and he cried a very private cry for a while.

Then he went outside and looked up at the clear black Nevada sky, as black as Terry's hair, and he said to the sky and whoever might be there listening: "We never really we never really *talked! Just talked!*"

Then he walked slowly back toward Littletown, his hands in his pockets. He would go down to San Francisco—hell!—to Frisco—with the three minstrels, and he would learn the secret from them, because they knew it and they'd tell him. If he was a good guy.

And he would wait for another four dollar turn on Terry, because there was no communication, none at all, with anyone, ever, and he was locked-in the same as everyone else, and all that mattered was laughing. So what the hell. . .he would laugh.

So, laughing, till his eyes hurt, he went back down the street. The sound of such hilarity did not reach very far in the night.

—Winnemucca, Nevada 1954
and Hollywood, 1964

MONA AT HER WINDOWS

When Mona was twenty-three, she had pleurisy, and the time in Women's Hospital had been violently peaceful: so calm and warm and tended that it made her shudder with pleasure to remember it. It was the one happy time—not counting growing up in Minnesota with Buddy and Eenor and the folks—she could remember. It was a period of placid contemplation of the way the world really was, and is.

It was a time in which the constant growing pressure of her ugliness came to her fully, completely. She had looked at the nurses, even the plain and unattractive ones, and had known they were more appealing than she would ever be. It was the days-long moment through which Mona told herself the truth. *I am not just ordinary, I am really quite unappetizing*. And she recognized the inevitable end result of having been born with the face she wore: she would never marry, she would perhaps never have a man (unless he was somehow deficient, for otherwise, why should he want *her*?) and she might never even experience the strange mystery of having a man enter her body. It was, at first, a realization so monstrous, so terrible in its ultimate thoroughness of destruction, that she cried. Not simple uncomplicated tears of sorrow, but a soulful emptying of her body that dried her, leaving her hacking, dry-sobbing, flushed and even sicker than she had been when admitted to the hospital. It was not a sorrow born of having been ill-treated, of being in pain, or of having lost something. It was that unnameable sorrow mixed with passionate fear at never having *had* anything to lose.

When she was released, she felt she must break away from the past, that she must begin a new existence, at the age of twenty-three, based upon the new truth she had discovered. This resolve was reinforced by the pitying stares of the homely nurses who said good-bye to her; women and girls who had hushed and soothed her during the nights of wretched crying. If these drabs could feel superior to her. . .then finally she knew her place, and her fate.

So Mona moved out of her apartment and quit her job. She closed her checking account and paid off her charges at the market and Macy's. She left the tag-ends of hopes and desires she had known till then, and went to find a new subsistence, in the realm of realization of futility.

Mona took an apartment on a busy corner of Seventh Avenue and Twenty-third Street, and she decorated it with Spartan efficiency. No television set and no record player; no parti-colored pillows to decorate the daybed; no bookshelves stocked with glossy flashy paperbacks and philosophical tracts from Anchor or Yale University Press; no clever pewter coffee mugs and no Lyonel Feininger prints on the walls. Just the necessities of life that keep a person breathing and free of sickness.

But the windows. . .

Ah, the windows!

Three seeing-out windows. Three constantly changing landscapes hung in the center of her walls. Three openings to the world. Three panoramic shadow plays, always new, always vivid. Into these three windows she poured all the unquenchable instincts a resigned soul could not damp.

She planted her flowerpots, and she set up the foam pillows on the floor, and day after day, night after night (when she was not at work in the catalogue section of the New York Public Library), she stared into the world.

Hidden, recording, devouring and ugly, she stared into other people's lives as they traversed from one side of her sight to the other, and then gone. She watched them with an intensity a casual observer might call psychotic. She studied the moles on the faces of delivery boys; she studied the rough-knuckled hands of cleaning women on their way home from swabbing office floors at five in the morning; she studied the exotic hatboxes and lustrous hairdos of the models, perhaps prostitutes, swirling and delighting their way away from passion; she learned the names of obscure freight companies and cartage firms from trucks roaring by; she absorbed the air and the beat and the life of the world, by osmosis and by rote.

As the months passed into a year, and that year gave way to a second, in the windows of her world, Mona found a particular pleasure in imagining herself one with the girls who lived their brief lives on the streets outside. A saucy brunette with a great flat leather portfolio under her arm would cross Mona's vision and in her window sanctuary Mona would merge with the brunette, knowing her feet were tired from having stood behind a perfume counter for eight hours. She would take heart, however, in the knowledge that now she was on her way to art school, where she would perfect her charcoal technique a little more. And one day I'll be a very good artist, and work for one of the big women's slicks, and one of the models will ask me for a date, and I'll go with him to the Chateaubriand, and then he'll ask me to. . .

As the brunette passed out of sight around the corner.

With the lights out in the apartment, and darkness providing a mummer's cloak, Mona picked up a slatternly blonde shuffling up Seventh Avenue, pausing at the light, and empathically she entered the blonde's head, feeling her hands sinking into the side pockets of the Alligator raincoat, wishing I was home in Cedar Rapids instead of going to meet Arnie, that stupe, that creep. But I suppose I'll marry him because if I don't, I'll *never* get those bills paid at Saks and Klein's. He's not very good-looking, but at least he can make it in the rack, and hell, what am I after, James Garner, or a meal ticket. . .? If only he didn't have that ridiculous astigmatism, those dopey glasses with the tortoise-shell frames! Well, hell, I can always make him go in for contact lenses after I get him. . .

Into the restaurant and out of sight of Mona.

It went this way, hour and hour and hour after hour. One girl, two girls, three, four and more, always more, coming down the Avenue, crossing Twenty-third Street, leaving buildings and entering bakeries, pausing at traffic lights and whistling through the twilight mistiness.

It was a whole new, vicarious, utterly satisfying life. And soon, Mona began to realize that she was better than all of them down there.

For *they* only had one life each, but she had thousands. There were worse fates than merely being ugly, and lonely. She knew *all* of those fates, because she was Everywoman, and experienced their brief walking-past lives more totally than any of them could. She was each happy girl, every sad girl, all the pretty ones, and for change the not-pretty ones. She thought their many thoughts, wore their many expressions, loved their many lovers, lived life to its fullest. She thrived. Yet there came a night. . .

In the dark painting that lived in her window, she saw, this night, a cheap-looking but sensuous Puerto Rican girl in a thigh-length black leather coat, beehive hairdo, smoky hose and overpainted face, strolling liquidly, languidly, close to the buildings. A pickup girl, a loose girl, a scarlet Miss looking for a five-dollar John.

Mona's pale eyes swooped down and slid inside the girl, knowing her soreness between the legs, knowing her weariness at having to make another ten tonight or they'll lock my bags in the room, and I'll have to find a flop somewhere till I can get my clothes out.

There was a stirring in the shadowed doorway, and the Puerto Rican girl (who was Mona) turned half toward the noise. A hand snaked out of the darkness and physically *away!* Mona was wrenched, back to her place high in the window, watching, terrified, mute, as the man half-pulled the tramp into the doorway.

Mona stared disbelieving as the alter ego that had been hers, a moment before, was thrown to the sidewalk. The man descended on the leather car coat, tore it open and, as Mona stared in horror, violated the streetwalker with an animal ferocity that forced Mona to bite her fist, stifle a scream, and finally, as the man arched upward in climax, faint painfully away from her viewport into reality.

It could only have been a few minutes of unconsciousness, for when she pulled herself to her knees on the foam cushions, the Puerto Rican girl was still sprawled on the sidewalk, half obscured by the doorway, her face hidden, her nyloned legs sticking out, awkwardly spread and limp, into the light from the streetlamps.

Mona closed the window softly, pulled the shade, and went to bed.

When day came, it seemed somehow silent in her streets, and though Mona tried to regain a oneness with her women going by, it was useless.

At eight o'clock that night—finally—she knew she had reached another junction of her existence. There *were* things worse than being ugly and lonely, and all of them were here, before these windows.

That night the windows were empty for the first time in years, but the streets had a new walker seeking whatever Fate chanced by first.

If there was a God for women who lived in windows, He would send an ugly boy with tortoise-shell glasses, rather than a ferocious animal.

The windows were dead eyes; life meant darkness and the streets of the world. Mona said hello.

—New York City, 1962

BLIND BIRD, BLIND BIRD, GO AWAY FROM ME!

Out of the night that covers me,
Black as the Pit from pole to pole,
I thank whatever gods may be
For my unconquerable soul.
WILLIAM ERNEST HENLEY
Invictus

There is a sound in that darkness. A soft, mewling sound, far out in the black, a small creature in pain, crying; vapors of night and distance obscure it, but that sound is terrible; a child afraid of the dark; yes, that sound no other sound can approach for pain and terror. The child, lost in the forest of the night, blind, hands out before his face, afraid to move, afraid to remain still, trapped, trembling, help me, help me! But if you go toward that pitiful pleading, somehow the voice seems deeper, older, more strangled by a darkness from within than the darkness without.

There. Up there, look up that flight of basement stairs, barely dimly seen by the crack of light shining under the door. A child crouched against the wooden panels, scratching feebly at the locked door, looking back over his shoulder, down into the basement. Another sound, tinny rasping counterpoint to the child's pathetic sobbing; a scuttling, furry sound, little claws against concrete, fearful gray creatures with snake-tails twitching, wire-thin whiskers moving spastically, bullet bodies moving quickstart and stop in the basement, coming to feed. With each new wave of movement from below, the child plunging deeper into hysteria, the voice rising shrilly, pleading with the mother beyond the locked door. . .

"Mommy, pl-please Mommy, let me in, let me in, Mommy, b-be guh-good, beee gooood, *Mommmee!*" Chittering shriek from below in the absolute darkness, the child flinging himself against the unyielding door, "*Mommmmmmee!*"

But the door remains closed, the child flattened against it, a painting on wood, terror contorting the small features into a gargoyle's insane face, and the blind darkness filling his mind till it bubbles froths churns like molten lava, searing the inside of his skull, running over and destroying all reason, coherence; pathetic infant, condemned to horror in the darkness; capital punishment, living death, entombment in fear; crime now lost in the mist of childhood, forgotten, tiny sin whose punishment razor-slashes the delicate lining of memory. This child will sleep with the lights on for many years.

Listen. The voice is deeper, down more in the throat, softer, more controlled by time, and the face alters, melts, shifts, runs like hot wax, that face framed by darkness. . .and comes to focus in time, another face.

MSgt. Arnott T. Winslow, US51403352, thirty-one years old, face pressed tightly against the rough plank door of a two-storey residence in the center of Bain-de-Bretagne, midway between Rennes and Nantes on the spearhead salient of General George S. Patton's 3rd Army. MSgt. Arnott T. Winslow, US Infantry, July 1944, hurled forward from his own past to press his face against the splintery dun-colored wood of a door in a waystop town midway between somewhere and nowhere. MSgt. Arnott T. Winslow, "Arnie" to his friends, formerly of Willoughby, Iowa, now wishing he were taffy that could slip between the slats of the unyielding barrier to his safety, a middling-warm day in July, in the midwest of lovely France.

Softly: "Let me in, let me in, let me in. . ." as a rattle of machinegun fire preceded, by an instant, the bite of masonry across the back of his neck. The Kraut gunner in the bell-tower was still chipping for an angle at him, but a ricochet might accomplish his mission for him.

Across the narrow cobblestoned street Arnie Winslow heard a tinkle of breaking window glass, and the muzzle of an M-1 rifle poked out, firing down the passage at the German troops spaced out in alleys, doorways, upstairs windows, rooftops. The rest of the patrol was in that building, cut off from escape on three sides by thick stone walls, and on the fourth by a town full of Elite Corps killers intent on keeping Winslow's patrol from getting back. With the intelligence that Bain-de-Bretagne was not—as the quisling had reported—empty of the enemy, evacuated in panic two days before. Twelve men were in that warehouse. Twelve of the fifteen who had come out on the patrol. Winslow made thirteen. Fourteen and fifteen lay sprawled in the weak, failing light of a French sundown. He could just see the inward-turned feet of Pfc. Coopersmith around the edge of the doorway, felled without murmur by a burst from a Schmizer burp-gun, loosed from a courtyard down the street. 2nd Lt. Thomas G. Benbow, formerly intercollegiate high-diving champion from the University of Utah, sprawled idiotically half-across a milk cart parked near the side of the warehouse. Idiotically, for the same covey of shots that had taken out Pfc. Coopersmith had done corrective surgery on Benbow's infectious grin, widening it from ear to ear, from nose to chin, in a bloody mash, leaving him with a Pagliacci resemblance to a circus clown. From where he was flattened against the door, Arnie could not see the bone-shattered cavern that opened the rear of Benbow's skull to the fresh air.

When they had cautiously slipped into the town, moved in two lines of skirmishers down the streets, it had seemed precisely as the little Vichy traitor had reported it: empty of all save the infirm and aged, left behind by not only the Germans, but by the collaborationist French who had fled from some inexplicable fear of the retribution Yanks were supposed to inflict on them. It had *seemed* a shoo-in. And then they had entered the passage between buildings; the first burst had dropped Pfc. Coopersmith and hurled Benbow like a Raggedy Andy doll against the warehouse, dumping him bloodily on the milk cart. . .and the patrol had dived—almost as one man—through the half-open door of the warehouse.

All but Winslow. MSgt. Arnott T. Winslow, US51403352, whose reflexes had hurled him in the opposite direction; brought him up short against the locked door of a house facing across the narrow street to the warehouse where his buddies now sporadically returned fire on the hordes of Nazi troops fly-specked through the town. They were ambushed. Trapped. Boxed in. But they were at least safe behind stone, while Arnie Winslow trembled flat against a locked door, murmuring softly to be let in, out of the light and out of the death.

"Arnie! You out there, Arnie!"

It was Truck. The push-faced Polack from Hoboken who had soldiered as corporal beside Winslow, all the way in from the spiked beach at Normandy. The voice was Truck, but the tone was Fear. Rabbit-warren Fear. Truck was inside the warehouse, and his shouts brought a cascade of hard-fire from a dozen concealed Kraut positions. Winslow could not afford to answer. The machine-gunner in the bell-tower of the church at the end of the passage knew where he was, but it was doubtful any of the others had him pegged. Otherwise he would have by now joined Coopersmith and Benbow. He remained silent.

He had to get inside that house. It was only a matter of time till the bell-tower assassin dusted that doorway effectively enough to pick him off. But the door was locked. He could not step back to blast the bolt through the door, for that would put him in plain sight from the street. He bumped his weight heavily against the door twice, three times. It bowed, but did not give.

There was only one way. If there were more ways, they weren't registering, and he had been in the doorway for almost two minutes now. He had to take the chance.

He hop-jumped half a dozen paces out into the street, a timorous creature, and then hurled himself like a battering ram back into the entranceway, smashing against the wooden door. The machine-gunner was a moment too slow. By the time he had tracked the big .30 caliber

J-34 to the new target, Arnie was on his return trip. The bigbeast rattle of spraying shots overrode the *thwack!* of Arnie's shoulder hitting the door, and puffs of dirt, chips of cobblestone exploded harmlessly as he slammed full against the bolted door. The door gave and splintered inward off its bolt as a fresh shower of shots ripped into the edge of the building, chasing him, seeking him, but not locating him.

Then, as the big air-cooled machine gun went berserk, firing hysterically at the empty doorway, he fell inside; with a fluid, almost instinctive movement, he slammed the door closed again, and fumbled for the bolt. It was half-torn from its screws, but it held, rattling into place as he palmed it home. Then he turned—

Into darkness.

That suddenly, that abruptly. The electricity of what had filled the past few moments had held light within his eyes, but now that he was momentarily safe, tension and fear and preoccupation were used up and the mind—magician master of misdirection—came fully to bear on what was inside that house. What was inside that house:

Darkness.

Nothingness.

Black chilled pressing-in heavy midnight blindness, a coal sack filled with dust; nothingness weighing down on his eyes, filming them with ink-shadows, flitting dim images. . .

Slowly his legs collapsed under him. Standing in quicksand, he began to sink with exaggerated slowness to the dirty floorboards of the anonymous hovel. A puppet whose usefulness has passed, his unseen manipulator snipped his strings and he fluttered into a heap, bundled in dark shrouds of fear, and a vagrant vision he had had for many years (and never remembered upon awakening) crawled back to him:

Thick winds, like ropes of sand, tore at him, the sound like tortured metal shrieking as it was rent. Arms flung up to the nightmare sky, whipped into cloud-and-dark froth, he stood on a barren plain. He was a scarecrow, or something very much like a scarecrow; an imbecile relation to a scarecrow. In the middleground of an empty plain, beaten by sound and hurricane winds, he was crucified on a shaft of night, under a gibbering sky. And as he stood unmoving, from out of that sky—riding a trough of shouting black wind—the blind bird plummeted toward him. It was an ink bird, a domino bird, a soot bird; blind and small and very frightened out in its storm; but he could not help it, could not bring it peace or security or comfort, and he had nothing to say to that blind bird, save to tell it to go away, to fly back up into the darkness. Blind bird, blind bird, go away from me! But it was a shivering, frightened little bird, and over his head it circled, all through that night, until at last he admitted he was afraid, too. The vision came with extraordinary clarity, for the first time in his life while he was awake, and he suddenly realized how many nights he had trembled in his bed, shivering with that pathetic, circling blind bird. And the question came to him unbidden, there in the pitch-darkness of that house, *Why do I remember it now?*

Why, indeed? Again, an answer leapt unbidden.

Less than a month before, the offensive had struck south from Normandy, leaving the flesh and the metal piled high in the fields, on the beaches, in the sea. He had been trotting along behind a deuce-and-a-half stacked high with cartridge cases, using the truck for cover across a two-mile open stretch currently in favor with the German mortar batteries. He had slung his M-1 over his shoulder and was folded down in upon himself, lighting the roach of his last cigarette, when the truck rolled its right front wheel across the exact center of an antitank mine. He had been a few paces farther behind (having ceased to dogtrot, trying to get the butt lit) and only that had saved him. All he knew was that the truck rose up in majestic fury, like a featherweight prop, sprouted blossoms of metal and flame, and exploded like a thousand fire-lilies. The concussion rather rudely hoisted him by the ass and shot-put him three hundred feet across the field and into a drainage ditch, without his once complaining. He was unconscious before he hit turf. He came to rest upside-down, legs twisted under his body (but, miraculously, unbroken), his back lofted in an aesthetic arch by his pack and the rifle which had whirled along with him. When the medics found him, he was sleeping as peacefully as any classic example of shock and shrapnel and whiplash and concussion and blast-burn could sleep. He was trundled back to the evacuation hospital and when the slight burns and flesh wounds had been treated, they had waited patiently for him to come out of the coma, hoping APCs would do the job and he could be trundled *back* into the line, because there was still *much* trouble out front. Every man was needed.

Arnie came out of it nicely, and sat up one morning as though refreshed from an extended snooze. Stretching his arms over his head and grunting with pleasure, he had heard the doctor ask, "Well, how do you feel?" and had gotten off the classic line, "What time is it?" The doctor had said, "About ten-thirty," and Arnie had said, "Blackout?" and the doctor had looked heavenward, because it was ten-thirty in the morning, not the evening, and Arnie's eyes were wide open.

They had bandaged his eyes, and he had lain there for close to a week, trapped in stifling darkness, and the soreness had passed, but the pools of thought had bubbled.

Memory within a memory:

Stealing dimes from his mother's purse. His father had gone to work, and she lay in bed, catching an extra hour before starting the housework. Silent Willoughby, Iowa morning. He knew at just what level of weariness her mind floated, and like a soldier in a movie he had stealthily opened the bedroom door just enough to slip through, had gone to his stomach on the rug, and pull-crawled himself across the room. Her big brown handbag stood on the dressing table bench, and smoothly he had lifted it down, dragged it noiselessly across the floor to the foot of the bed. (If she wakes up and looks out of the bedclothes, I'll be hidden by the foot of the bed and quiet; she'll go back to sleep.) Seven years old. Already accomplished. He had stolen forty cents in dimes. (She never inspects her change, never knows how much she has.) Always "she," seldom by name, why?

He had replaced the purse and turned to start the crawl back to the door, downstairs, outside to his bike, to Woolworth's for things worth forty cents he didn't really need. He had turned.

His mother was staring at him.

Breath clogged like the vacuum cleaner when it's full. Dust in his mouth, a haze through his brain, unbelievable fear. Her face was a mixture of fury and pity, sorrow and revenge.

Before he could move, she was out of the bed, the heels of her feet bed-red and horny, hitting the floor, and her soft hand sliced air and caught him across the cheek. "Why do you *do* it!" she moaned. He had hurt her, he knew it. That made it all the worse. He didn't *know* why! And she wasn't really asking. Then dragged by the collar to Daddy's clothes closet, poised on the lip of the mothball-smelling cavern, and the pit of his stomach turned to ice. "No, please, Mommy, nonono—"

Whipped inside, garbage hidden from view, door slammed and you'll stay in there till I find out what your father wants me to do with you I can't control you I don't know what to do with you, door slammed. Lock clicked as the skeleton key—maintained in that never-needed-to-be-locked door for just this purpose—turned turned quickly turned.

Back in there. Darkness. Oppressive, stuffed like a wad of cotton inside the toe of a sock. Ceiling invisible up there, pressing down, ready to flatten him. His little fist went into his mouth, cries floated to the surface of his mind but were never loosed; he was busy listening to someone else in the closet moaning piteously, whelp-cries for help, to be let out. He knew it was himself, but he could not feel himself making the muscular contractions needed for the sounds.

What fear in the Pit, in the darkness. Sounds of sightlessness, of terror at being closed in, unable to see. Indescribable. One memory melded to a thousand others, of basements (primarily! the most terrible of all!), of the trunk of the Plymouth once, of eyes open yet unseeing. . .memories. . .of other closets, of tiny hotel rooms where he slept better because the great neon OTE flashed on OTE and off OTE at regular intervals, metronomically, soothing him. . .memories. . .of beds with women in them, sometimes laughing, sometimes surly, sometimes uneasy, because he made love in the light, not in the faceless darkness they had come to trust, when their bodies and their egos were stripped naked for pleasure.

All of these memories, swirling: a paperweight globe of a pristine town that never existed, ankle-deep in snow, turned upside-down, shaken: thoughts swirling, memories like snow, cold, chilling, swirling.

Back from a memory within a memory, to merely a memory:

As Arnie had lain in that bed, the floodgates of his fears had been pried open. After years of having troweled the mud of forgetfulness over the scars, after years of subconsciously sinking the traumas in the silt of other experiences, maturity, pleasures, more pertinent fears. . .now freed, they thundered forth, and locked inside the bandages, he knew terror once more. He was blind!

The darkness that was deeper than darkness engulfed him, swallowed him whole, destroyed his senses and his reason, left him trembling and moaning like the child who had begged to be let out of the closet, who had pleaded to be taken out of that basement where the rats chittered below him.

And then one day, after a week in the evacuation hospital, the blindness had passed. That simply. They had removed the bandages when he had said he felt a prickling, and without any refocusing or salty tears, his eyesight had come back. It had been some sort of minor miracle. The doctor, less prone to muddy semantics, felt it was more temporary shock and psychosomatic than miraculous. But either way, he was pleased: with Arnie repple-deppled back into the line, it left the bed open for some new pile of human hamburger.

Arnie had been returned to his company and, so minor were the visible reminders of his wounds, within a few days he had almost totally forgotten the madness he had known while lying helpless without his eyes. Almost forgotten. Not quite, but almost.

Then the assault had consumed his attentions, and the simple business of remaining alive became vastly more menacing than any bolts of darkness from the past. The assault, the capture of the collaborationist, the order to dust out the town, the ambush, a burst of hacking fire from a Schmizer. . .

Another burst of hacking fire from the Schmizer down the street hauled him back to this moment in which he sat on his knees, legs collapsed under him like the segments of a carpenter's folding ruler, on the floor of the little French *maison de ville*. Back to this instant of absolute sightlessness, utter darkness, no-sight so much like the memories he had just flashed through.

And fear was reborn.

Consuming fear. Paralyzing fear. Stomach-numbing fear that left him crouched on the floor a mass of putty and milk. Whimpering. Soft tissue-paper whorls of sound from his chest. They came regularly, incapable of being captured in true fidelity by any human mechanism. They were the vocalizations of petrifying terror.

A floorboard creaked.

His whimpering halted, momentarily. A floorboard had creaked, but he had been stone-immobile. He listened, the blood pounding in his ears. A slight rasp, as of shoe sole against bare floor. It came from over his head.

He was not alone in the house.

(And why should he have thought he was? Every other building in this town seemed to be stinking with Nazi troops; why should he think this one was a sanctuary for lost Iowans?)

He could not move. The paralysis he felt at being trapped in the dark. It left him unable to function. He was shaking. Shivering. And the sound came again from above him. One man. . .two. . .a patrol. . .a barracks-full. . .he wanted to run. . .

The footsteps came again, gently. He sat in the middle of the room, looking up, the weight of the M-1 unfelt in his hands, and he could not protect himself. If there had been a sliver of light, a gleam, anything, he might have been able to pull himself together. . .but there was nothing. If there were windows in that room, they were boarded or bricked up. If there had been a smoldering sun dying on the horizon, it might have cast rays through the slats of the door, but (how long had he been there, remembering?) the sun had vanished and taken with it the day. Now it was night. Outside. Inside. Within his mind. He was alone with that other. Up there, in the dark.

Sound. Again. The other was coming for him. One? Two? How many? It had to be only one—he wrenched his mind forcibly from his terror to consider the logistics of the situation—and he was coming downstairs.

The one upstairs *had* to know he was here. The noise Arnie had made coming through the locked door would have given him all the warning he'd needed. But time had elapsed, and Arnie had made no sound, until he had begun whimpering, and the one (two, nine, nine hundred?) upstairs had waited, trying to ascertain how many had come through that door. Now the waiting was over, it was ended, and the stalking had begun.

The footsteps (yes, now he could tell, it was only one moving; perhaps there were more up there, but only one was moving toward him) reached the head of the stairs, lost to Arnie's right in the darkness. They began moving down, and there was the clank of metal on wood. The weapon striking the banister. Arnie tried to move his fingers, found them cold and unresponsive. He had to get under cover, not just sit there like a child in the middle of a playpen. He was sure meat, a lamb staked out for some hungry beast.

The footsteps descended, and Arnie could not even tell if the man was in sight. It was that dark. Or was most of the darkness behind his eyes, not really in the room? Had he gone blind again? Could the German see everything? He sat there waiting, and the steps came nearer, nearer, stopped.

A snap-bolt was thrown. It made a hard, unyielding sound in the room. Then there was a chuckle.

The burp-gun opened up at waist-level and slugs marched across the room in a straight line. Back and forth. The spray was a thorough one. It bit chunks out of the wooden walls, thundered into the door, sent flakes of wallpaper and debris cascading through the air. The German turned left and right in stately maneuver, cutting the room in half at the height any normal man would be standing. The fusillade seemed to go on indefinitely, and the crimson-flash of the muzzle brought a glare that revealed who was firing. Arnie stared across the room as the bullets snarled over his head. He did not move. He *could not* move. And as the trooper brought his burp-gun back and forth methodically, the muzzle flash showed Arnie a thickheaded, saturnine man with the top of his skull crammed tightly into a steel helmet, the pot down almost to the thick, unattractive eyebrows. The Nazi was grinning impishly. Chuckling. While the slugs thrummed and screamed overhead harmlessly.

Abruptly, the last slug tore through the wall of the house, and the last casing hit the bottom step on which the Nazi stood, and the room went silent. A sprinkle of plaster-dust made a fine, sifting noise. But it was silent. And dark again.

The rifle shot was a million times louder than anything ever heard in the world before. It had been silent, then the silence had been torn to shreds with a burp-gun's depredations, then silence again. And now the rifle shot.

The Nazi choked once; there was a watery gurgle as if someone had forgotten to turn a faucet off tightly, and with a metallic clatter of equipment and body, he fell forward, caught the edge of the banister and was whirled sidewise, tumbled the one step to the floor, and fell flat on his stomach.

Arnie suddenly realized he could feel the bucking of the M-1 in his hands, moments after the recoil had faded. He had killed the Nazi. Somehow. Without trying. Instinct, perhaps. Maybe it was someone else entirely. A reflex.

"Jeezus," he murmured, gently. The body at the foot of the stairs moved softly. Arnie got to his feet and blindly stumbled toward the sound. His right boot met an obstacle, and he reached down into that pit of shadow to touch the body. His hand encountered the face. His fingertip brushed an open eye. It was not moist. Curious. It was dry. Dead, this man was dead.

Click! Just that exactly, a switch of thought was turned off in Arnie Winslow's mind, and all his mouth-gagging fear came to asphyxiating proportions; the darkness built into a massive wave that swept over him; the wide-eyed shivering he had done as the hundreds of burp-gun slugs thundered just over his head; the death of this stranger; all built into an electrical current that turned off the switch; and the hammer that had been poised in his mind—suddenly struck!

Arnie Winslow fell forward across the body of the dead Nazi, unconscious. Blissfully, thankgod unconscious. His teeth were so tightly clenched, the enamel of one incisor chipped.

When he came up from the depths, breast-stroking with all his strength, he came awake in pieces. First his hands that held the rifle—under him, resting on something soft—and he tried to move them. They were under him. They would not move. But the soft something moved, it gave with the pressure. Then his legs, which bent at the knees, and he slid off the Nazi to the floor. Then his heart and his lungs and his chest, all went pumping back into action. Then his head. But his eyes remained dead. It was still dark all around him. But the fear had become a new creature, with new attributes; it had metamorphosed, and the paralysis was gone. He could move well enough—which he proved by standing up, supporting himself on the rifle and the banister which brushed him, which he grabbed—but he was trembling uncontrollably. He was locked in the hideous embrace of a twitching that threatened to shake his body apart. His head ached terribly. His mouth was dry, and it hurt.

The sound of rifle-fire from outside brought him to sudden awareness that nothing had changed. Truck and the others were still pinned down in that goddam warehouse, and the Krauts were intent on filling the building with corpses.

He knew there was nothing he could do, personally, to take the heat off them. Too many Germans. His only thought was of getting back to the lines, letting the main force know Bain-de-Bretagne was a deathtrap, and trying to send back a larger force to pry the patrol out of their bind. He thought of all this haphazardly, with stops and starts in his processes for the fear that gnawed at him. And all of it was afterthought. His first thought was: *It'll be lighter outside.*

Of such stuff are heroes made.

But when he had found his way back to the front door, and stuck his head out, a sense of impending doom had warned him and he had ducked back in just as a burst of automatic fire whined across the doorway. His friend in the bell-tower had taken no coffee breaks. He slammed the door. And was alone in the hole of black. The fear slammed him once more. Visions dark and terrible came and went. He was in the dark. The blind bird, the blind blind bird!

In a gesture he had long since stopped using, his fist went to his mouth. The child habit, back again. The man a child once more. *Help me. . .*

He began searching the house for other exits. There were no other doors. It was a town house, backed on three sides by the rear walls of other homes. The windows were bricked up. There was no skylight. The street was a cemetery waiting to receive his bones.

He lit a match. It was all the good and warm and fine and golden in the universe. His tongue came out of his mouth in pleasure at the sight of it, flickering there in his hand. He had not thought of it before, why, he didn't know. But here it was and here he was, and the light was all around him, washing him, laving him, reassuring him, and. . .he burned his fingers. He dropped the match and it went out.

There were three more in the folder. He wanted to light them all, all at once, and start a bonfire that would drive away the fears and the sharp-fanged things that lived in his fears of the dark. But that was insane. He struck another, brightly, quickly.

(And he suddenly realized he *was* just a bit mad.) The match burned out. . .

At which point he saw the metal ring in the floor, attached to the trapdoor. Trapdoor, basement, drainpipe, sewer, river, outlet, freedom, the American lines, freedom, light light light! A Chinese box within a box within a box within a great fog of darkness. He lit another match, and slinging the rifle across his back, he pulled the trapdoor ring. The huge wooden slab came up heavily, and he let it fall back with a crash. The pit opened before him. Darker than the darkness above. Most black of all hells. Infernally devoid of the slightest hint of light. That basement. There could be. . *.anything*. . .down there.

He stumbled back, the fear a great clot in his brain.

Black!

Black!

Oh, God how black! He could never go down there, could never never go down there! Madness waited, the fears of his childhood, damn you damn you, damn you the one I called "she," damn you!

Trembling!

Stumbling!

Incapable of halting himself, he stepped forward, his foot encountered emptiness and with a shriek he fell into the hole. He hit the stairs five times on his way to the bottom, and brought up short lying tangled, crying like an infant, at the bottom of the flight. He was down there in the pit. He was alone at the bottom. Silence. Darkness. Fearful empty!

He lay there for moments without duration, hours without relation to time, centuries ripped whole from the fabric of forever. He lay there, and knew this was the way it was going to be. There was no other way, so this was the way it would finally be. He listened.

Silence.

But the sound of water. Young fears came to join their elders. Water. The sewers ran under this house, under those streets, under this town, and down in those sewers he could find a way out, a way back. If he could become human enough to try it. But he was not a human, he was something named Arnie Winslow, six years old, maybe seven, and deathly afraid of the horrors that lurked in basements. He was crying. Tears burned his eyes, red burned, and ran down his cheeks, over his lips so he could taste the shame of them, and he was a boy of six, seven once more. He was a boy playing soldier, and as for those men in that warehouse, their names were already engraved on headstones. Because Arnie Winslow was not going down into the sewers. Oh, God, the very thought made his flesh pucker and wilt. The sewers.

The rattle of machine guns came distantly, down the stairwell. He could hear them dying. He could hear their bones decaying, their flesh rotting, the maggots eating their vitals. He could know what it was, and it meant nothing.

Given the choice of heroism and sanity, there is no man so brave that he will willingly plunge into death or madness. Heroes are made on the instant; quick men, who don't understand that the darkness always waits to swallow them. They are men unlike Arnie Winslow, lying at the bottom of the flight of stairs, dumped in sightlessly where monsters of the mind sit poised ready to spring, to feast on flesh of the soul.

He began scrabbling across the floor, toward the sound of the water. Fear was the Old Man of the Sea, riding him with hideous cackles and an unbreakable promise of death.

Time. . .does it crawl, too? Perhaps.

He found the lid of the water drain, and it was large enough to slip down through. It should have been too small, it should have been a tiny hole allowing only cellar water to escape; it should have been bolted shut by a large grille, it should have been a false entrance. It should have been, he wanted it to be. But it was large enough to allow him entrance without discomfort. Bodily discomfort. It should not have been so eager to swallow him. But it smiled and opened its maw, and he went down, and hung there above nothing, the rifle heavy across his shoulders, and fingertips left the edge of stone floor, and he dropped. It was less than two feet, but he fell for an eternity, and when he hit the water he screamed.

The knives slashed at his legs, and the cold steel pierced his tender six-, seven-year-old flesh and he screamed. It was a high, whining wail, carrying in its tone the erosive Doppler Effect of a train whistle whipping away into the night. Into this dreadful night that surrounded him. Waaaaaaaaaaa!

He crashed against the wall of the sewer main, and fell away from it as if it were molten. He tried to run, but the water had guillotined his coordination. He bumbled forward, and tried to find the matches in his pocket and got them out and just as simply dropped them. They were gone in an instant.

Now was forever down here.

He tried to walk forward, his hands out before him.

But it was no good. He was incapable of motion that made any sense. He was lost now. Out of the world and out of the light and doomed to rot down here in the filthy water that smelled of brackish remains. Urine, decaying vegetation, muck, sickly sweet smells of marshmallow and jacaranda that made his throat wheeze with the effort to keep the vomit down. The smell beat at him, and intermingled with the cold of the water, the flow of the stream, the darkness the ungodly all-pervasive darkness.

One foot moved out in front, then another slipping movement of the same foot in the mire under the water, then the other foot, and he was going. The tunnel sloped sharply downward, and the water climbed higher up his body. It lapped at his thighs, his groin, his waist, chest, shoulders, and suddenly the slope was too much for him, and he was slipping. The slime covering the bottom of the tunnel was thicker, slipperier, and before he could stop himself, he was moving forward against his own speed, and in an instant he'd lost balance. His arms flailed wildly, and he barely managed to get the M-1 over his head before he went under. He was struggling in a grotesque wet world, with grabless holds on nothing. He hand-over-handed to the surface, soaking the rifle in the process, and went under again. Garbage filled his mouth, and he was sick immediately, the weight of it ripping loose in his chest and thundering up into his mouth, just as he broke the surface. The drain was fouled a bit more by his own refuse, and then he was under again. Water filled his nose, his mouth, and he sputtered, gasped fighting to stay erect. The foul scummy water swirled around him, and he grew hysterical trying to free himself.

Then, in a moment, his feet touched bottom once more, and he came up. His head swam with the pounding ache of having vomited, and the smell that would not quit. He moved forward again, then paused as he thought he heard a sound.

Listening, ear cocked into the darkness. . .

Rasping little voices. Hundreds of little voices. The ones who lived here. He could hear their chittering metallic voices. They were all around him, up ahead, behind. Then something slick and wet and fast glided past him in the dark, and touched his hand. His mouth flew open and air bellowed up in his throat, and he screamed. So loud his ears popped, so long his throat went raw, so completely that he was left standing there empty of all but terror. The thing had giggled tinnily as it had passed him. Taunting him.

He wanted to flee, but there was no way out, no way to go but on. And then he heard the roar of a vehicle going overhead, and he knew he was under the street, and if he could hear them. . .could they not hear him?

He knew he could not howl again.

It had to be dammed up inside.

No escape valve.

So he moved forward. Pace after murky pace. His feet weighed half a ton each with the mud and clinging tendrils of nameless slimy things that clung to his barracks boots. But he moved on. He was incapable of thinking *why* he was moving forward, and the *how* was an enigma he would never solve.

But he went on, and it was a nightmare without end. It was forever wet and forever cold and forever dark, and he knew for certain that he would be in that stinking chill limbo forever and ever and ever.

And the voices all around him. He could not even see their eyes in the dark, but they were there. And then one of them landed with a heavy *plop!* on his shoulder.

He froze. Not voluntarily. He was smashed in the face by a numbing chunk of steel, and all movement left him. But he was not limp. He was brick-rigid. He could not move, could not even twitch, his body was frozen solid. The water rat moved idly about his shoulder, its thick, massive body a weight that bent him slightly. Its tail lashed at his shirt as its vile length hung down his back. The bullet-pointed face moved nearer Arnie's cheek, and he could feel the icy wire of its whiskers. The stench from it was incredible. It smelled like a thousand corpses rotting in a mass grave. The creature came nearer Arnie's face, and the fur was matted, stinking. Arnie could not have brushed the water rat off if he had had a thousand hands. The beast had its way. It was master of this nice, fine dry island.

Then, its head came up sharply, and it sniffed at Arnie's face. And it poised itself, as though to strike at something, but the whine wail shriek moan stopped it. The huge rat listened for a moment, as the shriek grew in intensity, and as it mounted to fill the cavern, the rat leaped high and arched out, disappearing in terror, into the water, and gone.

Arnie had no idea what the sound had been, but he was eternally grateful for its having come at that precise moment of absolute terror. But he never knew what it had been.

He hurried on down the tunnel, leaving his sound of fear where it had saved him.

There was more. Much more. Through miles of drainage sewer, among the floating schools of rats whose voices mingled so high he was deafened. Slipping and drinking the scum-clouded water. And always in darkness, always pounded by his fear that had grown to such proportions an entire section of his brain was closed off, numbed by the constant electrical level of horror and nausea.

Then he came to a tunnel-end, and he could hear the water rush to plunge over a precipice. It was a brief drop, but it was sufficient to tell him he'd found an outlet. When he came to the end of the passage, he found a huge metal grille, partially rusted, and in a frenzy of desperation he slammed it again and again with his hip, his shoulders, his back, till it broke away and dropped out.

He fell, gasping, into the murky stream, went under, came up and struck off spastically for the opposite side. When his feet could touch bottom, he dragged himself erect and hauled one foot after another, till he bumped against the far bank, and hauling himself like a sack of soaked meal, he fell face forward onto the thankgod ground. It was moist and cool, and he blessed it, blessed it, kissed the earth with his garbage-tainted lips.

There was more. Much more.

A sprint through a forest, crashing into trees, falling a hundred times, running full tilt into a thick limb that caught him full in the mouth and knocked him unconscious. When he came back to consciousness, his mouth was full of blood and two teeth had been shattered. His face felt like a pound of dogmeat. He stumbled erect, walked into the limb a second time, felt his head reverberate like a church bell and managed somehow to go on.

There was more. Much more. A crawl across a shelled no-man's-land littered with dead trucks and dead weapons and softer things that were attached to nothing at all. And once, yes, he was sure of it, once he heard a voice calling out to him in the darkness, "Help me. . .help me. . .I'm. . .where are m-my arms. . .help me. . ." but the voice was too much like no other voice he'd ever heard (he told himself) and he crawled on.

More. Into a mine field. He knew it was a mine field because the entrance to it was guarded by what had been a man. The left half of his face had been pushed in as though it were a paper cup, and in his outstretched hand, still clenched in the manner prescribed by the manual, was his bayonet, that he had been using to probe the ground for antipersonnel mines. It had probed too deeply, and now the hand would seek no more. The body with the pushed-in face was not too far from the hand for Arnie to know this was a mine field.

So he slid forward cautiously on his belly, probing with his own bayonet as the pushed-face Cerberus guarding the field had done. Somehow, he slid through. Darkness. All around.

And then, without his even realizing he had done it, he saw a body looming up out of the darkness, and he was crying again, letting it all out, holding nothing back, crying like the child inside all men. It was a sentry, and so pathetic were MSgt. Arnott T. Winslow's sobs that he never bothered to challenge him. He merely went forward and helped him to his feet. There could be no danger in an enemy who sounded like that.

He was in a company area, he didn't know which one, and someone said, "Hey, fellah, can you open your eyes?" and he realized he had crawled all the way from that sewer with his eyes so tightly closed they throbbed with pain. His eyes came unstuck slowly, and he was insane with delight to see a soft pink haze opening the sky like a brilliant blossom. It was daylight. It was rebirth. It was the world once more.

There was a lister bag hanging from a tripod, and he stumbled forward, managed to slump to his knees before it, and drank thirstily from the tap. They watched him, wondering what horrors had turned this man into little more than an animal. He could never tell them, they could never know, for perhaps their devils were spiders or snakes or hypodermic needles or some more nameless subliminal terror they would never have to face, if they were very very lucky. As lucky as Arnie Winslow had been *un*lucky.

It was not till much later, when the doctor had shaken his head and marveled at the stamina of this man who had crawled God only knew how far, to return to his own lines. With a broken jaw, with two teeth missing, with staved-in rib cage, with thousands of minor cuts, abrasions, holes in his flesh and loss of blood, with extreme shock shaking him like a high-tension wire in a hurricane, with exposure and loss of control of his hands. This was a remarkable creature, this creature the dog tags called MSgt. Arnott T. Winslow, US51403352.

And when the interrogation officer came to him in the field hospital, lying twitching and wide-eyed (as though he wanted to miss nothing of what went on in the light of day), only then did he remember why he had crawled all this way.

Truck and the patrol.

He told the G-2 and the man went away, and a while later he came back with another officer and they said things to Arnie Winslow.

"We don't have very accurate intelligence on that area."

"We're an advance spear of the front. We'd need at least a regiment out there. . ."

"Or a guide who could take us back the way you came."

Booming echoes of what they were saying cascaded back and forth in his skull. He could not believe he was hearing them correctly. All the pain and fear had been for nothing.

"Or at least a guide who knew the way. But we can't start till tonight. They'd shell our asses to bits if we tried it in daylight."

Arnie heard himself saying, "I'll take you back."

Through the darkness again. All the way back. Through the horror of the pit a second time.

The doctor interrupted. "This man isn't going anywhere. He's suffering from shock and three broken ribs and more minor afflictions than I have time to list. He's staying right here."

"I'll take you back. . ."

"Will he be able to travel by tonight, Doc?'"

"I strongly advise against it."

"I'll take you. . .I can do it. . ."

And they left him there, to sleep through the day, to give his mind and his body what little peace they could gather for the long night ahead.

Arnie Winslow closed his eyes and slept. He slept and dreamed of blind birds, aimless in a sullen sky. But he was able to help the flight now. It was not necessary to rid himself of fear, if he could merely learn to exist, to function *with* the fear.

He was still frightened, but he slept. There would always be the daylight.

—Hollywood, 1963

PASSPORT

His old man was drunk again. He was always that way, and Billy wondered why his Maw kept letting the old souse come back each time. It must be because of the old man's music; that was something nobody could resist.

Billy Wald stood in the corner of the room, his ten-year-old fingers lightly touching the peeling stucco of the wall, feeling the steady beat of the New Orleans day around him.

"An' when I come aroun', I wanna *find* ya here, not out cattin' round the streets with some other goddam. . ." The man's whiskey breath filled Billy's head with fumes, making the room seem indistinct, wavering. Billy Wald's father, a prune-faced man with eyes that were flaming rivets, stared balefully at the woman he had never married. The words dried up in his mouth, and as though it were compensation, his fist snaked out.

It caught the brown-haired woman below the eye, sent her back across the room, toppling the ironing board, sending the old cast-lead iron and its warming pan clattering to the floorboards. "And *that*. . .that, by God'll teach ya."

Billy felt the first strike. Felt the pain in his own young body, felt the blood quicken and the hatred boil up like swamp mud in a sinkhole. In a movement he was fastened to the thin man's leg, his teeth clenched through the filthy material of the pants.

A bellow of rage escaped the man, and his arm whipped over, and back, and down, like the roller coaster at the Park, and caught Billy across the back of the head.

Billy's lank brown hair flew up at the force of the strike, and the boy tumbled backward, brought up short against the wall, his eyes smarting, a throb drumming behind his ears.

The tall, thin—almost ghostlike—man stood gasping in the center of the room, his brown breath coming jaggedly through cracked lips. His eyes were wild, and his face was dense with the coarse stubble of a week's beard. He smelled of the New Orleans streets, and his shoes were heelless.

Why does Maw take him back all the time? The thought pounded round and round the track of the boy's mind.

"Stay 'way from me, ya little bastard, or I'll kick in your goddam bastard teeth!"

Bastard. Bastard. That was what the kids down in the lot called him. *Bastard.* That's what they said: Your old lady ain't married, and your old man stinks like old dead catfish been rottin' in the sun, and they toss him out inna gutter inna morning, cause he smells like piss on the floor. You're a bastard, bastard, bastard, and no real old man, just a wino, wino, wino! *That* was what they said, and he didn't know what it meant. Did it mean that his father never slept at home. . .except once in a while? Did it mean he didn't have the same last name as his father? His father's name was Joe Privalorio; but *his* name was Billy Wald. Was that what it meant? He wanted to know so badly. . .

His Maw was standing near the cupboard, her hand oddly steepled beneath her swollen eye. She watched the man who was his father by deed only, and Billy saw the fires of depthless hate swirl and mount and burn in her face. And they were mirrored in his own.

Then, and he knew it would happen just like this—because it *always* happened just like this, each time his father came back, came back drunk—the tired-faced, thin man went to the cupboard—shoving the woman away with a jab—and opened it.

Billy knew every movement, every action. And this was the good part.

This was the thing that made Maw let the old man keep coming around. This was the thing in his stomach that tickled and pounced and popped like hot soapsuds. This was the music that was coming. Joe Privalorio—some made fun and called him Provolone, some made it up that he was Mormon, from Utah, and they called him Provo—took down the battered, warped-bell cornet, the Three-Star, three-valve cornet, and without pucker or wetting of lips, put it to his mouth.

And then it started. . .

. . .ohGod then it started. . .

. . .and down in the streets jackhammer operators stopped work. . .

. . .and the pigeons shut up in the eaves. . .

. . .and the drunks sat up smiling in the gutters. . .

. . .and all the mouth organ punkeys stopped dancing and blowing their harmonicas for dimes on the sidewalk. . .

. . .and all the whores in their cribs stopped humping. . .

. . .and all New Orleans that could hear, well, they listened.

Because that was Slow Daddy Privalorio, old Provolone cheese, doing the only thing that kept him from being kicked to death by an irate saloonkeeper. Doing the only thing that kept him out of jail. Doing the only thing that made the woman he'd knocked up look at him again.

Doing the only thing that kept his son-in-deed-only from killing him.

He made some excellent music with a voice that spoke many languages.

Love and death. They're the cheapest things to a music man. They come and they go so fast, you'd think they wore roller-skates. (That's what his sounds said.)

That's the *real* music men. The men with it down low somewhere, just waiting till they take a stick in their hands, or put a horn to their lips. . .just waiting. Just waiting to bubble up like hot oil and spill out, and cover everything nicely. (That's what his sounds said.)

That's the real music men, the ones who feel it, and don't you know

I feel it, and don't you hear those winds blowing strong and spicy from the South, across my head, and down to my feet? Don't you feel the Earth tremble and the ground split, and everybody want to lie down and lock together? (*That's* what his sounds said.)

Billy Wald lay there in the angle of walls, watching, watching, powerfully watching—knowing this was what kept the world from crushing his old man to the pulp he should have been.

And before he knew what the word was, or what it could mean, he knew what that talent for musicing was to his old man. If he'd been older, he would have said it like this:

That's the only thing keeps him alive. It's the thing makes him a man and not a gobbet of human shit. It's the thing that makes him a man to my Maw, and to the people he mooches off. It's the only thing that gets him in anywhere.

That music. . .it's his passport.

He couldn't say it, but he knew it. He knew it right off, and the horn wasn't horn any more. It wasn't horn a bit. It was passport. To Billy Wald, horn was a sign of keeping that spicy world outside, off him. Off the music, off him. It was the ticket to being a man.

I know what it is, he might have said. *It's passport*.

And he watched the gobbet of human shit that was his father blow that horn till late into the night. Billy's Maw didn't move much, except to bring him some tomato bisque soup and crackers, and to give Daddy Joe a moist cloth to wipe away the sweat.

It grew slowly, the realization that the horn was the passport. It grew so slow, so soft, so slinky, that he was blowing it strong and hard before he knew it was going to be his life's work.

When he was seventeen, he left home. He couldn't stand it any more, with his Maw wrinkling, and shrinking, and breaking down slowly like a machine with worn-out parts. With his old man coming in one, two times a week, just for the bedroom. And beating her up, kicking him around. He just couldn't take it.

Mostly because he didn't know why he *did* take it.

He was tiny, and thin, and pale, but he was big enough to knock the crap out of Joe Privalorio; but he just couldn't. He'd make a fist and want to use it. . .but he couldn't hit the old man. He took a look, and he took a listen, and all he could hear was that music, far off and getting nearer.

So he went away; because that was the other side of putting up with it.

And after a while he found working on construction gangs broke his bones and broke his spirit; working the short-order grill made him sweat like a field hand, without even the pleasure of working in the sun, made him always stink of steam table grease. . .and he started to go to sloppy fat on his own bad food; and the turns driving a hack were just plain nerve-wracking, because nobody treated a cabdriver like a fellow human. So, he started with the horn.

He bought a battered-bell Three-Star out of the fly-specked window of a funky hock shop in Metairie. He didn't realize it, but it was exactly like Slow Daddy Joe's horn. He picked up three sidemen: one in Kansas City (a pure black guy with bad teeth, worse gums, and bewitched fingers) name of Jack Haddass Smith, who slumped over the piano as though round-shouldered, but whose rotten posture did not slow down his ten thousand hands; one in Van Buren, Indiana. . .an anti-Semitic Jew named Solly Gearhardt who was little, and dark and clever as hell with a walking bass, but who hated himself worse than any stalag commandant; one in Syracuse, New York. . .out of a gutter with his snare drum wrapped around his crewcut head, and a restaurant owner standing fists-on-hips above him, saying, "Your music's good, Carpenter, but I don't like your sass! And I don't like you likin' my wife!" That was Cappy Carpenter, the "capstone" they needed for the combo.

With those three, Billy tagged on the name "Billy Wald's Blue Notes" and they started making music.

That year—1949—the Army had it with Billy. He was 4F; bad eyes. Real bad. From getting slapped around a lot. So fucked-up that some nights he had to lean down to Cappy, in some smoky joint, and nudge the drummer in the neck.

"Hey, Cap, old trooper, there anything good out there?"

And Cappy would searchbeam the room, and give him back out of the corner of his mouth, "Man, there's a sophomore co-ed out there, table three, with a stack as high as Babel, and hair red-hot, like it was poured out of your horn."

Billy's eyes were bad, but his music was good. They worked and they worked steady. There was always a spot for them and they never once had to split the group or work a second job.

They never made the Astor Roof, but there were a few record sessions, some plush night spots, and a concert or two. The name Billy Wald was getting known.

"I tell you, Billy, we got a chance to be big. Really big. This A & R guy from Decca was down again last night, and *you* was here like the rest of us. *You* heard him!" Cappy Carpenter smacked a big wedge of hand across his blonde crewcut.

"No," Billy said, looking down at the horn, not looking at them at all. "No.

"There ain't gonna be no progressive stuff in this combo. We ain't ready yet." Outside the dressing room, sounds of the early dinner crowd filled the club.

Cappy slammed around the room, banging his fists into the dresser, the door, the walls, the chair. "Whattaya mean not ready?! For chrissakes, Billy, those last sides we cut were just on the border. We can't go on playin' Dixie all our life! There ain't no future. . ."

"No!" Billy shouted, looking up for an instant, then returning his glance to his lap and the horn.

Jack Haddass Smith sat up on the dirty bunk. He had been leaning against the wall, a cigarette growing shorter between his lips, his left eye closed against the sting of the smoke. "Billy," he said softly, as though afraid his voice might frighten. "Billy, I hate to admit it, brother, but I think Cap is right.

"Billy, everybody got to grow. They got to *change*, and if they don't. . ." He looked down, and dropped the cigarette butt down, and stepped on it.

Billy stood, his back to them, walked to the dirty back window, and scraped the size of a silver dollar clear with his fingernail. He stared out into the alleys, just thinking.

Solly Gearhardt scratched under his nose, and coughed.

He had a slight accent, middle-European, and unidentifiable. "Bill. I got to pudt in vit Jack an' Cappy. I tink we're long overdue. We could be makin' bedder money. . .bedder music. . .bedder every tingk. I—I've been meanin' to say sometingk to you about it for a long. . ." He mumbled to a stop, embarrassed.

Billy Wald stood at the window, staring at nothing, and they could hear his fingers drumming on the sill. "Not now," he said quietly. "Not now. Later, we'll talk. Later on when I can think, when I can figure out—"

Cappy exploded. "Shit, man! You're *always* stalling. What the fuck is it with you, Billy? Anything else, you're quick to jump, quick to take a risk, but this. . .you back off and piss'n'moan and sound like either a cranky fuckin' baby or a tired old horse's ass of an old fart! You. . .oh *shit!*"

He picked his sticks from the dressing table and stormed out of the dressing room, slamming the door. A minute later they heard the tentative practice paradiddles on the traps out front.

The other two sidemen looked at each other, realized they would get nowhere bracing him further, and vacated the dressing room quietly.

Billy turned away from the window, walked carelessly around the room, touching this, touching that, aimlessly. He sat down on the bunk, picked up the Three-Star, and stared at it. They had been playing Tony Hadley's Crescendo Casino for a week now, and the horn had never sounded better. Funny how an old cornet like that still had so much muscle.

It wasn't one of the modern three-valve snoot-jobs that blow sweet, and blow mellow, and don't have any zatz, or one of the screwloose jobs like Diz blows, aimed at the sky, or any of that sort of bizarre Pakistanian pocket trumpet. It was a real old-time Three-Star cornet, whirly and twirly, and battered like Bix's had been.

It had a dent in the bell that looked as if a Cro-Magnon had used it to bash in a skull. The valves stuck, no matter how much he greased them. The mouthpiece was black and stained. It looked exactly the way Slow Daddy Joe's cornet had looked, oh so long, long ago when the world was dim and softly-rounded, the way a child sees it. And full of hurt and loneliness, the way a child sees it.

Billy jerked to awareness, as though he had been asleep, and found he was running the ball of his thumb over the curve of the bell. He grinned lopsidedly, pushed his heavy horn-rims up the bridge of his nose with the same thumb, and got to his feet. He expelled a long sigh, that somehow ended with the word, "Sheee-zusss." He went out front.

It was the early show. Late January, and the crowds all seemed to be pink-cheeked and chilly as they huddled around their tables. The combo had eaten before they went into the first set, and Solly was complaining about a sour stomach as Billy climbed to the bandstand. "Oooh, whadt dee hell day godt in dose meatballs?" he was saying. "All I had was meatballs and spaghett. Day must of made dem with groun' glass fillin'."

Jack Haddass Smith looked up from the piano, a toothpick sticking out between the ugly baked beans of his teeth. He grinned. "Yeah, man, the onlyest trouble is—you had twelve them balls. That's 'nough to grind anybody."

Solly made a half-feint toward him with the stem of the bass and Jack ducked away, grinning. He let his big, square fingers flee across the keys and they all recognized it as the first few measures of "Skylark," done Billy's way. With a shape like the way Jackie Paris had done it.

Billy came up then, and he wasn't wearing his usual smile. The discussion in the dressing room was eating on him, and they could see it.

"Take it solo for ten, Jack."

Mr. Smith gave him a waggled two-fingers of agreement, and they swung into it. The audience was Christmas-residue unresponsive, but they didn't mind. They played as much for themselves as for the listeners at the tables.

Jack Haddass Smith beat off the initial melody, and set up the measures for the other three. Then Billy and Cappy came in together, the drums rat-tat-tatting solidly behind the Dixie wail of the Three-Star. Billy was short, but his torso was long, and when he hunched over the horn, talking to it, it seemed he was almost crippled. "Skylark" was a ballad, but they did it up-tempo.

His eyes were blue behind the thick horn-rims, and his hair was black. His nose was skewed off in the direction of Pittsburgh, and he wore a sport shirt open at the neck under his jacket. His hands seemed almost like those of a newborn baby's, soft and pink. That was Billy Wald, and it didn't matter what he looked like. Once he started playing.

The evening was no longer than most, no shorter than others. They played their set, and took their breaks, and no one in the combo again mentioned the change of style. No one bugged Billy. He sat on the stand steps, his arms holding the cornet down between his legs; he was thinking.

The final set. One-thirty, and the place was jammed and dimmed and the spots focused on the combo rattling out their noisy Dixie melodies. They swung off on "Royal Garden Blues," doubled back through "Chains, Chains, Chains," and took a whack at one of Billy's strangely titled originals. It was a solid old-style Memphis blues number, which Billy had titled (in progressive tone) "Through Melancholia, with Drum and Camera." They were halfway through the number, Solly running his snaking fingers up and down the bass, slapping it with a palm, twanging it like sixty, when an old man staggered into the joint. What were the odds. Yeah, right.

How he got in, even the owner, Tony Hadley, on the door, couldn't say. But somehow he slipped in when no one was watching. One moment the cleared dancing space on the floor was empty, and the next minute this funky old man was in the middle of it.

The spots on the combo washed the floor a bit, and there he was. . .clear as a bad dream. He was tall, but he looked like they'd decided to just stretch a little skin over the bones—not bother with fleshing him out. His hair was dirty gray, and spilling down his shoulders like an untalented amateur's scarecrow. His eyes were so black, and so deepset, he looked like a mugger had thumbed out the eyesockets, leaving only shadows.

His mouth worked at gumming a sentence, lips dry and thin; and he almost got a word out.

Billy Wald stopped blowing. It was, of course, because there are no good playwrights left in the world, Joe Privalorio. Fresh in from out of nowhere.

"Through Melancholia" died away as though it was ashamed to have been in the way while Billy yelled. And the sidemen stared at the old man. He was standing in the middle of the floor, weaving, tottering, almost ready to fall. Stinking drunk. What are the odds.

"Think ya smart up there, doncha?"

Nobody in the joint snagged a breath. Dinner dishes and forks stopped clattering. The music went far away, because it knew what was coming. But no one else knew.

"Think ya smart, doncha, ya little bastard. . ."

The bouncers came out of the kitchen, and started to muscle him down. Billy stepped quickly to the front of the platform, motioned them off. The old man staggered full into the spotlight, and Billy could see he was only halfway to dead. It was more than drink, much more. Truly going to die extremely soon. He had the old vegetable soup smell of death on him.

"Wald ya calls yaself! Billy *Wald*, ya gutterlittlebastard! Laid ya ole lady in the back room of the Mission Street Bar. . .Bar 'n' Grill n' you gotta be a li'l bastard with a name come on like Billy Wald!"

There was never anything like that in the whole world. Billy's hand turned white and trembly on the Three-Star, and when the stinking old rumpot started calling his Maw those names, he wanted to tear the old man's liver out and make him choke on it. But he stayed put, because he knew what was happening. And he felt *good* watching the old cocksucker dying, right there in the middle of the dance floor.

"Think ya can blow a horn, d'ya? Here, lemme show ya. . .I was the greatest horn man ever blew outta N'Walins. Gimme!"

He staggered to the podium, grabbed the Three-Star from Billy's shaking hand, pulled loose the mouthpiece, blew out the spit, and stood there. Just stood, half gone away in another world, with his legs apart, and his old back arched, and the pop of the mouthpiece slipped back in, and then the horn to his lips, and Billy didn't make a sound.

Billy didn't make a move.

Billy just stared, watching the old man die. Fuck'im! Croak, you old bastard sonofabitch!

No one thought the old man could do it. They waited to be embarrassed. But he pursed his gray, gray lips; and out it came.

Speaking many languages. Out it came. The first three notes were so goddamned familiar, Cappy had to look around, to make certain someone wasn't playing a record, or slipped Billy a new horn. . .

. . .because that was *Billy* blowing! All the way from the gut, that was Billy Wald.

Then they knew where Billy had gotten the talent, left there by some old rumdum. If this was Billy's old man—and they guessed it was, then there was no secret any more, where Billy had picked it up.

He was his old man's student. Whether he'd ever taken a lesson or not.

The old man played three choruses of "Beale St. Blues" as no one has ever heard it before or since, and even got Solly running his hand across the bass, till Cappy tossed him a look that said *Knock it off, shithead!*

Then he came to a stop, right in the middle of a bridge, and there was drool out of the corner of his mouth. His eyes were rheumy, and he stared at Billy from Hell.

"That's the end! That's all I'll ever play, Mr. Billy *Wald!*" he said. "Just *this!*" And took the sweet Three-Star and cracked it hard across the edge of the platform, denting the bell out of shape, caving the shank, pulling the mouthpiece loose and sending it off under a table.

Then he threw the thing at Billy's feet, staggered back a step or two with a bad laugh, coughed blood all over a guy and a woman at a ringside table, and dropped right on down dead in front of the bandstand, his hand and all its blue veins across Billy's shined brown cordovan shoes.

Billy fainted off the platform, and the bouncers carried both of them out back together. There was something poetic about it. Everybody said so.

In the dressing room he regained consciousness. He sat up, and an instant later he was crying. They all left the room because no one wanted to see that kinda shit happening. No one saw him rise and smash his hand against the metal door of the locker, beat his hands against his head. No one saw him writhe and suffer, and finally come to rest gasping. No one wanted to see that kinda shit.

It was not the work of a minute, nor the work of an hour; it took three hours. Three hours later, when he opened the door, the combo knew something had changed deep inside Billy Wald. As he left the darkness of the back room, he seemed to be a man stepping from an old familiar prison, into a fresh, clean, clear day. Something like that. He looked okay. Maybe. . .well, *refreshed.*

The Casino was dim, the crowds gone, the chairs ass-end up on the table. The three sidemen rose slowly, watching their leader come toward them.

He stopped at one table and stared at the broken metal that had been the Three-Star, the cornet that was exactly like his father's. He stared at it a moment, ran his hand across the ripped instrument, and smiled.

He came toward them, and the streaks of dirt and tears down his cheeks told them what he had gone through.

He stopped before them, and they watched carefully.

"It's all over now," he said.

Cappy Carpenter made a move to take his arm, but Billy shook him away. "It's all through; it's okay. I'm cool, honest. I'm free now. I guess I didn't even know I was tied up inside, but now I'm out of it. I cut it loose."

They smiled at him, and he jerked a thumb at the wreck of the Three-Star.

"Monday, we'll go out and pick me up a new weapon. I'm going to have to get in practice. . .

". . .as long as we're switchin' from Dixie to Progressive."

He smiled back at them, and the ghost drifted up, and up, and up, through the roof of the building, and left the Earth forever. Ugly, drunk, useless and mean, but at least, simply, the fuck *gone*.

The passport had been revoked. Further travel was forbidden.

—*New Orleans, 1956*

I CURSE THE LESSON AND BLESS THE KNOWLEDGE

Okay, if you'll for chrissakes stop leaning over my shoulder, I'll start it again. How the hell do you expect me to write this with you. . .*supervising* the damned thing? Listen, nuisance, one of the reasons I *became* a writer was because I swore I'd never work under someone's beady, watchful eyes ever again.

And here you are, telling me I haven't got it right, that it didn't happen that way at all. This is fiction, dammit, not real life. Fiction *turns* the mirror of reality; slightly, so things are seen in a new way.

That's unfair. I'm not lecturing, I'm merely explaining the way I write so you won't get all bent out of shape if I alter the facts. This isn't *supposed* to be one-for-one. It's supposed to be a story, and that means things will be changed.

Now I'll start it again, and you just shut up and stop *nuhdzing* me. And okay, okay, I won't call you Patti. (But I still think that's a super name for the young woman in the story.) Now. For the third time. I begin.

The first thing Katie ever said to me was, "How much is the school paying you to come here to speak today?"

I said, "Eight hundred dollars."

She looked shocked and awe-stricken for a moment and then said, "That's indecent. *No*body should make eight hundred dollars just for amusing a bunch of imbeciles for an hour and a half."

"I usually get fifteen hundred," I said.

"You're kidding. Just for standing up here and reading a couple of stories you wrote?"

"I've been told I read very well."

"So what? Dylan Thomas read better than you and he died broke."

"And an alcoholic to boot," I said. "Thank God I don't drink."

She started to turn away. The rest of the mob of students pressing in for autographs jammed into the space she'd vacated. I watched her as she walked away. "Hey!" I yelled. She stopped and turned around. She knew I meant her.

"Are you going with, engaged to, pregnant by, or hung up on?"

She thought about it for a moment. The mob ping-ponged their eyes between us, history in the making, before their very faces. "No," she said. "Why?"

"How'd you like to have a cup of coffee with me?"

The guy who had strolled up beside her looked as if he were about to get an enema with a thermite bomb. He started to take her arm, but she smiled and said, "Okay," and his hand never finished the grab.

She sat down in the first row of the empty auditorium and had a heated conversation with the guy who hadn't finished the grab. I tried to catch what they were saying, but the fans were babbling in my face and I've never been able to listen to two things at once. I signed their books as fast as I could—I was afraid she'd disappear—and as the last straggler moved away, fangs finally removed from my throat, charisma leaking out of my body with a soft hiss, I stepped off the stage and walked over to her.

Yes, I *know* I've made you sound cooler and hipper than you were that day. Yes, I *know* you went fumfuh fumfuh a lot. But this makes it sound better. So what if you've never read Dylan Thomas, what does that matter? Will you just sit back and let me get into this bloody thing!

They both stood up. The grabless guy didn't like me a lot; negative vibes hammered at me like the assault of noise made by one of those superpimp blacks in mile-hi platform wedgies who carry Radio Shack transistors with hundred and eighty decibel speakers, who boogie up and down Hollywood Boulevard blasting Kiwanis *schmucks* from Kankakee out of their white socks with the gain up full.

"Mr. Kane," Katie said, indicating the source of the negative emanations, "this is Joey. Joey, this is—"

He knew who I was. He'd sat through my lecture and my readings and had applauded. Until I'd hustled his girl, he'd been a faithful reader of my wonderful prose. I lose more fans that way. He didn't wait for the introduction, just thrust his hand forward and said, "Howdyado."

We shook. Solemnly. On such dumbass grounds as this did Menelaus and Paris get into one hell of a lousy relationship.

Nothing happened for a few seconds. Everyone waited for the Earth to stop jiggling on its axis. As usual, I was the one to move the action. "Well, listen, uh, Joey, it was nice meeting you." I turned to Katie. "Are you ready to go?" She almost gave Joey a look: the muscles in her neck moved slightly: but then she just nodded and said, "Okay." I smiled at Joey, very friendly, very magnanimous, and we walked away from him. I am very grateful blowguns and poisoned darts have never been marketed in this country by Wham-O.

The nameless nuisance in the background tells me I'm lying, and making Joey look like a jerk. That is true. Even though her affair with Joey was at an end at the time we met, she was still fucking him occasionally, and though I like to believe I'm very sophisticated about such things, I was born in 1934, which makes me forty-one, and I spent the greater part of my life as a sexist, not knowing I was doing anything wrong, and though I've had the error of my ways pointed out to me by a number of voluble women infinitely smarter and better-adjusted than myself, I cannot deny that the oink of the beast can occasionally be heard in the velvet tones I now affect. (Like an ex-drunk proselytizing for Alcoholics Anonymous, or a reformed head who's found Jesus, there are few things in this life as dichotomous, neither fish nor fowl, as an apostate male feminist. I try, but it's Fool's Gold, and I despise myself for the hypocrisy.)

Nonetheless, the truth of the matter is that Joey was a very good guy, and he urged her to have the cup of coffee with me. But I still hated him. He'd had his hands on her for two years, and I was jealous. And it's *my* story, dammit!

So we went to Yellowfingers where I ordered with all the aplomb of Gael Greene and Alexis Bespaloff melded into one unisexual gourmet.

"We'll have the spinach and mushroom salad for two, a sausage, cheese and ratatouille crêpe for the lady, and I'd like the fried baby and a cup of warm hair," I said, dimpling prettily. Katie broke up, the waitress stared at me with a charming mixture of nausea and loathing. "Make that a Croque Hawaiian and an iced tea," I said hurriedly. "And what would you like to drink?"

"A Coke."

At that instant I saw the future, "the evening spread out against the sky / Like a patient etherized upon a table." Gray and chill and inevitable. This moment during which I sit here writing it, as it hurtles down on me; I saw it then.

In a few minutes I would discover that Katie was eighteen, and I would discover that I was forty, nearly forty-one, she nearly nineteen, and she didn't even have to tell me how it was going to end. Damn you, Nabokov!

"Bring the lady a Coca-Cola," I said, and knocked my silverware into my lap trying to pull loose the napkin.

(It was *too* like that! Shut up and leave me alone; I feel like shit. Let me write, woman!)

The lunch went well. I snowed her like crazy. I was by turns serious, clever, amusing, controversial, urbane and Huck Finn. Her eyes were mostly green. Sometimes blue. Her hair fell over one side of her forehead in a soft sweep that paralyzed me.

I told her I was putting the make on her. She said, "You are?" She wasn't being coy, she simply didn't know that was what was happening. Lesson one for the old man trying to play grabass with (what the nuisance bitchily calls) "young stuff" (when she's trying to bug me): they don't do it that way these days. They are free—they assure me they're free. They just seem to raise invisible antennae and the libidinous message pulses off them. And in some marvelous, thaumaturgic progression of events without time or measure, like a fast wipe in a Chabrol film, *pow!* there they are in bed together, free and libidinous, everybody orgasming just the way Alex Comfort would have it, no effort, no hangups, no groping and no seduction. In the sweet and amoral world of the children there is no stalking, no hunting, no hustling; just the act, final and total and contained, as Merwin puts it, "one tone both pure and entire floating in the silence of the egg, at the same pitch as the silence."

I have no idea what I was thinking. It had been just another pain-in-the-ass speaking engagement; Price Junior College, an agro school that got confused and wound up with a bedroom-community commuter day-care babysitting population of twenty-five thousand acne-festooned urchins taking dingbat classes in Science Fiction, Artificial Flowers I, Bowling, Inert Gas Welding and Current Events in the Arts (which, so help me, Amen-Ra, turns out to be a course in how to be a good audience). Because it is essentially a free-tuition college for state residents—$6.50 per semester for students carrying 6 units or more, $2.50 for *shmucks* handling under 6 units—it is a refuge for post-puberty illiterates who would better serve the commonweal if they were out planting Ponderosa Pines in an effort to stem the floodtide of concrete threatening to pave over the entire state.

If, from these utterly objective and well-mannered remarks you get the impression that I have very little use for young girls, I am content in the knowledge that I absorbed Lord Alfred Korzybski's theories of General Semantics. I have but *nothing* to say to young girls. They're fine to look at, in the way I would look at a case filled with Shang dynasty glazes, but expecting to carry on a conversation with the average teenaged young lady is akin to reading Voltaire to a cage filled with chimpanzees. I'm certain they would feel the same alienation for me. I can live with that knowledge.

For instance. . .

Yes, I *realize* I'm digressing, nuisance! This is what is called background color. It lends depth to a story; it establishes character, motivation. *Please!* Do you mind?

As I was saying. For instance, one night I had a date with a certifiably mind-blowing, color-coded, lathe-turned, rhodium-plated gorgeous. I picked her up and she was wearing an evening dress that, had Lee Harvey Oswald turned around from his position crouched in front of that window in the Texas Schoolbook Depository, 1940 vintage Italian-made Mannlicher-Carcano in his mitt, and seen it, with her in it, would have burned out the clown's eyeballs and we'd be living in a much better country today. What I'm saying here, if you catch my drift, is that this female was a positive paralyzer.

Visions of sugar plums danced in my steamy gutter of a mind.

We went to The Magic Castle, which is a fornigalactic private club with dining room that specializes in showcasing the craft of the magician. We were carrying our drinks around the many fascinating rooms, and wandered into one where they had an Atwater-Kent setup that was playing tapes of old-time radio. *Amos'n'Andy, Jack Armstrong, Lux Presents Hollywood, Gangbusters*. And above the radio was a glass-fronted cabinet in which reposed half a dozen Captain Midnight secret decoder badges. I began enthusing over the nostalgic wonders of the little plastic-and-metal icons, and only paused in my panegyric when I caught the look of total noncomprehension on the face of my Helen of Troy. "Captain Midnight," I said. "He was on the radio in the Forties, when I was a kid. I used to lie on my stomach and listen to the program. It was sponsored by Ovaltine. I had a map of the Pacific Theatre of Operations on the wall. I used to mark the progress of the war with little maptacks with red heads on them." Absolute bewilderment on her face. "The war in the Pacific. Bataan, Corregidor, Saipan, Palau, Wake Island?" Nothing. "V-J Day?" More nothing. "World War II? It was in all the papers. 1941 through 1945."

She looked at me, perfection in every line and tremble, holding the Remy Martin of lust in the crystal snifters of her eyes, and she said, "World War II? I was born in nineteen—" and she named the year that coincided exactly with the date of the fire-bombing of my third marriage. I computed rapidly and came up with her age as not quite seventeen. I hastily ran the numbers through my terrified mind a second time and, even allowing for a recent birthday on her part, I was still in deep trouble. I removed the stinger from her paw very gingerly, smiled my brightest, and said, "It's time to go home now, dear." Fifteen minutes later she was inside her own home, safe and unsullied. Christ, I could have been arrested just for what I was *thinking*!

All of which brings me back to Katie, who was eighteen, and who was the exception to my loathing of young women that proved absolutely nothing. I was bananas over her from the git-go.

All of which totals up to make the point that we talked to each other. I got answers. Good answers. A marvel, this Katie. I didn't want to let her get away.

What do you mean: what impressed me most about you? The size of your tits, what do you think?

Don't hit me, I'm a sick man. I was only kidding, for God's sake!

All kinds of things impressed me. That look on your face like a depraved munchkin. The dumb imitations of Lily Tomlin you do. The word you made up for the feel of velvet against skin, *smoooodgee*. And what the hell do you think you're doing now? You're not going to put up that damned Christmas tree in here while I'm working? Can't you keep an eye on me from the living room? Oh, boy. Okay, okay, but if you make a sound I'll do a Jose Greco on your head.

I didn't want to let her get away. I knew I had to solidify the thing. I told her I had a few interesting errands to run, and did she want to come along before I returned her to Price and the parking lot where she'd left her car? She said okay, we finished eating, and left Yellowfingers.

She accompanied me to the post office to buy stamps for the office; to the hardware store to buy a half-dozen packages of gopher gassers as weaponry in my losing battle against the carnivorous rodents systematically gnawing my lawn and flowers to death; to the record shop to pick up the new sides by The Spinners and Grover Washington, Jr. And then I purposely made a detour through Bullock's Fashion Square so we could hit the bookstore. And there, right in front, between E.L. Doctorow's sensational RAGTIME and Deepak Chopra's SUCK UP THE FUZZY LOVE (or whatever), right on the front table, was a stack of my new book with my name in bright red letters. THOMAS KIRLIN KANE. "Oh, that's my new book," I said offhandedly, walking past the table as if it were a matter of absolutely no consequence. I wandered back to the "obscure stuff and incunabula" section, pretending to look for a book on quahogs (an edible clam) while surreptitiously watching her reactions as she picked up the book, read the cover, turned the book over, opened it and read the front flap copy, flipped to the back flap and saw my photograph, a stunner by Jill Krementz, showing me in thoughtful contemplation, pipe in mouth, finger up left nostril. She kept looking from the photo to me and back again, like an immigration official trying to penetrate a passport disguise, trying to see if Robert Vesco is *really* dumb enough to try sneaking back into the country posing as Leo Gorcey.

I couldn't find a book on quahogs. She came walking up beside me. I held my breath. This was the moment. Actually, there *is* no book on quahogs. "Jesus Christ," she said, "I didn't realize you were famous."

"You thought I was just another pretty *tuchis*?"

"I got to your lecture late. The auditorium was full, so I stood at the back with some friends. None of us knew who you were."

"So why'd you come up to talk to me?"

"I thought you were funny."

"Funny? *Funny!?!* A man stands up there and explains the Ethical Structure of the Universe, the Convoluted Nature of Life in the Cosmos, the Core Dichotomies of Love in a Loveless World. . .not to mention how to replace washers in leaking spigots. . .and you think he's *funny*?"

"I thought you had a nice *tuchis*, too."

Okay, so you *didn't* say that. You were slack-jawed that I was a world-famous author, come on, admit it. All right, you dumbshit nuisance, *don't* admit it, and will you fer chrissakes stop dropping that tinsel all over the typewriter! It's making the keys stick.

Then what happened. . .? Oh. Yeah. We went up to my house in the hills. Nice view, straight across the San Fernando Valley, above the smog line. Clear view to the Ventura Freeway and the pall of yellow-gray death produced by the thousand-wheeled worm. When people ask me if I find it hard living in Los Angeles with the smog, I tell them it doesn't hang where I am; but I have a dandy picture of the stuff killing all the Birchers out there in the Valley. It isn't a line that goes over very well in Ohio. But then, what can you expect from a state that lets the Kent State killers off without even rapping their pinkies?

She wandered around the house with her mouth hanging idly open. It's a super house. Like a giant toy shop furnished in Early Berserk. "My God," she murmured, passing me on her way toward the dining room with its posters from the Doug Fairbanks *Thief of Bagdad*, Errol Flynn *Sea Hawk* and Gary Cooper *Beau Geste* on the ceiling, "you really are famous."

She didn't want to break her date that night with her roommate and another girl friend. I took all three of them out. She mentioned she was going to look for work as a restaurant hostess. I left her at three in the morning, went home and masturbated till I went blind. Next morning, early, I called her and suggested she come to work for me, as an assistant to my office assistant. She said she didn't take charity. I said it wasn't charity, that I needed someone, that the work load was getting too much for Lynne, what with all the fan mail. She said she didn't believe me. I called Lynne out in Santa Monica. A guy answered. I said, "Let me talk to Lynne." After a second a muggy voice came on. "What time is it?" she asked. I told her. She groaned. "Call Katie," I said, on the verge of hysteria. "Tell her we need her." She wanted to know who Katie was. I told her the whole story. She continued groaning. I badgered her. She held out. I gave her a six dollar a week raise. She called Katie.

That day Katie came to work for me. She didn't go home. That night we fucked. I'd like to say we "made love" or that we "slept together" but the simple, unadorned truth of the matter is that I was blind with Technicolor passion and I went at her the way a troop of backpacking Boy Scouts fresh off the Gobi Desert would go at a six-pack of Hostess Twinkies. There is no firm memory anywhere in my head of what happened or how long it went on, though I keep getting a recurring vision of myself hanging upside-down from the shower curtain rod. That can't possibly be an accurate recollection.

She moved in two days later.

I ingratiated myself with her ex-roommate, her parents, her friends from Price, her hairdresser, and the mechanic who serviced her Fiat, just to be on the safe side.

That first month we went to Denver and Boulder on a lecture tour; I took her to New York (it was her first time out of the state) and turned her loose with my credit cards; and when she came back with a superb silver choker for me, and told me she'd bought it with her own money, I was hopelessly, desperately, irretrievably hooked through the gills. I put the ordering of Cokes with duck l'orange out of my mind. This was no kid, this was a woman; the one I'd been waiting for through three scungy marriages and forty-one lonely years. Thus doth Cupid make assholes of us all.

What's that? Oh, so I finally said something nice about you. It's *all* nice. Except the Coke thing, which I keep harping on because it's supposed to portend ugliness to come. I *know* it's not important. Look out, you're going to drop that ornament. . .oh shit, now look at it, all over the floor, and I'm barefoot. Merry Christmas, with me in Mt. Sinai, my foot rotting away from gangrene. No, don't get the vacuum, it'll tear it up inside. Get the broom and the dustpan. Nag, nag, nag: it's *my* gangrenous foot we're talking about here!

Okay, where the hell was I?

What do you mean, "get to when it started to go sour"? Oh. *That's* what you mean.

Well, it was a dynamite three months from the starting gate. We went everywhere, saw everything, did everything, and I started falling behind in the writing. So I had to spend a lot of time behind this typewriter. Katie started getting antsy. She wanted to go out and go to the beach, go water skiing, take a drive up the Coast to San Francisco.

I kept promising, but I was way behind and my publisher was screaming at me long distance from New York every day. Right on the tick of seven A.M., ten o'clock in New York, the phone would ring and it would be Norman, calling me a rancid pyramid of pig shit because he was missing printing deadlines. I would tell him I was working, which was true, but it wasn't coming fast enough.

So I was locked into the house. And Katie started hanging out at school longer each day, started going to evening rehearsals of "A Midsummer Night's Dream," took a flying lesson with some guy, spent lots of time in some restaurant with the "theatuh crowd" and I knew something was going on, though she kept volunteering the information that everything was cool and she loved me. She talked an awful lot of good trash at me.

Now understand something: as a card-carrying loner, I prefer, no I *insist* on a woman having her own thing. I definitely do not want a Stepford Wife, explaining the merits of Easy-Off Oven Cleaner or the manifest benefits of Preparation-H rectal suppositories while she's whipping up my favorite dessert with one hand and polishing the slate slabs in the entranceway with the other. I want a fully-realized human being who, unlike my mother who spent twenty-five years after my father died crying and wandering through life alone and stunned, can make it on her own. But. I am not a dip. I like to think I'm passing intelligent. And I don't mind if someone thinks I'm dumb, just as long as they don't *talk* to me as if they thought I was dumb. I knew something was up.

Yes, nuisance, I knew what was going down all the time. Not the specifics, but I knew there was a Baskerville hound out there on the moors, sniffing around your supple young boogie'ing body.

It wasn't till the fourth month that I learned his name was David.

Would that my name had been Goliath.

I don't remember how I found out that she'd been balling him. It doesn't matter.

I said it doesn't matter.

No, dammit, I don't want to write that part. Shut up, nuisance. . .

the tree is tipping. Hold it! Okay, now prop it up on the right. On the right. . .yeah, *there*. No, I'm not going into that part of it. We talked about it, you let something slip, he called here, I got tired of playing the game of I-know-nothing-and-everything's cool, whatever it was, I found out, and you laid all that crapola on me about how you were only nineteen and you needed to fly, to discover yourself, that it was the first relationship you'd ever had with someone who had a steady job, an occupation, a fully-established life that needed aerating and fertilizing and watering, and you were too young to handle responsibility for someone else's love and life, and I understood all that shit, but you want to know what I thought of?

I thought of that scene out of, I guess it was *Monkey Business*, where Groucho is carrying-on with Margaret Dumont and he begins dancing the shag, flinging his arms in the air, and he says, "I want to sing, I want to dance, I want to *hot cha cha*!" Well, I tried talking to you about it, and it didn't do any good; hell, yes, I knew you loved me, that it was good with us, but you were being torn in two directions at once, and it wasn't even that asshole David. Sure he was fucking you, but that wasn't what was important. Love ain't nothing but sex misspelled anyhow. That isn't where love comes from! I've *never* understood how some poor slob could permit his wife or lady friend to have a deep intellectual relationship with another man, and not think anything about it, but let him get meaty about it and the slob goes out of his pithecanthropoid mind. Love isn't meat in meat. It's all in the headwork. So David was only a convenient symptom. If he was good in bed and you enjoyed it, that's fine with me. I do the best I can. If you need supplements to your diet, well, McDonald's is on every street corner these days. But it was clear you wanted to cut and run because it was getting too thick, and you saw me as an older dude strapped to a typewriter, and you wanted to find out who Katie is.

So we had our little talk, Katie and me, and I suggested we ease off and just do our things as best we could, and if one or the other of us felt the need to partake of a greaseburger at some other fast-food counter, that was okay. And you said to me. . .no! *And Katie said to me*,

"What you're proposing is a mature, adult way of handling this thing; and since I'm neither mature nor adult, it just won't work. There's no way things are going to be copacetic for both of us." (I always wondered how you knew the word *copacetic*; that's a word from my generation, not yours.) "There's no way to avoid one of us getting wrecked, and I've decided it ought to be you, because you can handle it better than I. That's because you're a mature adult."

And you left. No, dammit. . .*Katie* left, and I put it all out of my mind in an hour. Don't say no one can put it out of his mind in an hour, God damn you, *I* did! I learned how to do it a long time ago. Just to mortar up that alcove where the hurt is. To brick it over and keep moving, just shuckin' and jivin'.

Yeah, Merry Christmas to you, too, kiddo.

I ain't mad. I curse the lesson and bless the knowledge. It'll be a long time again between hurts.

Hold everything. My name is David Feinberg and I did not write what you have just read. There is no Thomas Kirlin Kane. What you have just read was written by a woman. Her name is Patricia Katherine Feinberg. Her maiden name was Patti Brody. She is twenty years old. I am forty-three. We have been married for almost two years. She is the dearest person I have ever known and there is nothing in this life I need more than her love and support and presence in my world. For a while, when we first met, we had problems. Not so much between us, but from the outside, from people who saw us as a mismatch of "young stuff" and "dirty old man." We got past that after a great many aggravations. And how she remembered it all!

I have been in trimming the Christmas tree, which would decimate my mother if she were still alive, a good Jew like me; and I've heard Patti typing in here for days. But not till now has she suggested I come in and read what she's been writing. It's not her usual non-fiction stuff, it's a story. Her first fiction. I hope you enjoyed it. How she did it so much inside my head, writing it the way a man would write it, I'll never know. She wrote it a great deal more fairly than I would have, but for the record, I'm the one who orders Coke with *canard l'Orange*. How did she remember all this, all the detail, all the things I said in idle moments? I'm amazed.

But it's the best Christmas present I've ever received.

And have a happy yourself.

With love, from us, a terrific object lesson in beating the odds. Or, as Thomas Kirlin Kane would put it, everything's copacetic.

—Los Angeles, 1975

BATTLE WITHOUT BANNERS

When they first broke out of the machine shop, holding the guards before them, screwdrivers sharp and deadly against white-cloth backs covering streaks of yellow, they made for the South Tower, and took it without death. One of the hostage guards tried to break free, however, in the subsequent scuffle to liberate the machine gun from its gimbals and tracks, and Simon Rubin was forced to use the screwdriver on the man. They threw the body from the Tower as an example to the remaining three hostages, and had no further difficulties. In fact, the object lesson was so successful that it was the guards themselves that carried the cumbersome machine gun, with all its belts of ammunition, back down into the yard. The Tower was an insecure defensive position, interlocked as it was with the other three Towers and the sniping positions on the roofs of the main buildings. They had decided in advance to make it back down into the yard and there, with backs to the wall itself, to take their stand for as long as it took the second group to blow the gate.

Construction on the new drainage system had been underway for only two days, and the great sheets of corrugated sheet metal, the sandbags, the picks and shovels, all were stacked under guard near the wall. They were forced to gun down the man on duty to get into the shelter of the piles of material, but it didn't matter either way—if he lived or died—because they were going to take as many with them as they could, breakout or not.

Nigger Joe and Don Karpinsky set up the big-barreled machine gun and braced its sides as well as fore and aft with sandbags, digging it in so the recoil would not affect its efficiency.

Gyp Williams, who had engineered the break, took up a solid rifleman's position, flat out on his belly with legs spread and toes pointed out, the machine rifle braced against right shoulder and the left elbow dug deep into the brown earth of the yard, supporting the tripod grip. His brown eyes set deep into his black face were roaming things as he covered the wide expanse of the yard, waiting for the first assault; it had to come; he was the readiest ever.

Lew Steiner and the kid they called Chocolate made up the rest of the skirmish team, and they were busily unloading the homemade grenades and black powder bombs from the cotton-batting of the insulated box. . .when the first assault broke out of cover around the far wall of the Administration Building.

They came as a wave of white-winged doves, the ivory of their uniforms blazing against the hard cold light of the early morning. First came the sprayers, pocking the ground with little upbursts of dirt, and shredding the morning silence with the noise of their grease guns. Then a row of riflemen, and behind them half a dozen longarms with grenades, if needed.

"Away, they comin'!" Gyp Williams snapped over his shoulder. "Dig, babies!" and he got off the first burst of the defense, into their middle. Three of the grease gunners went down, legs everywhichway and guns tossed off like refuse, clattering and still chattering on automatic fire, pelting the wall with wasted lead. The second wave faltered an instant, and in that snatch of time Nigger Joe fed the belts to Karpinsky, who swung the big weapon back and forth, in even arcs, cutting them down right across the bellies. None of the riflemen made it a fifth of the distance across the empty yard. One of them went down kicking, and Karpinsky took him out on the next, lowered, arc.

"I am," Lew Steiner screamed, arching high to toss a black powder bomb, "*home free!*" It hit and exploded fifteen yards too short, but the effect was marvelous. The longarms caught up short and tried to turn.

"Bang

"Bang

"And bang," Gyp Williams grinned and murmured as he snapped off three sharp, short bursts, ending it for a trio of grenade carriers. And it was over that quickly, as the remaining grease gunners and three longarms fell, clambered, tripped, sprinted, raced back around the building.

"We done that thing." Gyp Williams rolled over on his back, aiming a thumb-and-finger pistol at his troops. "We sure enough, we done that thing."

"Send those guards outta here." Chocolate nodded his head at the hostages. Gyp agreed with a small movement of his massive head, and the three white-jacketed guards were shoved around the side of the enclosure, out into the open. For a moment they tensed, as though they expected to be shot down by the men in the tiny fort, but when no movement was made, they broke into a dead run, across the yard, arms waving, yelling to their compatriots that they were coming through.

The first burst of machinegun fire came from the North Tower and took one of them in mid-stride, making him miss his footing, leap and plunge in a half-somersault to crash finally onto the ground, sliding a foot and a half on the side of his face. The second burst cut down his partners. They tumbled almost into a loving embrace, piled atop one another.

Chocolate expelled breath through dry lips and asked, "Who's got the cigarettes?" Simon Rubin tossed him the pack and for a while they just lay there, smoking, alert, watching the bodies of the dead white guards who had been shot by their own men.

"Well," Gyp Williams commented philosophically, after a time, "*everybody* knows a white cat gets around niggers is gonna get contaminated. They just couldn't be trust, man. Dirty. Dir-ty."

"And kikes," Lew Steiner added. "Ding ding."

They settled down for the long wait, till the second group could blow the wall. They watched the shadows of the sun slither across the yard. Nothing moved. Warm, and nice, waiting. Quiet, too.

"How long you been in this prison?" Chocolate asked Simon Rubin. There was no answer for the space of time it took Rubin to draw in on the butt and expel smoke through his nostrils; then his long, horsey face drew down, character lines in the bony cheeks and around the deep-set eyes mapping new expressions. "As far back as I can remember," he replied carefully, thinking about it, "I suppose all of my life." Chocolate nodded lightly, turning back to the empty yard with a thin whistle of nervousness.

Something should happen. They all wanted it.

"When the hell they gonna blow that gate?" Nigger Joe murmured. He had been biting the inside of his full lower lip, chewing, biting again. "I thought they was gonna blow it soon's we got a position here. What the hell they doin' back in there?"

Gyp Williams motioned him to silence. "Quiet, willya. They'll get on it, you take it easy."

"I'm really scared." Don Karpinsky added a footnote. "It's like waiting for them to come and kill you. My old man told me about that at Belsen, how they came around and just looked at you, didn't say a word, just walked up and down, gauging you, looking to see if there was meat on you, and then later, boy oh boy, later they came back and didn't have any trouble picking you out, just walked up and down again, pointing, that one and that one and. . ."

"Can it." Gyp Williams hushed him. "Boy, you sure can *talk*!" He was silent a second, scrutinizing the young man, too young to need a shave every day, but old enough to be here behind the wall with them. Then, "What you in for, boy?"

Don Karpinsky looked startled, his face rearranging itself to make explanations, excuses, reading itself for extenuating circumstances, amelioration. "I, I, uh, I hurt some people."

Gyp Williams turned toward him more completely (yet kept a corner of his eye on the empty yard, where the bodies remained crumpled). "You *what*, you did *what*?"

"I just, uh, I *hurt* some people, with a, uh, with a bomb, see I made this bomb and when I tossed it I din't know there was any—"

"Whoa back, boy!" Gyp Williams pulled the young man's racethrough dialogue to a halt. "Go on back a bit. You made a *what*? A *bomb*?"

Karpinsky nodded dumbly; it was obvious he had never thought he would be censured here.

"Now what'n the hell you do *that* for, boy?"

Don Karpinsky turned to the belts of long slugs, neatly folded over themselves, ready for the maw of the machine gun. He would not, or could not, answer.

Simon Rubin spoke up. He had been listening to the interchange but had decided to let the young Karpinsky handle his own explanations. But now it needed ending, and since the young man had confided in him one rainy night in their cell, he felt the privileged communication might best be put to use here. "Gyp," he called the big black man's attention away from Karpinsky. It seemed to halt the next words from Gyp Williams's mouth.

"He bombed a church, Gyp. Some little town in Iowa. The minister was apparently some kind of a monster, got the local Male White Protestants convinced Jews ate *goyishe* children for Passover. They made it hell on the kid and his family. He was a chemistry bug, made a bomb, and tossed it. Killed six people. They threw him in here."

Gyp Williams seemed about to say something, merely clucked his tongue, and rolled over once more into a firing position. The only sound in the enclosure was the metallic sliding of the machine rifle's bolt as Gyp Williams made unnecessary checks.

Lew Steiner was asleep against the wall, his back propped outward by a sandbag, a black powder bomb in each hand, as though in that instant of snapping awake, he might reflexively hurl one of the spheroids more accurately, more powerfully than he had in combat.

"Whaddaya think, Gyp?" Chocolate asked. "You think they gonna try an' take us in daylight, or wait till t'night?" He was as young as Don Karpinsky, somewhere under twenty, but a reddish, ragged scar that split down his left cheek to the corner of his mouth made him seem—somehow—older, more experienced, more capable of violence than the boy who had bombed the small Iowa church.

Gyp Williams rose up on an elbow, gaining a better field of vision across the yard. He talked as much to himself as to Chocolate. "I don't know. Might be they'd be careful about waiting till dark. That's a good time for us as much as them. And when the other boys make the move to blow the gate, the dark'll be on our side, we can shoot out them searchlights. . ."

He chuckled, lightly, almost naïvely.

"What's so funny?" Nigger Joe asked, then turned as Simon Rubin asked, "Hey, Joe, I got a crick in my back, here, want to rub it out for me?" Nigger Joe acknowledged the request and slid across the dirt to Rubin, who turned his back, indicating the sore area. The Negro began thumbing it smooth with practiced hands, repeating, "Gyp, what's so funny?"

Gyp Williams's ruggedly handsome face went into a softer stage. "I remember the night they came for us, the caravan, about fifteen twenty cars, came on down to Littletown, all of them with the hoods, lookin' for the one who'd grabbed a feel off the druggist's wife. Man, they were sure pretty, all of them real black against the sky, just them white hoods showing them off like perfect targets.

"They's about ten of us, see, about ten, all laid out like I am now, out there on a little hill in the tall grass, watching them cars move on down. Show-offs, that's what they was. Show-offs, or they wouldn't've sat up on the backs of them convertibles, where we could see 'em so plain. No lights on the cars, all silent, but the white hoods, as plain as moonlight.

"We got about thirteen or fourteen of them cats before they figured they'd been ruined. I was just thinkin' 'bout it now, thinkin' 'bout them searchlights when they come on. Those white uniforms gonna be might fine to shoot at, soon's it gets dark." Then, without a break in meter, his tone became frenzied, annoyed, "When the hell they gonna blow that goddam *gate?*"

As if in reply, a long, strident burst from a grease gun, sprayed from the roof of the Administration Building, pocked the wall behind them, chewing out irregular niches in the brick. They were spattered with brick chips and mortar, dirt and whizzing bits of stone. Lew Steiner came rigidly awake, grasped the situation and ducked in a dummy-up cover, imitating the other five defenders.

They were huddled over that way, when they heard the whispering, chuckling whirr of helicopter rotors chewing the air. "They're coming over the wall in a 'copter!" Don Karpinsky shrieked.

Gyp Williams turned over, raising his sights on the machine rifle, bracing the barrel on an upright sheet of corrugated metal. "Lew! Get set, them bombs. . .they comin' over. . .Lew!"

But Steiner was lost in fear. It was silence he heard, frozen in silence, not the commanding voice of Gyp Williams. Gyp cursed tightly, eyes directed at the wall, scanning, tracking back and forth for the first sight of the guard chopper, coming with the tear gas or the thermite or a ten-second shrapnel cannister. "Joe! Joe, dammit, do somethin' about Lew, *you*, Joe!"

Nigger Joe slid across the ground, grasped Lew Steiner by the hair, and jerked him out of the snail-like fetal position he had assumed. Steiner still clutched the black smoke bombs, one in either fist, like thick, burnt rolls, snatched from an oven.

The colored man was unconcerned with niceties. He slapped Steiner heavily, the sound a counterpoint to the 'copter's rising comments. Lew Steiner did not want to come back from wherever he had gone to find peace and security. But the black man's palm would not be ignored. He bounced the work-pinkened flesh off Steiner's cheeks until the milky-blue of sight unseen had faded, and Steiner was back with them.

"Them bombs, Lew," Nigger Joe said, softly, with great kindness. "They comin' over the wall right'cheer behind us." Steiner's defection was already forgotten.

No more was said as Steiner rolled over, ready to meet the helicopter with his bombs. Chocolate and Don Karpinsky stayed with the fixed machine gun, prepared for a rear-guard attack in the face of the aerial threat. Nigger Joe and Simon Rubin lay on their backs, rifles pointed at the sky.

The whirlybird came over the wall fifty feet down the line, and Gyp Williams quickly readjusted himself for its approach. The machine was perhaps twenty feet over their heads, and came churning toward them rapidly, as though intent on low-level strafing. Gyp Williams loosed his first burst before the others, and it missed the mark by two feet. The helicopter came on rapidly, steadily. The six men lay staring at it, readying themselves, trying at the same time to find places for their naked bodies in the earth.

When it was almost directly overhead, Lew Steiner rose to a kneeling position and hurled first one black powder bomb, then the other, with tremendous force. The first bomb went straight, directly up into the air, passed over the cockpit of the machine, and tumbled back wobbling, to hit the top of the wall, bounce and explode on the other side. The reverberation could be felt in the wall and the ground, but no rifts appeared in the brick. The second bomb crashed into the side of the machine and a deafening roar split up the even sussuration of the 'copter's rotors. The machine tottered on its course, slipped sidewise and lost minor altitude, but was compensated, began to climb, and just as it hurled itself away in a slanting curve, a projectile tumbled dizzily, end-over-end from the machine.

Then the 'copter was gone, and they watched the projectile falling straight for them. Gyp Williams began screaming, "Fire, fire, hit it hit it hitithitithitit. . ." and they all poured flame into the sky, missing the tear gas bomb as it fell a few yards from their enclosure, exploded, and sent rolling clouds of tear gas straight toward them.

The vapors overwhelmed them; they felt the sting of the chemicals; their eyes went blood-red in an instant, and Don Karpinsky fell on his side, clutching his face, crying like an infant. Lew Steiner grabbed another bomb from somewhere, and hurled it at the empty yard, a motion of wanton fury and impotence that no one noticed, that had no effect. Gyp Williams refused to cry. He dug his broad face deep into the dirt.

The others recoiled, tried to protect themselves, but they knew the guards would attack in this moment of siege. They could hear them coming, rebel yells of victory and bloodlust shattering on the pane of the air. And over the battle cries, the malicious rattle of the machine gun as Chocolate sprayed the yard in steady, back-and-forth sweeps. Blind to everything, tears running out of his burning eyes, knowing only that he had the power to cut them down, the young man with the livid scar continued his barrage, building a wall of death the guards in their white uniforms could not penetrate.

And after a while, when the belts were exhausted, and the guards had gone back to cover, when the gas had blown away, stringers of mist on a late afternoon breeze some God had sent to prolong their passion, they all lay back with eyes crimson and streaming, knowing it had to be over soon, and hoping the second group would finally, please dear Lord, blow that frigging gate!

"Man, how long, how long," Nigger Joe spoke to the advancing dusk. "How long this gotta go on. It seem like I been livin' off misery all my life, you'd think it'd end sometime, not just keep goin' on and on and on."

Simon Rubin sat up and looked at him, and there was compassion in his lean, ascetic face.

"How many lives I gotta lead, steppin' down into the gutter for some 'fay cat? How many times I gotta be called 'Boy,' an' when'm I gonna get some memories I wanta put away to think back on, another time?" His eyes were lost in the twilight, set deep under bony eyebrow ridges, but his fierce voice was all around them, very soft but compelling. "Even in here they makin' me be somethin' I ain't. Even in here I'm tryin' to get away, get some life, what's left to me, and they got me down with my face in the dirt; they don't know. Man, they'll *never* know. I can remember every *one* them cats, makin' jokes, pokin' fun, sayin' things, a man's got to have *pride*, that's what matters, just his goddamn pride. They can have all the rest of it, just gimme the pride. An' when they come 'round takin' that too, then you gotta raise up and split some sonofabitch's head with a shovel. . ."

Simon Rubin's voice came sliding in on the semi-darkness, a cool soft fabric covering tiny sounds of crickets and metal clanking on metal from somewhere out there. "I know how you feel, Joe. There are a lot of us in that kind of ghetto.

"Only for some of us it gets worse, even when it gets better. You *knew* your kind of hate, but it was different for me."

Gyp Williams snorted in disgust. "Sheet, man, when you Jewish cats gonna come off that kick? When you gonna stop lyin' on yourself, man, that you been persecuted, so you know how a black man feels? Jeezus, you Jewish own most of the tenements up in Harlem. You as bad as any the rest of them cats." He turned away in suppressed fury, turning his anger on the machine rifle, whose bolt he snapped back twice quickly.

Simon Rubin began speaking again, as though by the continuing stream of words he could negate what Gyp Williams had said. "I wanted to get into dental college, but they had a quota on Jews. I didn't have the money or the name to be in that quota, so I went out for veterinary medicine. I got set back and set back so many times, I finally said to hell with it, and I changed my name, and had my nose fixed, and then I married a gentile.

"It even worked for a while." He smiled thinly, remembering, out of his not-very-Semitic face. "And then one night we had a fight about something, I don't remember what, and we went to bed angry, and in the middle of the night I turned to her and we started to make love, and when she was ready she began saying over and over in my ear, 'Now, you dirty kike, now, you dirty kike. . .'"

Simon Rubin buried his face in his hands.

Don Karpinsky asked, "Simon. . .?"

"So. . .so I know how you feel Joe," Simon finished. "I hated myself more than she could ever hate me; and when they sent me here for her, because of her, what I did to her, I gave them my name the way I came into the world with it. So I know, Joe, believe me, I *know*."

Nigger Joe started to turn away, his thoughts turned inward. He paused and looked directly at Simon Rubin: "I'm sorry you feel bad, Simon," he lamented, "it's just I been in chains four hundred years, and all that clankin' makes me hear not so good. I'm sorry you got troubles, man."

And their contest of agonies, their cataloguing of misery, their one-up of sorrow was cut short as the loudspeaker blared from across the yard, from the Administration Building.

"Hey! Hey over there!"

It was the main loudspeaker, mounted on the Administration Building, where the guards were waiting to come for them, holding out—it was now obvious—until their nerves were raw.

"Hey, Simon. . .Lew. . .all the rest of you. . .this is David, do you hear me, can you hear me, all of you?"

Gyp Williams fired off a long flaming burst, and they could hear the tinkle and shatter of window glass when it hit. It was an answer, of sorts.

"Listen, we can't blow the gate. We just can't do it, you guys."

Chocolate looked at his companions. "Hey! That's David, the one who was with the second group, what's he doin' in there with them?" Gyp Williams motioned him to silence. They listened.

"They've got the gate staked out, listen you men! They have it fixed so we can't get at it. Simon! Lew Steiner! All of you, Gyp, Gyp Williams, listen! They said they won't punish us if we go back to our cells. They said they won't demand payment, we can go right on like we were before, it's better this way, it isn't so bad, we know what we can do, we know what they won't let us do! Simon, Gyp, come on back, come on back and they won't make any trouble for us, we can go on the way we were before, don't rock the boat, you guys, *don't rock the boat!*"

Gyp Williams rose to both knees, somehow manhandling the heavy machine rifle against his chest, and he screamed at the top of his voice, throwing his head back so his very white teeth stood out like a necklace of sparkling gems in his mouth—"*Sellout bastards*!" and he fired, without taking his finger from the trigger, he fired and the flames and heat and steel and anguish went cascading across the yard, hitting unreceptive stone and gravel and occasionally one of the already dead would leap as a slug tore its cold flesh.

Finally, when he had made it clear what their answer was to be, he fell exhausted behind the sandbags, where he would die.

In that instant of minor silence, Simon Rubin said, "I'm going back." And he got up and walked across the yard, his head down, his hands locked behind his head.

Don Karpinsky began to cry, then, and Chocolate slid across to him, trying by his nearness to stop the fear and the fury of being too brave to live, too cowardly to die without tears. No one behind the barricade moved to shoot Simon Rubin. There was no point to it, no anger at him, only pity and a deep revulsion. And the guards in their immaculate white did not shoot him. Back in their world he was infinitely more valuable, as a symbol, a broken image, for the others who might try to free themselves another time.

They would point to him and say, "See Simon Rubin, *he* tried to rock the boat, and see what he's like?"

Behind the barricade Nigger Joe turned to Lew Steiner and the crying kid who had not fled with Simon Rubin.

"There, that's how much your people understand." He condemned them all.

And Lew Steiner said, "There were half a dozen of your boys in that second group, Joe. My back aches again, you feel like doing that thing?"

Nigger Joe chuckled lackadaisically, slid over and began thumbing Lew Steiner's back.

They were like that, waiting, when the final assault began. The high keening whine of a mortar shell came at them like the Doppler of a train passing on a track, and it landed far down at the end, where Chocolate caught it full, and split up like a ripe, dark pod. He was dead even as it struck, and the other four fell in a heap to protect themselves from screaming shrapnel.

When the ground had ceased to tremble, and they could see the world again, they tried not to look toward the end of the barricade, where a brown leg and a torn bit of cloth showed from under the heap of rubble, from under the fallen sheets of metal. They tried not to look, and succeeded, but Gyp Williams's face was now incapable of even that half-bitter, knowing smile he had offered before.

Another whining shell came across, struck the wall above them and exploded violently, with Lew Steiner's howl of pain matching it on a lower level.

The shard of twisted metal had caught him in the neck, ripping through and leaving him with a deep furrow, welling out wetly, black-red down his shirt and over the hand he raised to staunch the flow. Nigger Joe tore his shirt down the front and made a crude bandage. "It ain't bad, Lew, here, hold this on if you can."

The four of them turned back to see the first wave of white-uniformed guards breaking from the cover of the Administration Building and another group from around the end of the Laundry.

They came on like a wide-angled "V" with a longarm grenade hurler at the point. Gyp Williams turned loose with the machine rifle, and swept the first attackers; they fell, but one of them got off a grenade, and it sailed almost gracefully, a balloon of hard stuff, over and over into the enclosure. The earth split up and deafened them, and great chunks of steel and stone cascaded about them. It was enough to ruin the machine gun, and send Don Karpinsky tumbling over backward, his body saturated with tiny bits of steel and sand. He lay sprawled backward, eyes open at the sky of free darkening blue, over the wall he would never climb.

They huddled there, the three of them left—Gyp Williams, Nigger Joe, and Lew Steiner, still clutching the bloody rag to his neck.

The guards in their white uniforms would not let them go back to the cells. They knew the ones who were weak enough to keep from rocking the boat, and they knew the ones who had to be destroyed. These three were the last of the ones who had sought their freedom and their pride. They would be killed where they lay, when the ammunition had run out and all the strength was sapped from them, not only by the fighting, but by the ones who had betrayed them, the ones who had said it was better not to make trouble.

And as waves of faceless, soulless attackers streamed toward them across the dead-piled yard, no more intent on the particular men behind the barricade than they would have been about any other vermin who threatened them, Gyp Williams said it all for all three of them, and for the few strong ones who had found peace if not pride: "We all of us down in the dark. Some day, maybe. . .some day."

Then he managed somehow to get the machine rifle steadied, and he fired into the midst of them, screaming and running with their immaculate white uniforms the badges of purity and cleanliness.

But there were just too many of them.

There were *always*. . .

Just too damned many of them.

—New York City, 1961

A PATH THROUGH THE DARKNESS

In a summer heavy with sunshine and promises, I came to New York. It was the end of the confused times for me—and in many ways the beginning of a deeper bewilderment.

College had confused me with its confounding regimentation and inability to provide realities, answers; my family had exposed itself for the inelastic failure I had always unconsciously known it to be, love had been merely a high-flown word, an abstract concept whose meaning had changed with every pretty smile; I was, simply enough, a bewildered seeker.

New York magically held all my answers. On streets of purest gold I would seek my fortune, find it, and mold a life of meaning, achievement and satisfaction.

I took a room uptown across from Columbia University, in what had once been (thirty years before) a fashionable hotel. I paid ten dollars a week for a room with an unobstructed view of the air shaft, and cooking privileges I shared with two spinster schoolteachers, three college students, two Chinese exchange students and a constantly drunken Puerto Rican day-laborer. It was a quiet place, whose walls retained the odor of Cantonese cooking, Gallo wine and that never-to-be-forgotten smell of disinfectant mixed with urine. I had my radio, my books, my typewriter and a good bed. A single bed.

If I'd ever known anything that could be called happiness, this was it. . .languishing in a simplicity of existence that I rolled around in smugly, snugly, like a nesting baby or a happy-go-lucky terrier.

At first the writing came slowly, amateurishly, but in my fervor to write, and say what I had to say—to hell with the fact that others had said it all before me, far better; I *had* to write—I stayed behind the machine, working far into the nights, sleeping most of the mornings, then making the editorial rounds in the afternoon.

Again, it was the good life. Except for the loneliness.

There were friends, of course: Billy and Stella Soles who had come from California and subsisted on kidney bean soup, the publication of an amateur science fiction journal and endless bed-bouts; Aggie Vinson, a selling writer with a cool manner and a brotherly affection for my stumbling attempts at writing; Pernell Morris and his sister Beth, who ran a newsstand on Broadway and invited me over perhaps twice a week for a kosher meal; others.

But there was still the feeling I was walking alone, that I had no human goal toward which to work. That I was out there swinging by myself, and if it were to end tomorrow no one could really be troubled. The ripples would roll out and disappear, the water would close over and silence would replace me.

Perhaps that is the essence of loneliness: to feel that silence will replace you.

So when my money ran out, and I landed the job selling books and souvenirs in the Times Square bookshop (seven P.M. to three in the morning) I decided to throw a small blast. God knows my room wasn't large enough for the full Elsa Maxwell treatment, but nonetheless I invited everyone I had even remotely grown to know, and urged them to bring friends. It was the perfectly ordinary sort of thing one does when the loneliness gets too oppressive, too obstinately endless.

It was an ordinary thing, and when I think back on it I get uncharacteristically choked up, and I am chagrined at my callowness. It barks my shin on those protruding dream fantasies about going back in time five minutes before the event, and just *not doing it*. How I've wished for those precise five minutes to come again. Saved her. . .would it have saved her? I think not.

But it might have saved me.

They started arriving early, and the first ones were the Columbia students who wanted to souse-up their dates, lay them and get them back before Barnard curfew. They came with eighty-nine-cent bottles of Chianti and with routines borrowed from comedians' LPs. They were pretty much an empty lot, all sound and not a helluva lot of fury, but they made good background noise and as bookends they served the purpose of decoration.

At about nine o'clock Aggie arrived carrying a brown paper sack with a bottle of Pernod in it, and he flashed both the label and a secret smile as he retreated to a far corner. The label was the come-on and the secret smile said, *The dishwater booze is for the tourists, podnuh, but the goodies is for us.*

Billy and Stella blew in noisily, with a bowl of clam dip plastic-covered, and a box of stiff potato chips for dipping. Of all the horrors of the civilized world, I had decided clam, oyster and bleu cheese dips were the worst, and of the worst, Stella Soles's dips were the dippiest.

I beamed and thanked them. It smelled like decaying bodies.

Stella and Billy snuggled down on the sofabed and began pawing each other immediately. It was very much like the hippo and the dik-dik bird. Stella was perhaps six feet, three inches and *big*. . .really big, across the chest, across the shoulders, in the hips. . .a *big* woman. Billy was a gnat. He was barely five four, and wore his hair in a style reminiscent of Farmer Al Falfa. When he went at her, it was like watching a dwarf storm the Bastille. But they loved each other almost outrageously, and the whining sound of Stella calling, "*Bill*-ee. . .*Billll*-ee!" was a familiar sound in our building.

The mating call of the great musk ox.

The party was gasping for air, coming up for the second time only to sink for a third, and blessedly final, when the knock came at the door. I leaped to my feet with all the grace of a poled ox, and picked my way across the littered carpet—it was one of those parties where everyone dropped where they stood, usually in an orderly, out-of-the-way manner—and opened the door.

She had come with three fags, each dressed entirely in black, and next to their lean, hard-muscled litheness her tiny white-swathed figure was a shock.

Her face was so clear and direct, the features arranged as they might have been by a simpering cameo-carver who saw perfection in the face of disorder, I was truly startled. I had no idea who she was, but I instantly related to her, instantly desired her, instantly saw her image of me rise up and be greeted with attention. The three homosexuals with her distressed me, for I was very nearly pathological in my abhorrence for those of the gay set—but the girl was so arresting I let them pass.

She came into my single room, smiling like a street gamine, and found a place for herself and her retinue by the far window. It was too much; my eyes followed her as though I'd lost all volition or personal desire except to be near her, even if it was only by sight.

I followed them and started making introductions. . .for the first time in the evening they went badly. Inevitably they were set straight and she said her name was Stephie Cook, her friends were Blank, Blank and Blank Blank. Who the hell listened, who the hell cared what marcelled titles they had given themselves. That she was a queen of the fag set did not seem to offend me. Before, when I had run into a seemingly normal girl surrounded and attended by queers, I had drawn my own conclusions as to the girl's personality and sex habits. But with Stephie, somehow, it was entirely different. She was straight, I knew it, I could feel it, she was interested in me from the first, and I—by that weird alchemical nature of attraction—was completely in her power.

As the evening wore down, we gravitated toward one another on imbecile pretext: would you like a glass of Pernod? Do you work? Have you *really* read all these books? Where do you live?

The homosexuals seemed not to mind, smiling like indulgent *duennas* at Stephie as she nuzzled closer to me in a dim corner by the record player.

Sometime during the decaying last moments of the party, without either of us saying it aloud, we knew she would stay with me that night.

Aggie seemed to know, too. Perhaps it was that he knew me so well, took such a bemused view of my goings-on, and wished me well or perhaps he knew because he was also a writer who felt he had to *know* people to write honestly.

As he left, he raised the empty Pernod bottle in a pseudo-centurion salute, mumbled, "*Post hoc, ergo proctor hoc*," and grinned his way out of the room. Billy and Stella left soon after. They had been the last—the coeds and their spatula-handed paramours having checked out hours before, the three gay boys long since departed to their contorted repose—and when the door shut after them, we stared at each other from our seats without moving.

"Would you like a pair of my pajamas?" I asked. She nodded and gave me a look that was half-affection and half-trust. It was quite unlike anything I'd ever seen in a woman's face before.

I found my last laundry return had included only one pair of pajamas, so I offered her the tops. She took them, went down the hall to the bathroom and changed while I did the same in the room, and she returned as I was crawling into bed.

Wearing my oversized pajama tops, the sleeves rolled well above the wrists, the tails hanging down past her thighs, she was a Dresden doll figurine, come to life. It was an entirely commonplace, entirely believable and trite situation; I knew it had happened to a million other guys with a million other girls, but for me, it was the most astounding, the most hypnotizing experience of my life. In a matter of hours my loneliness had been ended.

She came to bed and we lay there talking for hours. We did not make love that night; we slept soundly, holding each other.

She lived in Brooklyn, and I would come running up out of the subway entrance, gathering speed as I raced down the half block to her building and—Doug Fairbanks–style—would bunch my muscles and leap, catching the railing of the little balcony that faced off her room. I would catch it, pull myself up and throw myself onto the balcony. It had all the demented romantic imagery of a Romeo seeking his Juliet.

It was our own personal route to one another. And then the French doors would open into the broom closet that she rented as a room. It was perhaps five feet across and twelve feet long, a narrow coffin of a room whose only advantage was that little balcony. Her bookshelf was on the wall over the racklike bed, and her bureau was shoved into a niche on the opposite wall. Posters of Eglevsky, Maria Tallchief and the Ballet Russe covered that wall opposite the bed; staring at us all through the short nights of muggy passion and unsatisfied demands.

In that room I grew to know Stephie more intimately than I had ever known anyone before. Not merely her body, which she gave rarely, unsatisfactorily, painfully. But her mind, and that commodity I had always thought was folly, her soul. But Stephie had a soul, one that at first confused me and invited attention; one that soon exposed itself for what it was—the soul of a demon.

Her thoughts were dark, strange, troubled.

She dwelled on facets of life that I had never even known existed. One night she sat smoking, her legs folded under her, and said:

"I saw a boy run over a cat today, with his bike."

I looked up from the book of Jackson Pollock prints we had gone in on together, not really hearing what she had said, but suddenly letting it filter through, and catching meaning from *her* intention to explain. "Oh?" I said.

"Yes," she explained, "he ran over it lengthwise, and the guts came out of its mouth like a pound of raw hamburger; its eyes were bulged and there was a tire track up its back and through the center of the spilled innards. Ants were—"

"*Jeezus*, Stephie!" I shouted. "For God's sake, what the hell is the matter with you?" I had a strong stomach, but this clinical attention to morbid detail gagged me.

She shrugged, got up and walked out onto the balcony, still smoking. She looked so tiny against the massed darkness of Brooklyn at night.

She was a tiny, delicate girl. Tiny. Delicate. Like a cell of botulism.

How had it happened? How had something so pure and innocent and—the word seems alien to me, but somehow appropriate—*charming* become so demented, so twisted and destructive? Could it have been me. . .could it have been that I had taken Stephie from paths she knew, paths that led deeper into the darkness of her own fears and past torments, and tried to lead her on a new path, out of the darkness? Was it that? Or is it preordained that some men will instinctively seek out those women who are worst for them, women who are good with other men but become evil in the hands of the wrong one? It tormented me, it haunted me, as the days went by and we continued to hurt each other in terrible, unnameable ways. Little ways that would have no meaning taken individually, but collectively painted a haunted canvas by Tchelitchew or Max Ernst.

There, existing in a chilly, tormented half-world of metamorphosed loneliness and vague desires, I sought ways to bedevil myself. I went far out of my way to discover trouble, to cultivate it, to urge its flagellant attentions on myself. Perhaps that was it: perhaps it was the smell of desperation and hopelessness on me that had attracted Stephie. Now, later, thinking on it, I have no doubt that a healthy man, someone not seeking the nit-picking of bits of destruction, would have avoided her.

Stephie was a Typhoid Mary, a plague-bearer, and only someone desiring illness would have rubbed up against her.

One night I had a date with her—it was my single night-off from the bookstore; usually I took the subway during the still hours after work; Times Square at three A.M. is another world, filled with weird types and wanderers who will *never* find their paths out of the darkness; riding to Brooklyn in that peculiarly No-Doz–chilled world was a surrealistic experience—and I had stopped off to buy her a trinket. It was a silver lavaliere; it had only cost a few dollars, but there was always this intense feeling in me that I might break through her wall of strange and disturbing distance with a word, a gift, a kiss, a gesture. I never did, of course, but the attempts were constantly being made.

I see them now as adolescent attempts to *buy* her, but at the time I thought they were unselfish. Was this a refusal on my part really to *give* of myself? Was it perhaps an attempt to gain without offering myself exposed? Did I sense she had the power to cut and hurt?

With the little silver pendant in its nest of cotton, the box tucked into my pocket, I vaulted to the balcony. The doors were locked.

I waited, sitting against the cold night with my back to the French doors, until early morning. I fell asleep that way, and only chance prevented the beat cop from seeing me there like some fetus-positioned cat-burglar. She didn't come home till almost three that afternoon. By then I was so sunk into a waiting stupor that even when she opened the French doors and I fell sidewise, half into her room, I didn't realize she had come back.

Her explanation: she had spent the night talking ballet with the "boys" at one of their co-op apartments; yes, she had known I would be there; no, she hadn't considered it important to phone me or leave a note; if she was gone she assumed I would leave, ride the long ride back to Manhattan, and be ready to see her another time.

We went for our blood test that week. She had to hold my hand when the doctor took the sample. I was poor, and wrote an uncle of mine in New Mexico, who owned a jewelry store, asking him for a ring. He sent a lovely but inexpensive modern band.

Why? Because it is far better to be lonely *with* someone than to be lonely alone.

I was frightened of Stephie, I knew it was all wrong, she was killing me by obscure, dangerous degrees, but I *needed* someone. And in that unfathomable way all those who seek to destroy themselves share, I wanted *her*. What was worst for me, I needed most. Still, I had no understanding of her; I didn't really know her, and we were both running headlong down that path into the darkness, hand-in-hand, knives in backs.

It was a little like going mad.

We went to an art movie on Lexington Avenue, midtown; a dark and depressing thing that seemed perfectly suited to my being with Stephie. As the weeks had gone by I had started smoking more, my thoughts were strange, devious, my work at the shop hadn't suffered because there wasn't that much imagination needed for it, but I was more easily upset, nastier to customers, shorter with the creeps who sought the clinical sex books; my nights alone were introspective, troubled. We were walking back to the subway on Lexington when we saw a crowd.

Stephie hurried me along and as we came abreast of them Stephie pointed up. Everyone was watching a ledge fifteen floors up. A man was standing there, his hands finger-spread against the sooty brick, his feet half-hanging over the edge.

His eyes held me. Even fifteen floors below him, I could see the whites, gigantic, milky, terrified. He didn't *want* to jump. . .whatever had driven him onto that ledge, he was like me, *he was me*. . .he wanted to fight it, but it had driven him there and he was held by it. But he wanted to live.

I glanced at Stephie, started to say something.

Her face.

How can I explain it so it will hold the impact it held for me then? How can I describe the expression of her face, the way she ground her teeth together, the contortion of her tiny features, the almost *purple light* across her cheekbones, the way her fists were clenched so tightly they went white. She *wanted* him to jump.

She didn't say a thing. I heard her. She was silent. *I heard her!*

Jump! she was saying, with her clenched teeth, her fists, that awful purple light playing across her face, *Jump!* The sight of him tumbling, going down, trying to fly the way falling men do with arms out, twitching. That was what she wanted to see. My throat went as dry as if I had chain-smoked for an hour straight. It was the most frightening thing I had ever seen.

I don't remember whether he fell, or was saved, or crawled back inside of his own volition, or whether we simply walked away. I don't remember. It didn't matter; just as what happened to me didn't matter. That guy up there was doomed—if not now, then sometime soon—just as I was. Something was destroying him, and something was destroying me. It didn't matter whether we fell now or later. It didn't matter. It had to happen.

Eight days before we were to go to City Hall—Billy and Stella were to be our witnesses—I learned who Stephie Cook was. I was allowed to discover how deep the layers of rust and decay on her soul were.

Jump!

We had been robbed at the bookstore on Broadway. . .well, almost robbed. Davey Haieff, the manager of the shop, was a rough number, who called the tourists and perverts who shopped for "different" books in our shop *kadodies*. We were just at the slack period of the evening, nine o'clock when most of the out-of-towners were free of dinner at the tourist traps and had made the eight-thirty curtain at the theaters. . .and we were loafing it.

That was when the four teenagers came in. They were like any other four teenagers you can see cruising Times Square, digging trouble. One of them meandered toward me in the back of the store, keeping his eyes on the showcase filled with Italian stilettos, Samurai swords, Solingen steel hunting knives—the sort of deadly looking but perfectly legal hardware sold to impress the yucks back home. I followed him, noticing that the other three hung around the raised cash register counter behind which Davey waited, watching, always watching everyone in the tiny shop.

"Can I interest you in a knife?" I asked the kid.

He was taller than me, by at least six inches, and the way he wore his T-shirt indicated he worked out on the parallel bars at the PAL gym. He looked more Bronx than Brooklyn; but they all looked pretty much the same, really. "Yeah, how 'bout that thing there." He jabbed a finger at the locked glass showcase, indicating a sixteen-inch Italian steel clasp-knife.

I grinned. This was my specialty. I could operate one of the clasp-knives by wrist action faster than any switchblade on the market, illegal though they were. We weren't allowed to sell switches or gravity or shake knives, so I had mastered the technique the better to push the merchandise we *could* sell.

Just as I unlocked the case, the other three made their move. I had the knife in my hand as one of them came up with an ironwood billy club and took a swing at Davey. I saw the action from the corner of my eye, and it was like a Mack Sennett comedy, sped up fifty-times normal.

Davey reached down, in and out, and up all in one fluid motion, and belted two of them with the rubber hose he kept there for just that purpose. They went down instantly, one of them open above the eyebrow with a five-inch gash that blinded him with his own blood. The third one bolted into the street.

My customer stood where he was. He had to, I had whipped open the knife and jammed it against his windpipe as I saw Davey move. It made a tiny indentation in the flesh, and he was still standing, staring wide-eyed at it when the cops came to take them away.

Davey told me to take the rest of the evening off.

I took the subway to Brooklyn and arrived just before ten o'clock—six hours earlier than usual. The balcony was vaulted, the doors thrown open and I bounded into the room carrying two popsicles, like something out of *The Thief of Bagdad.*

Stephie wasn't alone. She wasn't in bed, which made it worse.

A man would have driven me insane, I would have probably killed them both, I was so keyed up by the violence from the action in the shop. But it wasn't a man. I was stopped. I stopped. I was stopped, nothing but *stopped.* You understand what I am saying? Just stopped and stared and couldn't speak, and was so stopped I knew I was saying things to myself. Don't ask what I was saying, I have no idea.

Two girls lay on the bed, sucking on each other. Stephie sat naked, cross-legged on the floor, watching them with that same terrible expression she'd had while watching the man on the ledge.

One of the girls on the bed lay perfectly still as I came bursting in, playing possum, not stirring to draw attention. The other looked up and went white, deathly pale, the way I had written it a million times in my inadequate stories that avoided true confessions like this because they were improbable, written for sillyass housewives who would swallow *only* improbability. And I was part of it. They stared at me, all three of them. The first girl blankly, the second with fear—a puffy moth of a girl whose suntanned body seemed gross and fleshy to me—and Stephie, defiantly.

She wore a wedding ring. But not mine.

She wore a ring all right. On her little finger, left hand. A wedding ring—a lesbian's token of love and commitment. I was ill.

Had she been *on* the bed with one of them, it might have made some difference, then there would have been a reason, I could have rationalized. But *watching*. . .

I dropped the ridiculous popsicles and stumbled toward them, thinking I was moving back, away from them. The pudgy girl leaped off the bed, glistening with sweat, and flattened like a sack of brown sugar against the wall. "*Don't hit me*," she cried, "I can't stand pain. . .don't hit me!"

Stephie recrossed her legs in front of her, and her eyes were cold, dead, like a pair of gravestones. And at that moment, I understood. At that moment, school was out. What a complete, callow stupid hayseed I had been! She had used me as a cover, would have gone to the extreme of *marrying* me to cover. Why? What did I care? Her family, her job, the world in general, what did it matter? She had used me, and I was used up.

Then she sort of. . .lightly laughed. She let loose a Snow White giggle that sliced like a butcher's blade right through my stumbling consciousness and drained me of all energy. It was silly, and it hurt.

Watching.

She had been watching.

The one lying there still. Still as dead. If I lie silently here no one will hurt me. Fright. The room stank of it.

The other, against the wall. Terrified. Of me. The gross, hurting man. And my Stephie. . .watching.

Watching it all. Smiling endlessly.

Somehow, I got out of there, and back to Manhattan. Somehow.

Did I go by subway. . .was it underground or was I some sort of dead man on the way to the river Styx? Did I think about it, did I see that scene again and again? I don't know. I can't remember. Never!

I didn't know what to do.

I found Aggie and managed to tell it all, what I could tell, so driven out of my mind was I at the thought of her watching them on that bed. . .those *dykes*! He gave me a drink, and then called a girl he knew. She was a West Indian and she smelled of oregano. It couldn't have been worse.

Oddly, I kept feeling the doctor's needle in my arm, drawing the blood for the test, all through it. Everything was shaded in crimson.

I never saw Stephie again. The ultimate cliché for the ultimate hackneyed pain-story. Unfortunately, life is not a magazine story, with a sharp ending and a clear-cut moral; it drags on, there are sloppy ends, little after-touches, occasional phone calls, taperings-off that dull the edges of the most magnificent of tragedies. So it was with my Stephie, my woman-child and her Arctic chill. I later heard she had contracted tuberculosis and was suffering with it rather than asking her parents in New Jersey for money to see a doctor. Some called it grace under fire; I came to think of it as empty bravado, one more footfall on a path to self-destruction. She knew what she was doing. Stephie had chosen that way, all-knowing.

I missed her. Terribly. I was alone, once more, and now I was alone with the knowledge that Stephie and I were very much alike; the victims of the world; too weak to win.

I didn't even have the satisfaction of knowing I could use it as story-material. It wouldn't play; it was too much a tearjerker, too obviously probable to be a story; reality often stinks.

In any case—

Don't believe them. It's possible. You *can* keep a good man down.

—New York City and Chicago, 1960

A PRAYER FOR NO ONE'S ENEMY

"Did you get in?" He turned up the transistor. The Supremes were singing "Baby Love."

"None'a your damn business, man; a gentleman doesn't talk." The other one peeled a third stick of Juicy Fruit and folded it into his mouth. The sugary immediacy of it stood out for a moment, then disappeared into the wad already filling his left cheek.

"Gentleman? Shit, baby, you're a lotta stuff, but you aren't one of them there." He snapped fingers.

"D'jou check the plugs 'n' points like I said?"

He switched stations, stopped. The Rolling Stones were singing "I Can't Get No Satisfaction." "I took it into Cranston's, they said it was in the timing. Twenty-seven bucks."

"Plugs 'n' points."

"Oh, Christ, man, why don't you shine up awreddy. I'm *tellin'* you what Cranston said. He said it was in the timing, so why d'you keep sayin' plugs 'n' points?"

"Lemme use your comb."

"Use your own comb. You got scalp ringworm."

"Get stuffed! Lemme use your damn comb already!"

He pulled the Swedish aluminum comb out of his hip pocket and passed it over. The comb was tapered like a barber's comb. Gum stopped moving for an instant as the other pulled the gray shape through his long brown hair in practiced swirls. He patted his hair and handed the comb back. "Y'wanna go up to the Big Boy and get something to eat, clock the action?"

"You gonna fill the tank?"

"Fat chance."

"No, I don't wanna go up to the Big Boy and drive around and around like redskins at the Little Big Horn and see if that dopey-ass chick of yours is up there."

"Well, whaddaya wanna do?"

"I don't wanna go up to the Big Boy and go round and round like General Custer, that's for *damn* sure. . ."

"I got the picture. Round and round. Ha ha. Very clever. You oughta be in Hollywood, well what the hell do you *wanna* do?"

"You seen what's up at The Coronet?"

"I dunno, what is it?"

"That picture about the Jews in Palestine."

"Who's in it?"

"I dunno, Paul Newman I think."

"Israel."

"Okay, Israel, you seen it?"

"No, y'wanna see it?"

"Might as well, nothin' else happening around here."

"What time's your old lady come home?"

"She picks my father up at seven."

"That don't answer my question."

"Around seven-thirty."

"Let's make it. You got money. . .?"

"Yeah, for me."

"Jesus, you're a cheap bastard. I thought I was your tight close buddy?"

"You're a leech, baby."

"Turn off the radio."

"I'm gonna take it with me."

"So you ain't gonna tell me if you screwed Donna, huh?"

"None'a your damn business. You wanna tell me if you screwed Patti?"

"Forget it. Plugs 'n' points, you'll see."

"C'mon, we'll miss the first show."

So they went to see the picture about the Jews. The one that was supposed to say a very great deal about the Jews. They were both Gentile, and they had no way of knowing in advance that the picture about the Jews said nothing whatever about the Jews. In Palestine, or Israel, or wherever it was that the Jews were.

It wasn't even a particularly good film, but the exploitation had been cunning, and grosses for the first three days had been rewarding. Detroit. Where they make cars. Where Father Coughlin's Church of the Little Flower reposes in sanctified holiness. Population approximately two million; good people, strong like peasant stock. Where many good jazz men have started, blowing gigs in small roadhouses. Best barbecued spareribs in the world, at the House of Blue Lights. Detroit. Nice town.

The large Jewish Community had turned out to see the film, and though anyone who had been to Israel, or knew the first thing about how a *kibbutz* functioned, would have laughed it off the screen, for sheer emotionalism it struck the proper chords. With characteristic Hollywood candor, the film stirred a fierce ethnic pride, pointing out in broad strokes: *See, them little yids got guts, too; they can fight when they got to*. The movie was in the grand, altogether innocent tradition of cinematic flag-waving. It was recommended by *Parents' Magazine* and won a *Photoplay* gold medal as fare for the entire family.

The queue that had lined up to see the film stretched from the ticket booth across the front of the building, past a candy store with a window full of popcorn balls in half a dozen different flavors, past a laundromat, around a corner and three-quarters of the way down the block.

It was a quiet crowd. People in lines are always a quiet crowd. Arch and Frank were quiet. They waited, with Arch listening to the transistor, and Frank, Frank Amato, smoking and shuffling.

Neither paid much attention to the sound of engines roaring until the three Volkswagens screamed to a halt directly in front of the theater. Then they looked up, as the doors slammed open and out poured a horde of young boys. They were wearing black. Black turtle-neck T-shirts, black slacks, black Beatle boots. The only splash of color on them came from the yellow-and-black armbands, and the form of the swastika on the armbands.

Under the staccato directions of a slim Nordic-looking boy with very bright, wet gray eyes, they began to picket the theater, assembling in drill-formations, carrying signs neatly printed on a hand-press, very sturdy. The signs said:

THIS MOVIE IS
COMMUNIST-PRODUCED!
BOYCOTT IT!

GO BACK WHERE
YOU CAME FROM!
STOP RAPING AMERICA!

TRUE AMERICANS SEE
THROUGH YOUR LIES!

THIS FILM WILL CORRUPT
YOUR CHILDREN!
BOYCOTT IT!

and chanting, over and over: "Dirty little Christ-killers, dirty little Christ-killers, dirty little Christ-killers. . ."

In the queue was a sixty-year-old woman; her name was Lilian Goldbosch.

She had lost her husband Martin, her older son Shimon and her younger son Avram in the furnaces of Belsen. She had come to America with eight hundred other refugees on a converted cattle boat, from Liverpool, after five years of hopeless wandering across the desolate face of Europe. She had become a naturalized citizen and had found some stature as a buyer for a piece-goods house, but her reaction to the sight of the always-remembered swastika was that of the hunted Jewess who had escaped death—only to find loneliness in a new world. Lilian Goldbosch stared wide-eyed at them, overflowing the sidewalk, inundating her eyes and her thoughts and her sudden thismoment reality; arrogant in their militant fanaticism; and as one they came back to her—for they had never left her—terror, hatred, rage. Her mind (like a broken clock, whirling, spinning backward in time) sparklike leaped the gap of years, and her tired eyes blazed yellow.

She gave a wretched little scream and hurled herself at the tall blond boy, the leader with the gray eyes.

It was a signal.

The crowd broke. A low animal roar. Men flung themselves forward. Women were jostled, and then joined without reason or pausing to consider it. The muffled sound of souls torn by the sight of stalking (almost goose-stepping) picketers. Before they could stop themselves, the riot was underway.

A burly man in a brown topcoat reached them first. He grabbed the sign from one of the picketers, and with teeth grating behind skinned-back lips, for an instant an animal, hurled it into the gutter. Another man ripped into the center of the group and snapped a fist into the mouth of one of the boys chanting the slogan. The boy flailed backward, arms windmilling, and he went down on one knee. A foot on the end of gray sharkskin trousers—seemingly disembodied—lashed out of the melee. The toe of the shoe took the boy in the groin and thigh. He fell on his back, clutching himself, and they began to stomp him. His body curled inward as they danced their quaint tribal dance on him. If he screamed, it was lost in the roar of the mob.

Also in the queue were two high school boys.

They had been alone there, among all those people waiting. But now they were part of a social unit, something was happening. Arch and Frank had fallen back for an instant as others rushed forward;

others whose synapses were more quickly triggered by what they saw; but now they found their reactions to the violence around them swift and unthinking. Though they had been brushed aside by men on either side, cursing foully, who had left the line to get at the picketers, now they moved toward the mass of struggling bodies, still unaware of what was really taking place. It was a bop, and they felt the sting of participation. But in a moment they had collided with the frantic figure of Lilian Goldbosch, whose nails were raking deep furrows down the cheek of the tall, blond boy.

He was braced, legs apart, but did not move as she attacked him.

There was a contained, almost Messianic tranquility about him.

"Nazi! Nazi! Murd'rer!" she was mouthing, almost incomprehensibly. She slipped into Polish and the sounds became garbled with spittle. Her body writhed back and forth as she lashed out again and again at the boy.

Her arms were syncopated machines of hard work, destructive, coming up and down in a rhythm all their own, a rhythm of which she was unaware. His face was badly ripped, yet he did not move against her.

At that moment the two high school boys, faceless, came at the woman, one from either side; they took her by the biceps, holding her, protecting not the blond boy, but the older woman. Her movements went to spastic as she struggled against them frenziedly. "Let me, let go, let—" she struggled against them, flashing them a glance of such madness and hatred that for an instant they felt she must think them part of the picketing group, and then—abruptly—her eyes rolled up in her head and she fainted into Frank Amato's grasp.

"Thank you. . .whoever you are," the blond boy said. He started to move away, back through the rioting mob. It was as though he had *wanted* to take the woman's abuse; as though his purpose had been to martyr himself, to absorb all the hate and frenzy into his body, like a lightning rod sucking up the power of the heavens. Now he moved.

Arch grabbed him by the sleeve.

"Hold it a minute. . .hero! Not s'fast!"

The blond boy's mouth began to turn up in an insolent remark, but he caught himself, and instead, with a flowing, completely assured overhand movement, struck the younger boy's hand from his arm.

"My work's done here."

He turned, then, and cupped his hands to his mouth. A piercing whistle leaped above the crowd noises, and as the signal penetrated down through the mob, the swastika-wearers began to disengage themselves with more ferocity. One picketer kicked out, caught an older man in the shin with the tip of a tightly laced barracks boot, and shoved the man back into the crowd. Another boy jabbed a thumb into his opponent's diaphragm and sent the suddenly wheezing attacker sprawling, cutting himself off from further assault.

It went that way all through the crowd as the once-again-chanting picketers moved slowly but methodically toward their cars. It was a handsomely executed tactical maneuver, a strategic withdrawal of class and composure.

Once at the open car doors, they piled back against the black metal bugs, raising arms in an unmistakable *Heil!* and screamed, almost as one: "America always! To hell with the poisoners! Kill the Jews!"

Pop! Pop! With timing vaguely reminiscent of a Keystone Kops imbroglio, they heaved themselves into the vehicles, and were roaring down the street, around the corner, before the approaching growlers of the police prowl cars (summoned on a major 415) were more than a faint whine approaching from the distance.

On the sidewalk in front of the theater, people—for no other release was left to them—burst into tears and cursing.

Some kind of battle had been fought here—and lost.

On the sidewalk, someone had clandestinely chalked *the symbol.* No one moved to scuff it out. None of the picketers could have mooched the free time to do it; the obvious was obvious: someone in the queue had done it.

The subtlest, most effective poison.

Her apartment was an attempt to reassure her crippled spirit that possessions meant security, security meant permanence, and permanence meant the exclusion of sorrow and fear and darkness. She had thrust into every corner of the small one-bedroom apartment every convenience of modern technology, every possible knickknack and gimcrack of oddity, every utensil and luxury of the New World the rooms would hold. Here a 23" television set, its rabbit-ears askew against the wall. . .there a dehumidifier, busily purring at the silence. . .over there a set of Royal Doulton mugs, Pickwick figures smiling cherubically at their own ingenuousness. . .and a paint-by-the-numbers portrait of Washington astride a white stallion. . .a lemon glass vase overflowing with swizzle sticks from exotic restaurants. . .a stack of *Life*, *Time*, *Look* and *Holiday* magazines. . .a reclining lounge chair that vibrated. . .a stereo set with accompanying racks of albums, mostly Offenbach and Richard Strauss. . .a hide-a-bed sofa with orange and brown throw pillows. . .a novelty bird whose long beak, when moistened, dipped the creature forward on its wire rack, submerging its face in a glass of water, then pulled it erect, to repeat the performance endlessly. . .

The jerky movement of the novelty bird in the room, a bad cartoon playing over and over, was intended as reassurance of life still going on; yet it was a cheap, shadowy substitute, and instead of charming the two high school boys who had brought Lilian Goldbosch home, it unsettled them. It made them aware of the faint scent of decay and immolation here; a world within a world, a sort of superimposed precontinuum in which emotions had palpable massiveness, greater clarity.

The boys helped the still-shaken woman to the sofa, and sat her down heavily. Her face was not old, the lines were adornment rather than devastation, but there was a superimposition of pain on the tidy, even features. Cobwebs on marble. Her hair—so carefully tended and set every week by a professional, tipped, ratted, back-combed, pampered—was disheveled, limp, as though soaked with sweat. Moist stringlets hung down over one cheek. Her eyes, a light blue, altogether perceptive and lucid, were filmed by a milkiness that might have been tears, and might have been gelatinous anguish. Her mouth seemed moist, as though barely containing a wash of tormented sounds.

The years rolled back for Lilian Goldbosch. Once more she knew the sound of the enclosed van whose exhaust pipes led back into the prisoners' compartment, the awful *keee-gl keee-gl keee-gl* of the klaxon, rising above the frozen streets; frozen with fear of movement (if I stay quiet, they'll miss me, pass me by). The Doppler-impending approach of the van, its giant presence directly below the window, right at the curb, next to the face and the ears, and then its hissing passage as it swept away, a moving vacuum cleaner of living things, swallowing whole families. With eyes white eggshells in pale faces. And into the rear of that van, the exhaust whispering its sibilant tune of gas and monoxided forever. All this came back to Lilian Goldbosch as she shamefully spaded-over her memories of the past half hour. Those boys. Their armbands. Her fear. The crowd attacking. The way she had leaped at them. The madness. The fear.

The fear.

Again, the fear.

Burning, blazing through all of it: the fear!

That boy with his imperious blond good looks, the Aryan Superman: could he really know? Could he somehow, this American child born between clean sheets, with the greatest terror a failing mark in school, could he somehow know what that hated black swastika meant to her, to whole generations, to races of individuals who had worn yellow Stars of David and the word *Juden*, to shattered spirits and captured hearts who stood on alien roads as Stukas dived, or walked in desolate resignation to already filling mass graves, or labored across no-man's-lands with shellbursts lighting the way? Could he know, or was this something else. . .a new thing, that merely *looked* like the old sickness, the fear?

For the first time in more years than she cared to remember—had it been only twenty years since all of it?—Lilian Goldbosch had a surge of desire. Not the gilded wastes she had substituted for caring: not the pathological attention to hair in the latest frosted style, not the temporal acquisition of goods to fill empty rooms, not the television with its gray images, surrogates of life. A want. A need to know. A desire to find out.

Born of an old fear.

Was it the same. . .or something new?

She had to know. She was engulfed by desperation.

And with the desperation, a shocking realization that she could do something. What, she was not certain. But she had the sensation burning in her that if she could know this blond Gentile youth, could talk to him, this *goy*, could communicate with him, this stranger, she could find out the answers, know if the evil was coming again, or if it was just another lonely person, trapped within his skin.

"Will you boys do me a favor?" Lilian Goldbosch asked the two who had escorted her home. "Will you help me?"

At first they were confused, but as she talked, as she explained why she had to know, why it was important, they were drawn into a prospect of their times, and finally they nodded, a little hesitantly, the taller of the two saying, "I don't know if it'll do any good, but we'll try and find him for you."

Then they left. Down the stairs. While she went to wash the tears and streaked mascara from her young-old face.

Frank Amato was of Italian descent. He was a typical child of his times; transistorized, Sanforized, boss gear bomped groovy tuned-in on the music of the spheres, in a Continental belt-back slim-line hopsacking crease-resistant 14" tapered ineluctable reality that placed him in and of the teenage sub-culture.

Vietnam? Huh?

Voter registration in Alabama? Huh?

The ethical structure of the universe?

Huh?

Arch Lennon was a WASP. He had heard the term, but had never applied it to himself. He was a carbon-copy of Frank Amato. He lived day to day, Big Boy to Big Boy, track meet to track meet, and if there were sounds that went boomp in the night they were probably the old man getting up to haul another pop-top out of the Kelvinator.

Military junta? Huh?

Limited nuclear retaliation? Huh?

The infinitesimal dispensation of Homo sapiens in the disinterested cosmos?

Huh?

Standing down on the sidewalk outside Lilian Goldbosch's apartment, staring at each other.

"*That* was a smart move."

"Well, what the hell was I supposed to say? For chrissakes, she had aholda my arm I thought she was gonna bust it. That old lady's nuts."

"So why'd you promise her? Where the hell we gonna find that guy?"

"How should *I* know?"

"I gave my word."

"Big deal."

"Maybe not to you, but I gave it just the same."

"So we try and find that kid, right?"

"Uh. . ."

"What I thought. I gotta do all the brain work again. Jeezus, man, you are such a nit."

"D'jou get the license number of any of those cars?"

"Don't be a clown. No, I din't get the number. And even if I did, what'd we do with it?"

"DMV, wouldn't they tell us who it was registered to?"

"Sure. We're gonna walk into the Motor Vehicle Department just like James Bond, a couple of guys our age, and we're gonna say hey who owns this VW. Sure, I can picture it real good. You're a nit."

"So that's that."

"I wish."

"You got something else?"

"Maybe. One of those VWs had a sticker on the windshield. It was an emblem. Pulaski Vocational High School."

"So one of those guys goes to Pulaski. You know how many inmates they got over there? Maybe a million."

"It's a start."

"You're serious about this."

"Yeah, I'm serious about it."

"How come?"

"I dunno, she asked, an' I gave her my word. She's an old lady, it won't hurt anything to look a while."

"Hey, Frank?"

"What?"

"What's this all about?"

"I dunno, but those bastards were lousy, an' I gave my word."

"Okay, I'll help. But I gotta get home now, my folks oughta be back by now, and we can't do anything till tomorrow anyhow."

"Stay loose. See ya."

"See ya. Don't get in any trouble, double-oh-seven."

"Stick it."

They didn't know which one they would find, or even if they would recognize him when they did find him. But one of the wearers of the swastika attended Pulaski Vocational, and Pulaski Vocational went all year round. Summer, winter, night and day, it turned out students who knew more about carburetors, chassis dynamometers, metal lathes and printed circuitry than they did about THE CANTERBURY TALES, scoria and pumice, the theory of vectors and the fact that Crispus Attucks, a Negro, was the first American to fall in the Revolutionary War. It was a great gray stone Coventry of a school, where young boys went in unmarked, and emerged some years later all punched and coded to fit into the System, with fringe benefits and an approximate date of death IBM'd by the group insurance company.

Chances were good the boy—whichever boy it turned out to be—was still attending classes, even though it was summer, and Arch and Frank were free. So they waited, and they watched. And finally, they found one of them.

An acne-speckled, pudgy-hipped specimen in a baggy orange velour pullover.

He came out of the school, and Arch recognized him.

"There, the pear-shaped one, in the orange."

They followed him into the parking lot. The car he unlocked was a Monza, a late model. If they had been on the alert for a VW, they would have missed him.

"Hey!" Frank came up behind him. The pudgy turned.

He had beady little eyes, like a marmoset. The face was fleshy, with many small inflamed areas where he had shaved and the skin had broken out. There was a wasted look about him, as though he had been used up, and cast away. Even to Arch and Frank, the look of intense intelligence was missing from the pudgy's expression.

"Who're you guys?"

Arch did not like him. For a nameless reason, he did not like him. "Friends of a friend of yours."

Pudgy looked wary. He dumped his books into the back seat, not turning from them. He was getting set to jump inside the car and slam the door, and lock it, and pull out in a hurry. Pudgy was scared.

"Who's that, what friend?"

Frank moved slightly, to the side. It was almost a pavane, the maneuvering: Pudgy angled himself, his hand went toward the back of the front seat; Arch slid around the edge of the door. Frank's hand came up onto the roof of the car, near Pudgy's head. Pudgy's eyes got milky, fear bubbled up behind him, the taint was in his bloodstream.

"A tall kid, blond hair, you know," Frank said, his voice was deeper, a trifle threatening, "he was with you the other night at the movie, remember?"

Pudgy's right cheek tic'd. He knew what was happening. These were Jews. He made his move.

Arch slammed the door. It caught Pudgy at the forearm. He howled. Arch reached across and grabbed him by the ear. Frank sank a fist into Pudgy's stomach. The air whooshed out of Pudgy and left him flat, very flat, a cardboard cutout that they bundled into the front seat of the Monza, one on either side of him. They started the car, and rolled out of the parking lot. They would take him someplace. Someplace else. Pudgy would tell them who the blond Aryan had been, what his name was, where he could be found.

If they could pump enough air into him to produce sound.

Victor. Rohrer. Victor Rohrer. Blond, tall, solid with no extra flesh on his body, muscles very firm and tight, as though packed from the factory in plastic. Victor Rohrer. A face hewn from lignum vitae, from marble. Eyes chipped gray ice frost from lapis lazuli and allowed to die, harden into leaden cadaverousness. A languid body; without planes or angles; soft, downy-covered with barely visible blond hairs, each one a sensor, a feeler of atmospheres and temperatures, each one a cilium seeing and smelling and knowing the tenor of the situation. A Cardiff Giant, not even remotely human, something cold and breathing, defying Mendelian theories, defying heredity, a creature from another island universe. Muscled and wired, peering at a world of pain and confusion out of gray eyes that had seldom been blue with life. Lips thinned in expectation of silence. Victor. Rohrer. A creation of self, brought forth from its own mind for a need to exist.

Victor Rohrer, organizer of men.

Victor Rohrer, who had never known childhood.

Victor Rohrer, repository of frozen secrets.

Victor Rohrer, wearer of swastikas.

Patron of days and nights; singer of tuneless songs; visionary of clouds and nothingness; avatar of magics and unspoken credos; celebrant of terrors in nights of troubling, scary voices, endlessly threatening; architect of orderly destructions; Victor Rohrer.

"Who are you? Get away from me."

"We want you to talk to somebody."

"Punk filth!"

"Don't make me flatten you, wise guy."

"Don't try it; I don't like hurting people."

"*There's* one of the great laughs of our generation."

"Come on, Rohrer, get your ass in gear; somebody's waiting for you."

"I said: get away from me."

"We aren't goons, Rohrer, don't make us belt you around a little."

"It would take two of you?"

"If it had to."

"That isn't very sportsmanlike."

"Somewhichway, friend, you don't make us feel very sporty. Move it, or s'help me I'll lay this alongside your head."

"Are you from one of those street gangs?"

"No, we're just a coupla patriots doing a good deed."

"I'm tired'a talking. Get it going, Rohrer."

"You. . .you're *Jewish*, aren't you? You're a *Jew!*"

"I said get going, you bastard! Now!"

And they brought him to Lilian Goldbosch.

Wonder danced in her eyes. A dance of the dead in a bombed-out graveyard; a useless weed growing in a bog. She stared across the room at him. He stood just inside the door, legs close together, arms at his sides, his face as featureless as an expanse of tundra. Only the gray eyes moved in the face, and they did so liquidly, flowing from corner to corner, seeing what was there to be seen.

Lilian Goldbosch walked across the room toward him. Victor Rohrer did not move. Behind him, Arch and Frank closed the door softly. They stood like paladins, one on either side of the door. They watched—with intense fascination—what was happening in this silently humming room. As different worlds paused for an eternal moment.

They did not fully comprehend what it was, but so completely had the blond boy and the old woman absorbed each other's presence, that for now they—the ones who had effected the meeting—were gone, invisible, out of phase, no more a part of the life generated in the room than the mad little bird that dipped its beak in water, agonizingly straightened, rocked and dipped again, endlessly.

She walked up, very close to him. Where she had scratched him, his face was still marked. She reached up, involuntarily fascinated, and made as if to touch him. He moved back an inch, and she caught herself.

"You are very young."

It was said in appraisal, with a tinge of amazement, not a hue of poetry anywhere in it; an attempt to codify the reality of this creature, Victor Rohrer.

He said nothing, but a faint softness came to his mouth, as if he knew another truth. On another face, it might have been a sneer.

"Do you know me?" she asked. "Who I am?"

He was extremely polite, as if she were a supplicant and it had fallen to him to maintain decorum and form with her. "You're the woman who attacked me."

Her lips tightened. The memory was still fresh, an eroded fall on a volcanic hillside she had thought incapable of being ravaged again. "I'm sorry about that."

"I've come to expect it. From you people."

"My people. . ."

"Jews."

"Oh. Yes. I'm Jewish."

He smiled knowledgeably. "Yes, I know. It says everything, doesn't it?"

"Why do you do this thing? Why do you walk around and tell people to hate one another?"

"I don't hate you."

She stared at him warily; there had to be more. There was.

"How can one hate a plague of locusts, or a pack rat that lives in the walls? I don't hate, I'm merely an exterminator."

"Where did you get these ideas? Why does a boy your age fool around with this kind of thing, do you know what went on in the world twenty-five years ago, do you know all the sorrow and death this kind of thinking brought?"

"Not enough. He was a madman, but he had the right idea about the *Juden*. He had the final solution, but he made mistakes."

His face was perfectly calm. He was not reciting cant, he was delivering a theory he had worked out, logically, completely, finally.

"How did you get so much sickness in you?"

"It is a matter of opinion which of us is diseased. I choose to believe you are the cancer."

"What do your parents think of this?"

A hot little spot of red appeared high on his cheeks. "Their opinions are of very little concern to me."

"Do they know about what you do?"

"I'm getting tired of this. Are you going to tell these two punks to let me go, or will I have to put up with more abuse from you and your kind?" His face was getting slightly flushed now. "Do you wonder that we want to purge you, purify the country of your filth? When you constantly prove what we say is so?"

Lilian Goldbosch turned to the two boys by the door. "Do you know where he lives?" Arch nodded. "I want to see his mother and father. Will you take me there?" Again, Arch nodded. "He doesn't know. He doesn't understand. I can't find out from him. I'll have to ask there."

Flames burned up suddenly in Victor Rohrer's eyes. "You'll stay away from my home!"

"I'll get my purse," she said, softly.

He went for her. His hands came out and up and he was on her, hurling her backward, over a footstool, and they went into a heap, the woman thrashing frantically, and Victor Rohrer coldly, dispassionately trying to strangle her.

Arch and Frank moved quickly.

Frank grabbed Rohrer around the throat in a hammerlock, and without ceremony or warning, Arch lifted a marble ashtray from an end table and swung it in an arc. The ashtray smacked across the side of Victor Rohrer's head with an audible sound, and he suddenly tilted to the left and fell past Lilian Goldbosch.

He was not unconscious, Arch had pulled his punch, but he was dazed. He sat on the floor, moving his head as if it belonged to somebody else. The two high school boys attended the woman. She struggled to pick herself up, and they helped her to her feet.

"Are you okay?" Frank asked.

She leaned against Arch, and automatically her hand went to her hair, to tidy it. But the movement was only half-formed, as if all those narcissistic acts she had used to make her life livable were now frippery. Her breathing was jagged, and red marks circled her larynx where Rohrer had fastened on tightly.

"He is the complete Nazi," she said breathlessly. "He has eaten the Nazi cake, and digested it; he is one of them. It is the old fear, the same one, the very same one, come again. Dear God, we will see it again, the way it was before."

She began to sob. From an empty room within the structure of her soul, tears that had dried years before were called on, and would not come. Ludicrously, she rasped and wheezed, and when nothing came to her eyes, she swallowed hard and bit her lip. In a while she stopped.

"We must take him home," she said. "I want to talk to his parents."

They got Victor Rohrer under the arms, and they lifted him. He staggered and bobbled, but between them they got him downstairs and into the car. Arch sat in back with him, and Lilian Goldbosch stared straight ahead through the windshield, even when they finally pulled up in front of Rohrer's house in the suburb, Berkeley.

"We're here," Frank said to her. She started, and looked around slowly. It was a neat, unprepossessing house, set in a line among many such houses. It escaped a total loss of identity by a certain warmth of landscaping: dwarf Japanese trees dotting the front lawn, a carefully trimmed hedge that ran down the property line on one side, ivy holding fast to a corner of the house with several years of climbing having brought it just under the second-floor windows. An ordinary house, in an ordinary town.

"Okay, Rohrer, out."

Victor Rohrer went wild! His face contorted. The cold logical animosity of the cool reasoning racist was suddenly washed away. He began speaking in a thin, venomous tone, the words slipping out between knife-edge lips; they did not hiss, but they might as well have; he did not scream, but it had the same shocking effect.

"Kike filth. How much longer do you think you're going to be able to push people around like this? All of you, just like you, with your rotten poisonous filth, trying to take over, trying to tell people what to do; you ought to be killed, every one of you, slaughtered like pigs, I'd do it myself if I could. You'll see, your day is coming, the final day for you. . ."

It was rasped out with such intensity, Lilian Goldbosch sat straight, tensed, unable to move, it was a voice from the past. Her body began to tremble. It was the old fear, the one that years of war and years of peace had put in a grave she now found had always been too shallow. The corpse of that fear had clawed its way up out of the dirt and massed dead flesh of the communal grave, and was again walking the world.

Arch reached across and opened the door. He shoved Victor Rohrer before him. Frank and Lilian Goldbosch joined them as they walked up the front drive toward the little house.

"I've found my answer," Lilian Goldbosch said, terror in her voice. "It is the old fear, the terrible one, the one that destroys worlds. And he is the first of them. . .but there will be many more. . .many. . ."

Her eyes were dull as they reached the front door. Rohrer spun about, slapping Arch's hand off his arm. "You aren't going to meet them! I won't allow you in! This isn't a Jew-run town, I'll have you arrested for kidnapping, for breaking and entering. . ."

Lilian looked past him.

Past him, to the lintel of the door.

And the fear suddenly drained out of her face.

Victor Rohrer saw her expression, and half-turned his head. Arch and Frank looked in the direction of Lilian Goldbosch's stare. Attached to the lintel of the door, at a slant, was a tubular ornament of shiny brass. Near the top of the face of the ornament was a small hole, through which Arch and Frank could see some strange lettering.

Lilian Goldbosch said, "*Shaddai*," reached across Victor Rohrer and touched the tiny hole, then withdrew her hand and kissed the fingertips. Her face had been transformed. She no longer looked as though darkness was on its way.

HARLAN ELLISON
A PRAYER FOR NO ONE'S ENEMY

Victor Rohrer made no move toward her.

"That is a fine *mezuzah*, Victor," she said, softly, looking at him now with complete control of the situation. She started to turn away. "Come along, boys, I don't need to see Victor's parents now: I understand."

They stared at Rohrer. He suddenly looked like a hunted animal. All his cool polite self-possession was gone. He was sweating. Alone. He stood, suddenly, on his own doorstep, next to a tubular ornament on a right doorpost, alone. Afraid.

Lilian paused a moment, turned back to Victor Rohrer. "It is true no one has a happy childhood, Victor. But we all have to live, to go on. Yours must not have been nice, but. . .try to live, Victor. You aren't my enemy, neither am I your enemy."

She walked down the steps, turned once more and said, kindly, as an afterthought, "I will say a prayer for you."

Bewildered, Arch and Frank looked at Victor Rohrer for a long moment. They saw a man of dust. A scarecrow. An emptiness where a person had stood a moment before. This old woman, with incomprehensible words and a sudden sureness, had hamstrung him, cut the nerves from his body, emptied him like a container of murky liquid.

With a soft sound of panic, Victor Rohrer hurled himself off the front steps, and ran across the yard, disappearing in a moment. He was gone, and the three of them stood there, looking at the afternoon.

"What did you say to him?" Arch said. "That word you said. What was it?"

Lilian Goldbosch turned and walked to the car. They came and held the door for her. She was regal. When she looked up at the boys, she smiled. "*Shaddai.* The name of the Lord. From Deuteronomy."

Then she got in, and they closed the door. Out of sight of Lilian Goldbosch, where she sat calmly, waiting to be driven home, Arch and Frank stared at each other. Total confusion. Something had happened here, but they had no idea what it was.

Then they got in the car, and drove her home. She thanked them, and asked them to call on her again, any time. They could not bring themselves to ask what had happened, because they felt they should be smart enough to know; but they didn't know.

Outside, they looked at each other, and abruptly, just like that, everything that had gone before in their lives seemed somehow trivial. The dancing, the girls, the cars, the school that taught them nothing, the aimless days and nights of movies and cursing and picnics and drag races and ball games, all of it, seemed terribly inconsequential, next to this puzzle they had become part of.

"*Shuh-die*," Arch said, looking at Frank.

"And that other word: *muh-zooz*—what it was."

They went to see a boy they knew, in their class, a boy they had never had occasion to talk to before. His name was Arnie Sugarman, and he told them three things.

When they got back to Lilian Goldbosch's apartment, they knew something was wrong the moment they approached the door. It was open, and the sound of classical music came from within. They shoved the door open completely, and looked in.

She was lying half on the sofa, half on the floor. He had used a steam iron on her, and there was blood everywhere. They entered the room, avoiding the sight, avoiding the mass of pulped meat that had been her face before he had beaten her again, and again, and again, in a senseless violence that had no beginning and no end. The two high school boys went to the telephone, and Frank dialed the operator.

"Puh-police, please. . .I want to report a, uh, a murder. . ."

Lilian Goldbosch lay twisted and final; the terror that had pursued her across the world, through the years—the terror she had momentarily escaped—had at last found her and added her to the total that could never be totaled. She had found her answer, twenty-five years too late.

In the room, the only movement was a small bird with a comic beak that dipped itself in water, straightened, and then, agonizingly, repeated the process, over and over and over. . .

HARLAN ELLISON
A PRAYER FOR NO ONE'S ENEMY

Hunkered in an alley, where they would find him, Victor Rohrer stared out of mad eyes. Eyes as huge as golden suns, eyes that whirled with fiery little points of light. Eyes that could no longer see.

See his past, his childhood, when they had used names to hurt him. When his parents had been funny little people who talked with accents. When he had been friendless. . .for *that* reason.

For the reason of the *mezuzah* on the lintel. The little holy object on the lintel, the ornament that contained the little rectangle of parchment with its twenty-two lines of Hebrew from Deuteronomy.

Back behind huge garbage cans spilling refuse, in the sick-sweet rotting odor of the alley, Victor Rohrer sat with knees drawn up, staring at his limp hands, the way a fetus "sees" its limp, relaxed hands before its face. Quiet in there, inside Victor Rohrer. Quiet for the first time. Quiet after a long time of shrieking and sound and siren wails inside a skull that had offered no defense, no protection.

Victor Rohrer and Lilian Goldbosch, both *Juden*, both stalked; and on an afternoon in Detroit. . .

. . .both had answered with their lives a question that had never even existed, much less been asked, by two high school boys who now had begun to suspect. . .

. . .no one escapes, when night begins to fall.

—Detroit, Michigan, 1966

PUNKY & THE YALE MEN

"Love ain't nothing but sex misspelled," he had said, when he had left New York, for the last time. He had said it to the girl he had been sleeping with: a junior fashion and beauty editor with one of the big women's slicks. He had just found out she was a thirty-six-dollar-a-day cocaine addict, and it hadn't mattered, really, because he had gift-wrapped his love and given it to her, asking nothing in return except that she let him be near her.

And yet, when he asked her, that final day, why they had made love only once (with all her stray baby cats mewling in corners and walking over their intertwined bodies), she answered, "I was stoned. It was the only way I could hack it." And he had been sick. Even in his middle thirties, having been down so many dark roads that ended in nothingness, he had been hurt, had been destroyed, and he had gone away from her, gone away from that place, in that special time, and he had told her, "Love ain't nothing but sex misspelled."

It had been bad grammar for a writer as famous as Sorokin. But he was entitled to indulge. It had been a bad year. So he had left New York, for the last time, once again resuming the search that had no end; he had gone back to the studio in Hollywood, and had forgotten quite completely, knowing he would never return to New York.

Now, in another time, still seeking the punchline of the bad joke his life had become, he was back in New York.

Andy Sorokin came out of the elevator squinting, as though he had just stepped into dazzling sunshine.

Dazzling.

It was the forty-second-floor reception room of *Marquis* magazine and the most dazzling thing in it was the shadow-box display of Kodachrome transparencies from the pages of *Marquis*.

Dazzling:

Péche flambée at The Forum of The XII Caesars; tuxedoed and tuck-bow-tied stalwarts at a Joan Sutherland première; decorous girl stuff, no nylon and garter belt crotch shots; deep-sea fishing with marlin and mad-eyed bonita breaking white water; Yousuf Karsh character studies of two post-debs and a Louisiana racist politico; a brace of artily drawn cartoons; a Maserati spinning-out at the Nürburg Ring; Hemingway, Fitzgerald, Dorothy Parker, Nathanael West, others whose first work had appeared in the magazine; a soft-nosed Labrador Retriever in high grass, ostensibly retrieving a Labrador; two catamarans running before a gale.

Andy Sorokin was not dazzled. He squinted like a man suffering on the outside of a needle-thrust of heartburn.

The unlit cigarette hung from the exact center of his mouth, and he worked with his teeth at the spongy, now moist filter. Behind him, the elevator doors sighed shut, and he was almost alone in the reception room. He stood, still only two steps onto the deep-pile wall-to-wall, a man listening to silent songs in stone, as the nearly pretty receptionist looked up, waiting for *him* to come to *her*.

When he didn't, she pursed, she nibbled, and then she flashed her receptionist eyes. When he still paid no attention to her, she said firmly, projecting, "Yes, may I help you?"

Sorokin had not been daydreaming. He had been entirely *there*, assaulted by the almost pathological density of good taste in the reception room, beguiled by the relentless masculinity of the *Marquis* image as totemized in the Kodachromes, amused by an impending meeting that was intended to regain for him that innocence of childhood or nature he had somewhen lost, by the preposterous expedient of hurling him back into a scene, a past, he had fled—gladly—seventeen years before.

"I doubt it," he replied.

Steel shutters slammed down in her eyes. It had been a bitch of a day, lousy lunch, out of pills and the Curse right on time, and but *no room* in a day like today for some sillyass cigarette-nibbling smartass with funnys. It became unaccountably chill in the room.

Sorokin knew it had been a dumb remark. But it wasn't worth retracting.

"Walter Werringer, please," he said wearily.

"Your name?" in ice.

"Sorokin."

And she knew she had blown it. Ohmigod Sorokin. All day Werringer and the staff had been on tiptoes, like a basic training barracks waiting for the Inspector General. Sorokin, the giant. Standing here rumpled and nibbling a filter, and she had chopped him. The word was ohmigod. And but *no* way to recoup. If he so much as dropped a whisper to someone in editorial country, a whisper, the time for moving out of her parents' apartment on Pelham Parkway was farther off, the *Times* want ads.

She tried a smile, and then didn't bother. His eyes. How drawn and dark they were, like purse strings pulled tight closed. She should have guessed: those eyes: Sorokin.

"Right this way, Mr. Sorokin," she said, standing, smoothing her skirt across her thighs. There was a momentary flicker of reprieve: he looked at her body. So she preceded him down the corridor into editorial country, moving it fluidly. "Mr. Werringer and the staff have been expecting you," she said, turning to speak over her shoulder, letting the ironed-flat blonde discothèque hair sway back from her good left profile.

"Thank you," he said, wearily. It was a long quiet corridor.

"I really admired your book," she said, still walking. He had had fourteen novels published, she didn't say which one, which meant she had read none of them.

"Thank you."

She continued talking, saying things as meaningful as throat-clearings. And the terrible thing about it, was that from the moment

Andy Sorokin had entered the reception room, and she had thought *I blew it*, he had known everything that had passed through her mind. He had thought her thoughts, the instant she had thought them. Because she was a people, and that was Andy Sorokin's line. He was cursed with an empathy that often threatened to drive him up the wall, around the bend, down the tube and out of this world. He knew she had been playing it bitchily cool, then scared when she found out who he was, then trying to ameliorate it with her body and the hair-swirling. He knew it all, and it depressed him: to find out he was correct again. Once again. As always.

If just once they'd surprise me, he thought, following her mouth and words, her body. Thinking *this*, in preparation:

Here I am returning to New York, to the very core of The Apple, after summer solstice in L.A. (where the capris run to tight and the soma run to trembly), and it's returning to my past, to my childhood. Filthy, drizzly, crowded till I gag and scream for elbow room on the BMT, it's still where I came from, a glory—notably absent from The Coast. It doesn't even matter that the collar of my Eagle broadcloth looks as though caterpillars had shit in a sooty trail, after a day on the town; it doesn't matter that everyone snarls and bites in the streets; it doesn't matter that the service at the Teheran has been run into the toilet since Vincente went over the hill to The Chateaubriand; it doesn't matter that Whitey silenced Jimmy Baldwin the only way it could, by absorbing him, recognizing him, deifying him, making him the Voice of His People, driving him insane; it doesn't even matter that Olaf Burger up at Fawcett has grown stodgy with wealth and position; to hell with all the carping, dammit, it's New York, the hub of it all, the place where it all started again, and I've been so damned long on The Coast, in that Mickey Mouse scene hiya baby pussycat sweetheart lover. . .and even when I'm systemically inclined to believe sesquipedalian Thomas Wolfe (no, not that *Tom Wolfe, the* real *Tom Wolfe), I keep being amazed to find I* can *go home again, and again, and again.*

It is always New York, my Manhattan, where I learned to walk, where I learned all I know, and where it waits for me every time I come back, like a childhood sweetheart grown sexy with experience, yet still capable of adolescent charm. How bloody literary!

Sonofabitch, I love you, N'Yawk.

She was still gibbering, walking, and all he thought, every spun-out spiderweb sentence of it, only took a moment to whirl through his mind, before they arrived at the door to Walter Werringer's office, concluding with:

Even forty-two stories up in an editorial office, going in to see an important editor who wouldn't have paid me penny-a-word to carve the Magna Carta on his executive toilet wall before I went to Hollywood and became a Name, who now offers me an arm, a leg and a quivering thigh to go back down to Red Hook, Brooklyn and rewrite my impressions, seventeen years later, of juvenile delinquency, "Kid Gang Revisited," even this *is New York lovely. . .*

Oh, revenge, thy taste is groovy!

Thoughts of Andrew Sorokin, best-selling novelist, Hollywood scenarist, page 146 (vols. 5–6) of CONTEMPORARY AUTHORS [Born May 27, 1929, in Buffalo, New York; joined a gang of juvenile delinquents in Red Hook, Brooklyn, and posed as a member of the group for three months during 1948, gathering authentic background material for his first novel, CHILDREN OF THE GUTTERS.], and nominee for an Academy Award, as he stepped past an oiled-hipped receptionist into the outer office of Walter Werringer, editor of *Marquis* magazine: thoughts of Andrew Sorokin, if not recognized as a prophet in his own land, at least a prodigal returned to accept the huzzahs of the nobility. Time had passed, times had changed, and Andy Sorokin was back.

The receptionist spoke with purport to the trim and distant secretary in the outer office. "Frances. . .Mr. Sorokin." The secretary brightened, and the smile buttered across her lower face. "Oh, just a moment, Mr. Sorokin; Mr. Werringer is expecting you." She began clicking the intercom.

The receptionist did a little sensuality thing with her mouth as she touched Andy Sorokin's sleeve. "It was a pleasure meeting you, Mr. Sorokin."

He smiled back at her. "I'll stop to say good-bye on my way out." She was off the hook. He had done it purposely. One of his occasional gestures of humanity: why let her worry that he was going to cost her a job with a casual remark. It also meant he was going to ask for her number. Now all she had to decide was whether she would play it ingenue and let him ask, or hand him the pre-written note with the name and number on it, when he came back past her in the reception room. It was an infinitely fascinating game of ramifications, and Andy Sorokin knew she would play it with herself till he reappeared. She went, and he turned back as the secretary rose to usher him into the inner presence of Walter Werringer.

"Right this way, Mr. Sorokin," she said, standing, smoothing her skirt across her thighs. He looked at her body. She preceded him to the inner office door, moving it fluidly. *If just once they'd surprise me*, he thought.

Forty minutes later, they still had not discussed what Sorokin had come to discuss: the assignment. They had talked about Sorokin's career, from pulp detective and science fiction stories through the novels to Hollywood and the television, the motion picture scripts. The impending Oscar night, and Sorokin's nomination. They had discussed Sorokin's two disastrous marriages, his appraisal of Hollywood politics, the elegance of *Marquis*, the silliness of Sorokin's never having been in the pages of that elegant slick monthly. (But not the bitter weevil that nibbled Sorokin's viscera: that *Marquis* had never thought him worthy of acceptance before he had become famous and a Name.) They had discussed women, JFK, what had become of Mailer, the unreliability of agents, paperback trends, everything but the assignment.

And a peculiar posturing had sprung up between them.

Werringer stared at Andy Sorokin across a huge Danish coffee mug, steam fogging his bifocals, gulping with heavenly satisfaction. "Without joe I'd be dead," he said. He took another gulp, reinforcing his own stated addiction, and plonked the mug down on the desk blotter. "Ten, fifteen cups a day. Gotta have it." He liked to play the stevedore, rather than the literary lion. He enjoyed the role of the Hemingway more than that of the Maxwell Perkins. It was his posture, and as far as Sorokin was concerned, he was stuck with it. Yet it had an adverse effect on Sorokin, who had been what Werringer worked at seeming to be. (*Damn my empathy*, he thought. *Perversity incarnate!*) It had the effect of sending Sorokin into a pseudo-Truman Capote stance. Limp-wristed, campy, biting with bitchy aphorism and innuendo. Werringer was on the verge of mentally labeling Sorokin homosexual, even though the conclusion ran contrary to everything he knew of the writer, and the confusion only served to amuse Sorokin. But not too much.

"About this idea of yours, for me. . ." Sorokin finally broached it.

"Right. Yeah, let's get to it." Werringer crinkled his face in a Victor McLaglen roughsmile. He rummaged under a stack of manuscripts and pulled out a copy of Sorokin's first novel, sixteen years old in its original dust wrapper. CHILDREN OF THE GUTTERS. He fingered it as though it were some rare and moldering edition, a first folio "Macbeth," rather than a somewhat better than good fictionalized autobiography of three months Andy Sorokin had spent living a double-life, seventeen years before, when he had been young and provincial enough to think "experience" was a substitute for content or style. Three months with a kid gang, living in and running through the stinking streets, getting what he liked to call "the inside."

Now, seventeen years later, and Werringer wanted him to go back to those streets. After the army, after Paula and Carrie, after the accident, after Hollywood, after the last seventeen years that had given him so much, and stripped him so clean. Go back, Sorokin. Go back to it. If you can.

Werringer was doing the hairy-chested bit again. He tapped the book with a fingernail. "This has real guts, Andy. Real balls. I always felt that way about it."

"Call me Punky." Sorokin minced, smiling boyishly. "That's what they called me in the gang. Punky."

Werringer did a frowning thing. If Sorokin was a visceral realist out of the gutsy Robert Ruark school, why was he camping?

"Uh-huh, Punky, sure." He tried to get his feet under him, but wobbled a little. Sorokin tried not to snicker. "It has real plunge, real honesty in it, a helluva lot of depth," Werringer added, lamely.

Sorokin assumed a moue of displeasure, pure faggot: "Too bad it tiptoed through the bookstores," he said. "It was written to alter the course of Western Civilization, you know." Werringer paled. What was happening here? "You *do* know that, don't you?"

Werringer nodded dumbly, and took the remark at face value. He didn't know why he should feel as though he had just fallen down the rabbit hole, but the impression was overwhelming.

"Well, uh, what we'd like, what we *want*, for *Marquis*, is the same sort of ballz—uh, the same sort of highly emotional writing you put into this."

Sorokin felt his stomach tightening, now that the moment was with him. "What you want me to do, is go back down to Red Hook, to the same place I knew, and write about the way it is now."

Werringer banged a palm on the desk. "Exactly! The kids, what happened to them, where they are now. Did they wind up in the slammer, did they get married, go into the army, the whole story, seventeen years later. And the social conditions. Have the tenements been cleaned up? What about the low-rent housing projects? Has the Police Athletic League been of any use? What about racial tensions down there now, does it make for a different kind of kid gang, different rumbles, you know, the whole scene."

"You want me to go back down there."

Werringer stared. "Yeah, right, that's what we want. 'Kid Gang Revisited.' Something in depth."

The tension that had been growing in Sorokin now abruptly tightened like a fist. Go back down there. Go back to it, seventeen years later. "I was nineteen years old when I joined that gang," Andrew Sorokin said, half to himself. Werringer continued to stare. The man in front of him seemed to be in some sort of shock.

"I'm thirty-six now. I don't know—"

Werringer bit the inside of his lip. "We only want you to write it from the outside this time. You're no kid now, Andy. . .Mr. Soro—"

"But you don't want it to be a surface skimming, do you?"

"Well, no—"

"You want it to be guts and balls, right?"

"Yeah, right, we want—"

"You want it told the way it is, right? With realism, all the hip talk the kids talk?"

"Sure, that's part of—"

"You want me to find out what happened to all those kids I ran with, who didn't know I was studying them like bugs in a bottle. You want me to go down there seventeen years later and say, 'I'm the guy finked on you, remember me?' You want that, in essence that's what you want, isn't it?"

Werringer had the feeling now (sudden shifts with this man) that Sorokin was furious, was frightened, but furious. What the hell was going on?

"Well, yes, we want the truth, the inside, the way you did it the first time, but we don't want you to take any chances. We aren't. . .hell, we aren't *Confidential* or the *Enquirer*! We want—"

"You want me to go back in and let them take a whack at me!"

Aggression. Werringer reeled.

"Say, wait a minute we—"

"You expect a helluva story, and all the risks, and you want it *now*, right, Mr. Werringer?"

"What's the matter with you, Sorok—"

"Well, how the hell do you expect me to do it unless I go back down there and sink into it again, up to my GUTS, up to my BALLS, up to my EYEBALLS FOR CHRISSAKES! YOU DAMN DUMB DEADLINE-MEETER, YOU!"

Werringer shoved back from his desk, as though Sorokin might jump across and throttle him. His eyes were wide behind the bifocals, all out of shape and moist.

"It'll be my pleasure, Mr. Werringer," in a tone so soft and warm, relaxed at last. "How soon do you need it? And what length?"

Walter Werringer fumbled for his Danish coffee mug.

Sorokin had his hand on the door, when it opened inward, and two young men came through. The moment he saw them, prim and clean-scrubbed in their almost-identical dark blue suits, he knew they had come from the right families, had learned to dance at the age of six or seven at Miss Blesham's, or one of the other good salons, had been allowed that first quarter-snifter of Napoleon with "Dad," and had most certainly graduated from one of the right schools.

The one on the left, the taller of the two, with the straw-colored hair and polar twinkling blue eyes, entering the room with thumbs hooked into the decorative pockets of his vest, was an Andover man. Had to be.

The other, slightly shorter, perhaps only six feet, with shoes impeccably dullshined to avoid the vulgar ostentation of gloss, with flat brown hair parted straight back on the left side and brushed toward the rear of the skull in the European manner, whose eyes were of the lizard, *he* was Choate, surely, definitely, of course.

"Walter," Andover said, as he burst into the office, "we're breaking a little early today. Going over to The Algonquin for a few. Care to come along?"

Then he saw Sorokin, and stumbled to silence, in awe.

Werringer introduced them, with names Sorokin let slip out of his mind the instant they were spoken. He knew their names.

"Where did you go to school?" he asked them.

"Yale," said Andover.

"Yale," said Choate.

"Call me Punky," said Andrew Sorokin.

So they all went to The Algonquin for a few.

Choate scrabbled around in the bottom of the bowl. All the salted peanuts and little Cheerios and pretzels were gone. He gripped the bowl by its edge and banged it on the table. At The Algonquin, that was poor form.

"Succulents!" Choate howled.

The waiter came and took the bowl away from him like a nanny with an obstreperous infant. "Succulents, dammt," he slurred the word, only faintly.

"Andrew P. for Punky Sorokin, by God what a thrill and a half for overtime," said Andover, staring at Andy for the one billionth time since they had sat down. "A giant, you're a bloody giant, a flaming insti*tooo*tion! Y'know that? And here we are sitting right with you!"

Werringer had left two hours before. Evening was coming on. The two Yale men named Andover and Choate were just high enough to be playful. Andy was sober. He had tried, God knew he had tried, but he was still sober.

"Reality, that's what you deal in," said one of them. It didn't matter which was which. They both spoke from the same cultural mouth.

"Truth. Life. You know all there is to know about Life. An' I don't mean that Lucely, heh heh heeheehee. . ." he broke himself up completely, rolled around in the booth. Choate (or Andover, depending which had punned) shoved him away, roughly.

"You don't know what the hell you're talkin' about, Rob. Thass the one thing he *doesn't* know about. Life! The core of it, the heartmeat of it! We, who come from such austere backgrounds, even *we* know it better more truly than Andrew P. for Punky Sorokin sitting right there."

The other Yale man sat up, angry. "You shut up! This man is a giant. A flaming giant, and he *knows*, I tell you. He *knows* about the seamy side of Life."

"He never even touched it."

"He knows! He knows it all!"

"Fraud! Poseur!"

"Step owsside you bastard, I never knew you were such a bigoted crypto-Fascist bastard!"

Sorokin listened to them, and the fear he had known earlier that afternoon, when Werringer had sentenced him to going back down to Red Hook, returned. He had condemned himself to it, really, by what series of compulsions he did not want to examine, but here it was again. How did Choate know he was a fraud? How had Choate discovered the secret nubbin of fear in Andrew Sorokin's heart and soul?

"What, uh, what makes you say I'm a fraud?" he asked Choate. Choate's face had grown blotchy with drink, but he aimed a meaty finger at Sorokin and said, "I get spirit messages from the other world."

Andover took it as an affront. He shoved Choate roughly. "Owsside, bastard! Owsside, crypto-pinko!"

Sorokin wanted to get to the sober heart of it, though. "No, really, what makes you think I don't know reality?"

Choate took on the look of a pedant, and intoned sepulchrally. "Your first book'a short stories, you had a quote from Hemingway, remember it? You said it was your credo. Bushwah! 'There is no use writing anything that has been written before unless you can beat it. What a writer in our time has to do is write what hasn't been written before or beat dead men at what they have done.' I memorized it. It seemed to be valid. Bushwah!"

"Socialist, right-wing Birch muther-fugger!"

"Yes? So what makes you think I don't know what I'm talking about? That certainly doesn't prove your point."

"Ah!" Choate lifted a finger alongside his nose, like Santa Claus about to zoom up the chimney. Conspiratorial. "Ah! But your *fifth* book'a short stories, after you'd been out *there*"—he waved toward California—"you used *another* quote. You know what it was? Hah, you remember?"

Sorokin paused an instant to get it right, then recited. "'To reject one's own experiences is to arrest one's own development. To deny one's own experience is to put a lie into the lips of one's own life. It is no less than a denial of the Soul.' Oscar Wilde. What has that to do with proving your point?"

Choate was triumphant. "Fear. Cop-out. Your subconscious was squealing like a butchered pig. It knew you were a liar from the first, and were lying all the more in Hollywood. It knew! And so you had to say it to the world, so they could never accuse you of it. You don't know what Life is, what reality is, what truth is, what anydamnthing is!"

"I'm gonna push your rotten cruddy Tory face in!"

They wrestled around the other side of the booth, each too hammered to do the other any harm, as Sorokin thought about what Choate had said. Was it possible? Had he been trying to plead silently guilty to an unspoken charge?

When he had been a small child, he had been a petty thief. He had stolen things from the dime store. Not because he could not have bought them, because his family was too poor, but because he wanted them without having to pay for them, a sense of accomplishment, in a child's own strange philosophy. But he had always felt compelled to play with the new, stolen item, directly in front of his parents, that same night. So they could ask him where he got it, and he could risk their finding out he had stolen. If they did not press it, the stolen plaything was truly his; if they pressed it and he blurted he had stolen it, then he had to suffer a punishment he knew he deserved.

Was the inclusion of the Wilde quotation, as Choate suggested, another playing with a stolen toy in front of mommy and daddy, the world, his public?

Was it a manifestation of the fear he now felt? The fear that he had lost it, had always been in the process of losing it, could never regain it?

"Okay, dammit, I'm gonna show you the seamy side of Life! Now what about it, Mr. Punky? You wanna see the seamy side of Life?"

"He *knows* it, I tell ya!"

"Well, do you? Huh?"

"I'll have to make a phone call first. Cancel a dinner appointment." He sat, not moving, and they stared at one another like walruses contemplating the permanence of the sea.

"Well, do you, huh? If you do, put up or shut up." Choate was on the pinnacle of proving his point.

"Just shuddup, Terry, just shuddup; this man is not going to be chivvied and bullied and chockablocked by the likes of a McCarthy neo-Fascist demagogue such as yourself!" Andover was a tot drunker than Choate.

Sorokin was trembling inside. If anyone knew the seamy side of Life, it was Andrew Sorokin. He had run away at age fifteen, had been driving a dynamite truck in North Carolina by sixteen, working on a cat-cracker in West Texas age seventeen, at nineteen the gang, and his first book published at twenty. He had been in every scene imaginable from the sybaritic high life of the international jet set to uncontrolled LSD experimentation with Big Sur hippies. He had always wanted to believe he was with it, contemporary, of the times, in touch with the realities, *all* the myriad multicolored realities, no matter how strained or weird or demeaning.

And the question now before him: *has all this living degenerated into a search for kicks, is it a complex cop-out?* He slid out of the booth, and went to call Olaf Burger.

When he had gotten through the switchboard and all the interference, Burger's bushwhacker voice came across the line. "Yeah?"

"Didn't I tell you a million times that's no way to answer a phone? You should say, 'Massah Buhgah's awfiss, c'n ah helps yuh, bwana.'"

"Explain to me why I have to have a busy workday interrupted periodically by bigots, rednecks and kook writer sellouts from Smog Junction."

"'Cause you got such dear little Shirley Temple dimples, and you is a big paperback editor, and I burn for your body with a bright blue flame."

"What's on your alleged mind, nitwit?"

"Gotta call off the dinner."

"Janine'll parboil me. She made *patlijan moussaka* because you were coming. And dicing and braising lamb all day will not put her in a receptive frame of mind. At least give me an excuse."

"Two hotrock Ivy types from *Marquis* want to show me 'the seamy side of Life.'"

"That's not an excuse, that's a seizure of *petit mal.* You've got to be kidding."

There was a moment of serious silence from Sorokin. Then, in a different, slower voice he said, "I've got to do it, Olaf. It's important."

A corresponding moment of reorientation, the dual statement of a musical threnody. "You sound upset, Andy. Something happen? It's been three months since I've seen you, something biting on you again?"

Sorokin clicked his tongue against his teeth, seeking the words, finally deciding in an instant to put it baldly. "I'm trying to find out if I've got balls. Again."

"For the thousandth time."

"Yeah."

"When do you stop? When you get killed?"

"Give my love to Janine. I'll call you tomorrow. My treat at The Four Seasons, that ought to make up for it."

A pause. "Andy. . ."

Another beat of timelessness. "Uh-huh?"

"You're too expensive for the paperback line I edit, but there are a lot of others with a stock in you. Don't screw yourself up."

"Uh-huh."

Burger clicked off, and Andy Sorokin stood staring at the red plush of the phone booth for a long moment. Then he turned, exhaling breath in finality, and went back to a scene from Hogarth.

Andover was tapping the table over and over and over with his index finger, saying over and over and over, "You'll see, you'll see, you'll see. . ."

While Choate, who had rubbed carbon black from half a dozen spent matches on his cheeks, was flapping his arms tidily, and croaking over and over and over, "Nevermore, nevermore, nevermore. . ."

They took him to every paradise he had already known. All the places he had been when he was younger, all the predictable places. The Lower East Side. The Village. Spanish Harlem. Bedford–Stuyvesant.

And they grew more and more furious. They had sobered; the chill night air, the snow of winter's November, too many stop-offs where the liquor wasn't free; they were sobered. It had become a vendetta with both of the Yale men, not just Choate. Now Andover was with him, and they wanted to *show* the giant, Sorokin, something he had not seen before.

There were bars, and more bars, and dingy down-the-hole places where people sat murmuring into one another's libidos. And then a party. . .

Noise cascaded about him, a Niagara of watery impressions, indistinct conversational images. Snatches of flotsam carried down thunderingly past his ears" ". . .I went over to Ted Bates to ask them about those Viceroy residuals, and Marvy told me what the hell I'd gotten a trip to the Virgin Islands out of it and why didn't I stop bitching, and I told *him*, say, after that damned fruitcake director and his *fayguluh* crew got done letting me 'save' them from the gay life, I was so raw and miserable *double* residuals wouldn't of been enough to make up for all that weirdscene swinging, and besides, if they'd taken along some hooker they'd of had to pay her, too, so I should be getting extra consider—"

. . .beep, bip, boop, blah, bdip, chee chee chee. . .

". . .a gass! A real gass! The joint is laid out like an Arabian Nights kind of thing, with the waitresses in these transparent pants, and all the waiters in pasha turbans, and you lay on your side to eat, and I've got to admit it's hard as hell eating laying on your side, which is almost as bad as laying eating on your side heh heh, I swear I don't see how the hell they did it in those days, but the food is *ab*-solutely a gass, man. They've got this lemon drop soup, they call it *kufte abour* and it's a g—"

. . .bdoing, bupp, bupp, beep, bip, chee chee chee. . .

". . .this compendium of aborted hours and dead-end relationships is of minor concern, for at this moment, this very instant in weightless timeless time, this moment that I am about to describe minutely, all of what I have been through before this will outline itself. If not in particular, then in essence, hindsighted as it were, and what went before will be seen as merely a vapor trail of incidents one like another, building to this moment and. . .oh for CHRIST'S sake, Ginny, take your finger out of your nose. . ."

. . .bang bang bang, bding dong, clank, crunch, chee chee chee. . .

Technically, it might have been a party. Superficially it *resembled* a party, with too many people clogged into too small a space, a dingy loft off Jane Street in the Village. But there was more going on than just that.

The ritual dances of the friendly natives were being staged, both physically—as Simone and her husband's agent did a slow, extremely inept, psychosexual Skate—and emotionally—as Wagner Cole scathingly sliced up the peroxided poetess whose aspirations of literary immediacy were transparently *Saturday Review*—as well as ethnically—minor chittering of who-balled-who in the far corner by the rubber plant. The whole crowd was there, because it was Florence Mahrgren's birthday (wheeee!) and not just a dreamed-up reason for getting together.

Andy Sorokin stood against the fireplace wall, his margarita in his two cupped hands, talking to the whey-faced virgin Andover had found and brought to him. She was talking at him, about a bad movie made from one of his lesser novels.

"I never really thought Karin was completely bad," the virgin was saying. "And when they made the movie, I just *did not* like the way Lana Turner played the part."

Sorokin stared down at her benignly. She was very short, and large-bosomed. She wore a Rudi Gernreich and it had her pushed all up tight in front; she smiled with her lips but not her teeth. "That's very kind of you to say; there wasn't a great deal in the motion picture version to like, though I thought Frankenheimer's direction was nice."

She answered something totally irrelevant. He bore these conversations neatly or badly, depending on the final objective. In this case, it was getting the short, buxom virgin into the master bedroom; he gave it what charm he could spare.

Around them, like mist encircling a cleared space, the eye of a storm, the party pitched itself a noticeable degree higher in hysteria. Florence Mahrgren was hoisted on the shoulders of Bernbach & Barker (producers of three current Broadway hits) and carried around the room, as Ray Charles sang in the background, her skirt crumpled about her thighs, Bernbach & Barker improvising obscene happy birthday lyrics to the tune of their current success's theme song. Sorokin felt his gut tightening on him again. It never seemed to change, no matter how many times the people changed. They said the same stupid things, did the same senseless things, postured and played with themselves insipidly. He wanted either to screw the virgin or to get out of the party.

From another corner of the living room someone yelled, "Hey! How about Circle-Insult?" and before Andy could make for the door, the virgin had been snapped up by Andover, and she in turn had clutched his sleeve, and daisy-chain, they careened into the center of the maelstrom.

Circle-Insult. They were already forming the circle, everyone hunkering down cross-legged on the floor. The idle talented and the idle rich and the idle poor and the idle bored playing their games; affectation of innocence, the return to honesty in form—if not in content. Circle-Insult. The women sitting in the preordained postures, careless, nonchalant unawareness of lingerie and pale inner flesh flashed and gone and flashing again, beacons for the wanderers who would home there that night, keeping the coastline firmly in sight, keeping the final berth open to the lost and the needy. Charitable bawds.

They began playing Circle-Insult, the world's easiest game.

Tony Morrow turned to Iris Paine on his right. Tony to Iris: "You're the worst lay I've ever had. You don't move. You just lay there and let a guy, any guy, stick it in, and you whimper. Jeezus, you're a lousy lay."

Iris Paine turned to Gus Diamond on her right. Iris to Gus: "You smell bad. You have really vile bad breath. And you always stand too close when you talk to someone. You stink completely."

Gus Diamond turned to Bill Gardner on his right. Gus to Bill: "I hate niggers, and you are the most obnoxious nigger I ever met. You got no natural rhythm, and when we played tennis last weekend I saw you were hung smaller than me so stop trying to horse around with Betty, nigger, or you'll find your throat cut!"

Bill Gardner turned to Kathy Dineen on his right. Bill to Kathy: "You always steal outta these parties. One night you stole thirty-five bucks from Bernice's purse, and then split, and they called the cops but they never found out it was you. You're a thief."

Around and around and around. Circle-Insult.

Andy Sorokin stood as much of it as he could, then he rose and left, Andover and Choate trailing all quiet and sadly sober behind him. "You didn't like it," Choate said, following him down the stairs.

"I didn't like it."

"It wasn't the core of reality."

Sorokin smiled. "It wasn't even particularly seamy."

Choate shrugged. "I tried."

"How about The Ninth Circle?" Andover asked.

Sorokin stopped on the stairs, half-turned. "What's that?"

Choate grinned conspiratorially. "It's a joint, you know, a pub, a place." Sorokin nodded silently, bobbed his head and they followed him.

They took him to The Ninth Circle, which was a Village hangout, the way Chumley's had been a hangout when Andy had walked the weary streets. The way Rienzi's had been the spot to go and read *The Manchester Guardian* on a wooden hang-up pole, and sleep on Davey Rienzi's sandwich-cutting board when the rent was too much to make. The way there was always an in-hole for the colder children who couldn't bear to stand on street corners naked to the night.

And Choate and Andover—again—grew furious.

For the moment they entered the noisy, dingy bar with its inauspicious bullfight posters and sawdusty floor, a tall, skeletal man erupted from a seat tilted back against a wall, and dashed for Sorokin. "Andy! Andy Sorokin!"

It was Sid, big Sid, who had operated the tourist bus dodge on 46th Street and Broadway, in the days when Andy Sorokin had worked selling pornography in a bookshop on The Gay White Way. Cadaverously thin Sid, who had been one of the coterie of early-morning residents of Times Square, a closed society of those who were with it, as Andy had been.

Sid made a great fuss over Sorokin, pulling him to a table full of pretty girls and buffalo-moustached pickup men for the pretty girls. They reminisced about the old days before Sorokin had told his bosses at the bookshop to pick it and stick it, he was going to write. Before Sorokin had sold his books, gone in the army, married the women, made it in Hollywood. The old days before.

And the two Yale men grew furious at Punky.

Here they were, determined to show him the raw and pulsing inner heart of the seamy side of Life, and he was a familiar of all the types even *they* could not get to know. It was frustrating.

"So what are you doing these days?" Andy asked Sid. Sid flip-flopped a deprecatory hand. "Not much. I'm working a couple of hookers, you know, making a buck here and there." Andy grinned.

"Remember the night that chick wandered into the bookstore, and she wanted to get laid, and Freddy Smeigel started hustling her, and she pulled her skirt up to her chin and she was *sans* pants—"

Sid interrupted, "*What* pants?"

Andy grinned. "*Without*."

"Oh, yeah, tell it, g'wan, these guys'd laugh like hell."

Sorokin warmed to the story of the tourist woman from Sheboygan, and how they had quickly locked the front door and pulled the blind and she had pulled up her skirt again and let them look. She had done it half a dozen times, like a yo-yo on a string, just say the word and zip up went the dress. So they'd taken her next door into the record shop and Freddy had told her to do it for them, and she had done it zip again. So then they'd taken her around the block, upstairs of the Victoria Theatre, to the stockroom, and everyone had balled her.

Sorokin and Sid laughed over it, and Andover got nearly as furious as Choate. So they started drinking again, trying to resurrect their buzz of earlier that evening. Finally, when Andy had had enough of The Ninth Circle, he suggested they leave, and Sid handed him a card.

It said: LOTTE Call Sid 611 East 101st.

There was a phone number, and it had been scratched off, and another phone number written in, in ball-point. Sid laid an incredibly thin arm around Sorokin's shoulder. "It's one of my hustlers. Fourteen years old. Puerto Rican meat, but *too* much. You want a little bang, just call me, I'm usually around. On the house. Old times, like that."

Andy grinned, and shoved the card into the pocket of his Harris tweed jacket. "Take care, Sid. Nice seeing you again." And they left.

The two Yale men had an air of determination about them now, a frenzy almost. They would find a seamy side of Life to reveal to this wiseass giant, Sorokin, if they had to scour every grimy garbage can in the greater Manhattan area.

There is an infinitude of grimy garbage cans in the greater Manhattan area. They scoured many of them that night, that morning, winding up finally, stone-drunk, all three of them, in The Dog House Bar, a filth-pit of unspeakable emptiness, deep in the Bowery.

Sorokin sat across from the Yale men. Choate's face was once again blotchy with pink. Andover was giddy.

"Punky, pussycat." Andover smiled lopsidedly. "Luv'ya!" Choate sneered. The strain of surliness that lay close to the surface needed only a whisper of wind, a rustle of leaves, a murmur of direction, to come to the top.

"Cop-out," he mumbled. Then he swallowed hard. And his face went puce. "I'm going to whoopee," he mumbled.

His cheeks puffed out. There was a moist sound.

"You talk like a dumb *New Yorker* story," Andover said, very carefully. "Now if you were a *Playboy* story, you'd say puke, 'cause it's a realie word, and it has'a lotta reality, huh? And if you were a *Kenyon Review* story, you'd say vomit, because it has history behind it, roots, so t'speak. And if you were an *Esquire* story, you'd say upchuck, 'cause they're still trying to con everyone into thinking they're the voice of college. And if you were a *National Geographic* story—"

Choate slid sidewise in the booth, crab-style, and started out of the booth. "Ergh," he hummed soggily, "toil-ed?" Andy stood to help him.

Supporting Choate with an arm around his waist, and a hand under his armpit, Andy moved back through the crowded, smoke-dense bar, to the battered door marked GENTS. All around them, suddenly, Sorokin realized what a dismal, sinister place The Dog House Bar really was.

In a far corner sat a trio of men in black, all leaning hunkered down in, one next to the other, till they seemed to be one great black gelatinous mass. A wisp of conversation, like a sibilant ghost, hushed through the instant of silence, from that mass, to Sorokin: "Man, I gotta get off. . .gotta take a drive. . ."

Old junkies.

Back behind the jukebox, which was silent, lights faded, a tired harridan merely waiting for a john to slip a coin into her to show her jaded charms, a man and woman were doing something uncomfortable, the woman straddling the man's lap.

The booths were all filled. Groups of men in heavy sweaters, still feeling November with them, outside the fly-specked windows of the bar. Longshoremen, sandhogs, merchant mariners, night truckers; a group of Chinese over from Mott Street; hefty-thighed women clustered about one man with a pack of tarot cards; no one was clean. The smell of swine was in the room. Heavy, changing tone, first garlic, then sweat, then urine, it roiled overhead mixed layer on layer with cigarette and pipe smoke, occasionally clearing sufficiently to smell the acrid aroma of bad marijuana, too many seeds and stems to give any kind of a decent high. And dark. Dim shadows moving here and there, like plankton dark under a sea heavy with silt.

The hum of voices, all somnolent, no hilarity, not a laugh, not a snicker. The substitute was an occasional grunt, a forced sluggish thudding thrust of ughhh as of someone forcing a bowel movement, and usually from a woman, groped under a table. A place of base relationships.

The word immoral did not even apply. It was akin to the drunk who lay on the floor, propped against the wall between stacks of Coca-Cola cases, eyes wide yet unseeing, hands caked with unidentifiable filth, clothes shapeless and gray. An object of no identity, so sunk into alcoholism, addlewitted, that he was what the police called a wetbrain. The term drunk no longer applied, just as the term immoral did not apply. What Sorokin saw here, around him, poised holding Choate at the door of the toilet, was the final descent of man, to base needs.

He saw the world as it really was, as it was for him, also. The world that was unaffected by ambition or history or social graces. He saw the real side of life, which he had not seen for many years. He saw, God help him, the seamy side of Life.

The bar was full, down reflecting the length of the streaked backbar mirror. Elbow to elbow as four o'clock curfew raced toward them, bending and drinking, not even talking, getting as much inside as possible before night overtook them and they were sent out into the world alone.

A Negro came up to Sorokin, a heavy-faced Negro with conked reddish hair and bloodshot eyes, character gone from the face and replaced with weary cunning. He held up a pair of red plastic dice. "You go'n th' toilet baby? We got us a few fren'z heah, wanna do a thang'a craps, huh, howzabout?" and he laid his hand on Sorokin's backside. Sorokin stiffened.

"Forget it," he said, thickly. *Spade fag,* he thought, and was ill. *Of all the horrors Whitey has committed against the black man, homosexuality is the most perverse.*

The black man drew himself up, snorted a word, and went away, smelling strongly of Arrid and Jean Naté. Out of the corner of his eye, Sorokin saw him join another Negro in a side booth for two, and knew they were discussing that damn straight whitey muthuh by the toilet door.

And in that instant, Sorokin was satisfied. He knew at last, somehow and inexplicably, he had come of age. Late adolescence, the chase for masculinity, were found and over. He had seen all there was to see, and what he had done since he had left this milieu, was to seek responsibility. To mature was to belong; where you wanted to belong, surely, but to care about a life with continuity. He was suddenly whole. And free.

He opened the door and went through into the filthy bathroom with Choate.

The moment they entered the white-tiled toilet, Choate broke away, and fell down on his knees by the stand-up urinal. He began to vomit heavily, a rhinoceros sound deep from his stomach. Sorokin moved away from him, realizing his own bladder cried for emptying. He entered the stall, letting the swinging door slam hard behind him, and unzipped.

He began to urinate, thinking a codifying series of thoughts about the moment of realization he had just known. He barely heard the sound of the outer door open, the scuff of feet against the tiles, a heavy *thwack!* of something heavy hitting something yielding, and an almost immediate soft ughhh of gentle pain.

Sorokin, still urinating, peered outside the stall, pushing open the door in idle curiosity.

Two Negroes, the same two from the bar, were working Choate over. One had smashed Choate behind the ear with a white tennis sock filled with coins, and Choate was bleeding from the scalp, half-slumped into the vomit-filled urinal. The other one was groping for Choate's wallet.

Sorokin did not think about it. If he had, he would not have done it.

He charged out of the stall, head down, and plunged full-tilt into the Negro with the sockful of silver. It had been the Negro with the red plastic dice. He hit him at full speed, head against chest, hands pushing the black man sharply away from him. The Negro careened backward under the impact of the rush, and his head crashed against the white tiles with a sharp car-door crack. He sank to the floor instantly, eyes closed.

Sorokin turned, just in time to see the glint of honed steel as the second Negro flipped open the straight razor and set himself hard, slashing straight through in a flat arc from left shoulder across his body, like a good tennis player fielding a smash with a tight backhand. The razor silently hummed.

The black man caught Sorokin directly across the belly, and Sorokin felt it only as a tiny paper cut might feel. He plunged forward, still doing a ballet turn from the first Negro, unconscious against the tiles. Ingrained army infighting, learned at no small traumatic cost years before, leaped unbidden into Sorokin's reflexes. (You never forget how to swim, once you've learned. You never forget how to ride a bicycle, once you've learned. You never forget how to lay a woman, once you've learned. You never forget how to kill, once you've learned.)

He caught the Negro under the nose with the flat, hard edge of his palm, slamming back and up. The Negro's head whipped up as though on a wire, and he shrieked, high and piercingly, a woman's shriek. His knees buckled inward, and his arms flailed out to the sides. The straight razor went flying and clattered into a corner of the toilet, under the sink. The black man started to fall face-forward, and Sorokin realized he had not for a moment seen the black blood gushing out of the black man's black mouth onto his lower face. A torrent, a river, a dam burst of blood.

The Negro fell past Sorokin like a dropped sandbag. Empty and cold and heavily. He hit on his face, and lay silent, but the smear of blood ran across the white tiles. As he hit, something fell from his vest pocket, and tinkled away.

Sorokin knew the Negro was dead. One for certain, possibly two. He had to get out of there. He looked down, and the razor had cut through his Harris tweed jacket, through his shirt, through his undershirt, and through the top layers of his stomach's soft flesh. He was bleeding profusely, in a constantly welling red line, straight and clean and very, very neat. He touched it, and a bombshell went off in his head as shock set in. His eyes widened, and he said something but did not know what it was.

The thing that had fallen from the smashed Negro's vest winked up at him. It was one of the red plastic dice. It said two. Little white eyes in a clear red box.

Choate was still gasping and vomiting. Sorokin grabbed him up by the back of his jacket, and hauled him toward the door of the toilet. Behind him, neither black man moved, the scene of carnage just as it had been for almost a minute, an hour, forever.

They stumbled out of the toilet together, and Sorokin realized his fly was still open. He did the acceptable thing, and then zipped up his pants. He half-carried Choate toward the table.

Andover was making flirting, obscene gestures at the fat henna-rinsed sow locked in the over-shoulder embrace of a massive longshoreman, one booth away. *Oh, Jesus,* Sorokin thought, terror again bubbling up, *these two are going to get me killed!*

He pulled a ten-dollar bill from his side pocket, and threw it down on the table. Then he grabbed Andover and pulled him out of the booth before the sow could complain to her paramour. "Get the coats!" Sorokin ordered him.

Andover grabbed the coats, and with Sorokin hauling both of the drunken Yale men, they stumbled and fell out of The Dog House Bar. Punky wanted very much to get as far away from the scene in the toilet as possible.

For it was entirely probable that death lay stretched out on those filthy white tiles. The final crap-out.

The streets were cold and empty at four o'clock November.

The blood would not stop. He had torn up his undershirt, and stuffed it around his middle, but it had done no good. The undershirt was soaked deep brown from rotted blood.

He could not feel his legs, yet they continued to move, one in front of the other, a puppet conditioned to go on moving even when the puppet-master was dead. An improbable concept, a dead puppet-master, but flamingos were fine, as well. And papaya juice, sweet, cold, milky. There was a toy soldier once, that he had buried in the ground behind his parents' garage, in the town where he had been born, very long ago. He would go back and dig it up. When the whistle blew. Or before. If he could.

The two Yale men were drunk out of their skulls. They laughed and tittered and followed Punky where he led them, which was nowhere, plodding through fresh-fallen snow in the New York streets; he was in shock, and did not know it. The Yale men did not seem to find the dripping slash across Punky's belly very funny, but they didn't talk about it, so it probably didn't matter.

The heavy Harris tweed jacket (a new jacket, recently bought at Jack Breidbart's, on Sixth Avenue) was what had saved his life. It had absorbed much of the impact of that flat, whistling slash. Straight razor. Clean and true and deadly, made for death, not shaving.

And back there, in that toilet. If you strike a man hard enough under the nose, you will shatter the bridge and drive bone splinters into the brain, killing him instantly. And he will fall past you like a sandbag, like the Negro fell past Punky, so that you must sidestep, a *torero* who has made his kill. Back there, in that toilet.

And they walked the cold, chill, empty, screaming streets.

Punky put his hands in his pockets. He was cold, very cold. He felt a bit of cardboard. He pulled it out. It said: LOTTE   Call Sid   611 East 101st.

Punky yelled for a taxi. He yelled and yelled and yelled, his voice rising up spiraling among the icicle-frozen buildings of the Manhattan where he had come to get slashed, where he had come to find his manhood so late in his life, and found it, now dripping out on the white snow of the Manhattan that had always taken him back.

Then there was a taxi, and a long ride uptown, and Sid opening a tenement door, and a gorgeous black-haired Puerto Rican girl who said her name was Lotte, and she was only fourteen, but did someone wanna good fokk?

And time spun hazily by. The two Yale men had gotten laid, and were sleeping on two of the four beds in the apartment. And Sid had sampled his own merchandise, and he was sleeping off a methedrine high on the third bed, and Punky Sorokin was insanely sitting at a kitchen table, at 5:30 in the gray-rising morning, in the four-bed crib of a fourteen-year-old Puerto Rican whore named Lotte, playing gin rummy.

"Knock on six." He grinned boyishly, and bled.

She had serviced the other three, then returned to him and asked, "Wal, you nex', guy. You ready't fokk?"

He had smiled at her in friendliness, totally removed from the world around him, a child in shock, and touched his own bleeding belly. "Did you see I'm bleeding?" he had asked her, very matter-of-factly.

She had looked at it, and they had examined it together with intense care. She had said a few nice things about it, and he had thanked her. But he didn't want to fokk. But, he had asked, did she play gin rummy?

Knock or straight gin, she had wanted to know.

So they had sat down to play, over the oilclothed kitchen table. He liked Lotte a lot. She was a sweet child, and extremely pretty. All that black hair, done up in a high intricate style.

That went on for a long time, the timeless time of just playing, and the two of them smiling at one another. Until Punky decided to tell her things, and say what he had learned that night, and what was in his heart.

She listened, and was polite. She did not interrupt. And this is what Punky Sorokin said. . .

"You see before you a man eaten by worms. Envy, hungers most men don't even smell; lust, nameless things I want. To belong, someplace, to say what I have to say before I die, before I waste my years. All of it, pouring out of the tips of my fingers, like blood, needs. You sit here, and you live day to day and you sleep, get up, go eat, do things. But me, for me, each little thing should have been bigger, each book should have been better, all the riches, all the women, everything I want, just out beyond my reach, tormenting me. And even when I get the gold, when I get the story, when I do the movie, it still isn't what I want, it's something more, something bigger, something perfect. I don't know. I look every way, up and down the world, walking through rooms like something that's waiting for meat to come to it. I can't name it, can't say what it is, where I want it to come from. All I want to do, is *do*! At the peak of my form, at the fastest pace I can set. Running. Running till I drop. Oh, God, don't let me die till I've won."

Lotte, the fourteen-year-old Puerto Rican whore, stared at him across her cards. She laid the hand of gin rummy face-down on the kitchen-smelling oilcloth, and did not know what he was raving about. "Y'wanna can owf beer, hanh?"

In it, was all the gentleness, all the caring, all the concern AndyPunky had ever known. All the sweetness, all the warmth of someone who gave a damn. He started to cry. From far down inside him, it started up, building, great gasps of air, wrenching sobs. He lowered his head onto hands that were still bloody from the wounds dripping across his middle. His sobs were muffled, and the girl shrugged. She didn't, actually, give a fuck. She turned on the radio, and a Latin band was wailing:

¡*Vaya*!

There were streets and he was alone now. Punky had lost his two Yale men. They had showed him the seamy side of Life. Streets he walked on. At six o'clock in the New York morning. And he saw things. He saw ten things.

He saw a cabdriver sleeping in his front seat.

He saw a candy-maker opening his shop to work.

He saw a dog lifting its leg against a standpipe.

He saw a child in an alley.

He saw a sun that would not come up behind snow.

He saw an old, tired Negro man collecting cardboard flats behind a grocery store, and he told the old man I'm sorry.

He saw a toy store and smiled.

He saw pinwheels of violent color that cascaded and spun behind his eyes till he fell in the street.

He saw his own feet moving under him, leftrightleft.

He saw pain, red and raw and ugly in his stomach.

But then, somehow, he was in the Village, in front of Olaf Burger's apartment house, so he whistled a little tune, and thought he might go up to say hello. It was six-thirty.

So he went up and looked at the door for a while.

He whistled. It was nice.

Punky pressed the door buzzer. There was no answer. He waited an extremely long time, half-asleep, leaning there against the jamb. Then he pressed the buzzer again, and held it in. Somewhere deep in the apartment he could hear the distant, muffled locust hum of the buzzer. Then a shout. And then footsteps coming toward the door. The door was unlocked, slammed back on the police chain. Olaf's face, blurred by sleep, peering out of snooze-funk, furious, glared back at him.

"What the hell do you want at this—"

and stopped. The eyes widened at sight of all that blood. The door slammed shut, the chain was slipped, and the door opened again. Olaf stared at him, a little sick.

"Jesus Christ, Andy, what happened to you!"

"I fou—I found what I w-was looking for. . ."

They stared at each other, helpless.

Punky smiled once, gently, and murmured, "I'm hurt, Olaf, help me. . ." and fell sidewise, in through the doorway.

Was lost, and is found. The prodigal returned. Night and awakening. After a night of such length, opening of eyes, and a new awakening. The weavers, Clotho, Lachesis, Atropos. Atropos. She is the inflexible, who with her shears cuts off the thread of human life spun by Clotho, measured off by Lachesis.

Spun by Punky and his Yale men. Measured off by a fourteen-year-old Puerto Rican whore named Lotte in a four-bed pad in Harlem. Cut off by a Negro homosexual in The Dog House Bar in the Bowery.

Hospital white, hospital bright, and blood, instantblood, now downdropping from a bottle, and before the end, just before the end, Punky woke long enough to say, very distinctly, "Escape, please. . .escape. . ." and went away from there.

The doctor on Punky's right turned to the nurse on *his* right, and said, "He had enough."

Circle-Insult.

—New York City, 1964
and Los Angeles, 1965

harlan ellison

edgeworks.4

The Beast that Shouted Love at the Heart of the World

THE BEAST THAT SHOUTED LOVE AT THE HEART OF THE WORLD: CONTENTS

This one, with love, is for
MISS EUSONA PARKER,
who refused to believe
she was not my mother
and for
AHBHU
who refused to believe
I was not *his* mother.

FOREWORD

NEIL GAIMAN

I've been reading Harlan Ellison since I was a boy. I have known him as long, although by no means as well, as his wife, Susan—we met in Glasgow in 1985 at the same convention at which he first met and wooed his better half.

I interviewed him then for *Space Voyager*, a magazine for which I had written the previous two years, and which had, until that point, appeared perfectly healthy. The issue of the magazine that was to contain my interview with Harlan went to press. . .and the publisher pulled the plug on it, with the magazine half-printed, and fired the editor. I took the interview to an editor at another magazine. He paid me for it. . .and was fired the following day.

I decided at that point that it was unhealthy to write about Harlan, and retired the interview to a filing cabinet, in which it will sit until the end of the world. I cannot be responsible for the firing of any more editors, the closing of any more magazines.

There is no one in the world in any way like Harlan. This has been observed before, by wiser and abler people than I. This is true; and it is quite beside the point.

It has, from time to time, occurred to me that Harlan Ellison is engaged on a Gutzon Borglum-sized work of performance art—something huge and enduring. It's called Harlan Ellison: a corpus of anecdotes and tales and adversaries and performances and friends and articles and opinions and rumours and explosions and treasures and echoes and downright lies. People talk about Harlan Ellison, and they write about Harlan, and some of them would burn him at the stake if they could do it without getting into too much trouble; and some of them would probably worship at his feet if it weren't for the fact he'd say something that would make them go away feeling very small and very stupid. People tell stories in Harlan's wake, and some of them are true and some of them aren't, and some of them are to his credit and some of them aren't.

And that is also quite beside the point.

When I was ten I had a lisp, and was sent to an elocution teacher named Miss Webster who, for the next six years, taught me a great deal about drama and public speaking and, incidentally, got rid of the lisp somewhere in year one. She must have had a first name, but I've forgotten it now. She was magnificent—a stumpy, white-haired old theatrical lesbian (or so her pupils assumed) who smoked black cigarillos and was surrounded at all times by a legion of amiable but rather stupid Scottie dogs. She had huge bosoms, which she would rest on the table while she watched me recite the tongue-twisters and dramatic pieces I had been assigned. Miss Webster died about fifteen years ago, or so I was told by another ex-pupil of hers I met at a party some years back.

She is one of the very small number of people who have told me things for my own good that I've paid attention to. (There is, needless to say, a very large number of people—including, now I come to think of it, Harlan—who've told me perfectly sensible things for my own good that I've, for one reason or another, ignored completely.)

Anyway: I got to be fourteen years old and, one day, after a particularly imaginative interpretation of a Caliban speech, Miss Webster leaned back in her chair, lit a cigarillo with a flourish, and said, "Neil, dear. I think there's something you ought to know. Listen: to be eccentric, you must first know your circle."

And I—for once—heard, and listened, and understood. You can fuck around with the rules as much as you want to—*after* you know what the rules are. You can be Picasso after you know how to paint. Do it *your* way; but know how to do it *their* way first.

I've had a personal relationship with Harlan Ellison for much longer that I've known him. Which is the scariest thing about being a writer, because you make stories up and write stuff down and that's what *you* do. But people read it and it affects them or it whiles away a train journey, whatever, and they wind up moved or changed or comforted by the author, whatever the strange process is, the one-way communication from the stuff they read. And it's not why the stories were written. But it's true, and it happens.

I was eleven when my father gave me two of the Carr Wollheim BEST SF anthologies and I read "I Have No Mouth, and I Must Scream" and discovered Harlan. Over the next few years I bought everything of his I could find. I still have most of those books.

When I was twenty-one I had the worst day of my life. (Up to then, anyway. There have been two pretty bad days since. But this was worse than them.) And there was nothing in the airport to read but SHATTERDAY, which I bought. I got onto the plane, and read it crossing the Atlantic. (How bad a day was it? It was so bad I was slightly disappointed when the plane touched down gently at Heathrow without having, at any point on the journey, burst into flames or plunged flaming from the sky. That's how bad it was.)

And on the plane I read SHATTERDAY, which is a collection of mostly kick-ass stories—and introductions to stories—about the relationship between writers and stories. Harlan told me about wasting time (in "Count the Clock That Tells the Time"), and I thought, fuck it, I *could* be a writer. And he told me that anything more than twelve minutes of genuine personal pain was self-indulgence, which did more to jerk me out of the state of complete numbness I was in than anything else could have done. And when I got home I took all the pain and the fear and the grief, and all the conviction that maybe I *was* a writer, damn it, and I began to write. And I haven't stopped yet. SHATTERDAY, more or less, made me what I am today.

Your fault, Ellison. And again, quite beside the point.

So: THE BEAST THAT SHOUTED LOVE AT THE HEART OF THE WORLD, to which I bid you welcome.

My copy's the 1979 Pan (U.K.) edition: On the cover of this paperback, Blood's a purple thing that looks like a house-cat; Vic, behind him, is apparently a boy in his forties, and is, I think, hopping about on one leg. Still, most of Harlan's British covers had spaceships on them, so I mustn't grumble. And the back cover calls Harlan "The chief prophet of the New Wave in science fiction," attributing the opinion to *The New Yorker*.

Definition time, primarily for those of you born after 1970. *The New Wave*: a term, almost as unproductive as *Cyberpunk* would be, fifteen years on, used to describe a motley bunch of writers working in the latter half of the Sixties, loosely orbiting but not exclusively confined to *New Worlds* magazine in the Moorcock era and the original DANGEROUS VISIONS anthology, edited by the author of this collection. (If you want more information than that go and find a copy of the Clute-Nicholls ENCYCLOPEDIA OF SCIENCE FICTION, and check out the New Wave entry.)

Harlan may well have been "a prophet of the New Wave," but his foremost prophecy seems to have consisted of pointing out, in the introduction to this volume, that there was no such thing, just a bunch of writers, some of whom were pushing the edge of the envelope.

I never noticed the New Wave as anything particularly distinct or separate, when it was happening. It was Stuff to Read. Good stuff to read, even if it sometimes skirted the edge of incomprehensibility. I read it as I read all adult fiction, as a window into a world I didn't entirely understand: found Spinrad's BUG JACK BARRON a lot of fun, Moorcock's A CURE FOR CANCER addictive and curious. Ballard was distant and strange and made me think of stories told over the tannoy in far-off airports, Delany showed me that words could be beautiful, Zelazny made myths. And if they were the "New Wave" I liked it. But I liked most things back then. ("Yeah, that's your trouble, Gaiman," said Harlan, when I chided him recently for suggesting that someone I like should be sprinkled with sacred meal and then sacrificed, "you like everyone." It's true, mostly.)

I've digressed a little.

Fiction is a thing of its time, and as times change so does our take on the fiction. Consider the Reagan section of "Santa Claus vs. S.P.I.D.E.R."; consider Reagan's final smile "like a man who has regained that innocence of childhood or nature that he had somehow lost." Scary, in a way Harlan never intended, writing about the pompadoured Governor of California. Yet in another few years Reagan and his smile will have begun to lose meaning. He'll lose significance, become a name in the past for the readers, an odd historical name (I'm *just* old enough to know why the Spiro Agnew gag was funny), just as the who and the what and the why of the New Wave fade into the black. In a couple of his books James Branch Cabell footnoted the famous of his time—something that was viewed as (and was perhaps partly) an ironic comment—after all, who, today, would bother with an explanatory footnote of John Grisham[1] or John Major[2] or Howard Stern[3]? But Cabell's ironic footnotes are now useful information. Time passes. We forget. The bestselling novel in 1925 was (I am informed by Steve Brust) SOUNDINGS by A. Hamilton Gibbs. Huh? And *who*? Still, "Santa Claus. . ." works, and will keep working as long as there are B-movie spy plots to deconstruct; and as long as there is injustice.

It's true of the rest of the tales herein. They remain relevant; the only thing in the anthology that feels dated is the Introduction, as Harlan grooves to Jimi Hendrix and points to Piers Anthony as an underground writer. But hell, no one reads introductions anyway. (Admit it. You're not reading this, are you?)

And along with Spiro Agnew and A. Hamilton Gibbs and Howard Stern, the anecdotes and tales and the Legend in His Own Lifetime stuff about Harlan (most of which is, more or less, true-ish) and all the Gutzon Borglum stuff (and I ought to have given Gutzon, who carved the presidential faces into Mount Rushmore, his own footnote) will also be forgotten.

But the stories last. The stories remain.

"To be eccentric," says Miss Webster, dead for fifteen years, in the back of my head, her voice dry, her elocution perfect, "you must first know your circle." Know the rules before you break them. Learn how to draw, then break the rules of drawing. Learn to craft a story and *then* show people things they've seen before in ways they've never seen.

---

[1] Author of legal-based thrillers, popular in the early 1990s.

[2] British Conservative member of Parliament. Succeeded Margaret Thatcher as prime minister of England in 1991.

[3] I'm not quite sure. I think he's something on the radio.

That's what these stories are about. Some of them are quite brilliant, and they sparkle and glitter and shine and wound and howl, and some of them aren't; but in all of them you can see Harlan experimenting, trying new things, new techniques, new voices: craft and voices he'd later refine into the calm assurance of, say, DEATHBIRD STORIES, his examination of the myths we live by; into the stories of SHATTERDAY, in which he took apart, hard, the cannibalistic relationship between the writer and the story; or the bitter elegies of ANGRY CANDY.

He knew his circle; and he dared to go outside it.

Being preamble to Harlan is a strange and scary business. I take down the battered and thumbed and treasured paperbacks from the bookshelves and look at them, and there's Harlan on the back cover, with a pipe or a typewriter, and I wonder at how *young* he looks (it would be foolish to remark that Harlan is the youngest a-whisker-away-from-sixty-year-old I've ever met—it's patronizing and implies that it's a wonder that he's still in full possession of his faculties and capable of telling the Mah-jongg tiles apart; but he has a sense of wonder that's been beaten out of most people by the time they hit their twenties, and a certain cyclonic energy that puts me in mind of my eight-year-old daughter Holly, or of a particularly fiendish explosive device with a ferocious sense of humour; and more than that, he still has convictions and the courage of them); and I then realize the company I'm in, and I reread Stephen King's introduction to STALKING THE NIGHTMARE and watch Steve making the same points I'm trying so haltingly to make, that it's not about the personality, or the tales about Harlan, or even about Harlan the person. It's not about having the pleasure it gave me to hand Harlan the World Fantasy Award for Life Achievement, nor is it about the stunned expressions on the faces of the assembled banquetters, as they listened to his humble and gracious acceptance speech. (I lie through my teeth. Not humble. Not even very gracious. Very funny, though. And they *were* stunned).

Really, all it's about is a shelf of books, and a pile of stories, written as well as he could write them when he wrote them, which is *not* beside the point; which is, in fact, the whole point.

And Harlan continues to write, well, and passionately, and fiercely. (I commend to your attention his story "The Man Who Rowed Christopher Columbus Ashore" in the 1993 BEST AMERICAN SHORT STORIES collection—every bit as experimental as anything produced in the wildest excesses of the New Wave, and entirely successful. He knows his circle. He is willing to explore outside it.)

So: twelve stories follow.

These are not stories that should be forgotten; and some of you are about to read them for the first time.

Prepare to leave the circle, with a more-than-capable guide.

I envy you.

Neil Gaiman / December 1993

INTRODUCTION

The Waves in Rio

Standing in the hotel window staring out at the Atlantic Ocean, nightcrashing onto the Copacabana beach. Down in Brazil on a fool's mission, talking to myself. Standing in the window of a stranger whom I suddenly know well, while down the Avenida Atlantica in another window, one I know well, who has suddenly become a stranger.

Watching the onyx waves rippling in toward shore, suddenly facing out like green bottle glass, cresting white with lace, reaching, pawing toward shore, and spasming once finally, before vanishing into the sponge sand. I am a noble moron. I compose a poem.

My poem says, standing here, staring out across the works of man, wondering what the hell I'm doing here, an alien in a place he can never know. . .and there are the waves. Boiling across two thousand miles of emptiness in the terrible darkness, all alone, all the way from Lagos like the Gold Coast blacks who came, stacked belly-to-butt like spoons in the bellies and butts of alien ships. All that way, racing so far, to hurl themselves up on this alien beach, like me.

Now why in the name of reason would anyone, anything, travel that far. . .just to be alone?

Christ on the mountain looks down over Rio de Janeiro, arms spread, benediction silently flowing from stone lips. He was sculpted by an Italian, and brought to this mountain, staring off toward Sugar Loaf. There are lights hidden in Christ. Once a year—you know when—a remote switch is thrown at the other end of those lights, in the Vatican, and the Pope lights *Cristo Redentor*.

This is the Christ of the wealthy who live in the bauhaus apartments out along Leblon; the Christ of the blue carpet bettors at the Jockey Club; the Christ of those who dine on *fondue orientale* at the Swiss Chalet; the Christ of those who sail into Rio harbor on proud white yachts so proud and so white the sun blinds anyone staring directly at them. This is the Christ on the mountain.

Rio de Janeiro is a city of startling contrasts: from the yachts and the Jockey Club and the bauhaus apartments. . .to the shanty villages glued to the sides of the hills, where the poor scrabble for existence in their tropic paradise. *Favellas*, they are called. Down there below the big Christ, but above even the wealthy, the Gold Coast blacks have deposited their descendants, and the poor *mestizos* crowd one atop another in shanties built of corrugated shed roofing and wood slat that rots in the pulsing heat. They rise up in a crazy-quilt city above the city. And above them is a smaller hill. And on that hill they have erected another Christ. The Christ of the poor.

They are not noble morons. They are not writers who draw senseless parallels between the great white Christ on the mountain, and the little black Christ on the hill. They only know he is Christ the Redeemer. And though they have not enough *cruzeiros* to buy food for their rickety children, they have *centavos* to buy cheap tallow candles to set out on the altar of the street church. Christ will redeem them. They know it.

They are alone. In their own land, they are alone. Christ will never save them. Nor will men ever save them. They will spend their days like the waves from Africa, throwing themselves onto the beach of pitiless living.

They are no better than you or I.

I come to this book with clean hands, knowing I have done my work well. What happens with it from this point on, is all afterguessing.

I have drawn my parallels, have sighted down the gun, have sounded the clarion call. To what end?

Perhaps to codify finally for myself what my stories have been saying for the last few years: that man is building for himself a darkness of world that is turning him mad; that the pressures are too great, the machines too often break down, and the alien alone cannot make it. We must think new thoughts, we must love as we have never even suspected we can love, and if there is honor to violence we must get it on at once, have done with it, try to live with our guilt for having so done, and move on.

As with every book I've written, when the time comes for looking at it, I feel it is a good book, my best book. Later they tell me it is other things. That I meant something here I'd never thought about; and that I mucked-up that over there because I had neither the talent nor the insight. I cannot worry about that now. Later, perhaps, I'll worry and over-compensate, but right now, I am satisfied.

There are some things I want to say about these stories. Not all of them, because, as my editor at Avon, George Ernsberger, points out so correctly, "There isn't, really, something *interesting* to say about every story ever written—including, often, the very best ones." But the genesis and writing of *some* of these stories may be worthy of comment, if not for possible insights into the particular act of creation of *this* writer, then as craft notes for others passing this way.

The title story, "The Beast That Etcetera," was intended as an experiment. Consciously so. It was a serious stylistic and structural departure for me; and its warm reception by readers who were willing to go along with me to see if I could make my point, leads me to some conclusions about "avant-garde" writing, in general *and* in science fiction.

(It is not a sequential story. It is written in a circular form, as though a number of events were taking place around the rim of a wheel, simultaneously. The simultaneity of events around that wheel rim, however, occurs across the artificial barriers of time, space, dimension and thought. Everything comes together, finally, in the center, at the hub of the wheel.)

The "avant-garde" in speculative fiction these last two or three years has been plagued with a need on the part of certain critics and self-styled historians of the genre to categorize with the pigeon-hole label "New Wave." Any number of writers—no two of whom write anything alike—from Philip José Farmer to Thomas Disch, have been lumped into this clique of "New Wave writers." The list of those tagged with the appellation grows from moment to moment, and from journalist to journalist:

Aldiss, Brunner, Ballard, Sallis, Zelazny, Delany, Moorcock, Spinrad, Anthony, Wilhelm. . .everybody save Panshin and Niven (who, patently, are not), have at one time or another been pinned as "New Wave." And each has denied it.

Because of stories like "The Beast That Shouted Love at the Heart of the World," and because of the anthology DANGEROUS VISIONS, which I edited, I have also been lumped into this wholly artificial cul-de-sac.

For the record, and for those who need to be told bluntly, I do not believe there is such a thing as "New Wave" in speculative fiction (any more than there is something labeled with the abhorrent abbreviation "sci-fi," though I do not expect reviewers outside the genre to exercise enough taste to drop this convenient, though totally despicable, slang bastardization of a term presently unsuitable for that which the field has become). It is a convenient journalese expression for inept critics and voyeur-observers of the passing scene, because they have neither the wit nor the depth to understand that this richness of new voices is *many* waves: each composed of one writer.

Though I am wearied by the overuse of the phrase, "New Wave" is simply a manifestation of many writers doing their thing. To compare what I do with what Chip Delany does, is nonsense. To try drawing parallels between, say, Ballard's stories involving a codification of the "hero image" in our time, and Brian Aldiss's "acid-head war" stories, is insanity. To attempt a lumping-together of talents as divergent as the poetic Zelazny and the poetic Sallis, is insulting.

Yet there can be no denying that there is something happening: you don't know what the hell it is, do you, Mr. Jones, but you know it's happening, so you call it "New Wave," and that makes it easier to feel uneasy about, can you dig it, Mr. Jones?

Sure, there's something happening in this thing I call speculative fiction and you call science fiction and the clots call sci-fi. Just like there's something happening on college campuses and in rock music and up in Spanish Harlem and all over the place. What is happening is that a great many hip types are opening themselves more completely to all kinds of experiences and modes of expression. (Today, the person who out-of-hand denies anything experimental merely because it *is* experimental is not even considered square; he's merely pathetic. Like a tone-deaf, or a color-blind, or a tunnel-vision, or a rabid bigot.

There I was, down in Rio, at Hart Sprayger's dinner party, with all those glowing leading lights of sf, and Hart laid some Jimi Hendrix on the tape deck, and I was starting to groove behind it—having heard nothing since arriving in Rio but bad samba and worse bubble-gum music—and up walked the supposedly sharp wife of a science fiction "great," and she wrinkled her snout and said, "Oh, come on, you can't *really* like that noise?" I didn't answer. Why bother. She'll croak soon anyhow.)

So the thing that is happening is happening all at once. Spinrad is taking his long loud jab at the Establishment's use of power in BUG JACK BARRON, and ladylike Kate Wilhelm says fuck-you to the accepted modes of constructing a story and cops a well-deserved Nebula with "The Planners," and Carol Emshwiller and Piers Anthony become the writers to read in the underground, and frankly, who gives a damn which Sewell Peaslee Wright story in 1928 predicted aluminum wrap on sardine cans?

The reactionaries who are always with us. . .the terrified little children (no matter what their advanced age) who want to keep things as they are. . .who preach not merely censorship but Stalinist revisionism, in which entire topics become forbidden. . .these are the Mr. Jones's of sf. They prattle about "the sense of wonder," yet they are solidly entombed in concrete: the foundations of their pasts. They are locked into yesterday, while trying to corrupt our dreams of today and tomorrow. They tell us that these new writers, with their new ways of saying things, pollute the precious bodily fluids of science fiction. And they say they will launch a "holy war" against this "New Wave."

No chance, babies.

They rant to themselves. Every year, more and more, the readership of sf grows more knowledgeable, more aware of the demands of literary excellence. The fuddy-duddy yesterday can certainly be revered, for it contains the roots of our heritage in the form. But to revere is one thing, to totemize is another. To expect to hold up the future merely to let ghosts of yesterday feed on a today they don't own, is encystment. No one suggests the more traditional forms of sf be denied: there is always more than enough room for a full measure. And with craftsmen like Simak, Asimov, Niven, Clarke, Pohl and del Rey working, we will continue to find new lessons to learn, even in the traditional.

All we ask. . .no, the time for asking is well past; what we *demand* is equal time for the new voices. And these new voices are what the labelers have called the "New Wave."

It is the misnomer "avant-garde," already thirty-five years a hincty, outdated cliché. It would seem those dedicated to tomorrow would be willing to give free voice to those who envision *different* tomorrows, differently expressed.

One of these different modes of expression is the one I felt compelled to use in "The Beast." I've explained what that form needed to be, to tell my story the only way I felt it should be told. Yet when it appeared in magazine form, the editor felt it necessary to *add* explanatory lines, to *change* the form of the presentation. He felt it was too difficult for his audience to understand, as it appears in this volume. I cannot argue with this editor, so I will no longer write for him. He has said in correspondence that he conceives of his audience as being composed in large part of fourteen-year-old boys whose mommies thumb through the stories to make sure they are pure enough for their sons. Sadly, I do not write specifically for fourteen-year-old boys *or* their mommies. And so I expect a bit more erudition and concentration and cooperation from my readers. The editor knows I won't write for him, and he doesn't think it's enough of a loss to compensate for the aggravation I give him when he tinkers with the titles or content of my stories. It's probably better all around: there will now be a lotta mommies of fourteen-year-old boys who can sleep better, knowing Ellison is not loose, polluting their sons' precious bodily fluids.

But for you, who have bought this book, I wrote "The Beast That Shouted Love at the Heart of the World" without fetters or worries about kids and mommies. And I hope that freedom of creation sparks across to you in the reading.

. . .It occurs to me that I've gone on at considerably greater length than I'd intended, at greater length than I'd promised George Ernsberger I'd hold down to. I was going to relate the six-year-long chain of paranoid events that led to the writing of "Try a Dull Knife." I was damned anxious to talk about Robin Scott Wilson's Clarion College Workshop in Science Fiction & Fantasy, at which I wrote "Phoenix" and "The Pitll Pawob Division," while badgering my students to write a story a day. I wanted to try examining some of the reasons why "Shattered Like a Glass Goblin" is so reacted-to when I read it at college lectures. . .and why the drug crowd always bums me for having written it.

And most of all, I wanted to talk about "A Boy and His Dog." Oh, wow, that story.

But I don't have the space now. And I guess, really, I've lost the inclination.

Truly, what I feel is that anyone laying out hard cash for a book like this, deserves some new, specially-written-for-that-book material. But George is right: don't get out of hand.

I suppose, then, that the bottom line of what I've rambled on about here, ties the stories in with what I felt in Rio (and with "waves," of all kinds): the stories that are merely stories—what Vonnegut calls *foma*, harmless untruths—are for entertainment. The others are to tell you that as night approaches we are *all* aliens, down here on this alien Earth. To tell you that not Christ nor man nor governments of men will save you. To tell you that writers about tomorrow must stop living in yesterday and work from their hearts and their guts and their courage to tell us about tomorrow, before all the tomorrows are stolen away from us. To tell you no one will come down from the mountain to save your lily-white hide or your black ass. God is within you. Save yourselves.

Otherwise, why would you have traveled all this way. . .just to be alone?

Harlan Ellison / *Rio de Janeiro*
25 March 69

THE BEAST THAT SHOUTED LOVE AT THE HEART OF THE WORLD

After an idle discussion with the pest control man who came once a month to spray around the outside of his home in the Ruxton section of Baltimore, William Sterog stole a canister of Malathion, a deadly insecticide poison, from the man's truck, and went out early one morning, following the route of the neighborhood milkman, and spooned medium-large quantities into each bottle left on the rear doorstep of seventy homes. Within six hours of Bill Sterog's activities, two hundred men, women and children died in convulsive agony.

Learning that an aunt who had lived in Buffalo was dying of cancer of the lymph glands, William Sterog hastily helped his mother pack three bags, and took her to Friendship Airport, where he put her on an Eastern Airlines jet with a simple but efficient time bomb made from a Westclox TravAlarm and four sticks of dynamite in her three-suiter. The jet exploded somewhere over Harrisburg, Pennsylvania. Ninety-three people—including Bill Sterog's mother—were killed in the explosion, and flaming wreckage added seven to the toll by cascading skydown on a public swimming pool.

On a Sunday in November, William Sterog made his way to Babe Ruth Plaza on 33rd Street where he became one of 54,000 fans jamming Memorial Stadium to see the Baltimore Colts play the Green Bay Packers. He was dressed warmly in gray flannel slacks, a navy-blue turtleneck pullover and a heavy hand-knitted Irish wool sweater under his parka. With three minutes and thirteen seconds of the fourth quarter remaining to be played, and Baltimore trailing seventeen to sixteen on Green Bay's eighteen-yard line, Bill Sterog found his way up the aisle to the exit above the mezzanine seats, and fumbled under his parka for the U.S. Army surplus M-3 submachine gun he had bought for $49.95 from a mail-order armaments dealer in Alexandria, Virginia. Even as 53,999 screaming fans leaped to their feet—making his range of fire that much better—as the ball was snapped to the quarterback, holding for the defensive tackle most able to kick a successful field goal, Bill Sterog opened fire on the massed backs of the fans below him. Before the mob could bring him down, he had killed forty-four people.

When the first Expeditionary Force to the elliptical galaxy in Sculptor descended on the second planet of a fourth magnitude star the Force had designated Flammarion Theta, they found a thirty-seven-foot-high statue of a hitherto-unknown blue-white substance—not quite stone, something like metal—in the shape of a man. The figure was barefoot, draped in a garment that vaguely resembled a toga, the head encased in a skull-tight cap, and holding in its left hand a peculiar ring-and-ball device of another substance altogether. The statue's face was curiously beatific. It had high cheekbones; deep-set eyes; a tiny, almost alien mouth; and a broad, large-nostriled nose. The statue loomed enormous among the pitted and blasted curvilinear structures of some forgotten architect. The members of the Expeditionary Force commented on the peculiar expression each noted on the face of the statue. None of these men, standing under a gorgeous brass moon that shared an evening sky with a descending sun quite dissimilar in color to the one that now shone wanly on an Earth unthinkably distant in time and space, had ever heard of William Sterog. And so none of them was able to say that the expression on the giant statue was the same as the one Bill Sterog had shown as he told the final appeals judge who was about to sentence him to death in the lethal-gas chamber, "I love everyone in the world. I do. So help me God, I love you, all of you!" He was shouting.

Crosswhen, through interstices of thought called time, through reflective images called space; another then, another now. This place, over *there*. Beyond concepts, the transmogrification of simplicity finally labeled *if*. Forty and more steps sidewise but later, much later. There, in that ultimate center, with everything radiating outward, becoming infinitely more complex, the enigma of symmetry, harmony, apportionment singing with fine-tuned order in *this* place, where it all began, begins, will always begin. The center. Crosswhen.

Or: a hundred million years in the future. And: a hundred million parsecs beyond the farthest edge of measurable space. And: parallax warpages beyond counting across the universes of parallel existences. Finally: an infinitude of mind-triggered leaps beyond human thought.

There: Crosswhen.

On the mauve level, crouched down in deeper magenta washings that concealed his arched form, the maniac waited. He was a dragon, squat and round in the torso, tapered ropy tail tucked under his body; the small, thick osseous shields rising perpendicularly from the arched back, running down to the end of the tail, tips pointing upwards; his taloned shorter arms folded across his massive chest. He had the seven-headed dog faces of an ancient Cerberus. Each head watched, waiting, hungry, insane.

He saw the bright yellow wedge of light as it moved in random patterns through the mauve, always getting closer. He knew he could not run, the movement would betray him, the specter light finding him instantly. Fear choked the maniac. The specter light had pursued him through innocence and humility and nine other emotional obfuscations he had tried. He had to do something, get them off his scent. But he was alone on this level. It had been closed down some time before, to purge it of residue emotions. Had he not been so terribly confused after the killings, had he not been drowning in disorientation, he would never have trapped himself on a closed level.

Now that he was here, there was nowhere to hide, nowhere to escape the specter light that would systematically hunt him down. Then they would purge *him*.

The maniac took the one final chance; he closed down his mind, all seven brains, even as the mauve level was closed down. He shut off all thought, banked the fires of emotion, broke the neural circuits that fed power to his mind. Like a great machine phasing down from peak efficiency, his thoughts slackened and wilted and grew pale. Then there was a blank where he had been. Seven dog-heads slept.

The dragon had ceased to exist in terms of thought, and the specter light washed past him, finding nothing there to home in on. But those who sought the maniac were sane, not deranged as he was: their sanity was ordered, and in order they considered every exigency. The specter light was followed by heat-seeking beams, by mass-tallying sensors, by trackers that could hunt out the spoor of foreign matter on a closed-down level.

They found the maniac. Shut down like a sun gone cold, they located him, and transferred him: he was unaware of the movement; he was locked away in his own silent skulls.

But when he chose to open his thoughts again, in the timeless disorientation that follows a total shutdown, he found himself locked in stasis in a drainage ward on the 3rd Red Active Level. Then, from seven throats, he screamed.

The sound, of course, was lost in the throat baffles they had inserted, before he had turned himself back on. The emptiness of the sound terrified him even more.

He was imbedded in an amber substance that fit around him comfortably; had it been a much earlier era, on another world, in another continuum, it would have been simply a hospital bed with restraining straps. But the dragon was locked in stasis on a red level, crosswhen. His hospital bed was anti-grav, weightless, totally relaxing, feeding nutrients through his leathery hide along with depressants and toners. He was waiting to be drained.

Linah drifted into the ward, followed by Semph. Semph, the discoverer of the drain. And his most eloquent nemesis, Linah, who sought Public Elevation to the position of Proctor. They drifted down the rows of amber-encased patients: the toads, the tambour-lidded crystal cubes, the exoskeletals, the pseudopodal changers, and the seven-headed dragon. They paused directly in front and slightly above the maniac. He was able to look up at them; images seven times seen; but he was not able to make sound.

"If I needed a conclusive reason, here's one of the best," Linah said, inclining his head toward the maniac.

Semph dipped an analysis rod into the amber substance, withdrew it and made a hasty reading of the patient's condition. "If you needed a greater *warning*," Semph said quietly, "this would be one of the best."

"Science bends to the will of the masses," Linah said.

"I'd hate to have to believe that," Semph responded quickly. There was a tone in his voice that could not be named, but it undershadowed the aggressiveness of his words.

"I'm going to see to it, Semph; *believe it*. I'm going to have the Concord pass the resolution."

"Linah, how long have we known each other?"

"Since your third flux. My second."

"That's about right. Have I ever told you a lie, have I ever asked you to do something that would harm you?"

"No. Not that I can recall."

"Then why won't you listen to me *this* time?"

"Because I think you're wrong. I'm not a fanatic, Semph. I'm not making political hay with this. I feel very strongly that it's the best chance we've ever had."

"But disaster for everyone and everywhere else, all the way back, and God only knows how far across the parallax. We stop fouling our own nest, at the expense of all the other nests that ever were."

Linah spread his hands in futility. "Survival."

Semph shook his head slowly, with a weariness that was mirrored in his expression. "I wish I could drain *that*, too."

"Can't you?"

Semph shrugged. "I can drain *an*ything. But what we'd have left wouldn't be worth having."

The amber substance changed hue. It glowed deep within itself with a blue intensity. "The patient is ready," Semph said. "Linah, one more time. I'll beg if it'll do any good. Please. Stall till the next session. The Concord needn't do it *now*. Let me run some further tests, let me see how far back this garbage spews, how much damage it can cause. Let me prepare some reports."

Linah was firm. He shook his head in finality. "May I watch the draining with you?"

Semph let out a long sigh. He was beaten, and knew it. "Yes, all right."

The amber substance carrying its silent burden began to rise. It reached the level of the two men, and slid smoothly through the air between them. They drifted after the smooth container with the dog-headed dragon imbedded in it, and Semph seemed as though he wanted to say something else. But there was nothing to say.

The amber chrysalloid cradle faded and vanished, and the men became insubstantial and were no more. They all reappeared in the drainage chamber. The beaming stage was empty. The amber cradle settled down on it without sound, and the substance flowed away, vanishing as it uncovered the dragon.

The maniac tried desperately to move, to heave himself up. Seven heads twitched futilely. The madness in him overcame the depressants and he was consumed with frenzy, fury, crimson hate. But he could not move. It was all he could do to hold his shape.

Semph turned the band on his left wrist. It glowed from within, a deep gold. The sound of air rushing to fill a vacuum filled the chamber. The beaming stage was drenched in silver light that seemed to spring out of the air itself, from an unknown source. The dragon was washed by the silver light, and the seven great mouths opened once, exposing rings of fangs. Then his double-lidded eyes closed.

The pain within his heads was monstrous. A fearful wrenching that became the sucking of a million mouths. His very brains were pulled upon, pressured, compressed, and then purged.

Semph and Linah looked away from the pulsing body of the dragon to the drainage tank across the chamber. It was filling from the bottom as they watched. Filling with a nearly-colorless roiling cloud of smokiness, shot through with sparks. "Here it comes," Semph said, needlessly.

Linah dragged his eyes away from the tank. The dragon with seven dog heads was rippling. As though seen through shallow water, the maniac was beginning to alter. As the tank filled, the maniac found it more and more difficult to maintain his shape. The denser grew the cloud of sparkling matter in the tank, the less constant was the shape of the creature on the beaming stage.

Finally, it was impossible, and the maniac gave in. The tank filled more rapidly, and the shape quavered and altered and shrank and then there was a superimposition of the form of a man, over that of the seven-headed dragon. Then the tank reached three-quarters filled and the dragon became an underlying shadow, a hint, a suggestion of what had been there when the drainage began. Now the man-form was becoming more dominant by the second.

Finally, the tank was filled, and a normal man lay on the beaming stage, breathing heavily, eyes closed, muscles jumping involuntarily.

"He's drained," Semph said.

"Is it all in the tank?" Linah asked softly.

"No, none of it."

"Then. . ."

"This is the residue. Harmless. Reagents purged from a group of sensitives will neutralize it. The dangerous essences, the degenerate force-lines that make up the field. . .they're gone. Drained off already."

Linah looked disturbed, for the first time. "Where did it go?"

"Do you love your fellow man, tell me?"

"Please, Semph! I asked where it went. . .when it went?"

"And I asked if you cared at all about anyone else?"

"You know my answer. . .you know *me*! I want to know, tell me, at least what you know. Where. . .when. . .?"

"Then you'll forgive me, Linah, because I love my fellow man, too. Whenever he was, wherever he is; I have to, I work in an inhuman field, and I have to cling to that. So. . .you'll forgive me. . ."

"What are you going to. . ."

In Indonesia they have a phrase for it: Djam Karet—*the hour that stretches.*

In the Vatican's Stanza of Heliodorus, the second of the great rooms he designed for Pope Julius II, Raphael painted (and his pupils completed) a magnificent fresco representation of the historic meeting between Pope Leo I and Attila the Hun, in the year 452.

In this painting is mirrored the belief of Christians everywhere that the spiritual authority of Rome protected her in that desperate hour when the Hun came to sack and burn the Holy City. Raphael has painted in Saint Peter and Saint Paul, descending from Heaven to reinforce Pope Leo's intervention. His interpretation was an elaboration on the original legend, in which only the Apostle Peter was mentioned—standing behind Leo with a drawn sword. And the legend was an elaboration of what little facts have come down through antiquity relatively undistorted: Leo had no cardinals with him, and certainly no wraith Apostles. He was one of three in the deputation. The other two were secular dignitaries of the Roman state. The meeting did not take place—as legend would have us believe—just outside the gates of Rome, but in northern Italy, not far from what is today Peschiera.

Nothing more than this is known of the confrontation. Yet Attila, who had never been stopped, did not raze Rome. He turned back.

Djam Karet. The force-line field spewed out from a parallax center crosswhen, a field that had pulsed through time and space and the minds of men for twice ten thousand years. Then cut out suddenly, inexplicably, and Attila the Hun clapped his hands to his head, his mind twisting like rope within his skull. His eyes glazed, then cleared, and he breathed from deep in his chest. Then he signaled his army to turn back. Leo the Great thanked God and the living memory of Christ the Saviour. Legend added Saint Peter. Raphael added Saint Paul.

For twice ten thousand years—*Djam Karet*—the field had pulsed, and for a brief moment that could have been instants or years or millennia, it was cut off.

Legend does not tell the truth. More specifically, it does not tell *all* of the truth: forty years before Attila raided Italy, Rome had been taken and sacked by Alaric the Goth. *Djam Karet*. Three years after the retreat of Attila Rome was once more taken and sacked, by Gaiseric, King of all the Vandals.

There was a reason the garbage of insanity had ceased to flow through everywhere and everywhen from the drained mind of a seven-headed dragon. . .

Semph, traitor to his race, hovered before the Concord. His friend, the man who now sought his final flux, Linah, Proctored the hearing. He spoke softly, but eloquently, of what the great scientist had done.

"The tank was draining; he said to me, 'Forgive me, because I love my fellow man. Whenever he was, wherever he is; I have to, I work in an inhuman field, and I have to cling to that. So you'll forgive me.' Then he interposed himself."

The sixty members of the Concord, a representative from each race that existed in the center, bird-creatures and blue things and large-headed men and orange scents with cilia shuddering. . .all of them looked at Semph where he hovered. His body and head were crumpled like a brown paper bag. All hair was gone. His eyes were dim and watery. Naked, shimmering, he drifted slightly to one side, then a vagrant breeze in the wall-less chamber sent him back. He had drained himself.

"I ask for this Concord to affix sentence of final flux on this man. Though his interposition only lasted a few moments, we have no way of knowing what damage or unnaturalness it may have caused crosswhen. I submit that his intent was to overload the drain and thereby render it inoperative. This act, the act of a beast who would condemn the sixty races of the center to a future in which insanity still prevailed, is an act that can only be punished by termination."

The Concord blanked and meditated. A timeless time later they re-linked, and the Proctor's charges were upheld; his demand of sentence was fulfilled.

On the hushed shores of a thought, the papyrus man was carried in the arms of his friend, his executioner, the Proctor. There in the dusting quiet of an approaching night, Linah laid Semph down in the shadow of a sigh.

"Why did you stop me?" the wrinkle with a mouth asked.

Linah looked away across the rushing dark.

"Why?"

"Because here, in the center, there is a chance."

"And for them, all of them out there. . .no chance ever?"

Linah sat down slowly, digging his hands into the golden mist, letting it sift over his wrists and back into the waiting flesh of the world. "If we can begin it here, if we can pursue our boundaries outward, then perhaps one day, sometime, we can reach to the ends of time with that little chance. Until then, it is better to have one center where there is no madness."

Semph hurried his words. The end was rapidly striding for him. "You have sentenced them all. Insanity is a living vapor. A force. It can be bottled. The most potent genie in the most easily uncorked bottle. And you have condemned them to live with it always. In the name of love."

Linah made a sound that was not quite a word, but called it back. Semph touched his wrist with a tremble that had been a hand. Fingers melting into softness and warmth. "I'm sorry for you, Linah. Your curse is to be a true man. The world is made for strugglers. You never learned how to do that."

Linah did not reply. He thought only of the drainage that was eternal now. Set in motion and kept in motion by its necessity.

"Will you do a memorial for me?" Semph asked.

Linah nodded. "It's traditional."

Semph smiled softly. "Then do it for them; not for me. I'm the one who devised the vessel of their death, and I don't need it. But choose one of them; not a very important one, but one that will mean everything to them if they find it, and understand. Erect the memorial in my name to that one. Will you?"

Linah nodded.

"Will you?" Semph asked. His eyes were closed, and he could not see the nod.

"Yes. I will," Linah said. But Semph could not hear. The flux began and ended, and Linah was alone in the cupped silence of loneliness.

The statue was placed on a far planet of a far star in a time that was ancient while yet never having been born. It existed in the minds of men who would come later. Or never.

But if they did, they would know that hell was with them, that there was a Heaven that men called Heaven, and in it there was a center from which all madness flowed; and once within that center, there was peace.

In the remains of a blasted building that had been a shirt factory, in what had been Stuttgart, Friedrich Drucker found a many-colored box. Maddened by hunger and the memory of having eaten human flesh for weeks, the man tore at the lid of the box with the bloodied stubs of his fingers. As the box flew open, pressed at a certain point, cyclones rushed out past the terrified face of Friedrich Drucker. Cyclones and dark, winged, faceless shapes that streaked away into the night, followed by a last wisp of purple smoke smelling strongly of decayed gardenias.

But Friedrich Drucker had little time to ponder the meaning of the purple smoke, for the next day, World War IV broke out.

—Los Angeles, 1968

ALONG THE SCENIC ROUTE

The blood-red Mercury with the twin-mounted 7.6mm Spandaus cut George off as he was shifting lanes. The Merc cut out sharply, three cars behind George, and the driver decked it. The boom of his gas-turbine engine got through George's baffling system without difficulty, like a fist in the ear. The Merc sprayed JP-4 gook and water in a wide fan from its jet nozzle and cut back in, a matter of inches in front of George's Chevy Piranha.

George slapped the selector control on the dash, lighting YOU STUPID BASTARD, WHAT DO YOU THINK YOU'RE DOING and I HOPE YOU CRASH & BURN, YOU SON OF A BITCH. Jessica moaned softly with uncontrolled fear, but George could not hear her: he was screaming obscenities.

George kicked it into Overplunge and depressed the selector button extending the rotating buzzsaws. Dallas razors, they were called, in the repair shoppes. But the crimson Merc pulled away doing an easy 115.

"I'll get you, you beaver-sucker!" he howled.

The Piranha jumped, surged forward. But the Merc was already two dozen car-lengths down the Freeway. Adrenaline pumped through George's system. Beside him, Jessica put a hand on his arm. "Oh, forget it, George; it's just some young snot," she said. Always conciliatory.

"My masculinity's threatened," he murmured, and hunched over the wheel. Jessica looked toward heaven, wishing a bolt of lightning had come from that location many months past, striking Dr. Yasimir directly in his Freud, long before George could have picked up psychiatric justifications for his awful temper.

"Get me Collision Control!" George snarled at her.

Jessica shrugged, as if to say *here we go again*, and dialed CC on the peek. The smiling face of a fusco, the Freeway Sector Control Operator, blurred green and yellow, then came into sharp focus. "Your request, sir?"

"Clearance for duel, Highway 101, northbound."

"Your license number, sir?"

"XUPD 88321," George said. He was scanning the Freeway, keeping the blood-red Mercury in sight, obstinately refusing to stud on the tracking sights.

"Your proposed opponent, sir?"

"Red Mercury GT. '88 model."

"License, sir."

"Just a second." George pressed the stud for the instant replay and the last ten miles rewound on the Sony Backtracker. He ran it forward again till he caught the instant the Merc had passed him, froze the frame, and got the number. "MFCS 90909."

"One moment, sir."

George fretted behind the wheel. "*Now* what the hell's holding her up? Whenever you want service, they've got problems. But boy, when it comes tax time—"

The fusco came back and smiled. "I've checked our master Sector grid, sir, and I find authorization may be permitted, but I am required by law to inform you that your proposed opponent is more heavily armed than yourself."

George licked his lips. "What's he running?"

"Our records indicate 7.6mm Spandau equipment, bulletproof screens and coded optionals."

George sat silently. His speed dropped. The tachometer fluttered, settled.

"Let him go, George," Jessica said. "You know he'd take you."

Two blotches of anger spread on George's cheeks. "Oh, yeah!?!" He howled at the fusco, "Get me a confirm on that Mercury, Fusco!"

She blurred off, and George decked the Piranha: it leaped forward. Jessica sighed with resignation and pulled the drawer out from beneath her bucket. She unfolded the g-suit and began stretching into it. She said nothing, but continued to shake her head.

"We'll *see*!" George said.

"Oh, George, when will you ever grow up?"

He did not answer, but his nostrils flared with barely restrained anger.

The fusco smeared back and said, "Opponent confirms, sir. Freeway Underwriters have already cross-filed you as mutual beneficiaries. Please observe standard traffic regulations, and good luck, sir."

She vanished, and George set the Piranha on sleepwalker as he donned his own g-suit. He overrode the sleeper and was back on manual in moments.

"Now, you stuffer, *now* let's see!" 100. 110. 120.

He was gaining rapidly on the Merc now. As the Chevy hit 120, the mastercomp flashed red and suggested crossover. George punched the selector and the telescoping arms of the buzzsaws retracted into the axles, even as the buzzsaws stopped whirling. In a moment—drawn back in, now merely fancy decorations in the hubcaps. The wheels retracted into the underbody of the Chevy and the air-cushion took over. Now the Chevy skimmed along, two inches above the roadbed of the Freeway.

Ahead, George could see the Merc also crossing over to air-cushion. 120. 135. 150.

"George, this is crazy!" Jessica said, her face in that characteristic shrike expression. "You're no hot-rodder, George. You're a family man, and this is the family car!"

George chuckled nastily. "I've had it with these fuzzfaces. Last year. . .you remember last year? . . .you remember when that punk stuffer ran us into the abutment? I swore I'd never put up with that kind of thing again. Why'd' you think I had all the optionals installed?"

Jessica opened the tambour doors of the glove compartment and slid out the service tray. She unplugged the jar of anti-flash salve and began spreading it on her face and hands. "I *knew* I shouldn't have let you put that laser thing in this car!" George chuckled again. Fuzzfaces, punks, rodders!

George felt the Piranha surge forward, the big reliable Stirling engine recycling the hot air for more and more efficient thrust. Unlike the Merc's inefficient kerosene system, there was no exhaust emission from the nuclear power plant, the external combustion engine almost noiseless, the big radiator tailfin in the rear dissipating the tremendous heat, stabilizing the car as it swooshed along, two inches off the road-bed.

George knew he would catch the blood-red Mercury. Then one smartass punk was going to learn he couldn't flout law and order by running decent citizens off the Freeways!

"Get me my gun," George said.

Jessica shook her head with exasperation, reached under George's bucket, pulled out his drawer and handed him the bulky .45 automatic in its breakaway upside-down shoulder rig. George studded in the sleeper, worked his arms into the rig, tested the oiled leather of the holster, and when he was satisfied, returned the Piranha to manual.

"Oh, God," Jessica said, "John Dillinger rides again."

"Listen!" George shouted, getting more furious with each stupidity she offered. "If you can't be of some help to me, just shut your damned mouth. I'd put you out and come back for you, but I'm in a duel. . .can you understand that? I'm in a duel!" She murmured a yes, George, and fell silent.

There was a transmission queep from the transceiver. George studded it on. No picture. Just vocal. It had to be the driver of the Mercury, up ahead of them. Beaming directly at one another's antennae, using a tightbeam directional, they could keep in touch: it was a standard trick used by rods to rattle their opponents.

"Hey, Boze, you not really gonna custer me, are you? Back'm, Boze. No bad trips, true. The kid'll drop back, hang a couple of biggies on ya, just to teach ya a little lesson, letcha swimaway." The voice of the driver was hard, mirthless, the ugly sound of a driver used to being challenged.

"Listen, you young snot," George said, grating his words, trying to sound more menacing than he felt, "I'm going to teach *you* the lesson!"

The Merc's driver laughed raucously.

"Boze, you *de*-mote me, true!"

"And stop calling me a bozo, you lousy little degenerate!"

"Ooooo-weeee, got me a thrasher this time out. Okay, Boze, you be custer an' I'll play arrow. Good shells, baby Boze!"

The finalizing queep sounded, and George gripped the wheel with hands that went knuckle-white. The Merc suddenly shot away from him. He had been steadily gaining, but now as though it had been springloaded, the Mercury burst forward, spraying gook and water on both sides of the forty-foot lanes they were using. "Cut in his afterburner," George snarled. The driver of the Mercury had injected water into the exhaust for added thrust through the jet nozzle. The boom of the Merc's big, noisy engine hit him, and George studded in the rear-mounted propellers to give him more speed. 175. 185. 195.

He was crawling up the line toward the Merc. Gaining, gaining. Jessica pulled out her drawer and unfolded her crash-suit. It went on over the g-suit, and she let George know what she thought of his turning their Sunday Drive into a kamikaze duel.

He told her to stuff it, and did a sleeper, donned his own crash-suit, applied flash salve, and lowered the bangup helmet onto his head.

Back on manual he crawled, crawled, till he was only fifty yards behind the Mercury, the gas-turbine vehicle sharp in his tinted windshield. "Put on your goggles. . .I'm going to show that punk who's a bozo. . ."

He pressed the stud to open the laser louvers. The needle-nosed glass tube peered out from its bay in the Chevy's hood. George read the power drain on his dash. The MHD power generator used to drive the laser was charging. He remembered what the salesman at Chick Williams Chevrolet had told him, pridefully, about the laser gun, when George had inquired about the optional.

Dynamite feature, Mr. Jackson. Absolutely sensational. Works off a magneto hydro dynamic power generator. Latest thing in defense armament. You know, to achieve sufficient potency from a CO_2 *laser, you'd need a glass tube a mile long. Well, sir, we both know* that's *impractical, to say the least, so the project engineers at Chevy's big Bombay plant developed the "stack" method. Glass rods baffled with mirrors—360 feet of stack, the length of a football field. . .plus end-zones. Use it three ways. Punch a hole right through their tires at any speed under a hundred and twenty. If they're running a GT, you can put that hole right into the kerosene fuel tank, blow them off the road. Or, if they're running a Stirling, just heat the radiator. When the radiator gets hotter than the engine, the whole works shuts down. Dynamite. Also. . .and this is with proper CC authorization, you can go straight for the old jugular. Use the beam on the driver. Makes a neat hole. Dynamite!*

"I'll take it," George murmured.

"What did you say?" Jessica asked.

"Nothing."

"George, you're a family man, not a rodder!"

"Stuff it!"

Then he was sorry he'd said it. She meant well. It was simply that. . .well, a man had to work hard to keep his balls. He looked sidewise at her. Wearing the Armadillo crash-suit, with its overlapping discs of ceramic material, she looked like a ferryflight pilot. The bangup hat hid her face. He wanted to apologize, but the moment had arrived. He locked the laser on the Merc, depressed the fire stud, and a beam of blinding light flashed from the hood of the Piranha. With the Merc on air-cushion, he had gone straight for the fuel tank.

But the Merc suddenly wasn't in front of him. Even as he had fired, the driver had sheered left into the next forty-foot-wide lane, and cut speed drastically. The Merc dropped back past them as the Piranha swooshed ahead.

"He's on my back!" George shouted.

The next moment Spandau slugs tore at the hide of the Chevy. George slapped the studs, and the bulletproof screens went up. But not before pingholes had appeared in the beryllium hide of the Chevy, exposing the boron fiber filaments that gave the car its lightweight maneuverability. "Stuffer!" George breathed, terribly frightened. The driver was on his back, could ride him into the ground.

He swerved, dropping flaps and skimming the Piranha back and forth in wide arcs, across the two lanes. The Merc hung on. The Spandaus chattered heavily. The screens would hold, but what else was the driver running? What were the "coded optionals" the CC fusco had mentioned?

"Now see what you've gotten us into!"

"Jess, shut up, shut up!"

The transceiver queeped. He studded it on, still swerving. This time the driver of the Merc was sending via microwave video. The face blurred in.

He was a young boy. In his teens. Acne.

"Punk! Stinking punk!" George screamed, trying to swerve, drop back, accelerate. Nothing. The blood-red Merc hung on his tailfin, pounding at him. If one of those bullets struck the radiator tailfin, ricocheted, pierced to the engine, got through the lead shielding around the reactor. Jessica was crying, huddled inside her Armadillo.

He was silently glad she was in the g-suit. He would try something illegal in a moment.

"Hey, Boze. What's your slit look like? If she's creamy'n'nice I might letcha drop her at the next getty, and come back for her later. With your insurance, baby, and my pickle, I can keep her creamy'n'nice."

"Fuzzfaced punk! I'll see you dead first!"

"You're a real thrasher, old dad. Wish you well, but it's soon over. Say bye-bye to the nice rodder. You gonna die, old dad!"

George was shrieking inarticulately.

The boy laughed wildly. He was up on something. Ferro-coke, perhaps. Or D4. Or merryloo. His eyes glistened blue and young and deadly as a snake.

"Just wanted you to know the name of your piledriver, old dad. *You* can call me Billy. . ."

And he was gone. The Merc slipped forward, closer, and George had only a moment to realize that this Billy could not possibly have the money to equip his car with a laser, and that was a godsend. But the Spandaus were hacking away at the bulletproof screens. They weren't meant for extended punishment like this. Damn that Detroit iron!

He had to make the illegal move *now*.

Thank God for the g-suits. A tight turn, across the lanes, in direct contravention of the authorization. And in a tight turn, without the g-suits, doing—he checked the speedometer and tach—250 mph, the blood slams up against one side of the body. The g-suits would squeeze the side of the body where the blood tried to pool up. They would live. If. . .

He spun the wheel hard, slamming down on the accelerator. The Merc slewed sidewise and caught the turn. He never had a chance. He pulled out of the illegal turn, and their positions were the same. But the Merc had dropped back several car-lengths. Then from the transceiver there was a queep and he did not even stud in as the Police Copter overhead tightbeamed him in an authoritative voice:

"XUPD 88321. Warning! You will be in contravention of your dueling authorization if you try another maneuver of that sort! You are warned to keep to your lanes and the standard rules of road courtesy!"

Then it was queeped, and George felt the universe settling like silt over him. He was being killed by the system.

He'd have to eject. The seat would save him and Jessica. He tried to tell her, but she had fainted.

How did I get into this? he pleaded with himself. *Dear God, I swear if you get me out of this alive I'll never never never go mad like this again. Please God.*

Then the Merc was up on him again, pulling up *alongside*!

The window went down on the passenger side of the Mercury, and George whipped a glance across to see Billy with his lips skinned back from his teeth under the windblast and acceleration, aiming a .45 at him. Barely thinking, George studded the bumpers.

The super-conducting magnetic bumpers took hold, sucked Billy into his magnetic field, and they collided with a crash that shook the .45 out of the rodder's hand. In the instant of collision, George realized he had made his chance, and dropped back. In a moment he was riding the Merc's tail again.

Naked barbarism took hold. He wanted to kill now. Not crash the other, not wound the other, not stop the other—*kill the other!* Messages to God were forgotten.

He locked-in the laser and aimed for the windshield bubble. His sights caught the rear of the bubble, fastened to the outline of Billy's head, and George fired.

As the bolt of light struck the bubble, a black spot appeared, and remained for the seconds the laser touched. When the light cut off the black spot vanished. George cursed, screamed, cried, in fear and helplessness.

The Merc was equipped with a frequency-sensitive laserproof windshield. Chemicals in the windshield would "go black," opaque at certain frequencies, momentarily, anywhere a laser light touched them. He should have known. A duelist like this Billy, trained in weaponry, equipped for whatever might chance down a Freeway. Another coded optional. George found he was crying, piteously, within the cavern of his bangup hat.

Then the Merc was swerving again, executing a roll and dip that George could not understand, could not predict. Then the Merc dropped speed suddenly, and George found himself almost running up the jet nozzle of the blood-red vehicle.

He spun out and around, and Billy was behind him once more, closing in for the kill. He sent the propellers to full spin and reached for eternity. 270. 280. 290.

Then he heard the sizzling, and jerked his head around to see the back wall of the car rippling. *Oh my God,* he thought, in terror, *he can't afford a laser, but he's got an inductor beam!*

The beam was setting up strong local eddy currents in the beryllium hide of the Chevy. He'd rip a hole in the skin, the air would whip through, the car would go out of control.

George knew he was dead.

And Jessica.

And all because of this punk, this rodder fuzzface!

The Merc closed in confidently.

George thought wildly. There was no time for anything but the blind plunging panic of random thought. The speedometer and the tach agreed. They were doing 300 mph.

Riding on air-cushions.

The thought slipped through his panic.

It was the only possibility. He ripped off his bangup hat, and fumbled Jessica's loose. He hugged them in his lap with his free hand, and managed to stud down the window on the driver's side. Instantly, a blast of wind and accelerated air skinned back his lips, plastered his cheeks hollowly, made a death's head of Jessica's features. He fought to keep the Chevy stable, gyro'd.

Then, holding the bangup hats by their straps, he forced them around the edge of the window where the force of his speed jammed them against the side of the Chevy. Then he let go. And studded up the window. And braked sharply.

The bulky bangup hats dropped away, hit the roadbed, rolled directly into the path of the Merc. They disappeared underneath the blood-red car, and instantly the vehicle hit the Freeway. George swerved out of the way, dropping speed quickly.

The Merc hit with a crash, bounced, hit again, bounced and hit, bounced and hit. As it went past the Piranha, George saw Billy caroming off the insides of the car.

He watched the vehicle skid, wheelless, for a quarter of a mile down the Freeway before it caught the inner breakwall of the Jersey Barrier, shot high in the air, and came down turning over. It landed on the bubble, which burst, and exploded in a flash of fire and smoke that rocked the Chevy.

At three hundred miles per hour, two inches above the Freeway, riding on air, anything that broke up the air bubble would be a lethal weapon. He had won the duel. That Billy was dead.

George pulled in at the next getty, and sat in the lot. Jessica came around finally. He was slumped over the wheel, shaking, unable to speak.

She looked over at him, then reached out a trembling hand to touch his shoulder. He jumped at the infinitesimal pressure, felt through the g- and crash-suits. She started to speak, but the peek queeped, and she studded it on.

"Sector Control, sir." The fusco smiled.

He did not look up.

"Congratulations, sir. Despite one possible infraction, your duel has been logged as legal and binding. You'll be pleased to know that the occupant of the car you challenged was rated number one in the entire Central and Western Freeway circuits. Now that Mr. Bonney has been finalized, we are entering your name on the dueling records. Underwriters have asked us to inform you that a check will be in the mails to you within twenty-four hours.

"Again, sir, congratulations."

The peek went dead, and George tried to focus on the parking lot of the neon-and-silver getty. It had been a terrible experience. He never wanted to use a car that way again. It had been some other George, certainly not him.

"I'm a family man," he repeated Jessica's words. "And this is just a family car. . .I. . ."

She was smiling gently at him. Then they were in each other's arms, and he was crying, and she was saying that's all right, George, you had to do it, it's all right.

And the peek queeped.

She studded it on and the face of the fusco smiled back at her. "Congratulations, sir, you'll be pleased to know that Sector Control already has fifteen duel challenges for you.

"Mr. Ronnie Lee Hauptman of Dallas has asked for first challenge, and is, at this moment, speeding toward you with an ETA of 6:15 this evening. In the event Mr. Hauptman does not survive, you have waiting challenges from Mr. Fred Bull of Chatsworth, California. . .Mr. Leo Fowler of Philadelphia. . .Mr. Emil Zalenko of. . ."

George did not hear the list. He was trying desperately, with clubbed fingers, to extricate himself from the strangling folds of g- and crash-suits. But he knew it was no good. He would have to fight.

In the world of the Freeway, there was no place for a walking man.

—Clarion State College,
Clarion, Pennsylvania, 1968
and Los Angeles, 1969

The Author wishes to thank Mr. Ben Bova, formerly of the Avco Everett Research Laboratory (Everett, Massachusetts), for his assistance in preparing the extrapolative technical background of this story.

PHOENIX

I buried Tab in a shallow grave beneath the shifting red sands. It wasn't deep enough to keep the hysterical night beasts from finding his corpse and tearing it to the bones, but it made me feel better. At first I couldn't face Marga and her swine husband, but when it came time to move on, I had to redistribute the packs—loading as much of what Tab had been carrying as we could into our three rucksacks—and the first glances of their naked hatred were easy to handle. But ten more miles of trekking across that devil underfoot, that stinking blood desert, dissipated some of their vigor; they knew, as I knew. . .we had to hang together. It was the only way to get out alive.

The sun hung above us like a great eye, punched by a sharp flaming stick. . .a bloody, dripping eye that turned the stinking desert red around us. Illogically, I wanted a good cup of coffee.

Water. I wanted water, too. And lemonade. With ice all the way up to the top of the glass. Ice cream. Maybe on a stick. I shook my head. . .I was buzzing.

Red sands. It was a painting we were dragging across, not a reality. Sand was yellow ocher; sand was brown; sand was gray; it wasn't red. Unless you poke the sun in the eye and let it bleed all over the earth. I wished I was back at the University. There was a water cooler just down the hall from my office. I missed that water cooler. I could remember it clearly. The aluminum cool of it, the step-pedal and the arc of water. Oh, God, I couldn't think of anything but the squat beautiful water cooler.

What the hell was I doing out here!

Looking for a legend.

A legend that had already cost me every cent I'd ever saved, every coin I'd ever squirreled up in an account for emergency. This wasn't an emergency—it was stark staring lunacy. An insanity that had taken the life of my friend, my partner. . .Tab. . .gone. . .heat stroke, gasping, tearing at himself, eyes bulging, tongue protruding, the face turning black and the blood vessels spasming in his temples. . .I tried not to think about it, and could think of nothing else. His face, stretched back in a death rictus, was all I could see, wavering before me in the air, like heat-devils on the endless horizon, that face just an instant before I spilled red sand over it. And left him for whatever unclean creatures could live on this desert.

"Are we going to stop?"

I turned to look back at Marga's husband. He had a name, but I kept forgetting it. I *wanted* to keep forgetting it. He was a stupid, weak bastard, with long straight hair that picked up all the moisture from his scalp, and dripped it in oily drops down the back of his neck. He brushed the hair straight back from his receding hairline and it hung like a sleek mat, curling around his ears. His name was Curt, or Clark, or something. I didn't really *want* to know. I didn't really *want* to picture him on top of her in a cool white bed somewhere, with an air conditioner humming, their bodies soldered together by passion. I didn't want to know this sonofabitch, but he was there, lagging half a dozen paces behind me. Bent almost double by the rucksack.

"We'll stop soon," I said, and kept moving.

It should have been you, you bastard, not Tab!

In the lee of an improbable rock outcropping, in the middle of the nowhere freezing nothing, we set up the little chemical stove, and Marga cooked us an evening meal. Meat, tasteless, pre-packaged, a bad commercial choice for an expedition like this—another example of her swine husband's ineptitude. I chewed it and chewed it, and wanted to cram it in his ear. Some kind of pudding. The last of the water. I waited for the swine to offer a suggestion that we should boil out our own urine. I waited, but he didn't know that little fact, fortunately for him.

"What are we going to do tomorrow?" he whined.

I didn't answer him.

"Eat your food, Grant," Marga said, not looking up. She knew I was getting pushed to an extreme none of us would like. Why the hell didn't she tell him we'd known each other before? Why didn't she say something to break the back of all that silence? How much longer could this deranged charade go on?

"No, I want to *know!*" the swine demanded. He sounded like a petulant child. "It was *you* that got us into this! Now you've got to get us out of it!"

I ignored him. The pudding tasted like butterscotch mortar paste.

The bastard heaved his empty pudding tin at me.

"Answer me!"

I went for him. Right across the stove, and down on top of him with my knee in his throat. "Listen, baby boy," I didn't recognize my own voice, "stop clanging on my ears. I've had enough of you. Had enough the first day out. If we come back from this up to our asses in money, you'll tell everyone it was you that did it. If we bust out or die here, you'll blame me. So now we know what choices you've got, and don't let me hear any mouth about it. Just lay there, or eat your pudding, or *die*, you egg-eyed cockroach, but don't *demand*, or I'll stave in your windpipe!"

I'm not sure he understood a word of what I said. I was almost frothing, crazy with hate and heat, slurring my words. He was starting to black out.

Marga pulled me off him.

I slunk back to my place and stared off at the stars. There weren't any. It wasn't that kind of night.

Hours later, she slid over to my side. I wasn't sleeping, despite the bone-cold and the need to be under a thermal blanket in my sleeping bag. I *wanted* to be cold: to freeze my hatred, to chill my self-loathing, to drop the temperature on the killing rage building within me. She sat there a moment, staring down at me, trying to ascertain in the dark if I had my eyes open. I opened them and said, "What do you want?"

"I want to talk to you, Red."

"About what?"

"About tomorrow."

"Nothing to talk. Either we make it or we don't."

"He's frightened. You have to allow him—"

"Nothing. I have to allow him not a thing. The way I read it, I've allowed him just about everything I can already. Don't expect a nobility out of me that your own husband doesn't possess. I wasn't that well brought-up."

She bit her lower lip. She was in pain, I knew it, I'd have given anything to reach out and touch her hair, it might have helped, I didn't do it. "He'd gone wrong so many times, Red. So many business deals that just went wrong in his hands. He thought this might be his chance. His last main chance. You've got to understand. . ."

I sat up. "Lady, I was like a slave at a galley oar. You know that, don't you? You know you had me by the ears. All tight, all wrapped up. But I wasn't high enough up in the sanctified holy order for you, was I? I didn't wear the purple robe of position! I was a working stiff, a professor. . .a nice guy to roll around with when there wasn't anything at stake. But along came the swine with the golden tooth—"

"Red, stop it!"

"Stop it, sure. Anything you say." I flopped down and rolled over, my back to her, my face toward the rock. She didn't move for a long time. I thought she might have fallen asleep. I wanted to reach her, somehow, but I knew I'd slammed whatever doors there ever were between us. Finally, she tried again, in a softer voice.

"Red, is it going to be all right?"

I rolled over and stared up at her. There wasn't enough light to see her features. It was easier to be civil to a silhouette. "I don't know. If your husband hadn't shorted us on supplies—that was all I asked of him for a one-third share, recall. . .just supplies—if he hadn't shorted us, Tab wouldn't have died, and we'd have a better chance. He was the one knew best how to follow the magnetic grid. I can do it, but it was *his* invention, he knew the fine working, down to the last quarter mile. If we're lucky, if we're close enough *now* so any course errors I make don't carry us off at an extreme angle, we might still blunder into it. Or maybe there'll be another tremor. Or maybe we'll hit an oasis. I wouldn't bet on any of them. It's all in the hands of the gods. Pick a half a dozen, use the stove for an altar, and start worshipping now. Maybe by morning we'll have amassed enough good will from on high to pull us through."

She went away from me, then. I lay there, thinking of nothing in particular. When she lay down beside him, he whimpered and turned to her in his sleep. Like a child, I wanted to cry. But it wasn't that kind of night, either.

All the legends of the lost continent I'd ever heard, ever since I'd been a child. All of them, about golden cities and the incredible people who moved there, and the staggering science lost to us forever when the continent had sunk and the sea had claimed it. I'd been fascinated, as any child is fascinated by the strange, the unknown, the magical. No one ever loses that. And as I'd pursued a career in archeology, the tantalizing clues, the constant references. Finally, finding the theory that perhaps what had been a sea in that dim and wondrous past was now a desert. The dead sands merely the bottom of a long-sunk ocean.

Tab had been the first real link with the dream. He had been a loner, even at the University. Though he had tenure, he'd been considered something of a dreamer; a good enough man in his field, but always postulating some insane fantasy theory about time-warp fields and the past never dying. We had become friends. Nothing so strange. He needed someone. . .I needed someone. It is possible for men to feel love for one another, and nothing sexual in it. Perhaps there was more than that. He was my friend. I never probed it more deeply than that.

And finally Tab had shown me his device. His temporal seismograph. His theory was wild, constructed on mathematics and lofty logic that I never found even suggested by any of the standard texts. He said time had weight. That the heaviness of centuries could permeate both living matter and dead rock. That when time evaporated—chronoleakage, he called it—even something as immense as a continent would rise. It explained, in a crazy way I could never have explained to my dust-encrusted pedantic contemporaries, the continual re-formation of the face of the earth. I suggested perhaps we could find the source of the legends, that perhaps. . .

Tab had laughed, clapped his hands like a small boy, and we'd started work on the project. Finally, it had all begun to fall into place. There were seismic tremors logged in desert areas I'd already selected as potentialities.

We'd finally been convinced: it was happening.

The lost continent was at last rising.

We'd known we needed financing. It had been not only unavailable to us. . .it had been considered a mad scheme by two madmen. . .and our careers had been thrown into jeopardy. Finally, the swine husband had come forward. He'd sounded like a man with the golden touch of success. I hadn't known to whom he was married. We'd made our deal. We would supply the science, the expertise, the search party. He would finance. And when we had left for the dig locale, he had sprung her on me.

For Tab, I couldn't back out. Now Tab was dead, and I was out on the edge of lingering death with the two people I hated most in the world.

That day's walk of fire was no worse than the day before. It was bad enough.

Just after mid-day, the beasts set upon us.

We were entering the area of strongest tremors, according to the magnetic grid. I knew I could be as much as three hundred miles off, but the readings were strong. I was paying close attention to Tab's machine—that tiny and magnificent little device he'd wasted his life to bring to reality—when Marga called my attention to the black dots on the horizon. We stopped and watched as they grew slowly larger. After a time we were able to make out that it was a pack of. . .*something*.

Then, still later, with a growing fear, we were able to make out individual shapes. I was at once terrified and elated. Whatever they were, they weren't any kind of creature I'd ever known to exist on the face of the earth, at least not in civilized times. They came loping toward us, flat-out at an incredible speed. And when they were close enough for us to see finally what they *were*. . .Marga began screaming with a naked and deranged horror that I could not fault. They made the flesh on my neck prickle. Her husband tried to run, but there was nowhere to run. We were trapped in the open. Then they set upon us, and began tearing flesh.

I used the collapsible shovel, locking it at its full length, swinging it around me in an arc that caught one of the filthy things and almost severed its ugly, misshapen head from its neck. Spittle and blood and bits of fur coated me. I was blind with terror, and the sound of their dog-voices in my ears blotted out everything but the shrieking of Marga as they tore her apart.

Finally, somehow, I drove them off. Stinking corpses littered the sand around me like garbage, some of the dog-things still heaving their slashed breasts with pumped blood breathing. I went around and killed the last ones hanging on.

Then I found her. She was not quite dead. She had barely enough left in her to ask me to take care of him. . .her husband. She went away from me for the last time.

We went on, her man and myself. We went on, and I don't know that I thought a coherent thought from that moment on. But we went on. The next day, we found it.

It rose up out of the scarlet sands. Six months before, we might have passed directly over its towers and domes, and never known that beneath our boots the lost continent of mythology was rising steadily toward the light. Six months from now, its streets and lowest recesses might be totally free of the whirling sands. It had risen like a bubble through water.

Ruined, destroyed, shattered, a great and silent testimony to a race that had been here before us, that had played whatever inevitable drama those magic men had devised, only to end its days in dust and oblivion. I understood what had happened to the dog-beasts. It had not been natural disaster that had ended the life of the wonder city, the magic continent on which we now stood. There were unmistakable signs of a war. Our radioactivity detector was clicking furiously. I could not even laugh wryly at their stupidity. The sight of such grandeur, cast aside so senselessly, made my throat tighten. Yes, time was circular. Men repeated their mistakes.

Her husband stared, awe and a kind of illiterate wonder in his coarse face. "Water!" he mumbled urgently. "Water!"

He started running toward the city.

I called to him. I called. Softly. Let him go. Let him run toward whatever dream castles he thought might offer him sanctuary. I watched him go, and followed slowly.

It might have been the radiation that killed him, or the pockets of poison gas from under the earth that surely still pulsed there in the dead streets of the magic city. When I finally managed to track a path into the city, using my radiation detector to avoid the areas of densest radioactivity, I found him. Bloated, blackened, swollen in the last rigors of a death that could not have been awful enough to satiate my need to see him twisted on the rack of his last moments.

I took a few unarguable bits of proof; relics, artifacts, devices unknown to any of the gray, wise heads at all the universities. I started back. I would make it. I knew I would make it. I was alone. I had things that would keep me moving. For Tab, for her. . .even for him. I would get back to Atlantis, and tell them that time was, indeed, circular. That New York City had risen.

—Clarion State College,
Clarion, Pennsylvania, 1968

ASLEEP: WITH STILL HANDS

Beneath the Sargasso Sea: the Sleeper.

Waiting for their mutual tomorrow: Leaf and Laurrayne.

Peace, on Earth. So much peace.

And Abbott, going to kill six hundred years.

Leaf's Force, opaqued and committed to slaughter, raced for the chart coordinates where the Sleeper had been planted, six hundred years before. Inside the assault vehicle—restored from its display case in the Smithsonian—Abbott turned suddenly, as the sound of the tracker alarms went off on the plot-board. For a fleeting instant he saw his face washing across the polished bulkhead, blurred by his movement, but nonetheless *him*: chocolate brown, bright eyes, freckles, a particular kind of nose.

"Lock in!" he ordered the 1st Lieutenant.

The 1st Lieutenant palmed three huge buttons on the plot-board, the scanner screen shifted intensities, and out of the sea-murk and slime-fog of the Sargasso appeared the coalescing image of an outdated but powerful seaskimmer, bearing down on them.

"Reading!" Abbott demanded.

"Course coordinate to sweep our bow."

"What kind of time?"

"Minute and a half. . .maybe."

Abbott slammed the chart rack with his hand. For the first time since they had slipped out of what had been the Pensacola Sub Pens, he was furious with anger, furious with the possibility that they might not make it, might not get to the Sleeper first, might not turn him off first, might lose the opening jump of the war to Laurrayne's Force.

He turned back to the six men in the vehicle. "First stays on scanner; the rest of you link up with me."

The Commander of Leaf's Force dropped into a gelatin-trough and closed his eyes. The other five team-members did the same, adjusting their seats to trough, and sliding back down into the enclosing yellow-green substance.

Immediately, Abbott felt his mind being touched by the five. He lined them in behind his own focus, and held the force in readiness as he probed softly, sweetly, toward the seaskimmer and Laurrayne's Force. When he had dwindled the probe to a stress-point, he left the probe and traced back along its length to his focus. Then, with the power of the five men, he hurled himself down the probe, crackling, rushing, invisibly striking the stress-point.

The stress-point was in the mind of one of Laurrayne's men, and as the mental force-beam struck, instantly charring out the man's skull, burning out the eyes, Laurrayne's Commander slammed down his own mental barrier and expanded it to enclose his men. It was barely in time to save them.

The burned-out corpse still stood erect, the empty black eyesockets flashing power that ripped and crackled through the seaskimmer. The force-beam of Abbott's mind, powered to the fifth, leaped and burned from the face of the dead man. The corpse jerked with the power it contained, and the arms flapped wide and without volition, the legs rubbered and twisted as the head tossed loosely on its neck, spume of deadly power emanating from the eyes, burning, charring.

Safe within the mind barrier erected by their Force Leader, Laurrayne's men stared in horror at what had become of their companion. Laurrayne's Force Leader turned away, and then swallowed hard. He spoke to his men with difficulty. "Link up with me, we'll stop it."

There were eight left alive in the seaskimmer. They joined minds, and short-circuited the force-beam. The empty husk of the corpse dropped instantly. The stench of corrupt flesh was high in the seaskimmer. One of the men gagged. "*Tense in there!*" the Leader snapped, and full intensity from the man's mind was sent resurging into the common pool.

The Leader tried to track back down the path of the force-beam focus, but Abbott had already mazed it, and somewhere out over the sea the stalking evaporated.

Laurrayne's Force now had the task of rectifying their course. The dead man had burned out whole banks of controls. The seaskimmer was plunging wildly out of control, deeper into the Sargasso Sea.

While they tried to bring themselves back to optimum efficiency, hoping to regain time, Abbott was urging his team toward the coordinates where the Sleeper had been sent down, so long before.

Abbott unlinked and spoke his orders smoothly, softly, urging his team back to their positions. The troughs were re-chaired and the team-members took their places. Abbott watched. They were moving sluggishly, reluctantly.

He continued watching.

"Okay, what is it?"

They turned and stared at him. No one spoke. "Open up. Let me in." They shied from his stare, but one by one opened their minds to his probe. He went in, touched lingeringly for an instant, then withdrew. He saw what was in their minds.

"I know. But we have to do it."

They didn't react.

"Don't let it slow us down. Keep alert." He went back into each of their minds and smoothed the places where their horror lay: horror at what they had seen their mental power do to the Laurrayne team-member. Smoothed, their efficiency rose and they went at their controls, sending the vehicle deeper into the fog-shrouded Sargasso, seeking the place of the Sleeper.

Abbott blanked himself off, and thought about it. Leaf had found him leading group therapy classes at Klock Institute; sessions filled with men and women bored with their existences, surfeited with ennui and longing for answers that would not be the same as the one they had all invariably found: suicide.

Leaf had come to him and had opaqued Abbott's thoughts so the Sleeper could no longer monitor him. And then he had told him about war. About the value of war. The necessity of war, to make man Man again. And Abbott had listened, had cleaved to Leaf's philosophy, because he had been exposed to the consequences of continued peace. But he had had the feeling that had he not agreed with Leaf, had he not decided to head up Leaf's assault force, the man would have killed Abbott on the spot.

Now. . .where was he? What was he doing?

Did he believe it, still. . .? Now that they had actually made contact, had actually burned out a man's head, had actually used him as an instrument of death. Did he still think of Leaf and Laurrayne as saviors of mankind. . .or were they precisely what the Sleeper had been created to prevent.

He didn't know. Now. And he wanted to know, needed to know. Desperately.

The vehicle, with a boring mole locked in its belly, moved deeper into the seaweed-clogged vastness of the Sargasso.

Beneath the Sea, the Sleeper waited, having no way of knowing that his time was nearing its end, that men were coming to turn him off, that once again war would walk the world.

And Abbott, the instrument of their destiny, needed to know.

In the world, before Laurrayne and Leaf, it had been different. It was not that much changed, yet, but if the Force reached the Sleeper. . .

Before they had come, it had been different:

Only two men knew the secret of making thoughts opaque. The first was Pieter Kalder, the man who had serendipitously stumbled on the technique. He was an old man, almost bald, who had bitten his nails since childhood, refining the process to such an elegance that now he worked only at the corners of his fingernails, closest to the quick.

The other was his assistant, a teddy bear of a man, short and round with a nervous habit of nodding continuously through someone else's question as though proving attentiveness all along the way.

He never considered himself a happy man.

But then, neither did Kalder.

But the teddy bear had found a measure of meaning in working with the brilliant Kalder. The teddy bear's name was Albert Ophir, and he contributed the refraction mathematics to the technique. Their method had been in existence for seventeen years before the right parties happened upon them. By that time Kalder and Ophir were in other places than where they had been, and they were doing other things.

No one had cared what they had found. Because it had not mattered; after a while, even to them.

Because at that time there had been peace in the world for six hundred years.

And for six hundred years there had been no progress.

Then, by chance, one of the right parties stumbled on the technique, or more precisely, the records of the technique. Before he could tie down his lines of communication, the other right party learned of what had been found.

The first of the right parties, after six hundred years, and after seventeen years, was a man named Laurrayne. He was huge through the shoulders, bearlike in his love, with an enormous appetite. He thrived on life and the living of it.

The other right party was a thoughtful, skintight man named Leaf who wrote poetry and sang in a sweet, distant voice. He was well on in years and had refused the youth restoratives, feeling—perhaps properly—that a man should reconcile himself to growing old gracefully, without trying to avoid the inevitable.

These men were the right parties to take note of the technique for making thoughts opaque because these men were (though not the first in six hundred years) fired with the desire to start war on Earth again. To begin the holocaust of random slaying and senseless theft of what belonged to other nations and parties. To recommence global hostilities that would plunge every man into his personal hell of fear and distrust.

Which had been impossible for six hundred years while the Sleeper sat with still hands and closed eyes in his cavern of steel beneath the Sargasso Sea, monitoring the thoughts of the world, keeping the peace.

Laurrayne and Leaf chose to be enemies.

For how else could war be effected if there were no combatants, no opposite sides, no antagonists?

And they sought out Kalder and Ophir.

For how else could Man begin to resume his climb of Progress to his Destiny, if there were no wars to spur creativity and challenge his abilities? If the monitoring of the Sleeper could not be ended so that Man might once again bash the brains of other men, and think his thoughts of tomorrow, dream his dreams of the stars?

They were right parties to choose up sides, and to seek out the formulators of the technique, because they so believed what needed to be done was a holy chore, that they were able to dismiss the thoughts of Kalder and Ophir from their minds before the sweep of the Sleeper's monitor could pin it in their heads. They were perhaps lucky, but then perhaps they were destined, for they cleared their minds and when the Sleeper's monitor touched them they were pink and clean and fresh as the souls of newborn infants—of which there were a regulated number each year.

Right, because they were able to seek out Kalder and Ophir, one to each, without having to harbor the thoughts of *why* they were doing what they were doing.

And when Laurrayne found Kalder, in Vienna, he was able to put the technique into instant use, making his own thoughts opaque; thereby putting him beyond the retaliatory powers of the Sleeper. Even as Leaf had done, only days before, when he had located Ophir in Greenland, and had obtained the secret from him.

After which, each man killed his informant with dispatch and an absolute minimum of pain. Of course.

After which, each set about opaqueing the thoughts of a carefully selected force of men; men who would form the nuclei of armies that would eventually lock in mortal combat, once again sending the glorious sound of death across the land.

But first, before Man's Destiny could be fulfilled, the Sleeper had to be shut off, had to be silenced in his silent task, six hundred years on the job. Laurrayne and Leaf chose their men carefully, and using the charts to be found in certain places, sent their special forces out to locate the Sleeper beneath the Sargasso. To end his eternal life, and close down his prying mind.

And all of it while the Sleeper watched; closed eyes and silent, with still hands beneath the Sargasso.

Abbott was dreaming. A dream from another life, drawn up through the quicksand of his unconscious, some reincarnated otherlife worn within another body. He had consciously sought this dream, had ordered it up on the instant, to examine it and with it help himself examine what he was doing now, in this time, in this place.

It was a dream of war.

Learned and remembered through the memory of his flesh that had been another man's flesh, impregnated with how-it-was before the flesh had been assigned to him. He was remembering the past, and how it had been with war.

The dream began with pithecanthropoids and their clubs, their first thrown stones. The dream progressed through bow and arrow, through sword and mace and quarterstaff; the dream was of arbalest and great thundering catapults. The dream was of blowguns and flintlock rifles, of grenades and bayonets, of tanks and triplanes, of jets and atomic bombs and napalm, of heat-seeking missiles and bacteria. Then the dream faltered, as the flesh remembered the fourth world war, and what it was like after that fourth, and how they had not learned, even then. He dreamed. . .

He was ambushed by a garbage-reeking roverpak of Yahoos as he maneuvered the Healy between the shellholes on Fountain Avenue, just past Vine. Bartok had passed around the rumor there were cans of New

England clam chowder and anchovy paste still intact amid the ruins of the Hollywood Ranch Market. Of course, he had been lying; no such thing. But he *had* found a jar of Beluga caviar. It had been kicked under a pile of lath and plaster, the label almost entirely ripped away. He had recognized it instantly and slipped it into his tucker-bag along with several charred magazines: a perfectly readable issue of *McCall's*, half a *Popular Science*, and a one-shot someone had published on The Beatles, shortly before the war. He could only vaguely recall ever having heard The Beatles, but the magazine was good for a few laughs, which in itself made the item worth at least a pint of canned blackberries. Other than these, the store had been empty. Gutted and ransacked a hundred times over. The stink of ambushed looters had forced him to tie a bandanna across his lower face.

The engine of the Healy had been missing badly for close to a week—since the attack on the Hollywood Bowl—and Leonardo da Vinci was away on a fresh-meat forage somewhere in Topanga Canyon, so he would have to wait for the mechanic's return for the necessary repairs. It was the snapping and popping of the exhaust as he tooled out of the Ranch Market, that had awakened the roverpak.

They swarmed out into the street as he sped slalom-style up Fountain, avoiding the shellholes with practiced skill. As he first saw them, his immediate instinct was to deck the accelerator and drive straight through them. But he had tried that once. . .and the damage to the Healy had been close to unrepairable. It had taken a forage as far southwest as Anaheim to locate a windscreen for the little four-banger. And a can of British racing green was almost non-existent by this time.

So he killed them, instead.

He pulled the oilskin cover off the brace-mounted Thompson, threw off the safety, and sprayed the street. The gimbals—at best jerry-rigged conveniences added by Sgt. York when the mountings were already in work—squeaked and jerked, but held. He knocked out half a dozen with the first bursts, and the rest scattered for cover. He took one huge, grizzled Yahoo (obviously the bastard had been eating long pig, it showed in the face, it always did when they turned ghoul) on the fly, as he dove for a ditch; the ghoul did an intricate one-and-a-half gainer before he hit, split, and lay twitching. Two more ran flat-out in front of him, failing to see the crater yawning before them, and as they dropped, and he sped past, he caught a glimpse of the deadly green bacterial mist that still hung in a wispy pool at the bottom; the two Yahoos would not be coming back up from the crater. Then he was through them, and the angry hornet pinging of their small arms fire was behind him. He whistled the Jazztet changes on Tadd Dameron's "Hi-Fly" all the way back to the Capitol Tower; and later that week he helped Thomas Jefferson and Henry David Thoreau chart out a new World Peace Constitution. . .

Abbott dreamed on.

Memories from six hundred years of history books. The history of man and his wars.

Another dream, long after the first had melded into peace, and another war, and another peace, and then an answer that had come to mankind when it seemed his last hope was gone. The Sleeper. . .

"Abbott!"

Leaf's Force Leader came up from his reveries of war and peace, to see his six crew-members staring at him.

"You were talking in your sleep."

He swallowed and nodded. They went back to their controls. The vehicle was moving more slowly now. He rose from the gelatin-trough and checked the plot-board. Ten minutes. They would cross the coordinates in ten minutes.

"First, stay on point. You, you, and you, come with me." He moved out of the control section, entered the dropshaft and allowed himself to be drawn down to the storage level. Behind him, the three team-members drifted smoothly down.

By the time they had settled, Abbott had dilated the hatch into the chamber where the mole was dogged to the deckplates. It was as large as the entire seaskimmer Laurrayne's Force had employed, tractor-treaded and auger-nosed. It loomed there in the semi-darkness of the unused storage chamber, its twin head-beams dark (Abbott had a swift flash of the dead, burned-out eyes of the man they had killed). Like a great metal insect, some silvered potato bug grown immense.

He palmed the lights brighter in the chamber, and ordered the three team-members up the side of the mole, and into the conning hatch.

Then he followed. When they were all securely snugged into their pressure suits and strapped into the formfits, Abbott hooked up with the First. "Give me a reading."

The returned thought, from the mind of the 1st Lieutenant, was like the thin, reedy wind that blows through the lofts of cathedrals. "I make it six minutes. Do you want the bays opened now?"

Abbott decided not. "Hold them closed till we're directly over the coordinates, then release from your board. Keep linked up with me through the operation."

He received acknowledgment, and settled back. It was six minutes dead time. He linked with the three men in the mole and prescribed six minutes sleep. They fell instantly down through the layers of readiness and were fully, deeply asleep. Abbott plunged after them, having set his consciousness to awaken him in five minutes, twenty-eight seconds.

They would need to remain awake for the full time of the operation; this respite now would serve to freshen them. But it did nothing to freshen Abbott. The dreams of his reincarnated flesh began again, picking up where they had left off. . .

Dreams of war, and the peace that always followed. There had been a fifth war, and a sixth, and somehow the antagonists always seemed to pull back just at the very edge of total extinction. And then they tried another way: personal combat. Save the nations of fine young men. Send out the heads of state. If the men at the top had to do their own slaying, perhaps war would become a trifle less attractive to them, the fat killers of children. . .Abbott's flesh remembered:

When the President of All-Americas came into the arena, he was greeted with a rising tide of catcalls, boos and murderous hisses. He dragged his spiked net through the dust behind him, and ignored the hail of freezi-hot tins being hurled from the groundling bleachers.

He walked about aimlessly, waiting for his opponent to emerge from the ready-tank at the opposite end of the packed-earth arena. He looked up into the sky. It was a chill day, a hell of a day for a summit meeting. The brinksmanship pennons were all whipping sharply in a brisk breeze from the. . .he cocked his head and estimated. . .east end of the arena. He looked toward the ready-tank again, but Dmitri Gregorovich Potamkin, Chairman of the Communist Republic, Khan of the Freely Liberated Chinese Red Star States, Premier of the Hemisphere of the People's Proletariat Protectorate, was late.

Glenn O. Dawzman, Chief of State of All-A, smiled a secret smile and twitched his steel-mesh net in a gesture of defiance at the smartmoney boxes that had wagered heavily in favor of the Russkichink boss. It was going to be a good day in commodities, steel, luxury shares, and communications. If he won. He thought it likely. He now fully believed the reports his Secretary of State had brought him in the White House that morning, reports fresh from CIA men double-covered at Potamkin's training camp in the Urals. Reports that Potamkin had looked slow, uncoordinated, that the Russkichink was growing faint of heart. It was going to be a smashing victory for Democracy and the American Way of Life today.

Glenn Dawzman knew Heaven was on his side.

A roar went up from the prole sections.

Potamkin lumbered out of the ready-tank, brandishing a short sword and carborundum shield. Dawzman swallowed heavily. He had thoughts of his childhood in Texas. Potamkin looked in fine shape, a great black bear of a man, a thick mat of dark wiry hair covering his chest and belly like fur, all white teeth bared in brutal humor, eyes deep-set beneath shag-brows that made him resemble some sort of *yeti*.

Dawzman revised his theories about the day's forthcoming contest. It might be a stalemate. It might even conceivably be a diplomatic setback. All-A might have to relinquish its claims to the Sudan. It might even be preamble to a huge and stately funeral: GOD DIES IN OFFICE. He read the fax headlines in the sudden blind space behind his eyes, where he had just now this instant suddenly found himself alone with fear and the future. . .what might be a short future, indeed.

Politics was hell on an older man.

He crouched, and Potamkin came on.

He swirled his net, Potamkin lunged abruptly, the short sword came straight on, and he whipped the net over the blade. Spikes struck blade and sparks flew. . .

Abbott's flesh was pinged by his consciousness. He came riding up out of sleep and memory, running data on the peace that was not peace, the wars that followed, and ending once again with the Sleeper.

"Okay, everybody up!" His men jumped to the command.

The bays opened. The dogs de-magnetized, and the mole dropped straight down out of the belly of the larger vehicle.

They were in the Sargasso now, plummeting down through a miasma of seaweed, debris, and absolute utter stygian blackness. He cut on the head-lamps. They shone out into nothingness. "Give me a reading on the bottom."

One of his team-members consulted a dial. "Coming up fast. . .300. . .360. . .410. . .480. . .500. . ."

And then Abbott screamed. The linkage with his 1st Lieutenant had suddenly blown in a corona of heat and pain and sudden silence. "Laurrayne's Force just blasted the vehicle," he told them. He did not pass along his sensory impressions of that last instant of life the First had known, as Laurrayne's Force Leader had swept him with destruction.

They were on their own now, and above them somewhere the other Force was dropping down to intercept.

Abbott felt gratitude as they struck bottom.

Oh my god, what am I doing? he thought.

The team-member at the chart board said they were directly over the coordinates. "Should I begin a shaft?" Abbott nodded, realizing he was losing control of his operation, that these men sensed surely that his mind was in a turmoil.

The chart board man made a hole in the air with his forefinger and the boring engineer caught it. He tapped out inclining instructions on the control panel. The mole rose up on its base, tilted its body forward, and the machine began to move forward as the engineer threw home the switch that started the screw-bit nose turning slowly. It made very little noise.

"Sandhog," Abbott called the engineer, "give me a fifty degree shaft for six miles, then increase to full ninety, got it?"

The sandhog okayed, and they moved forward. The screw nose touched silt, spewed it out on both sides of the mole, and bit deeper. It began whining. The black mud flew up and back in fan-wedges, and the mole began to descend on tractor-treads down the track of the shaft it was boring for itself.

Abbott could no longer restrain the thought; he opaqued it from his crew, but he dealt with it now, finally: beneath him, hundreds of miles down, somewhere in the silent stone center of his world, a man sat asleep, silently reading the thoughts of all men, keeping them from that endless pastime war. Abbott now knew he would make it. . .Laurrayne's Force notwithstanding. He felt the certainty in him. Even if it was ego-delusion, still he had to react to it. (If Laurrayne's Force destroyed him before he got to the Sleeper, it wouldn't matter, it would all be ended. But there was only one other possibility: he *would* make it. And he had to think about that.)

He had, finally, to think about the Sleeper.

Down there.

The Sleeper had been a man. No one now remembered his name, it didn't matter. But his name had been Blanos. Paul Vevery Blanos. He had been a theologian. A philosopher. He had worked in the name of rationality, sanity, all the days of his life.

He had been the original architect of the Pacem In Terrus Congress in Basel which had led inevitably to The World Council. He had written volumes on the joy and logic of peace; his nine-volume history of war took thirty years of research and analysis to write; and when the ninth and final volume was published, it was the final word on the subject. From that moment onward, anyone who ever cared to speak of war or peace had to refer to Blanos.

What few knew—even the heads of state who called him friend—was that Paul Blanos was one of a group known only to each other as Eleven Concerned. Blanos and ten other good men, captains of industry, world-famous philanthropists, personalities, founders of dynasties and founders of trusts in the name of the advancement of Man. Between them, in their not insubstantial ways, they had staved off innumerable conflicts, merely by the pressure of their wealth, power and sensibleness.

When Blanos's helicopter was sabotaged by a fanatic of the newly-revived *thuggee* cult, it was the Eleven Concerned who moved with quicksilver speed to save him.

The body and the brain were dead.

There was no medical room for discussion. Dead.

The Eleven Concerned had ways, however.

They carried off the remains of Blanos, and they hooked those remains into a machine. Blanos lived. No, not really. Blanos dreamed. He could not be brought fully back to life, but he could be brought to that intermediate stage so dreamlike in its nature.

Eleven Concerned secreted what had been the glory of Blanos in a shockproof underground chamber, and there Blanos continued his work. Eleven Concerned released it through the next twenty years as posthumous findings from the seemingly endless files of the great Blanos. Then they found the machine had altered Blanos.

He was part man, part dreamer, part machine.

He was something new.

Though they had no name for him, though they still called him Blanos, the man who was dead and sleeping in the machine had become the Sleeper.

He could monitor their thoughts.

He never communicated with them, he sought no two-way thoroughfare of exchange, but he read them. And he tested his own powers. They burgeoned.

Until finally he *did* communicate with them.

He told them what they must do with his body.

Eleven Concerned began the most incredible excavating operation since the Great Pyramid of Cheops. They sank a shaft, and they built a cavern, and they set the Sleeper in his dreamer's chair, down down down in the center of the world, deep under the Sargasso Sea, where no one could reach him. And the Sleeper began the monitoring that would never cease. Eleven Concerned then informed the world that it had a guardian angel, that it was now forbidden to start war, for the Sleeper was there, on duty every waking and sleeping moment of every one of their lives, and the least little thought in their heads about war, or what it took to make a war, or how you got yourself stupidly into a posture that could only be alleviated by war, would result in some tender smoothing in the mind. And the war would be stopped at its first germinating stage.

The world reacted badly.

It tried to start wars.

It got not far at all.

The Eleven were no longer Concerned.

It had been so for six hundred years. Even for the times when *other* Concerneds decided it was necessary to get to the Sleeper, and turn him off. They had been smoothed. And Man had lived in peace for six hundred years, while the Sleeper dreamed his dreams that had their termini in the souls and skulls of men far over his head, walking the world.

Then had come Kalder and Ophir.

And they had begotten the technique.

And the technique had called into focus Leaf and Laurrayne.

Who had sent out Forces. Forces that were now plunging down a shaft in the earth, toward a Sleeper who had no idea they were coming; a Sleeper who still dreamed his Blanos philosophy dreams of the good world, where good men lived a good life.

Coming toward him, Abbott; antichrist, assassin, mechanic of shutdown, stayer of centuries, savior of mankind, dealer in realities, emissary of power, killer of the dream. Force Leader. Going down. Wondering.

Laurrayne's Force caught up with them shortly after Abbott had noted their rate of descent and the angle of the shaft was approaching seventy-five degrees. There was a short, sharp squawk—a chicken being beheaded—and one of the team-members fell over his controls. Smoke poured out of his loosely hanging mouth. Abbott slammed a barrier around them, and instantly felt the cascading power of the Laurrayne Force Leader's mind.

Abbott knew it had to be done here, it had to be ended now, they could not drag it all the way down the shaft to the Sleeper. It had to be settled finally here, in the pit leading to the center of the earth. He ordered the remaining two to link with him. They were only three, against at least half a dozen—maybe more—but he had to do what he could. Now!

Abbott flung himself against the force-beam, struck it, rode with the power of it for an instant, then shifted direction and began racing back up the line toward the Laurrayne Force Leader's mind. So intense was the attack that Abbott was able to gain half the distance back to its focus before the Laurrayne Leader knew he was there, on his way. He snapped up his own barrier.

It was what Abbott had counted on.

He plunged on, struck the barrier and diffused. The barrier became black with the spread of oily thought. The Laurrayne Leader could not think out past it. He was trapped within the fortress of his own protection.

And his Force kept coming, down the shaft.

Abbott waited, pressure-suited, mind elsewhere, in the night-black shaft. When he saw the first light of the Laurrayne attack vehicle, he strung the imploder in its cat's cradle, across the mouth of the shaft. Then he ran back to the mole, a mile down the shaft.

His movements had been controlled by the plot-board in the mole. Movements programmed and predictable as the jerking of a dead frog's leg under an electric shock. His body had been plugged in, and the mole's thinktank had used him, a somnambulist, a zombie, a robot, while his mind still locked in oily dark across the rounded surface of the Laurrayne Leader's barrier.

Back in the mole, Abbott waited.

Too late, the Laurrayne Force Leader realized he had been outmaneuvered. *He* had worked entirely with thought, and Leaf's man had struck instantly back to the basics of what they were all trying to do. War. Personal combat. Hand-to-hand fighting. Not locked in the safety of minds across miles, but right out there, in the dirt, stringing an imploder.

In the instant before the Laurrayne attack vehicle struck the imploder, the Leader ruefully thought, "You win," at his opponent, and then there was a deafening *absence* of sound from up the shaft, and the force-beam winked out.

Abbott had won. He had understood the nature of war much more clearly than his opponent. He had had the roots of memory upon which to draw for nourishment. He had reincarnated his flesh through dreams and had remembered what it was to do the job by hand.

"Let's get out of here," he told his men.

The mole began its burrowing again, and in the vehicle Abbott cried silently.

When they broke through the wall of blue and shining stone, they found themselves in a chamber that seemed not to have been constructed by the hand of a man. The workmanship was beyond anything Abbott had ever seen. When he yanked off his breather mask, he saw his face, brown and tense, clearly reflected in the amazingly beautiful walls. How he knew there would be air here to breathe. . .he was always to wonder.

The floor was of a green metallic substance that seemed at first to show great depth—as though looking down through seawater—and then extreme shallowness—as though light was buried just beneath the reflective surface. Near the opening they had gouged in the rock wall, a circular platform of the same material, yet somehow denser, more potent, a deeper green, rested not quite on the floor. It was suspended less than an inch above the shallow-depth green of the flooring. On the platform was a chair of intricate design. The most notable thing about the chair, however, were the candles set in heavy golden balls—set at the runic points of a sextagram.

That was notable. And one other thing.

In the chair sat the Sleeper.

Encased in a metal and glass helmet attached to a collar that was too large for the shrunken body—a collar and helmet whose weight no living man could have long supported—the Sleeper sat dead, dreaming. Monitoring. Keeping the peace.

The control console that measured invisible stresses and fluxes seemed as dead as the man. . .silent and dark. His hands rested heavily on the arms of the chair. He did not move.

Behind him, Abbott and one of the two remaining team-members moved closer. Their pressure-suits seemed now terribly warm in this centuries-sealed cavern. The gigantic boring-nose cone of the mole was silent at last. The standby lights flashed orange. Light flooded out of the cavern, illuminating the pale-blue rock of the shaft they had just dug.

And the Sleeper dreamed.

The keeper of the peace.

The team-member walked slowly forward, amazement in his face. "This is him," he said, softly. The myth was in fact a reality. He started to step up onto the platform, reaching out to touch the robe the Sleeper wore.

The robe that seemed to cover something other than a human body; after six hundred years, what lay beneath that robe was certainly not human, not any longer.

"Get away from there!"

The team-member jerked back at the sudden sound of Abbott's raised voice. He drew back, looking sheepish.

"Get back in the mole. Set up for reverse, we'll be going right back the way we came."

The team-member started back to the hole in the cavern wall, then stopped. Abbott turned to look at him. The man was smiling, his face flushed with something like delight. His eyes were bright. "We did it, dammit! We really did it. This is the starting over, isn't it? This is where we get another chance!"

Abbott felt his throat close. He could not speak. He motioned the man back to the mole with a peremptory gesture.

When he was alone in the chamber, he turned back to the Sleeper. Thoughts of corpses with eyes that spewed death were in his head. Thoughts of rubble-strewn city streets and Yahoos that were animals that had been men. Thoughts of gaping mouths with smoke pouring out. Thoughts of great men standing naked with their fear in arenas that substituted for war. Thoughts of implosions that sucked sound and life from the air. *Oh my god,* he thought, *oh my dear sweet god, tell me.*

But Abbott had taken Leaf for his god, and Leaf had taken allegiance to the god of war. So Abbott was alone. With the Sleeper, who could not monitor him, could not help him by smoothing him. Abbott was where he had wanted to be, functioning as a man again. And he was terribly afraid. Afraid to do nothing, to return to the surface and leave the Sleeper turned on. Afraid to turn him off and let man seek his destiny. Afraid to make that decision for all the men who would come after.

He walked forward, and it was as if ghosts came to observe him, in that cavern out of time and space, where the peace had been kept for six hundred years; ghosts of all the men who had died, and silent staring eyes of men who had died of natural causes without having been burst like pods by shot and shell, who said silently, *We lived our full number of days. . .why are you doing this?*

He looked down at the control console. It was really quite simple, when he studied it. Simple, as all great art is simple. Uncomplicated and direct.

And he did what he had to do.

The mole hunched its way back up the shaft, and long before they reached the ocean bottom, Leaf had made his contact. He was jubilant, and congratulated Abbott. The war would start later that day, and of course Leaf would have the jump, for Laurrayne was still waiting.

In the mole, the team-members congratulated one another, for Leaf had said all monitoring had ceased on Earth. The Sleeper had been shut down. And they now confided in Abbott that they had been instructed that if he faltered in his task they were to have killed him and gone on without thinking about it. Leaf had implanted that in their minds; he was skillful, that fine man.

But now they assured Abbott that though they had had momentary doubts about his carrying it through, they could see that he was the strongest, the most conscientious of them all, and they were privileged to be serving under him in this Great Cause.

Abbott thanked them, and sat by himself to think.

To think of what he had done down there, in the Sleeper's chamber.

To think of his sudden thoughts back there. Not of the world, of the war, of the ones who would die now and the ones who would continue to die as long as man walked his world; not even of himself, or of Leaf, or of what had had to be done to get them there. His thoughts had been of the Sleeper.

Of the dead man who had continued on even after his body had turned to dust beneath the robe. Of the man who had spent lifetimes beyond his own lifetime that men could live in peace.

And he had turned him off.

No. Not quite.

The controls had been simple. Simple enough to re-route in something like a möbius circuit, feeding back in on itself; a closed circuit that began and ended with the Sleeper. He still thought his thoughts of peace, still monitored in a sweeping wave that went out and out and out—yet never really left him—and would never again encounter thoughts of war, because all he would be receiving would be his own thoughts of peace.

The Sleeper would continue to dream. And now, at last, there might be happiness in him, if he could still feel happiness somewhere in the mind that was no longer human. Because now he would believe man had finally grown accustomed to peace, had bred war out of his system, was content, and happy, and productive.

Down there, the Sleeper would dream eternally, while overhead man would destroy himself again and again, and who could say which way was the better?

Only Abbott would know, and he would spend all the rest of his days remembering. Remembering what had been, what was, and what seemed to be. . .for the Sleeper. He had made his decision—and had it both ways.

But it made it no easier for him.

Terror waited for Abbott at the end of the shaft.

Terror, and the new world.

And down there. . .

The only one who cared. Now helpless, duped by the least of the ones he had sought to save.

Asleep: with still hands.

—Los Angeles
and Santa Monica, 1968

SANTA CLAUS VS. S.P.I.D.E.R.

☛ *I*

It was half-past September when the red phone rang. Kris moved away from the warm and pliant form into which he had been folded, belly to back, and rubbed a hand across sticky eyes. The phone rang again. He could not make out the time on the luminous dial of his wrist watch. "What is it, honey?" mumbled the blonde woman beside him. The phone rang a third time. "Nothing, baby. . .go back to sleep," he soothed her. She burrowed deeper under the covers as he reached for the receiver, plucking it out of the cradle in the middle of a fourth imperative.

"Yeah?" His mouth tasted unhappy.

A voice on the other end said, "The King of Canaan needs your service."

Kris sat up. "Wait a minute, I'll take it on the extension." He thumbed the HOLD button, slipped out of the bed even as he racked the receiver and, naked, padded across the immense bedroom in the dark. He found his way through the hall and into the front office, guiding his passage only by the barest touch of fingertips to walls. He pulled the bronze testimonial plaque from the little people away from the wall, spun the dial on the wall safe, and pulled it open. The red phone with its complex scrambler attachment lurked in the circular opening.

He punched out code on the scrambler, lifted the receiver and said, "The king fears the devil, and the devil fears the Cross." Code and counter-code.

"Kris, it's S.P.I.D.E.R.," said the voice on the other end.

"Shit!" he hissed. "Where?"

"The States. Alabama, California, D.C., Texas. . ."

"Serious?"

"Serious enough to wake you."

"Right, right. Sorry. I'm still half-asleep. What time is it?"

"Half-past September."

Kris ran a hand through his thick hair. "Nobody any closer for this one?"

"Belly Button was handling it."

"Yeah. . .and. . .?"

"He floated to the top off the coast of Galveston. He must have been in the Gulf for almost a week. They packed plastic charges on his inner thighs. . ."

"Okay, don't describe it. I'm mad enough at being shook out of sleep. Is there a dossier?"

"Waiting for you at Hilltop."

"I'll be there in six hours."

He racked the receiver, slammed the safe port and spun the dial. He shoved the plaque back in place on the wall and stood with his balled fist lying against the bronze. Faint light from a fluorescent, left burning over one of the little people's drafting tables, caught his tensed features. The hard, mirthless lines of his face were the work of a Giacometti. The eyes were gun-metal blue, and flat, as though unseeing. The faintly cruel mouth was thinned to an incision. He drew a deep breath and the muscle-corded body drew up with purpose.

Then, reaching over to his desk, he opened a drawer and rang three times, sharply, on a concealed button set into the underside of the drawer. Down below, in the labyrinth, PoPo would be plunging out of his cocoon, pulling on his loincloth and earrings, tapping out the code to fill the egress chamber with water.

"Peace on Earth. . ." Kris murmured, starting back for the bedroom and his wet suit.

☛ *II*

PoPo was waiting in the grotto, standing on a let-down shelf beside the air tanks. Kris nodded to the little one and turned his back. PoPo helped him into his rig, and when Kris had cleared the mouthpiece, adjusted the oxygen mixture. "Keeble keeble?" PoPo inquired.

"Sounds like it," Kris replied. He wanted to be on his way.

"Dill-dill neat peemee," PoPo said.

"Thanks. I'll need it." He moved quickly to the egress chamber which had been filled and emptied. He undogged the wheel and swung the port open. A few trickles of Arctic water hit the basalt floor. He turned. "Keep the toy plant going. And look into that problem on tier 9 with CorLo. I'll be back in time for the holidays."

He put one foot over the sill, then turned and added, "If everything goes okay."

"Weeble zexfunt," said PoPo.

"Yeah, no war toys to you, too." He stepped inside the egress chamber, spun the wheel hard to dog it, and signaled through the lucite port. PoPo filled the chamber and Kris blew himself out.

The water was black and sub-zero. The homing light on the sub was his only comfort. He made it to the steel fish quickly, and within minutes was on his way. Once he had passed the outer extreme of the floe, he surfaced, converted to airborne, blew the tanks that extruded the pontoons, and taxied for a takeoff. Aloft, he made ramjet velocity and converted again.

Three hundred miles behind him, somewhere below the Arctic Ocean, PoPo was rousing CorLo from his cocoon and chiding the hell out of him for putting European threading on all the roller skates, thereby making all the American keys useless.

☛ III

Hilltop was inside a mountain in Colorado. The peak of the mountain swung open, allowing Kris's VTOL (the sub, in its third conversion) to drop down onto the target pad.

He went quickly to the secret place.

The Taskmaster was waiting for him with the dossier. Kris flipped it rapidly: eidetic memory.

"S.P.I.D.E.R. again," he said softly. Then, with an inquiring tone, "It means

> SOCIETY FOR
> POLLUTION,
> INFECTION AND
> DESTRUCTION OF
> EARTHMEN'S
> RESOURCES

is that it?" The Taskmaster shook his head. Kris mmmm'ed. "Well, what are they up to this time? I thought we'd put them out of commission after that anthrax business in the Valley of The Winds."

The Taskmaster tilted back in his plastic chair. The multi-faceted eyeball-globes around the room picked up pinpoints of brilliance from the chair and cast them over the walls in a subtle light-show. "It's as you read there. They've taken over the minds of those eight. What they intend to do with them, as puppets, we have no idea."

Kris scanned the list again. "Reagan, Johnson, Nixon, Humphrey, Daley, Wallace, Maddox, and—who's this last one?—Spiro Agnew?"

"Doesn't matter. We can usually keep them out of trouble, keep them from hurting themselves. . .but since S.P.I.D.E.R. got into them, they've been running amuck."

"I've never even heard of most of these."

"How the hell could you, up there, making toys."

"It's the best cover I've ever had."

"So don't get crabby, just because you never see a newspaper. Take my word for it: these are the names this season."

"Whatever happened to that whatwashisname. . .Willkie?"

"Didn't pan out."

"S.P.I.D.E.R.," Kris said again. "Does it stand for

SPECIAL
POLITBURO
INTENT ON
DESTROYING
EVERYBODY'S
RACE

?" The Taskmaster shook his head again, a bit wearily.

Kris rose and pumped the Taskmaster's hand. "From the dossier, I suggest the best place to start is with this Daley, in Chicago."

The Taskmaster nodded. "That's what COMPgod said, too. You'd better stop down and see the Armorer before you leave. He's cobbled up a few swell new surprises for you."

"Will I be working that dumb red suit again?"

"As a spare, probably. It's a little early for the red suit."

"What time is it?"

"Half-past September."

 ***IV***

When Kris emerged from the dropshaft, Miss Seven-Seventeen's eyes grew round. He came toward her, with the easy, muscled stride that set him so far apart from the rest of the agents. (Most of them were little more than pudgy file-clerks; where had she ever gotten the idea that espionage was a line of work best suited to Adonises? Surely from the endless stream of bad spy novels that had glutted the newsstands; what a shock when she had discovered that pinching the trigeminal nerve to cause excruciating pain, or overpowering an enemy by cupping both hands and slapping both of his ears simultaneously were tactics as easily employed by men who resembled auks, as by beefcake contest winners. Tactics equally as effective when struck by gobbets of mud as by Rodin statues.) But Kris. . .

He came up to her desk, and stared down silently until she dropped her eyes. Then, "Hello, Chan."

She could not look at him. It was too painful. The Bahamas. That night. The gibbous moon hanging above them like an all-watching eye as the night winds played a wild accompaniment counterpoint to their insensate passion, the lunatic surf breaking around them on the silver sands. The goodbye. The waiting. The report from upstairs that he had been lost in Tibet. She could handle none of it. . .now. . .with him standing there. . .a thick, white scar across the breastbone, now hidden by his shirt, but known to her nonetheless, a scar made by Tibor Kaszlov's saber. . .she knew every inch of his flesh. . .and she could not answer. "Well, answer, stupid!" he said.

He seemed to understand.

She spoke into the intercom, "Kris is here, sir." The red light flashed on her board, and without looking up she said, "The Armorer will see you now."

He strode past her, seemingly intent on walking into the stone wall. At the last possible instant it slid back smoothly and he disappeared into the Armorer's workshop. The wall slid back and Seven-Seventeen suddenly realized she had been fisting so tightly that her lacquered nails had drawn blood from her palm.

The Armorer was a thickset, bluff man given to tweeds and pipes. His jackets were made specially for him on Savile Row, with many pockets, to hold the infinitude of gadgets and pipe tools he constantly carried.

"Kris, good to see you." He took the agent's hand and pumped it effusively. "Mmm. Harris tweed?"

"No, as a matter of fact it's one of those miracle fibers," Kris replied, turning smoothly to show the center-vent, depressed-waist, Edwardian-styled, patch-pocket jacket. "Something my man in Hong Kong whipped up. Like it?"

"Elegant," the Armorer said. "But we aren't here to discuss each other's sartorial elegance, are we?"

They had a small mutual laugh at that. Divided evenly, it took less than ten seconds. "Step over here," the Armorer said, moving toward a wall-rack where several gadgets were displayed on pegboard. "I think you'll find these most intriguing."

"I thought I wasn't supposed to use the red suit this time," Kris said tartly. The red suit was hung neatly on a teakwood valet near the wall.

The Armorer turned and gave him a surprised look. "Oh? Who told you that?"

Kris touched the suit, fingered it absently. "The Taskmaster."

The Armorer's mouth drew down in a frown. He pulled a pipe from a jacket pocket and thrust it between his lips. It was a Sasieni Fantail with an apple bowl shape, seriously in need of a carbon-cake scraping. "Well, let us just say the Taskmaster occasionally fails to follow his own lines of communication." He was obviously distressed, but Kris was in no mood to become embroiled in inter-office politics.

"Show me what you've got."

The Armorer pulled a small penlight-shaped gadget off one of the pegboards. There was a clip on its upper end for attaching to a shin pocket. "Proud of this one. I call it my deadly nightshade." He lit the pipe with a Consul butane lighter, turning up the flame till it was blue, just right for soldering.

Kris took the penlight-shaped gadget and turned it over and over. "Neat. Very compact."

The Armorer looked like a man who has just bought a new car, about to ask a neighbor to guess how much he had paid for it. "Ask me what it does."

"What does it do?"

"Spreads darkness for a radius of two miles."

"Great."

"No, really. I mean it. Just twist the clip to the right—no, no, don't do it now, for Christ's sake! you'll blot out all of Hilltop—when you get in a spot, and you need an escape, just twist that clip and pfizzzz you've got all the cover you need for an escape." The Armorer blew a dense cloud of pipe smoke: It was Murray's Erinmore Mixture, very aromatic.

Kris kept looking at the suit. "What's new with *that?*"

The Armorer pointed with the stem of the pipe. It was a mannerism. "Well, you've got the usual stuff: the rockets, the jet-pack, the napalm, the mace and the Mace, the throwing knives, the high-pressure hoses, the boot-spikes, the .30 calibre machine guns, the acid, the flammable beard, the stomach still inflates into a raft, the flamethrower, the plastic explosives, the red rubber nose grenade, the belt tool-kit, the boomerang, the bolo, the bolas, the machete, the derringer, the belt-buckle time bomb, the lockpick equipment, the scuba gear, the camera and Xerox attachment in the hips, the steel mittens with the extensible hooks, the gas mask, the poison gas, the shark repellent, the Sterno stove, the survival rations and the microfilm library of one hundred great books."

Kris fingered the suit again. "Heavy."

"But in addition," the Armorer said happily, "this time we've really extended ourselves down here in Armor—"

"You're doing a helluva job."

"Thanks, sincerely, Kris."

"No, I mean *really!*"

"Yes, well. In addition, this time the suit has been fully automated, and when you depress this third button on the jacket, the entire suit becomes inflatable, airborne, and seals for high-level flight."

Kris pulled a sour face. "If I ever fall over I'll be like a turtle on its back."

The Armorer gave Kris a jab of camaraderie, high on the left biceps. "You're a great kidder, Kris." He pointed to the boots. "Gyroscopes. Keep you level at all times. You *can't* fall over."

"I'm a great kidder. What else have you got for me?"

The Armorer stepped to the peg-board and pulled off an automatic pistol. "Try this."

He depressed a button on the control console and the east wall of the Armory dropped, revealing a concealed firing range behind it. Silhouette targets were lined up at the far end of the tunnel.

"What happened to my Wembley?" Kris asked.

"Too bulky. Too unreliable. Latest thing, you're holding: a Lassiter-Krupp laser explosive. Sensational!"

Kris turned, showing his thinnest side to the mute silhouettes. He extended and locked his right arm, bracing it with left hand around right wrist, and squeezed the trigger. A beam of light and a sibilant hiss erupted from the muzzle of the weapon. At the same instant, down the tunnel, all ten of the silhouettes vanished in a burst of blinding light. Shrapnel and bits of stone wall ricocheted back and forth in the tunnel. The sound of their destruction was deafening.

"Jesus God in Heaven," Kris murmured, turning back to the Armorer, who was only now removing the glare-blast goggles. "Why didn't you warn me about this stupid thing! I can't use one of these. . .I have to be surreptitious, circumspect, unnoticed. This bloody thing would be fine to level Gibraltar, but it's ridiculous for hand-to-hand combat. Here, take it!"

He thrust the weapon at the Armorer.

"Ingrate!"

"Give me my Wembley, you lunatic!"

"Take it, it's there on the wall, you short-sighted slave of the Establishment!"

Kris grabbed the automatic, and the deadly nightshade. "Send the suit care of my contact in Montgomery, Alabama," he said, hurrying toward the door.

"Maybe I will, and maybe I won't, you moron!"

Kris stopped and turned. "Listen, man, dammit, I can't stand here and argue with you about firepower. I've got to save the world!"

"Melodrama! Lout! Reactionary!"

"Cranky bastard! And I hate your damned blunderbuss, that's what. . .I *hate* the stupid loud thing!"

He reached the wall, which slid back, and dashed through. Just before it closed completely, the Armorer threw down his pipe, smashed it with his foot and screamed, "And I hate that faggy jacket of yours!"

☛ *V*

Chicago, from the Shore Drive, looked like one immense burning garbage dump. They were rioting again on the South Side. And from the direction of Evanston and Skokie could be seen twin spiraling arms of thick, black smoke. In Evanston the D.A.R. was looting and burning; in Skokie the D.A.R. had joined with the women of the W.C.T.U. from Evanston, and the offices of a paperback pornographer were being razed. The city was going insane.

Kris drove the rental birdcage Maserati into Ohio Street, turned right onto the underground ramp of the motel, and let the attendant take it. Carrying only his attaché case, he made for the fire exit leading up to the first floor of the motel. Once inside the stairwell, however, he turned to the blank wall, used his sonic signaler, and the wall pivoted open. He hurried inside, closed the wall, and threw the attaché case onto the double bed. The

WAITING

light was glowing on the closed-circuit television. He flicked the set on, stood in front of the camera, and was pleased to see that his Chicago contact, Freya, was wearing her hair long again.

"Hello, Ten-Nineteen," he said.

"Hello, Kris. Welcome to the Windy City."

"You've got big troubles."

"How soon do you want to start? I've got Daley pinpointed."

"How soon can I get to him?"

"Tonight."

"Soon enough. What are you doing at the moment?"

"Not much."

"Where are you?"

"Down the hall."

"Come on over."

"In the after*noon*!?!"

"A healthy mind in a healthy body."

"See you in ten minutes."

"Wear the *Réplique*."

☛ *VI*

Dressed entirely in black, the Wembley in an upside-down break-away rig, its butt just protruding from his left armpit, Kris pulled himself across the open space between the electrified fence and the dark, squat powerhouse, his arms and legs crablike in the traditional infantryman's crawl.

Inside that building, Daley had been pinpointed by Ten-Nineteen's tracking equipment. He had been there for almost two days, even through the riots.

Kris had asked Freya what he was up to, there in the powerhouse. She had not known. The entire building was damped, impenetrable to any sensors she had employed. But it was S.P.I.D.E.R. business, whatever it was—that had to be for dead certain. For a man in his position to be closeted away like that, while his city went up in flames—that had to be for *dead* certain.

Kris reached the base of the powerhouse. He slid along its face till he could see the blacked-over windows of the el above him. They were nearly a foot over his head. No purchase for climbing. He had to pull a smash&grab. He drew three deep breaths, broke the Wembley out of its packet and pulled the tape wound round the butt. It came loose, and he taped the weapon into his hand. Then three more deep breaths. Digging hard he dashed away from the building, thirty feet into the open, sucked in breath again, spun, and dashed back for the powerhouse. Almost at the face of the building he bent deeply from the knees, pushed off, and crossed his arms over his head as he smashed full into the window.

Then he was through, arching into the powerhouse, performing a tight somersault and coming down with knees still bent, absorbing the impact up through his hips. Glass tinkled all around him, his blacksuit was ripped raggedly down across the chest. His right arm came out, straight, the Wembley extended.

Light suddenly flooded the powerhouse. Kris caught the scene in one total impression: everything.

Daley was hunched over an intricate clockwork mechanism, set high on a podiumlike structure at the far end of the room. Black-light equipment throughout the room still glowed an evil rotting purple. Three men, wearing skintight outfits of pale green, were starting toward him, pulling off black-light goggles. A fourth man still had his hand on the knife-switch that had raised the interior lights. There was more.

Kris saw great serpentine connections running from Daley's clockwork mechanism, snaking across the floor to hookups on the walls. A blower system, immense and bulky, dominated one entire wall. Vats of some bubbling dark substance, almost like liquid smoke, ranked behind the podium.

"Stop him!" Daley screamed.

Kris had only a moment as the three men in green came for him. And in that instant he chose to firm his resolve for what was certainly to come. He always had this instant, on every assignment, and he had to prove to himself that it was right, what he must do, however brutal. He chose, in that instant, to look at Daley; and his resolve was firmed more eloquently than he could have hoped. This was an evil old man. What might have been generous old age in another man, had been cemented into lines of unspeakable ugliness. This man was evil incarnate. Totally owned by S.P.I.D.E.R.

The three green men lumbered forward. Big men, heavily muscled, faces dulled with malice. Kris fired. He took the first one in the stomach, spinning him back and around, into one of his companions, who tried to sidestep, but went down in a twist of arms and legs as the first green man died. Kris pumped three shots into the tangle and the arms and legs ceased moving, save for an occasional quiver. The third man broke sidewise and tried to tackle Kris. He pulled back a step and shot him in the face. The green man went limp as a Raggedy Andy doll and settled comically onto his knees, then tumbled forward onto the meat that had been his head.

As though what had happened to his companions meant nothing to the fourth man, he stretched both arms out before him—zombielike—and stumbled toward Kris. The agent disposed of him with one shot.

Then he turned for Daley.

The man was raising a deadly-looking hand weapon with a needle-muzzle. Kris threw himself flat-out to the side. It was only empty space that Daley's weapon burned with its beam of sizzling crimson energy. Kris rolled, and rolled, and rolled right up to the blower system. Then he was up, had the Wembley leveled and yelled, "Don't make me do it, Daley!"

The weapon in Daley's hand tracked, came to rest on Kris, and the agent fired at that moment. The needle-nosed weapon shattered under the impact of the steel-jacketed round, and Daley fell backward off the podium.

Kris was on him in a moment.

He had him up on his feet, thrust against the podium, and a two-fingered paralyzer applied to a pressure point in the clavial depression before Daley could regain himself. Daley's mouth dropped open with the pain, but he could not speak. Kris hauled him up on the podium, a bit more roughly than was necessary, and threw him down at the foot of the clockwork mechanism.

It was incredibly complex, with timers and chronographs hooked in somehow between the vats of bubbling smoke and the blower system on the wall. Kris was absorbed in trying to understand precisely what the equipment *did*, when he heard the sigh at his feet. He glanced down just in time to see something so hideous he could not look at it straight on, emerge from Daley's right ear, slither and scuttle onto the floor of the podium, and then explode in a black puff of soot and filth. When Kris looked again, all that remained was a dusty smear; what might be left should a child set fire to a heap of powdered magnesium and potassium nitrate.

Daley stirred. He rolled over on his back and lay gasping. Then he tried to sit. Kris knelt and helped him to a sitting position.

"Oh, my God, my God," Daley mumbled, shaking his head as if to clear it. The evil was gone from his face. Now he was little less than a kindly old gentleman who had been sick for a very very long time. "Thank you, whoever you are. Thank you."

Kris helped Daley to his feet, and the old man leaned against the clockwork mechanism.

"They took me over. . .years ago," he said.

"S.P.I.D.E.R., eh?" Kris said.

"Yes. Slipped inside my head, inside my mind. Evil. Totally evil. Oh, God, it was awful. The things I've done. The rotten, unconscionable things! I'm so ashamed. I have so much to atone for."

"Not you, Your Honor," said Kris, "S.P.I.D.E.R. *They're* the ones who'll pay. Even as this one did." The black splotch.

"No, no, no. . .*me*! I did all those terrible things, now *I* have to clean it all up. I'll tear down the South Side slums, the Back o' the Yards squalor. I'll hire the best city planners to make living space for all those black people I ignored, that I used shamefully for my own political needs. Not soulless high-rises wherein people stifle and lose their dignity, but decent communities filled with light and laughter. And I'll free the Polacks! And all the machine politics I used to use to assign contracts to inadequate builders. . .I'll tear down all those unsafe buildings and have them done right! I'll disband the secret gestapo I've been gathering all these years, and hire only those men who can pass a stringent police exam that will take into account how much humanitarianism they have in them. I'll landscape everything so this city will be beautiful. And then I'll have to give myself up for trial. I hope I don't get more than fifty years. I'm not that young any more."

Kris sucked on a tooth reflectively. "Don't get carried away, Your Honor."

Then he indicated the clockwork machine.

"What was this all about?"

Daley looked at the machine with loathing. "We'll have to destroy it. This was my part of the eight-point plan S.P.I.D.E.R. put into operation twenty-four years ago, to. . .to. . ."

He stumbled to a halt; a confused, perplexed look spread over his kindly features. He bit his lower lip.

"Yes, go on," Kris urged him, "to do what? What's S.P.I.D.E.R.'s master plan? What is their goal?"

Daley spread his hands. "I—I don't know."

"Then tell me. . .who *are* they? Where do they come from? We've battled them for years, but we have no more idea of who they are than when we started. They always self-destruct themselves like that one—" he nodded toward the sooty smear on the podium, "—and we haven't been able to capture one. In fact, you're the first pawn of theirs that we've ever captured alive."

Daley kept nodding all through Kris's unnecessary explanation. When the agent was finished, he shrugged. "All I remember—whatever it was in my head there, it seems to have kept me blocked off from learning anything very much—all I remember is that they're from another planet."

"Aliens!" Kris almost shouted, instantly grasping what Daley had said. "An eight-point plan. The other seven names on the list, and yourself. Each of you taking one phase of a master plan whose purpose we do not as yet understand."

Daley looked at him. "You have a genuine gift for stating the obvious."

"I like to synthesize things."

"Amalgamate."

"What?"

"Nothing. Forget it. Go on."

Kris looked confused. "No, as a matter of fact, *you* go on. Tell me what this equipment here was supposed to do."

"It's still doing it. We haven't shut it off."

Kris looked alarmed. "How do we shut it off?"

"Push that button."

Kris pushed the button, and almost immediately the vats stopped bubbling, the smoke-like substance in the vats subsided, the blowers ceased blowing, the clockwork machine slowed and stopped, the cuckoo turned blue and died, the hoses flattened, the room became silent. "What *did* it do?" Kris asked.

"It created and sowed smog in the atmosphere."

"You're kidding."

"I'm *not* kidding. You don't really think smog comes from factories and cars and cigarettes, do you? It cost S.P.I.D.E.R. a fortune to dummy up reports and put on a publicity campaign that it was cars and suchlike. In actuality, I've been spreading smog into the atmosphere for twenty-four years."

"Sonofagun," Kris said, with awe. Then he paused, looked cagey, and asked, "Tell me, since we now know that S.P.I.D.E.R. are aliens from outer space, does it mean

> *S*CABROUS,
> *P*REDATORY
> *I*NVADERS
> *D*ETERMINED TO
> *E*LIMINATE
> *R*ATIONALITY

?" Daley stared at him. "Don't ask *me*; no one tells me anything."

Then he jumped down off the podium and started for the door to the powerhouse. Kris looked after him, then picked up a crowbar, and set about destroying the smog machine. When he had finished, sweating, and surrounded by crushed and twisted wreckage, he looked up to see Daley standing by the open door leading outside.

"Something I can do for you?" he asked.

Daley smiled wistfully. "No. Just watching. Now that I'm a nice fellah again, I wanted to see my last example of random, brutal violence. It's going to be so quiet in Chicago."

"Tough it out, baby," Kris said, with feeling.

 ***VII***

The eight-point plan seemed to tie together in Alabama. Wallace. But Wallace was off campaigning for something or other, and apparently the eight-point plan needed his special touch (filtered through the even gentler touch of a S.P.I.D.E.R. operative, inside his head) to be tied together. Kris decided to save Wallace for the last. Time was important, but Freya was covering for Daley and the death of the smog machine in Chicago, and frankly, time be hanged! This looked like the last showdown with S.P.I.D.E.R., so Kris informed Hilltop he was going to track down and eradicate the remaining seven points of the plan, with Wallace coming under his attention around Christmastime. It would press Kris close, but he was sure PoPo was on the job at the factory; and what had to be done. . .had to be done. It was going to be anything but easy. He thought wistfully of his Arctic home, the happily buzzing toy factory, the way Blitzen, particularly, nuzzled his palm when he brought the sugar cubes drenched in LSD, and the way the little mothers flew when they got loaded.

Then he pulled his thoughts away from happier times and cooler climes, setting out to wreck S.P.I.D.E.R. He took the remaining seven in order. . .

☛ *VIII REAGAN: CAMARILLO, CALIFORNIA*

Having closed down all the state mental institutions on the unassailable theory that nobody was really in need of psychiatric attention ("It's all in their heads!" Reagan had said at a $500-a-plate American Legion dinner only six months earlier), Kris found him in the men's toilet on the first floor of the abandoned Camarillo state facility, combing his pompadour.

Reagan spun around, seeing Kris's reflection in the mirror, and screamed for help from one of his zombie assistants, a man in green, who was closeted in a pay toilet. (Inmates had been paid a monthly dole in Regulation Golden State Scrip, converted from monies sent to them by married children who didn't want their freako-devo-pervo relatives around; this Scrip could be used to work the pay toilets. Reagan had always believed in a pay-as-you-go system of state government.)

Kris hit the booth with a savate kick that shattered the door just as the man in green was emerging, the side of his shoe collapsing the man's spleen. Then the agent hurled himself on Reagan, in an attempt to capture him, subdue him, and somehow keep the S.P.I.D.E.R. symbiote within Reagan's head from self-destructing. But the devilishly handsome Reagan abruptly pulled away and as Kris watched, horrified, he began to shimmer and change shape.

In moments it was not Reagan standing before Kris, but a seven-headed Hydra, breathing from its seven mouths a) fire, b) ammonia clouds, c) dust, d) broken glass, e) chlorine gas, f) mustard gas and g) a combination of halitosis and rock music.

Three of the heads (c, e, & f) lunged forward on their serpentine necks, and Kris flattened against the toilet wall. His hand darted into his jacket and came out with a ball-point pen. He shook it twice, anti-clockwise, and the pen converted into a two-handed sword. Wielding the carver easily, Kris lay about him with vigor, and in a few minutes the seven heads had been severed.

Kris aimed true for the heart of the beast, and ran it through. The great body thumped over on its side, and lay still. It shimmered and changed back into Reagan. Then the black thing scampered out of his ear, erupted and smeared the floor tiles with soot.

Later, Reagan combed his hair and applied pancake makeup to the glare spots on his nose and cheekbones, and moaned piteously about the really funky things he had done under the stupefying and incredibly evil direction of S.P.I.D.E.R. He swore he didn't know what the letters of the organization's name stood for. Kris was depressed.

Reagan then showed him around the Camarillo plant, explaining that *his* part of the eight-point plan was to use the great machines on the second and third floors to spread insanity through the atmosphere. They broke up the machines with some difficulty: much of the equipment was very hard plastic.

Reagan assured Kris he would work with Hilltop to cover the demise of the second phase of the eight-point plan, and that from this day forward (he raised a hand in the Boy Scout salute) he would be as good as good could be: he would bring about much-needed property tax reform, he would stop *nuhdzing* the students at UCLA, he would subscribe to the *L.A. Free Press, The Avatar, The East Village Other*, the

Berkeley Barb, *Horseshit*, *Open City* and all the other underground newspapers so he could find out what was *really* happening; and within the week he would institute daily classes in folk dancing, soul music and peaceful coercion for members of the various police departments within the state.

He was smiling like a man who has regained that innocence of childhood or nature that he had somehow lost.

☛ IX JOHNSON: JOHNSON CITY, TEXAS

Kris found him eating mashed potatoes with his hands, sitting apart from the rest of the crowd. He looked like hell. He looked weary. There was half an eaten cow on a spit, turning lazily over charcoal embers. Kris settled down beside him and passed the time of day. He thought Kris was with the party. He belched. Then Kris snapped a finger against his right temple, and dragged his unconscious form into the woods.

When Johnson came around, he knew it was all over. The S.P.I.D.E.R. symbiote scuttled, erupted, smeared on the dead leaves—it was now the middle of October—and Johnson said he had to hurry off to stop the war. Kris didn't know which war he was referring to, but it sounded like a fine idea.

"Tell me," said Kris, earnestly, "does S.P.I.D.E.R. mean

SECRET
PREYERS
INVOLVED IN
DEMOLISHING
EVERYTHING
RIGHT-MINDED

or is it something even more obscure?"

Johnson spread his hands. He didn't know.

Johnson told him his part of the eight-point plan was fomenting war. And butchering babies. But now that was all over. He would recall the troops. He would let all the dissenters out of prison. He would retool for peace. He would send grain to needy nations. He would take elocution lessons. Kris shrugged and moved on.

☛ X HUMPHREY & NIXON: WASHINGTON, D.C.

It was a week after the election. One of them was President. It didn't matter. The other one was shilling for the opposition, and between them they'd divided the country down the middle. Nixon was trying to get a good shave, and Humphrey was trying to learn to wear contact lenses that would make his eyes look bigger.

"You know, Dick, the trouble is, basically, I got funny little eyes, like a bird, y'know?"

Nixon turned from the mirror on the office wall and said, "You should complain. I've got five o'clock shadow and it's only three-thirty. Hey, who's that?"

Humphrey turned in the easy chair and saw Kris.

"Goodbye, S.P.I.D.E.R.," Kris said, and fired sleep-darts at each of them.

Before the darts could hit, the black things scuttled, erupted and smeared. "Damn!" Kris said, and left the office without waiting for Nixon and Humphrey to regain consciousness. It would be a week or two before that happened, in any case. The Armorer wasn't yet on-target when it came to gauging how long people stayed under with these darts. Kris left, because he knew their parts of the eight-point plan were to confuse issues, to sow confusion and dissension in the atmosphere. Johnson had told him that much. Now they would become sweet fellahs, and the President would play like he had a watchbird watching him, saying no-no.

Christmas was fast a-coming. Kris was homesick.

☛ XI

S.P.I.D.E.R. tried to kill Kris in Memphis, Detroit, Cleveland, Great Falls and Los Angeles. They missed.

XII MADDOX: ATLANTA, GEORGIA

It was too ugly to describe. It was the only S.P.I.D.E.R. pawn that Kris had to kill. With a little gold ax-handle: a souvenir of Maddox's famous restaurant. Kris destroyed the nigger-hating machine, Maddox's part in the eight-point plan, and ate fried chicken all the way to Montgomery, Alabama.

XIII WALLACE: MONTGOMERY, ALABAMA

The red-suited Santa Claus trudged across the open square in front of the Montgomery state building, clanging his little brass bell. The Santa Claus was fat, jolly, bearded, and possibly the deadliest man in the world.

Kris looked around him as he plowed through the ankle-deep snow. The state buildings were clustered around the perimeter of the circular square, and he had a terrible prickling feeling up and down his spine. It might have been the cumbersome suit with all its equipment, so confining it made him sweat even in the midst of December 24th cold and whiteness. His boots were soaking wet from the snow, his pace measured, as he climbed the State House steps. . .watching.

Everything was closed down for the holidays. All Alabama state facilities. Yet there was movement inside the city. . .last-minute shoppers hurrying to fulfill their quotas as happy consumers. . .children scurrying here and there, seeming to be going somewhere, but probably just caroming. (Kris always smiled when he saw the kids; they were truly the only hope; they had to be protected; not cut off from reality, but simply protected; and the increasing cynicism in the young had begun to disturb him; yet it seemed as though the young activists were fighting against everything S.P.I.D.E.R. stood for, unconsciously, but doing a far better job than their elders.)

A man, hurrying past, down the steps, bundled to the chin in a heavy topcoat, glanced sidewise, squinting, and ignored the outstretched donation cup the Santa Claus proffered. Kris continued on up.

The tracking devices inside the fur-tasseled hat he wore now bleeped and the range-finding trackers were phasing higher as Kris neared Wallace. It was going to be a problem getting into the building. But then, if it weren't for problems making it necessary to carry such a surfeit of equipment in the red suit, Santa Claus would be a thin, svelte figure. "Ho ho ho," Kris murmured, expelling puffs of frosty air.

As he reached the first landing of the State House, Kris began the implementation of his plan to gain access. Fingertipping the suit controls in the palm of his right mitten, he directed the high-pressure hoses toward a barred window on the left wing of the State House. Once they had locked-in directionally, Kris coded the tubes to run acid and napalm, depressed the firing studs, and watched as the hoses sprayed the window with acid, dissolving bars and glass alike. Then the napalm erupted from the hoses in a burning spray, arcing over the snow and striking the gaping hole in the face of the State House. In moments the front of the State House was burning.

Kris hit the jet-pack and went straight up. When he was hovering at two hundred feet, he cut in the rockets and zoomed over the State House. The rockets died and Kris settled slowly, then cut out the jet-pack. He was on the roof. . .unseen. The fire would keep their attention. At this stage in the eradication of the eight-point plan they would be expecting him, but they wouldn't know it would be this formidable an assault force.

The geigers were giving a hot reading from the North Wing of the State House. His seven-league boots allowed him to leap over in three strides, and he packed plastic charges along the edges of the roof, damping them with implosion spray so the force of their blast would be directed straight down. Then he set the timer and leaped back to the section of roof where his trackers gave him the strongest Wallace reading. Extending the hooks in his mittens, he cut a circular patch in the roof, then burned it out with acid. It hung in its place. Suddenly, the plastic charges went off on the roof of the North Wing, and under cover of the tumult, he struck! He used the boot-spikes to kick in the circular patch he'd cut in the roof. The circular opening had cut through the roofing material; now he used the flamethrower to burn through the several layers of lath and plaster and beaming, till all that stood between him and entrance was the plaster of the ceiling. He withdrew a grenade from the inner pockets of the capacious suit, pulled the pin, released the handle, and dropped it into the hole. There was a sharp, short explosion, and when the plaster dust cleared he was free to leap down inside the Alabama State House.

Kris jumped, setting the boots for light bounce.

He jumped into a readily waiting group of green-suited zombies. "Ho ho ho!" Kris chortled again, opening up with the machine guns. Bodies spun and flopped and caromed off walls, and seconds later the reception squad was stacked high in its own seepage of blood.

They had barricaded the doors to the room. Kris now had no time for lockpicks. He pulled off his red rubber nose and hurled it. The doors exploded outward in a cascading shower of splintered toothpickery. He plunged through the smoke and still-flying wreckage, hit the hallway, turned to follow the pinging urgency of his trackers. Wallace was moving. Trying to get away? Maybe.

Hauling out the bolo knife, he dashed forward again. Green-suited zombies came at him from a cross-corridor and he hacked his way through them without pause. A shot spanged off the wall beside his ear and he half-turned, letting a throwing-knife drop into his hand from its oiled sheath. The marksman was half-in, half-out of a doorway down the corridor. Kris let the knife slide down his palm, caught it by the tip, and in one quicksilver movement overhanded it. The knife just scored the edge of the doorjamb and buried itself in the zombie's throat. He disappeared inside the room.

The trackers were now indicating a blank wall at the end of a cul-de-sac. Kris came on at it, full out, his suit's body armor locked for ramming. He hit the wall and went right through. Behind the blank face of the cul-de-sac was a stone stairway, leading down into the darkness. Zombies lurked on those stairs. The .30 cal's were good enough for them; Kris fled down the stairs, firing ahead of him. The zombies peeled away and fell into darkness.

At the bottom he found the underground river, and saw the triangular black blades of shark dorsals.

Still murmuring ho ho ho, Kris dove headfirst into the stygian blackness. The water closed over him, and nothing more could be seen, save the thrashing of sharks.

Less than an hour later, the entire Alabama State House and much of the public square went straight up in a hellfire explosion of such ferocity that windows were knocked out in slat-back houses of po' darkies in Selma.

☛ *XIV*

She was lightly scraping her long painted fingernails down his naked back. He lay prone on the bed, occasionally reaching to the nightstand for a pull on the whiskey and water. The livid scars that still pulsed on his back seemed to attract her. She wet her full lips, and her naked, large-nippled breasts heaved as she surveyed his body.

"He fought to the end. The sonofabitch was the only one of the eight who really *liked* that black thing in his head. Really, genuinely evil. Worst of the bunch; no wonder S.P.I.D.E.R. picked him to ramrod the eight-point plan." He buried his face in the pillow, as though trying to blot out the memory of what had gone before.

"I waited three and a half months for you to come back," the blonde said, tidying her bosom. "The least you could do is tell me where you *were*!"

He turned over and grabbed her. He pulled her down to him and ran his hands over her lush flesh. She seemed to burn with a special heat. Much, much later, some time in mid-January, he released her, and said, "Baby, it's just too goddam ugly to talk about. All I'll say is that if there had been *any* chance of saving that Wallace mother from his own meanness, I'd have taken it."

"He was killed?"

"When the underground caverns blew. Sank half the state of Alabama. Funny thing was. . .it sunk mostly Caucasian holdings. All the ghettos are still standing. The new governor—Shabbaz X. Turner—has declared the entire state a disaster area, and he's got the Black Cross organized to come in and help all the poor white folks who were refugee'd by the explosion. That bastard Wallace must have had the entire state wired."

"Sounds dreadful."

"Dreadful? You know what that fink had as his part of the eight-point plan?"

The girl looked at him wide-eyed.

"I'll tell you. It was his job—through the use of tremendously sophisticated equipment—to harden the thought-processes of the young, to age them. To set their concepts like concrete. When we exploded all that devil's machinery, suddenly everyone started thinking freely, digging each other, turning to one another and realizing that the world was in a sorry state, and that what they'd been sure of, a moment before, might just possibly be in question. He was literally turning the young into old. And it was causing aging."

"You mean we don't age naturally?"

"Hell no. It was S.P.I.D.E.R. that was making us get older and older, and fall apart. Now we'll all stay the way we are, reach an age physically of about thirty-six or -seven, and then coast on out for another two or three hundred years. And oh yeah, no cancer."

"That too?"

Kris nodded.

The blonde lay on her back, and Kris traced a pattern on her stomach with his large, scarred hands. "Just one thing," the blonde said.

"Yeah, what's that?"

"What was S.P.I.D.E.R.'s eight-point plan all about? I mean, aside from the individual elements of making everyone hate everyone else, what were they trying for?"

Kris shrugged. "That, and what the name S.P.I.D.E.R. means, we may never know. Now that their organization has been broken up. Shame. I would've liked to've known."

And you will know, a voice suddenly said, inside Kris's head. The blonde rose up off the bed and withdrew a deadly stinger pistol from beneath the pillow. *Our agents are everywhere*, she said, telepathically.

"You!" Kris ejaculated.

Since the moment you returned, after Christmas. While you were recuperating from your wounds, lying there unconscious, I slipped in—having trailed you from Alabama—that's why you never found evidence that Wallace's symbiote had self-destructed—I slipped in and invaded this poor husk. What made you think you had beaten us, fool? We are everywhere. We came to this planet sixty years ago—check your history; you'll find the exact date. We are here, and here we stay. For the present to wage a terrorist war, but soon—to take everything for ourselves. The eight-point plan was our most ambitious to date.

"Ambitious!" Kris sneered. "Hate, madness, cancer, prejudice, confusion, subservience, smog, corruption, aging. . .what kind of filth are you?"

We are S.P.I.D.E.R. the voice said, while the blonde held the needle on him. *And once you know what S.P.I.D.E.R. stands for, you will know what our eight-part plan was intended to do to you poor, weak Earthmen.*

Watch! The voice was jubilant.

And the S.P.I.D.E.R. symbiote crawled out of her ear and darted for Kris's throat. He reacted instantly, spinning off the bed. The symbiote missed his throat by micro-millimeters. Kris hit the wall, shoved off with a bare foot and dove back onto the bed, scrambling around the blonde, grabbing her hand, and directing the needle of the weapon at the symbiote. It scuttled for cover, even as the lethal blast seared across the bedsheets. Then Kris grabbed for the deadly nightshade, on the bedstand beside him, and hurled it.

Instantly, all of the underground toy-making complex was awash in darkness.

He felt the blonde jerk in his grasp, and he knew that the S.P.I.D.E.R. symbiote had fled back to its one place of safety. Inside her. He had no choice but to kill her. But she threw the needle away, and he was locked there in eternal darkness, on the bed, holding her body as it struggled to free itself; and he was forced by his nakedness to kill her using the one weapon God had given him when he came into the world.

It was a special weapon, and it took almost a week to kill her.

But when it was over, and the darkness had cleared, he lay there thinking. Exhausted, ten pounds lighter, weak as a kitten, and thinking.

Now he knew what S.P.I.D.E.R. meant.

The symbiote was small, black, hairy, and scuttled on many little legs. The eight-point plan was intended to make people feel bad. That simple. It was to make them feel simply crummy. And crummy people kill each other. And people who kill each other leave a world intact enough for S.P.I.D.E.R.

All he had to do was delete the periods.

 *XV*

The time/motion studies came in the next week. They said that the deliveries this past holiday had been the sloppiest on record. Kris and PoPo shuffled the reports and smiled. Well, it would be better next year. No wonder it was so sloppy this year. . .how effective was a Santa Claus who was really an imposter? How effective could Santa Claus be when he was PoPo and CorLo, the one standing on the other's shoulders, wearing a red suit three sizes too big for them? But with Kris laid up from saving the world, they had had no choice.

There were complaints coming in from all over.

Even from Hilltop.

"PoPo," Kris said, when the phones refused to cease clanging, "I'm not taking any calls. They want me, they can reach me at Antibes. I'm going off to sleep for three months. They can reach me in April sometime."

He started out of the office just as CorLo ran in, a wild expression on his face. "Geeble gip freesee jim jim," CorLo said. Kris slumped back into his seat.

He dropped his head into his hands.

Everything went wrong.

Dasher had knocked-up Vixen.

"The shits just won't let you live," Kris murmured, and began crying.

—Los Angeles, 1968

EDITOR'S NOTE: *the astute reader will be quick to notice that Mr. Ellison's story has one small flaw in it. The insidious eight-point plan totally ignores the Republican vice-presidential candidate, Mr. Spiro Agnew. Apparently the Author forgot him. Apparently the Author was not the only one.*

TRY A DULL KNIFE

It was *pachanga* night at The Cave. Three spick bands all going at once, each with a fat momma shaking her meat and screaming *¡Vaya!* The sound was something visible, an assault in silver lamé and screamhorn. Sound hung dense as smog-cloud, redolent as skunk-scent from a thousand roaches of the best shit, no stems or seeds. Darkness shot through with the quicksilver flashes of mouths open to show gold bridgework and dirty words. Eddie Burma staggered in, leaned against a wall and felt the sickness as thick as cotton wool in his throat.

The deep scar-burn of pain was bleeding slowly down his right side. The blood had started coagulating, his shirt stuck to his flesh, but he dug it: it wasn't pumping any more. But he was in trouble, that was the righteous truth. Nobody can get cut the way Eddie Burma'd been cut and not be in deep trouble.

And somewhere back out there, in the night, they were moving toward him, coming for him. He had to get through to—who? Somebody. Somebody who could help him; because only now, after fifteen years of what had been happening to him, did Eddie Burma finally know what it was he had been through, what had been done to him. . .what was *being* done to him. . .what they would certainly do to him.

He stumbled down the short flight of steps into The Cave and was instantly lost in the smoke and smell and twisting shadows. Ethnic smoke, Puerto Rican smells, lush shadows from another land. He dug it; even with his strength ebbing, he dug it.

That was Eddie Burma's problem. He was an empath. He felt. Deep inside himself, on a level most people never even know exists, he felt for the world. Involvement was what motivated him. Even here, in this slum nightclub where intensity of enjoyment substituted for the shallow glamour and gaucherie of the uptown boîtes, here where no one knew him and therefore could not harm him, he felt the pulse of the world's life surging through him. And the blood started pumping again.

He pressed his way back through the crowd, looking for a phone booth, looking for a toilet, looking for an empty booth where he could hide, looking for the person or persons unknown who could save him from the dark night of the soul slipping toward him inexorably.

He caromed off a waiter, Pancho Villa moustache, dirty white apron, tray of draft beers. "Hey, where's the *gabinetto*?" he slurred the request. His words were slipping in their own blood.

The Puerto Rican waiter stared at him. Uncomprehending. "*¿Perdón?*"

"The toilet, the *pissoire*, the can, the head, the crapper. I'm bleeding to death, where's the potty?"

"Ohhh!" meaning dawned on the waiter. "*¡Excusados. . .atavio!*" He pointed. Eddie Burma patted him on the arm and slumped past, almost falling into a booth where a man and two women were groping one another darkly.

He found the door to the toilet and pushed it open. A reject from a Cuban superman film was slicking back his long, oiled hair in an elaborate pompadour before the foggy mirror. He gave Eddie Burma a passing glance and went back to the topography of his coiffure. Burma moved past him in the tiny room and slipped into the first stall.

Once inside, he bolted the door, and sat down heavily on the lidless toilet. He pulled his shirt up out of his pants, and unbuttoned it. It stuck to his skin. He pulled, gently, and it came away with the sound of mud squished underfoot. The knife wound ran from just below the right nipple to the middle of his waist. It was deep. He was in trouble.

He stood up, hanging the shirt on the hook behind the door, and pulled hanks of toilet paper from the gray, crackly roll. He dipped the paper in a wad, into the toilet bowl, and swabbed at the wound. Oh, God, *really* deep.

Then nausea washed over him, and he sat down again. Strange thoughts came to him, and he let them work him over:

This morning, when I stepped out the front door, there were yellow roses growing on the bushes. It surprised me; I'd neglected to cut them back last fall, and I was certain the gnurled, blighted knobs at the ends of the branches—still there, silently dead in reproach of my negligence—would stunt any further beauty. But when I stepped out to pick up the newspaper, there they were. Full and light yellow, barely a canary yellow. Breathing moistly, softly. It made me smile, and I went down the steps to the first landing, to get the paper. The parking lot had filled with leaves from the eucalyptus again, but somehow, particularly this *morning, it gave the private little area surrounding and below my secluded house in the hills a more lived-in, festive look. For the second time, for no sensible reason, I found myself smiling. It was going to be a good day, and I had the feeling that all the problems I'd taken on—all the social cases I took unto myself—Alice and Burt and Linda down the hill—all the emotional cripples who came to me for succor—would shape up, and we'd all be smiling by end of day. And if not today, then certainly by* Monday. *Friday, the latest.*

I picked up the paper and snapped the rubber band off it. I dropped the rubber band into the big metal trash basket at the foot of the stairs, and started climbing back up to the house, smelling the orange blossoms and the fine, chill morning air. I opened the paper as I climbed, and with all the suddenness of a freeway collision, the morning calm vanished from around me. I was stopped in mid-step, one leg raised for the next riser, and my eyes felt suddenly grainy, as though I hadn't had enough sleep the night before. But I had.

The headline read: EDWARD BURMA FOUND MURDERED.

*But. . .*I *was Eddie Burma.*

He came back from memories of yellow roses and twisted metal on freeways to find himself slumped against the side of the toilet stall, his head pressed to the wooden wall, his arms hanging down, the blood running into his pants top. His head throbbed, and the pain in his side was beating, hammering, pounding with a regularity that made him shiver with fear. He could not sit there, and wait.

Wait to die, or wait for them to find him.

He knew they would find him. He knew it.

The phone. He could call. . .

He didn't know whom he could call. But there had to be someone. Someone out there who would understand, who would come quickly and save him. Someone who wouldn't take what was left of him, the way the others would.

They didn't need knives.

How strange that *that* one, the little blonde with the Raggedy Ann shoebutton eyes, had not known that. Or perhaps she had. But perhaps also the frenzy of the moment had overcome her, and she could not simply feed leisurely as the others did. She had cut him. Had done what they all did, but directly, without subtlety.

Her blade had been sharp. The others used much more devious weapons, subtler weapons. He wanted to say to her, "Try a dull knife." But she was too needing, too eager. She would not have heard him.

He struggled to his feet, and put on his shirt. It hurt to do it. The shirt was stained the color of teak with his blood. He could barely stand now.

Pulling foot after foot, he left the toilet, and wandered out into The Cave. The sound of "Mamacita Lisa" beat at him like gloved hands on a plate glass window. He leaned against the wall, and saw only shapes moving moving moving in the darkness. Were they out there? No, not yet; they would never look here first. He wasn't known here. And his essence was weaker now, weaker as he died, so no one in the crowd would come to him with a quivering need. No one would feel it possible to drink from this weak man, lying up against a wall.

He saw a pay phone, near the entrance to the kitchen, and he struggled toward it. A girl with long dark hair and haunted eyes stared at him as he passed, started to say something, then he summoned up strength to hurry past her before she could tell him she was pregnant and didn't know who the father was, or she was in pain from emphysema and didn't have doctor money, or she missed her mother who was still in San Juan. He could handle no more pains, could absorb no more anguish, could let no others drink from him. He didn't have that much left for his own survival.

My fingertips (he thought, moving) *are covered with the scars of people I've touched. The flesh remembers those touches. Sometimes I feel as though I am wearing heavy woolen gloves, so thick are the memories of all those touches. It seems to insulate me, to separate me from mankind. Not mankind from* me, *God knows, because they get through without pause or difficulty—but* me, *from mankind. I very often refrain from washing my hands for days and days, just to preserve whatever layers of touches might be washed away by the soap.*

Faces and voices and smells of people I've known have passed away. But still my hands carry the memories on them. Layer after layer of the laying-on of hands. Is that altogether sane? I don't know. I'll have to think about it for a very long time, when I have the time.

If I ever have the time.

He reached the pay phone; after a very long time he was able to bring a coin up out of his pocket. It was a quarter. All he needed was a dime. He could not go back down there, he might not make it back again. He used the quarter, and dialed the number of a man he could trust, a man who could help him. He remembered the man now, knew the man was his only salvation.

He remembered seeing him in Georgia, at a revival meeting, a rural stump religion circus of screaming and Hallelujahs that sounded like !H!A!L!L!E!L!U!J!A!H! with dark black faces or red necks all straining toward the seat of God on the platform. He remembered the man in his white shirt sleeves, exhorting the crowd, and he heard again the man's spirit message.

"Get right with the Lord, before *he* gets right with *you*! Suffer your silent sins no longer! Take out your truth, carry it in your hands, give it to me, all the ugliness and cesspool filth of your souls! I'll wash you clean in the blood of the lamb, in the blood of the Lord, in the blood of the truth of the word! There's no other way, there's no great day coming without purging yourself, without cleansing your spirit! I can handle all the pain you've got boiling around down in the black lightless pit of your souls! Hear me, dear God hear me. . .I am your mouth, your tongue, your throat, the horn that will proclaim your deliverance to the Heavens above! Evil and good and worry and sorrow, all of it is mine, I can carry it, I can handle it, I can lift it from out of your mind and your soul and your body! The place is here, the place is me, give me your woe! Christ knew it, God knows it, *I* know it, and now *you* have to know it! Mortar and trowel and brick and cement make the wall of your need! Let me tear down that wall, let me hear all of it, let me into your mind and let me take your burdens! I'm the strength, I'm the watering place. . .come drink from my strength!"

And the people had rushed to him. All over him, like ants feeding on a dead beast. And then the memory dissolved. The image of the tent revival meeting dissolved into images of wild animals tearing at meat, of hordes of carrion birds descending on fallen meat, of small fish leaping with sharp teeth at helpless meat, of hands and more hands, and teeth that sank into meat.

The number was busy.

It was busy again.

He had been dialing the same number for nearly an hour, and the number was always busy. Dancers with sweating faces had wanted to use the phone, but Eddie Burma had snarled at them that it was a matter of life and death that he reach the number he was calling, and the dancers had gone back to their partners with curses for him. But the line was still busy. Then he looked at the number on the pay phone, and knew he had been dialing himself all that time. That the line would always *always* be busy, and his furious hatred of the man on the other end who would not answer was hatred for the man who was calling. He was calling himself, and in that instant he remembered who the man had been at the revival meeting. He remembered leaping up out of the audience and taking the platform to beg all the stricken suffering ones to end their pain by drinking of his essence. He remembered, and the fear was greater than he could believe. He fled back to the toilet, to wait for them to find him.

Eddie Burma, hiding in the refuse room of a sightless dark spot in the netherworld of a universe that had singled him out for reality. Eddie Burma was an individual. He had substance. He had corporeality. In a world of walking shadows, of zombie breath and staring eyes like the cold dead flesh of the moon, Eddie Burma was a real person. He had been born with the ability to belong to his times; with the electricity of nature that some called charisma and others called warmth. He felt deeply; he moved through the world and touched; and was touched.

His was a doomed existence, because he was not only an extrovert and gregarious, but he was truly clever, vastly inventive, suffused with humor, and endowed with the power to listen. For these reasons he had passed through the stages of exhibitionism and praise-seeking to a state where his reality was assured. Was very much his own. When he came into a room, people knew it. He had a face. Not an image, or a substitute life that he could slip on when dealing with people, but a genuine reality. He was Eddie Burma, only Eddie Burma, and could not be confused with anyone else. He went his way, and he was identified as Eddie Burma in the eyes of anyone who ever met him. He was one of those memorable people. The kind other people who have no lives of their own talk about. He cropped up in conversations: "Do you know what Eddie said. . .?" or "Guess what happened to Eddie?" And there was never any confusion as to who was the subject under discussion.

Eddie Burma was a figure no larger than life, for life itself was large enough, in a world where most of those he met had no individuality, no personality, no reality, no existence of their own.

But the price he paid was the price of doom. For those who had nothing came to him and, like creatures of darkness, amorally fed off him. They drank from him. They were the succubi, draining his psychic energies. And Eddie Burma always had more to give. Seemingly a bottomless well, the bottom had been reached. Finally. All the people whose woes he handled, all the losers whose lives he tried to organize, all the preying crawlers who slinked in through the ashes of their non-existence to sup at his board, to slake the thirsts of their emptiness. . .all of them had taken their toll.

HARLAN ELLISON
TRY A DULL KNIFE

Now Eddie Burma stumbled through the last moments of his reality, with the wellsprings of himself almost totally drained. Waiting for them, for all his social cases, all his problem children, to come and finish him off.

I live in a hungry world, Eddie Burma now realized.

"Hey, man! C'mon outta th'crapper!" The booming voice and the pounding on the stall door came as one.

Eddie trembled to his feet and unbolted the door, expecting it to be one of them. But it was only a dancer from The Cave, wanting to rid himself of cheap wine and cheap beer. Eddie stumbled out of the stall, almost falling into the man's arms. When the beefy Puerto Rican saw the blood, saw the dead pale look of flesh and eyes, his manner softened.

"Hey. . .you okay, man?"

Eddie smiled at him, thanked him softly, and left the toilet. The nightclub was still high, still screaming, and Eddie suddenly knew he could not let *them* find this good place, where all these good people were plugged into life and living. Because for *them* it would be a godsend, and they would drain The Cave as they had drained him.

He found a rear exit, and emerged into the moonless city night, as alien as a cavern five miles down or the weird curvature of another dimension. This alley, this city, this night, could as easily have been Transylvania or the dark side of the moon or the bottom of the thrashing sea. He stumbled down the alley, thinking. . .

They have no lives of their own. Oh, this poisoned world I now see so clearly. They have only the shadowy images of other lives, and not even real *other lives—the lives of movie stars, fictional heroes, cultural clichés. So they borrow from me, and never intend to pay back. They borrow, at the highest rate of interest. My life. They lap at me, and break off pieces of me. I'm the mushroom that Alice found with the words* EAT ME *in blood-red on my id. They're succubi, draining at me, draining my soul. Sometimes I feel I should go to some mystical well and get poured full of personality again. I'm tired. So tired.*

There are people walking around this city who are running on Eddie

Burma's drained energies, Eddie Burma's life-force. They're putt-putting around with smiles just like mine, with thoughts I've second-handed like old clothes passed on to poor relatives, with hand movements and expressions and little cute sayings that were mine, Scotch-taped over their own. I'm a jigsaw puzzle and they keep stealing little pieces. Now I make no scene at all, I'm incomplete, I'm unable to keep the picture coherent, they've taken so much already.

They had come to his party, all of the ones he knew. The ones he called his friends, and the ones who were merely acquaintances, and the ones who were using him as their wizard, as their guru, their psychiatrist, their wailing wall, their father confessor, their repository of personal ills and woes and inadequacies. Alice, who was afraid of men and found in Eddie Burma a last vestige of belief that males were not all beasts. Burt, the box-boy from the supermarket, who stuttered when he spoke, and felt rejected even before the rejection. Linda, from down the hill, who had seen in Eddie Burma an intellectual, one to whom she could relate all her theories of the universe. Sid, who was a failure, at fifty-three. Nancy, whose husband cheated on her. John, who wanted to be a lawyer, but would never make it because he thought too much about his clubfoot. And all the others. And the new ones they always seemed to bring with them. There were always so many new ones he never knew. Particularly the pretty little blonde with the Raggedy Ann shoebutton eyes, who stared at him hungrily.

And from the first, earlier that night, he had known something was wrong. There were too many of them at the party. More than he could handle. . .and all listening to him tell a story of something that had happened to him when he had driven to New Orleans in 1960 with Tony in the Corvette and they'd both gotten pleurisy because the top hadn't been bolted down properly and they'd passed through a snowstorm in Illinois.

All of them hung to his words, like drying wash on a line, like festoons of ivy. They sucked at each word and every expression like hungry things pulling at the marrow in beef bones. They laughed, and they watched, and their eyes glittered. . .

HARLAN ELLISON
TRY A DULL KNIFE

Eddie Burma had slowly felt the strength ebbing from him. He grew weary even as he spoke. It had happened before, at other parties, other gatherings, when he had held the attention of the group, and gone home later, feeling drained. He had never known what it was.

But tonight the strength did not come back. They kept watching him, seemed to be *feeding* at him, and it went on and on, till finally he'd said he had to go to sleep, and they should go home. But they had pleaded for one more anecdote, one more joke told with perfect dialect and elaborate gesticulation. Eddie Burma had begun to cry, quietly. His eyes were red-rimmed, and his body felt as though the bones and musculature had been removed, leaving only a soft rubbery coating that might at any moment cave in on itself.

He had tried to get up; to go and lie down; but they'd gotten more insistent, had demanded, had ordered, had grown nasty. And then the blonde had come at him, and cut him, and the others were only a step behind. Somehow. . .in the thrashing tangle that had followed, with his friends and acquaintances now tearing at one another to get at him, he had escaped. He had fled, he did not know how, the pain of his knifed side crawling inside him. He had made it into the trees of the little glen where his house was hidden, and through the forest, over the watershed, down to the highway, where he had hailed a cab. Then into the city. . .

See me! See me, please! Just don't always come and take. Don't bathe in my reality and then go away feeling clean. Stay and let some of the dirt of you rub off on me. I feel like an invisible man, like a drinking trough, like a sideboard dripping with sweetmeats. . .Oh God, is this a play, and myself unwillingly the star? How the hell do I get off stage? When do they ring down the curtain? Is there, please God, a man with a hook. . .?

I make my rounds, like a faith healer. Each day I spend a little time with each one of them. With Alice and with Burt and with Linda down the hill; and they take from me. They don't leave anything in exchange, though. It's not barter, it's theft. And the worst part of it is I always needed that, I always let *them rob me. What sick need was it that gave them entrance to my soul? Even the pack rat leaves some worthless object when it steals a worthless object. I'd take anything from them: the smallest anecdote, the most used-up thought, the most stagnant concept, the puniest pun, the most obnoxious personal revelation. . .anything! But all they do is sit there and stare at me, their mouths open, their ears hearing me so completely they empty my words of color and scent. . .I feel as though they're* crawling into me. *I can't stand any more. . .really* I *can't.*

The mouth of the alley was blocked.

Shadows moved there.

Burt, the box-boy. Nancy and Alice and Linda. Sid, the failure. John, who walked with a rolling motion. And the doctor, the juke-box repairman, the pizza cook, the used-car salesman, the swinging couple who swapped partners, the discothéque dancer. . .all of them.

They came for him.

And for the first time he noticed their teeth.

The moment before they reached him stretched out as silent and timeless as the decay that ate at his world. He had no time for self-pity. It was not merely that Eddie Burma had been cannibalized every day of the year, every hour of the day, every minute of every hour of every day of every year. The awareness dawned unhappily—in that moment of timeless time—that he had let them do it to him. That he was no better than they, only different. They were the feeders—and he was the food. But no nobility could be attached to one or the other. He needed to have people worship and admire him. He needed the love and attention of the masses, the worship of monkeys. And for Eddie Burma that was a kind of beginning to death. It was the death of his unself-consciousness; the slaughter of his innocence. From that moment forward, he had been aware of the clever things he said and did, on a cellular level below consciousness. He was aware. Aware, aware, aware!

And awareness brought them to him, where they fed. It led to self-consciousness, petty pretensions, ostentation. And that was a thing devoid of substance, of reality. And if there was anything on which his acolytes could not nourish, it was a posturing, phony, *empty* human being.

They would drain him.

The moment came to a timeless climax, and they carried him down under their weight, and began to feed.

When it was over, they left him in the alley. They went to look elsewhere.

With the vessel drained, the vampires moved to other pulsing arteries.

—Los Angeles, 1963, 1965, 1968

THE PITLL PAWOB DIVISION

Mourg radiated with annoyance. The work was piling up, and the division was understaffed, and he knew—as certainly as there was vapor for all—that before his next shedding, they would ship in more of those.

He radiated, he revolved, and he thrommed. But the aperture glowed, even as he knew it would, and one of *them* stood there. . .blinking, waving *its* appendages, and mouthing (he had learned the word from an earlier one of *them)* meaningless sounds. Ah, oh, there was a sound he'd heard before: he recognized the way the face aperture formed it, and the vibrations *it* made in the vapor. He felt the sound with his da-linquers, yes it was the same sound.

"Help!"

Mourg ignored *it*. He was vaporizing in his lower right quadrant, and an attempt at handling this one would only dissipate him further. He floated into a pocket and sucked deeply of vapor, till his lower right quadrant throbbed and he felt a tremor of guilt at his own gluttony. (How odd, Mourg jelled, that we use the term vapor for so many things: for life-essence, for the vanishment of the life-essence, for the newborn if columned, for brakinge, and for Thom. . .but he's a pain in the g. But it was an old jell, one Mourg had jelled many times before, and the relavator marked it in his log, penalizing Mourg for repetition. Mourg grew even more annoyed.)

"Unclean," Mourg insulted the relavator, sending the impression through three warps and a pinking so it would not be logged against him.

Furiously annoyed now—both for the logging and for the necessity of guile—Mourg settled back inside the great blue egg with *that*. The *it* that was *that* was now all crimped up with *its* appendages wrapped around itself, twitching in a most unsightly manner. Mourg felt his gorge become buoyant. Fives, but *they* were uggle uggle ugly!

Girding himself, Mourg pflenged and became solid. The *it* gave a high-pitched sound and scuttled backward to the very wall of the egg, *its* round things in the top of *its* front bulging. As head of the division, Mourg was expected to deal with this sort of reaction. He had yearned all the best texts on the subject—Zitmowse on Instability In Solid And Gaseous Life-Forms, T-Shremp on Pflenging With Care, that exomorph, what was his name, from 884 on Dealing With Others—and he considered himself rather an adept at getting the job done.

He assumed something like the shape of *it*.

It blubbered: apparently the shape was not close enough.

Mourg tried talking to *it* in *its* sounds. "Ik thik cleen beebay maykyoo uhlilmohr thik ik." It didn't work. *It* blubbered worse, a pink thing falling out of *its* sound-aperture and vibrating madly.

It's unhinged, apparently, Mourg jelled. (He was not logged; the jell applied to repetitive work—all in the line of duty.)

Mourg removed the hair and the wheels, and *it* seemed to like the appearance better. Mourg riffled *its* memory-tracks and found the proper sound-patterns.

"Hey, guy, take it easy. Nobody's going to hurt you."

That settled down, stopped twitching, ceased whimpering, vibrated a good deal less. Colors came and went on *its* face, and Mourg, responding to the stimulus, flashed a few itself. *It* vomited.

Apparently *it* didn't mind red or green or gold, but crem and bidny made *it* ill. Mourg ceased flashing. "Now don't get all nervous again, guy. Everything's fine."

"Where am I?" *it* asked, softly. *Its* upper sound-aperture trembled.

"The egg," Mourg said.

It drained a saline solution from *its* round things.

Mourg ascertained—through six affirming techniques—that *it* was unhappy at *its* environment. Mourg tried to make *it* a little more at ease. Mourg pflenged the egg, himself, and *that*.

Now it was a tall green jungle of stalks that rose up into the bright yellow sunlight. The balloon thing drifted down toward them. Mourg was squatter and naked. *It* was changed, too.

And *it* yelled and cried and flung *it*self about in a manner that made Mourg crosshatched and tepid. "Oh, come *on* now," Mourg said with annoyance, "now you're just being cranky, dammit!"

He dimmed it all, re-pflenged, and decided—as *that* would sound—to hell with it. Mourg pflenged the egg back.

It was going the way it always went with *these*. The division was littered with them, cluttered with them, festooned with them.

"Okay, okay," Mourg sounded. He had dealt with *these* long enough to know *they* were only testy little babies. Give *them* what *they* needed, and *they* kept quiet, and went back and told all the others *they'd* done this or done that, had had such and such an experience.

Mourg had given *them* a lot of things.

Noses. Women. Fire. God. Thought. Reproductive organs. An apple. Wheels. Olih (though they still hadn't figured out how to use it). Dogs. Numbers. Dreams. Fat. Safety pins. And he gave *this* what *it* needed, and sent *it* back. With relief.

Then Mourg pflenged, vastened, thrillip'd, exhaled, carbed, moved, de-ligged, orkrorlened, adumbrated, extruded, drank deeply of vapor, and slid off through his own cryonic metabolism (very nearly like peristalsis) for a little sleep.

He was roused from his slumbers less than a nanosecond later by his superior, fraught with a polymorphic fixation, Sid, who screamed silently, invoking the wrath of Five, and other dires, demanding to know what Mourg had done with *that*.

Gave *it* what *it* needed, Mourg went blue and in.

And what was that, this time, Sid in'd.

It wanted the universe.

HARLAN ELLISON
THE PITLL PAWOB DIVISION

Sid did a thing that was like a shrug, and pflenged, leaving behind the comment, One of these days *they* are going to want something worthwhile.

Mourg tried to get back to sleep, but it was difficult. He kept wheeling back to Sid's comment, and decided finally that *they* could have the universe, silly thing really *wasn't* worth much. But what if *they* ever *did* wise up?

—*Clarion State College,*
Clarion, PA, 1968

THE PLACE WITH NO NAME

This is how legends are born.

Perhaps it was because Norman had never suffered from an excess of oily, curly hair that he had been unable to make it as a gigolo. Or as Norman had phrased it: "I can't stand patent-leather on my hair or my feet." So he had taken the easy way out: Norman Mogart had become a pimp.

Er, let's make the semantics more palatable. (In an era of garbage collectors who are Sanitation Disposal Engineers, truck drivers who are Transportation Facilitation Executives, and janitors who are Housing Maintenance Overseers, a spade is seldom a spade, Black Panthers please note.) Norman Mogart was an Entertainment Liaison Agent.

Pfui. Norman was a pimp.

Currently marketing a saucy item titled Marlene—a seventeen-year-old Puerto Rican voluptuary with a childlike delight in the carnal act and an insatiable craving for Juicy Fruit gum—Norman was doing nicely. Succinctly put, Norman was doing just whiz-bang. His alpaca coat had a velvet collar; his Porsche had recently been re-bored; his Diners Club account was up to date; and his $32-a-day habit was nicely in hand.

Norman Mogart was also an Artificial Stimulant Indoctrinaire.

Pfui. Norman was a junkie.

It is not true that cocaine addicts are more sensual than common garden-variety hopheads, vipers, stashhounds, potheads, speed freaks, crystal-spaceouts, pill-droppers, acid-heads or blastbabies. It's just that coke hits like paresis after a while, and when a member of the opposite sex begins to put on (as they used to say around the Brill Building) "the bee," the cocaine sniffer just doesn't have the wherewithal to say no.

Consequently, when Marlene—live wire that she was—felt compelled to snuggle up to her entrepreneur, Norman was too weak with happy to resist. It was this inability—nay, rather this *elasticity* of moral fiber—on Norman's part, that brought about his terrible trouble, and the sudden pinching need for the bread to get turned on with. Marlene chose to snuggle up under a bush in Brooklyn's fabled Prospect Park, unfortunately, and it was one of New York's Finest (not to mention chicken-est) who felt honor-bound to bust her, chiefly because he had been called on the carpet only that morning by his Captain for having been caught catnapping (with pillow and alarm clock) in the rear of a police ambulance. The bust left Norman with not only his pants down, but his source of income cut off.

Three weeks and six hundred and seventy-two dollars later, Norman was out of money and out of dust. His connects smelled the nature of his impecunity and magically dried up. Norman was in a sorry way.

There comes a point in the downward slide of the human condition when a man ceases to be a man. He may still walk erect, but it is principally a matter of skeletal arrangement, not ethics. Norman had reached that point. . .and passed it: screaming. Like the Doppler effect of a train whistle as it fades past a fixed point. Norman was going insane. The hunger was no longer even localized; withdrawal was an entity in itself. It clung to him like dark mud, it filled his mouth with rust. In a movie theater where he had fled to catch a few moments of peace and Chaplin's *City Lights*, he smelled the sick sweat pungency of someone in the darkness tuning in on grass, and he wanted very much to puke. Instead, he lit his eighty-five-dollar GBD, the pipe Elyse had given him for his birthday, the year before she had gone off and married one of her tricks, a canning company executive from Steubenville, Ohio. The aromatic curlicues of tobacco blotted it out a trifle, and Norman was able to continue on his thorny path to furious darkness, unimpeded by the scents of lesser joys.

Inevitably, it came down to finding another hooker—for the ravishing Marlene had been sent to the Women's House of Detention at Sixth and Greenwich Avenues for a big one-twenty, it being her second bust. It came down to finding a new hooker, or boosting a drug store for its till and drug supplies. But: Norman was a Constitutionally Incapacitated Swashbuckler.

Pfui. Norman was a goddam coward.

As for the former solution, it was luck-out there, as well: there were no other girls on the turf worth handling. For in his own way, and in his own pattern, Norman was a dealer in quality goods. Cheap or tawdry merchandise was a stink in his nostrils, inevitably bringing on a loss of reputation. In Norman's line of work, either solution was written in the hieroglyphics of bankruptcy.

Thus, view Norman Mogart, hung between the torture posts of his limitations and his desires. Swinging gently in a breeze of desperation.

The only climate that could have forced Norman to do what he did.

He accosted the woman as she turned to lock her car. It had been the only empty space on Hudson Street, and Norman had known if he lurked for only a few moments in the dark doorway of the Chinese hand laundry, someone coming home late to one of the apartment buildings on Christopher or Bleecker would pull into it. He had been in the doorway no more than five minutes when the woman pulled in, backed and filled, and cut the ignition.

As she emerged, and turned to lock the door, Norman struck. He had a short length of pipe in his topcoat pocket, and he came up on her silently, and jammed it into the small of her back. "A gun, lady."

The woman didn't react as Norman had expected. With one sweeping movement she spun on the toe of her right foot, brought her arm around and directed the muzzle of the "gun" to the side. In two seconds Norman Mogart was grappling with a woman who had taken a course in street self-defense at the West Side YMHA. Norman found himself lifted on a stout hip, slung into the car, and sliding down its side. Then the woman kicked him. It was a very professional kick. It caught Norman directly under the heart and sent slivers of black glass up through his body into his brain. The next part he remembered only dimly: he grabbed her leg, pulled it out from under her and she fell with her skirt up around her hips, and her coat up around her skirt. Then he beat her solidly seven or eight times in the face with the length of pipe.

When the glass had dissolved in his brain and body, he was sitting on the dirty bricks of Hudson Street, half on top of a mound of dead meat.

He was still sitting there, a few minutes later, not quite believing what he had done, when the prowl car's searchlight speared him.

Norman Mogart scrambled to his knees and scuttled around the car. He dropped the pipe—which was now sticky—and crouching low, ran for his life. He ran into a man coming out of a narrow doorway leading up to cold-water flats, and caromed off him. He threw the man away from him and ran up Hudson Street. He kept running, with the squad car behind him, siren shrieking, gumball machine flickering angry red, searchbeam jabbing for him. He ran into Jane Street and kept going till he found a doorway. He ducked into the doorway and ran up a flight of stairs. And another flight. And another. And then he climbed a ladder and came out through a trapdoor on the roof of a Greenwich Village tenement. It was a roof that locked with other roofs, and he fled across the roofs, catching himself in wash hung on poles-and-rope, and screamed because he didn't know what it was.

Then he found a fire escape, and clattered down the iron steps till he came to the drop-ladder, and it squeaked rustily, and he climbed down, dropping into another alley. Then he ran up another street, and onto Seventh Avenue, and across Seventh Avenue, dodging between cars. Then he was on another street, and he walked with head bowed, hands in topcoat pockets, praying he had lost them.

Light pooled on the sidewalk, and he looked up.

The light came from a trip lamp in the window of the store, and the sign it illuminated said:

Norman Mogart hesitated only a moment. He pulled open the door, and stepped into the shop. It was empty. There was a brown, leathery, wizened little man with pointed ears standing in the exact center of the empty shop.

Yes, the shop was one of those.

"You're early," said the little man.

Norman Mogart was suddenly frightened. There was the unmistakable rattle of lunacy in the little man's voice. He stared for a long moment, feeling his gorge rise. Then he turned and reached out for the doorknob, knowing it was just there, under his questing fingers. There was no door.

"You're almost ninety seconds early," the little man murmured. "We'll have to wait, or throw everything out of phase."

Norman Mogart backed up, kept backing up, backed through the space where the door should have been, the wall should have been, the sidewalk outside the shop should have been, the street should have been. They weren't there. He was still inside the shop, whose dimensions seemed to expand as he moved. "You better let me out of here, crazy old man," Norman said quaveringly.

"Ah. It's time." The little old man hurried toward Norman. Norman turned and ran. Across a faceless, empty plain of existence. He kept running. There were no rises, no dips, no features to the surrounding terrain. It was as though he were in some enormous television studio set of limbo, running and running across an empty plain.

Finally, he slipped, exhausted, to the floor of the shop, and the little old man scampered up to him. "Ah. Fine. Now it's time."

He sat down cross-legged before Norman Mogart. Norman noticed with some alarm that though the little old man was sitting in a lotus position, quite comfortably, there was almost a foot of empty air between his bottom and the floor. The little man was sitting on the air.

Norman shut his eyes tightly. The little old man began talking to

Norman as though he had *just* entered the shop, not as though he had been ninety seconds early.

"Welcome, Mr. Mogart. So you want to escape. Well, that's what I sell here. Escape. Inside."

Norman opened his eyes.

"Who are you?"

"A humble shopkeeper."

"No, c'mon now, who *are* you?"

"Well, if you press me. . ."

The little man shimmered, and changed form. Norman shrieked. The form shimmered again, became the little old man. "Will you settle for what I'm showing you?"

Norman bobbled his head eagerly.

"Ah. Well, then, *do* you or do you *not* wish to escape, Mr. Mogart? I can guarantee that if you refuse my offer, the police will apprehend you in a matter of minutes."

Norman hesitated only a second, then nodded.

"Ah. Good. Then we have an arrangement. And, with all my heart, I thank you." Norman had only a moment to consider the peculiar tone in the little old man's voice.

Then he began to dissolve.

He looked down and saw his legs beginning to fade away. Slowly. Without pain. "Wait a second, wait hold it!" Norman implored. "Are you a demon? A devil, some kind of thing like that? Am I going to Hell? Hey, wait a minute, if I'm going to Hell, I shoulda made a bargain. . .what do *I* get?. . .Hey, hold on, I'm fading away. . .Are you a gnome or an elf, or what?. . .Hey, what are you. . .!?!"

All that were left in the shop were Norman's eyes, his ears, his lower lip and a patch of hair. And even as these faded, the little old man said, "You can call me Simon."

And then, like the Cheshire cat, Norman Mogart faded away completely, hallucinating for an instant that the little old man had added, "Or Peter. It doesn't matter. . ."

At first, in that painful introductory moment upon returning to consciousness, Norman Mogart knew only that he was looking straight up. He was lying on his back, in a springy bed of some growth, the .30-06 Husqvarna still held at high-port across his chest and one shoulder—but he was flat-out on his back. As that first moment stretched like warm taffy, drawing itself out until it had become one minute or five or ten, strange thoughts faded away: thoughts of another life, of a pain that burned in him, a pain that was now gone, to be replaced by a pain of quite another sort, of a woman, of running, of a little man. . .of an image that faded faded faded away to be replaced by. . .what? His senses crept timorously back to him, each carrying an allotted burden of *new* memories, replacing those old ones, now fading and gone; depositing the new memories in suddenly cleared spaces, and they fit snugly, as though they belonged, settling to rest in his mind.

He was staring straight up, through the interlaced boughs of half a dozen jacarandas, and while he lay there, senses settling carefully back in their niches, he dwelled on flesh that faded and how lovely the blossoms seemed.

Had it been night, in a cold place? Here it was day, and warm. So warm. Had it rained here? Yes.

It *had* been raining. Heavily, he supposed, for the ground on which he lay gave off a moist and repellent squishing when he moved; his clothes were soaked through to the skin; his hair lay matted along his forehead; the stock and barrel of the hunting rifle were beaded with rain that had clashed with cosmoline and encysted itself.

He realized, finally, that the knapsack was still in place on his back, that he must have fallen straight back when he collapsed, and that now it was a painful hump which forced him to lie in a tortured arched condition. He slipped sidewise, and received immediate ease from the pain.

Still he looked up, seeing the huge leafy fronds that had collected their water greedily, and seeing the strange birds that came to slake their thirst at those informal watering-places. One bird he saw. . .

He had never known it, true so true; he had hardly lent credence to the native stories: he had heard it was so, that there were jungle birds of brilliant plumage whose colors ran in the rain, but he had snickered at the thought. Very often, too often (and if *once* too often, then he was a fool on a fool's errand!), the natives were like children, much rather believing their fancy made-up tales than the truth. Yet here it was, above him, nonchalant, and here—in this wonderland that was certainly no Wonderland—it was true. So who were the children, after all?

He stared up at the wild-eyed huge-billed creature and saw its colors, like a Madras print, running, flowing, melding one into another, red and yellow and green. And he marveled.

Beside him, in the rain-swollen pool, the jacaranda blossoms clotted like sour flesh, sucking at the flow of clear water. *Cocaine? What did that mean? Not him, perhaps some other.*

Now he felt rested, and with the thought, as punctuation, the mad-eyed bird leapt howling into the slate sky. He rose awkwardly, steadying himself on this root, that bole, stiffly, shifting the rick-rack between his shoulder blades. He seemed to rise up and up, a scarecrow, an exceptionally thin man, until he stood unsteadily, staring at the world. Then he looked down, and his reflection, jigsawed by bright blossoms, looked back. He did not recognize himself for a long moment. The body seemed all wrong. He remembered *another* body, in a cold place, and fear, and the hurt that lived in that other body. . .then he recognized himself.

He did not know how long he had lain there, the fever rising higher in him, then abating, then rising once more, a volcanic heat that rose and fell to no discernible rhythm. . .but the burns and sores were better this day. He felt he could go on alone without balming himself with herbs. (He had begun to suspect, in any case, that one of the herbs, he did not know which, was poisoning him further.) (There, *that* was a thought that belonged to this body, not the other.) (Yet the rifle had gotten no lighter: rueful thought.) (Cocaine?)

Before him, the jungle presented its unknown face, many-eyed, uncaring, but ready for him to take that first step away from this clearing, that rain-pool; it would sense the intrusion of this Norman Mogart who was nothing to that ageless green. (My name is Harry Timmons, Jr. My name is) Norman Mogart sighed.

And then, if he persisted, as the White Man always persists, unable to distinguish between folly and futility, the jungle would come for him with claw and tendril and the inhaled hacking cough of the swamp.

He was frightened by strangeness, both within him and around him. (God himself, he felt, would be frightened here!) But he knew that somewhere beyond the gray-green rotting carcass of this jungle, somewhere back where neither the peons nor the *Indios* would go, where they all feared a place, a Place With No Name, a place outside thought or memory, he would find the one he sought. He would find the fabled bringer of fire, the one still known as Prometheus, chained to his rock, his liver eaten out and rejuvenated. And that. . .*that* was enough to drive him on against fears a thousandfold more potent than this, merely terrifying, jungle. Or the strangeness within him.

He struck off, by the compass still south by southwest, machete and thick-soled boots beating a way for his long, wiry frame. In the chittering depths of that green denseness he seemed too slight, too terrified to find anything as great as that which he sought. His small blue eyes behind the wire-framed lenses of his glasses seemed so watery, so fragile, so astigmatic, they could never recognize grandeur, even if it were to present itself. But he was here, and he was moving, and somewhere behind these dew-cupping fronds, he would come to the legend-that-lived. He had to believe that, *keep* believing it.

It had not been an easy thing, this trek through the rain forest; the feverish drifting upon the waters of the mesa lake where the plane had crashed, killing the others instantly, spitting itself upon the drogued *fuienta,* plunging with a near-living gasp into the eroded bottom. He remembered with the delirium of heat and pain and the nausea of water fever, finding the *piragua* floating on the edge of the lake. Half-drowned, he had plunged his body into the lean, fire-blackened slit and descended into the darkness of nonthinking. The water, lapping against the seamed side of the dugout, had lulled his muted consciousness. He had sought and found a euphoric state of nonfeeling like that proffered by the peyote of the *serpentes* who see the secret colors of God upon the wind and the night, melting into the chiaroscuro of the jungle night.

(But if he could remember all that, even through the delirium, why did his thoughts continue to scatter and fall past alien memories that he was this other, this small man on a brick street in the cold?)

He kept moving.

And what was it the *Indios* said about him? About Harry Tim—Norman Mogart? He had heard the story from them in a dozen accents. That he was mad to go to the Place With No Name. And what was it those superstitious wise ones said about. . .*him?* About the legend.

The first time it was among the *Cholos,* when he could barely find the breath to pursue such an impossible tale. Who else but Norman Mogart would have seen in the semblance of the snake totem the identity of the legends that found their way through the *Rig-Veda,* the *Osai nai Komata?* Who else? Why, even the twenty references in the *Heiji Monogatari,* that warrior epic of half a world away. . .all these fitted piece-by-piece to the final pattern.

Now, fevered, moving, skin mottled by the three varieties of diploid fungus so common to the tableland, he knew that his eyes would become the color of llama milk, and his ears become muffled to the sounds of the insinuating fronds in a matter of days; but in that time he might see the thing he had come to see, if it existed.

The *Cholos* had promised him—with fear—as had the *Zenos*—with ridicule—and the *Huilichachas*—with disbelief—that he would find Him. If he went where the colors of the *Yoatl* ran like paint, if he went seven times seven meters, there. . .trapped in the cleft of the living rock. . .He rested, eyes filled with the black tears of fever and pain.

It was not a vulture that assailed Him, of course. No vulture that tore at his vitals. This they told him. That was the Western version; the distorted version of the legend of the fire-bringer. Only He, Huipoclapiol, was the bringer not of fire, but of lies; not the searing brand of truth, but the greater revelation of falsehood, and for this his spleen was ripped from his quivering viscera by the mad-eyed Yoatl, whose plumage colors ran like rainbow blood over His brown, immortal body.

And now he had found the bleeding color-bird, and so he knew the rest of it must be true.

Sunk within his own madness (how far into fire-dreams am I gone, he wondered, knowing only one out of six images was of the real world, all others products of the fever, the pain, even this other life I seem to have led, yet know I never led) he faintly heard the sound. . .a mad sound from beyond the green. . .

Eyes burning bright, he hacked through a cat's cradle of vines, found himself abruptly on a ridge, and looked down to see the sound and what made it. The dull, droning, faraway mad sound of living death. There went the wide brown swath, like an ocean breaker, a ribbon road of desolation and roiling, hungering tumult. The *marabunta*! The warrior ants, the hell-that-moves, the mouth that never knows filling, the army ants that sweep all before them until they inexplicably vanish back into the jungle to wait their time once more.

He stared down at them, far off, feeling a cold return to sanity. No man could look on the face of such total destruction and not burn away the fever of madness; so much death at once cannot be escaped, even by doorways that lead to delusion. For a very long time he stared down into the valley, watching the moving, always moving billion-legged worm that devoured the world as it went. Then, shivering with the knowing of how small he was, how easily this jungle could take him and kill him, he turned away, and sought again the safety of the jungle. The *marabunta* were moving in a line with him, away from him, but they were far off, they were no immediate threat. Merely a reminder (that indescribable sound still drifting back to him) that he was only alone, only a man, and there were greater gods awake in the land.

Had he not been hallucinating in blue and yellow, he would never have found the entrance to the Place With No Name.

The fever had gotten worse, the fungi that now matted his arms and legs seemed in a race with him, to establish sovereignty of his body before he found what he sought. His most paralyzing fear was of the fungus covering his eyes.

And then he began hallucinating, circles of light emanating from each leaf, from every mote of dust, from the sun, from each outcropping of rock. A million circles, pulsing in blue and yellow, filling his world with empty bubble shapes, through which he slogged, half-conscious. Then he came to a ring of low hills, there in the jungle, high atop the mesa. He started around the foothills, hoping for a break that would carry him through, in blue and yellow.

The passage was overgrown with foliage, and he would never have seen it, had it *not* been radiating circles of light. It was, in fact, the only point in his vision that was clear. Almost like a pathway through his delirium. He cleared the vegetation with his machete, and pried away several jagged chunks of rock that had fallen to block the passage. It was quite dark inside.

Norman Mogart took a step inside, then another. Stood waiting. Heard silence. Drew breath. Stepped again. Walked forward with fear. With hope. Saw nothing. Hung his machete on his belt. Slung his rifle. Extended his hands. Felt the walls of the passage. Narrower. Wider. Moving forward. Deeper and deeper into the mountain. Farther.

Saw light far ahead. Hurried toward it. Marveled that the circles of light had left him. Came to the mouth of the passage. Stepped out. Saw Him.

Mogart was on a wide ledge that circled almost completely around the inside of the mountain. Below him, far below him, he could make out what had surely been the throat of what-was-now-obviously not a mountain but a dormant volcano. And all the way across the volcano, on the wide ledge directly across from him, Prometheus was chained to the rock.

Norman Mogart started around the ledge, keeping his eyes alternately on his destination, that incredible figure bent backward over the rock outcrop, and where his feet were placing themselves.

As he neared the figure, he began to realize that if it was a man, it was a man such as had never existed on this Earth. Prometheus was very brown, almost a walnut shade. His eyes, which were closed, were vertical slits. Around the mouth, which was little more than a horizontal gash running completely across the lower face, were tiny fleshy tendrils. They reminded Mogart of the spiny whiskers of a catfish. The tendrils moved in slight, quivering random patterns.

Prometheus was bent backward over a rock, arms spread and webbed-fingered hands (with more tendrils on the knuckles) pulled down on either side. Huge faceted bolts of a blue metal had been driven through the wrists, into the rock. A chain of the same metal circled the nipped-in waist and was itself bolted to the rock. Bolts had been driven through the flipper-like feet.

Even as he neared, a scream from the sky brought his eyes up, and he saw the *Yoatl* dive straight down, and with mad-eyed purpose it landed on the chest of the creature. (Mogart realized, suddenly, that this—man?—had altogether too many ribs in the huge chest.) The bird arched its neck and drove its beak into the walnut flesh. It came away red with blood, and Mogart could now make out the scar tissue that covered the body of the chained creature.

He yelled, then. As loud as he could. The bird gave him a quizzical stare, then flapped away into the sky. At the sound of Mogart's voice, Prometheus raised his head and looked across the ledge.

He saw Mogart, moving toward him hurriedly.

Then he began to cry.

Mogart came to his side rapidly. He tried to speak, but he had no idea what to say.

Then the chained figure spoke. In a tongue Mogart could not understand.

"I don't know. . .what you're saying. . ."

The figure closed his eyes a moment, then mumbled something to himself, as though running through a litany of some sort, and finally said, "Your words. This is right."

"Yes. Yes, now I can understand. . .are you. . .?"

The man's face broke into a smile. A tortured, painful smile of relief and passion. "So the Justice finally sent you. My time is done. I'm very grateful to you."

Norman Mogart did not know what he meant.

"A moment," the figure said, and closed its eyes in concentration. "Now. Touch me."

Mogart hesitated. The mute appeal in the eyes of the walnut man urged him, and he reached out and touched the flesh of the chained man.

There was an instant of disorientation, and when he could focus again, he found himself alone on the ledge, now chained where the walnut figure had been. And he was alone. Quite alone. Chained in the place of Prometheus; himself having become the fire-bringer.

That night, after the *Yoatl* had come again and again to him, he had his first dream. A dream that lived in fire. And this was the dream:

They had been lovers. And from their love had come compassion. For the creatures of that primitive world. They had brought the fire of knowledge; against all the rules of the Justices they had interfered with the normal progress of another world. And so they had been sentenced. The one to a fate chained to a rock in a place no man would ever visit. The other to a public death.

They were immortal, so they would live forever and suffer forever. They radiated in a strange way, so the *Yoatl* came to feed, and to run like paint as a result.

But now their sentences were at an end.

So the Justice had selected two. One was even now exchanging places with the other, and Norman Mogart had taken the place of the one men had come to call Prometheus. Of the other. . .he had been an alien, even as Prometheus had been. He had brought the next step in wisdom for the savages of this world. At the same time, though for the savages they were millions of years apart: for time had no meaning to these aliens.

Now, the lovers were freed. They would return and start again, for they had paid their penances.

Norman Mogart lay out on the rock, eyes closed, thinking of the two men who had loved each other, and him, and all the creatures of this world. He thought of them as they returned to *another* Place With No Name.

He thought of himself, and was in pain, and could not be entirely unhappy. How long it would last, he had no idea, but it was not a completely unsatisfactory way to mark out eternity.

And he thought of the man the Justice had found to take the place of that other, and he knew that when April came around again, he would be given his crown of thorns.

For that was how legends came to be born in the minds of savages, even in the Place With No Name.

—Cupertino, CA, *1964 and*
Los Angeles, *1968*

WHITE ON WHITE

He had wakened in the immense circular bed, feeling the satin sheets against his naked body. His face had been turned to the open French doors, and the first sight he had seen that morning was the vibrant Aegean, cerulean and mysterious, below the balcony of the villa. Then he had turned, and the Countess lay watching him from across the faraway expanse of too many years of high living. Her eyes, like the Sea, were cerulean and mysterious.

"What do I see in you?" she asked softly.

It was a question tinged with self-hatred and a grim realization that she was, inescapably, what she had allowed her hedonism to let her become. Paul sat up in bed, ruffling a hand through his blond hair. He gave her the rugged and knowing look—the one that had worked so well on the ex-wife of the deposed Southeast Asian premier—and answered her without words.

"You genuinely are a swine, Paul," she said.

There was affection in her tone.

So he reached across, and paid his dues for that day, making ferocious love to her while his mind strayed in a waking dream: the same dream he had always dreamed. Of one woman, a constant woman, from whom he would never have to flee. Knowing all the while that his pattern—like hers—had been sternly and exquisitely set by too many years at the wrong trade.

And when he lay back again on his own side of the bed, looking out at the Sea and working the worm of the word *gigolo* through the under-layers of his mind, she said, "I'm sick of Greece. I want to go away."

Paul slipped out of the bed and walked quickly onto the balcony. Where would it be this time? Paris; Côte d'Azur; Marrakech; Stowe, Vermont for the skiing? It didn't matter. Wherever, it was with *whom-ever* and for *how long*, till the woman—whichever woman it was to which he'd attached himself—grew tired of him, snarled "ladies' man" and threw him out. Somewhere, Paul knew, there was a woman, a special woman. . .one who would see beyond the hard, flat, tanned musculature to the soul he knew he possessed. However withered and atrophied it might be, still it was there, and one day, somewhere, he would find her, and she would keep him. Forever.

That day they left Athens and the villa.

The Countess had decided she needed adventure. Not riding to the hounds in Sussex, not tobogganing in the Swiss Alps, not stalking gazelle in Kenya; she had decided this time it was to be Nepal. Everest.

Not the highest summit, not even the southern face where the dilettantes used grapnel and piton to climb their easy climbs and return, winded, to armchairs in the club, where they could lie about their bravery. A foothill. Something wild and somewhat less than tortuous, where a Countess and her fancy man could taste the bite of the wind, trek the snow, and feel they had not been unplugged completely from life.

Their Sherpa was a withered old specimen, but adjudged honest to a fault and steadfast in the most harrowing circumstances. So they took him on, and began the climb.

But even sophisticated forays across the near edge of danger can go wrong, and somewhere beyond the fifth plateau the freak storm hit them, sending them deeper into their parkas, hurling a barrage of heavy snow against their snow-goggles, terrifying both the Countess and her tall, rugged Paul.

He dreamed of warmer climes, and knew when they got down from this insane coventry of white that he would be finished with her. Or her with him.

They made camp against the rock-wall of a modest outcropping, high up on the massif, the hide of the tent whistling and clapping around them as they huddled together and drank coffee from tin cups.

"This was stupid," he said.

"I *like* being stupid," she answered viciously. "I can afford all manner of stupidities."

It began the argument, and it spiraled up and up till he knew if he remained in the tent with her that when the Sherpa came to them from his own tent in the morning, she would be dead.

So he bundled tightly and stalked out onto the ledge, and followed it a few yards around the face of the massif. A few yards was all it took. He was immediately lost. The tents were gone in the frantic whiteness of the raging storm.

He felt terror rising in him, and for the first time realized precisely where he was, and what he was doing. He stumbled forward, hands out before him, trying to find at least the rock-wall, to follow it back. It, too, had vanished. Snow clotted his goggles, and he brushed them clean only to have them mass over again. He went to his knees, and had he known how to cry, he would have done so.

On hands and knees, he crawled.

For a very long time.

Then, through the sweeping gale he saw a break in the snow, a moment of lessened frenzy, and there was a cave. He pulled himself forward, and crawled into the shelter. The cave was not deep, but it was dark and it was protected. He lay up against the wall of the cave for moments, until he could regain his breath. Then he thumbed up the goggles and let the hood of the fur parka fall back from his head.

He looked around.

The cave was somehow very still, despite the epileptic writhing of the storm outside and its damned-soul shriek. In the far corner of the cave, something stirred. Paul blinked several times, the ice that had formed on his eyelashes weighing the lids. He could not make out what it was over there.

Then it rose.

He was incapable of screaming. The sound froze deep in his throat, even as the world around him froze.

The great white creature shambled toward him, and he could make out its form now. It was gigantic, fully eight feet tall, massive through the body, with legs as thick as tree trunks. Covered with silken white hair, a pelt of fur as deep and thick as a sheepskin rug. Where the face should have been, a travesty of humanity peered out through ingots of black fire. A nose more like that of an orangutan than a human. A mouth as wide as a gnome's. The creature stood over him, and Paul lay there paralyzed.

Then the thing stooped and gathered him up. It brought him close, and he could smell the awful stink of its breath. His mind fled from thinking of what it had been eating to smell like that.

Then it began to murmur. Deep sounds, musical sounds, warm sounds, from somewhere in its belly.

And with eyes that widened, then closed in a fear of encroaching insanity, Paul knew he had at last found the constant woman, the faithful woman, the one to whom he must belong, forever.

The creature was taken with him, and the sound of the Countess laughing *ladies' man* rang in his head. The *yeti* held him close, protecting him from the storm as they lumbered out of the cave, up the mountain and into the lost night of eternity.

The logic was inescapable: anthropologists should have suspected, should have known for a certainty: if there was such a thing as an Abominable Snowman. . .

He had been intuitively right. There *was* love eternal.

—Onboard American Airlines
Flight 322, LA to NY,
30,000 feet in the air, 1968

RUN FOR THE STARS

I

They found him looting what was left of the body of a fat shopkeeper. He was hunkered down with his back to the blasted store-front, picking through the hundred pockets of the dead merchant's work-bib.

He didn't hear them come in. The scream of the Kyban ships scorching the city's streets mingled too loudly with the screams of the dying.

They crept up behind him, three men with grimy faces and determined stares. The roar of a power terminal exploding somewhere across the city covered the crackle of their boots in the powdered and pebbled concrete that littered the floor. They stopped, and a man with blond hair nodded to the other two. They grabbed him suddenly, twisting his hands up behind his back, bringing a sharp, surprised scream from him.

Bills and change tinkled from his hands, scattered across the rubble-strewn floor.

Benno Tallant twisted his head painfully and looked up at the men holding him. "Lemme go! He was dead! I only wanted to get enough money to buy food with! Honest to God, lemme go!" Tears gathered in the corners of his eyes from the pains in his twisted arms.

One of the men holding him—a stocky, plump man of indeterminate age and a lisping speech said snappishly, "In case you hadn't noticed, lootie, this is a grocery you were robbing. There's food all over the shop. Why not use that?"

He gave the arm he held another half-twist.

Tallant bit his lip. There was no use arguing with these men; he couldn't tell them the money was to get narcotics. They would kill him and that would be the end of it. This was a time of war, the city was under siege from the Kyben, and they killed looters. Perhaps it was better that way; in death the insatiable craving for the dream-dust would stop, and he would be free. Even dead he would be free.

Free, to walk without the aid of the dream-dust; free, to lead a normal life. Yes, that was what he wanted, to be free. . .he would never touch the dream-dust again, if he came out of this alive.

And the pusher was probably dead, anyhow.

The thought of death—as it usually did—sent chills coursing down through his legs, numbing his muscles. He sagged in their grip.

The pig-faced man, who had not spoken, grunted in disgust. "This the best we can do, for Christ's sake? There's *got* to be someone in the group better for this job. Look at the miserable little slob, he's practically jelly."

The blond man shook his head. He was obviously the leader of the group. A patch of high forehead was miraculously clean among the filth and grime of his skin; he rubbed his hand over his forehead now, blotting away the clean area. "No, Shep, I think this is our man."

He turned to Tallant, stooped down and studied the quaking looter. He put his hand to Tallant's right eye, and spread the lids. "A junkie. Perfect." He stood up, added, "We've been looking for you all day, fellah."

"I never saw you before in my life, what do you want with me? Lemme go, willya!" They were taking too long to kill him—something was wrong.

His voice was rising in pitch, almost hysterically. Sweat poured down over his face as though a stream had been opened at the hairline.

The tall, blond man spoke hurriedly, glancing over his shoulder. "Come on, let's get him out of here. We'll let Doc Budder go to work on him." He motioned them to lift the quaking man, and as he rose, added, "There's a good five hours' work there," and he patted Tallant's lean stomach.

The lisping man named Shep said, "And those yellow bastards up there may not give us that long."

The pig-faced man nodded agreement, and as though to punctuate their feelings, a woman's high-pitched scream struck through the fast-falling dusk. They stopped, and Tallant thought he might go mad, right there, right in their arms, because of the scream, and these men, and no dust, and the entire world shattering around him. He wanted very badly to lie down and shiver.

He tried to slump again, but the pig-faced man dragged him erect.

They made their way through the shop, kicking up fine clouds of concrete dust and stepping on bits of plasteel that crackled beneath their feet. They paused at the shambles of the storefront, and peered into the gathering darkness.

"It's going to be a rough four miles back," the lisping man said; and the tall, blond leader silently nodded agreement.

Outside, the explosion of a fuel reservoir superimposed itself over the constant blast and scream of Kyban attack. . .and the mere scream of human death.

The silence fell for an instant. . .the deadly silence of the battlefield that only signifies new horrors preparing. . .then before the new breath could be drawn, a screaming missile whined overhead and ripped through the face of an apartment building across the street. Metalwork and concrete flew in all directions, shattering on the blasted pavement, sending bits of stuff cascading over them.

They watched with tight faces for an instant; then, hauling their human burden, slipped quietly and quickly into the evening.

Behind them, the fat shopkeeper lay amidst the debris of his store, dead, safe, and uncaring.

II

Benno Tallant awoke during the operation, his throat burning with dryness, his head swimming in fatigue. He saw his stomach open, the bare organs—slick and wet in their own pulsing blood—staring up nakedly at him. A grizzled little man, with sharp spikes of white beard dotting his cheeks, was carefully settling a knobbed and calibrated block of metal into the flesh. He caught a glimpse of the operating lamp's idiot glare above him, and promptly fainted again.

When he awoke the second time, he was in a cold, cold room, lying naked to the groin on an operating table, his head slightly higher than his feet. The red, puckered scar that ran from the bottom of his rib cage to the inside of his thigh stared up at him. It reminded him of a crimson river coursing through desert land. The pin-head gleam of a metal wire-tip stuck up in the center of the scar. Abruptly, he remembered.

They stopped his screaming by forcing a wadded-up towel into his mouth.

The tall blond man from the ruined shop stepped into Tallant's arc of vision. He had washed the filth from his face, and he wore a dun-colored military uniform, with the triple studs of a Commander on the lapel. The man stared closely at Tallant for a moment, noting the riot of emotions washing the looter's face.

"I'm Parkhurst, fellow. Head of Resistance, now that the President and his staff are dead." He waited for the convulsions of Tallant's face to cease. They continued, the eyes growing larger, the skin turning red, the neck tendons stretching taut.

"We have use for you, mister, but there isn't much time left. . .so if you want to stay alive, calm down."

Tallant's face eased into quiet.

They pulled the towel from Benno Tallant's mouth and for a moment his tongue felt like thick, prickly soup. The picture of his stomach, split and wet, came back to him once more. "*What was that?* What have you done to me? Why do this to me?" He was crying; the tears oozed out of the corners of his eyes, running ziggily down his cheeks into the corners of his mouth, and down his chin again.

"I wonder that, too," said a voice from Tallant's left. He turned his head painfully, small shafts of pain hitting him at the base of the neck. He saw the grizzled man with the spiky beard. It was a doctor; the doctor who had been inserting the metal square in Tallant's stomach the first time he had awakened. Tallant assumed this was Doc Budder.

The nearly bald man continued, "Why this sniveling garbage, Parkhurst? There are a dozen men left in the post who would've volunteered. We would have lost a good man, but at least we'd know the thing was being carried by someone who could do the job."

He caught his breath as he finished speaking; a thick, phlegmy cough made him steady himself on the edge of the operating table. "Too many cigarettes. . ." he managed to gasp, as Parkhurst helped him to a chair across the room.

Parkhurst shook his head and pointed at Tallant. "The best possible job can be done by somebody who's afraid of the thing. By someone who will run. The running will take time, and that's all that will be left to ensure our living till we get to Earth, or another outpost. What do you think, Doc?

"Do you have any doubt this man will run?"

Doc Budder rubbed the bristling stubble on his chin. It rasped in the silence of the room. "Mmm. I guess you're right, Parkhurst—you usually *are*—it's just that. . ."

Parkhurst cut him off with friendly impatience. "Never mind, Doc. How soon can we have this one up and around?"

Doc Budder wheezingly hoisted himself from the chair. He coughed once more, deeply, said, "I had the epidermizer on him. . .he's knitting nicely. I'll put it back on him but, uh, say, Parkhurst, y'know, all those cigarettes, my nerves are a little jumpy. . .I wonder, uh, would you have a little, uh, something to sort of steady me?" A hopeful gleam appeared in the old man's eyes, and Tallant recognized it at once for what it really was. The old man was a junkie, too. Or a winehead. He couldn't name the specific poison, but there was the same unnatural craving eating at Doc Budder that he suddenly realized was eating at him, also.

Parkhurst shook his head firmly. "Nothing, Doc. We have to keep you right on hand in case something goes. . ."

"Goddam it, Parkhurst, I'm not a ward of the state! I'm a doctor, and I have a right to—"

Parkhurst turned away from staring at Tallant, staring at Tallant but thinking of Doc Budder. “Look, Doc. This is a bad time for everybody. This is rough on all of us, Doc, but my wife got burned down in the street when the Kyben struck three days ago, and my kids were burned in the school. Now I know it’s rough on you, Doc, but if you don’t so help me God stop bugging me for your whiskey, I’m going to kill you, Doc. I’m going to kill you.”

He had spoken softly, pacing his words for full effect and clear understanding, but the desperation in his voice was apparent. The tones of a man with a terrible anguish in him, and a terrible burden on his shoulders. He would not humor the old man any longer.

“Now. How soon can we get him out of here, Doc?”

Doc Budder’s eyes swept across the room hopelessly, and his tongue washed his lips. He spoke hurriedly, nervously.

“I’ll—I’ll put the epidermizer back on it. It should be set in another four hours. There’s no weight on the organs; it was a clean insertion. He shouldn’t feel a thing.”

Benno listened closely. He still didn’t know what had been done to him, what the operation had been about, and his overwhelming terror at this whole affair had been sublimated in the little tableau between Budder and Parkhurst. But now he ran a shaking hand over the scar.

The fear was gagging him, and he felt the nervous tics starting in his inner upper arm and his cheek. Doc Budder wheeled a slim, tentacled machine to the operating table, and lifted a telescoping arm from the shaft. On the end was a small rectangular nickel-steel box with a small hole in it. Budder threw a switch, and a shaft of light struck out from the hole, washed the scar.

Even as he watched, the wound seemed to lose color, pucker more. He couldn’t feel the thing they had put in his stomach, but he knew it was there.

A sudden cramp hit him.

He cried in pain.

Parkhurst’s face turned white. “What’s the matter with him?”

The words came out so quickly, they were one word.

Doc Budder pushed aside the telescoping arm of the epidermizer, leaned over Tallant, who lay there breathing with difficulty, his face wrenched into an expression of utter pain. "What's the matter?"

"It hurts—it—*here*—" He indicated his stomach. "Pain, all over here, hurts like hell. . .*do something*!"

The fat little doctor stepped back with a sigh. He slapped the telescoping arm back into position with a careless motion. "It's all right. Self-induced cramp. I didn't think there'd be any deleterious after-effects.

"But," he added, with a malicious glance at Parkhurst, "I'm not as good a doctor, as sober and upstanding a doctor, as the Resistance could use, if it had its choice, so you never know."

Parkhurst waved a hand in annoyance. "Oh, shut up, Doc."

Doc Budder pulled the sheet up over Tallant's chest, and the looter whined in pain. Budder snarled down at him. "Shut up that goddammed whining, you miserable slug. The machine's healing you through the sheet. You haven't got a thing to worry about. . .right now. There are women and kids out there. . ." he waved toward the boarded-up window ". . .suffering a lot worse than you!"

He turned toward the door, Parkhurst following, lines of thought slicing across the blond man's forehead.

Parkhurst stopped with a hand on the knob. "We'll be back with food for you later." He turned back to the door, then added, not looking at Tallant, "Don't try to get out. Aside from the fact that there's a guard on the door—and that's the only way out unless you want to go to *them* through the window—aside from that, you might open that incision and bleed to death before we could find you."

He clicked the light switch, stepped out, and closed the door behind himself. Tallant heard voices outside the door, softly, as though coming through a blanket of moss, and he knew the guard was standing ready outside.

Tallant's thoughts weren't deterred by the darkness. He remembered the dream-dust, and the pains shot up in him again; he remembered the past, and his mouth chocked up; he remembered awakening during the operation, and he wanted to scream. The darkness did not interfere with Benno Tallant's thoughts.

They became luminous and the next six hours were a bright, thinking hell.

III

The lisping man, Shep, came for him. He had cleaned up, also, but there were fine tracings of dirt around his nose, and under his nails, and in the lines of pocketing beneath his eyes. He had one thing in common with the other men Tallant had seen; he was weary, to the core.

Shep shot the telescoping arm of the epidermizer into its shank hole, and rolled the machine back against the wall. Tallant watched him carefully, and when Shep turned down the sheet, examining the now-gone thin, white line that had been the incision, Benno raised himself on his elbows, and asked, "How's it going outside?" His tones were friendly, the way a child trying to make up to someone who has been angry with him is friendly.

Shep raised his gray eyes and did not answer.

He left the room, reappeared a few minutes later with a bundle of clothes. He threw them on the operating table next to Tallant, and helped the looter sit up. "Get dressed," he said shortly.

Tallant sat up, and for a moment the crawling of his belly-hunger for the dream-dust made him gag. He hung his head down and opened his mouth, making retching noises deep in his throat. But he was nausea-dry, and nothing came.

He straightened up and put a shaking hand through his brown hair. "L-listen," he began, speaking confidentially to the Resistance man, "do y-you know where I can lay my hands on some dream-dust? I-I can make it worth your while, I've got—"

Shep turned on him, and the lisping man's hand slammed against Tallant's face, leaving a burning red mark. "No, mister, *you* listen to *me*. In case you don't know it, there's a Kyban battle armada on its way across space, headed directly for Deald's World. We've only been hit by an advance scout party, and they've nearly demolished the planet as it is.

"About two million people are dead out there, buddy. Do you know how many people that is? That's almost the entire population of this planet.

"And you sit there asking me to get you your snuff!

"If I had any say in the matter, I'd kick you to death right here, right now.

"Now you get into those goddammed clothes, and don't say another word to me, or so help me bleeding Jesus I'm not responsible for what happens to you!"

He turned away, and Tallant stared after him. There was no fight in him, merely a desire to lie down and cry. Why was this happening to him? He'd try anything to get the dust now. . .it was getting bad inside him. . .real bad. . .and he'd tried to stay out of the fighting. . .he'd only been getting the money from that shop to find a pusher. . .why were they badgering him. . .what had they *done* to him?

"*Get dressed!*" Shep shouted, the cords in his neck tightening, his face screwing into an expression of rage.

Tallant hurriedly slipped into the jumper and hood, the boots, and buckled the belt around himself.

"Come on." Shep prodded him off the table.

Tallant stood up, nearly fell; he clung to Shep in terror, feeling the unsteadiness washing through him.

Shep shrugged his hands off, commanded, "Walk, you slimy, yellow bastard! *Walk*!"

He walked, and they went down the hall, into another sealed-tight compartment, and Tallant realized they must be underground.

He walked slightly behind Shep, knowing there was no place else to go, and the lisping man seemed to pay him no attention; knowing the looter would follow.

Through the walls—and through the very ground, Tallant estimated—he could hear the reverberations of shock bombs hitting the planet. He knew only vaguely what was happening.

The Earth-Kyban War had been a long and costly battle—they had been fighting for sixteen years—but this was the first time a Kyban fleet had broken through this far into the Terran dominion.

But it had obviously been a sudden, sneak attack, and Deald's World was the first planet to be hit. He had seen the devastation, while aboveground, and he knew that if these men were alive and working to defend Deald's World, they were the last pocket of the Resistance left.

But what did they want with him?

Shep turned right down a corridor, and palmed a loktite open. He stepped aside and Tallant walked into what appeared to be a communications room.

High banks of dials and switches, tubes and speaker rigs covered the walls. Parkhurst was there, holding a hand-mike carelessly, talking to a technician.

The blond man turned as Tallant stepped through. He nodded to himself, as though setting everything right in his mind, as though satisfied that all was going as planned, now that the looter was here. "We thought you'd like to know what this is all about." He hesitated. "We owe you that, at any rate."

The technician waved his hand in a circle, one finger extended, indicating they had started something turning, perhaps indicating the batteries were being warmed.

Parkhurst pursed his lips for a moment, then said almost apologetically, "We don't hate you, fellow." Tallant realized that they had not even bothered to find out his name yet. "We have a job to do," Parkhurst continued, half-watching Tallant, half-watching the technician, "and more is at stake than you or me or the life of anyone left here on Deald's World. Much more.

"We had a job to do, and for the job we needed a certain type of man. You fit the bill so beautifully, you'll never quite know. There was no premeditation; it just happened to be you. If it hadn't been you, it would have been someone *like* you." He shrugged with finality.

Tallant felt the shivers beginning. He stood quaking, wishing he had just a sniff of the dust, just a miserable sniff. He wasn't interested in all this high-flown patriotic gabble Parkhurst was throwing at him; all he wanted was to be let alone, let back out there, even if the Kyben *were* burning the planet, just to get back out there. Perhaps he could find a cache of the dust. . .because he knew he wouldn't get it from these men. If Doc Budder couldn't get his hootch, then they wouldn't give Tallant any dream-dust.

Yes, that was it. He knew it now. It was a plot, a conspiracy to keep him from his beloved dust. He had to have it, he was *going* to have it—but he would wait, he would be sly and cautious, and wait till these madmen were out of the way, till they weren't watching, then he would get away. There were no Kyben aboveground, it was only a foul, despicable plot to keep him from his beloved dust. His eyes narrowed.

Then the memory of the metal thing in his stomach jerked him instantly to reality. Tallant stood quaking. He had still not gotten over his terror at seeing the metal thing placed in his stomach.

His sallow face was dotted with sweat and streaked with dirt, though they had washed him several times during the six hours it had taken the scar to heal.

He was a lean man; the gray tuberous sort of man who always brings the wolf or pack-rat to mind. Brown hair and small, deep-set eyes. A face that seemed to taper to a rodentlike tip.

"What—what are you going to do with me now?" He touched himself lightly, almost fearfully, on the stomach. "What is that thing you did to me?"

A high, keening whine broke from one of the many speakers on the wall, and the tight-lipped technician gestured wildly at Parkhurst, finally tapping him on the shoulder. Parkhurst turned to the technician, and the man gave him a go-ahead signal. Parkhurst motioned Tallant to silence, motioned Shep to stand close by the shaking looter.

Then he spoke into the hand-mike. A bit too clearly, a bit too loudly, as though he were speaking to someone a great distance away, as though he wanted every word precise and easily understood.

"This is the headquarters of Resistance on Deald's World. We are subjects of Earth, and we are speaking to the Kyban fleet.

"Are you listening? This call is being broadcast over all tight beams, so we are certain you receive us. We'll wait ten minutes for you to rig up a translator and to hook in with your superiors, so they can hear this announcement.

"This is of vital importance to you Kyban, so we suggest as soon as you've translated what I've just said, you make the proper arrangements, and contact your officers."

He signaled the technician to cut off.

Then Parkhurst once again turned to Tallant. "They'll translate. They'll have to. . .they knew the best way to attack, so they must have had contact with Earth Traders, or Terran ships that went too far into the Coalsack. They will be able to decipher us."

Tallant ran a thin hand up his neck. "What are you going to do with me? What are you going to do?" He felt hysteria building in him, but could not stop the flow of words. *He was afraid!* "This isn't fair! You've got to tell me!" His voice became shrill. Shep moved in closer behind him, clasped the looter's arm above the elbow. Tallant stopped just as another torrent of words was about to burst forth.

Parkhurst spoke unhurriedly, quietly, trying to calm Tallant. "This is the advance guard of a gigantic Kyban fleet, mister. We're sure of that because there are almost fifty ships in the force that attacked us. If that's what they are using for an advance scout, the fleet must be the largest assembled during the War.

"It's obvious they intend to crush right through, the sheer force of weight breaking through all the Earth defenses, and perhaps strike at Earth itself.

"This is the big push of the War for the Kyben, and there is no way to get word to Earth. Our inverspace transmitters went when they burned down the transpoles at the meridian. There's no way to warn the home planet. They're defenseless if all the outer colonies go—as they surely will if this fleet gets through.

"We've got to warn Earth. And the only way we can do it, and with luck save the lives of the few thousands left alive on Deald's World, is to stall for time. That's why we needed a man like you. You."

Then he fell silent, and they waited silently.

The only sounds in the room were the click and whisper of the blank-faced machines, the tight, sobbing breaths of Benno Tallant.

Finally the big wall-chronometer had ticked away ten minutes, and the technician signaled Parkhurst once more.

The blond man took up the hand-mike again, and began speaking quietly, earnestly, knowing he was no longer dealing with subordinates, but the men in power up there above the planet; speaking as though each word were the vital key to a great secret.

"We have placed a bomb on this planet. A sun-bomb. I'm sure you know what that means. The entire atmosphere will heat, right up to the top layers of the stratosphere. Not quite enough to turn this world into a nova, but well enough above the point where every living thing will perish, every bit of metal heat to incandescence, the ground scorched through till nothing can ever grow again. This world, all of us, all of *you*, will die.

"Most of your fifty ships have landed. The few that remain in the sky can not hope to escape the effects of this bomb, even if they leave now. And if they do—you are being tracked by radar—we will set the bomb off without a moment's hesitation. If you wait, there is another possibility open to you."

He tossed a glance at the technician, whose eyes were fixed on a bank of radar screens with one pip in the center of each. The technician shook his head, and Tallant realized they were waiting to see if their story was accepted. If one of those pips moved out away from the planet, it would mean the Kyben did not believe, or thought it was a bluff.

But the Kyben obviously could not chance it. The pips remained solidly fastened to the center of the screens.

Then Tallant's eyes suddenly widened. What Parkhurst had said was finally penetrating. He *knew* what the blond man meant! He *knew* where that bomb was hidden. He started to scream, but Shep's hand was over his mouth before the sound could escape, could go out over the transmitter to the Kyben.

He became violently ill. Shep drew away from him, cursing softly, pulling a rag from a console top to wipe himself off. Tallant continued to vomit in dry, wracking heaves, and Shep moved back swiftly to catch him as he fell.

The lisping man eased Tallant onto a console bench, and continued daubing at his spattered uniform.

Tallant knew he was on the verge of madness.

He had lived by his wits all his life, and it had always been the little inch someone would allow him that had afforded the miles he had attained. But there was no inch this time. Bewildered, he realized he could not take advantage of the weakness or the politeness of these men, as he had taken advantage of so many others. These men were hard, and ruthless, and they had planted a sun-bomb—My God In Heaven!—a *sun*-bomb in his stomach!

He had once seen stereos of a sun-bomb explosion.

He threw up again, this time falling to the floor.

Through a fog he heard Parkhurst continue: "We repeat, don't try to take off. If we see one of your ships begin to blast, we'll trigger the bomb. We give you one alternative to total destruction. To destruction of this planet you will need so desperately for storage, refueling and supply for your fleet. One alternative."

He paused, looked around the communications room, which had suddenly seemed to grow so crowded. He seemed a bit embarrassed, perhaps by the obvious histrionics of the tense situation. Parkhurst licked his lips and went on carefully, "Let us go. Let the Earthmen on this planet blast away, and we promise not to set off the bomb. After we have left the atmosphere, we will set the bomb on automatic, and leave it for you to find yourselves. If you doubt we have actually done as I say, take a stabilization count with whatever instruments you have to detect neutrino emission.

"That should convince you instantly that *this is no bluff!*

"We will tell you this, however. There is one way the bomb may be deactivated. You can find it in time, but not till we have gotten away. It is a gamble you will have to take. The other way. . .there is no gamble at all. Only death.

"If you don't comply, we set off the bomb. If you do accede to our demands, we will leave at once, and the bomb will be set to automatic, and will go off at a designated time. It's armed with a foolproof time-device, and it can't be contained by any neutrino-dampers.

"That is our conditioned demand. We'll wait for your answer no more than an hour. At the end of that time, we trigger the bomb, even if we are to die!

"You can reach us over the band on which you are receiving this message."

He motioned to the technician, who threw a switch. A bank of lights went dark, and the transmitter was dead.

Parkhurst turned to Tallant, lying shivering in his own filth. His eyes were very sad, and very tired. He had to say something, and it was obvious what he said would be cruel, terrifying.

Don't let him say it, don't let him say it, don't let him say it, Benno Tallant kept repeating in the maddened confines of his mind. He screwed his eyes shut, put his slippery fists to them to ensure the darkness, perhaps blotting out what Parkhurst would say.

But the blond man spoke.

"Of course," he said quietly, "that end of it *may* be a bluff. I may be lying. There may *not* be any way to damp that bomb. Even after they find it."

IV

Tallant had been in such bad shape, they had had to lock him in the operating room, after removing everything breakable. Shep had been for strapping Tallant to the table, but Parkhurst and the pig-faced man—an ex-baker turned sniper named Banneman—were against it.

They left Benno Tallant in the room, while the hour elastically drew itself out. Finally, Shep palmed the loktite open and came in to find the looter lying on his side in the room, his legs drawn up near his chest, his hands down over his knees, the wide, dark eyes staring unseeingly at the limp, relaxed fingers.

He drew a pitcherful of water from a tap in the next room, and threw it on Tallant's face. The looter came out of his almost trancelike state with a wail and a start. He looked up, and memories flooded back at once. And the dust hunger.

"J-just a sniff. . .just a s-sniff is all I want. . .*please*!"

Shep stared at the weakling with a mixture of disgust and livid hopelessness. "This is the savior of Earth!" He spat on the floor.

Tallant's guts were untwisting. His mouth was dry then foully wet then dry again. His head ached and his muscles were constricted. He wanted that dust more than anything, he *had* to have it. They had to *help* him. He whined, and crawled toward Shep's boots.

The lisping man drew back. "Get on your feet. They expect the answer any minute."

Tallant got to his feet painfully, steadying himself on the operating table. They had the table bolted to the floor, but he had managed to bend two of its legs in his frantic, screaming drive to get out, to get to the dust.

"Come on," Shep said.

Shep led the shivering, drooling Tallant to the communications room once more, and when Parkhurst saw the state of disintegration coming over Tallant, he spoke quietly to Doc Budder. The spike--chinned old man nodded, and slipped past Tallant, out the door. Tallant stared around the room with blank eyes, till Doc Budder came back.

The old man held a snow-white packet, and Tallant recognized it for what it was. Dream-dust. "Gimme, gimme, gimme, please, ya gotta give it to me, give it, give me. . ."

He extended shaking, pale hands, and his twitching fingers sought the packet. Doc Budder, recognizing another addict was getting his craving, while *he* suffered without his own poison, held the packet back, taunting Tallant for a moment.

The addict struggled toward the old man, almost fell on him, his breath ragged and drool slipping out of his mouth. "Gimme, gimme, gimme, gimme. . ." His voice was a whisper, fervent, pleading.

The Doc laughed shrilly, enjoying the game, but Parkhust snapped,

"Let him alone, Doc. I said let him have his dope!"

The Doc threw the packet to the floor, and Tallant was on hands and knees in an instant, scrabbling for it. He had it in his hands, and he ripped the packet open with his teeth.

He struggled across the floor on his knees, to the comm-console and ripped a piece of paper from a pad. He folded it one time, and let the white dream-dust filter out of the packet, into the trough of paper.

Then he turned to the wall, crouching down so they could not see what he was doing, and inhaled the dust through each nostril.

Even as the dust slid up his nasal passages, the hunger died, the strength returned to him, the pressure eased from the base of his skull, his hands stopped trembling.

When he turned back he was no longer a shambles.

He was only a coward.

"How much longer?" Banneman asked from across the room, carefully keeping his eyes from Tallant.

"Any minute now," the technician answered from behind his commask. And as though his words had been a signal, the squawk-boxes made a static sound, and the rasp of a translating machine broke the silence of the room.

It was in a cold, metallic voice, product of changing Kyban to English.

"We accept. You have the bomb, as our instruments indicate, so we allow you seven hours to load and leave." That was the message, that was all.

But Tallant's heart dropped in his body. If the alien instruments showed an increase in neutrino emission, it could only mean his last hope was gone. The Resistance *did* have the bomb, and he knew where it was.

He was a walking bomb. He was walking death!

"Let's get moving," Parkhurst said, and started toward the corridor.

"What about me?" Tallant's voice rose again and he grasped at Parkhurst's sleeve. "Now that they'll let us go, you don't need me any more, do you? You can take that—that *thing* out of me!"

Parkhurst looked at Tallant wearily, an edge of sadness in his eyes. "Take care of him, Shep. We'll need him, seven hours from now." And he was gone.

Tallant remained with Shep, as the others left. He turned to the lisping man, and cried out, "What? Tell me! What?"

Then Shep explained it all to Tallant.

"You're going to be the last man on Deald's World. Those Kyban have tracing machines to circle down on centers of neutrino emission. They would find it in a moment if it were in one place. But a moving human being isn't always in one place. They'll never suspect it's in a human being.

"They'll think we're all gone. But you'll still be here, with the bomb. You're our insurance policy.

"Parkhurst controls the bomb as long as he's on the planet, and it won't go off. But as soon as he leaves, he sets it on automatic, and it goes off in the time allotted to it.

"That way, if an alien ship tries to follow us, tries to take off, the bomb explodes. If they *don't* take off, and don't find it in time, it goes off anyhow."

He was so cool in explaining, so uncaring that he was condemning Tallant to death, that Benno Tallant felt the strength of his dream-dust rising in him, felt anguish and fury at being used as a dupe and a walking bomb.

"What if I just turn myself in to them and let them cut it out with surgery, the same way you put it in?" Tallant said snappishly, with momentary bravery.

"You won't," Shep answered smugly.

"Why not?"

"Because they won't bother being as gentle as we were. The first detachment of Kyban foot-soldiers that trace the bomb to you will pin you to the ground and let an attaché slice you open."

He watched the horror that passed across Tallant's face. "You see, the longer you keep running, the longer it takes them to find you. And the longer it takes them to find you, the better chance we have of getting back to warn Earth. So we had to pick a man who was so stinking cowardly, he would keep running. . .because his whole nature depended on running. . .on staying alive.

"No, you'll keep running, fellow. That's why Parkhurst picked you. You'll run, mister, and never stop!"

Tallant drew himself up, and *screamed,* "My name is Tallant. Benno Tallant. Do you understand I have a name! I'm Tallant, Benno, Benno, Benno, Tallant!"

Shep grinned nastily and slumped down on the console bench. "I don't give a flying damn *what* your name is, fellow. Why do you think we never asked you your name?

"Without a name, you'll be all the easier to forget. This isn't an easy thing to do—for Parkhurst and the others—they have feelings and scruples about you, fellow.

"But I don't. A dream-duster just like you assaulted my wife before—before—" He stopped, and his eyes raised to the ceiling. Aboveground, the Kyben sat, waiting. "So I sort of figure it all evens out. I don't mind seeing a dustie like you die, at all. Not at all."

Tallant made a break for the door, then, but Shep had his rifle up, and a sharp crack slammed it into the small of Benno Tallant's back. The looter slumped to the floor, writhing in pain, crying out.

Shep slipped back to his seat.

"Now we'll just wait about seven hours," he said quietly. "Then you become real valuable, fellow. Real valuable. Y'know, you've got the life of the Kyban fleet in your belly."

He laughed, and laughed some more, and Benno Tallant thought he would go mad from the sounds of underground laughter. He just wanted to lie down. And die.

But that would come later.

The rocket field was silent at last. The noise of loading the few remaining thousands of Dealders had crashed back and forth for seven hours, and the ships had gone up in great clouds of fumes and exhaust trailings. Now the last ship was finished, and Benno Tallant watched as

Parkhurst lifted the little girl. She was a tiny girl with yellow braids, and she clutched a plastic toy. Parkhurst held her an instant longer than necessary, staring at her face, and Tallant saw compassion and sorrow for his own dead children coursing across the blond man's face. But he felt no sympathy for Parkhurst.

They were leaving him here to die in the most frightening way possible.

Parkhurst hoisted the little girl, set her inside the ship's plug-port, where the other hands received her. He began to swing up himself.

He paused with one hand on the swing-rail. He turned and looked at Tallant, standing with shaking hands at his sides, like a lost dog, pleading not to be left behind.

It was difficult for him, Tallant could tell. The man was not a murderer; he felt this was the only possible solution to the problem.

He had to warn Earth. But Tallant could feel no companionship. My God! They were condemning him to turn into a sun. . .

"Look, mister, it's like this. We're not as stupid as the Kyben think. They assume we'll blast and leave the bomb here. We'll be in our pokey little ships, they'll find and damp the bomb, then take off and wipe us out somewhere in space. All canned and ready to be burned.

"But they're wrong, Tallant. We made sure they wouldn't find that bomb.

"In time, with their neutrino-detectors, they could get the sun-bomb. But not if the carrier is moving. We *had* to find a man like you, Tallant. A coward, a runner.

"You're the only assurance we have that we'll make it to an Earth outpost to warn the mother world. I—I can't say anything to you that will make you think any better of us; don't you think I've burned over and over in my mind for what I'm doing? Get that look off your face, and say something!"

Tallant stared silently ahead, the fear draining down and around in him like poison rotting his legs.

"Somehow, even though I know you'll die, and I know I'm sentencing you to death, I look on you with pride. Can you understand anything as strange as that, mister? Can you understand that even though I've used the life in you the way I'd use the power of a robot-truck, I'm prideful because I *know* you'll keep them away from you for a long, long time, and I will be able to save these few people left, save the Earth.

"Can you understand that?"

Tallant broke. He grabbed Parkhurst's sleeve. "Oh, please, please, in the name of God, take me with you! Don't leave me here! I'll die. . . I'll. . .die. . ."

Parkhurst firmly disengaged Tallant's hand, his face tense.

Tallant fell back. "But why? Why do you hate me? Why do you want me to die?" Sobs caught in the looter's throat.

The Resistance leader's face became grim. "No, don't *think* that! Please, don't think that! I didn't even know you when we found we needed a man like you for this, mister. I hate your type, that's true, but there's no reason for me to hate *you*!

"You're a hero, mister. When—if—we get through this, a monument will be set up for you. It's no good, and it won't help you, but it will be set up.

"In the past seven hours I've schooled myself to despise you. I have to, mister, or I'd never leave you here. I'd stay in your stead, but that wouldn't do any good. I wouldn't have the same desire to run. I'm tired; my wife, my kids, they're all dead. *I* want to die, I just want to die. But, but, *you*—you want to live, and you'll run till they can't find you, and that will give us the time we need!

"I've taught myself to think of you as some sort of refuse of the human race.

"And," he added, in lost frantic justification, "you've helped me think of you that way. Look at yourself!"

Tallant knew what Parkhurst meant. He *was* garbage, he *was* a coward, he *would* run. He could almost picture his own slight body shaking as though under an ague, the sweat rolling off him, the fear a live thing around his body, his eyes large and white-ringed as they looked for a way out. Tallant knew he was a coward. It didn't help any.

He didn't want to die like this!

"So," Parkhurst finished, "I hate you because I *have* to hate you, mister. And because I hate you, because I hate myself, and *not* you, I've done this to you. And because you are what you are, you'll run and hide from those Kyban so that we can get to a relay station, and warn Earth they're coming."

He began to swing up into the ship again, when Tallant once more clutched his arm.

The coward had pleaded all through these last hours, and even now he knew no other way. A lifetime of sowing had reaped for him a harvest of spinelessness.

"At least, at least tell me, *is* there a way to damp the bomb. Can it be done? You told *them* that it could!" The childish eagerness of his expression caused Parkhurst's face to wrinkle with disgust.

"There isn't a bone in your body, is there?"

"Answer me! *Tell me*!" Tallant shouted. Faces appeared whitely at the ports of the spaceship.

"I can't tell you, mister. If there were, if you knew for certain, you'd be off to the Kyban lines right now. But if you think it'll go off when they touch it, you'll wait a long time." He shook the man's hand loose and pulled himself up into the ship.

The port began to slide home, and Parkhurst stopped it for a second, his voice softening as he said:

"I know you. Goodbye, Benno Tallant. I wish I could say God bless you."

The port slid shut. Tallant could hear it being dogged, and the whine of the atomic motors starting up. He ran away from the blast area in wild blindness, seeking the protection of the bunkers set back from the blast pit. The bunkers beneath which the Resistance had their headquarters.

He stood at the filtered window, watching the thin line of exhaust trailings disappearing into the night sky.

He was alone.

The last man on Deald's World.

He remembered what Parkhurst had said: *I don't hate you. But this has to be done. It has to be done, and you will have to do it. But I don't hate you.*

And here he was, alone with a planet of attacking Kyben he had never even seen, and a total-destruction bomb in his stomach.

V

After they were gone, after the last drop of exhaust trail had been lost in the starry night sky, Tallant stood by the open door of the bunker, staring across the emptiness of the field. They had left him; all his begging, all his appeals to their humanity, all his struggling, all of it had been for nothing. He was lost, lost out here in space, with the emptiness of the field and the emptiness of his heart.

The chill winds from the ocean came rippling across the field, caught him in their wake, and smoothed over him. He felt the hunger rising once more.

But this time, if nothing else, he could drown himself in dream-dust. That was it! He would send himself into a dust stupor, and lie there in heaven till the bomb went off, killing him.

He found the trapdoor, lifted it, and went down into the Resistance headquarters.

A half-hour, throwing supplies around, smashing into lockers, breaking open cabinets, and he had found Doc Budder's supply of medicinal dream-dust. Nurmo-heroinyte concentrate; the dream-dust that had found him, made him a slave after one small sampling when he was twenty-three years old. That had been a long time before this, and he knew this was his only rest now.

He sniffed away a packet, and felt himself getting stronger, healthier, more fierce. Kyben? Yes, bring them on! He could fight the entire armada single-handed. Then let those lousy sonofabitching Earthies try to come back. Deald's World would be his, he would be the king, the master of the universe!

He strutted back up the stairs, slammed back the trapdoor, the white packets in his jumper pocket.

Tallant saw his first Kyban then.

They were swarming across the rocket field, hundreds of them. They were average-sized, more than five feet tall, less than six, all of them. They looked almost human—but golden-skinned; and their fingers ended in silky tentacles, six of them to a hand.

Abruptly, the resemblance to normal humans terrified Tallant. Had they been grotesque, it would be something else; he could despise and hate them as monsters. But these Kyben were, if anything, handsomer than humans.

He had never seen them before, but he had heard the screams that had echoed through the city's canyons. He had heard a girl getting the flesh flayed off her back, and in his own way he had felt sorry for her. He remembered he had wished she might die from loss of blood. Wounds like that would only take three or four hours to kill her. With the Kyben, that would have been the quickest, least painful way.

Yet they looked very much like humans. But golden.

Suddenly Tallant realized he was trapped. He was caught in one of the bunkers, with no protection, no weapon, no way out. They would find him, and kill him, not realizing he had the bomb in him. They would not ask whether or not he carried a bomb. . .that was too ridiculous to consider.

That was why Parkhurst had done it. It was too ridiculous to consider.

They were looking for a sun-bomb, and that bomb—according to the logic of a searcher—would be in some obscure hiding place. In the ocean, under a thousand tons of dirt, in a cave. But not in a human being. A human being was the last thing they might consider.

Nobody could be cruel enough to plant a sun-bomb in a human being.

That was why Parkhurst had done it.

He looked around the bunker wildly. There was only the one exit. And the field was crawling with Kyben—furious enough at having been outfoxed to gut the first Earthie they found.

He watched them getting larger and larger in the filtered window.

As he watched, he noticed something further about them. They all wore suits of insulating mail, and each carried a triple-thread blastick. They were armed to kill, not to capture prisoners. He was trapped!

Tallant felt the fury of desperation welling up in him again. As it had when he had first learned he carried the sun-bomb. Not only to be boxed-in this way—to be a human bomb—but to have to keep running. He knew the Kyben were ruthless. They would already have started scouting for the bomb with ship-based emission detectors, spiraling over the planet in ever-decreasing circles, narrowing in on the bomb.

When they found it was not stationary, they would know it was in a living carrier. They would close in relentlessly, then. He was trapped!

But if these common foot-soldiers on the field got to him, he wouldn't even get *that* far, far enough to run. They would scorch him and laugh over his charred carcass. If they had that long to laugh. The bomb was certain to go off if he died—Parkhurst had said as much.

He had to get away.

Parkhurst was right. The only escape was in flight.

If he could stay alive long enough, he might be able to figure a way of dampening the bomb himself.

Or he had to keep away from them long enough to get to the Kyban commanding officers. It was the only chance. If he kept running, and avoided them entirely—the bomb would detonate eventually. He had to get to the men in charge, and have *them* remove the bomb without triggering it.

He would outsmart Parkhurst and his filthy bunch of survivors. He would not *let* himself get caught, unless it was by the right persons, in high places. Then he would offer his services to the Kyban, and help them hunt down the Earthmen, and kill them.

After all, what did he owe Earth?

Nothing. Nothing at all. They had tried to kill him, and he would make them pay. He would *not* die! He would live with his beloved dream-dust forever. Forever!

If he could remain alive that long, he would be able to think his way out of the Kyban camp. *That* was the answer!

Yes, that was it.

But now one Kyban foot-soldier was dodging, broken-field running, and now he was at the door of the bunker, and now he was inside, his triple-thread blastick roaring, spraying flame and death around the bunker.

Tallant had been beside the window, behind the door. Now he slammed the door, so the others on the field could not see what was happening, and he found a new strength, a strength he had not known he possessed.

He dove low from behind the Kyban soldier, tackling him. The soldier fell, the blastick jarred from his hands, and Benno Tallant was up, stamping the alien's face in. One, two, three, four and the alien was dead, his head a pulped mass.

Then Tallant knew what to do.

He dragged the soldier by his feet to the edge of the trapdoor, lifted it, and shoved the Kyban through. The body went clattering down the stairs, and landed with a thump.

Tallant grabbed up the blastick and slipped in before any more soldiers could appear. He let the trapdoor slam shut, knowing it would not be seen unless there was a thorough search; there was no reason to expect that, as they believed all Earthmen had left the planet. This was a reconnaissance mission, and there would be no search.

He desperately hoped.

He crouched down, beneath the trapdoor, the blastick ready in his hands, ready to smear off the face of anyone who lifted the door.

Overhead he heard the sound of shouts, and the door of the bunker crashed open against the wall. He heard the rasp and roar of more blasticks being fired, and then the sound of voices in the sibilant hiss of the Kyban tongue. He heard boots stomping around above him, and men searching. Once a foot stepped directly on the trapdoor, and little bits of dust and dirt filtered through around the edges, and he thought he was caught then.

But a shout from outside brought grudging answer from the soldiers, and they trooped out, leaving the bunker deserted.

Tallant lifted the door to make certain, and when he saw it was clear, lifted it higher to look through the filtered window. The Kyben were moving off in the other direction.

He decided to wait till they had gone. Night was upon the land, and he wanted to get away.

While he waited, he sniffed a packet of dust.

He was God again!

He made it as far as the Blue Marshes before another patrol found him.

He had been moving—unawares—in the most perfect escape pattern imaginable, circling outward, so that any Kyban ships tracking overhead with emission detectors could not pinpoint him. Eventually, of course, they would see that the target was not in the same place, and then they would recognize what the Earthmen had done.

He kept moving.

It was a totally cloudless, moonless night, with the stark black tips of the Faraway Mountains rising up beyond the marsh clingers and vines. The smell of the night was clean and quick, till he stepped off the land, and entered the Marshes. Then all the rot of the eternities swam up to offend his nostrils.

Tallant's stomach heaved, and for a moment he wondered if vomiting would set the bomb off. Then he recalled having been sick before, and knew action of that sort could not trigger the weapon.

He stepped into the swirling, sucking blue-black mud, and instantly felt it dragging down, down at his boots. He lifted the blastick above his head for leverage, and stepped high, pulling up each foot with a muted, sucking *thwup!* as he slowly moved.

The Marshes were filled with animal life, and whether vicious or harmless, they all made their voices heard. The noises swelled as he trod deeper into the dankness, as though some unimaginable insect telegraphy was warning the inhabitants that outside life was approaching. Ahead of him, and slightly to the left, he heard the deep-throated roar of a beast, and he knew it was big.

The fear began to ring his belly once more, and he found himself muttering, "Why me?" over and over again, in a dull monotone that somehow helped him keep going. As he moved, the subtle phosphorescence of the blue-black muck swirled, coating his lower legs and boots with glowing tips, and each step left a moment's round-edged hole in the stuff. Which was quickly sucked closed.

It was as he was scrambling over a rotted stump, fallen across the open way, having set his blastick in the crotch of a bush on the other side, that the beast broke out of the clinging matted vines, and trumpeted its warning at him.

Tallant froze. One foot in the air, the other shoved into a niche in the stump, his hands holding his full weight. His eyes opened wide, and he saw the dark gray bulk of the animal all at once.

It was almost triangular. A smooth thorax rose to an almost idiotically tiny head, set at the apex of the triangle. The back was a long slope that tapered to the ground. Its eight legs were set under it, almost as a kickplate might be set under a bookcase.

Two tiny red eyes gleamed through the mist of the Blue Marshes, set above a square snout and a fanged mouth that slobbered ooze. The beast stood silent for a moment. Then muted coughs left its throat, and its imbecilic head rose an inch on the non-existent neck.

It sniffed the breeze, it sniffed the mist, it sniffed the spoor of Benno Tallant. It took one step, two, faltering, as though trying to decide whether advance was recommended. Tallant stared at the animal, unable to move from its path, a cold wash of complete terror hinging him to the stump as if it were the one solid form in the universe.

The beast trumpeted again, and lumbered forward.

Its scream struck out into the night, and the blast of fire that ripped at its gray hide came from nowhere. The beast rose on its back sets of legs, pawing at the sky. Another *scheeee* of power and the flames bit at the animal's tiny head.

For an instant the thing was wrapped in flame and smoke, then it exploded outward. Blood spilled through the leaves and vines, covering

Tallant with warm, sticky liquid. Bits of flesh cascaded down, and he felt one slippery bit go sliding down his cheek.

His stomach twisted painfully in him, but the explosion unstuck him. He was not alone in the Marshes.

Since he was the last *man* on Deald's World, there was only one other answer.

Kyben? *Kyben!*

Then he heard their voices above the trembling sounds of the Marshes. They were around a bank of bushy trees, about to burst into the clearing where the scattered hulk of the beast lay, quivering, even in death.

Tallant felt a strange quivering in himself. He found a sudden inexplicable identification with the beast, lying out there in the open. That beast had been more man than he. It had died, in its brutishness, but it had not turned and run away. He knew the animal had no mind, and yet there was something. . .*something*. . .in the beast's death that made him feel altered, changed, matured. He could never tell what it had been, but when the animal had died, he knew he would never give up to the Kyben. He was still terribly frightened—the habits of a lifetime could not change in a moment—but there was a difference now. If he was going to die, he was going to make sure he died on his feet—not in the back as he ran away.

The Kyben came into view. They moved out from his left, almost close enough for him to touch them. They moved across the clearing, and he knew they had not seen him. But they had mechanisms that could trace the bomb's emissions, and in a few moments they would get his track. He had to do something—and quickly.

The five Kyben moved to the dead animal, obviously too engrossed in examining their kill to study their detectors. Tallant reached for the blastick in the crotch of the tree.

He slipped on the stump, and his hand collided with the metal of the weapon. It clattered free from the tree, and fell with a splash into the mud.

One of the Kyben whirled, saw Tallant, and screamed something softly deadly to his companions, bringing his own instrument up. A blast of blue power streaked through the space between them, and Tallant hesitated only an instant. It was almost an instant too long. The blast-beam seared across his back, barely touching him, ripping wide his jumper's covering, scorching his flesh.

He screamed in agony, and dove headfirst into the muck himself, both trying to extinguish the fires of hell that arched on his back, and trying to find the weapon that had disappeared into the mire.

He fell solidly into the stuff, and felt it closing over his head. It was a pool of mud deeper than he had thought.

The stuff clogged his throat, and he struck out blindly. His hands broke to the top, and he suddenly realized this might be his only way out.

He tried to reach bottom, found it with his flailing feet, and dragged himself across the pool, gagging with each step. He felt the land rising under him, and stuck his head out momentarily.

The Kyben were still in front of him, but they were turned away slightly, thinking he was still in the same position, that perhaps he had drowned.

He knew immediately that he had to kill them all, and before they could call in to their superiors, or the game was up. The moment the Kyban Command knew there was a human left on the planet, they would realize where the bomb was hidden. Then any chance he had of surviving was gone.

He saw one of the Kyben—a tallish one with golden hair clipped into an extremely exaggerated flattop—turning toward him, his blastick at the ready. Then the adrenaline pumped through Tallant's veins, and he saw the beast, and for the first time in his life—knowing the dream-dust had worn off, but not really caring—he moved with aggression. He started running.

Lifting his feet high, he pounded around the rim of the pool, spraying blue mud and slime in every direction. The suddenness of the movement surprised the Kyban, and he failed to bring the blastick into play.

In a moment, Tallant was on him, the drive of his rushing advance bowling the Kyban over. Tallant's foot came down with a snap, and he felt the alien's neck snap under the pressure of his boot.

Then he had the blastick in his arms, fumbling for the fire stud, and raw power was blueing out, in a wide arc, catching the remaining four members of the patrol.

Their screams were short, and their bodies spattered the Marshes for fifty feet. Tallant stared down at the raw, pulsing husks that had been aliens a minute before, and leaned against a tree.

God, God, God. . .he murmured over and over in his mind's desertland, and felt the nausea rising again. He thought of the dust for a moment. Of the packets in his sealed jumper pocket, but felt no need for it now.

Somehow, the fire was up in him.

The killer instinct was rising in the coward.

Tallant struck out again, a fresh weapon in his hands.

By now the Earthmen were far away in their ships, and the Kyben still feared the bomb would trigger if they tried to take off; Tallant *knew* they had not tried to leave Deald's World by one fact only:

The bomb in his middle had not exploded yet.

But time was dripping away.

VI

That night, Tallant killed his twentieth and thirtieth Kyben.

The second set of five went as he left the Blue Marshes. Ambushed from behind a huge, snout-like rock, they went down bubbling.

Single reconnaissance men died by knife and by club at Tallant's hands as he made his way through the fields of swaying, unharvested Summerset that lay on the outskirts of Xville. They walked slowly through the fields, another five-man team, just their shoulders and heads showing above the tall burnished stalks of grain. Occasionally Tallant, from where he crouched below sight-level in the field, saw the snout of a blastick poke up from the Summerset. It was hardly difficult at all to drag each one down in his turn as the alien passed nearby.

The first one's skull shattered like a plastic carton, as Benno Tallant swung the end of the blastick viciously. Even as the Kyban sank down nearly atop him, the looter felt a rugged thrill course down his veins; there was a pleasure he had never known in this sort of guerrilla warfare. From the first team-member he had taken the long, scythe-shaped knife with its inlaid tile handle.

It had worked wondrously well on the other four.

Kyban blood was yellow. He wasn't surprised.

By the time dawn slid glowingly up on the horizon, Tallant knew the Kyben were aware of his presence. What it meant, who he was, what he was doing on Deald's World. . .none of those answerables might have occurred to them as clearly as he phrased them, but thirty Kyben had by that time died before the blue power of his blastick or the curve of his knife. And eventually they would be found where they had fallen; they would be reported missing; they would not check in.

Then the Kyban Command would know they were not alone on the planet.

All through the night he had heard robot patrol scouts circling overhead, trying to track down the neutrino emission of the bomb, and several times two or three had homed in on him. But at two miles radius they merely circled, waiting to pinpoint by ground search. But before the troops could close in, he had made good his escape, and they circled helplessly, awaiting new instructions.

It seemed about the time for them to realize the bomb was in a moving carrier. What that carrier was, and the reason thirty troops were dead, would soon show themselves to be the same: a man alive on the planet.

The robot patrol scouts circled and buzzed overhead, and for a moment Tallant wondered how *they* had gotten aloft when a ship could not. Then he answered his question with the logical reason. The robots were just that—robots. Operating from mechanical means. The ships were inverspace ships, operating from warp-mechanisms. And it was obviously the warp pattern that set the bomb off.

So he could be easily tracked, but the Kyben could not leave, to chase and destroy the Earthies.

Tallant's fist balled and his dirt-streaked face twisted in a new kind of hatred as he thought of the men who had left him here to die. Parkhurst and Shep and Doc Budder and the rest. They who had left him here to this!

He was fooling them. He was staying alive!

But wasn't that what they had wanted? Hadn't they chosen properly? Wasn't he running to stay alive, allowing them to escape to warn Earth? What did he care for Earth? What had it ever given him?

He swore then, in a voiceless certainty deeper than mere frustration and anger, that he would do more than survive. He would come out of this ahead. He wasn't sure *how*. . .but he would.

As the light of morning reached him through the jagged opening in the front of the building, where he lay on the floor, he vowed he would not die here on this—someone else's—battlefield.

He rose to his feet, and looked out through the blasted plasteel face of the building. The capital city of Deald's World stretched below him, and to the right.

In the center, towering higher than any building, was the command ship of the Kyban fleet.

Somehow, in the darkness, with the newly-acquired stealth of a Marsh animal, he had passed the outgoing Kyban troop lines, and was behind their front. He was inside the circle. Now he had to take advantage of that.

He sat down for a moment to think of his only way out.

Before the looting Kyban soldier stepped into the room, he had arrived at the solution. He had to get to that Kyban ship, and get inside. He had to find a Kyban surgeon. It might be death, but it was a *might*; any other way it was a certainty.

He stood up to go, to skulk through the alleys of Xville to the ship, when the double-chinned, muscled Kyban came up the partially-ruined stairs, and stopped cold in the entrance of the room, amazement mirrored on his puttied features. An Earthie. . .here on conquered ground!

He dragged his blastick from its sheath, aimed it, and fired dead range at Tallant's stomach.

The shaft of blue light caught Tallant as he rocketed sideways. It seared at his flesh, and he felt an all-consuming wave of pain rip down through him. He had side-stepped partially, and the blast had taken him high on the right arm. He was horribly convulsed by agony for an instant, then. . .

He could not feel his right arm.

Tallant was moving through a fog of pain, and in a moment, before the Kyban could fire again, had grabbed the blastick with his left hand. The little man felt a strange power coursing through him, and he dimly recognized it as the power of hatred; the hatred of all other men, all other beings, that had displaced his cowardice.

He ripped at the blastick violently, and the alien was yanked toward him, thrown off-balance.

As the bewildered Kyban stumbled past, losing his hold on his own weapon, Tallant brought up a foot, and sent it slamming into the alien's back.

The yellow outworlder staggered forward, arms thrown out wildly, tripped over the rubble clogging the floor, and pitched headfirst through the rift in the wall.

Tallant limped to the hole and watched him fall, screaming.

"Aaaaaaaaaaaaaaaarghhhhh!" and the sound of it whistled back up through the city's canyon, till it vanished with an audible thud thirty floors below. That scream, held and piercing, was more than a death knell. It was a signal. The area was a great sounding-board, and every foot of that screaming descent had been recorded on the walls and in the stones of the city.

The Kyben would be here shortly. Their comrade could not have directed them to their goal more effectively had he planned it.

Then Tallant realized something:

He had only one arm.

His eyes seemed to swing down without his willing them; he could feel no pain now; the blastick had cauterized the stump immediately. There would be no infection, there would be no more pain, but he was neatly amputated at the biceps. His eyes moved slightly and he gagged at the sight.

With one arm, what could he *hope* to accomplish?

How could he stay alive?

Then he heard the raised voices of the Kyben coming through the building; he knew they would investigate from where their comrade had fallen. He moved with wooden legs, feeling the fight draining out of him, but moving nonetheless.

Moving in a reflexive pattern of survival. . .recognizing his only chance was to get to that Kyban flagship towering in the center of Xville. He had arrived at the lone chance, the final chance available to him, after close inspection of all paths out of this situation. That chance was almost certainly death, but the *almost* was a shade no other chance held.

His legs carried him out of the room, down a back flight of stairs, endlessly, endlessly down and somewhere along the way—probably in the room itself, but he could not quite remember—he carried the blastick. Then there was a time, as he wound down the interminable stairs, when he did not have the blastick. And even later, as he saw the big number 14 on the wall by the door, he had it again. As the numbers decreased, as 10 melted to 5 to 3, he realized he had come thirty flights. . .entirely in shock.

When he was on the first floor, the front of the building was surrounded by Kyben, staring and motioning at the body of their comrade. Tallant looked away; he had thought himself inured to death, but the Kyban had died in a particularly unpleasant manner.

He shifted the blastick in the crook of his arm—the one arm left—and huddled back against the wall. There were three tortuous miles of ruined city and piled rubble between him and the flagship. (And once he was there, he had no assurance that the thing he sought would even be there!) Not to mention the entire land-army of the Kyban fleet, a horde of robot patrol scouts that must surely have realized the bomb was being carried by a man, and his own wounds.

He leaned the blastick against the wall, and felt gingerly at the stump of his arm. There was no pain, and the raw, torn end had been neatly, completely, like a bit of putty smoothed over, cauterized. He felt fine otherwise, though the night in the Blue Marshes had brought him a kink in the right leg, forcing him into an unconscious limp.

There was still a chance to make it.

At that moment he heard the public address system in the scout ship that circled the building. It boomed down, flooding the streets with sound, in English:

"EARTHMAN! WE KNOW YOU ARE HERE! GIVE YOURSELF UP BEFORE YOU DIE! EVEN IF YOU CONTROL THE BOMB, WE WILL FIND YOU AND KILL YOU. . .FIND YOU AND KILL YOU. . .FIND YOU AND KILL YOU. . ."

The robot scout ship moved off across the city, the same message broadcast over and over, till Tallant felt each word burning into his brain. *Find you and kill you, find you and kill you. . .*

His breath came in short gasps, and he stumbled back against the wall, feeling its stony coolness under his hands. He closed his eyes, and drank deeply of emptiness. The path of cowardice was a twisting one. He had found that out. But though it might occasionally cross the road of bravery, it always passed back to the other path.

Tallant was frightened. He reached for his dream-dust.

Time was growing short and Tallant could feel it in his gut.

He had no way of knowing whether the bomb was nearing triggering time, but there was a vague, prickling sensation throughout his body that he interpreted as danger. The bomb might go off at any second, and that would be the end of it. Benno Tallant tightened his single fist into a painful ball; his rodent-like face drew down into an expression of blind fury, and the lines about his closed eyes grew deeper as he screwed his eyes tighter. He squeezed them till he heard a muted roaring in his ears; then he swore to himself he would come out ahead in this situation! Somehow, although he knew no possible way it could come true, he was going to beat the lousy Earthies who had done this to him. He was going to get to that flagship. . .and when he did! He was going to win.

Not by cutting the corners the way a coward would. . .the way he had been doing it for years. . .but the way a winner does it, the way *he* was going to do it.

He hefted the blastick and turned to go.

The Kyben knew now that the bomb was in a human's hands. Not in a human's stomach—that they could *not* know—but in a human's hands. For their target had moved, shifted, eluded them all through the night. Obviously it was not buried or fastened down. Hidden in the best possible place. . .in a moving target. They were after him, and the net would be closing down. But there were a few things in his favor.

The most important of which was the fact that he had killed a number of patrolmen out in the fields, in the Marshes, and they would center their search in that area. They would not realize he had come through the sewer system into the capital city during the night.

He was safe for a while.

Even as Tallant thought that, as he moved toward the basement stairs of the ruined building, a Kyban officer, resplendent in sand-white uniform and gold braid, came through the door in front of him.

The alien was unarmed, but in an instant he had whipped out the dress knife, and was making passes in the air before Tallant's face. That same feeling of urgency, of strength from some unknown pool within him, boiled up in Tallant. The officer was too close for Tallant to use the long blastick, but he still had the arc-shaped knife from the night before. He dropped the blastick softly into a pile of ash and slag-dust, ducked as the Kyban blade whistled past his ear, and leaped for the officer, before the other's tentacled hand could whip back around.

With his one hand fingers-out, Tallant reached the Kyban, drove the thin fingers deep into the alien's eyes. The officer let out a piercing shriek as his eyeballs watered into pulp, and the prongs of Tallant's hand went into his head. Then, before the Kyban could open his mouth to shriek again, before he could do anything but wave his hands emptily in the air, feeling his eyes running down his cheeks, Benno Tallant drew his own scythe-shaped blade from his belt, and slashed the alien's neck with one sidearm swipe.

The officer fell in a golden-blooded heap, and Tallant grabbed up his blastick, charging through the hall of the building, reaching the door that led to the basement, slamming it behind him, and plunging into the darkness of the building's depths.

Overhead he could hear the yells of Kyban foot-soldiers discovering their officer, but he didn't wait to have them discover him. Keeping careful track of which direction he faced, he felt around the floor of the basement till he contacted the sealplug that led to the sewers. He had come up through that polluted dankness the night before, seeking momentary rest, and fresh air.

He had climbed to the top of the building to see how the enemy was displaced, and fallen asleep—against his will. Now he was back to the sewers, and the sewers would carry him to the one lone chance for life he could imagine.

He ran his suddenly strong fingers around the edge of the sealing strip, and pried up the heavy lid with one hand.

He grimaced in the darkness. He *had* to pry it up with one hand. . .that was all they had left him.

Another moment and the port sighed up, counter-balanced, and Tallant slid himself over the lip, the blastick stuck through his belt. He kept himself wedged against the side of the hole, a few feet above the darkly swirling water of the sewer, and grabbed for the lid. The sealplug sighed down, and Tallant let himself drop.

The knife slid from his belt, fell into the water and was gone in an instant. He hit the tunnel wall as he fell, and came down heavily on one leg, tightening it, sending a pain shooting up through his left side.

He regained his footing by clawing at the slimy walls of the tunnel, and braced himself, legs spread wide apart against the dragging tide of the sewer water.

He kept pulling himself along the wall till he found a side-tunnel that headed in the proper direction. Just as he turned the corner, he saw the sealplug open, far back down the tunnel's length, and a searchbeam flooded the water with a round disc of light. They had suspected his means of escape already.

"Sssisss sss sss kliss-isss!" He heard the sibilance of the Kyban speech being dragged down the hollowness of the tunnel to him. They were coming down into the sewers after him.

He had to hurry. The net was tightening. He knew he had a good chance of getting away, even though they had light and he had none.

They would have to try *all* the tunnels, but he would not; he would keep going in one direction, inexorably.

The direction that led to the gigantic Kyban flagship.

VII

It was a short run from the sewer plug that exited by the service entrance of what had been a department store. A short run, and he was hidden by the shadow of the monstrous spaceship fin. A guard stood by the ramp; guards stood at each ramp; Tallant circled.

He found a loading ramp, and the guard slumped against the shining skin of the deep-space ship. Tallant took a step toward the alien, realized he'd never make it in time.

The same strange urge to strike rose up in Benno Tallant, showing him a way he would not have considered the day before. He could not use the blastick—too noisy; he had lost the scythe-knife; he was too far away to throw a boot and hope it would stun the guard.

So he walked out, facing the guard, coughing.

Carefully, nonchalantly, as though he had every right to be there. And as the guard heard the coughing, looked up, and amazedly watched Tallant stalking toward him. . .Benno Tallant waved a greeting, and began to whistle.

The guard watched for a second.

The second was long enough.

Tallant had his hand around the alien's neck before the guard could raise an alarm. One leg behind the Kyban's, and he was atop the guard. The butt of the blastick shattered the flat-featured face, and the way was clear.

Tallant crouched as he walked up the ramp. Late morning light filtered across his back, and he held the cumbersome blastick with one hand on the trigger-stock, the weapon shoved under his armpit. He sprinted quickly up the ramp, slid his hand down the stock to the handle. The inside of the ship was cool and moist and dark.

Kyba was a cooler planet, and a moister planet, and a darker planet.

But all three congealed into a feeling of dank oppression that made Tallant wonder bleakly whether it was worth it; whether life was so important suddenly, that he should keep on moving, and not just lie down.

He saw what must have been a freight shaft, and stepped into it. There was no drag, and he pressed a button on the inner wall of the hollow tube. The suck was immediately generated, drawing him up through the ship.

He let himself slow by scraping his heels against the inner wall, at each layer of the ship, seeking the one escape factor he hoped was on board.

He saw no one. The ship's complement had been cut to the dregs, obviously. Every able-bodied Kyban sent planetside to search for the bomb.

Here was the bomb. . .walking through the mother ship.

Tallant began to sweat as he rose in the shaft; if he had figured incorrectly, if what he thought was aboard, was *not* aboard, he was doomed. He was. . .he saw what he wanted!

The Kyban was walking down a hall, directly in Tallant's line of sight as he peered from the freight tube. He wore a long white smock, and though Tallant had no way of knowing for certain, he was sure the apparatus hanging about the alien's neck was the equivalent of an electrostethoscope.

This Kyban was a doctor.

Tallant propelled himself from the shaft, landed on the plasteel deck of the ship with legs spread, the blastick wedged between body and armpit, his hand tight to the trigger-stock.

The Kyban doctor stopped dead, staring at this man who had come from nowhere. The alien's eyes roved up and down Tallant's body, stopping for a long moment at the stump of the right arm.

Tallant moved toward the doctor, and the Kyban backed up warily.

"English," Tallant asked roughly. "You speak English?"

The doctor stared silently at Tallant, and the Earthman squeezed a bit harder on the trigger-stock, till his knuckles went white with the strain of not firing.

The Kyban doctor nodded simply.

"There's got to be an operating room around here," Tallant went on, commandingly. "Take me there. Now!"

The doctor watched the man silently, till Tallant began to advance. Then he suddenly realized—Tallant could see the dawning realization in alien eyes—that this desperate creature must *need* him for something, and would not—under *any* circumstances—shoot. Tallant saw the realization on the alien's flat-featured face, and an instant reciprocal fury possessed him.

He backed the alien to the wall, and gripped the blastick farther down its length. Then he swung it, hard!

The muzzle cracked across the Kyban's shoulder, and he let out a muted moan. Tallant hit him again, in the stomach; a third time across the face, opening a gash that ran to the temple. Had the Kyban not been nearly bald, his hair would have been matted with blood.

The alien sank back against the wall, began to slide down. Tallant kicked him just below the double-jointed knee, straightening the doctor up.

"You'll stay alive, Doc. . .but don't try your stamina against mine. I've been up all night, running from your foot-soldiers. And right along now I'm getting pretty edgy. So you just walk ahead of me, and we'll see that operating room of yours."

The golden-skinned outworlder hesitated a fraction of a second, and Tallant brought his knee up with a snap. The medic screamed, then. High and piercing. Tallant knew the sound would carry through the ship, so he kicked out at the alien, driving him before the blastick.

"Now you get this straight, fella," Tallant snarled. "You're going to walk ahead of me, right straight to that operating room, and you're going to do a little surgery on me. . .and one move, so help me God, *one move* that seems unlikely, and I take off the top of your yellow skull. Now *move it*!"

He jabbed the blastick hard into the Kyban's back, and the medic tottered off down the hall.

They were passing a utility rack—loaded with leg chains and head braces and manacles, used by the Kyben to keep prisoners in tow—when the Kyban sergeant struck. He had heard the scream, come out of the wardroom, and positioned himself in the alcove behind the utility rack, waiting for Tallant and the doctor to come his way. The attack was too hurried, however; and as the sergeant lunged for Tallant, and wrenched the blastick from his hand to ensure the medic's safety, Tallant whirled away, and smashed the glass of the utility rack.

In a moment his reflexes had taken over, and he bore no slightest resemblance to the quivering Benno Tallant who had cried to Parkhurst for his life. Now he was an avenging devil. His hand closed about a long, heavy-link leg chain, and brought it whistling free from its pincers and through the air with a snap.

The chain caught the Kyban sergeant along the base of the skull, and the outworlder choked out a sibilant nothing as his brain was smashed in its case.

He fell frontwards, crashing against the medic who had been reaching for the dropped blastick, and they tumbled to the plasteel floor together.

The chain was imbedded in the Kyban's head.

Tallant took a short step and brought his booted foot down with a crunch on the medic's hand. Hard enough to discourage the alien's reaching. . .but not hard enough to impair his surgical ability.

Tallant spotted a service revolver halfway drawn from its snugger on the Kyban sergeant's belt, and he drew the sleek little sliver-nosed pistol, pointing it at the medic.

"This is better.

"Let's go."

The medic got to his feet with difficulty, groaning as he rose. He knew now that Tallant was more dangerous than an entire army. The

Earthman was desperate, really desperate, and he knew why: this must be the one who had the bomb. The Commandant had been talking about this man the night before, when they had realized a man was still alive on Deald's World.

He had taken a great deal of punishment, and he knew the Earthie would continue to deal it out; not enough to kill him, but the pain would be very great.

The Kyban doctor was no hero.

The operating room was inevitable.

"And take your comrade with you," Tallant added.

The medic grabbed up the sergeant's feet and dragged him behind as he walked toward the operating room. The trail of blood was faintly golden against the plasteel floor plates. Tallant kicked the blastick into the alcove. They might not come down through this corridor too soon, still looking as they were for him, outside the city.

The operating room was inevitable.

Tallant refused to take even a local anesthetic. He sat propped up on the operating table, the silver-shaft revolver pointed directly at the medic. The Kyban stared at the cylinder of the gun, saw the little capsules in their chambers, thought of how they were fired through the altering mechanism, how they came out as raw energy, and he wielded the electroscalpel with care.

Tallant's face became beaded with sweat as the incisions were made; though he hardly felt the electric beam cut through the flesh.

But as the layers of flesh that had been the scar peeled back, and he again saw his innards, wet and pulsing, he remembered the first time.

Things had changed, *he* had changed since Doc Budder had put the bomb in his belly. Now he was nearing the end of the path. . .starting a new one.

In twenty minutes it was over.

Tallant had guessed correctly.

The bomb could *not* be set off under cautious operating conditions. Parkhurst had made great mention of the inverspace drive's warp field setting it off, and of the bomb detonating of its own accord when the time came. But when it had come to mention of the Kyben removing it, he had threatened Tallant only with being cut to ribbons. Perhaps it had been Parkhurst's subconscious way of offering Tallant a chance; perhaps it had just been an oversight in the Resistance leader's explanation. . .but in either case, the operation had been completed successfully, and the bomb was out.

Tallant watched carefully as the Kyban put an alien version of an epidermizer on the wound. He watched steadily for a half-hour as the scar built up.

Then he was whole again, and the danger had been extracted from his belly.

He stared at the medic carefully, said in level tones:

"Graft the bomb to my stump."

The medic's dark eyes opened wider; he blinked rapidly, and Tallant repeated what he had said. The medic backed away, knowing what purpose Tallant had in mind—or *thinking* he knew, which was the same thing as far as Tallant was concerned.

It took ten minutes of pistol-whipping for Tallant to realize the medic would go only so far, and no farther. The physician would *not* graft the total destruction sun-bomb to the stump of Tallant's right arm.

. . .at least. . .not under his own will.

The idea dawned slowly, but when formed was clear and whole and practicable. Tallant reached into his jumper pocket, extracted one of the last two packets of dream-dust. He bent down, and under pressure, made the half-conscious Kyban sniff it. He got the entire packet, the full, demolishing dose into the alien's nostrils. Then he settled back to wait, remembering the first time he had met the dream-dust.

The memory flooded back, and he recalled that the first, imprudent whiffing had made him a confirmed addict; it was powerful that way.

When the medic awoke, he would be an addict. . .would do *anything* for that last packet nestling in Tallant's jumper pocket.

The Earthman knew he would never again be God—or at least till he could locate more dust—but it was worth it, for what he had in mind. *More* than worth it.

He waited, knowing they would not be disturbed. The Kyben were out looking for him, and the emissions of the ship around him would confuse the robot scouts; he was safe for the time being. And when the medic awoke, he would do *anything* Tallant wanted.

Tallant wanted only one thing.

The sun-bomb grafted to his arm, where he could detonate it in an instant.

There had been no pain. The same force that had ripped Tallant's arm to atoms, had deadened the nerve ends. The bomb was set into the flesh slightly, a block at the end of the stump. With a simple wire hookup that would detonate under several circumstances:

If Tallant consciously triggered the bomb.

If anyone tried to remove the bomb against his will.

If he died, and his heart stopped.

The Kyban doctor had done his work well. Now he huddled, shaking under the effects of total dust addiction, moaning, begging Tallant for the last packet.

"Sure, mister, you can have the snuff." He held the clear plastic packet between two fingers, so the Kyban could see both the revolver and the dust at once. "But first, first. First you take me updecks to meet your Commandant."

The Kyban's eyes were golden slits, but they widened now as he tried to comprehend what the Earthie meant. He had thought he knew what the man was after. . .to get rid of the bomb and leave Deald's World. But now. . .

He was confused, terrified. What was this insatiable hunger that clawed at him, and made his every nerve a burning wire? The Earthman had done it to him, and somehow, he knew that little white packet held the end of his hunger.

He hardly realized he had led the Earthman to the bridge, but when he looked again, they were there, and the Commandant was staring wide-eyed at them, demanding an explanation. Needing none, really.

Then, as the doctor watched, Tallant raised the revolver and fired. The shot took away half the Commandant's face, and he spun sidewise, spraying himself across the port. The body tumbled to the floor and rolled a few inches, to the edge of the dropshaft. Tallant walked past the doctor, and calmly nudged the body over with his boot. The body hung there a split instant, then dropped out of sight as quickly as a stone down a well.

There was only one more step to take.

Tallant walked over to the doctor, examining him carefully as he came nearer. The man was a typical Kyban. . .a bit shorter than most, with a protruding stomach, and a head that would be quite bald in a few years.

His skin was the aging off-gold of the Kyban race, and his face was strong. Strong, that is—Tallant noted—with the exception of the infinitesimal tic in the cheek and lower lip, the hunger lines about the mouth and eyes. The good doctor was now an addict, and that suited Tallant just fine.

He found a weird pleasure in having bent this man so simply to his design. He found the events of the past day invigorating, now that they were over.

And as the face of the doctor grew larger in his eyes, Benno Tallant took stock of himself. The bad in him—and he was the first to admit it was there, festering deeper than any superficial nastiness—had not changed one bit. It had not become good, it had not tempered him into mellow thoughts through his trials, it had left him only harder. It had matured itself.

For years, as he skulked and begged, as he weaseled and cheated, his strength of amorality had been going through an adolescence. Now it was mature. Now he had direction, and he had purpose. Now he was no longer a coward, for he had faced all the death the world could throw at him, and had bested it. He had outsmarted the Earthmen, he had outmaneuvered the Kyben. He had bested the foot-soldiers in the field, and the mathematicians in the bunkers. He had lived through the bomb, and the attack of the aliens, and the night of terror and all it held otherwise. He had come through the Marshes, and the fields, and the city, to this final place.

To this cabin of the fleet ship.

But he was not the Benno Tallant the Earthmen had found the day before, looting a dead shopkeeper. He was another man entirely. A man whose life had taken the one possible turn it could. . .for the other turn—*death*—was a stranger to him.

Benno Tallant shoved the doctor ahead of him, to the banks of controls.

He paused, turning the shaking addict to him. He stared into the golden slits, and the golden face, and realized with consummate pleasure that he did not hate these aliens who had tried to find him and cut out his belly; he admired them, for they were engaged in taking what they wanted.

No, he didn't hate *them*.

"What is your name, my good old friend?" he asked cheerily.

The doctor's hand, tentacle-ended, came up quivering, to beg for the last packet. Tallant slapped the hand away; he did not hate the outworlders, but he had no room for sympathy. All of that decency and compassion was gone—burned away by the blast of hell in the bombed-out building, eaten away by the cruelty of his fellow Earthmen. He was hard now, and reveled in it.

"Your name!"

The doctor's tongue quivered over the word: "Norghese."

"Well, Doctor Norghese, you and I are going to be ever such good friends, you know that? You and I are going to do big things together, aren't we?"

In the quivering, chill-raked body of the little doctor, Tallant knew he had a slave from this time on. He clapped the alien about the shoulders.

"Find me the communications rig in this mess, Doc."

The alien pointed it out, and on command, threw the switch that connected Tallant to the troops in the field, to the ships that were settled all across Deald's World, to the skeleton crew of the ship in which he stood.

He lifted the speak-stick, and stared at it for a moment. He had considered blowing up the fleet, ordering it to return home, a number of things.

But that had been the day before when he had been Tallant the Trembling.

This was today.

And he was a new Benno Tallant.

He spoke sharply and shortly.

"This is the last man on Deald's World, my Kyban friends. I'm the man your superiors have finally realized carried the sun-bomb.

"Hear me now!

"I still carry it. But now I control it. I can set it off at any moment, and kill us all. . .even in space. Believe that the power of this bomb is incalculable. If you doubt me, I will let you speak to Doctor Norghese of the mother ship, in a few moments, and he will verify what I've said.

"But you have no reason to fear me. . .or what I can do. I'm going to offer you a deal far superior to anything you had as mere Kyban soldiers on conquest missions for your home world.

"I offer you the chance to become conquerors in your own right. Now that you've been away from home for years, and are weary of battle, I'll offer you the chance to come home not just as tin heroes, but as warriors with money and worlds at your command.

"Does it matter to you who leads this fleet? As long as you conquer the galaxies? I don't think it does!"

He paused, knowing they would see it his way. They would have to see it that way. Planetary allegiance only went so far, and he could turn this home-hungry planetful of foot-soldiers into the greatest conquering force ever known.

"Our first destination is. . ." he paused, knowing he was hewing a destiny he could never escape, ". . .Earth!"

He handed the speak-stick to the doctor, shoved him once to indicate he wanted verification of what he had said, listened for a moment to make sure the doctor's sibilant monotone in English was appropriate.

Then he walked to the viewport, and stared out as the dusk fell again across the city of Xville, and the fields of slowly ripening Summerset, and beyond them the Marshes and the Faraway Mountains.

He watched it all. . .Deald's World. . .and made a vow that his revenge would be long and detailed.

Then something Parkhurst had said, oddly enough, leaped to mind as appropriate for this time and this place and his new life:

I don't hate you. But this has to be done. It has to be done, and you will have to do it. But I don't hate you.

He thought the thoughts, and knew they were true.

He didn't hate anyone now. He was above that; he was Benno Tallant, and now there was no need for the dust; he was cured.

He turned away from the port and looked about at the ship that would mold his destiny, knowing he was free of Deald's World, free of the dust. He needed neither now.

Now he was God on his own.

—*New York, 1958*

ARE YOU LISTENING?

There are several ways I wanted to start telling this. First, I was going to begin it:

I began to lose my existence on a Tuesday morning.

But then I thought about it and:

This is my horror story.

. . .seemed like a better way to begin. But after thinking it over (I've had a devil of a lot of time to think it over, believe you me), I realized both of those were pretty melodramatic, and if I wanted to instill trust and faith and all that from the outset, I had just better begin the way it happened, and tell it through to now, and then make my offer, and well, let you decide for yourself.

Are you listening?

Perhaps it all began with my genes. Or my chromosomes. Whichever or whatever combination made me a Casper Milquetoast prototype, that or those are to blame, I'm sure. I woke up a year ago on a Tuesday morning in March, and knew I was the same as I had been for hundreds of other mornings past. I was forty-seven years old, I was balding, my eyes were good—and the glasses I used only for reading. I slept in a separate room from my wife Alma, and I wore long underwear—chiefly because I've always picked up a chill quickly.

The only thing that might possibly be considered out-of-the-ordinary about me is that my name is Winsocki.

Albert Winsocki.

You know, like the song. . .

"Buckle down Winsocki, you can win Winsocki if you'll only buckle down. . ." Very early in life I was teased about that, but my mild nature kept me from taking offense, and instead of growing to loathe it, I adopted it as a sort of personal anthem. Whenever I find myself whistling something, it is usually that.

However—

I woke up that morning, and got dressed quickly. It was too cold to take a shower, so I just dabbed water on my wrists and face, and dressed quickly. As I started down the stairs, Zasu, my wife's Persian, swept past between my legs. Zasu is a pretty stable cat, and I had never been quite snubbed before, though the animal *had* taken to ignoring me with great skill. But this morning of which I speak, she just swarmed past, and not even a meowrll or a spit. It was unusual, but not remarkable.

But just an indication of what was to come.

I came into the living room, and saw that Alma had laid out my paper on the arm of the sofa, just as she had done for twenty-seven years. I picked it up in passing, and came into the dinette.

My orange juice was set out, and I could hear Alma in the kitchen beyond. She was muttering to herself as usual. That is one of my wife's unpleasant habits, I'm afraid. At heart she is a sweet, dear woman, but when she gets annoyed, she murmurs. Nothing obscene, for goodness sake, but just at the bare threshold of audibility, so that it niggles and naggles and bothers. She *knew* it bothered me, or perhaps she didn't, I'm not sure. I don't think Alma was aware that I really *had* any likes or dislikes of any real strength.

At any rate, there she was, muttering and murmuring, so I just called out, "I'm down, dear. Good morning." Then I turned to the paper, and the juice. Acidic.

The paper was full of the same sort of stuff, and what else could orange juice be but orange juice?

However, as the minutes passed, Alma's mutters did not pass away. In fact, they got louder, more angry, more annoyed. "Where *is* that man? He *knows* I despise waiting breakfast! Now look. . .the eggs are hard. Oh, where *is* he?"

This kept up for some time, though I repeatedly yelled in to her, "Alma, *please* stop, I'm here. I'm down, can't you understand?"

Finally, she came storming past, and went through into the living room. I could hear her at the foot of the stairs—hand on banister, one foot flat on the first step—yelling up to no one at all, "Albert! *Will* you come down? Are you in the bathroom again? Are you having trouble with your kidneys? Shall I come up?"

Well, that was too much, so I laid aside my napkin, and got up. I walked up behind her and said, just as politely as I could, "Alma. What is the matter with you, dear? I'm right here."

It made no impression.

She continued howling, and a few moments later stalked upstairs. I sat down on the steps, because I was sure Alma had lost her mind, or her hearing had gone, or something. After twenty-seven happily married years, my wife was dreadfully ill.

I didn't know what to do. I was totally at a loss. I decided it would be best to call Dr. Hairshaw. So I went over and dialed him, and his phone rang three times before he picked it up and said, "Hello?"

I always felt guilty calling him, no matter what time of the day it was—he had *such* an intimidating tone—but I felt even *more* self-conscious this time, because there was a decidedly muggy value to his voice. As though he had just gotten out of bed.

"Sorry to wake you at this hour, Doctor," I said quickly. "This is Albert Winso—"

He cut me off with, "Hello? Hello?"

I repeated, "Hello, Doctor? This is Al—"

"Hello there? Anyone there?"

I didn't know what to say. It was probably a bad connection, so I screamed as loud as I could. "Doctor, this is—"

"Oh, *hell!*" he yelled, and jammed down the receiver.

I stood there for a second with the handpiece gripped tightly, and I'm dreadfully afraid an expression of utter bewilderment came over my face. Had everyone gone deaf, today? I was about to re-dial, when Alma came down the stairs, talking out loud to herself.

"Now *where* on Earth can that man have gone? Don't tell me he got up and went out without any breakfast? Oh well, that's less work for me today."

And she went right smack past me, staring right *through* me, and into the kitchen. I plonked down the receiver and started after her. This was *too* much! During the past few years Alma had lessened her attentions to me, even at times seemed to ignore me; I would speak and she would not hear, I would touch her and she would not respond. There had been increasingly more of these occasions, but this was too much!

I went into the kitchen and walked up behind her. She did not turn, just continued scouring the eggs out of the pan with steel wool. I screamed her name. She did not turn, did not even break the chain of humming.

I grabbed the pan from her hands and banged it as hard as I could on the stove-top (something remarkably violent for me, but I'm sure you can understand that this was a remarkable situation). She did not even start at the noise. She went over to the icebox and took out the cube trays. She began to defrost the box.

That was the last straw. I slammed the pan to the floor and stalked out of the room. I was on the verge of swearing, I was so mad. What kind of game *was* this? All right, so she didn't want to make my breakfast; so that was just one more little ignoring factor I had to put up with. All right, so why didn't she just *say so*. But this folderol was too much!

I put on my hat and coat and left the house—slamming the door as hard as I could.

I glanced at my pocket-watch, and saw the time had long since passed for me to catch my bus to the office. I decided to take a taxi, though I wasn't quite sure my budget could afford the added strain. But it was a necessity, so I walked past the bus stop, and hailed a cab as it went past. Went past is correct. It zipped by me without even slowing. I had seen it was empty, so why didn't the cabbie stop? Had he been going off duty? I supposed that was it, but after eight others had whizzed by, I was certain something was wrong.

But I could not discern what the trouble might be. I decided, since I saw it coming, to take the bus anyhow. A young girl in a tight skirt and funny little hat was now waiting at the stop, and I looked at her rather sheepishly, saying, "I just can't figure out these cabmen, can you?"

She ignored me. I mean, she didn't turn away as she would to some masher, nor did she give me a cursory glance and not reply. I mean, she didn't know I was there.

I didn't have any more time to think about it, because the bus stopped, and the girl got on. I started up the steps, and barely made it for the bus driver slammed the doors with a wheeze, catching the tail of my coat.

"Hey! I'm caught!" I yelled, but he paid no attention. He watched in his rear view mirror as the girl swayingly strode to a seat, and he started to whistle. The bus was crowded, and I didn't want to make a fool of myself, so I reached out and pulled his pants leg. Still, he didn't respond.

That was when the idea started to form.

I yanked my coattail loose, and I was so mad I decided to make him *ask* for his fare. I walked back, expecting any moment to hear him say, "Hey, you. Mister. You forgot to pay your fare." Then I was going to respond, "I'll pay my fare, but I'll report you to your company, too!"

But even that tiny bit of satisfaction was denied me, because he continued to drive, and his head did not turn. I think that made me angrier than if he had insulted me; what the hell was going on? Oh, excuse me, but that was what I was thinking, and I hope you'll pardon the profanity, but I want to get this across just as it happened.

Are you listening?

Though I shoved between an apoplectic man in a Tyrolean hat and a gaggle of high school girls, when disembarking, though I nudged and elbowed and shoved them, just desperately *fighting* to be recognized, no one paid me the slightest heed. I even—I'm so ashamed now that I think of it—I slapped one of the girls on her, uh, her behind, so to speak. But she went right on talking about some fellow who was far out of it, or something like that.

It was most frustrating, you can imagine.

The elevator operator in my office building was asleep—well, not *quite*, but Wolfgang (that's his name, and he's not even German, isn't that annoying?) always *looked* as though he was sleeping—in his cage. I prodded him, and capered about him, and as a final resort cuffed him on the ear but he continued to lie there against the wall, with his eyes shut, perched on his little pull-down seat. Finally, in annoyance, I took the elevator up myself, after booting him out onto the lobby tiles. By then I had realized, of course, that whatever strange malady had befallen me, I was to all intents and purposes, invisible. It seemed impossible that even if I were invisible, that people should not notice their backsides being slapped, or their bodies being kicked onto the tiles, or their elevators stolen, but apparently such was precisely the case.

I was so confused by then—but oddly enough, not in the slightest terrified—I was half belligerent, and half pixilated with my own limitless abilities. Visions of movie stars and great wealth danced before my eyes.

And disappeared as rapidly.

What good were women or wealth if there was no one to share it with you? Even the women. So the thoughts of being the greatest bank robber in history passed from me, and I resigned myself to getting out—if out was the proper term—getting out of this predicament.

I left the elevator on the twenty-sixth floor, and walked down the hall to the office door. It read the same as it had read for twenty-seven years:

Rames & Klaus
Diamond Appraisers
JEWELRY EXPERTS

I shoved open the door, and for a second my heart leaped in my throat that perhaps till now it had all been a colossal hoax. For Fritz Klaus—big, red-faced Fritz with the small mole beside his mouth—was screaming at me.

"Winsocki! You dolt! How many times have I told you when they go back in the pinch-bags, pull tight the cords! A hundred thousand dollars on the floor for the scrubwoman! Winsocki! You imbecile!"

But he was not screaming at me. He was screaming, that was all. But really, it was no surprise. Klaus and George Rames never actually talked to me. . .or even bothered to shout at me. They knew I did my job—had, in fact, been doing it for twenty-seven years—with method and attentiveness, and so they took me for granted. The shouting was all part of the office.

Klaus just had to scream. But he was directing his screams at the air, not at me. After all, how *could* he be screaming at me? I wasn't even there.

He went down on his knees, and began picking up the little uncut rough diamonds he had spilled, and when he had them all, he went down farther on his stomach, so his vest was dirtied by the floor, and looked under my bench.

When he was satisfied, he got up and brushed himself off. . .and walked away. As far as he knew, I was working. Or in his view of the world, was I just eliminated? It was a puzzler, but no matter. . .I was not there. I was gone.

I turned around and went back down the hall.

The elevator was gone.

I had to wait a long time till I could get to the lobby.

No cars would stop for my ring.

I had to wait till someone else on that floor wanted down.

That was when the real horror of it all hit me.

How strange. . .

I had been quiet all my life. I had married quietly and lived quietly and now, I had not even the one single pleasure of dying with a bang. Even that had been taken from me. I had just sort of snuffed out like a candle. How or why or when was no matter. I had been robbed of that one noise I had thought was mine, inevitable as taxes. But even that had been deprived me. I was a shadow. . .a ghost in a real world. And for the first time in my life, all the bottled-up frustrations I had never known were banked inside me, burst forth. I was shocked through and down with horror, but instead of crying, I did not cry.

I hit someone. I hit him as hard as I could. In the elevator there. I hit him full in the face, and I felt his nose skew over, and blood ran darkly on his face, and my knuckles hurt, and I hit him again, so my hand would slide in the blood, because I was Albert Winsocki and they had taken away my dying. They had made me quieter still. I had never bothered anyone, and I was hardly noticed, and when I would finally have had someone mourn for me, and notice me, and think about me as myself alone. . .I had been robbed!

I hit him a third time, and his nose broke.

He never noticed.

He left the elevator, covered with blood, and never even flinched.

Then I cried.

For a long time. The elevator kept going up and down with me in it, and no one heard me crying.

Finally, I got out and walked the streets till it was dark.

Two weeks can be a short time.

If you are in love. If you are wealthy and seek adventure. If you have no cares and only pleasures. If you are healthy and the world is fine and alive and beckoning. Two weeks can be a short time.

Two weeks.

Those next two weeks were the longest in my life. For they were hell. Alone. Completely, agonizingly alone, in the midst of crowds. In the neoned heart of town I stood in the center of the street and shrieked at the passing throngs. I was nearly run down.

Two weeks of wandering, sleeping where I wanted to sleep—park benches, the honeymoon suite at the Waldorf, my own bed at home—and eating where I wanted to eat—I took what I wanted; it wasn't stealing, precisely; if I hadn't eaten, I would have starved—yet it was all emptiness.

I went home several times, but Alma was carrying on just nicely without me. Carrying on was the word. I would never have thought Alma could do it, particularly with the weight she had put on the past few years. . .but there he was.

George Rames. My boss. I corrected myself. . .my ex-boss.

So I felt no real duty to home and wife.

Alma had the house and she had Zasu. And, it appeared, she had George Rames. That fat oaf!

By the end of two weeks, I was a wreck. I was unshaved, and dirty, but who cared? Who could see me. . .or would have cared had they been able to!

My original belligerence had turned into a more concrete antagonism toward everyone. Unsuspecting people in the streets were pummeled by me as I passed, should the inclination strike me. I kicked women and slapped children. . .I was indifferent to the moans and cries of those I struck. What was their pain compared to *my* pain—especially when none of them cried. It was all in my mind. I actually *craved* a scream or whine from one of them. For such an evidence of pain would have been a reminder that I was in their ken, that at least I existed.

But no such sound came.

Two weeks? Hell! Paradise Lost!

It was a little over two weeks from the day Zasu had snubbed me, and I had more or less made my home in the lobby of the St. Moritz-On-The-Park. I was lying there on a couch, with a hat I had borrowed from a passerby over my eyes, when that animal urge to strike out overcame me. I swung my legs down, and shoved the hat back on my head. I saw a man in a trenchcoat leaning against the cigar counter, reading a newspaper and chuckling to himself. That cruddy dog, I thought, what the hell is *he* laughing about?

It so infuriated me, I got up and lunged at him. He saw me coming and sidestepped. I, of course, expected him to go right on reading even when I swung on him, and his movement took me by surprise. I went into the cigar case and it caught me in the stomach, knocking the wind from me.

"Ah-ah, buddy," the man in the trenchcoat chastised me, waggling a lean finger in my face. "Now that isn't polite at all, is it? To hit a man who can't even see you."

He took me by the collar and the seat of my pants and threw me across the lobby. I went flailing through a rack of picture postcards, and landed on my stomach. I slid across the polished floor and brought up against the revolving door.

I didn't even feel the pain. I sat up, there on the floor, and looked at him. He stood there with his hands on his hips, laughing uproariously at me. I stared, and my mouth dropped open. I was speechless.

"Catching flies, buddy?"

I was so amazed, I left my mouth open.

"Y-you, you can *see* me!" I was whooping. "You can *see* me!"

He gave a rueful little snort, and turned away. "Of course I can." He started to walk away, then stopped and said, over his shoulder, "You don't think I'm one of *them*, do you?" He crooked his thumb at the people rushing about in the lobby.

It had never dawned on me.

I had thought I was alone in this thing.

But here was another, like me!

Not for a second did I consider the possibility that he could see me where the others could not, and still be a part of their world. It was apparent from the moment he threw me across the lobby that he was in the same predicament *I* was. But somehow, he seemed more at ease about it all. As though this were one great party, and he the host.

He started to walk away.

I scrambled to my feet as he was pressing the button for the elevator, wondering why he was doing that. The elevator couldn't stop for him if it was human-operated, as I'd seen it was.

"Uh, hey! Wait a minute there—"

The elevator came down, and an old man with baggy pants was running it. "I was on six, Mr. Jim. Heard it and come right down."

The old man smiled at the man in the trenchcoat—Jim it was—and Jim clapped him on the shoulder. "Thanks, Denny. I'd like to go up to my room."

I started after them, but Jim gave Denny a nudge, and inclined his head in my direction, with a disgusted expression on his face. "Up, Denny," he said.

The elevator doors started to close. I ran up.

"Hey! Wait a second. My name is Winsocki. Albert Winsocki, like the song. *You* know, buckle down Win—"

The doors closed almost on my nose.

I was frantic. The only other person (*persons*, I realized with a start) who could see me, and they were going away. . .I might search and never find them.

I was *so* frantic, in fact, I almost missed the easiest way to trace them. I looked up and the floor indicator arrow was going up, up, up to stop at the tenth floor. I waited till another elevator came down, with the ones who could not see me in it, and tossed out the operator. . .and took it up myself.

I had to search all through the corridors of the tenth floor till I heard his voice through a door, talking to the old man.

He was saying, "One of the newer ones, Denny. A boor, a completely obnoxious lower form of life."

And Denny replied, "Chee, Mr. Jim, I just like to sit an' hear ya talk. Wit' all them college words. I was real unhappy till you come along, ya know?"

"Yes, Denny, I know." It was a condescending tone of voice if ever I'd heard one.

I knew he'd never open the door, so I went looking for the maid from that floor. She had her ring of keys in her apron, and never even noticed me taking them. I started back for the room, and stopped.

I thought a moment, and ran back to the elevator. I went downstairs and climbed into the booth where the bills were paid, where all the cash was stored. I found what I was after in one of the till drawers. I shoved it into my coat pocket, and went back upstairs.

At the door I hesitated. Yes, I could still hear them babbling. I used the master key to get inside.

When I threw open the door, the man named Jim leaped from the bed and glared at me. "What are you doing in here? Get out at once, or I shall *throw* you out!"

He started toward me.

I pulled what I had gotten from the till drawer from my pocket, and pointed it at him. "Now just settle back, Mr. Jim, and there won't be any trouble."

He raised his hands very melodramatically, and shuffled backward till his knee-backs caught the edge of the bed and he sat down with a plop.

"Oh, take down your hands," I said. "You look like a bad western movie." His hands came down self-consciously.

Denny looked at me. "What's he doin', Mr. Jim?"

"I don't know, Denny; I don't know," Jim said slowly, with thought. His eyes were trained on the barrel of the snub-nosed revolver I held. His eyes were frightened.

I found myself shaking. I tried to hold the revolver steady, but it wavered in my hand as though I were inside the eye of a tornado. "I'm nervous, fellow," I said, partly to let him note it, as if he hadn't already, and half to reassure myself that I was master of the situation. "Don't make me any worse than I am right now."

He sat very still, his lowered hands folded in his lap.

"For two weeks now, I've been close to going insane. My wife couldn't see or hear or feel me. No one in the street could. No one for two weeks. It's like I'm dead. . .and today I found you two. You're the only ones like me! Now I want to know what this is all about. What's happened to me?"

Denny looked at Mr. Jim, and then at me.

"Hey is he cuckoo, Mr. Jim? You want I should slug him, Mr. Jim?"

The old man would never have made it.

Jim saw that much, to his credit.

"No, Denny. Sit where you are. The man wants some information. I think it's only fair I give it to him." He looked at me. His face was soft, like a sponge.

"My name is Thompson, Mr—ah—Mr. what-did-you-say-your-name-was?"

"I didn't, but it's Winsocki. Albert Winsocki. Like in the song. You remember the song, yeah?"

"Oh yes; Mr. Winsocki. Well." His poise and sneering manner were returning as he saw he at least had the edge on me in information. "The reason for your current state of non-noticeability—you aren't really insubstantial, you know—that gun could kill me. . .a truck could run us down and we'd be dead—the reason is very complex. I'm afraid I can't give you any scientific explanations, and I'm not even sure there are any. Let's put it this way. . ."

He crossed his legs, and I steadied the gun on him. He went on. "There are forces in the world today, Mr. Winsocki, that are invisibly working to make us all carbon copies of one another. Forces that crush us into molds of each other. You walk down the street and never see anyone's face, really. You sit faceless in a movie, or hidden from sight in a dreary living room watching television. When you pay bills, or car fares or talk to people, they see the job they're doing, but never you.

"With some of us, this is carried even farther. We are so unnoticeable about it—wallflowers, you might say—all through our lives, that when these forces that crush us into one mold work enough to get us where they want us, we just—poof!—disappear to all those around us. Do you understand?"

I stared at him.

I knew what he was talking about, of course. Who could fail to notice it in this great machined world we'd made for ourselves. So that was it. I had been made like everyone else, but had been so negative a personality to begin with, it had completely blanked me out to everyone. It was like a filter on a camera. Put a red filter on and everything red was there—but not there. That was the way with me. The cameras in everyone had been filtered against me. And Mr. Jim, and Denny, and—

"Are there more like us?"

Mr. Jim spread his hands. "Why, there are dozens, Winsocki. Dozens. Soon there will be hundreds, and then thousands. With things going the way they are. . .with people buying in supermarkets and eating in drive-ins and this new subliminal TV advertising. . .why, I'd say we could be expecting more company all the time.

"But not me," he added.

I looked at him, and then at Denny. Denny was blank, so I looked back at Thompson. "What do you mean?"

"Mr. Winsocki," he explained patiently, but condescendingly, "I was a college professor. Nothing really brilliant, mind you, in fact I suppose I was dullness personified to my students. But I knew my subject. Phoenician Art, it was. But my students came in and went out and never saw me. The faculty never had cause to reprimand me, and so after a while I started to fade out. Then I was gone, like you.

"I wandered around, as you must still be doing, but soon I realized what a fine life it was. No responsibility, no taxes, no struggling for existence. Just live the way I wish, and take what I want. I even have Denny here—he was a handyman no one paid attention to—as my friend and manservant. I like this life, Mr. Winsocki. That was why I was not too anxious to make your acquaintance. I dislike seeing the status quo upset."

I realized I was listening to a madman.

Mr. Jim Thompson had been a poor teacher, and had suffered my fate. But where I had been turned—as I now realized—from a Milquetoasted hum-drummer to a man cunning enough to find a revolver and adventurous enough to use it, he had been turned into a monomaniac.

This was his kingdom.

But there were others.

Finally, I saw there was no point talking to him. The forces that had cupped us and crushed us till we were so small the rest of the world could not see us, had done their work all too well on him. He was lost. He was satisfied with being unseen, unheard, unknown.

So was Denny. They were complacent. More than that. . .they were overjoyed. And during this past year I have found many like them. All the same. But I am not like that. I want out of here. I want you to see me again.

I'm trying desperately, the only way I know how.

It may sound stupid, but when people are daydreaming, or unfocused on life, so to speak, they may catch sight of me. I'm working on that. I keep whistling and humming. Have you ever heard me? The song is "Buckle Down Winsocki."

Have you ever caught sight of me, just out of the corner of your eye, and thought it was a trick of your imagination?

Have you ever thought you heard a radio or TV playing that song, and there was no radio or TV?

Please! I'm begging you! Listen for me. I'm right here, and I'm humming in your ear so you'll hear me and help me.

"Buckle Down Winsocki," that's the tune. Can you hear it?

Are you listening?

—New York, 1958

S.R.O.

Bart Chester was walking down Broadway when it materialized out of black nothing.

He was giving Eloise the line, with the, "No, honest to *God*, Eloise, I mean if you come over to my place, we'll have just *one*—s'help me, just *one*—then we'll be off to the show." He was acutely aware there might not be any show that night, chiefly because there was no money that night, but Eloise didn't know that. She was a sweet girl and Bart didn't want to spoil her with luxuries.

Bart was just figuring mentally how many it would take to get Eloise's mind off a show and onto more earthy matters, when the whine began.

Like a thousand generators spinning at top-point efficiency the sound crawled up the stone walls encasing Times Square; bouncing back and back, reverberating thunderously amid the noise of Broadway, causing heads to turn, eyes to lift.

Bart Chester turned his head, lifted his eyes, and was one of the first to see it shimmer into existence. The air seemed to pinken and waver, like heat lightning far off. Then the air ran like water. It may have been in the eyes, or actually in the air, but the air did run like water.

The sly gleam faded from Bart Chester's eyes, and he never did get that "little one" with Eloise. He turned away from her splendid charms, realizing, knowing, sensing that he had a place in what was coming.

Others must have felt the same way: traffic on the sidewalks was slowing, people turning to stare into the evening darkness.

The coming was rapid. The air quivered a bit more, and a form began to take shape, as a ghost emerging from mist. The shape was long, and cylindrical, protruberant and shining. It materialized over Times Square.

Bart took three rapid steps to the edge of the sidewalk, his eyes searching into the glare of neon, trying to see more of that weird structure. People jostled him and a knot began to form, as though he were a catalyst for some chemical action.

The thing (and Bart Chester had been in show business too long to jump at snap labels) hung there, suspended by hangings of nothing, as if waiting. It stretched up, out between the trench of buildings, towering a good ten feet over the tallest one. The structure—whatever it was—appeared to be over nine hundred feet high. It hung above the ground, over the traffic island dividing Broadway and Seventh Avenue, the flickering of a million lights coloring its smooth tube body.

Even as he watched, the seemingly unbroken skin of the structure parted and a flat plate emerged from a circular aperture. The plate was dotted with small holes, and in another instant a thousand metallic filaments pushed through the holes. Rigidly, they vibrated in the air.

Newspaper stories of the last few years, coupled with a natural childlike credulity, joined. *Migod,* thought Chester, and somehow knew his assumption was correct, *they're testing the atmosphere!* When he had said this to himself, the greater implication struck him: *it's a spaceship! That—that thing came from another planet! Another planet?*

It had been many months since the Emery Bros. Circus, in which Bart had sunk all his ready cash, had folded. It had been many months since Bart had paid his rent, and not many less since he'd had three full meals in one twenty-four-hour period. He was desperately looking for an angle. Any angle!

Then, with the blood of the innate entrepreneur coursing through him, beating fiercely, a running torrent of greed as hot as lava, he thought joyously: *Good God, what an attraction this would make!*

Concessions. Balloons saying "Souvenir of the Spaceship." Popcorn, peanuts, Cracker Jacks, binoculars, pennants! Food! Hot dogs, candied apples; what a pitch! What a perfect pitch!

If I can get to it first, he added, mentally clicking his fingers.

He hardly saw the wildly gesturing policeman using his call box. He hardly heard the mixed screams and murmurs of the thronging crowds watching the metal filaments weaving their patterns. He elbowed back through the crowd.

Faintly, through the rising crowd noise, he heard Eloise moaning his name. "Sorry, baby," he yelled over his shoulder, putting his elbow into a fat woman's diaphragm, "but I've been hungry too long to pass up a sweet deal like this!

"Excuse me, ma'am. Pa'rm me, Mac. Excuse me, I'd like to get—uh—through here. Uh! Thanks, Mac," and he was at the drugstore door. He adjusted his bow tie for a moment, muttering low to himself, "Ohboyohboyohboy! Just looka this, little Bartie Chester! You're gonna make a millyun bucks! Yessir!"

He scrabbled for change as he slid into the booth. In another few minutes he had placed the long-distance call collect—to Mrs. Charles Chester in Wilmington, Delaware. He heard the phone ringing at the other end, then his mother's voice, "Yes, hello?" and he started to say, "Hey! Ma!" but the operator's voice cut through.

"Will you accept the charges, Mrs. Chester?"

When she had said yes, Bart threw himself into it. "Hello, hello, *Ma*! How ya?"

"Why, Bart, how wonderful to hear from you. It's been so long! Just those few postcards!"

"Yeah, yeah, I know, Ma," he cut her off, "but things have been really jumpin' for me here in New York. Look, Ma, I need some money."

"Well. . .how much, Bart? I can let you have. . ."

"I'll need a couple hunnerd, Ma. It's the biggest—so help me God—the *biggest* goddam deal I ever—"

"*Bart!* Your language! And to your mother!"

"Sorry, Ma, really sorry, but this is so hot it's burnin' my pinkies! Honest to—" he caught himself quickly, "—gosh! Ma, I need the dough like I never did before. I can get it back to you in a few months, Ma! Pleeze, Ma! I never asked ya for nothin' before!"

The next two minutes were a gradual wearing-down period in which Mrs. Charles Chester promised to go to the bank and get the last two hundred in sight. Bart thanked her most graciously. He ignored the operator's snide interjections to his mother about waiting for charges *she* would have to pay, then he was off the line and back on another.

"Hello, Erbie? This is Bart. Look, I got a deal on that is without a doubt the most—*wait* a minute, for Christ's sake, willya—this is the greatest thing ever hit the—"

Five minutes and five hundred dollars later: "Sandy, baby? Who's *this*? Who ya think? This's Bart! Bart Ches—HEY! don't hang up! This is a chance for you to make a millyun; a sweet honest-to-God millyun! Now here's what I want. I wanta borrow from you—"

Fifteen minutes, six phone calls, and four thousand five hundred and twenty dollars later, Bart Chester bolted from the drug store, just in time to see the tentacled plate receding into the ship, the skin closing again.

Eloise was, of course, gone. Bart didn't even notice.

The crowds were by this time overflowing into the streets—though everyone was careful not to get under the structure—and traffic was blocked to a standstill all up the avenue. Motorists were perched on car hoods, watching the machine.

Fire trucks had been drawn up, somehow. Rubber-overcoated firemen stood about biting their lower lips and shaking their heads ineffectually. *I've gotta get in there; get the edge on any other promoters!* Visions of overflowing coffers of gold danced in Bart Chester's head.

As he was pushing through the crowd, back to the curb, he saw the police cordon forming. The beefy, spectacled cop was joining hands with a thin, harassed-looking bluecoat, as Chester got to them.

"Sorry, buddy, you can't go in there. We're shooin' everyone out now," the fat officer said, over his shoulder.

"Look, officer, I *gotta* get in there." At the negative shake from the cop, Chester exploded, "Look—I'm Bart Chester! You know, Star Cavalcade of 1954, the Emery Bros. Circus—I produced 'em! I *got* to get in there!" He could tell he was making no impression whatsoever.

"Look, you've got to—Hey! Inspector! Hey, over here!" He waved frantically, and the short man in the drab overcoat paused as he headed toward the squad car pool.

Taking care not to step on the microphone cables being laid along the street, he walked toward the crowd. Chester said to the cops, "Look, I'm a friend of Inspector Kesselman. Inspector," he said imploringly, "I've got to get in there. It's real important. Maybe a promotion!"

Kesselman began to shake his head no, then he looked at Chester with narrowed eyes for a moment, remembering free tickets to fights, and reluctantly bobbed his head in agreement. "Okay, come on," he said, with obvious distaste, "but stay close."

Chester ducked under the restraining arms of the cops, following the little man around the shadow of the structure.

"How's the promoting business, Chester?" asked the Inspector as they walked.

Bart felt his head grow light and begin to float off his shoulders. *That* was precisely the trouble: "Lousy," he said.

"Come over some night for dinner, if you get the time," added the Inspector, in a tone that suggested Bart turn down the invite.

"Thanks," said Bart, carefully walking around the huge machine's shadow in the street.

"Is it a spaceship?" asked Chester, in almost a childlike tone. Kesselman turned and looked at him strangely.

"Where in Hell did you get *that* idea from?" he asked.

Chester shrugged his shoulders, "Oh, just them comic books I been readin'." He smiled lopsidedly.

"You're crazy," said Kesselman, shaking his head as he turned away.

Two hours later, when the last firemen had come down from the ladders, shaken their heads in failure and said, "Sorry, these acetylene torches don't even get the metal smoky," and walked away, Kesselman still looked at Chester with annoyance and said, "You're crazy."

An hour later, when they had ascertained definitely that machine gun bullets did not even dent the structure, he was less sure, but he refused to call the scientists Chester suggested. "Goddammit, Chester, this is *my* business, not yours, now either you keep your trap shut, or I'll boot you out beyond the cordon!" He gestured meaningfully at the throbbing crowds straining against the joined hands of the police. Chester subsided, confident they would do as he had suggested, eventually.

Eventually was one hour and fifty minutes later when Kesselman threw up his hands in despair and said, "Okay, get your goddam experts in here, but do it fast. This thing might settle any minute.

"Or," he added sarcastically, looking at the grinning Bart Chester, "if there's monsters in this thing, they may start eating us any minute now."

It was a spaceship. Or at any rate, it was from *someplace* else.

The gray-faced scientists clucked knowingly to each other for a while; one of the braver experts climbed a fire ladder and tested the ship in some incomprehensible manner, and then they concurred.

"It is our opinion," said the scientist with the three snatches of hair erupting from an otherwise bald head, "that this vehicle—am I speaking clearly enough for you reporters?—this vehicle is from somewhere off Earth. Now whether," he pointed out, while the others nodded in agreement, "this is a spaceship, or as seems more likely from the manner in which it appeared, a dimension-spanning device, I am not certain.

"But," he concluded, making washing movements with his hands, "it is definitely of extraterrestrial origin." He spelled the six-syllable word, and the reporters went whooping off to the telephones.

Chester grabbed Kesselman by the arm. "Look, Inspector, who has say-so—jurisdikshun—*you* know—over this thing? I mean, who would have say-so about entertainment rights and like that?" Kesselman was looking at him as though he were insane. Chester started another sentence, but the screams from the crowd drowned him out. He looked up quickly.

The skin of the spaceship was opening again.

By the time the crowds had streamed into the crosstown streets, terror was universally mirrored on every face, but mingled with an overwhelming sense of the wonder of it all. New Yorkers were once again torn between their native desire to watch, and a fear of the unknown.

Chester and the stubby-legged Inspector found themselves walking backward, taking short steps, fearful steps, as they looked upward. *Don't let them be monsters,* Chester was almost praying. *Or that beautiful meal-ticket'll be knocked off by the militia!*

The spaceship was motionless; it had not altered its original position by an inch. But a platform was extending. A transparent platform, so clear and so thin, it seemed almost invisible. Six hundred feet up the ship's length, between two huge ribbed knobs extending as though they were growths, the platform slid out over Times Square.

"Get some guns on that thing!" bellowed Kesselman at his men. "Get up in those buildings!" He pointed at two skyscrapers between which the spaceship hovered.

Chester stared at the ship in fascination as the platform extended—then stopped. As he watched, a note was sounded. It rose in his mind, audibly, yet soundlessly. He cocked his head to one side, listening. He could see the police, and slowly returning pedestrians, doing the same. "Whutzat?" he asked.

The sound built, climbing from the hollow arch at the bottom of his feet, to the last inch of each strand of hair on his head. It overwhelmed him and his sight dimmed for a moment, to be replaced by bursting lights and flickering shadows. In an instant his vision cleared, but he knew it had been a preamble. He knew—again without reason—the sound had come from the ship. He turned his eyes to the platform once more, just in time to see the lines begin their forming.

He could never quite describe what they were, and the only thing he knew for certain was that they were beautiful. The lines were suspended in air and of colors he had never known existed. They were parallel and crossed streamers that lived between the reds and blues of Earth. They were alien to his sight, yet completely arresting. He could not take his eyes from their wavering, shifting, formations.

Then the colors began to seep. Like running paints the lines melted, forming, forming, forming in the air above the platform. The colors intermingled and blended; soon a backdrop of shades blotted out the skin of the ship.

"What—what is it?" he heard Kesselman ask, faintly.

Before he could answer, *they* came out.

The beings appeared and stood silent for an instant. They were all different in bodily appearance, yet somehow Chester knew they were all alike underneath. As though they had donned coverings. In the instant they stood there, motionless, he knew each by name. The purple-furred one on the left, he was Vessilio. The one with stalks growing where his eyes should have been, he was Davalier. The others, too, all bore names, and oddly, Chester knew each one intimately. They did not repulse him, for all their alienness. He knew Vessilio was stalwart and unflinching in the face of duty. He knew Davalier was a bit of a weakling, prone to crying in private. He knew all this and more. He *knew* each one, personally.

Yet they were all monstrous. Not one was shorter than forty feet. Their arms—when they had arms—were well-formed and properly sized for their bodies. Their legs, heads, torsos the same. But few had arms and legs and torsos. One was a snail-shape. Another seemed to be a ball of coruscating light. A third changed form and line even as Chester watched, pausing an instant in a strangely unidentifiable middle stage.

Then they began moving.

Their bodies positioned and swayed. They moved around one another, intricately. Chester found himself enthralled. They were magnificent! Their motions, their actions, their attitudes in relation to one another, were glorious. More, they told a story. A deeply interesting story.

The lines shifted, the merged colors changed. The aliens went through involved panoramas of descriptive motion.

Not for a second did Chester consider he might stop watching them. They were something so alien, so different, yet so compelling, he knew he must watch them or forever lose the knowledge they were imparting with their movements.

When the soundless note had sounded again, the colors had faded, the aliens were gone and the platform had slid back, the spaceship was quiet and faceless once more. Chester found himself breathing with difficulty. They had been—well, literally breathtaking!

He glanced at the huge clock on the Times Building. Three hours had elapsed in the space of a second.

The murmurs of the crowd, the strange applause for a performance they could not have fully understood, the feel of Kesselman's hand on his arm, all faded away. He heard the Inspector's voice, so whispery in his ear, "Good Lord, how marvelous!" Even that was out of his range now.

He knew, as he had known everything else, just what the ship was, who the aliens were, what they were doing on Earth. He heard himself saying it, quietly, almost with reverence:

"That was a play. They're actors!"

They *were* magnificent, and New York learned it only shortly before the rest of the world got wind of the news. Hotels and shops suddenly found themselves deluged by the largest tourist crowds in years. The city teemed with thousands of visitors, drawn from all over the Earth, who wished to witness the miracle of The Performance.

The Performance was always the same. The aliens came out onto their platform—their stage, really—every evening at precisely eight o'clock. They were finished by eleven.

During the three hours they maneuvered and postured, they filled their appreciative audiences with mixtures of awe and love and suspense such as no other acting group had ever been able to do.

Theaters in the Times Square area were forced to cancel their evening performances. Many shows closed, many switched to matinee runs and prayed. The Performance went on.

It was uncanny. How each person who watched enraptured could find identification, find meaning; though everyone saw something a little different; though no words were spoken; though no comprehensible motions were made.

It was uncanny. How they could see the actors do the exact same things, over and over, each Performance, and never tire of it—come back to see it again. It was uncanny, yet beautiful. New York took The Performance to its heart.

After three weeks, the army was called away from the ship—which had done nothing but produce The Performance regularly each evening—to quell a prison riot in Minnesota. In five weeks Bart Chester had made all the necessary arrangements, shoestring-fashion, and was praying things wouldn't fizzle as they had with the Emery Bros. Circus. He was still going without meals, moaning to those who would listen, "What a lousy racket this is—but I got a deal on now that's—"

In seven weeks Bart Chester had begun to make his first million.

No one would pay to watch The Performance, of course. Why should they when they could stand in the streets and see it? But there was still the unfathomable "human nature" factor with which to contend.

There were still those who would rather sit in a gilded box seat, balcony style, hung from the outside of a metropolitan skyscraper (insured by Lloyd's, to be sure!), than stand in a gutter.

There were still those who felt that popcorn and chocolate-covered almonds made preparation of watching more pleasant. There were still those who felt the show was *common* if they did not have a detailed program.

Bart Chester, whose stomach had begun to bulge slightly beneath his new charcoal-gray suit, took care of those things.

Bart Chester Presents flowed in elegant script across the top of the programs, and beneath it, simply, The Performance. It was rumored up and down the street that Bart Chester was the new Sol Hurok, and a man which it is whom we must all definitely watch!

During the first eight months of The Performance, he made back all the borrowed money he had invested in building-face leases and construction work. Everything from there on out was reasonably clear profit. The confection and souvenir concessions he leased for a fifty percent cut of the gross to the people who supplied ball games and wrestling matches.

The Performance went on, regularly, as an unquestionable smash hit.

VARIETY said: ETs SOCKO IN PLUSH REVUE!

The *Times* was no less ebullient with its praise:

". . .We found The Performance on Times Square as refreshing and captivating at its first anniversary as it was on its opening night. Even the coarse commercial interests which have infected it could not dim the superlativeness of the. . ."

Bart Chester counted his receipts and smiled; and grew just a little fat for the first time in his life.

The two thousand, two hundred and eighty-ninth Performance was as brilliant and as satisfying as the first, the hundredth, or the thousandth. Bart Chester sat back in his plush seat, only vaguely aware of the stunning girl beside him. Tomorrow she would be back, trying to get a break in some off-Broadway production, but tomorrow The Performance would still be there, pouring money into his pockets.

The major part of his mind concentrated, held in awe and wonder at the intricacy and glory of the actors' movements. A minor segment was thinking, as it always did with him.

Wonderful! Marvelous! A true spec'tcle like The New Yorker *said!* All around him, like perspiration on a huge beast, the Chester Balconies clung to their buildings. The inexpensive seats between 45th and 46th Streets, the higher-priced boxes festooning façades all the way up to the Times Building. *One of these days those slobs'll break down and I'll be able to build on the Times, too!* he thought.

Over six years; what a run! Beats South Pacific! *Dammit, wish I could have made all that in gate receipts.*

He frowned mentally, thinking of all the people watching from the streets. For free! The crowds were still as huge as the first day. People never seemed to tire of seeing the play. Over and over they watched it, enraptured, deep in it, not even noticing the flow of time. The Performance always satisfied, always enchanted.

They're fabulous players, he thought. *Only*. . .

The thought was half-formed. Nebulous. Annoying, but strangely strangely annoying—there was no reason why he should feel qualms.

Oh well.

He concentrated on the play. It really took little concentration, for the actors spoke directly to the mind; their charming appeal was to a deeper and clearer well than mere appreciation.

He was not even aware when the tone of the play changed. At one point the actors were performing a strangely exotic minuet of movement. A second later, they were all down near the front of the platform.

"That isn't in the play!" he said, incredulously, the mood broken. The beautiful girl beside him grabbed at his sleeve.

"What d'ya mean, Bart?" she asked.

He shook her hand off in annoyance. "I've seen this show hunnerds of times. Right here they all get around that little humpbacked birdthing and stroke it. What're they staring at?"

He was correct. The actors were looking down at their audience who had begun to applaud nervously, sensing something was wrong. The aliens watched with stalks, with cilia, with eyes. They were staring at the people in the streets, on the balconies, seeming to see them for the first time since they'd arrived. Something was very wrong. Chester had felt it first—perhaps because he had been there from the beginning. The crowds were beginning to sense it also. They were milling in the streets, uncertainly.

Chester found his voice tight and high as he said, "There's—there's something *wrong!* What're they doing?"

When the platform sank slowly down the face of the ship, till finally one of the actors stepped off into the empty space beside the machine, he began to realize.

It was only after the first few moments, when the horror of the total carnage he knew was coming had worn off, he found himself staring fascinated as the little, forty-foot, humpbacked bird-thing strode through Times Square, that he knew.

It had been a wonderful show, and the actors had appreciated the intense interest and following of their audience. They had lived off the applause for over six years. They were artists without a doubt.

And up to a point, they had *starved* for their art.

—New York, 1956

WORLDS TO KILL

I

Clasping the jeweled hilt of the stone kris with both hands, the Rt. Rev. Mr. Push, exalted high priest of the One Authentic Temple of God, Inc., raised it slowly heavenward, point downward, perfectly straight and parallel to his naked and painted body. When his extended elbows formed the outside points of a diamond, and the brown-stained blade was just above his head, he began to intone the sacred litany. The sound of it was picked up by the loudspeaker mike hanging around his neck, and was thrown out across the great stadium.

Even so, it was difficult making out the words where the cripple sat, across the huge tiered bowl, in the 2.50 seats. A candy butcher was shrieking, "Koola! Frynuts! Cold Koola! Hot Frynuts!" at the end of his row, and the high priest's sacred sing-song was drowned out by the commercial.

Hunkered down, legless, on his rolling cart, the leather-tanned man lifted the binoculars to his eyes again, and sighted across the bowl to the sacrificial altar, trying to lip-synch the few words he was able to make out, with the precise mouth movements of the high priest.

The litany came to an end and the crowd shouted its responses with religious enthusiasm. The legless man on the cart tracked the binoculars rapidly across the crowd, and then brought their unblinking sight back to the high priest as he arched back slightly, rib cage suddenly becoming prominent with the effort, and drove straight down, hard, with the kris, into the red circle that had been painted over the naked girl's heart.

As the kris sank to the jeweled hilt the crowd roared, leaping to its feet, throwing sacrificial roses into the air.

On his cart, the cripple holstered his binoculars and finished his popcorn. The crowd blocked off his view of everything but their straining bodies. The voices went up and seemed to become too shrill to have emanated from human throats.

When the bedlam quieted, the legless man asked two of the nearest enthusiasts if they would lift his cart down off the seat. When they had set him in the aisle, he propelled himself with difficulty up the aisle to the exit portal, and down the ramp. Behind him another virgin was being sacrificed.

Outside the stadium, scooting along smoothly with a pair of padded wooden blocks strapped over his hands, the cripple made for a freight expressway moving like quicksilver through the suburban stadium section.

Crates of goods, force-locked in position to avoid theft or spillage, hissed past him on the maximum-speed strip, as he came abreast of a checkloading station. The clocker, a man of indeterminate age chewing on a chocolate ring, did not bother to look up as the cripple propelled himself up the short metal ramp with a forceful rowing motion. But when the little cart stopped in front of the clocker's bubble—a pie-wedge opened in its force-field so he could get the dubious benefits of the sticky moist breeze blowing across the expressways—he looked down from his seat and his eyes narrowed.

"Excuse me," the cripple asked politely, "would you do me a kind of a favor, please?"

The clocker did things with his mouth, cleaning out the bits of nuts the chocolate ring had deposited between his teeth. "What?"

A short, harsh syllable.

"I, uh, can't afford a passenger slipway, and I was wondering if you'd let me ride the freightway down to the 147th Street Oval. . .?"

The clocker was shaking his head. "No."

"You wouldn't even have to lock me on," the cripple insisted. "I can do a thing with the wheels, they've got a vacuum base. It wouldn't be any bother."

The clocker turned away.

"I'd really appreciate it," the cripple pressed him.

The clocker turned back, eyes narrowed again, mouth hard. "Against the rules, bo, you know that. Don't wanna discuss't. Just slipaway."

The cripple's deeply tanned face grew tense, jaw muscles moved softly, and his anger extended itself through his features to his nose, which quivered like an animal's. "Some helluva way to treat a bo," he said snappishly. "How the hell you think I got shortn'd this way, you bastard! I worked the slips, same's you. Now I give both my legs and I come an' ask another workman same's I was, an' what I get? Dumped on, is what it is. You bastard, all I asked was for a ride down'ta the Oval, that such a big damn thing?"

The clocker looked shocked, and suddenly chagrined.

"Hey, I'm sorry, bo."

The cripple did not reply. He slipped the wooden blocks back on his hands and started to turn himself around. The clocker got down off his seat, which regained its original shape, sighing softly. The clocker came and stood in front of the little cart. "No, hey, I'm really sorry, bo. It's, you know, they get you locked in with rules. Hell, I'll put you on a slip, just gimme a minute."

The cripple nodded brusquely, as though only now getting his due.

The clocker opened the access lock and walked ahead of the cart as the cripple rolled after him. The elevator dropped them down just below the level of the works, and they moved across under the maximum-speed and mid-range slipways. They came up through the loading lock between the mid-range and slow-speed slips, and the clocker got down on his knees and made ready to shove the cart onto the slowest slipway.

"Thanks," the cripple said with a smile.

HARLAN ELLISON
WORLDS TO KILL

The clocker made a forget-it motion with his hand, and nudged him onto the slipway. As the cripple slid away, the clocker stood up and called after him, "Hey, sorry, bo!"

Three miles down the slipway, the cripple shifted slips more adroitly than the clocker would have thought possible. He held his position on the mid-range slipway for a quarter mile, then shifted again. Now on the maximum-speed freightway, with the whining of the works making it impossible for any spy equipment of the priest's police to pick up his words, he rubbed back the flap of flesh on his right biceps that concealed the communications device, and began to report:

"Okay. Final stuff. Feed it directly to the machine. The preliminary judgments seem to be accurate. They've reached a seven stage in technology, but socially they're doing maybe four. Strong myth and religious ties. Wide open for a crash-in tactic, I think. No, make that a certainty. Couch the attack in a religious way, maybe the fall of a sun god, or a second coming kind of thing. That'll put them into a temporary panic and first penetration can be effected with minimal losses. Now I'm going to feed you the coded stuff for precision, but the one thing I couldn't code-up is the barbarism thing they've got going here. Really a bunch of animals, just under the surface. That may be our strongest weapon, so code what you can of it, and let the analyzer extrap the rest. You can get Arnak's troops ready, and tell Folger we'll need light to medium armor on the cruisers, probably nothing any heavier. Except I've got a long list of special stuff Nord'll have to rig up for particular jobs. Okay now, I'll wait for your signal for clear on the machine. . ."

He rode the express freightway another three miles, in silence, waiting.

When it came, it was a sharp jamming buzz, and he began to speak in a flat, emotionless voice, into his biceps:

"Invasion ET commence ourtime five slant two five slant zero nine-er slant thirteen hundred hours. . ."

He had long since passed the 147th Street Oval by the time he had finished transmitting; his words had gone out through the atmosphere, directed through space in a line as straight as a thought, which was by no means straight. Curlicued and doubled-back, the transmission had been picked up by doggie stations and boosted even farther.

In another star-system altogether, the transmission had been received and acknowledged.

On the freightway, the legless cripple rose from his cart, stretched his legs and changed his clothes quickly. When he slipshifted, back down to the low-speed strip, he was dressed as a kelp fisherman in from the fields, wearing country bumpkin clothing.

He disappeared without a trace into the amusement suburb. It was twelve days histime till the planet was scheduled to die.

II

Natives called the planet Reef. Its origins in slang went back to the first Terran explosion outward, when the immigrants, sick to death of space and wandering, had foundered on that bright planet of a blue-white star. Reef, on which they had built a world for themselves. Reef, on the verge of being invaded.

A manta was dropped down first. It sowed the winds with an alienation dust that drove every man from every other man, that sent husbands quivering from their wives and mothers from their children. The people of Reef broke into tiny communities of one frightened soul each. Then the fireballs came down, and the people trembled in fear and superstition.

Then came Folger's cruisers. The medium-class stock took out the military installations and the railheads, the shipping ports and the single space center. The lightweights ranged up and down the planet slicing communications lines, blacking out television and radio, playing search-and-destroy with any pockets of possible organized resistance (as reported by the advance scout, the legless cripple, the man known as Jared). Then the troop platforms were skimmed in, and Arnak's commandos spun their spiderwebs down, waiting for the word to downdrop. Through the early morning sky the great circular black platforms rode the winds, the cilia-thin spiderwebs hanging down like sensory-feelers of some gigantic sea creature.

The commandos waited.

The psycheprobe stations were dropped in seventy previously specified locations, hit the planet at full acceleration and shucked their protective hulls on impact. They drove straight down through the crust of the planet; linking up in a network of overriding thought-patterns, the broadcast went out, jamming normal brain-signals.

In varying intensities the psycheprobes washed the minds of the invaded with hopelessness, shame, cowardice, depression, terror, paranoia, nausea, weariness, hunger, a desire to return to the womb, a realization that there was never, ever any such return possible for them. . .and back through the cycle again.

The commandos dropped.

ET of Commencement was 5/25/09/1300 hours.

In the flagship *Tempest*, Jared received the Planetary Secure signal of 5/27/09/0644 hours. It had taken forty-one hours and forty-four minutes to initiate, execute and complete the subjugation of the planet called Reef. It was the one hundred and seventy-fourth planet Jared had conquered for a client.

On the bridge of the *Tempest*, the circular hull was studded with two hundred highly sophisticated two-way viewing screens showing every phase of the securing operation.

Jared had been watching the screens; now he turned to the humanoid with the squid's head, and said softly, "Pay me."

Ram, unquestioned ruler of thirty million squid humanoids existing on a dark planet of Reef's sun, a being who had lived his life in various kinds of darkness, turned to the leathery-tanned man and his one great eye blinked quickly.

The tentacles that draped down over his chest and back twirled and fretted. "You do a magnificent job, Jared," his tentacle-semaphore twined.

"Pay me," Jared repeated.

Ram twined. "The job is not completed."

"You heard the Secure signal. You owe me the final half of your payment. Make it, Ram."

The squid-creature's rear tentacles made a plaited statement to a second squid-being near the dropshaft. Ram's lieutenant saluted with a roll, and stepped off into the dropshaft.

"He will return in a moment with the cases."

"Thank you, Ram." Jared turned back to his screens.

Ram watched him for long moments, then stepped up beside him. Jared was not a tall man; the squid-being stood a full head above him. Ram was barely capable of forming human speech, his vocal apparatus composed almost entirely of vibrating membranes. Yet he fancied himself a cosmopolite, and it pleased him to make the attempt. With a hideous parody of the speech of men, he ventured, "Yooo errr fummmm Earssss orrrginnnyyy, hiiii mmmm towwww?"

Jared kept his eyes on screen 113, where commandos were separating women from men into force-screened compounds. "Yes. I'm an Earthman. Originally."

But his tone was not one to encourage conversation. Had Ram been of Earth, he would have recognized the tone. But as he was not, "Whudddizzziddd Iygggonnnn Earssss?"

Jared turned slowly.

He stared at Ram until the alien's tentacles began a reflexive twining. He did not answer, and in a few moments Ram moved away, twining behind Jared's back, "Arrogant polyp! Mercenary!"

Ram's lieutenant lifted into view, followed by two alien squids carrying metal cases. They were set down at Ram's feet, and he was just looking up, focusing the great eye, when Jared came to him. "Open them," the leathery spacer said. Ram waggled to his lieutenant.

The lieutenant undulated the command to the two squid troopers with the caskets, at the same time handing an unscrambler to one of them. The instrument was used on the force-bead locks and the caskets hissed open pneumatically.

Jared looked down into the cases, first one, then the other.

"Thank you, Ram," he said.

HARLAN ELLISON
WORLDS TO KILL

"One year's production of The Metal," Ram said softly, slowly, with movements like seaweed in a gentle warm ocean current. "Enough of The Metal to light a planet for a thousand years. Enough to power a million cruisers to the edge of infinity. Enough to buy a world."

"It bought you Reef," Jared said.

"This half. . .and the other half. . .two years' production of my world. The most valuable export we have ever had. What will you do with all of it?"

Jared looked at him coldly. The silence grew. Ram turned away.

Jared took the unscrambler and thumbed in a new setting. Then without another look at The Metal within the cases, he sealed them, the lids lowering on their pneumatic rods. "Aren't you curious whether I short-changed you?" Ram waggled, his interpretation tentacle signaling wry good humor.

Jared smiled at him with a noticeable lack of warmth. "You wouldn't cheat me, Ram. You want to hire me again. To conquer Signa II."

Ram's lieutenant made a frantic movement. A movement of consternation. Ram silenced him with a wave.

The squid creature took a step toward Jared.

"Yes. Yes, I do."

Jared turned back to the screens. He pointed to screen 50. "Look, Ram. The end is coming to Reef."

On the screen the sky of Reef had turned yellow with day. In the distance the red sun was a blur. Down out of that crimson sky Ram's chosen Governor was dropping, his human body drawn up inside the soft ruff of its squid head. The one great eye, its central orb gleaming green and bright, the Governor was dropping down from a squid cruiser riding safely within an attack wedge of Jared's invasion force. The Governor was descending to take control of the conquered planet from Jared's mercenaries. His squid flesh glowed with the black and red tints of joy.

Ram's tentacles touched Jared on the shoulder.

The man who conquered worlds for a price turned half to him. Ram spoke with the intentness pattern.

"Now I have two worlds in this system. Signa II is next. Then Gola, Karthes, Vale and Kalpurnika. My people will rule the system. We lie in the center of the hub of the trade lines. Half of everything is yours as payment. Jared?"

The mercenary wore a garment very much like a tunic. His arms were bare. Now he rubbed one muscular forearm with the stiffened fingers of his other hand. He did not respond to Ram's words; there was something of unliving stone in his expression.

"I know you've done it for other worlds," Ram pressed on. "My reports on your work were thorough. That is why I came to you. I know you've done jobs for clients several times in the same system. I *need* the other five to strengthen my position in this galaxy. They'll take Reef back if—"

Jared spoke with no intonation, flat and final. "No."

"But why?"

Jared walked away from him, then.

Ram stared after him for a few moments, then stalked after him suddenly lashing out with tentacles that encircled the mercenary's waist and chest. He spun him around and hissed, "Yooo doooo sissss forrrr meeee!"

Jared's movements were almost too quick to see; grasping the thick ropes of the tentacles circling his waist in one hand, and the tentacles around his chest with the other, he dipped and spun out of their encircling grasp. Then he planted himself firmly, and contracted his body in a peculiar manner, literally lifting the squid creature off his feet, whirling and hurling him across the bridge. It was an unexpected and artful maneuver, and Ram careened through the air toward a bulkhead. At the beginning of the movement his legs and arms and tentacles had been a twisted mass, but instinctively he withdrew his body into the ruff of the squid head, and as he struck the wall his tentacles touched first, absorbing the shock. The humanoid body dropped down out of the squid head and he touched down on the deck no more unsettled than he had been before Jared had thrown him.

Jared aimed a finger at the alien. "I took your commission for one job, one job only, Ram. I've done my job, you've paid me. The contract is fulfilled. Go take possession of your conquered province."

Ram betrayed no sign of fury at the Earthman's words. He walked quickly to the dropshaft and disappeared. The remaining squids stood immobile, as though waiting for a command from the Earthman. He did not speak.

Then the lieutenant signaled his men and they went downship after Ram.

Not long after, Jared saw the shuttle ship of Ram and his group drop out of the *Tempest*. He followed it down on screens 71-5, his face frozen without expression.

But much later, when Arnak's commandos had been withdrawn and Ram's Governor had brought in his own holding forces, Jared's face was a field of emotions, watching the wholesale slaughter in the force-screened compounds.

In a matter of hours three-fourths of the population of Reef was dead, the remaining millions already being routed to work-areas.

Jared fed the coursecomp a route back, and went away from there.

He left the screens burning, showing space and not-space, showing stars and whirling pinwheels of galaxies.

He drenched himself in the loneliness of darkness.

The cases of The Metal remained unmoved on the bridge.

Jared took no calls on the bridge; alone, watching nothing as the *Tempest* stretched itself between the scene on his last commission and the return base.

Downship, the staff found it difficult to speak to one another. They were loyal, but there were times when their employer took on assignments they could not reconcile with even their basest motives.

It was night.

It was always night.

There was seldom anything but silence in the night.

III

Pocked, but faceless, the bulk of Jared's moon grew ever greater. Somehow, it was less a home than a return base for him. He watched it emptily, two hundred times in two hundred screens. He was compelled to close his eyes.

As they approached the snuff-out barrier that invisibly closed Jared's moon off from the rest of the universe, there on the dark edge of nowhere, he coded the signals for entry.

The crust of the blasted moon-surface rolled back and the *Tempest* entered. The moon closed over the flagship. The rest of the rolling stock was already berthed. Jared left the ship, entered one of the dropshafts ranked to one side of the mooring docks, and was sucked up to the city level.

The core of Jared's moon had been artificially hollowed. The machine had been planted in the center. Around the core of the machine Jared's city had been built. An impregnable fortress.

He went straight to his town house, where he tore off his clothes, bathed, and let the mecks massage and relax him. Then he slept for twenty-six hours.

When he arose, he punched out breakfast, though it was artificial night in the city. All around him, above and below him, the sound of the machine, vague and satisfied, hummed in the walls. The machine was thinking. He sat on the edge of a chair and ate the breakfast.

Then he turned off the airjets that had been his bed, bathed again, and went downstairs to check what his staff had put on the memory-corders. There were six items, all coded priority.

One: a delegation from the Galactic Sodality had arrived two months previous with formal complaints to be lodged.

Two: a client from Kim. Commission: to conquer the sea-world Wah-whiting in the same solar system.

Three: a client from the Clan of Seven. Commission: to conquer the three remaining worlds in the String of Ten who would not join the Clan.

Four: an ex-client, the Ragish of Tymalle, seeking return of a portion of his payment due to an almost successful insurrection. Payment: the miracle drug Y-Kappa.

Five: a client from Bunyan IV. Commission: to conquer the woman-ruled world of Khaine in the nearby star-system.

Six: a representative of the conquered planet EElax. Commission: regain the planet for the deposed government.

He programmed them Four, Six, Three, Two, One, Five. The memorycorder assured him each of the delegations had been thoroughly searched and okayed; they had been billetted comfortably, waiting for Jared's return from the Reef job.

He sat in the office of his town house, amid the heavy oak furniture transshipped from Earth years before. He sat silently, smoking, thinking about Reef.

The slaughter had been ghastly, even greater than he had supposed—but not greater than the machine had predicted. Having fed Ram's nature, and the nature of the invasion rationale, into the machine, the prediction had been on the decimal point. The machine was always right.

Jared remembered when he had begun organizing his invasion and conquest project. The first job, a small one, utilizing ancient (and nearly forgotten) guerrilla techniques had netted him enough capital to begin the construction of the machine. It had purchased the services of the scientific staff he needed. The first prototype of the machine had been workable enough to provide plans for the second job. And from that conquest had come the first base, and troops. The organization had expanded steadily, its reputation spreading throughout the star-groups. Ten years before, he had begun the core job on the moon of this dark star's only planet. Now, closed off and untouchable, he was sought out by hundreds of clients every year. Some he interviewed, most he turned away. Of the ones seen, only a handful ever had their propositions fed into the machine. And of those scant few, only one or two were ever taken on as clients.

But when the bargain had been struck, Jared had carried off his end without failure. One hundred and seventy-four worlds had changed hands through the world-killing talents of Jared, his troops, and his machine.

The city was now a large city, the machine had restructured itself and added to its own bulk; his equipment was the most advanced, his techniques the most effective. For hire. Jared, the world-killer. At first his price had been staggering sums in Galactic Funds. But as the years had passed, less and less he had accepted money.

One job might bring huge stores of an anti-death drug, another ownership of an ore planetoid, still another the placement of a certain government official. Random payments, random selection of clients, totally without form or direction. Only the name of Jared persisted, cloaked almost in legend, feared and hated.

Jared heard the sound of footsteps coming through the reception hall. He looked up as Denna Gill appeared at the head of the short flight of stairs leading down into the oak-beamed living room.

"Welcome back," the alien said.

He came down the stairs, his furball body atop its three long ostrich legs bobbing up and down. The two great, limpid eyes looked at Jared with concern. The alien's "face" was roughly humanoid in arrangement, but more closely approximated that of an intelligent bird in demeanor.

"You don't look well."

Jared slumped in the big armchair. He shoved the memorycorder pickup away from him. It rolled to its niche in the paneled wall, the wall opened, the machine rolled in, the panel closed. It was an Eighteenth Century living room again. "I'm just a little tired."

"How did it go?"

"Well enough, I suppose."

"I take it the machine was correct?"

"Ram brought it right out on the decimal point."

Gill settled down his legs till his perfectly round fuzzy head was on a level with Jared's. "You expected it."

"Doesn't mean I had to enjoy watching it."

"No. It doesn't mean that."

They sat in silence for a moment. Then Jared drew in a deep breath, shifted the conversation, and asked, "This delegation from the Sodality. Who's on it?"

"Becker from Earth, Stieglitz from Alpha-C Nine, that young one, what's his name, Mosey, Morrissey. . ."

"Mosier, French I think; from the Crab?"

"That's the one."

"Anyone else?"

"The usual. Representatives of frightened planets."

"You don't sound particularly worried."

"I fed it to the machine."

"And?"

Gill bobbled his head in a movement of dismissal. "Unimportant."

"I see we finally got Bunyan IV to come in."

"We've been pushing them for three years. When you bought the cake for Cooper they had to do something. It was a nice maneuver."

"Don't remind me of the cost."

"But they're here, that's what counts. Think we can get what we want from them?"

"They want Khaine. They have to have it. I think they'll bite. What does the machine say?"

"No extrap on it yet."

Jared rose. "Let's start the clown-show."

The human and his companion walked out through the living room. Down a passage behind a concealed panel, to a monorail whose single track vanished in the dimness of a tunnel carved from the dead heart of the moon. In the little car, Jared passed his hand across a glowing plate and the monorail vehicle shot out of its berth. The trip lasted only seventy seconds, ending in a low cave where a dropshaft hissed softly.

Jared and Gill descended in the dropshaft and stepped off at the vacuum-lock behind the reception chamber. They passed through the lock and Jared swung the center-pin panel around. They entered the reception chamber.

A hundred million million reflections of themselves flooded back at them, washed in the silvery light of the incredible diamond that was the reception chamber.

In a position where every delegate or potential client might truly be an assassin sent by a conquered world to rid the universe of the man who hired himself out to kill worlds for a price, Jared had made it as difficult as possible for the dispensers of vengeance.

His payment for the conquest of Isopia had been the nearly impossible delivery of a diamond one-eighth of a mile in diameter. A diamond from the Glass Mountains of Isopia, selected by his geologists for this purpose. Who could kill a man when there were a hundred million million possibilities?

Jared and Gill seated themselves behind the interview consoles, and Gill signaled for the first client to be dropped down to them.

The Ragish of Tymalle and his group entered from the far end of the diamond, through a panel similar to the one Jared and Gill had used. They were a long way off, but their images cascaded and slipped and bounced across the chamber. Inside a diamond, they faced Jared.

It took Jared three minutes to explain clearly why even a partial return of the payment for the conquest the Ragish had commissioned was impossible. Jared made it forcefully apparent that he took no responsibilities for the inability of a client to hold what had been won for him. The Ragish and his group departed.

He took one minute to turn down the commission of the EElaxian government-in-exile.

One minute to turn down the commission from the Clan of Seven. With a ray of hope: come see me again in four years Earthtime.

One minute to dispatch the delegation from Kim. A bogus client that had somehow passed inspection. The kill attempt was a clever one, but the three aliens were vaporized even as they released the search/seek/kill missiles from their ornate brocaded clothing.

Then the neatly-tailored group from the Galactic Sodality entered.

Becker, their spokesman, was a large-bodied man with a full white beard. He instinctively induced resonances of kindness, wisdom, honesty. Santa Claus.

Jared knew him, and distrusted him.

Though they were at the far end of the diamond, pickups in the walls bounced their voices clearly to Jared.

"Good evening," Becker began.

"I understand you have a complaint to lodge, Mr. Becker." Jared spoke softly, but the dismissal of protocol obviously shocked Becker.

"Why, uh, that's why we've come."

"Then let's get to it."

Becker called for some files from a young man behind him, apparently Mosier of the Crab Nebula. He extended them toward Jared, far down the glimmering chamber. It was ludicrous gesture, and Becker drew back his hand. "We have specifics enumerated herein."

"Say it, Mr. Becker. My time is short."

"This policy of conquest of yours must end. We of the Galactic Sodality have come together in a spirit of peace and harmony; our purpose is to bring unity to the known universe. There have been war and conquest since man left Earth. . ."

"I know my history, Mr. Becker. Perhaps better than you. I've made so much of it, after all."

"Arrogance can be the death of you!"

"Hypocrisy can be yours!"

Becker stammered for a moment.

"Let me put it to you bluntly, Mr. Becker. You and your Sodality, from which in the past two years I've received applicants from nine worlds. Your spoken wish for peace is a laudable one. It may not be the best thing for me personally or commercially, but I can sympathize with it intellectually. If you get what you say you want, I'm out of business. That doesn't appeal to me particularly. But it's still a lofty concept.

"Unfortunately, you're a fraud, Mr. Becker, as is your Galactic Sodality. The nomenclature doesn't matter. Galactic Sodality. United Worlds. Planetary Nexus. I've seen them come and go. Under stress, any one of the signatories to your pact would turn on the rest of you and employ me, if they thought they had a chance of taking over the starways. Not the least of them is Earth, for which we are all supposed to harbor a deep and instinctive affection. Your ball of mud is no more honest and valuable than any other, Becker. In fact, I've had feelers from clients on Earth as regards Alpha-C Nine. Mr. Stieglitz, are you there in the group. . .?"

A tall, thin Niner stepped forward. His bright red flesh was pulsing with fury. "I'm here!"

"You might inquire of Mr. Becker about that. The most recent feeler was from President Spaak himself. It was done through a Swiss Neutrality Combine on Proxima-C One."

There was an immediate and heated exchange between Becker and the Niner. Jared ordered them out of the diamond.

With the warning that any attempt at mounting an attack on Jared's moon would be greeted with the same enthusiasm Jared brought to any commission he undertook.

When they were gone, the Earthman sank back in his chair. Gill watched him closely.

"Do you want to break for a while?"

Jared shook his head. "Let's get to the meat."

The delegation from Bunyan IV was dropped in, and made its application. Jared listened and when the delegate had concluded he fed the additional facts into the machine through the console. It came back, as he had hoped, affirmative.

"I'll take the job."

"At what cost?" the client asked.

"The highest possible, of course," Jared replied.

IV

It was not that Khaine was an amazon world, nor even that women dominated. It had been made obvious, however, centuries before, that women ruled better than men. Thus, the government of Khaine was almost entirely female, with "the High" a woman elected by a combination of popular vote and computer selection. The High Irina was the current ruler of the planet: part president, part queen, part spokesman of a senate; very much a woman.

She discovered the presence of Jared on Khaine only three months histime after he had arrived.

They trapped him in the Park of Cats, there in the center of the capital city of Khaine, Jerusalem.

A mixed male and female unit of intelligence rangers staked out the park and began moving toward the center. Jared had been posing as a nightclub comedian, a fat man with a fluffy ring of white hair that circled his head. The disguise deflated and peeled easily. He was stripped down to a skinsuit, night-black and oiled, by the time the first of the rangers found him. They were under orders to take him alive. He swung up into a tree, sending the Khainesque cats shrieking from the branches. He hurled himself forward, from tree to tree, as they tried to make out his direction in the dark.

Then they brought in the kliegs and the flamers, and burned down the trees in the direction he was heading. They had him trapped in the feather-topped trees, the lights on him, when he vanished.

High above them, against the night sky, a bright blue dot appeared, flickered for a moment, then winked out.

Jared reappeared on the left bank of the Ganges River that divided Jerusalem in two parts. He now wore a breathing apparatus over his face, and a weapons belt was slung around his waist.

He took a reading from an instrument on his wrist, then he dove into the river. Down into its polluted darkness he swam, the special light goggles allowing only the most inadequate view through the water.

Near the bottom of the River, one of the guards from the intelligence rangers caught him blipping on his screen and came up to meet him. Jared met the man with an extended trident-spear. The guard caught the steel in his chest and disappeared tumbling awkwardly into the darkness.

Jared found the waterlock to the chamber without difficulty, and blew it with equal ease. When he had pumped out the access chamber he unshipped his weapon and undogged the entry portal. There was silence in the chamber. Jared consulted the instrument on his wrist and turned to his right, feeling along the solid metal wall. Suddenly, it slipped back, and he was looking into a control room floor-to-ceiling with dials and circuit indicators. The woman had her back to him.

"It can't do what my machine can do," Jared said.

The woman turned suddenly, dropping a group of thin metal strips on a ring.

"You dropped your phasers."

The woman was lovelier than the dossier photo-block Jared had studied. Lovelier, but not prettier. Just lovelier, in a way no facsimile could capture. Hers was a face that had been pretty in youth, but as she had grown older the prettiness had fought a battle with the accumulation of wisdom, the encroachment of character. Merely pretty had lost. Now she was lovelier.

"Who are you. . .how did you. . .?"

"The source that let you know I was on Khaine is the same source that told me where your control chamber was to be found." He added after a moment, "I've always felt espionage was a two-edged sword. It usually cuts both ways at the same time. Jeopardy is the operable word, I believe."

She went for a button on a wall. He caught her before she had reached it. She spun him around as he grabbed her arm. He felt her apply the leverage and tried to check himself, but she used his inertia against him and he went up against the wall, and rebounded.

She went for the button again.

He fired and the beam sizzled past her, blowing the button, the circuit, and half the wall out.

The concussion pitched her sidewise and she struck her neck on the edge of a components cabinet. Her eyes rolled up and she fell to the deck.

Jared rose slowly, and went to her.

She was only unconscious.

He snapped a breather on her, hoisted her over his shoulder and left the control chamber.

Rising up through the river, he could not tell if she had stopped breathing. It was not till he had disassembled them, beamed them, and reassembled them in the observation center of the *Tempest* that he called in the surgeon and was told she would be all right.

They were three days out from Khaine, heading for the moon,

when she came up from under the sedatives.

She looked around, instantly grasped where she was, and tried to escape. Jared had her put under again. It would not do to have the High Irina of Khaine die in the airless, colorless spaces of not-space.

Gill was waiting. He looked worried. It was not an expression a human would hold if he were worried, but Gill was a Mexla and Jared knew his moods. He was worried.

"What if she won't cooperate?"

"I don't expect her to want to."

Gill sank and rose on his legs. "Then how the hell—"

"No, not a brainscan; and not drugs. I've got to make her want to do it."

"How the hell—"

"You said that: if you haven't something constructive, pass off and let me get on with it."

"Jared, my God, what if. . .what if. . ." He could not even frame the thought. It was much too dangerous, much too horrible a thought.

Jared touched the alien gently. "Gill, we've come this far. If we're wrong now, if all of your 'what ifs' are so. . .if somewhere along the way it went bad and we never knew it. . .then we are what they say we are. If we've done it right, then it'll work out all right."

Gill bobbled in a resigned manner. "You going to see the machine now?"

Jared nodded. "Is it programmed?"

Gill walked him to the dropshaft. "Up to the top."

Jared touched him again, gently ruffling his fur. "Be at peace, old friend." Then said, "No way back now."

He dropped down through the center of the moon, till he came to the force-locks that separated men from the machine. He unscrambled them, with the only unit that worked—a unit phased in with his brain wave patterns.

The great port opened, and Jared passed in to speak to the machine. It had been many years since he had been summoned down for a consultation.

Now he stood before it, as it rose up out of sight in the gut of the moon. He stood before the metal brain he had caused to be built, to serve him as he killed worlds for profit.

"Hello, Jared," the machine said.

"It's been a long time," Jared answered. He went to the formfit chair the machine kept for him. He sat down and oddly, for the first time in years, he was totally relaxed. Talking to the machine was exactly like talking to Gill, for the machine had selected the voice-prints of the little alien as his own. The gentle warmth of Gill's tones came from the air around Jared, but it was the voice of the machine, faintly oiled and cool in the caverns.

"Did you bring the High?"

"Yes, I brought her. You're certain it was a necessity for the invasion?"

"Have I ever been wrong?"

Jared chuckled softly. "If you have, I've no way of checking you."

The machine chittered to itself as though considering. "Is it that you think perhaps you've given too much power to a machine, mine creator?"

"It isn't seemly for a machine to mock its master."

"Sorry. Only asking."

"No, it's not that I think you have too much power, it's that I'm afraid if you blow a circuit somewhere, and reroute buggy, we may all wind up saying, 'Yes, massa' to the robots."

"I have no desire to rule men. I am content."

Jared let it lie. The machine could not lie, it could not obfuscate. But it might program itself for a specious truth.

"You're worried about the invasion of Khaine," the machine pin-pointed Jared's problem.

"You haven't told me much this time."

"There are reasons. You set me only one chore, Jared. I am directed to the fulfillment of that chore, I have to do what is necessary. Till now we have been in the first phase of the program. Now we are about to enter the second, the most difficult phase. There was only one weak link."

"And that was. . .?"

The machine waited. "You."

Jared's eyes widened. Many things suddenly became clear to him. He sank down in the formfit, his mind a whirling cyclone of disorder.

Finally, he said, "So now we need the High Irina."

The machine answered quickly. "Yes. *We* need her, and *you* need her. Men often become too much like their machines, Jared. Then they blame the machines for dehumanizing them. For fifteen years I have worked on the program with you. And you worked on it alone for seven years before I was built. Twenty-two years, Jared, a large part of any man's life. Larger than most for yours, because the task you've set yourself is destined to kill you. You've become too much like me. Yes, we need the High."

They talked on, for many hours.

Then Jared dropped up to his city, where Gill met him. Jared looked exhausted. He was able to smile at the alien for a moment before he whispered. "Take me home, Gill. I need sleep."

Then he slumped down and the Mexla took him through the tunnels to the town house, where he stripped him and sent him to sleep on the restful jets of warm air.

And then the alien went to his own home.

But he did not sleep.

V

Gill could not understand it. After the machine had made it an imperative that Jared, himself, personally, run the recon mission to Khaine, and personally capture the High Irina himself, there was no place in the incredibly simple invasion plan for her use.

The machine had only told them that much, at the outset of the commission. *Capture the High Irina.* So Jared had risked his life and had done it. Then Jared had gone down below and had his talk with the machine, and said nothing about it.

But the next day they had had their battle plan, and the High Irina's only place in it was that the machine insisted she be on board the *Tempest* to witness the invasion in all of its phases.

Gill was nervous, worried. It seemed wrong. There *was* something wrong, terribly wrong.

Now, as they watched the final stages of the mop-up, as the client from Bunyan IV chuckled like a madman beside them, Gill checked the force-bonds on the High, and wished they had never accepted the commission.

She had not spoken throughout the campaign. It had been a one-day affair; Khaine was terribly vulnerable. Now it was killed, even as she watched.

Jared had paid no attention to her, but had taken his position before the two hundred screens and supervised the slaughter. She had not spoken when they turned the skyline of Jerusalem glowing red, nor when the city winked out of existence. She had not spoken when they ran the strafing missions with the stukas across the plandar refineries nor when they made a glass-sided crater of the mountain armaments base. She watched silently, and when the Planetary Secure signal came through, she closed her eyes and sank back against her bonds.

The client from Bunyan IV—tall and thin as something out of an Earth legend, with knobs at the joints, a nose sharp as a letter opener, and eyes slitted and green—turned to Jared as the world-assassin said, "That's it, Seventeen. The job is done."

"Fine, just fine," said the alien, snapping his joints with delight. He had laughed hysterically throughout the operation. Jared despised him.

"One more tiny thing, though," Seventeen said, palming out a razor-disc. He turned to the High, where she sat force-shackled. "Goodbye, my Irina."

He cracked back in three sharp stages cocking his arm to spin off the disc. Irina stared at him coldly. She was not frightened.

"No!"

The word cracked as sharply as had Seventeen's joints. Seventeen swiveled his long head in stages. Jared was staring at him evenly. The wire-thin arm with the razor-disc did not lower.

"I said: no."

HARLAN ELLISON
WORLDS TO KILL

Seventeen laughed with the shrieking high sound of a lunatic. "This is the High Irina, assassin. She is the only one who could lead a counter-attack against me. It is that she must die. Now!" He jerked back.

"I haven't been paid yet, Seventeen."

"In good time, assassin."

"Now."

"First I attend myself to final things first."

"Don't make me kill you, Seventeen," Jared said, behind him. The client from Bunyan IV snapped back in stages, and saw the weapon in Jared's hand.

"What is this?"

"I want to be paid now. Right now."

Seventeen tried to keep his eyes on both Gill and Jared at the same time. The fuzzy alien was working his way around the bridge slowly. Seventeen could tell he was being stalked, but he did not know why.

"You never told me what it is that is payment."

Jared nodded toward the woman.

"No!" The word was Jared's word, said as loud and with as much imperativeness as the world-killer had said it, a moment before.

Jared moved closer, aiming the weapon and realigning himself so the beam would miss vital instruments behind Seventeen. "She's mine. That's my payment. Kill her and I call back my units. In three days we can be at Bunyan IV; what you saw here can be repeated there."

Seventeen lowered the disc.

"She is yours."

Jared's reply was pleasant. "Thank you, Seventeen. Now go take possession."

The client from Bunyan IV dropped out of sight, and in the screens a few minutes later the shuttleship dropped out of the *Tempest* in a similar manner. Then Jared spoke to Gill.

"Relay the transfer affirmative. Let them take it now."

Gill rose on his legs and went to pass ownership of Khaine to the Bunyan IV fleet hanging just outside the detector range of the conquered planet.

Irina watched as the alien ships dropped down through the atmosphere of her planet. Now. . .she averted her eyes.

Finally, when she looked up, Jared was watching her. "You should have let him kill me," she said in a low and level voice. "You'll never have a secure moment while I live." Jared put away his weapon.

"You'll talk to a friend of mine," Jared said.

And he turned away from her.

When they returned to Jared's moon, she tried to kill him as the force-bonds were removed. It was an abortive effort, and Gill managed to get the sedative-spray into her skull without too much thrashing around.

When she woke, she was in the caverns, in the formfit, in the presence of the machine.

Then the machine proved to her that Jared paid a far higher price for his conquests than did any of his clients. The machine opened channels in her brain that had always been blocked by environment and loyalties and age.

Then she knew who Jared really was, and what he was doing. . .

"It was a futile, noble idea," the machine said. "It was doomed from the start; until I was created. Then it stood a chance. Twenty-two years. Now it is a possibility. Order in the known universe. Worlds linked to worlds by mutual respect and mutual ethic. Now it is a possibility. We have conquered each world in a manner to give Jared's clients possession—but not permanent possession. When the time comes, because of the manner of conquest and because of the stresses we have set up in a master program, all the parts will fall into place. Each invader will fall, but in a way that will link the worlds in reliance upon one another. Cogs in a great galactic machine. Not like their petty Sodalities and Unions, but a great humanistic structure that will serve all men as individuals and all worlds as entities."

Irina, no longer the High, listened to it all, her mind absorbing the truth of the machine because it had been at last opened to truth.

"Jared's loneliness is that he knows he must do this job alone, for it is the only way it *can* be done. And if he fails, or if he dies in the process, his name will live on in the memory of the million worlds as the greatest villain the universe ever spawned. It is now an additional part of my task to keep him sane, keep him honest, keep him alive, so the job can be done. Each payment he took was an aid to getting the master program implemented. Even you. Most importantly, you."

Irina rose.

The machine added only, "Not just as his woman, if you decide to stay. But to learn all he knows, to take over for him if he dies. And if there is time, to give him children who can do the job after him. This is one secret that must be shared with silence. Only the alien Gill knows, and he cannot help Jared."

She left the chamber, dropped up and was met by the fuzzy Mexla. "Will you stay?" he asked her.

"I'll stay," she said, and then paused, as if she wanted to say something else. "Not now," she finally said. "Another time, when I can say what I have to say."

Gill took her to him, where he slept. And he left her there, watching him as he turned in his sleep, thinking awful thoughts of death and futility. And she looked at him, not loving him, perhaps never loving him, not really liking him, for she could never like the man who had showed her the sights in the two hundred screens, but willing to stay; wondering in the silent words she had not been able to speak to Gill:

Why should this god be any more successful than all the other gods who have failed?

But across the empty reaches of space there was no answer, only silent attention from the million worlds that waited to become parts of a master universe, or to curse till eternity the names of those who killed planets for profit.

—New York, 1968

SHATTERED LIKE A GLASS GOBLIN

So it was there, eight months later, that Rudy found her; in that huge and ugly house off Western Avenue in Los Angeles; living with them, *all* of them; not just Jonah, but all of them.

It was November in Los Angeles, near sundown, and unaccountably chill even for the fall in that place always near the sun. He came down the sidewalk and stopped in front of the place. It was gothic hideous, with the grass half-cut and the rusted lawnmower sitting in the middle of an unfinished swath. Grass cut as if a placating gesture to the outraged tenants of the two lanai apartment houses that loomed over the squat structure on either side. (Yet how strange. . .the apartment buildings were taller, the old house hunched down between them, but *it* seemed to dominate *them*. How odd.)

Cardboard covered the upstairs windows.

A baby carriage was overturned on the front walk.

The front door was ornately carved.

Darkness seemed to breathe heavily.

Rudy shifted the duffel bag slightly on his shoulder. He was afraid of the house. He was breathing more heavily as he stood there, and a panic he could never have described tightened the fat muscles on either side of his shoulderblades. He looked up into the corners of the darkening sky, seeking a way out, but he could only go forward. Kristina was in there.

Another girl answered the door.

She looked at him without speaking, her long blonde hair half-obscuring her face; peering out from inside the veil of Clairol and dirt.

When he asked a second time for Kris, she wet her lips in the corners, and a tic made her cheek jump. Rudy set down the duffel bag with a whump. "Kris, please," he said urgently.

The blonde girl turned away and walked back into the dim hallways of the terrible old house. Rudy stood in the open doorway, and suddenly, as if the blonde girl had been a barrier to it, and her departure had released it, he was assaulted, like a smack in the face, by a wall of pungent scent. It was marijuana.

He reflexively inhaled, and his head reeled. He took a step back, into the last inches of sunlight coming over the lanai apartment building, and then it was gone, and he was still buzzing, and moved forward, dragging the duffel bag behind him.

He did not remember closing the front door, but when he looked, some time later, it was closed behind him.

He found Kris on the third floor, lying against the wall of a dark closet, her left hand stroking a faded pink rag rabbit, her right hand at her mouth, the little finger crooked, the thumb-ring roach holder half-obscured as she sucked up the last wonders of the joint. The closet held an infinitude of odors—dirty sweat socks as pungent as stew, fleece jackets on which the rain had dried to mildew, a mop gracious with its scent of old dust hardened to dirt, the overriding weed smell of what she had been at for no one knew how long—and it held her. As pretty as pretty could be.

"Kris?"

Slowly, her head came up, and she saw him. Much later, she tracked and focused and she began to cry. "Go away."

In the limpid silences of the whispering house, back and above him in the darkness, Rudy heard the sudden sound of leather wings beating furiously for a second, then nothing.

Rudy crouched down beside her, his heart grown twice its size in his chest. He wanted so desperately to reach her, to talk to her. "Kris. . .

please. . ." She turned her head away, and with the hand that had been stroking the rabbit she slapped at him awkwardly, missing him.

For an instant, Rudy could have sworn he heard the sound of someone counting heavy gold pieces, somewhere off to his right, down a passageway of the third floor. But when he half-turned, and looked out through the closet door, and tried to focus his hearing on it, there was no sound to home in on.

Kris was trying to crawl back farther into the closet. She was trying to smile.

He turned back; on hands and knees he moved into the closet after her.

"The rabbit," she said, languorously. "You're crushing the rabbit." He looked down, his right knee was lying on the soft matted-fur head of the pink rabbit. He pulled it out from under his knee and threw it into a corner of the closet. She looked at him with disgust. "You haven't changed, Rudy. Go away."

"I'm outta the army, Kris," Rudy said gently. "They let me out on a medical. I want you to come back, Kris, please."

She would not listen, but pulled herself away from him, deep into the closet, and closed her eyes. He moved his lips several times, as though trying to recall words he had already spoken, but there was no sound, and he lit a cigarette, and sat in the open doorway of the closet, smoking and waiting for her to come back to him. He had waited eight months for her to come back to him, since he had been inducted and she had written him telling him, *Rudy, I'm going to live with Jonah at The Hill.*

There was the sound of something very tiny, lurking in the infinitely black shadow where the top step of the stairs from the second floor met the landing. It giggled in a glass harpsichord trilling. Rudy knew it was giggling at *him*, but he could discern no movement from that corner.

Kris opened her eyes and stared at him with distaste. "Why did you come here?"

"Because we're gonna be married."

"Get out of here."

"I love you, Kris. Please."

She kicked out at him. It didn't hurt, but it was meant to. He backed out of the closet slowly.

Jonah was down in the living room. The blonde girl who had answered the door was trying to get his pants off him. He kept shaking his head no, and trying to fend her off with a weak-wristed hand. The record player under the brick-and-board bookshelves was playing Simon & Garfunkel, "The Big Bright Green Pleasure Machine."

"Melting," Jonah said gently. "Melting," and he pointed toward the big, foggy mirror over the fireplace mantel. The fireplace was crammed with unburned wax milk cartons, candy bar wrappers, newspapers from the underground press, and kitty litter. The mirror was dim and chill. "*Melting!*" Jonah yelled suddenly, covering his eyes.

"Oh shit!" the blonde girl said, and threw him down, giving up at last. She came toward Rudy.

"What's wrong with him?" Rudy asked.

"He's freaking out again. Christ, what a drag he can be."

"Yeah, but what's *happening* to him?"

She shrugged. "He sees his face melting; that's what he says."

"Is he on marijuana?"

The blonde girl looked at him with sudden distrust. "Mari—? Hey, who *are* you?"

"I'm a friend of Kris's."

The blonde girl assayed him for a moment more, then by the way her shoulders dropped and her posture relaxed, she accepted him. "I thought you might've just walked in, you know, maybe the Laws. You know?"

There was a Middle Earth poster on the wall behind her, with its brightness faded in a long straight swath where the sun caught it every morning. He looked around uneasily. He didn't know what to do.

"I was supposed to marry Kris. Eight months ago," he said.

"You want to fuck?" asked the blonde girl. "When Jonah trips he turns off. I been drinking Coca-Cola all morning and all day, and I'm really horny."

Another record dropped onto the turntable and Stevie Wonder blew hard into his harmonica and started singing, "I Was Born To Love Her."

"I was engaged to Kris," Rudy said, feeling sad. "We was going to be married when I got out of basic. But she decided to come over here with Jonah, and I didn't want to push her. So I waited eight months, but I'm out of the army now."

"Well, *do* you or *don't* you?"

Under the dining room table. She put a satin pillow under her. It said: *Souvenir of Niagara Falls, New York.*

When he went back into the living room, Jonah was sitting up on the sofa, reading Hesse's MAGISTER LUDI.

"Jonah?" Rudy said. Jonah looked up. It took him a while to recognize Rudy.

When he did, he patted the sofa beside him, and Rudy came and sat down.

"Hey, Rudy, where y'been?"

"I've been in the army."

"Wow."

"Yeah, it was awful."

"You out now? I mean for good?"

Rudy nodded. "Uh-huh. Medical."

"Hey, that's good."

They sat quietly for a while. Jonah started to nod, and then said to himself, "You're not very tired."

Rudy said, "Jonah, hey listen, what's the story with Kris? You know, we was supposed to get married about eight months ago."

"She's around someplace," Jonah answered.

Out of the kitchen, through the dining room where the blonde girl lay sleeping under the table, came the sound of something wild, tearing at meat. It went on for a long time, but Rudy was looking out the front window, the big bay window. There was a man in a dark gray suit standing talking to two policemen on the sidewalk at the edge of the front walk leading up to the front door. He was pointing at the big, old house.

"Jonah, can Kris come away now?"

Jonah looked angry. "Hey, listen, man, nobody's *keeping* her here. She's been grooving with all of us and she likes it. Go ask her. Christ, don't bug *me*!"

The two cops were walking up to the front door.

Rudy got up and went to answer the doorbell.

They smiled at him when they saw his uniform.

"May I help you?" Rudy asked them.

The first cop said, "Do you live here?"

"Yes," said Rudy. "My name is Rudolph Boekel. May I help you?"

"We'd like to come inside and talk to you."

"Do you have a search warrant?"

"We don't want to search, we only want to talk to you. Are you in the army?"

"Just discharged. I came home to see my family."

"Can we come in?"

"No, sir."

The second cop looked troubled. "Is this the place they call 'The Hill'?"

"Who?" Rudy asked, looking perplexed.

"Well, the neighbors said this was 'The Hill' and there were some pretty wild parties going on here."

"Do you hear any partying?"

The cops looked at each other. Rudy added, "It's always very quiet here. My mother is dying of cancer of the stomach."

They let Rudy move in, because he was able to talk to people who came to the door from the outside. Aside from Rudy, who went out to get food, and the weekly trips to the unemployment line, no one left The Hill. It was usually very quiet.

Except sometimes there was a sound of growling in the back hall leading up to what had been a maid's room; and the splashing from the basement, the sound of wet things on bricks.

It was a self-contained little universe, bordered on the north by acid and mescaline, on the south by pot and peyote, on the east by speed and redballs, on the west by downers and amphetamines. There were eleven people living in The Hill. Eleven, and Rudy.

He walked through the halls, and sometimes found Kris, who would not talk to him, save once, when she asked him if he'd ever been heavy behind *anything* except love. He didn't know what to answer her, so he only said, "Please," and she called him a square and walked off toward the stairway leading to the dormered attic.

Rudy had heard squeaking from the attic. It had sounded to him like the shrieking of mice being torn to pieces. There were cats in the house.

He did not know why he was there, except that he didn't understand why *she* wanted to stay. His head always buzzed and he sometimes felt that if he just said the right thing, the right way, Kris would come away with him. He began to dislike the light. It hurt his eyes.

No one talked to anyone else very much. There was always a struggle to keep high, to keep the *group high* as elevated as possible. In that way they cared for each other.

And Rudy became their one link with the outside. He had written to someone—his parents, a friend, a bank, someone—and now there was money coming in. Not much, but enough to keep the food stocked, and the rent paid. But he insisted Kris be nice to him.

They all made her be nice to him, and she slept with him in the little room on the second floor where Rudy had put his newspapers and his duffel bag. He lay there most of the day, when he was not out on errands for The Hill, and he read the smaller items about train wrecks and molestations in the suburbs. And Kris came to him and they made love of a sort.

One night she convinced him he should "make it, heavy behind acid" and he swallowed fifteen hundred mikes cut with Methedrine, in two big gel caps, and she was stretched out like taffy for six miles. He was a fine copper wire charged with electricity, and he pierced her flesh. She wriggled with the current that flowed through him, and became softer yet. He sank down through the softness, and carefully observed the intricate wood-grain effect her teardrops made as they rose in the mist around him. He was downdrifting slowly, turning and turning, held by a whisper of blue that came out of his body like a spiderweb. The sound of her breathing in the moist crystal pillared cavity that went down and down was the sound of the very walls themselves, and when he touched them with his warm metal fingertips she drew in breath heavily, forcing the air up around him as he sank down, twisting slowly in a veil of musky looseness.

There was an insistent pulsing growing somewhere below him, and he was afraid of it as he descended, the high-pitched whining of something threatening to shatter. He felt panic. Panic gripped him, flailed at him, his throat constricted, he tried to grasp the veil and it tore away in his hands; then he was falling, faster now, much faster, and *afraid*!

Violet explosions all around him and the shrieking of something that wanted him, that was seeking him, pulsing deeply in the throat of an animal he could not name, and he heard her shouting, heard her wail and pitch beneath him and a terrible crushing feeling in him. . .

And then there was silence.

That lasted for a moment.

And then there was soft music that demanded nothing but inattention. So they lay there, fitted together, in the heat of the tiny room, and they slept for some hours.

After that, Rudy seldom went out into the light. He did the shopping at night, wearing shades. He emptied the garbage at night, and he swept down the front walk, and did the front lawn with scissors because the lawnmower would have annoyed the residents of the lanai apartments (who no longer complained, because there was seldom a sound from The Hill).

He began to realize he had not seen some of the eleven young people who lived in The Hill for a long time. But the sounds from above and below and around him in the house grew more frequent.

Rudy's clothes were too large for him now. He wore only underpants. His hands and feet hurt. The knuckles of his fingers were larger, from cracking them, and they were always an angry crimson.

His head always buzzed. The thin perpetual odor of pot had saturated into the wood walls and the rafters. He had an itch on the outside of his ears he could not quell. He read newspapers all the time, old newspapers whose items were embedded in his memory. He remembered a job he had once held as a garage mechanic, but that seemed a very long time ago. When they cut off the electricity in The Hill, it didn't bother Rudy, because he preferred the dark. But he went to tell the eleven.

He could not find them.

They were all gone. Even Kris, who should have been there somewhere.

He heard the moist sounds from the basement and went down with fur and silence into the darkness. The basement had been flooded. One of the eleven was there. His name was Teddy. He was attached to the slime-coated upper wall of the basement, hanging close to the stone, pulsing softly and giving off a thin purple light, purple as a bruise. He dropped a rubbery arm into the water, and let it hang there, moving idly with the tideless tide. Then something came near it, and he made a sharp movement, and brought the thing up still writhing in his rubbery grip, and inched it along the wall to a dark, moist spot on his upper surface, near the veins that covered its length, and pushed the thing at the dark-blood spot, where it shrieked with a terrible sound, and went in and there was a sucking noise, then a swallowing sound.

Rudy went back upstairs. On the first floor he found the one who was the blonde girl, whose name was Adrianne. She lay out thin and white as a tablecloth on the dining room table as three of the others he had not seen in a very long while put their teeth into her, and through their hollow sharp teeth they drank up the yellow fluid from the bloated pus-pockets that had been her breasts and her buttocks. Their faces were very white and their eyes were like soot-smudges.

Climbing to the second floor, Rudy was almost knocked down by the passage of something that had been Victor, flying on heavily ribbed leather wings. It carried a cat in its jaws.

He saw the thing on the stairs that sounded as though it was counting heavy gold pieces. It was not counting heavy gold pieces.

HARLAN ELLISON

SHATTERED LIKE A GLASS GOBLIN

Rudy could not look at it; it made him feel sick.

He found Kris in the attic, in a corner breaking the skull and sucking out the moist brains of a thing that giggled like a harpsichord.

"Kris, we have to go away," he told her. She reached out and touched him, snapping her long, pointed, dirty fingernails against him. He rang like crystal.

In the rafters of the attic Jonah crouched, gargoyled and sleeping. There was a green stain on his jaws, and something stringy in his claws.

"Kris, please," he said urgently.

His head buzzed.

His ears itched.

Kris sucked out the last of the mellow good things in the skull of the silent little creature, and scraped idly at the flaccid body with hairy hands. She settled back on her haunches, and her long, hairy muzzle came up.

Rudy scuttled away.

He ran loping, his knuckles brushing the attic floor as he scampered for safety. Behind him, Kris was growling. He got down to the second floor and then to the first, and tried to climb up on the Morris chair to the mantel, so he could see himself in the mirror, by the light of the moon, through the fly-blown window. But Naomi was on the window, lapping up the flies with her tongue.

He climbed with desperation, wanting to see himself. And when he stood before the mirror, he saw that he was transparent, that there was nothing inside him, that his ears had grown pointed and had hair on their tips; his eyes were as huge as a tarsier's and the reflected light hurt him.

Then he heard the growling behind and below him.

The little glass goblin turned, and the werewolf rose up on its hind legs and touched him till he rang like fine crystal.

And the werewolf said with very little concern, "Have you ever grooved heavy behind *anything* except love?"

"Please!" the little glass goblin begged, just as the great hairy paw slapped him into a million coruscating rainbow fragments all expanding consciously into the tight little enclosed universe that was The Hill, all buzzing highly contacted and tingling off into a darkness that began to seep out through the silent wooden walls. . .

—Milford, Pike County,
Pennsylvania, 1967

A BOY AND HIS DOG

N.B. Though the story that follows has been reprinted widely, has won a number of literary awards, and has been made into a motion picture you may have seen, it was never intended to stand alone. It is the third section of a novel-in-progress whose overall title is BLOOD'S A ROVER. *And though considerable time has passed since this novella first appeared in print, the full story of Blood and Vic (and one important other who does* not *appear in this section) has yet to be told. But I'm on the job.*

—Harlan Ellison

I

I was out with Blood, my dog. It was his week for annoying me; he kept calling me Albert. He thought that was pretty damned funny. Payson Terhune: ha ha.

I'd caught a couple of water rats for him, the big green and ocher ones, and someone's manicured poodle, lost off a leash in one of the downunders.

He'd eaten pretty good, but he was cranky. "Come on, son of a bitch," I demanded, "find me a piece of ass."

Blood just chuckled, deep in his dog-throat. "You're funny when you get horny," he said.

Maybe funny enough to kick him upside his sphincter asshole, that refugee from a dingo-heap.

"Find! I ain't kidding!"

"For shame, Albert. After all I've taught you. Not 'I *ain't* kidding.' I'm *not* kidding."

He knew I'd reached the edge of my patience. Sullenly, he started casting. He sat down on the crumbled remains of the curb, and his eyelids flickered and closed, and his hairy body tensed. After a while he settled down on his front paws, and scraped them forward till he was lying flat, his shaggy head on the outstretched paws. The tenseness left him and he began trembling, almost the way he trembled just preparatory to scratching a flea. It went on that way for almost a quarter of an hour, and finally he rolled over and lay on his back, his naked belly toward the night sky, his front paws folded mantislike, his hind legs extended and open. "I'm sorry," he said. "There's nothing."

I could have gotten mad and booted him, but I knew he had tried. I wasn't happy about it, I really wanted to get laid, but what could I do? "Okay," I said, with resignation, "forget it."

He kicked himself onto his side and quickly got up.

"What do you want to do?" he asked.

"Not much we *can* do, is there?" I was more than a little sarcastic. He sat down again, at my feet, insolently humble.

I leaned against the melted stub of a lamppost, and thought about girls. It was painful. "We can always go to a show," I said. Blood looked around the street, at the pools of shadow lying in the weed-overgrown craters, and didn't say anything. The whelp was waiting for me to say okay, let's go. He liked movies as much as I did.

"Okay, let's go."

He got up and followed me, his tongue hanging, panting with happiness. Go ahead and laugh, you eggsucker. No popcorn for *you*!

Our Gang was a roverpak that had never been able to cut it simply foraging, so they'd opted for comfort and gone a smart way to getting it. They were movie-oriented kids, and they'd taken over the turf where the Metropole Theater was located. No one tried to bust their turf, because we all needed the movies, and as long as Our Gang had access to films, and did a better job of keeping the films going, they provided a service, even for solos like me and Blood. *Especially* for solos like us.

They made me check my .45 and the Browning .22 long at the door. There was a little alcove right beside the ticket booth. I bought my tickets first; it cost me a can of Oscar Mayer Philadelphia Scrapple for me, and a tin of sardines for Blood. Then the Our Gang guards with the bren guns motioned me over to the alcove and I checked my heat. I saw water leaking from a broken pipe in the ceiling and I told the checker, a kid with big leathery warts all over his face and lips, to move my weapons where it was dry. He ignored me. "Hey you! Motherfuckin', toad, move my stuff over the other side. . .it goes to rust fast. . .an' it picks up any spots, man, I'll break your bones!"

He started to give me jaw about it, looked at the guards with the brens, knew if they tossed me out I'd lose my price of admission whether I went in or not, but they weren't looking for any action, probably understrength, and gave him the nod to let it pass, to do what I said. So the toad moved my Browning to the other end of the gun rack, and pegged my .45 under it.

Blood and me went into the theater.

"I want popcorn."

"Forget it."

"Come on, Albert. Buy me popcorn."

"I'm tapped out. You can live without popcorn."

"You're just being a shit."

I shrugged: sue me.

We went in. The place was jammed. I was glad the guards hadn't tried to take anything but guns. My spike and knife felt reassuring, lying-up in their oiled sheaths at the back of my neck. Blood found two together, and we moved into the row, stepping on feet. Someone cursed and I ignored him. A Doberman growled. Blood's fur stirred, but he let it pass. There was always *some* hardcase on the muscle, even on neutral ground like the Metropole.

(I heard once about a get-it-on they'd had at the old Loew's Granada, on the South Side. Wound up with ten or twelve rovers and their mutts dead, the theater burned down and a couple of good Cagney films lost in the fire. After that was when the roverpaks had got up the agreement that movie houses were sanctuaries. It was better now, but there was always somebody too messed in the mind to come soft.)

It was a triple feature. *Raw Deal* with Dennis O'Keefe, Claire Trevor, Raymond Burr and Marsha Hunt was the oldest of the three. It'd been made in 1948, eighty-six years ago; god only knows how the damn thing'd hung together all that time; it slipped sprockets and they had to stop the movie all the time to re-thread it. But it was a good movie. About this solo who'd been japped by his roverpak and was out to get revenge. Gangsters, mobs, a lot of punching and fighting. Real good.

The middle flick was a thing made during the Third War, in '92, twenty-seven years before I was even born, thing called *Smell of a Chink*. It was mostly gut-spilling and some nice hand-to-hand. Beautiful scene of skirmisher greyhounds equipped with napalm throwers, jellyburning a Chink town. Blood dug it, even though we'd seen this flick before. He had some kind of phony shuck going that these were ancestors of his, and *he* knew and *I* knew, he was making it up.

"Wanna burn a baby, hero?" I whispered to him. He got the barb and just shifted in his seat, didn't say a thing, kept looking pleased as the dogs worked their way through the town. I was bored stiff.

I was waiting for the main feature.

Finally it came on. It was a beauty, a beaver flick made in the late 1970s. It was called *Big Black Leather Splits*. Started right out very good. These two blondes in black leather corsets and boots laced all the way up to their crotches, with whips and masks, got this skinny guy down and one of the chicks sat on his face while the other one went down on him. It got really hairy after that.

All around me there were solos playing with themselves. I was about to jog it a little myself when Blood leaned across and said, real soft, the way he does when he's onto something unusually smelly, "There's a chick in here."

"You're nuts," I said.

"I tell you I smell her. She's in here, man."

Without being conspicuous, I looked around. Almost every seat in the theater was taken with solos or their dogs. If a chick had slipped in there'd have been a riot. She'd have been ripped to pieces before any single guy could have gotten into her. "Where?" I asked, softly. All around me, the solos were beating-off, moaning as the blondes took off their masks and one of them worked the skinny guy with a big wooden ram strapped around her hips.

"Give me a minute," Blood said. He was really concentrating. His body was tense as a wire. His eyes were closed, his muzzle quivering. I let him work.

It was possible. Just maybe possible. I knew that they made really dumb flicks in the downunders, the kind of crap they'd made back in the 1930s and '40s, real clean stuff with even married people sleeping in twin beds. Myrna Loy and George Brent kind of flicks. And I knew that once in a while a chick from one of the really strict middle-class downunders would cumup, to see what a hairy flick was like. I'd heard about it, but it'd never happened in any theater *I'd* ever been in.

And the chances of it happening in the Metropole, particularly, were slim. There was a lot of twisty trade came to the Metropole. Now, understand, I'm not specially prejudiced against guys corning one another. . .hell, I can understand it. There just aren't enough chicks anywhere. But I can't cut the jockey-and-boxer scene because it gets some weak little boxer hanging on you, getting jealous, you have to hunt for him and all he thinks he has to do is bare his ass to get all the work done for him. It's as bad as having a chick dragging along behind. Made for a lot of bad blood and fights in the bigger roverpaks, too. So I just never swung that way. Well, not *never*, but not for a long time.

So with all the twisties in the Metropole, I didn't think a chick would chance it. Be a toss-up who'd tear her apart first: the boxers or the straights.

And if she *was* here, why couldn't any of the other dogs smell her. . .?

"Third row in front of us," Blood said. "Aisle seat. Dressed like a solo."

"How's come *you* can whiff her and no other dog's caught her?"

"You forget who I am, Albert."

"I didn't forget, I just don't believe it."

Actually, bottom-line, I guess I *did* believe it. When you'd been as dumb as I'd been and a dog like Blood'd taught me so much, a guy came to believe *everything* he said. You don't argue with your teacher.

Not when he'd taught you how to read and write and add and subtract and everything else they used to know that meant you were smart (but doesn't mean much of anything now, except it's good to know it, I guess).

(The reading's a pretty good thing. It comes in handy when you can find some canned goods someplace, like in a bombed-out supermarket; makes it easier to pick out stuff you like when the pictures are gone off the labels. Couple of times the reading stopped me from taking canned beets. Shit, I *hate* beets!)

So I guess I *did* believe why he could whiff a maybe chick in there, and no other mutt could. He'd told me all about *that* a million times. It was his favorite story. History he called it. Christ, I'm not *that* dumb! I knew what history was. That was all the stuff that happened before now.

But I liked hearing history straight from Blood, instead of him making me read one of those crummy books he was always dragging in. And *that* particular history was all about him, so he laid it on me over and over, till I knew it by heart. . .no, the word was *rote*. Not *wrote*, like writing, that was something else. I knew it by rote, means you got it word-for-word.

And when a mutt teaches you everything you know, and he tells you something rote, I guess finally you *do* believe it. Except I'd never let that leg-lifter know it.

II

What he'd told me rote was:

Over sixty-five years ago, in Los Angeles, before the Third War even got going completely, there was a man named Buesing who lived in Cerritos. He raised dogs as watchmen and sentries and attackers. Dobermans, Danes, schnauzers and Japanese akitas. He had one four--year-old German shepherd bitch named Ginger. She worked for the Los Angeles Police Department's narcotics division. She could smell out marijuana. No matter how well it was hidden. They ran a test on her: there were 25,000 boxes in an auto parts warehouse. Five of them had been planted with marijuana sealed in cellophane, wrapped in tin foil and heavy brown paper, and finally hidden in three separate sealed cartons. Within seven minutes Ginger found all five packages. At the same time that Ginger was working, ninety-two miles farther north, in Santa Barbara, cetologists had drawn and amplified dolphin spinal fluid and injected it into Chacma baboons and dogs. Altering surgery and grafting had been done. The first successful product of this cetacean experimentation had been a two-year-old male Puli named Ahbhu, who had communicated sense-impressions telepathically. Cross-breeding and continued experimentation had produced the first skirmisher dogs, just in time for the Third War. Telepathic over short distances, easily trained, able to track gasoline or troops or poison gas or radiation when linked with their human controllers, they had become the shock commandos of a new kind of war. The selective traits had bred true. Dobermans, greyhounds, akitas, pulis and schnauzers had become steadily more telepathic.

Ginger and Ahbhu had been Blood's ancestors.

He had told me so, a thousand times. Had told me the story just that way, in just those words, a thousand times, as it had been told to him. I'd never believed him till now.

Maybe the little bastard *was* special.

I checked out the solo scrunched down in the aisle seat three rows ahead of me. I couldn't tell a damned thing. The solo had his (her?)

cap pulled way down, fleece jacket pulled way up.

"Are you sure?"

"As sure as I can be. It's a girl."

"If it is, she's playing with herself just like a guy."

Blood snickered. "Surprise," he said sarcastically.

The mystery solo sat through *Raw Deal* again. It made sense, if that was a girl. Most of the solos and all of the members of roverpaks left after the beaver flick. The theater didn't fill up much more, it gave the streets time to empty, he/she could make his/her way back to wherever he/she had come from. I sat through *Raw Deal* again myself. Blood went to sleep.

When the mystery solo got up, I gave him/her time to get weapons if any'd been checked, and started away. Then I pulled Blood's big shaggy ear and said, "Let's do it." He slouched after me, up the aisle.

I got my guns and checked the street. Empty.

"Okay, nose," I said, "where'd he go?"

"Her. To the right."

I started off, loading the Browning from my bandolier. I still didn't see anyone moving among the bombed-out shells of the buildings. This section of the city was crummy, really bad shape. But then, with Our Gang running the Metropole, they didn't have to repair anything else to get their livelihood. It was ironic; the Dragons had to keep an entire power plant going to get tribute from the other roverpaks; Ted's Bunch had to mind the reservoir; the Bastinados worked like fieldhands in the marijuana gardens; the Barbados Blacks lost a couple of dozen members every year cleaning out the radiation pits all over the city; and Our Gang only had to run that movie house.

Whoever their leader had been, however many years ago it had been that the roverpaks had started forming out of foraging solos, I had to give it to him: he'd been a flinty sharp mother. He knew what services to deal in.

"She turned off here," Blood said.

I followed him as he began loping, toward the edge of the city and the bluish-green radiation that still flickered from the hills. I knew he was right, then. The only things out here were screamers and the access dropshaft to the downunder. It was a girl, all right.

The cheeks of my ass tightened as I thought about it. I was going to get laid. It had been almost a month, since Blood had whiffed that solo chick in the basement of the Market Basket. She'd been filthy, and I'd gotten the crabs from her, but she'd been a woman, all right, and once I'd tied her down and clubbed her a couple of times she'd been pretty good. She'd liked it, too, even if she did spit on me and tell me she'd kill me if she ever got loose. I left her tied up, just to be sure. She wasn't there when I went back to look, week before last.

"Watch out," Blood said, dodging around a crater almost invisible against the surrounding shadows. Something stirred in the crater.

Trekking across the nomansland I realized why it was that all but a handful of solos or members of roverpaks were guys. The War had killed off most of the girls, and that was the way it always was in wars. . .at least that's what Blood told me. The things getting born were seldom male *or* female, and had to be smashed against a wall as soon as they were pulled out of the mother.

The few chicks who hadn't gone downunder with the middle-classers were hard, solitary bitches like the one in the Market Basket; tough and stringy and just as likely to cut off your meat with a razor blade once they let you get in. Scuffling for a piece of ass had gotten harder and harder, the older I'd gotten.

But every once in a while a chick got tired of being roverpak property, or a raid was got-up by five or six roverpaks and some unsuspecting downunder was taken, or—like this time, yeah—some middle-class chick from a downunder got hot pants to find out what a beaver flick looked like, and cumup.

I was going to get laid. Oh boy, I couldn't wait!

III

Out here it was nothing but empty corpses of blasted buildings. One entire block had been stomped flat, like a steel press had come down from Heaven and given one solid wham! and everything was powder under it. The chick was scared and skittish, I could see that. She moved erratically, looking back over her shoulder and to either side. She knew she was in dangerous country. Man, if she'd only known *how* dangerous.

There was one building standing all alone at the end of the smashflat block, like it had been missed and chance let it stay. She ducked inside and a minute later I saw a bobbing light. Flashlight? Maybe.

Blood and I crossed the street and came up into the blackness surrounding the building. It was what was left of a YMCA.

That meant "Young Men's Christian Association." Blood had taught me to read.

So what the hell was a young men's christian association? Sometimes being able to read makes more questions than if you were stupid.

I didn't want her getting out; inside there was as good a place to screw her as any, so I put Blood on guard right beside the steps leading up into the shell, and I went around the back. All the doors and windows had been blown out, of course. It wasn't no big trick getting in. I pulled myself up to the ledge of a window, and dropped down inside. Dark inside. No noise, except the sound of her, moving around on the other side of the old YMCA. I didn't know if she was heeled or not, and I wasn't about to take any chances. I bowslung the Browning and took out the .45 automatic. I didn't have to snap back the action—there was always a slug in the chamber.

I started moving carefully through the room. It was a locker room of some kind. There was glass and debris all over the floor, and one entire row of metal lockers had the paint blistered off their surfaces; the flash blast had caught them through the windows, a lot of years ago. My sneakers didn't make a sound coming through the room.

The door was hanging on one hinge, and I stepped over—through the inverted triangle. I was in the swimming pool area. The big pool was empty, with tiles buckled down at the shallow end. It stunk bad in there; no wonder, there were dead guys, or what was left of them, along one wall. Some lousy cleaner-up had stacked them, but hadn't buried them. I pulled my bandanna up around my nose and mouth and kept moving.

Out the other side of the pool place, and through a little passage with popped light bulbs in the ceiling. I didn't have any trouble seeing. There was moonlight coming through busted windows and a chunk was out of the ceiling. I could hear her real plain now, just on the other side of the door at the end of the passage. I hung close to the wall, and stepped down to the door. It was open a crack, but blocked by a fall of lath and plaster from the wall. It would make noise when I went to pull it open, that was for certain. I had to wait for the right moment.

Flattened against the wall, I checked out what she was doing in there. It was a gymnasium, big one, with climbing ropes hanging down from the ceiling. She had a squat, square, eight-cell flashlight sitting up on the croup of a vaulting horse. There were parallel bars and a horizontal bar about eight feet high, the tempered steel all rusty now. There were swinging rings and a trampoline and a big wooden balancing beam. Over to one side there were wall-bars and balancing benches, horizontal and oblique ladders, and a couple of stacks of vaulting boxes. I made a note to remember this joint. It was better for working out than the jerry-rigged gym I'd set up in an old auto wrecking yard. A guy has to keep in shape, if he's going to be a solo.

She was out of her disguise. Standing there in the skin, shivering. Yeah, it was chilly, and I could see a pattern of chicken-skin all over her. She was maybe five-six or -seven, with nice tits and kind of skinny legs. She was brushing out her hair. It hung way down the back. The flashlight didn't make it clear enough to tell if she had red hair or chestnut, but it wasn't blonde, which was good, and that was because I dug redheads. She had nice tits, though. I couldn't see her face, the hair was hanging down all smooth and wavy and cut off her profile.

The crap she'd been wearing was thrown around on the floor, and what she was going to put on was up on the vaulting horse. She was standing in little shoes with a kind of funny heel on them.

I couldn't move. I suddenly realized I couldn't move. She was nice, really nice. I was getting a real big kick out of just standing there and seeing the way her waist fell inward and her hips fell outward, the way the muscles at the side of her tits pulled up when she reached to the top of her head to brush all that hair down. It was really weird the kick I was getting out of standing and just staring at a chick do that. Kind of very, well, woman stuff. I liked it a lot.

I'd never ever stopped and just looked at a chick like that. All the ones I'd ever seen had been scumbags that Blood had smelled out for me, and I'd snatch'n'grabbed them. Or the big chicks in the beaver flicks. Not like this one, kind of soft and very smooth, even with the goose bumps. I could have watched her all night.

She put down the brush, and reached over and took a pair of panties off the pile of clothes and wriggled into them. Then she got her bra and put it on. I never knew the way chicks did it. She put it on backwards around her waist, and it had a hook on it. Then she slid it around till the cups were in front, and kind of pulled it up under and scooped herself into it, first one, then the other; then she pulled the straps over her shoulder. She reached for her dress, and I nudged some of the lath and plaster aside, and grabbed the door to give it a yank.

She had the dress up over her head, and her arms up inside the material, and when she stuck her head in, and was all tangled there for a second, I yanked the door and there was a crash as chunks of wood and plaster fell out of the way, and a heavy scraping, and I jumped inside and was on her before she could get out of the dress.

She started to scream, and I pulled the dress off her with a ripping sound, and it all happened for her before she knew what that crash and scrape was all about.

Her face was wild. Just wild. Big eyes: I couldn't tell what color they were because they were in shadow. Real fine features, a wide mouth, little nose, cheekbones just like mine, real high and prominent, and a dimple in her right cheek. She stared at me really scared.

And then. . .and this is really weird. . .I felt like I should *say* something to her. I don't know what. Just something. It made me uncomfortable, to see her scared, but what the hell could I do about *that*, I mean, I was going to rape her, after all, and I couldn't very well tell her not to be shrinky about it. She was the one cumup, after all. But even so, I wanted to say hey, don't be scared, I just want to lay you. (That never happened before. I never wanted to *say* anything to a chick, just get in, and that was that.)

But it passed, and I put my leg behind hers and tripped her back, and she went down in a pile. I leveled the .45 at her, and her mouth kind of opened in a little o shape. "Now I'm gonna go over there and get one of them wrestling mats, so it'll be better, comfortable, uh-huh? You make a move off that floor and I shoot a leg out from under you, and you'll get screwed just the same, except you'll be without a leg." I waited for her to let me know she was onto what I was saying, and she finally nodded real slow, so I kept the automatic on her, and went over to the big dusty stack of mats, and pulled one off.

I dragged it over to her, and flipped it so the cleaner side was up, and used the muzzle of the .45 to maneuver her onto it. She just sat there on the mat, with her hands behind her, and her knees bent, and stared at me.

I unzipped my pants and started pulling them down off one side, when I caught her looking at me real funny. I stopped with the jeans. "What're *you* lookin' at?"

I was mad. I didn't know why I was mad, but I was.

"What's your name?" she asked. Her voice was very soft, and kind of furry, like it came up through her throat that was all lined with fur or something.

She kept looking at me, waiting for me to answer.

"Vic," I said. She looked like she was waiting for more.

"Vic what?"

I didn't know what she meant for a minute, then I did. "Vic. Just Vic. That's all."

"Well, what're your mother and father's names?"

Then I started laughing, and working my jeans down again. "Boy, are you a dumb bitch," I said, and laughed some more. She looked hurt. It made me mad again. "Stop lookin' like that, or I'll bust out your teeth!"

She folded her hands in her lap.

HARLAN ELLISON
A BOY AND HIS DOG

I got the pants around my ankles. They wouldn't come off over the sneakers. I had to balance on one foot and scuff the sneaker off the other foot. It was tricky, keeping the .45 on her and getting the sneaker off at the same time. But I did it.

I was standing there buck-naked from the waist down and she had sat forward a little, her legs crossed, hands still in her lap. "Get that stuff off," I said.

She didn't move for a second, and I thought she was going to give me trouble. But then she reached around behind and undid the bra. Then she tipped back and slipped the panties off her ass.

Suddenly, she didn't look scared any more. She was watching me very close and I could see her eyes were blue now. Now this is the really weird thing. . .

I couldn't do it. I mean, not exactly. I mean, I *wanted* to fuck her, see, but she was all soft and pretty and she kept *looking* at me, and no solo I ever met would believe me, but I heard myself *talking* to her, still standing there like some kind of wetbrain, one sneaker off and jeans down around my ankles. "What's *your* name?"

"Quilla June Holmes."

"That's a weird name."

"My mother says it's not that uncommon, back in Oklahoma."

"That where your folks come from?"

She nodded. "Before the Third War."

"They must be pretty old by now."

"They are, but they're okay. I guess."

We were just frozen there, talking to each other. I could tell she was cold, because she was shivering. "Well," I said, sort of getting ready to drop down beside her, "I guess we better—"

Damn it! That damned Blood! Right at that moment he came crashing in from outside. Came skidding through the lath, and plaster, raising dust, slid along on his ass till he got to us. "*Now* what?" I demanded.

"Who're you talking to?" the girl asked.

"Him. Blood."

"The dog!?!"

Blood stared at her and then ignored her. He started to say something but the girl interrupted him. "Then it's true what they say. . .you can all talk to animals. . ."

"You going to listen to her all night, or do you want to hear why I came in?"

"Okay, why're you here?"

"You're in trouble, Albert."

"Come on, forget the mickeymouse. What's up?"

Blood twisted his head toward the front door of the YMCA. "Roverpak. Got the building surrounded. I make it fifteen or twenty, maybe more."

"How the hell'd they know we was here?"

Blood looked chagrined. He dropped his head.

"Well?"

"Some other mutt must've smelled her in the theater."

"Great."

"Now what?"

"Now we stand 'em off, that's what. You got any better suggestions?"

"Just one."

I waited. He grinned.

"Pull your pants up."

IV

The girl, this Quilla June, was pretty safe. I made her a kind of a shelter out of wrestling mats, maybe a dozen of them. She wouldn't get hit by a stray bullet, and if they didn't go right for her, they wouldn't find her. I climbed one of the ropes hanging down from the girders and laid out up there with the Browning and a couple of handfuls of reloads. I wished to God I'd had an automatic, a bren or a Thompson. I checked the .45, made sure it was full, with one in the chamber, and set the extra clips down on the girder. I had a clear line-of-fire all around the gym.